THE SOUTHERN WOMAN

THE SOUTHERN WOMAN

SELECTED FICTION

ELIZABETH SPENCER

Introduction by Afia Atakora

MODERN LIBRARY

NEW YORK

2021 Modern Library Trade Paperback Edition

Published in the United States by Modern Library, an imprint
of Random House, a division of Penguin Random House LLC,
New York.

MODERN LIBRARY and the TORCHBEARER colophon are
registered trademarks of Penguin Random House LLC.

Originally published in hardcover in the United States by
Modern Library, an imprint of Random House, a division of
Penguin Random House LLC, in 2001.

Some of the stories in this work were originally published in
*The Atlantic, The Kenyon Review, McCall's, New Canadian Stories, The
New Yorker, North American Review, Ontario Review, Prairie Schooner,
The Southern Review,* and *Texas Quarterly.* In addition, some have
appeared in *The Light in the Piazza and Other Italian Tales*
(Jackson: University Press of Mississippi, 1996), *Jack of Diamonds*
(New York: Viking Penguin, 1988) and *The Stories of Elizabeth
Spencer* (New York: Doubleday, 1981).

LIBRARY OF CONGRESS CATALOGUING-IN-PUBLICATION DATA
Spencer, Elizabeth
The southern woman: selected fiction/Elizabeth Spencer.
p. cm.
ISBN 978-0-593-24118-9
Ebook ISBN 978-0-593-24119-6
1. Southern States—Social Life and customs—Fiction. 2. Italy—
Social life and customs—Fiction. 3. Women—Southern States—
Fiction. 4. Women—Italy—Fiction. I. Title
PS3537.P4454 S68 2001
813'.54—dc21   00-054612

Printed in the United States of America on acid-free paper

modernlibrary.com
randomhousebooks.com

246897531

For Samuel S. Vaughan, in appreciation

CONTENTS

INTRODUCTION

AFIA ATAKORA

If you have not heard of Elizabeth Spencer, it's alright. You were not meant to. Before being invited to write this introduction to her works, I had not heard of her, either.

Spencer is not often enough named where she belongs, among that pantheon of Southern writers, the Faulkners and Twains. Frankly, Spencer is rarely even listed among the demigods, made lesser, of course, because their stories, like hers, are by, for, and about women. Think Flannery O'Connor, Kate Chopin, Eudora Welty. Though I daresay that Elizabeth Spencer is in a category of her own, to be set apart from certain Southern writers, from certain Southern traditions.

To say that she was silenced is to perhaps give too much credit to the literary establishment and not enough credit to the indelible draw of storytelling to a natural-born storyteller. Still, after Elizabeth Spencer earned the unanimous vote of the 1957 Pulitzer judges for her novel *The Voice at the Back Door*, the Pulitzer board refused to formally name her the winner. Asterisk, no prize for fiction was awarded that year.

For *The Voice at the Back Door*, Spencer drew inspiration from a real civil rights case. In the fictional telling, a Black man stands falsely accused of a crime. A white man is called upon to defend him in the heart of the segregated South. If this sounds familiar, do keep in mind that by 1957 Spencer's novel had already won the Pulitzer and been robbed of it too. Harper Lee's *To Kill a Mockingbird* was not yet published, and would not win its own Pulitzer until 1960. You've surely heard of Harper Lee, we've told and retold *To*

Kill a Mockingbird, we teach it to children. And perhaps it is precisely this—that the lesson of *Mockingbird* is a child's lesson with straightforward evils and simple solutions that made it more palatable a parable to the Pulitzer committee, the literary establishment, the American reader skimming the shelves. We'd rather the tidy morality play, the simple schoolyard lesson: Just don't be racist. Spencer offered a question that begged a response, an open-ended indictment of a segregated society steeped in racism, a country self-destructively committed to the systems that perpetuate violence and hate. The Pulitzer committee deemed that we were not ready to hear what Spencer had to say about racism in America, no matter how well she had rendered it—or precisely because she had rendered it too well.

Silenced? No. Spencer continued to write, widely, prolifically from the central nervous system of America and beyond. She had tapped into a vein and, of the pure essence collected there, drew out all the stories of pride, of sin, of neglected promise and tainted legacy. Rather than silenced, one might say she was hushed.

———

In truth, I came ready to read this collection with one eye shut the way one might cringe through an old Disney film, bracing for racism, ready with reflexive apologies, "It was a different time."

But both of my eyes popped open when I got to the story "Sharon." Reader, I said "Wow." Out loud. Because Spencer weaves a spell, performs a sleight of hand which makes you convinced you are falling in love with Sharon—Sharon being the name of the plantation, like *Gone With the Wind*'s Tara—in a knowing wink to that strange old Southern preoccupation with the personification of land and objectification of people. But you are not falling in love with the land, or even the ghost of the mistress who owned it, Miss Eileen. You are falling in love with the woman behind it all, the new mistress, whether she wants to be or not. Like the narrator's uncle, you have gone and fallen in love with the Black maid Melissa. Like him, you feel for her and you can't ever truly know her. You discover this, as the narrator does, as an outside observer glimpsing what looks like love through a window. But do you believe equal love can exist between a white man and his Black maid in the fraught, segregated South that has been presented to you, seamless and spare, in these few exquisite pages? Spencer does not tell you what to think, instead, like an impressionist painter, she provides you with a hundred tiny dots of rich detail, a veritable Seurat of Southern life. The image you see is your own, of your own making and in your own likeness. And just like that, Spencer has you, because she's told you something about the South and something about yourself, too, and all your complicated preconceived notions.

"Politically correct" is a loaded term, "woke," another. By the powers vested in me, by the same literary establishment that hands out prizes and asterisks, I am pleased to declare Elizabeth Spencer as neither. What some of these stories might lack in respectful terminology they make up for in sumptuous language and innate empathy, which kind of makes you wonder why some of those other old Southern writers have such a hard time writing "Other" people as just that, people. The most enduring image in "Sharon" is its final one, suggesting that for all that segregation, that great legacy of "othering," the white South and its Black history are indelibly intertwined, a complicated miscegenation of hate, and love, too.

Product of her time, Spencer might be, but she makes smart, gorgeous use of that time. Her writing embodies the tell-it-like-it-is vigor that we like to think is the spirit of America, though we've usually got it wrong, got it soiled. But "tell-it-like-it-is" as written by Spencer is pure, distilled, admirable. She evokes the romantic allure of the prideful South and makes those of us who can view it only from the outside envious.

"Rebel" is a loaded term, too, particularly as it relates to the South, to America, to civil war and civil liberties. To Black, to white. Elizabeth Spencer is a rebel.

Now, Americans, we love us a good rebel, with a caveat, a rebel with an asterisk attached, so long as that rebel is for us, not against us. Us, that limited pronoun, meaning us white males, us exceptional Americans, us the literary establishment.

Elizabeth Spencer's stories are not for us. I suspect they are for herself, a working out of the world around her, like painting the same still life over and over from different angles, no agenda, no embellishment, just an attempt to render the image a little more accurately. A little closer to the truth each time.

The truth can be damning. The girls who own the point of view in many of Spencer's Southern stories are finding that out. They are "Daughters of the Confederacy," daughters of "a different time," markedly coming of age as white women in the Jim Crow–era South and in the long shadow of slavery. They are precocious. They ask impolite questions. Their genteel mamas hush them. They refuse to be hushed. But these girls are not Scout needing their hands held by Atticus Finch to understand empathy. Spencer's girls are full-bodied and full-throated. They, like all of her characters, are flawed and real.

We meet one such child, Maybeth, in "The Little Brown Girl." Similar to the daughter in "Sharon," Maybeth lives on an old plantation ruled by a Mama and Daddy who don't have much patience for her curiosity. Maybe the Black workers have more sympathy or maybe they don't have the social standing to shoo her away; whatever the case, Maybeth finds an affinity with the adult Black help, in particular Jim Williams, who appears in her world only part of the year, to tend her father's cotton. Between them they invent the idea of a little girl, an imaginary friend for the lonesome Maybeth, a daughter for the markedly solitary Jim, a whole person whose existence they can almost convince themselves to believe in.

Jim Williams might be a mythic Negro, but he is not a "magical" one. And in a different writer's telling, Jim's deception would be the object lesson, and Maybeth would be the white savior in training. Not so in Spencer's stories. That touch of Southern gothic magic stirs up the ghost of the Little Brown Girl, standing like a shared thought between Maybeth and Jim. We understand Maybeth's longing for a playmate, and even the inherited idea that she might buy herself a brown one. But this literally haunting narrative makes only the barest hint at why Jim yearns for the spirit of a little brown daughter.

Spencer may summon up a ghost, but after she lets the ghost's very existence speak for itself. There's a dark sorrow there that our narrator and our writer both know they can't get at, and they both wisely take a step back from the stories that aren't theirs to tell. Spencer's strength lies in knowing what is hers: the rich dialect, the lush landscapes, and the stories of her youth made as real as she can render them, a goal that goes entirely against the sensibilities of that same upbringing. Elizabeth Spencer won't be hushed, either.

Still, if Spencer is the titular Southern Woman, then the departure of her settings from her native Mississippi—to Europe, to Canada, to the North—make up a clear trajectory. Her South had rejected her and she went on to write the way exiles do: from other places, a distance which makes the heartbeat of home pulse even louder.

This is perhaps why Spencer's most celebrated story, the one you've probably heard of, "The Light in the Piazza," is not set in the South at all but in Italy. Certainly, on the face of it, this novella is her most palatable work—no Negroes here—so palatable in fact that it became a 1962 film and a 2003 Broadway musical. The film, with Olivia de Havilland as Margaret Johnson, a debutante outside her prime, is well cast. De Havilland, after all, was made famous for her role as Scarlett O'Hara's bestie and earned an Oscar nomination for Best Supporting Actress (asterisk, she lost to Hattie McDaniel as Mammy).

On the page, Margaret Johnson might as well be the middle-aged version of Scarlett's pal, or her 1950s descendant, anyway, and her mannerly witticisms about her three-month sojourn to work on her tan in postwar Italy could easily serve as the Southern Woman's travel guide. But the heart of the novella is Margaret's relationship with her adult daughter, who has "the mental age of a child of ten."

This story is bold for its time, bold for any time, exploring the interiority of an older woman, who desperately protects her child and yet has a guilty yearning to be free of her. That Clara is an adult with special needs is handled with care. Spencer never makes fun of Clara, never makes her magical or beatific; in fact, much of Clara's perceived limitations are told secondhand through her mother's need to explain her. Margaret does so with the full breadth of her Winston-Salem–bred dignity, a compulsion that quickly comes undone in the space of one Italian summer, so that "The Light" refers to the new way in which Margaret might see her daughter, removed from American definitions of capability, of pride, of success.

What the adaptation leaves behind on the page, and what has been hushed in Spencer's work time and time again, is this key criticism of the homeland. Margaret has to be away from America to gain this new perspective, remove herself from her deep roots and from the capitalist sensibilities for which her absent husband, Noel, is the perfect stand in. He gave up on Clara long ago. In the midst of the "communist scare," his "every experience found immediate reference in his business." And "When," Margaret wonders, "had money come to seem to him the very walls that keep out the storm?"

"I'm going to do it." Margaret sees the light. "Without Noel."

When Spencer returns to the Americas, she is older, wiser, and she inhabits older, wiser characters. Her later works continue to pick at the established seams of female identity, and even Up North, and elsewhere, that Southern magic is the scalpel. In a master class of spare storytelling, "Owl" tells of a wife disappointed that the appearance of an ominous bird is not a foretelling of her husband's untimely death after all. In "I, Maureen" a similar spousal near-death experience leads to a breathtakingly honest rendering of mental illness and a pyrrhic victory with echoes of *Medea*.

As Maureen tells it, "I could have been a witch, an evil spirit."

Her estranged husband rails, "I don't know why you ever had to turn into a spirit at all! Just a woman, a wife, a mother, a human being—! That's all I ever wanted."

"Believe me," says Maureen, *"I don't know either."*

The beauty and the brutality in Spencer's stories is precisely this: You can't know where she means to take you. It is almost as if she doesn't know where she means to take herself, as though she pushes forth, and pushes forth and arrives at the truth quite as stunned about it as you are.

There is the sense of walking in on someone at their most vulnerable, naked. The shock is not in the nudity but in the fact that they don't immediately grab a towel, it is in the way they refuse to be ashamed. So here we are, Spencer seems to shrug and say in her stories, you might as well go ahead and get an eyeful.

—

AFIA ATAKORA is the author of *Conjure Women*, a Southern gothic novel exploring the lives of emancipated slaves in the immediate aftermath of the Civil War. She holds an MFA from Columbia University, where she was the recipient of the De Alba Fellowship. Atakora was born in the United Kingdom and raised in New Jersey, where she now lives.

THE SOUTH

THE LITTLE BROWN GIRL

Maybeth's father had a business in the town, which was about a mile from where they lived, but he had about forty acres of land below the house that he planted in cotton and corn. The land was down the hill from the house and it was on two levels of ground: twenty acres, then a bluff covered with oak sprouts and vines, then a lower level, which stretched to the property line at the small creek. You could see it all from the house—the two fields and the creek, and other fields beyond the creek—but from the upper field you could just see as far as the willows along the creek bank.

For nine months of the year, Maybeth's father hired a Negro named Jim Williams to make the crop. Jim would work uptown in the mornings and come in the afternoons around two o'clock— a black, strapping Negro in blue overalls, stepping light and free and powerful on the road from town. He would go around the house to the back to hitch up the black mule in spring, or file on the hoe blade in summer, or drag a great dirty-white cotton sack to the field in the fall. Spring, summer, and fall they saw him come, until he became as much a part of the household as Maybeth or Brother or Lester Junior or Snookums, the cook; then, after the last pound of cotton was weighed in the cold fall twilight, the Jim they knew would vanish. In winter, they sometimes spoke to a town Negro as Jim, and he would answer back, pleasant as you please, but it was no use pretending he was the same. The cotton stalks stood black and sodden in the field, and the cornstalks broke from the top, and there was nothing for a little girl to do in the afternoons but grow all hot and stuffy by the fire or pester Mother for things to eat or study schoolbooks sometimes. There wasn't anybody much to play with out where they lived.

At last, the spring day would come when Maybeth could leap away from the school bus and the ugly children in the bus, and run up the drive to the house, then down the hill, under the maple trees, to the field. Jim would be in the field, plowing with the middle-buster, and she would get to follow behind him for the first time in the year. Jim did a lot of funny things out there in the field. Up ahead, where the rows ended at the top of the bluff, Jim sometimes stopped when he had pulled the plow out of the ground, and while the black mule circled in the trace chains he would fling up his head and sing out, rich and full, as loud as he could sing, "Ama-a-zi-in' grace—" The air would quiver for the next line to come, but Jim would be well into the field by then, driving the plow down the furrow with a long, swinging stride.

Once, Maybeth tried to tell him the next line. "It goes 'How sweet the sound,' Jim," she said, trying to put her little shoes in Jim's broad tracks.

But all Jim Williams said was, "Git up, Jimson Weed!" Other times, he called the mule Daisy Bell, and that was funny, too, because the mule's name was Dick, and Dick was a man mule, Maybeth was sure. But when she told Jim that, he only said, "Lawd, Lawd," as though she had told him something he had never heard before, or something he had only half heard when she said it. You couldn't tell which.

But most of the time Maybeth was asking Jim questions. When she got like that with Mother, Mother would finally say, "Now, what on earth made you think of that?" Daddy would laugh at her questions and say, "I don't know, honey." But Jim knew the answer to everything. He knew why the jaybird bounced on the air when he flew and why the mule swept his nose along the ground when he turned and why the steel plow slid out of the earth as clean as when it entered. Sometimes Maybeth knew that Jim was making up, but most of the time she believed him word for word, like the catechism in Sunday School.

One spring afternoon, a few days before Maybeth's seventh birthday, Jim was sporting a new red bandanna in the back pocket of his overalls. Even before Maybeth reached him, she spotted it, and she asked about it first thing.

"My little girl give me that," he said. He spoke in his making-up voice, but he looked perfectly straight-faced.

Maybeth hurried very fast behind him. "Aw, Jim, you ain't got a little girl, have you? How old is she?"

"She be eight nex' fall," he said, very businesslike. "Gee, mule."

"How big is she?"

"She jes' 'bout your size, honey."

A little brown girl in a starched blue-and-white checked dress stepped smiling before Maybeth's eyes. From then on, Maybeth's questions all went in one direction, and if Jim had any peace, it was only because he was Jim.

"When will I get to see her, Jim? When will she come and play with me?"

"Some day nex' week, I reckon."

"What day next week?"

"Long 'bout the middle part of the week, I spec'."

"Aw, you're just foolin', Jim. Aren't you just foolin'?"

"Ama-a-zi-in' grace—" sang Jim Williams as the black mule turned in the trace chains against a low and burning cloud. And that night, when Jim had eaten his supper in the kitchen and gone, the little brown girl in the blue-and-white checked dress stayed on.

"Mother, guess what Jim told me today," said Maybeth, opening her arithmetic book before the fire. "He said he had a little girl. She's coming and play with me."

"Oh, honey, Jim's just fooling you. Jim hasn't got any children, has he, Lester?"

"Not that I ever heard of," said Daddy. "It's a good thing, too—the way he drinks and carries on every Saturday night."

"He's fooling you," said Mother.

Maybeth bent quickly to her sums. "I know it," she said.

And in a way she had known it all along. But in another way she hadn't known it, and the not knowing still remained along with the knowing, and she never thought it out any further. Nothing was changed, and she and the little brown girl played together before she went to sleep at night, in dull moments at school, and when she was being quiet on the bus, riding home with the noisy children. The little girl was the first thing to ask questions about when she ran to the field after school, the warm sun on her yellow hair, and her feet already uncomfortable to be out of their shoes.

The first thing, that is, until the Friday came when Maybeth was seven. It was a perfect birthday. Under her plate at breakfast that morning she found two broad silver dollars. The class sang "Happy Birthday" to her in school, and that night Snookums, the cook, who usually finished work in the afternoon, returned from her house to cook supper, and they all had fried chicken and rice and gravy and a coconut birthday cake.

Maybeth ran into the kitchen to show her silver dollars to Snookums and Jim. "Look, Snookums! Look, Jim!" she said.

"Lawd-ee!" said Snookums. She was a young, bright Negro with a slim waist and straight black hair.

"My, *my!*" said Jim. "That's ringin' money, ain't it, Snookums?"

"Lawd-ee!" said Snookums.

"Which you druther have, Snookums," said Jim, "ringin' money or foldin' money?"

The door was open to the dining room, and Maybeth heard her big brother laugh and holler back, "Either one'll do to buy Saturday-night liquor, won't it?"

Jim and Snookums just fell out laughing, and Maybeth somehow felt ashamed.

After supper, she put the two silver dollars in a little box inside a bigger box and put them in the very back right-hand corner of her drawer in the bureau.

The next day was Saturday, and it rained, so Jim stayed in the barn and shelled corn for the chickens, and Maybeth watched.

"I *wuz* gwine bring my little girl to play with you nex' week," said Jim.

Maybeth was stricken. "How come you can't, Jim? Oh, how come you can't?"

"She ain't got no fine dress like you is. She ain't got nothin' 'cept one ole brown dress. She say she shame to come."

Maybeth broke the stubborn grains of corn from a cob one at a time, and her heart beat very fast. "Have you sure 'nough got a little girl, Jim?"

Jim did not answer. "There's dresses at the Jew store," he went on mournfully. "But they's nigh onto two dollars. Take the nigger long time to make up that money."

A few minutes later, Maybeth was hurrying back to the house in the rain.

She took the two silver dollars out of the little box within the larger box, and ran back to the barn.

"What you fixin' to do?" Jim Williams asked, holding the two coins in his open palm and cutting his eyes toward her.

"For the dress," Maybeth said. "You know. For your little girl's dress, Jim."

"Your daddy ain't gwine like you playin' around with this money," he said.

"He ain't going to know," said Maybeth.

"You *sure?*" he asked, snapping shut the three clasps on his little leather purse.

"I'm not going to tell him," said Maybeth.

"Gwine git her a yalla dre-ess," sang Jim softly, and the corn poured out of his fingers in rich handfuls and rattled against the side of the scuttle as fast as the rain on the tin roof.

Maybeth did not know why she had given Jim the money. It was like when you are playing mud pies by yourself and you get real salt and pepper for the pies, or when you are dressing up to play lady and you make a mess of all the closets and cedar chests trying to get something real and exactly right—the high-heeled button shoes or the hat with the plume. She and Jim were playing that Jim had a little girl. But when the playing was over, Jim did not give the money back, and, of course, she did not really know that she had expected him to, so she never asked. And because she wasn't exactly sure what money meant, her sorrow centered on the two little empty boxes in the corner of the dresser drawer.

She thought of them with an empty feeling when she rode to school on Monday morning in the pickup with Daddy and saw a yellow dress in the Jew-store window. When she rode back from school on the bus, she looked again, and something went queer inside her, because the yellow dress was gone.

Maybeth ran so hard down the hill to the field that afternoon that the pound of her feet shook her all over and she could hardly stop running at the fence. All the way home in the bus, all the way through the yard and down the hill, she could picture Jim plowing with the little girl in the yellow dress behind him in the furrow, and they would look up when Maybeth came. From the fence, she could see that Jim was plowing down at the far corner, where the land was lowest; he was almost through busting the upper field. She could just see the top of his head following Dick's flapping ears up the slope. Maybeth crawled through the barbed wire and caught a snag in her dress. When she had pulled it free, and looked up, Jim was in full view on the higher ground, and he was alone.

Maybeth came slowly out of the maple shade into the hot sun. As she crossed the rows, the clods made her stumble once or twice. She fell in behind him at last.

"I tore my dress. See?" she said, holding up the snagged hem.

He glanced back, the sweat big on his temples and catching the sun on his cheek. "Sho' did," he said. "You shorely did."

They were back beside the bluff before she asked, "How come your little girl didn't come today, Jim?"

He had stopped, with the plow in the new furrow, to cut himself a plug of tobacco. He jerked his kinky head toward the creek. "She down there," he said.

"Down there?"

"She shame to come till you come. She say she gwine set in the bushes and watch for you. She be comin' on in a minute now."

Maybeth ran to the edge of the bluff, among the honeysuckle

vines, and stared and stared down toward the low willows along the creek bank, until their sharp spring green blurred in her eyes.

"Where, Jim, where?"

Jim hooked the lines over the plow handle. "Whoa, mule," he said. He walked away from her along the edge of the bluff and stood on the highest point, bigger than anything from sky to sky. He pointed.

"See," he said, and his tone was infinite. "Look yonder. She setting on the groun'. See. She done crossed her legs."

"Has she got on a—a yellow dress?"

"Yes'm! Yes'm! You sees her! You sees her sho'!"

"Is she sitting under that bigges' clump of willow, right over yonder? Sitting cross-legged?"

"Yes'm! That's right! By that bigges' clump."

"Sort of with one hand on the ground?"

"Yes, ma'am! You sees her sho'!"

Then, in two strides, he was back at the plow. "She'll come. My little girl'll come. Gee, mule. She knows we done seen her, and she'll come. Gee up, sir!"

The plow ran into the earth, and Maybeth, still standing on the bluff, could hear from somewhere the creak of the harness, and the tearing of little roots as the soft ground was severed. She stood staring, and the green blur beyond the lower field fanned out and then closed together around the shape of something—was it something?—like a still image under the willow trees. Humming to himself, Jim Williams passed farther down the slope, but Maybeth stayed on the bluff, as motionless as the fluted honeysuckle bloom beside her hand and the willows across the lower field standing up in the windless air.

She saw something move under the willows.

Maybeth began to walk, and then she began to run, faster and faster. The rows, with their heavy chunks of clodded earth, flew beneath her, trying to trip her, to keep her from the hill and the white house on the hill and Mother.

She caught her breath a little in the yard, and then she went in and found Mother in the kitchen, drinking some water.

"Why, precious, why are you so hot?" Mother said. "Why did you come back from the field?"

How could you tell about the yellow dress and something coming alive beneath the willows? "I—I got hungry," said Maybeth.

Mother gave her a piece of cold corn bread and sent her out on the back steps. There was a sound around the corner of the house. A Bantam rooster stepped toward her on the flagstone walk. Maybeth jumped up, trembling, and flung the muffin to him and ran into the house, through one room and another.

"Mother!" she called. "Mother!"

"In here, honey."

When she came into the room, her mother looked up at her. Then she laid aside her darning basket and took Maybeth into her arms and rocked her in the rocking chair.

THE ECLIPSE

Anybody would have noticed them, they were both so pretty. The young lady was immaculate and fresh, out of choice, or perhaps you could say out of disdain for people who weren't; gloves snow white and stocking seams straight—she would stay just so all summer. The boy with her might or might not. He was small but growing, possibly about twelve years old, and could reach a new phase any minute. He was by nature blond and bright as a daisy, and soap and water had been recently at work, for the tuft of hair at his crown was springing erect again, strand by strand. What had made him content to scrub so well? She, obviously, was the answer.

She rode backward for the time being (later they would swap), reading a slick-paged magazine, and he looked out the window, but remarks occurred to them; they exchanged glances as though by signal. His feet were reassuring: honest, puppylike, clumsy. One thought pleasantly of them bare below rolled blue jeans, splotched with dust and watermelon juice. From behind the magazine page she drank in the soft-cut lines of his profile. Her eyes fell away the instant before he caught her staring. Somebody could come very near to them without their noticing. Somebody did. "Dorothy Eavers! Don't you remember *me*?"

The train passed through a landscape that looked empty, partly because they were moving so fast; it gave them only a slight rocking motion as a sign of its power. Since the interior of the sealed air-conditioned coach was not cluttered by the sound of rails, there was no need for the woman to shout, much less get up and cross the aisle. But she had done both. Never mind; the two traveling companions recovered almost at once. She was not a threat. By some feat, the immaculate girl was even able to recall her name.

"Ina Pearl! I didn't see you."

"Well, I saw *you*. The reason it took me so long, I couldn't believe my eyes. Not that you've changed a bit, now that I see you up close. I just didn't know you lived down here any more. I didn't know you had a little boy, either. I declare! He's almost as tall as you."

"But he's not mine! This is my student, my pupil."

"Music!" said Ina Pearl. "It always just thrilled me to death to hear you play. But weren't you going to New York and go on the stage?"

Dorothy Eavers winced. This came of college-girl exchanges, confidences given that would be quoted with no regard for accuracy.

"I never thought of the stage," she said. "I had hoped to do concert work, but I couldn't make a go of it. I took a job teaching public school music in Stilton. Quite a change! I give some private lessons, too—to Weston, for instance." She touched his hair. "I wasn't good enough for New York, I guess."

"Oh, now, I bet you were, too!" cried Ina Pearl.

"The funny thing is I give more concerts now than I ever did," said Dorothy Eavers. "Weston, here"—her smile at the boy, meeting his eyes, was like a wink of agreement on Ina Pearl—"Weston has put me in my place. I'm his accompanist. No one can get enough of hearing him sing. We're going to New Orleans now to audition for this famous boys' choir—oh, I'm sure you've heard of them. They—"

"Do you know," Ina Pearl inquired of her, comfortably regarding Weston, "since I saw you last, I've had two? They're just about his size. One might be a little bit bigger and the other a little bit littler. Sing! You couldn't make them stop yelling long enough to *sing* anything."

Having thus established her children as indubitably superior to boys who did stop yelling and sing, she went on to tell everything else about them. Weston knew himself out of it now. He turned his attention from the fleet landscape and examined her, this talkative intruder. She was nothing like Miss Eavers. He went through an appalling catalogue of her faults, arriving at the conclusion that she wasn't in the least attractive. When she opened her purse and took out her compact, powder sprinkled into an unwholesome tangle of junk. Her fingernails were painted bright, and three of them were chipped. He could think of other, even worse things that probably were wrong with her, too—he had got quite a supply from watching his mother—and from every single one of them Miss Eavers was absolutely free, which was why everybody back in town said she was "stuck-up."

Oh, he had heard them talking. From the upstairs window after supper, sitting where they said he oughtn't to, because the screen might not be strong enough, he had heard them.

"Stuck-up thing!" (Mother.)

"Got mighty pretty ankles, Miss Mamie." (Mr. Harry Buford, from across the street.)

"Bob Nabors begged her for a date, like several others when she first came, but Bob especially. . . . Just crazy about her. Why would it hurt to give him a date? She thinks because she's lived in New York and knows about music." (Mother.)

Cigar glow down in the dark. (Mr. Harry, thinking about her.) "Maybe she likes 'em older, more mature."

"I got nothing against her. I just wish Weston wasn't quite so enthusiastic. He ought not to put all of his time on music." (Daddy.)

"She's stuck-up, if you ask me. Just plain stuck-up." (Mother.)

From the window in the dark, Weston could look up into the clean, brilliant September sky. He knew better than anybody. Miss Eavers was no more stuck-up than a star.

When the woman called Ina Pearl got off at the next station stop, they did not converse about her.

"Where's this?" asked Weston, leaning out.

"Picayune, I think," said Miss Eavers.

"I wouldn't like to live here, either," said Weston.

"What do you mean, 'either'?"

"Either here or Stilton." He did not choose to watch the exit of Ina Pearl from his life—how she was greeted by two little boys with suckers in their jaws, how she scrambled into a car beside a man in shirt sleeves. Weston looked ahead of him. His mouth was softly closed; his lashes were thick as June grass; his summer freckles lingered just below the skin, like a thin wash of gold. He waited to move on again. "Or any place else in Mississippi," he murmured.

Miss Eavers glanced up in something like alarm from the enameled page of the latest musical arts magazine. She occasionally felt twinges of her responsibility for him, but their relationship had galloped from the first, and except to instruct him in range, scales, breathing, voice projection, and allied matters, she had never exerted her natural authority.

"But you've never been out of it!" she exclaimed.

He did not accept the reproof, if that was what it was. He had got his idea from her, after all, if never in so many words.

"I'm going out now," he said superbly.

He was obviously headed for a lot of trouble.

—

The first he knew of it, the trouble had already happened. It was at the audition—for that hour they had talked about for so long did finally, actually, roll around. Weston's fine concluding high note had been sent aloft to fade, he had heard his little discreet applause from the handful of listeners who sat in the auditorium with their notebooks out, and he had made his little bow. He and Miss Eavers were leaving the stage of the auditorium when she and her music books brushed past him into the wings. A man was coming into the wings from another direction, stooping to enter a small door that opened into the backstage area from the auditorium itself. A short flight of steps brought him quickly level with them.

"Dorothy Eavers!" he said. "I couldn't believe it."

"Sh-h-h!" said Miss Eavers, a bit teacherish. "You'll have to whisper."

"When I came through the door and saw you up there on the stage, I said, 'I'm right back in college and late for convocation.' You always played the Alma Mater."

"I saw you when you came in. From the corner of my eye. Can you imagine! I recognized you right away."

Weston was hurt. That she could have been free to notice any-body while he was singing, even out of the corner of her eye! And where had she been looking all the other times she accompanied him? Oh, he was very hurt.

Some quality in the season, in the spring air that was so much heavier this far south than what they had left in Stilton, liberated him. He felt he was dreaming, so he did not try to be polite. He certainly did not want to go along while Miss Eavers had lunch with this newspaperman she used to go to college with. He said he would go back to the hotel; he took advantage of an artist's right to weari-ness. He would go by himself, too. He had got around Jackson, after all, more than once; he knew that cities, like mechanical toys, never gave you any problem you couldn't figure out. He did not wave good-by when he parted from them on St. Charles Avenue, though he felt sure that she had turned and was looking back anxiously, had turned and turned again, until the man's big hand pressed her back below the shoulder blades and she moved on. "If anything should happen to him . . ." He did not hear her say it, but if she was saying anything, that was it—not "But I want to be with Weston." Just let a man who wasn't from Stilton come along and she became exactly like all the others *in* Stilton. Maybe she was stuck-up after all. He was tremendously successful in reaching the hotel.

The only thing he was not successful in doing was staying alone in his room. He had absolutely nothing to say to himself. If he didn't mind being alone at home, in Stilton, it was only because somebody was always wondering about him. He went down into the lobby and wandered about among the palms. He bought some chewing gum, some Life Savers, and a pack of cigarettes, just to see how it felt. He sat down at a desk in the writing room and wrote, on a picture post-card of the hotel, "I have slipped away from Miss Eavers and to-night I am going to some HOT SPOT. Oh, boy!"

Then he could not think of anybody to address it to. A year ago, there would have been three or four. But now they all knew the truth: He Sang. It was her fault that he couldn't make the card sound right. Oh, hadn't she been awful? She had cut him off from every-body except herself; then she had gone off and left him. He tore the card in two and went to buy a newspaper. He sat on the edge of a sofa, sinking down between the armrest and the big leather cushion. The paper was all about a world as troubled as his own, though much less concentrated.

"See anything good, sonny?"

There was a man sitting at the far end of the sofa from him. He spoke with a Northern accent and he was whacking away on a stick of gum.

"Want to read it?" Weston asked.

"No, thanks. Already seen it. Just making conversation. Killing time. You meeting someone?"

"I was meeting my teacher. But she won't come now."

"I thought boys always wanted to get away from their teachers. Maybe you're teacher's pet. Or maybe your teacher's a pet. Ha-ha!"

Weston had never actually heard anybody say "Ha-ha!" before. He had read it lots of times, mainly in the funny paper. This gave him confidence. "I'm just crazy about Miss Eavers," he confided mournfully. "Only she's so much older than I am that naturally we can't get married. She likes me a lot, though. She won't give anybody in town a date, but when I come to take a lesson, that makes her happy. I know it does. She says so. I can sing real well, see? Miss Eavers says if I'm not a genius, I'm the closest thing to it she's ever heard sing. We came down to New Orleans to audition me for this real famous boys' choir. Everybody at home just knows I'll get in. I can make people cry. Then, this morning, right while I was singing, this man her own age came in. She'd already met him a long time ago, and—" He found the next too grisly to relate.

"Now she's gone off with him," said the man, as easy as that. "So you didn't get the prize?"

"The what?"

"Did you win the money? Did they take you on? You know what I mean."

"Oh, the choir director. I don't know. He said for us all to come back this afternoon and they would tell us which ones. But I don't care about it. It was all on account of her I was doing so well."

"Look, now, kid, you can't look at it that way. You gotta get in there and win, see? By golly, maybe you *are* a genius. All you gotta do is get in there and show 'em."

"It would make her feel a lot worse if I didn't," said Weston, though it had never seriously entered his head that they wouldn't take him. Too many people had told him how good he was, some even from Out of the State. He was greatly in demand for civic clubs and had given a concert in Jackson. "However, I will," he added.

"That's the spirit."

The Northern man, who was waiting for space on an airplane to Denver, Colorado, took him to the hotel drugstore and bought him a sandwich and an ice-cream soda. Then he seemed to forget that Weston was there at all. Perhaps longer conversations than the one they had exchanged were unknown to him. He hauled himself back to attention by means of a tremendous yawn. "I think you're really stuck on this schoolteacher, kid."

Weston did not answer.

"Yes, sir, got a real old-timey crush. But she's perfectly right, you know—going off with that fellow her own age. Look at it from her standpoint. Anyway, you got to learn to be realistic. Y'know, if I've got a motto, that's it. *Be Real-isstic!*" The man leaned close to pronounce this thoroughly, and revealed very bad breath and tartar more than halfway down each tooth.

"Thank you for the chicken salad sandwich and chocolate ice-cream soda," said Weston. "I better hurry on back now. I hope you have a nice trip and all. Good-by."

He walked hastily out of the drugstore, bumping into stools. He wished he had not told the Yankee man anything. He had turned out to be just as bad as Mother and Daddy. Never mind. Weston *did* sing better than anybody else, and he had only to go to the auditorium and hear them say so.

When he rejoined Miss Eavers outside the auditorium that afternoon, she was alone. She looked as cool as ever, in her spring silk dress that had something like water lilies printed on it, and her new little curly straw hat. She had bought all this for their trip, just as he had not worn until now his blue-and-beige checked flannel coat and gabardine trousers. His underwear was new, too, if anybody wanted to know. Miss Eavers held her long spring wrap over her arm, but otherwise she looked just the same as when she walked away with the man she used to know in college. Maybe her forehead was a little rosy and her hair shaken a bit forward, as though by a breeze or agitation, but this might have resulted naturally from having said to the man, "I have to hurry on back now," and leaving him with a disappointed feeling, just as Weston had left the Yankee in the drugstore. At any rate, neither of them told each other about it.

"Hello, Miss Eavers."

"Weston." She touched his lapel, which he knew to be perfectly straight. "They say we can go in and have a seat. In a few minutes they'll tell us who has been chosen."

He held the door for her.

———

Going back, they had the lounge car to themselves most of the time. It got dark along about Picayune, and Weston tried to think of some way to make Miss Eavers not notice when they got to Stilton, so that they could go on to Chicago together in the coach with the soft gray rugs and the green easy chairs and the lamplight, and maybe never come home at all. She could change her printed silk dresses for black satin. It would be as simple as that. Better and better night clubs would pay them more and more. They would show the world.

The fact was that the director of the boys' choir had not chosen Weston after the audition; worse still, he had not mentioned him at all. But now that Weston and Miss Eavers had been through every detail of the audition four times and had decided that the director, if not actually crazy, knew nothing about his job, he began to feel drowsy and comforted, just as he felt after any other kind of misfortune—a bump on the head, for instance. In Chicago, they all came around to his dressing room to shake hands.

Presently, in the swaying twilight where they so comfortably were, he became aware that Miss Eavers was talking. He even knew that she had begun to speak after a sigh. "I had such a good time today. It was a wonderful surprise to see Frank. I hadn't seen him in years. He took me to such a nice place to eat. We had good food.

Later, we rode out along the lake in his car. We had a lot to talk about. I want to live like that. I want somebody nice, who knows where to go and what to order, to ask me out every now and then. I miss that kind of thing in Stilton." She sighed again, and the two sighs formed the proper setting around her words.

He leaned toward her. She must be told right away about Chicago. He finished splendidly, drawing out his wallet. "You didn't know, but Daddy gave me fifty dollars extra, to have in reserve in case we needed it. So we've got a start, see?"

"Weston." Her face had the expression he could always bring to ladies' faces in every audience by singing one of the old ones, like "Old Black Joe" or, more successful yet, "Danny Boy." He had even made her cry. She reached across and caught his hand. "Weston." She said it again.

He looked down at her hand on his; it might as well have been the chilly white touch of an aunt. She even patted. He knew then they would not be going to Chicago, let alone trying to sing in night clubs. They would get off when the train stopped at Stilton.

"We planned this trip for two months," he said, "and you went off with the first man that came along."

"Oh, Weston, do try to look at it from my standpoint."

"All this time you made me think I could sing better than anybody else in the world."

"I thought you could. You can! I still think you can!"

She was going to have answers to everything, and he would have to believe them. All that, too, came of her being older.

He left Miss Eavers and began to wander as freely as a chimpanzee on the loose through the dark, night-traveling train. When they reached the outskirts of Stilton, just at the point where he knew that the train broke over the rise and all the watchers at the station could see, he had found the right way to release the emergency brakes. Having previously read, on a printed card beside the handle, all the penalties that pertained to this action, along with the directions on how to perform it, he was not surprised at the wrath of the conductor, or at how more and more officials kept appearing from various distances along the train. When at last they pulled into the Stilton station, even the engineer came down from the engine to join the others, all on account of Weston. He could tell the engineer by the great big cuffs on his gloves.

The conductor hauled Weston down the steps by one arm. Not until then did Miss Eavers appear. "Where's yer husband, lady? Is his daddy here?" they all asked her, but she only shook her head in a dazed way, as though there had really been a wreck. She never did tell them that she wasn't anything but his music teacher.

Then everybody left off speaking to her, because Weston's father was there, saying, "I'm his daddy. You don't mean *he* did it? You don't say! You *don't* say!" He could not have been happier if he were making eggnog on Christmas morning. He lighted a cigar and offered others to the conductor and the engineer and the stationmaster, and cheerfully signed all the papers about how he would have to pay the twenty-five-dollar fine. After the train left, all the men who had come down to meet it hung around the station for a long time, talking. They all could tell about similar things they had done, and all of them said that when they were boys they had wanted to stop a train some way or other but never had. Mr. Robert Littleton had tried to flag one once, but it hadn't paid any attention. Finally, Daddy and Weston went home together.

"How did you stop her, son?" Daddy asked on the way home. "How did you reach the handle?"

"I stood on a suitcase in the car platform," Weston said.

It was quite some time before anybody thought to ask him how he had done in the music contest.

The next afternoon, Miss Eavers called to say that he had not come to his music lesson and that she thought he might be sick, but his mother said no, he wasn't sick, but he wasn't in the house right then and he would call her later. Weston was there, however. He was lying flat on his stomach on the glider on the side porch, listening to every word, but he was incapable, through something that seemed a good deal like laziness, of opening his mouth to say so.

———

In the following days, he rallied. He sang for the Kiwanis Club at Scott's Hotel on Friday, as scheduled, and, the next week, went with

Miss Eavers to Clinton, Mississippi, to give a program for the Junior Chamber of Commerce. But the weather kept getting hotter. School sped inexorably toward June. What had it all meant? Nothing could completely focus his attention. He took to playing the radio, listening to any old thing.

During May, some newspaperman came up all the way from New Orleans twice to see Miss Eavers; the postmistress said that letters were being exchanged. Nobody was surprised when she resigned from the school in June. The only question was how Weston would "take it"; to everybody's relief, Weston did not seem overly concerned. As a matter of fact, he believed himself to be secretly glad of it, though only in a minor way, like finishing typhoid shots. Whenever he had wanted to do something, it seemed he always had a lesson or a program. Naturally, he couldn't put *all* of his time on music.

So neither anybody nor anything warned him about the anguish that struck him like chills and fever one hot summer night when he awoke wondering, *How did she get home?*

Nobody had seen her leave the station that night they got back. (What would she have to say to men who swapped stories while they waited around to meet the train, or to railroad conductors, or to the engineer in his big dirty gloves?) She had simply withdrawn. He saw her now, carrying the suitcase through all the poor parts of Stilton, at last turning into the pretty street where she lived. Now she passed alone under the trees, sweet as an arrow, and started up the walk to her rooming house. The yard around her rested fragrant and damp with spring; the bridal wreath hung whiter than moonlight. The porch was wooden and hollow, but she did not make much noise crossing it, and in a bit of moonlight she saw where to fit her key. She turned sideways to get the suitcase through. Then she closed the door behind her. The house was big and dark and quiet; lots of people lived there, but he knew where her room was—right above the front porch. The street said nothing, all its length. In the yard, the flowers did not stir. No light came on.

From the town he watched—from just what point he did not know, but he knew he watched—and no light ever came on. She might as well have walked through the false front of a house and fallen a mile, the way they did in movie cartoons. She might as well have died on the stair.

Miss Eavers! Miss Eavers! Oh, wait, wait, wait, wait, wait!

On the hot, coverless July bed Weston lay, and a tongue of lightning flickered in the far sky.

FIRST DARK

When Tom Beavers started coming back to Richton, Mississippi, on weekends, after the war was over, everybody in town was surprised and pleased. They had never noticed him much before he paid them this compliment; now they could not say enough nice things. There was not much left in Richton for him to call family— just his aunt who had raised him, Miss Rita Beavers, old as God, ugly as sin, deaf as a post. So he must be fond of the town, they reasoned; certainly it was a pretty old place. Far too many young men had left it and never come back at all.

He would drive in every Friday night from Jackson, where he worked. All weekend, his Ford, dusty of flank, like a hard-ridden horse, would sit parked down the hill near Miss Rita's old wire front gate, which sagged from the top hinge and had worn a span in the ground. On Saturday morning, he would head for the drugstore, then the post office; then he would be observed walking here and there around the streets under the shade trees. It was as though he were looking for something.

He wore steel taps on his heels, and in the still the click of them on the sidewalks would sound across the big front lawns and all the way up to the porches of the houses, where two ladies might be sitting behind a row of ferns. They would identify him to one another, murmuring in their fine little voices, and say it was just too bad there was nothing here for young people. It was just a shame they didn't have one or two more old houses, here, for a Pilgrimage— look how Natchez had waked up.

One Saturday morning in early October, Tom Beavers sat at the counter in the drugstore and reminded Totsie Poteet, the drugstore clerk, of a ghost story. Did he remember the strange old man who used to appear to people who were coming into Richton along the Jackson road at twilight—what they called "first dark"?

"Sure I remember," said Totsie. "Old Cud'n Jimmy Wiltshire used to tell us about him every time we went 'possum hunting. I could see him plain as I can see you, the way he used to tell it. Tall, with a top hat on, yeah, and waiting in the weeds alongside the road ditch, so'n you couldn't tell if he wasn't taller than any mortal man could be, because you couldn't tell if he was standing down in the ditch or not. It would look like he just grew up out of the weeds. Then he'd signal to you."

"Them that stopped never saw anybody," said Tom Beavers, stirring his coffee. "There were lots of folks besides Mr. Jimmy that saw him."

"There was, let me see . . ." Totsie enumerated others—some men, some women, some known to drink, others who never touched a drop. There was no way to explain it. "There was that story the road gang told. Do you remember, or were you off at school? It was while they were straightening the road out to the highway—taking the curves out and building a new bridge. Anyway, they said that one night at quitting time, along in the winter and just about dark, this old guy signaled to some of 'em. They said they went over and he asked them to move a bulldozer they had left across the road, because he had a wagon back behind on a little dirt road, with a sick nigger girl in it. Had to get to the doctor and this was the only way. They claimed they knew didn't nobody live back there on that little old road, but niggers can come from anywhere. So they moved the bulldozer and cleared back a whole lot of other stuff, and waited and waited. Not only didn't no wagon ever come, but the man that had stopped them, he was gone, too. They was right shook up over it. You never heard that one?"

"No, I never did." Tom Beavers said this with his eyes looking up over his coffee cup, as though he sat behind a hand of cards. His lashes and brows were heavier than was ordinary, and worked as a veil might, to keep you away from knowing exactly what he was thinking.

"They said he was tall and had a hat on." The screen door flapped to announce a customer, but Totsie kept on talking. "But whether he was a white man or a real light-colored nigger they couldn't say. Some said one and some said another. I figured they'd been pulling on the jug a little earlier than usual. You know why? I never heard of *our* ghost *saying* nothing. Did you, Tom?"

He moved away on the last words, the way a clerk will, talking back over his shoulder and ahead of him to his new customer at the same time, as though he had two voices and two heads. "And what'll it be today, Miss Frances?"

The young woman standing at the counter had a prescription already out of her bag. She stood with it poised between her fingers, but her attention was drawn toward Tom Beavers, his coffee cup, and the conversation she had interrupted. She was a girl whom no ordinary description would fit. One would have to know first of all who she was: Frances Harvey. After that, it was all right for her to be a little odd-looking, with her reddish hair that curled back from her brow, her light eyes, and her high, pale temples. This is not the material for being pretty, but in Frances Harvey it was what could sometimes be beauty. Her family home was laden with history that nobody but the Harveys could remember. It would have been on a Pilgrimage if Richton had had one. Frances still lived in it, looking after an invalid mother.

"What were you-all talking about?" she wanted to know.

"About that ghost they used to tell about," said Totsie, holding out his hand for the prescription. "The one people used to see just outside of town, on the Jackson road."

"But why?" she demanded. "Why were you talking about him?"

"Tom, here—" the clerk began, but Tom Beavers interrupted him.

"I was asking because I was curious," he said. He had been studying her from the corner of his eye. Her face was beginning to show the wear of her mother's long illness, but that couldn't be called change. Changing was something she didn't seem to have done, her own style being the only one natural to her.

"I was asking," he went on, "because I saw him." He turned away from her somewhat too direct gaze and said to Totsie Poteet, whose mouth had fallen open, "It was where the new road runs close to the old road, and as far as I could tell he was right on the part of the old road where people always used to see him."

"But when?" Frances Harvey demanded.

"Last night," he told her. "Just around first dark. Driving home."

A wealth of quick feeling came up in her face. "So did I! Driving home from Jackson! I saw him, too!"

—

For some people, a liking for the same phonograph record or for Mayan archaeology is enough of an excuse to get together. Possibly, seeing the same ghost was no more than that. Anyway, a week later, on Saturday at first dark, Frances Harvey and Tom Beavers were sitting together in a car parked just off the highway, near the spot where they agreed the ghost had appeared. The season was that long, peculiar one between summer and fall, and there were so many crickets and tree frogs going full tilt in their periphery that their voices could hardly be distinguished from the background noises, though they both would have heard a single footfall in the grass. An edge of autumn was in the air at night, and Frances had put on a tweed jacket at the last minute, so the smell of moth balls was in the car, brisk and most unghostlike.

But Tom Beavers was not going to forget the value of the ghost, whether it put in an appearance or not. His questions led Frances into reminiscence.

"No, I never saw him before the other night," she admitted. "The Negroes used to talk in the kitchen, and Regina and I—you know my sister Regina—would sit there listening, scared to go and scared to stay. Then finally going to bed upstairs was no relief, either, because sometimes Aunt Henrietta was visiting us, and *she'd* seen it. Or if she wasn't visiting us, the front room next to us, where she stayed, would be empty, which was worse. There was no way to lock ourselves in, and besides, what was there to lock out? We'd lie all night like two sticks in bed, and shiver. Papa finally had to take a hand. He called us in and sat us down and said that the whole thing was easy to explain—it was all automobiles. What their headlights did with the dust and shadows out on the Jackson road. 'Oh, but Sammie and Jerry!' we said, with great big eyes, sitting side by side on the sofa, with our tennis shoes flat on the floor."

"Who were Sammie and Jerry?" asked Tom Beavers.

"Sammie was our cook. Jerry was her son, or husband, or something. Anyway, they certainly didn't have cars. Papa called them in. They were standing side by side by the bookcase, and Regina and I were on the sofa—four pairs of big eyes, and Papa pointing his finger. Papa said, 'Now, you made up these stories about ghosts, didn't you?' 'Yes, sir,' said Sammie. 'We made them up.' 'Yes, sir,' said Jerry. 'We sho did.' 'Well, then, you can just stop it,' Papa said. 'See how peaked these children look?' Sammie and Jerry were terribly polite to us for a week, and we got in the car and rode up and down the Jackson road at first dark to see if the headlights really did it. But we never saw anything. We didn't tell Papa, but headlights had nothing whatever to do with it."

"You had your own *car* then?" He couldn't believe it.

"Oh no!" She was emphatic. "We were too young for that. Too young to drive, really, but we did anyway."

She leaned over to let him give her cigarette a light, and saw his hand tremble. Was he afraid of the ghost or of her? She would have to stay away from talking family.

Frances remembered Tommy Beavers from her childhood— a small boy going home from school down a muddy side road alone, walking right down the middle of the road. His old aunt's house was at the bottom of a hill. It was damp there, and the yard was always muddy, with big fat chicken tracks all over it, like Egyptian writing. How did Frances know? She could not remember going there, ever. Miss Rita Beavers was said to order cold ham, mustard, bread, and condensed milk from the grocery store. "I doubt if that child ever has anything hot," Frances's mother had said once. He was always neatly dressed in the same knee pants, high socks, and checked shirt, and sat several rows ahead of Frances in study hall, right in the middle of his seat. He was three grades behind her; in those days, that much younger seemed very young indeed. What had happened to his parents? There was some story, but it was not terribly interesting, and, his people being of no importance, she had forgotten.

"I think it's past time for our ghost," she said. "He's never out so late at night."

"He gets hungry, like me," said Tom Beavers. "Are you hungry, Frances?"

They agreed on a highway restaurant where an orchestra played on weekends. Everyone went there now.

From the moment they drew up on the graveled entrance, cheerful lights and a blare of music chased the spooks from their heads. Tom Beavers ordered well and danced well, as it turned out. Wasn't there something she had heard about his being "smart"? By "smart," Southerners mean intellectual, and they say it in an almost condescending way, smart being what you are when you can't be anything else, but it is better, at least, than being nothing. Frances Harvey had been away enough not to look at things from a completely Southern point of view, and she was encouraged to discover that she and Tom had other things in common besides a ghost, though all stemming, perhaps, from the imagination it took to see one.

They agreed about books and favorite movies and longing to see more plays. She sighed that life in Richton was so confining, but he assured her that Jackson could be just as bad; *it* was getting to be like any Middle Western city, he said, while Richton at least had a sense of the past. This was the main reason, he went on, gaining confidence in the jumble of commonplace noises—dishes, music, and a couple of drinkers chattering behind them—that he had started coming back to Richton so often. He wanted to keep a connection with the past. He lived in a modern apartment, worked in a soundproof office—he could be in any city. But Richton was where he had been born and raised, and nothing could be more old-fashioned. Too many people seemed to have their lives cut in two. He was earnest in desiring that this should not happen to him.

"You'd better be careful," Frances said lightly. Her mood did not incline her to profound conversation. "There's more than one ghost in Richton. You may turn into one yourself, like the rest of us."

"It's the last thing I'd think of you," he was quick to assure her.

Had Tommy Beavers really said such a thing, in such a natural, charming way? Was Frances Harvey really so pleased? Not only was she pleased but, feeling warmly alive amid the music and small lights, she agreed with him. She could not have agreed with him more.

———

"I hear that Thomas Beavers has gotten to be a very attractive man," Frances Harvey's mother said unexpectedly one afternoon.

Frances had been reading aloud—Jane Austen this time. Theirs was one house where the leather-bound sets were actually read. In Jane Austen, men and women seesawed back and forth for two or three hundred pages until they struck a point of balance; then they got married. She had just put aside the book, at the end of a chapter, and risen to lower the shade against the slant of afternoon sun. "Or so Cud'n Jennie and Mrs. Giles Antley and Miss Fannie Stapleton have been coming and telling you," she said.

"People talk, of course, but the consensus is favorable," Mrs. Harvey said. "Wonders never cease; his mother ran away with a brush salesman. But nobody can make out what he's up to, coming back to Richton."

"Does he have to be 'up to' anything?" Frances asked.

"Men are always up to something," said the old lady at once. She added, more slowly, "In Thomas's case, maybe it isn't anything it oughtn't to be. They say he reads a lot. He may just have taken up with some sort of idea."

Frances stole a long glance at her mother's face on the pillow. Age and illness had reduced the image of Mrs. Harvey to a kind of caricature, centered on a mouth that Frances could not help comparing to that of a fish. There was a tension around its rim, as though it were outlined in bone, and the underlip even stuck out a little. The mouth ate, it took medicine, it asked for things, it gasped when breath was short, it commented. But when it commented, it ceased to be just a mouth and became part of Mrs. Harvey, that witty tyrant with the infallible memory for the right detail, who was at her terrible best about men.

"And what could he be thinking of?" she was wont to inquire when some man had acted foolishly. No one could ever defend accurately the man in question, and the only conclusion was Mrs. Harvey's; namely, that he wasn't thinking, if, indeed, he could. Although she had never been a belle, never a flirt, her popularity with men was always formidable. She would be observed talking marathons with one in a corner, and could you ever be sure, when they both burst into laughter, that they had not just exchanged the most shocking stories? "Of course, *he*—" she would begin later, back with the family, and the masculinity that had just been encouraged to strut and preen a little was quickly shown up as idiotic. Perhaps Mrs. Harvey hoped by this method to train her daughters away from a lot of sentimental nonsense that was their birthright as pretty Southern girls in a house with a lawn that moonlight fell on and that was often lit also by Japanese lanterns hung for parties. "Oh, he's not like that, Mama!" the little girls would cry. They were already alert for heroes who would ride up and cart them off. "Well, then, you watch," she would say. Sure enough, if you watched, she would be right.

Mrs. Harvey's younger daughter, Regina, was a credit to her mother's long campaign; she married well. The old lady, however, never tired of pointing out behind her son-in-law's back that his fondness for money was ill-concealed, that he had the longest feet she'd ever seen, and that he sometimes made grammatical errors.

Her elder daughter, Frances, on a trip to Europe, fell in love, alas! The gentleman was of French extraction but Swiss citizenship, and Frances did not marry him, because he was already married—that much filtered back to Richton. In response to a cable, she had returned home one hot July in time to witness her father's wasted face and last weeks of life. That same September, the war began. When peace came, Richton wanted to know if Frances Harvey would go back to Europe. Certain subtly complicated European matters, little understood in Richton, seemed to be obstructing Romance; one of them was probably named Money. Meanwhile, Frances's mother took to bed, in what was generally known to be her last illness.

So no one crossed the ocean, but eventually Tom Beavers came up to Mrs. Harvey's room one afternoon, to tea.

Though almost all her other faculties were seriously impaired, in ear and tongue Mrs. Harvey was as sound as a young beagle, and she could still weave a more interesting conversation than most people who go about every day and look at the world. She was of the old school of Southern lady talkers; she vexed you with no ideas, she tried to protect you from even a moment of silence. In the old days, when a bright company filled the downstairs rooms, she could keep the ball rolling amongst a crowd. Everyone—all the men especially—got their word in, but the flow of things came back to her. If one of those twenty-minutes-to-or-after silences fell— and even with her they did occur—people would turn and look at her daughter Frances. "And what do you think?" some kind-eyed gentleman would ask. Frances did not credit that she had the sort of face people would turn to, and so did not know how to take advantage of it. What did she think? Well, to answer that honestly took a moment of reflection—a fatal moment, it always turned out. Her mother would be up instructing the maid, offering someone an ash-tray or another goody, or remarking outright, "Frances is so timid. She never says a word."

Tom Beavers stayed not only past teatime that day but for a drink as well. Mrs. Harvey was induced to take a glass of sherry, and now her bed became her enormous throne. Her keenest suffering as an invalid was occasioned by the absence of men. "What is a house without a man in it?" she would often cry. From her eagerness to be charming to Frances's guest that afternoon, it seemed that she would have married Tom Beavers herself if he had asked her. The amber liquid set in her small four-sided glass glowed like a jewel, and her diamond flashed; she had put on her best ring for the company. What a pity no longer to show her ankle, that delicious bone, so remarkably slender for so ample a frame.

Since the time had flown so, they all agreed enthusiastically that Tom should wait downstairs while Frances got ready to go out to dinner with him. He was hardly past the stair landing before the old lady was seized by such a fit of coughing that she could hardly speak. "It's been—it's been too much—too *much* for me!" she gasped out.

But after Frances had found the proper sedative for her, she was calmed, and insisted on having her say.

"Thomas Beavers has a good job with an insurance company in Jackson," she informed her daughter, as though Frances were incapable of finding out anything for herself. "He makes a good appearance. He is the kind of man"—she paused—"who would value a wife of good family." She stopped, panting for breath. It was this complimenting a man behind his back that was too much for her—as much out of character, and hence as much of a strain, as if she had got out of bed and tried to tap-dance.

"Heavens, Mama," Frances said, and almost giggled.

At this, the old lady, thinking the girl had made light of her suitor, half screamed at her, "Don't be so critical, Frances! You can't be so critical of men!" and fell into an even more terrible spasm of coughing. Frances had to lift her from the pillow and hold her straight until the fit passed and her breath returned. Then Mrs. Harvey's old, dry, crooked, ineradicably feminine hand was laid on her daughter's arm, and when she spoke again she shook the arm to emphasize her words.

"When your father knew he didn't have long to live," she whispered, "we discussed whether to send for you or not. You know you were his favorite, Frances. 'Suppose our girl is happy over there,' he said. 'I wouldn't want to bring her back on my account.' I said you had to have the right to choose whether to come back or not. You'd never forgive us, I said, if you didn't have the right to choose."

Frances could visualize this very conversation taking place between her parents; she could see them, decorous and serious, talking over the fact of his approaching death as though it were a piece of property for agreeable disposition in the family. She could never remember him without thinking, with a smile, how he used to come home on Sunday from church (he being the only one of them who went) and how, immediately after hanging his hat and cane in the hall, he would say, "Let all things proceed in orderly progression to their final confusion. How long before dinner?" No, she had had to come home. Some humor had always existed between them—her father and her—and humor, of all things, cannot be betrayed.

"I meant to go back," said Frances now. "But there was the war. At first I kept waiting for it to be over. I still wake up at night sometimes thinking, I wonder how much longer before the war will be over. And then—" She stopped short. For the fact was that her lover had been married to somebody else, and her mother was the very person capable of pointing that out to her. Even in the old lady's present silence she heard the unspoken thought, and got up nervously from the bed, loosing herself from the hand on her arm, smoothing her reddish hair where it was inclined to straggle. "And then he wrote me that he had gone back to his wife. Her family and his had always been close, and the war brought them back together. This was in Switzerland—naturally, he couldn't stay on in Paris during the war. There were the children, too—all of them were Catholic. Oh, I do understand how it happened."

Mrs. Harvey turned her head impatiently on the pillow. She dabbed at her moist upper lip with a crumpled linen handkerchief; her diamond flashed once in motion. "War, religion, wife, children—yes. But men do what they want to."

Could anyone make Frances as angry as her mother could? "Believe what you like then! You always know so much better than I do. *You* would have managed things somehow. Oh, you would have had your way!"

"Frances," said Mrs. Harvey, "I'm an old woman." The hand holding the handkerchief fell wearily, and her eyelids dropped shut. "If you should want to marry Thomas Beavers and bring him here, I will accept it. There will be no distinctions. Next, I suppose, we will be having his old deaf aunt for tea. I hope she has a hearing aid. I haven't got the strength to holler at her."

"I don't think any of these plans are necessary, Mama."

The eyelids slowly lifted. "None?"

"None."

Mrs. Harvey's breathing was as audible as a voice. She spoke, at last, without scorn, honestly. "I cannot bear the thought of leaving you alone. You, nor the house, nor your place in it—alone. I foresaw Tom Beavers here! What has he got that's better than you and this place? I knew he would come!"

Terrible as her mother's meanness was, it was not half so terrible as her love. Answering nothing, explaining nothing, Frances stood without giving in. She trembled, and tears ran down her cheeks. The two women looked at each other helplessly across the darkening room.

———

In the car, later that night, Tom Beavers asked, "Is your mother trying to get rid of me?" They had passed an unsatisfactory evening, and he was not going away without knowing why.

"No, it's just the other way around," said Frances, in her candid way. "She wants you so much she'd like to eat you up. She wants you in the house. Couldn't you tell?"

"She once chased me out of the yard," he recalled.

"Not really!"

They turned into Harvey Street (that was actually the name of it), and when he had drawn the car up before the dark front steps, he related the incident. He told her that Mrs. Harvey had been standing just there in the yard, talking to some visitor who was leaving by inches, the way ladies used to—ten minutes' more talk for every forward step. He, a boy not more than nine, had been crossing a corner of the lawn where a faint path had already been worn; he had had nothing to do with wearing the path and had taken it quite innocently and openly. "You, boy!" Mrs. Harvey's fan was an enormous painted thing. She had furled it with a clack so loud he could still hear it. "You don't cut through my yard again! Now, you stop where you are and you go all the way back around by the walk, and don't you ever do that again." He went back and all the way around. She was fanning comfortably as he passed. "Old Miss Rita Beavers' nephew," he heard her say, and though he did not speak of it now to Frances, Mrs. Harvey's rich tone had been as stuffed with wickedness as a fruitcake with goodies. In it you could have found so many things: that, of course, he didn't know any better, that he was poor, that she knew his first name but would not deign to mention it, that she meant him to understand all this and more. Her fan was probably still somewhere in the house, he reflected. If he ever opened the wrong door, it might fall from above and brain him. It seemed impossible that nowadays he could even have the chance to open the wrong door in the Harvey house. With its graceful rooms and big lawn, its camellias and magnolia trees, the house had been one of the enchanted castles of his childhood, and Frances and Regina Harvey had been two princesses running about the lawn one Saturday morning drying their hair with big white towels and not noticing when he passed.

There was a strong wind that evening. On the way home, Frances and Tom had noticed how the night was streaming, but whether with mist or dust or the smoke from some far-off fire in the dry winter woods they could not tell. As they stood on the sidewalk, the clouds raced over them, and moonlight now and again came through. A limb rubbed against a high cornice. Inside the screened area of the porch, the swing jangled in its iron chains. Frances's coat blew about her, and her hair blew. She felt herself to be no different from anything there that the wind was blowing on, her happiness of no relevance in the dark torrent of nature.

"I can't leave her, Tom. But I can't ask you to live with her, either. Of all the horrible ideas! She'd make demands, take all my time, laugh at you behind your back—she has to run everything. You'd hate me in a week."

He did not try to pretty up the picture, because he had a feeling that it was all too accurate. Now, obviously, was the time she should go on to say there was no good his waiting around through the years for her. But hearts are not noted for practicality, and Frances stood with her hair blowing, her hands stuck in her coat pockets, and did not go on to say anything. Tom pulled her close to him—in, as it were, out of the wind.

"I'll be coming by next weekend, just like I've been doing. And the next one, too," he said. "We'll just leave it that way, if it's O.K. with you."

"Oh yes, it is, Tom!" Never so satisfied to be weak, she kissed him and ran inside.

He stood watching on the walk until her light flashed on. Well, he had got what he was looking for; a connection with the past, he had said. It was right upstairs, a splendid old mass of dictatorial female flesh, thinking about him. Well, they could go on, he and Frances, sitting on either side of a sickbed, drinking tea and sipping sherry with streaks of gray broadening on their brows, while the familiar seasons came and went. So he thought. Like Frances, he believed that the old lady had a stranglehold on life.

Suddenly, in March, Mrs. Harvey died.

———

A heavy spring funeral, with lots of roses and other scented flowers in the house, is the worst kind of all. There is something so recklessly fecund about a south Mississippi spring that death becomes just another word in the dictionary, along with swarms of others, and even so pure and white a thing as a gardenia has too heavy a scent and may suggest decay. Mrs. Harvey, amid such odors, sank to rest with a determined pomp, surrounded by admiring eyes.

While Tom Beavers did not "sit with the family" at this time, he was often observed with the Harveys, and there was whispered speculation among those who were at the church and the cemetery that the Harvey house might soon come into new hands, "after a decent interval." No one would undertake to judge for a Harvey how long an interval was decent.

Frances suffered from insomnia in the weeks that followed, and at night she wandered about the spring-swollen air of the old house, smelling now spring and now death. "Let all things proceed in orderly progression to their final confusion." She had always thought that the final confusion referred to death, but now she began to think that it could happen any time; that final confusion, having found the door ajar, could come into a house and show no inclination to leave. The worrisome thing, the thing it all came back to, was her mother's clothes. They were numerous, expensive, and famous, and Mrs. Harvey had never discarded any of them. If you opened a closet door, hatboxes as big as crates towered above your head. The shiny black trim of a great shawl stuck out of a wardrobe door just below the lock. Beneath the lid of a cedar chest, the bright eyes of a tippet were ready to twinkle at you. And the jewels! Frances's sister had restrained her from burying them all on their mother, and had even gone off with a wad of them tangled up like fishing tackle in an envelope, on the ground of promises made now and again in the course of the years.

("Regina," said Frances, "what else were you two talking about besides jewelry?" "I don't remember," said Regina, getting mad.

"Frances makes me so mad," said Regina to her husband as they were driving home. "I guess I can love Mama and jewelry, too. Mama certainly loved *us* and jewelry, too.")

One afternoon, Frances went out to the cemetery to take two wreaths sent by somebody who had "just heard." She drove out along the winding cemetery road, stopping the car a good distance before she reached the gate, in order to walk through the woods. The dogwood was beautiful that year. She saw a field where a house used to stand but had burned down; its cedar trees remained, and two bushes of bridal wreath marked where the front gate had swung. She stopped to admire the clusters of white bloom massing up through the young, feathery leaf and stronger now than the leaf itself. In the woods, the redbud was a smoke along shadowy ridges, and the dogwood drifted in layers, like snow suspended to give you all the time you needed to wonder at it. But why, she wondered, do they call it bridal *wreath*? It's not a wreath but a little bouquet. Wreaths are for funerals, anyway. As if to prove it, she looked down at the two she held, one in each hand. She walked on, and such complete desolation came over her that it was more of a wonder than anything in the woods—more, even, than death.

As she returned to the car from the two parallel graves, she met a thin, elderly, very light-skinned Negro man in the road. He inquired if she would mind moving her car so that he could pass. He said that there was a sick colored girl in his wagon, whom he was driving in to the doctor. He pointed out politely that she had left her car right in the middle of the road. "Oh, I'm terribly sorry," said Frances, and hurried off toward the car.

That night, reading late in bed, she thought, I could have given her a ride into town. No wonder they talk about us up North. A mile into town in a wagon! She might have been having a baby. She became conscience-stricken about it—foolishly so, she realized, but if you start worrying about something in a house like the one Frances Harvey lived in, in the dead of night, alone, you will go on worrying about it until dawn. She was out of sleeping pills.

She remembered having bought a fresh box of sedatives for her mother the day before she died. She got up and went into her mother's closed room, where the bed had been dismantled for airing, its wooden parts propped along the walls. On the closet shelf she found the shoe box into which she had packed away the familiar articles of the bedside table. Inside she found the small enameled-cardboard box, with the date and prescription inked on the cover in Totsie Poteet's somewhat prissy handwriting, but the box was empty. She was surprised, for she realized that her mother could have used only one or two of the pills. Frances was so determined to get some sleep that she searched the entire little store of things in the shoe box quite heartlessly, but there were no pills. She returned to her room and tried to read, but could not, and so smoked instead and stared out at the dawn-blackening sky. The house sighed. She could not take her mind off the Negro girl. If she died . . . When it was light, she dressed and got into the car.

In town, the postman was unlocking the post office to sort the early mail. "I declare," he said to the rural mail carrier who arrived a few minutes later, "Miss Frances Harvey is driving herself crazy. Going back out yonder to the cemetery, and it not seven o'clock in the morning."

"Aw," said the rural deliveryman skeptically, looking at the empty road.

"That's right. I was here and seen her. You wait there, you'll see her come back. She'll drive herself nuts. Them old maids like that, left in them old houses—crazy and sweet, or crazy and mean, or just plain crazy. They just ain't locked up like them that's down in the asylum. That's the only difference."

"Miss Frances Harvey ain't no more than thirty-two, -three years old."

"Then she's just got more time to get crazier in. You'll see."

—

That day was Friday, and Tom Beavers, back from Jackson, came up Frances Harvey's sidewalk, as usual, at exactly a quarter past seven in the evening. Frances was not "going out" yet, and Regina had telephoned her long distance to say that "in all probability" she should not be receiving gentlemen "in." "What would Mama say?" Regina asked. Frances said she didn't know, which was not true, and went right on cooking dinners for Tom every weekend.

In the dining room that night, she sat across one corner of the long table from Tom. The useless length of polished cherry stretched away from them into the shadows as sadly as a road. Her plate pushed back, her chin resting on one palm, Frances stirred her coffee and said, "I don't know what on earth to do with all of Mama's clothes. I can't give them away, I can't sell them, I can't burn them, and the attic is full already. What can I do?"

"You look better tonight," said Tom.

"I slept," said Frances. "I slept and slept. From early this morning until just 'while ago. I never slept so well."

Then she told him about the Negro near the cemetery the previous afternoon, and how she had driven back out there as soon as dawn came, and found him again. He had been walking across the open field near the remains of the house that had burned down. There was no path to him from her, and she had hurried across ground uneven from old plowing and covered with the kind of small, tender grass it takes a very skillful mule to crop. "Wait!" she had cried. "Please wait!" The Negro had stopped and waited for her to reach him. "Your daughter?" she asked, out of breath.

"Daughter?" he repeated.

"The colored girl that was in the wagon yesterday. She was sick, you said, so I wondered. I could have taken her to town in the car, but I just didn't think. I wanted to know, how is she? Is she very sick?"

He had removed his old felt nigger hat as she approached him. "She a whole lot better, Miss Frances. She going to be all right now." Then he smiled at her. He did not say thank you, or anything more. Frances turned and walked back to the road and the car. And exactly as though the recovery of the Negro girl in the wagon had been her own recovery, she felt the return of a quiet breath and a steady pulse, and sensed the blessed stirring of a morning breeze. Up in her room, she had barely time to draw an old quilt over her before she fell asleep.

"When I woke, I knew about Mama," she said now to Tom. By the deepened intensity of her voice and eyes, it was plain that this was the important part. "It isn't right to say I *knew*," she went on, "because I had known all the time—ever since last night. I just realized it, that's all. I realized she had killed herself. It had to be that."

He listened soberly through the story about the box of sedatives. "But why?" he asked her. "It maybe looks that way, but what would be her reason for doing it?"

"Well, you see—" Frances said, and stopped.

Tom Beavers talked quietly on. "She didn't suffer. With what she had, she could have lived five, ten, who knows how many years. She was well cared for. Not hard up, I wouldn't say. Why?"

The pressure of his questioning could be insistent, and her trust in him, even if he was nobody but old Miss Rita Beavers' nephew, was well-nigh complete. "Because of you and me," she said, finally. "I'm certain of it, Tom. She didn't want to stand in our way. She never knew how to express love, you see." Frances controlled herself with an effort.

He did not reply, but sat industriously balancing a match folder on the tines of an unused serving fork. Anyone who has passed a lonely childhood in the company of an old deaf aunt is not inclined to doubt things hastily, and Tom Beavers would not have said he disbelieved anything Frances had told him. In fact, it seemed only too real to him. Almost before his eyes, that imperial, practical old hand went fumbling for the pills in the dark. But there had been much more to it than just love, he reflected. Bitterness, too, and pride, and control. And humor, perhaps, and the memory of a frightened little boy chased out of the yard by a twitch of her fan. Being invited to tea was one thing; suicide was quite another. Times had certainly changed, he thought.

But, of course, he could not say that he believed it, either. There was only Frances to go by. The match folder came to balance and rested on the tines. He glanced up at her, and a chill walked up his spine, for she was too serene. Cheek on palm, a lock of reddish hair fallen forward, she was staring at nothing with the absorbed silence of a child, or of a sweet, silver-haired old lady engaged in memory. Soon he might find that more and more of her was vanishing beneath this placid surface.

He himself did not know what he had seen that Friday evening so many months ago—what the figure had been that stood forward from the roadside at the tilt of the curve and urgently waved an arm to him. By the time he had braked and backed, the man had disappeared. Maybe it had been somebody drunk (for Richton had plenty of those to offer), walking it off in the cool of the woods at first dark. No such doubts had occurred to Frances. And what if he told her now the story Totsie had related of the road gang and the sick Negro girl in the wagon? Another labyrinth would open before her; she would never get out.

In Richton, the door to the past was always wide open, and what came in through it and went out of it had made people "different." But it scarcely ever happens, even in Richton, that one is able to see the precise moment when fact becomes faith, when life turns into legend, and people start to bend their finest loyalties to make themselves bemused custodians of the grave. Tom Beavers saw that moment now, in the profile of this dreaming girl, and he knew there was no time to lose.

He dropped the match folder into his coat pocket. "I think we should be leaving, Frances."

"Oh well, I don't know about going out yet," she said. "People criticize you so. Regina even had the nerve to telephone. Word had got all the way to her that you came here to have supper with me and we were alone in the house. When I tell the maid I want biscuits made up for two people, she looks like 'What would yo' mama say?'"

"I mean," he said, "I think it's time we left for good."

"And never came back?" It was exactly like Frances to balk at going to a movie but seriously consider an elopement.

"Well, never is a long time. I like to see about Aunt Rita every once in a great while. She can't remember from one time to the next whether it's two days or two years since I last came."

She glanced about the walls and at the furniture, the pictures, and the silver. "But I thought you would want to live here, Tom. It never occurred to me. I know it never occurred to Mama . . . This house . . . It can't be just left."

"It's a fine old house," he agreed. "But what would you do with all your mother's clothes?"

Her freckled hand remained beside the porcelain cup for what seemed a long time. He waited and made no move toward her; he felt her uncertainty keenly, but he believed that some people should not be startled out of a spell.

"It's just as you said," he went on, finally. "You can't give them away, you can't sell them, you can't burn them, and you can't put them in the attic, because the attic is full already. So what are you going to do?"

Between them, the single candle flame achieved a silent altitude. Then, politely, as on any other night, though shaking back her hair in a decided way, she said, "Just let me get my coat, Tom."

She locked the door when they left, and put the key under the mat—a last obsequy to the house. Their hearts were bounding ahead faster than they could walk down the sidewalk or drive off in the car, and, mindful, perhaps, of what happened to people who did, they did not look back.

Had they done so, they would have seen that the Harvey house was more beautiful than ever. All unconscious of its rejection by so mere a person as Tom Beavers, it seemed, instead, to have got rid of what did not suit it, to be free, at last, to enter with abandon the land of mourning and shadows and memory.

A SOUTHERN LANDSCAPE

_____

If you're like me and sometimes turn through the paper reading anything and everything because you're too lazy to get up and do what you ought to be doing, then you already know about my home town. There's a church there that has a gilded hand on the steeple, with the finger pointing to Heaven. The hand looks normal size, but it's really as big as a Ford car. At least, that's what they used to say in those little cartoon squares in the newspaper, full of sketches and exclamation points—"Strange As It Seems," "This Curious World," or Ripley's "Believe It or Not." Along with carnivorous tropical flowers, the Rosetta stone, and the cheerful information that the entire human race could be packed into a box a mile square and dumped into Grand Canyon, there it would be every so often, that old Presbyterian hand the size of a Ford car. It made me feel right in touch with the universe to see it in the paper—something it never did accomplish all by itself. I haven't seen anything about it recently, but then, Ford cars have got bigger, and, come to think of it, maybe they don't even print those cartoons any more. The name of the town, in case you're trying your best to remember and can't, is Port Claiborne, Mississippi. Not that I'm *from* there; I'm from *near* there.

Coming down the highway from Vicksburg, you come to Port Claiborne, and then to get to our house you turn off to the right on State Highway No. 202 and follow along the prettiest road. It's just about the way it always was—worn deep down like a tunnel and thick with shade in summer. In spring, it's so full of sweet heavy odors, they make you drunk, you can't think of anything—

you feel you will faint or go right out of yourself. In fall, there is
the rustle of leaves under your tires and the smell of them, all sad
and Indian-like. Then in the winter, there are only dust and bare
limbs, and mud when it rains, and everything is like an old dirt-
dauber's nest up in the corner. Well, any season, you go twisting
along this tunnel for a mile or so, then the road breaks down into
a flat open run toward a wooden bridge that spans a swampy creek
bottom. Tall trees grow up out of the bottom—willow and cypress, gum and sycamore—and there is a jungle of brush and
vines—kudzu, Jackson vine, Spanish moss, grapevine, Virginia
creeper, and honeysuckle—looping, climbing, and festooning the
trees, and harboring every sort of snake and varmint underneath.
The wooden bridge clatters when you cross, and down far below
you can see water, lying still, not a good step wide. One bank is
grassy and the other is a slant of ribbed white sand.

Then you're going to have to stop and ask somebody. Just say,
"Can you tell me where to turn to get to the Summerall place?"
Everybody knows us. Not that we *are* anybody—I don't mean that.
It's just that we've been there forever. When you find the right
road, you go right on up through a little wood of oaks, then across a
field, across a cattle gap, and you're there. The house is nothing
special, just a one-gable affair with a bay window and a front
porch—the kind they built back around fifty or sixty years ago. The
shrubs around the porch and the privet hedge around the bay window were all grown up too high the last time I was there. They
ought to be kept trimmed down. The yard is a nice flat one, not
much for growing grass but wonderful for shooting marbles. There
were always two or three marble holes out near the pecan trees
where I used to play with the colored children.

Benjy Hamilton swore he twisted his ankle in one of those same
marble holes once when he came to pick me up for something my
senior year in high school. For all I know, they're still there, but
Benjy was more than likely drunk and so would hardly have needed
a marble hole for an excuse to fall down. Once, before we got the
cattle gap, he couldn't open the gate, and fell on the barbed wire
trying to cross the fence. I had to pick him out, thread at a time, he

was so tangled up. Mama said, "What were you two doing out at the gate so long last night?" "Oh, nothing, just talking," I said. She thought for the longest time that Benjy Hamilton was the nicest boy that ever walked the earth. No matter how drunk he was, the presence of an innocent lady like Mama, who said *"Drinking?"* in the same tone of voice she would have said *"Murder?"* would bring him around faster than any number of needle showers, massages, ice packs, prairie oysters, or quick dips in December off the northern bank of Lake Ontario. He would straighten up and smile and say, "You made any more peach pickle lately, Miss Sadie?" (He could even say "peach pickle.") And she'd say no, but that there was always some of the old for him whenever he wanted any. And he'd say that was just the sweetest thing he'd ever heard of, but she didn't know what she was promising—anything as good as her peach pickle ought to be guarded like gold. And she'd say, well, for most anybody else she'd think twice before she offered any. And he'd say, if only everybody was as sweet to him as she was. . . . And they'd go on together like that till you'd think that all creation had ground and wound itself down through the vistas of eternity to bring the two of them face to face for exchanging compliments over peach pickle. Then I would put my arm in his so it would look like he was helping me down the porch steps out of the reflexes of his gentlemanly upbringing, and off we'd go.

It didn't happen all the time, like I've made it sound. In fact, it was only a few times when I was in school that I went anywhere with Benjy Hamilton. Benjy isn't his name, either; it's Foster. I sometimes call him "Benjy" to myself, after a big overgrown thirty-three-year-old idiot in *The Sound and the Fury,* by William Faulkner. Not that Foster was so big or overgrown, or even thirty-three years old, back then; but he certainly did behave like an idiot.

I won this prize, see, for writing a paper on the siege of Vicksburg. It was for the United Daughters of the Confederacy's annual contest, and mine was judged the best in the state. So Foster Hamilton came all the way over to the schoolhouse and got me out of class—I felt terribly important—just to "interview" me. He had just graduated from the university and had a job on the paper in Port

Claiborne—that was before he started work for the *Times-Picayune* in New Orleans. We went into an empty classroom and sat down.

He leaned over some blank sheets of coarse-grained paper and scribbled things down with a thick-leaded pencil. I was sitting in the next seat; it was a long bench divided by a number of writing arms, which was why they said that cheating was so prevalent in our school—you could just cheat without meaning to. They kept trying to raise the money for regular desks in every classroom, so as to improve morals. Anyway, I couldn't help seeing what he was writing down, so I said, "'Marilee' is all one word, and with an 'i,' not a 'y.' 'Summerall' is spelled just like it sounds." "Are you a senior?" he asked. "Just a junior," I said. He wore horn-rimmed glasses; that was back before everybody wore them. I thought they looked unusual and very distinguished. Also, I had noticed his shoulders when he went over to let the window down. I thought they were distinguished, too, if a little bit bony. "What is your ambition?" he asked me. "I hope to go to college year after next," I said. "I intend to wait until my junior year in college to choose a career."

He kept looking down at his paper while he wrote, and when he finally looked up at me I was disappointed to see why he hadn't done it before. The reason was, he couldn't keep a straight face. It had happened before that people broke out laughing just when I was being my most earnest and sincere. It must have been what I said, because I don't think I *look* funny. I guess I don't look like much of any one thing. When I see myself in the mirror, no adjective springs right to mind, unless it's "average." I am medium height, I am average weight, I buy "natural"-colored face powder and "medium"-colored lipstick. But I must say for myself, before this goes too far, that every once in a great while I look Just Right. I've never found the combination for making this happen, and no amount of reading the make-up articles in the magazines they have at the beauty parlor will do any good. But sometimes it happens anyway, with no more than soap and water, powder, lipstick, and a damp hairbrush.

———

My interview took place in the spring, when we were practicing for the senior play every night. Though a junior, I was in it because they always got me, after the eighth grade, to take parts in things. Those of us that lived out in the country Mrs. Arrington would take back home in her car after rehearsal. One night, we went over from the school to get a Coca-Cola before the drugstore closed, and there was Foster Hamilton. He had done a real nice article—what Mama called a "write-up." It was when he was about to walk out that he noticed me and said, "Hey." I said "Hey" back, and since he just stood there, I said, "Thank you for the write-up in the paper."

"Oh, that's all right," he said, not really listening. He wasn't laughing this time. "Are you going home?" he said.

"We are after 'while," I said. "Mrs. Arrington takes us home in her car."

"Why don't you let me take you home?" he said. "It might—it might save Mrs. Arrington an extra trip."

"Well," I said, "I guess I could ask her."

So I went to Mrs. Arrington and said, "Mrs. Arrington, Foster Hamilton said he would be glad to drive me home." She hesitated so long that I put in, "He says it might save you an extra trip." So finally she said, "Well, all right, Marilee." She told Foster to drive carefully. I could tell she was uneasy, but then, my family were known as real good people, very strict, and of course she didn't want them to feel she hadn't done the right thing.

That was the most wonderful night. I'll never forget it. It was full of spring, all restlessness and sweet smells. It was radiant, it was warm, it was serene. It was all the things you want to call it, but no word would ever be the right one, nor any ten words, either. When we got close to our turnoff, after the bridge, I said, "The next road is ours," but Foster drove right on past. I knew where he was going. He was going to Windsor.

Windsor is this big colonial mansion built back before the Civil War. It burned down during the 1890s sometime, but there were still twenty-five or more Corinthian columns, standing on a big open space of ground that is a pasture now, with cows and mules and calves grazing in it. The columns are enormously high and you can see some of the iron grillwork railing for the second-story gallery clinging halfway up. Vines cling to the fluted white plaster surfaces, and in some places the plaster has crumbled away, showing the brick underneath. Little trees grow up out of the tops of columns, and chickens have their dust holes among the rubble. Just down the fall of the ground beyond the ruin, there are some Negro houses. A path goes down to them.

It is this ignorant way that the hand of Nature creeps back over Windsor that makes me afraid. I'd rather there'd be ghosts there, but there aren't. Just some old story about lost jewelry that every once in a while sends somebody poking around in all the trash. Still it is magnificent, and people have compared it to the Parthenon and so on and so on, and even if it makes me feel this undertone of horror, I'm always ready to go and look at it again. When all of it was standing, back in the old days, it was higher even than the columns, and had a cupola, too. You could see the cupola from the river, they say, and the story went that Mark Twain used it to steer by. I've read that book since, *Life on the Mississippi,* and it seems he used everything else to steer by, too—crawfish mounds, old rowboats stuck in the mud, the tassels on somebody's corn patch, and every stump and stob from New Orleans to Cairo, Illinois. But it does kind of connect you up with something to know that Windsor was there, too, like seeing the Presbyterian hand in the newspaper. Some people would say at this point, "Small world," but it isn't a small world. It's an enormous world, bigger than you can imagine, but it's all connected up. What Nature does to Windsor it does to everything, including you and me—there's the horror.

But that night with Foster Hamilton, I wasn't thinking any such doleful thoughts, and though Windsor can be a pretty scary-looking sight by moonlight, it didn't scare me then. I could have got right out of the car, alone, and walked all around among the columns, and whatever I heard walking away through the weeds would not have scared me, either. We sat there, Foster and I, and never said a word. Then, after some time, he turned the car around and took the road back. Before we got to my house, though, he stopped the car by the roadside and kissed me. He held my face up to his, but outside that he didn't touch me. I had never been kissed in any deliberate and accomplished way before, and driving out to Windsor in that accidental way, the whole sweetness of the spring night, the innocence and mystery of the two of us, made me think how simple life was and how easy it was to step into happiness, like walking into your own rightful house.

———

This frame of mind persisted for two whole days—enough to make a nuisance of itself. I kept thinking that Foster Hamilton would come sooner or later and tell me that he loved me, and I couldn't sleep for thinking about him in various ways, and I had no appetite, and nobody could get me to answer them. I half expected him at play practice or to come to the schoolhouse, and I began to wish he would hurry up and get it over with, when, after play practice on the second night, I saw him uptown, on the corner, with this blonde.

Mrs. Arrington was driving us home, and he and the blonde were standing on the street corner, just about to get in his car. I never saw that blonde before or since, but she is printed eternally on my mind, and to this good day if I'd run into her across the counter from me in the ten-cent store, whichever one of us is selling lipstick to the other one, I'd know her for sure because I saw her for one half of a second in the street light in Port Claiborne with Foster Hamilton. She wasn't any ordinary blonde, either—dyed hair was in it. I didn't know the term "feather-bed blond" in those days, or I guess I would have thought it. As it was, I didn't really think anything, or say anything, either, but whatever had been galloping along inside me for two solid days and nights came to a screeching halt. Somebody in the car said, being real funny, "Foster Hamilton's got him another girl friend." I just laughed. "Sure has," I said. "Oh, Mari-leee!" they all said, teasing me. I laughed and laughed.

I asked Foster once, a long time later, "Why didn't you come back after that night you drove me out to Windsor?"

He shook his head. "We'd have been married in two weeks," he said. "It scared me half to death."

"Then it's a mercy you didn't," I said. "It scares *me* half to death right now."

Things had changed between us, you realize, between that kiss and that conversation. What happened was—at least, the main thing that happened was—Foster asked me the next year to go to the high school senior dance with him, so I said all right.

I knew about Foster by then, and that his reputation was not of the best—that it was, in fact, about the worst our county had to offer. I knew he had an uncommon thirst and that on weekends he went helling about the countryside with a fellow that owned the local picture show and worked at a garage in the daytime. His name was A. P. Fortenberry, and he owned a new convertible in a sickening shade of bright maroon. The convertible was always dusty— though you could see A.P. in the garage every afternoon, during the slack hour, hosing it down on the wash rack—because he and Foster were out in it almost every night, harassing the countryside. They knew every bootlegger in a radius of forty miles. They knew girls that lived on the outskirts of towns and girls that didn't. I guess "uninhibited" was the word for A. P. Fortenberry, but whatever it was, I couldn't stand him. He called me into the garage one day—to have a word with me about Foster, he said—but when I got inside he backed me into the corner and started trying it on. "Funny little old girl," he kept saying. He rattled his words out real fast. "Funny little old girl." I slapped him as hard as I could, which was pretty hard, but that only seemed to stimulate him. I thought I'd never get away from him—I can't smell the inside of a garage to this good day without thinking about A. P. Fortenberry.

When Foster drove all the way out to see me one day soon after that—we didn't have a telephone in those days—I thought he'd come to apologize for A.P., and I'm not sure yet he didn't intend for me to understand that without saying anything about it. He certainly put himself out. He sat down and swapped a lot of Port Claiborne talk with Mama—just pleased her to death—and then he went out back with Daddy and looked at the chickens and the peach trees. He even had an opinion on growing peaches, though I reckon he'd given more thought to peach brandy than he'd ever given to orchards. He said when we were walking out to his car that he'd like to take me to the senior dance, so I said O.K. I was pleased; I had to admit it.

Even knowing everything I knew by then (I didn't tell Mama and

Daddy), there was something kind of glamorous about Foster Hamilton. He came of a real good family, known for being aristocratic and smart; he had uncles who were college professors and big lawyers and doctors and things. His father had died when he was a babe in arms (tragedy), and he had perfect manners. He had perfect manners, that is, when he was sober, and it was not that he departed from them in any intentional way when he was drunk. Still, you couldn't exactly blame me for being disgusted when, after ten minutes of the dance, I discovered that his face was slightly green around the temples and that whereas he could dance fairly well, he could not stand up by himself at all. He teetered like a baby that has caught on to what walking is, and knows that now is the time to do it, but hasn't had quite enough practice.

"Foster," I whispered, "have you been drinking?"

"Been *drinking*?" he repeated. He looked at me with a sort of wonder, like the national president of the W.C.T.U. might if asked the same question. "It's so close in here," he complained.

It really wasn't that close yet, but it was going to be. The gym doors were open, so that people could walk outside in the night air whenever they wanted to. "Let's go outside," I said. Well, in my many anticipations I had foreseen Foster and me strolling about on the walks outside, me in my glimmering white sheer dress with the blue underskirt (Mama and I had worked for two weeks on that dress), and Foster with his nice broad aristocratic shoulders. Then, lo and behold, he had worn a white dinner jacket! There was never anybody in creation as proud as I was when I first walked into the senior dance that night with Foster Hamilton.

Pride goeth before a fall. The fall must be the one Foster took down the gully back of the boys' privy at the schoolhouse. I still don't know quite how he did it. When we went outside, he put me carefully in his car, helped to tuck in my skirts, and closed the door in the most polite way, and then I saw him heading toward the privy in his white jacket that was swaying like a lantern through the dark, and then he just wasn't there any more. After a while, I got worried that somebody would come out, like us, for air, so I got out and went to the outside wall of the privy and said, "Foster, are you all right?"

I didn't get any answer, so I knocked politely on the wall and said, "Foster?" Then I looked around behind and all around, for I was standing very close to the edge of the gully that had eroded right up to the borders of the campus (somebody was always threatening that the whole schoolhouse was going to cave off into it before another school year went by), and there at the bottom of the gully Foster Hamilton was lying face down, like the slain in battle.

What I should have done, I should have walked right off and left him there till doomsday, or till somebody came along who would use him for a model in a statue to our glorious dead in the defense of Port Claiborne against Gen. Ulysses S. Grant in 1863. That battle was over in about ten minutes, too. But I had to consider how things would look—I had my pride, after all. So I took a look around, hiked up my skirts, and went down into the gully. When I shook Foster, he grunted and rolled over, but I couldn't get him up. I wasn't strong enough. Finally, I said, "Foster, Mama's here!" and he soared up like a Roman candle. I never saw anything like it. He walked straight up the side of the gully and gave me a hand up, too. Then I guided him over toward the car and he sat in the door and lighted a cigarette.

"Where is she?" he said.

"Who?" I said.

"Your mother," he said.

"Oh, I just said that, Foster. I had to get you up someway."

At that, his shoulders slumped down and he looked terribly depressed. "I didn't mean to do this, Marilee," he said. "I didn't have any idea it would hit me this way. I'm sure I'll be all right in a minute."

I don't think he ever did fully realize that he had fallen in the gully. "Get inside," I said, and shoved him over. There were one or two couples beginning to come outside and walk around. I squeezed in beside Foster and closed the door. Inside the gym, where the hot lights were, the music was blaring and beating away. We had got a real orchestra specially for that evening, all the way down from Vicksburg, and a brass-voiced girl was singing a 1930s' song. I would have given anything to be in there with it rather than out in the dark with Foster Hamilton.

I got quite a frisky reputation out of that evening. Disappearing after ten minutes of the dance, seen snuggling out in the car, and gone completely by intermission. I drove us away. Foster wouldn't be convinced that anybody would think it at all peculiar if he reappeared inside the gym with red mud smeared all over his dinner jacket. I didn't know how to drive, but I did anyway. I'm convinced you can do anything when you have to—speak French, do a double back flip off a low diving board, play Rachmaninoff on the piano, or fly an airplane. Well, maybe not fly an airplane; it's too technical. Anyway, that's how I learned to drive a car, riding up and down the highway, holding off Foster with my elbow, marking time till midnight came and I could go home without anybody thinking anything out of the ordinary had happened.

When I got out of the car, I said, "Foster Hamilton, I never want to see you again as long as I live. And I hope you have a wreck on the way home."

Mama was awake, of course. She called out in the dark, "Did you have a good time, Marilee?"

"Oh yes, ma'am," I said.

Then I went back to my shed-ceilinged room in the back wing, and cried and cried. And cried.

———

There was a good bit of traffic coming and going out to our house after that. A. P. Fortenberry came, all pallid and sober, with a tie on and a straw hat in his hand. Then A.P. and Foster came together. Then Foster came by himself.

The story went that Foster had stopped in the garage with A.P. for a drink before the dance, and instead of water in the drink, A.P. had filled it up with grain alcohol. I was asked to believe that he did this because, seeing Foster all dressed up, he got the idea that Foster was going to some family do, and he couldn't stand Foster's family, they were all so stuck-up. While Foster was draining the first glass, A.P. had got called out front to put some gas in a car, and while he was gone Foster took just a little tap more whiskey with another glassful of grain alcohol. A.P. wanted me to understand that Foster's condition that night had been all his fault, that instead of three or four ounces of whiskey, Foster had innocently put down eighteen ounces of sheer dynamite, and it was a miracle only to be surpassed by the resurrection of Jesus Christ that he had managed to drive out and get me, converse with Mama about peach pickle, and dance those famous ten minutes at all.

Well, I said I didn't know. I thought to myself I never heard of Foster Hamilton touching anything he even mistook for water.

All these conferences took place at the front gate. "I never saw a girl like you," Mama said. "Why don't you invite the boys to sit on the porch?"

"I'm not too crazy about A. P. Fortenberry," I said. "I don't think he's a very nice boy."

"Uh-*huh*," Mama said, and couldn't imagine what Foster Hamilton was doing running around with him, if he wasn't a nice boy. Mama, to this day, will not hear a word against Foster Hamilton.

I was still giving some thought to the whole matter that summer, sitting now on the front steps, now on the back steps, and now on the side steps, whichever was most in the shade, chewing on pieces of grass and thinking, when one day the mailman stopped in for a glass of Mama's cold buttermilk (it's famous) and told me that Foster and A.P. had had the most awful wreck. They had been up to Vicksburg, and coming home had collided with a whole carload of Negroes. The carnage was awful—so much blood on everybody you couldn't tell black from white. They were both going to live, though. Being so drunk, which in a way had caused the wreck, had also kept them relaxed enough to come out of it alive. I warned the mailman to leave out the drinking part when he told Mama, she thought Foster was such a nice boy.

The next time I saw Foster, he was out of the hospital and had a deep scar on his cheekbone like a sunken star. He looked handsomer and more distinguished than ever. I had gotten a scholarship to Millsaps College in Jackson, and was just about to leave. We had a couple of dates before I left, but things were not the same. We would go to the picture show and ride around afterward, having a conversation that went something like this:

"Marilee, why are you such a nice girl? You're about the only nice girl I know."

"I guess I never learned any different, so I can't help it. Will you teach me how to stop being a nice girl?"

"I certainly will not!" He looked to see how I meant it, and for a minute I thought the world was going to turn over, but it didn't.

"Why won't you, Foster?"

"You're too young. And your mama's a real sweet lady. And your daddy's too good a shot."

"Foster, why do you drink so much?"

"Marilee, I'm going to tell you the honest truth. I drink because I like to drink." He spoke with real conviction.

So I went on up to college in Jackson, where I went in for serious studies and made very good grades. Foster, in time, got a job on the paper in New Orleans, where, during off hours, or so I understood, he continued his investigation of the lower things in life and of the effects of alcohol upon the human system.

It is twenty years later now, and Foster Hamilton is down there yet.

Millions of things have happened; the war has come and gone. I live far away, and everything changes, almost every day. You can't even be sure the moon and stars are going to be the same the day after tomorrow night. So it has become more and more important to me to know that Windsor is still right where it always was, standing pure in its decay, and that the gilded hand on the Presbyterian church in Port Claiborne is still pointing to Heaven and not to Outer Space; and I earnestly feel, too, that Foster Hamilton should go right on drinking. There have got to be some things you can count on, would be an ordinary way to put it. I'd rather say that I feel the need of a land, of a sure terrain, of a sort of permanent landscape of the heart.

SHIP ISLAND

THE STORY OF A MERMAID

The French book was lying open on a corner of the dining room table, between the floor lamp and the window. The floor lamp, which had come with the house, had a cover made of green glass, with a fringe. The French book must have lain just that way for two months. Nancy, coming in from the beach, tried not to look at it. It reminded her of how much she had meant to accomplish during the summer, of the strong sense of intent, something like refinement, with which she had chosen just that spot for studying. It was out of hearing of the conversations with the neighbors that went on every evening out on the side porch, it had window light in the daytime and lamplight at night, it had a small, slanting view of the beach, and it drew a breeze. The pencils were still there, still sharp, and the exercise, broken off. She sometimes stopped to read it over. "The soldiers of the emperor were crossing the bridge: *Les soldats de l'empereur traversaient le pont.* The officer has already knocked at the gate: *L'officier a déjà frappé*—" She could not have finished that sentence now if she had sat right down and tried.

Nancy could no longer find herself in relation to the girl who had sought out such a good place to study, had sharpened the pencils and opened the book and sat down to bend over it. What she did know was how—just now, when she had been down at the beach, across the boulevard—the sand scuffed beneath her step and shells lay strewn about, chipped and disorderly, near the water's edge. Some shells were empty; some, with damp drying down their backs, went for short walks. Far out, a long white shelf of cloud indicated a distance no gull could dream of gaining, though the gulls spun tirelessly up, dazzling in the white light that comes just as morning vanishes. A troop of pelicans sat like curiously carved knobs on the tops of a long series of wooden piles, which were spaced out at intervals in the water. The piles were what was left of a private pier blown away by a hurricane some years ago.

Nancy had been alone on the beach. Behind her, the boulevard glittered in the morning sun and the season's traffic rocked by the long curve of the shore in clumps that seemed to burst, then speed on. She stood looking outward at the high straight distant shelf of cloud. The islands were out there, plainly visible. The walls of the old Civil War fort on the nearest one of them, the one with the lighthouse—Ship Island—were plain today as well. She had been out there once this summer with Rob Acklen, out there on the island, where the reeds grew in the wild white sand, and the water teemed so thick with seaweed that only crazy people would have tried to swim in it. The gulf had rushed white and strong through all the seaweed, frothing up the beach. On the beach, the froth turned brown, the color of softly moving crawfish claws. In the boat coming home through the sunset that day, a boy standing up in the pilothouse played "Over the Waves" on his harmonica. Rob Acklen had put his jacket around Nancy's shoulders—she had never thought to bring a sweater. The jacket swallowed her; it smelled more like Rob than he did. The boat moved, the breeze blew, the sea swelled, all to the lilt of the music. The twenty-five members of the Laurel, Mississippi, First Baptist Church Adult Bible Class, who had come out with them on the excursion boat, and to whom Rob and Nancy had yet to introduce themselves, had stopped giggling and making their silly jokes. They were tired, and stood in a huddle like sheep; they were shaped like sheep as well, with little shoulders and wide bottoms—it was somehow sad. Nancy and Rob, young and trim, stood side by side near the bow, like figureheads of the boat, hearing the music and watching the thick prow butt the swell, which the sunset had stained a deep red. Nancy felt for certain that this was the happiest she had ever been.

Alone on the sand this morning, she had spread out her beach towel and stood for a moment looking up the beach, way up, past a grove of live oaks to where Rob Acklen's house was visible. He would be standing in the kitchen, in loafers and a dirty white shirt and an old pair of shorts, drinking cold beer from the refrigerator right out of the can. He would eat lunch with his mother and sister, read the paper and write a letter, then dress and drive into town to help his father in the office, going right past Nancy's house along the boulevard. Around three, he would call her up. He did this every day. His name was Fitzrobert Conroy Acklen—one of those full-blown Confederate names. Everybody liked him, and more than a few—a general mixture of every color, size, age, sex, and religion—would say when he passed by, "I declare, I just love that boy." So he was bound to have a lot of nicknames: "Fitz" or "Bobbie" or "Cousin" or "Son"—he answered to almost anything. He was the kind of boy people have high, undefined hopes for. He had first seen Nancy Lewis one morning when he came by her house to make an insurance call for his father.

Breaking off her French—could it have been the sentence about "l'officier"?—she had gone out to see who it was. She was expecting Mrs. Nattier, their neighbor, who had skinny white freckled legs she never shaved and whose husband, "off" somewhere, was thought not to be doing well; or Mrs. Nattier's little boy Bernard, who thought it was fun to hide around corners after dark and jump out saying nothing more original than "Boo!" (once, he had screamed "Raw head and bloody bones!" but Nancy was sure somebody had told him to); or one of the neighbor ladies in the back—old Mrs. Poultney, whom they rented from and who walked with a cane, or Miss Henriette Dupré, who was so devout she didn't even have to go to confession before weekday Communion and whose hands, always tucked up in the sleeves of her sack, were as cold as church candles, and to think of them touching you was like rabbits skipping over your grave on dark rainy nights in winter up in the lonely wet-leaf-covered hills. Or else it was somebody wanting to be paid something. Nancy had opened the door and looked up, and there, instead of a dozen other people, was Rob Acklen.

Not that she knew his name. She had seen boys like him down on the coast, ever since her family had moved there from Little Rock back in the spring. She had seen them playing tennis on the courts back of the hotel, where she sometimes went to jump on the trampoline. She believed that the hotel people thought she was on the staff in some sort of way, as she was about the right age for that—just a year or so beyond high school but hardly old enough to work in town. The weather was already getting hot, and the season was falling off. When she passed the courts, going and coming, she saw the boys out of the corner of her eye. Were they really so much taller than the boys up where they had moved from, up in Arkansas? They were lankier and a lot more casual. They were more assured. To Nancy, whose family was in debt and whose father, in one job after another, was always doing something wrong, the boys playing tennis had that wonderful remoteness of creatures to be admired on the screen, or those seen in whiskey ads, standing near the bar of a country club and sleekly talking about things she could not begin to imagine. But now here was one, in a heavy tan cotton suit and a light blue shirt with a buttoned-down collar and dark tie, standing on her own front porch and smiling at her.

Yet when Rob called Nancy for a date, a day or two later, she didn't have to be told that he did it partly because he liked to do nice things for people. He obviously liked to be considerate and kind, because the first time he saw her he said, "I guess you don't know many people yet?"

"No, because Daddy just got transferred," she said—"transferred" being her mother's word for it; fired was what it was. She gave him a Coke and talked to him awhile, standing around in the house, which unaccountably continued to be empty. She said she didn't know a thing about insurance.

Now, still on the beach, Nancy Lewis sat down in the middle of her beach towel and began to rub suntan lotion on her neck and shoulders. Looking down the other way, away from Rob's house and toward the yacht club, she saw a man standing alone on the sand. She had not noticed him before. He was facing out toward the gulf and staring fixedly at the horizon. He was wearing shorts and a shirt made out of red bandanna, with the tail out—a stout young man with black hair.

Just then, without warning, it began to rain. There were no clouds one could see in the overhead dazzle, but it rained anyway; the drops fell in huge discs, marking the sand, and splashing on Nancy's skin. Each drop seemed enough to fill a Dixie cup. At first, Nancy did not know what the stinging sensation was; then she knew the rain was burning her. It was scalding hot! Strange, outlandish, but also painful, was how she found it. She jumped up and began to flinch and twist away, trying to escape, and a moment later she had snatched up her beach towel and flung it around her shoulders. But the large hot drops kept falling, and there was no escape from them. She started rubbing her cheek and forehead and felt that she might blister all over; then, since it kept on and on and was all so inexplicable, she grabbed her lotion and ran up the beach and out of the sand and back across the boulevard. Once in her own front yard, under the scraggy trees, she felt the rain no longer, and looked back curiously into the dazzle beyond the boulevard.

"I thought you meant to stay for a while," her mother said. "Was it too hot? Anybody would be crazy to go out there now. There's never anybody out there at this time of day."

"It was all right," said Nancy, "but it started raining. I never felt anything like it. The rain was so hot it burned me. Look. My face—" She ran to look in the mirror. Sure enough, her face and shoulders looked splotched. It might blister. I might be scarred for life, she thought—one of those dramatic phrases left over from high school.

Nancy's mother, Mrs. Lewis, was a discouraged lady whose silky, blondish-gray hair was always slipping loose and tagging out around her face. She would not try to improve herself and talked a lot in company about her family; two of her uncles had been professors simultaneously at the University of North Carolina. One of them had written a book on phonetics. Mrs. Lewis seldom found anyone who had heard of them, or of the book, either. Some people asked what phonetics were, and others did not ask anything at all.

Mrs. Lewis now said to her daughter, "You just got too much sun."

"No, it was the rain. It was really scalding hot."

"I never heard of such a thing," her mother said. "Out of a clear sky."

"I can't help that," Nancy said. "I guess I ought to know."

Mrs. Lewis took on the kind of look she had when she would open the handkerchief drawer of a dresser and see two used, slightly bent carpet nails, some Scotch Tape melted together, an old receipt, an unanswered letter announcing a cousin's wedding, some scratched negatives saved for someone but never developed, some dusty foreign coins, a bank deposit book from a town they lived in during the summer before Nancy was born, and an old telegram whose contents, forgotten, no one would dare now to explore, for it would say something awful but absolutely true.

"I wish you wouldn't speak to me like that," Mrs. Lewis said. "All I know is, it certainly didn't rain here."

Nancy wandered away, into the dining room. She felt bad about everything—about quarreling with her mother, about not getting a suntan, about wasting her time all summer with Rob Acklen and not learning any French. She went and took a long cool bath in the big old bathroom, where the bathtub had ball-and-claw feet painted mustard yellow and the single light bulb on the long cord dropped down one mile from the stratosphere.

What the Lewises found in a rented house was always outclassed by what they brought into it. Nancy's father, for instance, had a china donkey that bared its teeth in a great big grin. Written on one side was "If you really want to look like me" and on the other "Just keep right on talking." Her father loved the donkey and its message, and always put it on the living room table of whatever house they were in. When he got a drink before dinner each evening he would wander back with glass in hand and look the donkey over. "That's pretty good," he would say just before he took the first swallow. Nancy had often longed to break the donkey, by accident—that's what she would say, that it had all been an accident—but she couldn't get over the feeling that if she did, worse things than the Lewises had ever imagined would happen to them. That donkey would let in a flood of trouble, that she knew.

After Nancy got out of the tub and dried, she rubbed Jergens Lotion on all the splotches the rain had made. Then she ate a peanut-butter sandwich and more shrimp salad left over from supper the night before, and drank a cold Coke. Now and then, eating, she would go look in the mirror. By the time Rob Acklen called up, the red marks had all but disappeared.

———

That night, riding down to Biloxi with Rob, Nancy confided that the catalogue of people she disliked, headed by Bernard Nattier, included every single person—Miss Henriette Dupré, Mrs. Poultney, and Mrs. Nattier, and Mr. Nattier, too, when he was at home—that she had to be with these days. It even included, she was sad to say, her mother and father. If Bernard Nattier had to be mean—and it was clear he did have to—why did he have to be so corny? He put wads of wet, chewed bubble gum in her purses—that was the most original thing he ever did. Otherwise, it was just live crawfish in her bed or crabs in her shoes; anybody could think of that. And when he stole, he took things *she* wanted, nothing simple, like money—she could have forgiven him for that—but cigarettes, lipstick, and ashtrays she had stolen herself here and there. If she locked her door, he got in through the window; if she locked the window, she suffocated. Not only that, but he would crawl out from under the bed. His eyes were slightly crossed and he knew how to turn the lids back on themselves so that it looked like blood, and then he would chase her. He was browned to the color of dirt all over and he smelled like salt mud the sun had dried. He wore black tennis shoes laced too tight at the ankles and from sunup till way past dark he never thought of anything but what to do to Nancy, and she would have liked to kill him.

She made Rob Acklen laugh. She amused him. He didn't take anything Nancy Lewis could say at all to heart, but, as if she was something he had found on the beach and was teaching to talk, he, with his Phi Beta Kappa key and his good level head and his wonderful prospects, found everything she told about herself cute, funny, absurd. He did remark that he had such feelings himself from time to time—that he would occasionally get crazy mad at one of his parents or the other, and that he once planned his sister's murder down to the last razor slash. But he laughed again, and his chewing gum popped amiably in his jaws. When she told him about the hot rain, he said he didn't believe it. He said, "Aw," which was what a boy like Rob Acklen said when he didn't believe something. The top of his old white Mercury convertible was down and the wind rushed past like an endless bolt of raw silk being drawn against Nancy's cheek.

In the ladies' room mirror at the Beach View, where they stopped to eat, she saw the bright quality of her eyes, as though she had been drinking. Her skirts rustled in the narrow room; a porous white disc of deodorant hung on a hook, fuming the air. Her eyes, though blue, looked startlingly dark in her pale skin, for though she tried hard all the time, she never seemed to tan. All the sun did, as her mother was always pointing out, was bleach her hair three shades lighter; a little more and it would be almost white. Out on the island that day, out on Ship Island, she had drifted in the water like seaweed, with the tide combing her limbs and hair, tugging her through lengths of fuzzy water growth. She had lain flat on her face with her arms stretched before her, experiencing the curious lift the water's motion gave to the tentacles of weed, wondering whether she liked it or not. Did something alive clamber the small of her back? Did something wishful grope the spiral of her ear? Rob had caught her wrist hard and waked her—waked was what he did, though to sleep in the water is not possible. He said he thought she had been there too long. "Nobody can keep their face in the water that long," was what he said.

"I did," said Nancy.

Rob's brow had been blistered a little, she recalled, for that had been back early in the summer, soon after they had met—but the changes the sun made on him went without particular attention. The seasons here were old ground to him. He said that the island was new, however—or at least forgotten. He said he had never been there but once, and that many years ago, on a Boy Scout picnic. Soon they were exploring the fort, reading the dates off the metal signs whose letters glowed so smoothly in the sun, and the brief summaries of what those little boys, little military-academy boys turned into soldiers, had endured. Not old enough to fill up the name of soldier, or of prisoner, either, which is what they were—not old enough to shave, Nancy bet—still, they had died there, miserably far from home, and had been buried in the sand. There was a lot more. Rob would have been glad to read all about it, but she wasn't interested. What they knew already was plenty, just about those boys. A bright, worried lizard ran out of a hot rubble of brick. They came out of the fort and walked alone together eastward toward the dunes, now skirting near the shore that faced the sound and now wandering south, where they could hear or sometimes glimpse the gulf. They were overlooked all the way by an old white lighthouse. From far away behind, the twenty-five members of the adult Bible class could be overheard playing a silly, shrill Sunday School game. It came across the ruins of the fort and the sad story of the dead soldiers like something that had happened long ago that you could not quite remember having joined in. On the beach to their right, toward the gulf, a flock of sandpipers with blinding-white breasts stepped pecking along the water's edge, and on the inner beach, toward the sound, a wrecked sailboat with a broken mast lay half buried in the sand.

Rob kept teasing her along, pulling at the soft wool strings of her bathing suit, which knotted at the nape and again under her shoulder blades, worrying loose the damp hair that she had carefully slicked back and pinned. "There isn't anybody in that house," he assured her, some minutes later, having explored most of that part of the island and almost as much of Nancy as well, having almost, but not quite—his arms around her—coaxed and caressed her down to ground level in a clump of reeds. "There hasn't been in years and years," he said, encouraging her.

"It's only those picnic people," she said, holding off, for the reeds would not have concealed a medium-sized mouse. They had been to look at the sailboat and thought about climbing inside (kissing closely, they had almost fallen right over into it), but it did have a rotten tin can in the bottom and smelled, so here they were back out in the dunes.

"They've got to drink all those Coca-Colas," Rob said, "and give out all those prizes, and anyway—"

She never learned anyway what, but it didn't matter. Maybe she began to make up for all that the poor little soldiers had missed out on, in the way of making love. The island's very spine, a warm reach of thin ground, came smoothly up into the arch of her back; and it was at least halfway the day itself, with its fair, wide-open eyes, that she went over to. She felt somewhat historical afterward, as though they had themselves added one more mark to all those that place remembered.

Having played all the games and given out the prizes, having eaten all the homemade cookies and drunk the case of soft drinks just getting warm, and gone sight-seeing through the fort, the Bible class was now coming, too, crying "Yoohoo!" to explore the island. They discovered Rob hurling shells and bits of rock into the surf, while Nancy, scavenging a little distance away, tugged up out of the sand a shell so extraordinary it was worth showing around. It was purple, pink, and violet inside—a palace of colors; the king of the oysters had no doubt lived there. When she held it shyly out to them, they cried "Look!" and "Ooo!" so there was no need for talking to them much at all, and in the meantime the evening softened, the water glowed, the glare dissolved. Far out, there were other islands one could see now, and beyond those must be many more. They had been there all along.

Going home, Nancy gave the wonderful shell to the boy who stood in the pilothouse playing "Over the Waves." She glanced back as they walked off up the pier and saw him look at the shell, try it for weight, and then throw it in the water, leaning far back on his arm and putting a good spin on the throw, the way boys like to do—the way Rob Acklen himself had been doing, too, just that afternoon.

"Why did you do that?" Rob had demanded. He was frowning; he looked angry. He had thought they should keep the shell—to remember, she supposed.

"For the music," she explained.

"But it was ours," he said. When she didn't answer, he said again, "Why did you, Nancy?"

But still she didn't answer.

———

When Nancy returned to their table at the Beach View, having put her lipstick back straight after eating fish, Rob was paying the check. "Why not believe me?" she asked him. "It was true. The rain was hot as fire. I thought I would be scarred for life."

It was still broad daylight, not even twilight. In the bright, air-conditioned restaurant, the light from the water glazed flatly against the broad picture windows, the chandeliers, and the glasses. It was the hour when mirrors reflect nothing and bars look tired. The restaurant was a boozy, cheap sort of place with a black-lined gambling hall in the back, but everyone went there because the food was good.

"You're just like Mama," she said. "You think I made it up."

Rob said, teasing, "I didn't say that. I just said I didn't believe it." He loved getting her caught in some sort of logic she couldn't get out of. When he opened the door for her, she got a good sidelong view of his longish, firm face and saw the way his somewhat fine brows arched up with one or two bright reddish hairs in among the dark ones; his hair was that way, too, when the sun hit it. Maybe, if nobody had told him, he wouldn't have known it; he seemed not to notice so very much about himself. Having the confidence of people who don't worry much, his grin could snare her instantly— a glance alone could make her feel how lucky she was he'd ever noticed her. But it didn't do at all to think about him now. It would be ages before they made it through the evening and back, retracing the way and then turning off to the bayou, and even then, there would be those mosquitoes.

Bayou love-making suited Rob just fine; he was one of those people mosquitoes didn't bite. They certainly bit Nancy. They were huge and silent, and the minute the car stopped they would even come and sit upon her eyelids, if she closed her eyes, a dozen to each tender arc of flesh. They would gather on her face, around her nose and mouth. Clothlike, like rags and tatters, like large dry ashes of burnt cloth, they came in lazy droves, in fleets, sailing on the air. They were never in any hurry, being everywhere at once and always ready to bite. Nancy had been known to jump all the way out of the car and go stamping across the grass like a calf. She grew sulky and despairing and stood on one leg at a time in the moonlight, slapping at her ankles, while Rob leaned his chin on the doorframe and watched her with his affectionate, total interest.

Nancy, riddled and stinging with beads of actual blood briar-pointed here and there upon her, longed to be almost anywhere else—she especially longed for New Orleans. She always talked about it, although, never having been there, she had to say the things that other people said—food and jazz in the French Quarter, beer and crabs out on Lake Pontchartrain. Rob said vaguely they would go sometime. But she could tell that things were wrong for him at this point. "The food's just as good around here," he said.

"Oh, Rob!" She knew it wasn't so. She could feel that city, hanging just over the horizon from them scarcely fifty miles away, like some swollen bronze moon, at once brilliant and shadowy and drenched in every sort of amplified smell. Rob was stroking her hair, and in time his repeated, gentle touch gained her attention. It seemed to tell what he liked—girls all spanking clean, with scrubbed fingernails, wearing shoes still damp with white shoe polish. Even a fresh gardenia stuck in their hair wouldn't be too much for him. There would be all sorts of differences, to him, between Ship Island and the French Quarter, but she did not have much idea just what they were. Nancy took all this in, out of his hand on her head. She decided she had better not talk any more about New Orleans. She wriggled around, looking out over his shoulder, through the moon-light, toward where the pitch-black surface of the bayou water showed in patches through the trees. The trees were awful, hung with great spooky gray tatters of Spanish moss. Nancy was re-minded of the house she and her family were living in; it had re-cently occurred to her that the peculiar smell it had must come from some Spanish moss that had got sealed in behind the paneling, between the walls. The moss was alive in there and growing, and that was where she was going to seal Bernard Nattier up someday, for him to see how it felt. She had tried to kill him once, by filling her purse with rocks and oyster shells—the roughest she could find. She had read somewhere that this weapon was effective for ladies in case of attack. But he had ducked when she swung the purse at him, and she had only gone spinning round and round, falling at last into a camellia tree, which had scratched her. . . .

"The Skeltons said for us to stop by there for a drink," Rob told her. They were driving again, and the car was back on the boulevard, in the still surprising daylight. "What did you say?" he asked her.

"Nothing."

"You just don't want to go?"

"No, I don't much want to go."

"Well, then, we won't stay long."

The Skelton house was right on the water, with a second-story, glassed-in, air-conditioned living room looking out over the sound. The sofas and chairs were covered with gold-and-white striped satin, and the room was full of Rob's friends. Lorna Skelton, who had been Rob's girl the summer before and who dressed so beautifully, was handing drinks round and saying, "So which is your favorite bayou, Rob?" She had a sort of fake "good sport" tone of voice and wanted to appear ready for anything. (Being so determined to be nice around Nancy, she was going to fall right over backward one day.)

"Do I have to have a favorite?" Rob asked. "They all look good to me. Full of slime and alligators."

"I should have asked Nancy."

"They're all full of mosquitoes," said Nancy, hoping that was O.K. for an answer. She thought that virgins were awful people.

"Trapped, boy!" Turner Carmichael said to Rob, and banged him on the shoulder. Turner wanted to be a writer, so he thought it was all right to tell people about themselves. "Women will be your downfall, Acklen. Nancy, honey, you haven't spoken to the general."

Old General Skelton, Lorna's grandfather, sat in the corner of the living room near the mantel, drinking a scotch highball. You had to shout at him.

"How's the election going, General?" Turner asked.

"Election? Election? What election? Oh, the election! Well—" He lowered his voice, confidentially. As with most deaf people, his tone went to extremes. "There's no question of it. The one we want is the one we know. Know Houghman's father. Knew his grandfather. His stand is the same, identical one that we are all accustomed to. On every subject—this race thing especially. Very dangerous now. Extremely touchy. But Houghman—absolute! Never experiment, never question, never turn back. These are perilous times."

"Yes, sir," said Turner, nodding in an earnestly false way, which was better than the earnestly impressed way a younger boy at the general's elbow shouted, "General Skelton, that's just what my daddy says!"

"Oh yes," said the old man, sipping scotch. "Oh yes, it's true. And you, missy?" he thundered suddenly at Nancy, making her jump. "Are you just visiting here?"

"Why, Granddaddy," Lorna explained, joining them, "Nancy lives here now. You know Nancy."

"Then why isn't she tan?" the old man continued. "Why so pale and wan, fair nymph?"

"Were you a nymph?" Turner asked. "All this time?"

"For me I'm dark," Nancy explained. But this awkward way of putting it proved more than General Skelton could hear, even after three shoutings.

Turner Carmichael said, "We used to have this crazy colored girl who went around saying, 'I'se really white, 'cause all my chillun is,'" and of course *that* was what General Skelton picked to hear. "Party's getting rough," he complained.

"Granddaddy," Lorna cried, giggling, "you don't understand!"

"Don't I?" said the old gentleman. "Well, maybe I don't."

"Here, Nancy, come help me," said Lorna, leading her guest toward the kitchen.

On the way, Nancy heard Rob ask Turner, "Just where did you have this colored girl, did you say?"

"Don't be a dope. I said she worked for us."

"Aren't they a scream?" Lorna said, dragging a quart bottle of soda out of the refrigerator. "I thank God every night Granddaddy's deaf. You know, he was in the First World War and killed I don't know how many Germans, and he still can't stand to hear what he calls loose talk before a lady."

"I thought he was in the Civil War," said Nancy, and then of course she knew that that was the wrong thing and that Lorna, who just for an instant gave her a glance less than polite, was not going to forget it. The fact was, Nancy had never thought till that minute which war General Skelton had been in. She hadn't thought because she didn't care.

It had grown dark by now, and through the kitchen windows Nancy could see that the moon had risen—a moon in the clumsy stage, swelling between three-quarters and full, yet pouring out light on the water. Its rays were bursting against the long breakwater of concrete slabs, the remains of what the hurricane had shattered.

After saying such a fool thing, Nancy felt she could not stay in that kitchen another minute with Lorna, so she asked where she could go comb her hair. Lorna showed her down a hallway, kindly switching the lights on.

The Skeltons' bathroom was all pale blue and white, with handsome jars of rose bath salts and big fat scented bars of rosy soap. The lights came on impressively and the fixtures were heavy, yet somehow it all looked dead. It came to Nancy that she had really been wondering about just what would be in this sort of bathroom ever since she had seen those boys, with maybe Rob among them, playing tennis while she jumped on the trampoline. Surely the place had the air of an inner shrine, but what was there to see? The tops of all the bottles fitted firmly tight, and the soap in the tub was dry. Somebody had picked it all out—that was the point—judging soap and bath salts just the way they judged outsiders, business, real estate, politics. Nancy's father made judgments, too. Once, he argued all evening that Hitler was a well-meaning man; another time, he said the world was ready for communism. You could tell he was judging wrong, because he didn't have a bathroom like this one. Nancy's face in the mirror resembled a flower in a room that was too warm.

When she went out again, they had started dancing a little—a sort of friendly shifting around before the big glass windows overlooking the sound. General Skelton's chair was empty; he was gone. Down below, Lorna's parents could be heard coming in; her mother called upstairs. Her father appeared and shook hands all around. Mrs. Skelton soon followed him. He was wearing a white jacket, and she had on a silver cocktail dress with silver shoes. They looked like people in magazines. Mrs. Skelton held a crystal platter of things to eat in one hand, with a lace handkerchief pressed between the flesh and the glass in an inevitable sort of way.

In a moment, when the faces, talking and eating, the music, the talk, and the dancing swam to a still point before Nancy's eyes, she said, "You must all come to my house next week. We'll have a party."

A silence fell. Everyone knew where Nancy lived, in that cluster of old run-down houses the boulevard swept by. They knew that her house, especially, needed paint outside and furniture inside. Her daddy drank too much, and through her dress they could perhaps clearly discern the pin that held her slip together. Maybe, since they knew everything, they could look right through the walls of the house and see her daddy's donkey.

"Sure we will," said Rob Acklen at once. "I think that would be grand."

"Sure we will, Nancy," said Lorna Skelton, who was such a good sport and who was not seeing Rob this summer.

"A party?" said Turner Carmichael, and swallowed a whole anchovy. "Can I come, too?"

Oh, dear Lord, Nancy was wondering, what made me say it? Then she was on the stairs with her knees shaking, leaving the party, leaving with Rob to go down to Biloxi, where the two of them always went, and hearing the right things said to her and Rob, and smiling back at the right things but longing to jump off into the dark as if it were water. The dark, with the moon mixed in with it, seemed to her like good deep water to go off in.

———

She might have known that in the Marine Room of the Buena Vista down in Biloxi, they would run into more friends of Rob's. They always ran into somebody, and she might have known. These particular ones had already arrived and were even waiting for Rob, being somewhat bored in the process. It wasn't that Rob was so bright and witty, but he listened and liked everybody; he saw them the way they liked to be seen. So then they would go on to new heights, outdoing themselves, coming to believe how marvelous they really were. Two fraternity brothers of his were there tonight. They were sitting at a table with their dates—two tiny girls with tiny voices, like mosquitoes. They at once asked Nancy where she went to college, but before she could reply and give it away that her school so far had been only a cow college up in Arkansas and that she had gone there because her daddy couldn't afford anywhere else, Rob broke in and answered for her. "She's been in a finishing school in Little Rock," he said, "but I'm trying to talk her into going to the university."

Then the girls and their dates all four spoke together. They said, "Great!"

"Now watch," said one of the little girls, whose name was Teenie. "Cootie's getting out that little ole rush book."

Sure enough, the tiniest little notebook came out of the little cream silk bag of the other girl, who was called Cootie, and in it Nancy's name and address were written down with a sliver of a gold pencil. The whole routine was a fake, but a kind fake, as long as Rob was there. The minute those two got her into the ladies' room it would turn into another thing altogether; that she knew. Nancy knew all about mosquitoes. They'll sting me till I crumple up and die, she thought, and what will they ever care? So, when the three of them did leave the table, she stopped to straighten the strap of her shoe at the door to the ladies' room and let them go on through, talking on and on to one another about Rush Week. Then she went down a corridor and around a corner and down a short flight of steps. She ran down a long basement hallway where the service quarters were, past linen closets and cases of soft drinks, and, turning another corner and trying a door above a stairway, she came out, as she thought she would, in a night-club place called the Fishnet, far away in the wing. It was a good place to hide; she and Rob had been there often. I can make up some sort of story later, she thought, and crept up on the last bar stool. Up above the bar, New Orleans–style (or so they said), a man was pumping tunes out of an electric organ. He wore rings on his chubby fingers and kept a handkerchief near him to mop his brow and to swab his triple chins with between songs. He waved his hand at Nancy. "Where's Rob, honey?" he asked.

She smiled but didn't answer. She kept her head back in the shadows. She wished only to be like another glass in the sparkling row of glasses lined up before the big gleam of mirrors and under the play of lights. What made me say that about a party? she kept wondering. To some people it would be nothing, nothing. But not to her. She fumbled in her bag for a cigarette. Inadvertently, she drank from a glass near her hand. The man sitting next to her smiled at her. "I didn't want it anyway," he said.

"Oh, I didn't mean—" she began. "I'll order one." Did you pay now? She rummaged in her bag.

But the man said, "What'll it be?" and ordered for her. "Come on now, take it easy," he said. "What's your name?"

"Nothing," she said, by accident.

She had meant to say Nancy, but the man seemed to think it was funny. "Nothing what?" he asked. "Or is it by any chance Miss Nothing? I used to know a large family of Nothings, over in Mobile."

"Oh, I meant to say Nancy."

"Nancy Nothing. Is that it?"

Another teaser, she thought. She looked away from his eyes, which glittered like metal, and what she saw across the room made her uncertainties vanish. She felt her whole self settle and calm itself. The man she had seen that morning on the beach wearing a red bandanna shirt and shorts was standing near the back of the Fishnet, looking on. Now he was wearing a white dinner jacket and a black tie, with a red cummerbund over his large stomach, but he was unmistakably the same man. At that moment, he positively seemed to Nancy to be her own identity. She jumped up and left the teasing man at the bar and crossed the room.

"Remember me?" she said. "I saw you on the beach this morning."

"Sure I do. You ran off when it started to rain. I had to run, too."

"Why did you?" Nancy asked, growing happier every minute.

"Because the rain was so hot it burnt me. If I could roll up my sleeve, I'd show you the blisters on my arm."

"I believe you. I had some, too, but they went away." She smiled, and the man smiled back. The feeling was that they would be friends forever.

"Listen," the man said after a while. "There's a fellow here you've got to meet now. He's out on the veranda, because it's too hot in here. Anyway, he gets tired just with me. Now you come on."

———

Nancy Lewis was always conscious of what she had left behind her. She knew that right now her parents and old Mrs. Poultney, with her rent collector's jaw, and Miss Henriette Dupré, with her religious calf eyes, and the Nattiers, mother and son, were all sitting on the back porch in the half-light, passing the bottle of 6-12 around, and probably right now discussing the fact that Nancy was out with Rob again. She knew that when her mother thought of Rob her heart turned beautiful and radiant as a sea shell on a spring night. Her father, both at home and at his office, took his daughter's going out with Rob as excuse for saying something disagreeable about Rob's father, who was a big insurance man. There was always some talk about how Mr. Acklen had trickily got out of the bulk of his hurricane-damage payments, the same as all the other insurance men had done. Nancy's mother was probably responding to such a charge at this moment. "Now, you don't know that's true," she would say. But old Mrs. Poultney would say she knew it was true with *her* insurance company (implying that she knew but wouldn't say about the Acklen company, too). Half the house she was renting to the Lewises had blown right off it—all one wing—and the upstairs bathroom was ripped in two, and you could see the wallpapered walls of all the rooms, and the bathtub, with its pipes still attached, had got blown into the telephone wires. If Mrs. Poultney had got what insurance money had been coming to her, she would have torn down this house and built a new one. And Mrs. Nattier would say that there was something terrible to her about seeing wallpapered rooms exposed that way. And Miss Henriette Dupré would say that the Dupré house had come through it all ab-so-lootly intact, meaning that the Duprés had been foresighted enough to get some sort of special heavenly insurance, and she would be just longing to embark on explaining how they came by it, and she would, too, given a tenth of a chance. And all the time this went on, Nancy could see into the Acklens' house just as clearly—see the Acklens sitting inside their sheltered game room after dinner, bathed in those soft bug-repellent lights. And what were the Acklens saying (along with their kind of talk about their kind of money) but that they certainly hoped Rob wasn't serious about that girl? Nothing had to matter if he wasn't serious. . . . Nancy could circle around all of them in her mind. She could peer into windows, over-hearing; it was the only way she could look at people. No human in the whole human world seemed to her exactly made for her to stand in front of and look squarely in the eye, the way she could look Bernard Nattier in the eye (he not being human either) before taking careful aim to be sure not to miss him with a purseful of rocks and oyster shells, or the way she could look this big man in the red cummerbund in the eye, being convinced already that he was what her daddy called a "natural." Her daddy liked to come across people he could call that, because it made him feel superior.

As the big man steered her through the crowded room, threading among the tables, going out toward the veranda, he was telling her his life story all along the way. It seemed that his father was a terri-bly rich Yankee who paid him not to stay at home. He had been in love with a policeman's daughter from Pittsburgh, but his father broke it up. He was still in love with her and always would be. It was the way he was; he couldn't help being faithful, could he? His name was Alfred, but everybody called him Bub. The fellow his father paid to drive him around was right down there, he said, as they stepped through the door and out on the veranda.

Nancy looked down the length of the veranda, which ran along the side of the hotel, and there was a man sitting on a bench. He had

on a white jacket and was staring straight ahead, smoking. The highway curled around the hotel grounds, following the curve of the
shore, and the cars came glimmering past, one by one, sometimes
with lights on inside, sometimes spilling radio music that trailed up
in long waves and met the electric-organ music coming out of the
bar. Nancy and Bub walked toward the man. Bub counseled her
gently, "His name is Dennis." Some people in full evening dress
were coming up the divided walk before the hotel, past the canna
lilies blooming deeply red under the high, powerful lights, where
the bugs coned in long footless whirlpools. The people were drunk
and laughing.

"Hi, Dennis," Bub said. The way he said it, trying to sound confident, told her that he was scared of Dennis.

Dennis's head snapped up and around. He was an erect, strong,
square-cut man, not very tall. He had put water on his light brown
hair when he combed it, so that it streaked light and dark and light
again and looked like wood. He had cold eyes, which did not express anything—just the opposite of Rob Acklen's.

"What you got there?" he asked Bub.

"I met her this morning on the beach," Bub said.

"Been holding out on me?"

"Nothing like that," said Bub. "I just now saw her again."

The man called Dennis got up and thumbed his cigarette into
the shrubbery. Then he carefully set his heels together and bowed.
It was all a sort of joke on how he thought people here behaved.
"Would you care to dance?" he inquired.

Dancing there on the veranda, Nancy noticed at once that he
had a tense, strong wrist that bent back and forth like something
manufactured out of steel. She also noticed that he was making her
do whatever it was he called dancing; he was good at that. The
music coming out of the Fishnet poured through the windows and
around them. Dennis was possibly even thirty years old. He kept
talking the whole time. "I guess he's told you everything, even about
the policeman's daughter. He tells everybody everything, right in
the first two minutes. I don't know if it's true, but how can you tell?

If it wasn't true when it happened, it is now." He spun her fast as a top, then slung her out about ten feet—she thought she would certainly sail right on out over the railing and maybe never stop till she landed in the gulf, or perhaps go splat on the highway—but he got her back on the beat and finished up the thought, saying, "Know what I mean?"

"I guess so," Nancy said, and the music stopped.

The three of them sat down together on the bench.

"What do we do now?" Dennis asked.

"Let's ask her," said Bub. He was more and more delighted with Nancy. He had been tremendously encouraged when Dennis took to her.

"You ask her," Dennis said.

"Listen, Nancy," Bub said. "Now, listen. Let me just tell you. There's so much money—that's the first thing to know. You've got no idea how much money there is. Really crazy. It's something, actually, that nobody knows—"

"If anybody knew," said Dennis, "they might have to tell the government."

"Anyway, my stepmother on this yacht in Florida, her own telephone—by radio, you know—she'd be crazy to meet you. My dad is likely off somewhere, but maybe not. And there's this plane down at Palm Beach, pilot and all, with nothing to do but go to the beach every day, just to pass away the time, and if he's not there for any reason, me and Dennis can fly just as good as we can drive. There's Alaska, Beirut—would you like to go to Beirut? I've always wanted to. There's anything you say."

"See that Cad out there?" said Dennis. "The yellow one with the black leather upholstery? That's his. I drive."

"So all you got to do," Bub told her, "is wish. Now, wait—now, think. It's important!" He all but held his hand over her mouth, as if playing a child's game, until finally he said, "Now! What would you like to do most in the world?"

"Go to New Orleans," said Nancy at once, "and eat some wonderful food."

"It's a good idea," said Dennis. "This dump is getting on my nerves. I get bored most of the time anyway, but today I'm bored silly."

"So wait here!" Nancy said. "So wait right here!"

She ran off to get Rob. She had all sorts of plans in her head.

But Rob was all taken up. There were now more of his friends. The Marine Room was full of people just like him, lounging around two big tables shoved together, with about a million 7-Up bottles and soda bottles and glasses before them, and girls spangled among them, all silver, gold, and white. It was as if while Nancy was gone they had moved into mirrors to multiply themselves. They were talking to themselves about things she couldn't join in, any more than you can dance without feet. Somebody was going into politics, somebody was getting married to a girl who trained horses, somebody was just back from Europe. The two little mosquito girls weren't saying anything much any more; they had their little chins glued to their little palms. When anybody mentioned the university, it sounded like a small country the people right there were running *in absentia* to suit themselves. Last year's Maid of Cotton was there, and so, it turned out, was the girl horse trainer—tall, with a sheaf of upswept brown hair fastened with a glittering pin; she sat like the mast of a ship, smiling and talking about horses. Did she know personally every horse in the Southern states?

Rob scarcely looked up when he pulled Nancy in. "Where you been? What you want to drink?" He was having another good evening. He seemed to be sitting up above the rest, as though presiding, but this was not actually so; only his fondness for every face he saw before him made him appear to be raised a little, as if on a special chair.

And, later on, it seemed to Nancy that she herself had been, among them, like a person who wasn't a person—another order of creature passing among or even through them. Was it just that nothing, nobody, could really distract them when they got wrapped up in themselves?

"I met some people who want to meet you," she whispered to Rob. "Come on out with me."

"O.K.," he said. "In a minute. Are they from around here?"

"Come on, come on," she urged. "Come on out."

"In a minute," he said. "I will in a minute," he promised.

Then someone noticed her pulling at his sleeve, and she thought she heard Lorna Skelton laugh.

She went racing back to Bub and Dennis, who were waiting for her so docilely they seemed to be the soul of goodness, and she said, "I'll just ride around for a while, because I've never been in a Cadillac before." So they rode around and came back and sat for a while under the huge brilliant overhead lights before the hotel, where the bugs spiraled down. They did everything she said. She could make them do anything. They went to three different places, for instance, to find her some Dentyne, and when they found it they bought her a whole carton of it.

The bugs did a jagged frantic dance, trying to climb high enough to kill themselves, and occasionally a big one crashed with a harsh dry sound against the pavement. Nancy remembered dancing in the open air, and the rough salt feel of the air whipping against her skin as she spun fast against the air's drift. From behind she heard the resonant, constant whisper of the gulf. She looked toward the hotel doors and thought that if Rob came through she would hop out of the car right away, but he didn't come. A man she knew passed by, and she just all of a sudden said, "Tell Rob I'll be back in a minute," and he, without even looking up said, "O.K., Nancy," just like it really was O.K., so she said what the motor was saying, quiet but right there, and definitely running just under the splendid skin of the car, "Let's go on for a little while."

"Nancy, I think you're the sweetest girl I ever saw," said Bub, and they drove off.

She rode between them, on the front seat of the Cadillac. The top was down and the moon spilled over them as they rode, skimming gently but powerfully along the shore and the sound, like a strong rapid cloud traveling west. Nancy watched the point where the moon actually met the water. It was moving and still at once. She thought that it was glorious, in a messy sort of way. She would have liked to poke her head up out of the water right there. She could feel the water pouring back through her white-blond hair, her face slathering over with moonlight.

"If it hadn't been for that crazy rain," Bub kept saying, "I wouldn't have met her."

"Oh, shut up about that goofy rain," said Dennis.

"It was like being spit on from above," said Nancy.

The needle crept up to eighty or more, and when they had left the sound and were driving through the swamp, Nancy shivered. They wrapped her in a lap robe from the back seat and turned the radio up loud.

———

It was since she got back, since she got back home from New Orleans, that her mother did not put on the thin voile afternoon dress any more and serve iced tea to the neighbors on the back porch. Just yesterday, having nothing to do in the hot silence but hear the traffic stream by on the boulevard, and not wanting a suntan, and being certain the telephone would not ring, Nancy had taken some lemonade over to Bernard Nattier, who was sick in bed with the mumps. He and his mother had one room between them over at Mrs. Poultney's house, and they had stacks of magazines—the *Ladies' Home Journal, McCall's, Life,* and *Time*—piled along the walls. Bernard lay on a bunk bed pushed up under the window, in all the close heat, with no breeze able to come in at all. His face was puffed out and his eyes feverish. "I brought you some lemonade," said Nancy, but he said he couldn't drink it because it hurt his gums. Then he smiled at her, or tried to—it must have hurt even to do that, and it certainly made him look silly, like a cartoon of himself, but it was sweet.

"I love you, Nancy," he said, most irresponsibly.

She thought she would cry. She had honestly tried to kill him with those rocks and oyster shells. He knew that very well, and he, from the moment he had seen her, had set out to make her life one long torment, so where could it come from, a smile like that, and what he said? She didn't know. From the fever, maybe. She said she loved him, too.

Then, it was last night, just the night before, that her father had got drunk and made speeches beginning, "To think that a daughter of mine . . ." Nancy had sat through it all crouched in the shadows on the stair landing, in the very spot where the moss or old seaweed back of the paneling smelled the strongest and dankest, and thought of her mother upstairs, lying, clothed, straight out on the bed in the dark, with a headache and no cover on and maybe the roof above her melted away. Nancy looked down to where her father was marching up to the donkey that said, "If you really want to look like me—Just keep right on talking," and was picking it up and throwing it down, right on the floor. She cried out, before she knew it— "Oh!"—seeing him do the very thing she had so often meant to do herself. Why had he? Why? Because the whiskey had run out on him? Or because he had got too much of it again? Or from trying to get in one good lick at everything there was? Or because the advice he loved so much seemed now being offered to him?

But the donkey did not break. It lay there, far down in the tricky shadows; Nancy could see it lying there, looking back over its shoulder with its big red grinning mouth, and teeth like piano keys, still saying the same thing, naturally. Her father was tilting uncertainly down toward it, unable, without falling flat on his face, to reach it. This made a problem for him, and he stood thinking it all over, taking every aspect of it well into account, even though the donkey gave the impression that not even with a sledgehammer would it be broken, and lay as if on some deep distant sea floor, toward which all the sediment of life was drifting, drifting, forever slowly down. . . .

Beirut! It was the first time she had remembered it. They had said they would take her there, Dennis and Bub, and then she had forgotten to ask, so why think of it right now, on the street uptown, just when she saw Rob Acklen coming along? She would have to see him sometime, she guessed, but what did Beirut have to do with it?

"Nancy Lewis," he said pleasantly, "you ran out on me. Why did you act like that? I was always nice to you."

"I told them to tell you," she said. "I just went to ride around for a while."

"Oh, I got the word, all right. About fifty different people saw you drive off in that Cadillac. Now about a hundred claim to have.

Seems like everybody saw those two characters but me. What did you do it for?"

"I didn't like those Skeltons, all those people you know. I didn't like those sorority girls, that Teenie and Cootie. You knew I didn't, but you always took me where they were just the same."

"But the point is," said Rob Acklen, "I thought you liked me."

"Well, I did," said Nancy Lewis, as though it all had happened a hundred years ago. "Well, I did like you just fine."

They were still talking on the street. There had been the tail of a storm that morning, and the palms were blowing. There was a sense of them streaming like green flags above the low town.

Rob took Nancy to the drugstore and sat at a booth with her. He ordered her a fountain Coke and himself a cup of coffee. "What's happened to you?" he asked her.

She realized then, from what he was looking at, that something she had only half noticed was certainly there to be seen—her skin, all around the edges of her white blouse, was badly bruised and marked, and there was the purplish mark on her cheekbone she had more or less powdered over, along with the angry streak on her neck.

"You look like you fell through a cotton gin," Rob Acklen continued, in his friendly way. "You're not going to say the rain over in New Orleans is just scalding hot, are you?"

"I didn't say anything," she returned.

"Maybe the mosquitoes come pretty big over there," he suggested. "They wear boxing gloves, for one thing, and, for another—"

"Oh, stop it, Rob," she said, and wished she was anywhere else.

It had all stemmed from the moment down in the French Quarter, over late drinks somewhere, when Dennis had got nasty enough with Bub to get rid of him, so that all of Dennis's attention from that point onward had gone exclusively to Nancy. This particular attention was relentless and direct, for Dennis was about as removed from any sort of affection and kindness as a human could be. Maybe it had all got boiled out of him; maybe he had never had much to get rid of. What he had to say to her was nothing she hadn't heard before, nothing she hadn't already been given more or less to understand from mosquitoes, people, life-in-general, and the rain out of the sky. It was just that he said it in a final sort of way—that was all.

"I was in a wreck," said Nancy.

"Nobody killed, I hope," said Rob.

She looked vaguely across at Rob Acklen with pretty, dark blue eyes that seemed to be squinting to see through shifting lights down in the deep sea; for in looking at him, in spite of all he could do, she caught a glimmering impression of herself, of what he thought of her, of how soft her voice always was, her face like a warm flower.

"I was doing my best to be nice to you. Why wasn't that enough?"

"I don't know," she said.

"None of those people you didn't like were out to get you. They were all my friends."

When he spoke in this handsome, sincere, and democratic way, she had to agree; she had to say she guessed that was right.

Then he said, "I was having such a good summer. I imagined you were, too," and she thought, He's coming down deeper and deeper, but one thing is certain—if he gets down as far as I am, he'll drown.

"You better go," she told him, because he had said he was on his way up to Shreveport on business for his father. And because Bub and Dennis were back; she'd seen them drift by in the car twice, once on the boulevard and once in town, silenter than cloud, Bub in the back, with his knees propped up, reading a magazine.

"I'll be going in a minute," he said.

"You just didn't realize I'd ever go running off like that," Nancy said, winding a damp Coca-Cola straw around her finger.

"Was it the party, the one you said you wanted to give? You didn't have to feel—"

"I don't remember any party," she said quickly.

Her mother lay with the roof gone, hands folded. Nancy felt that people's mothers, like wallpapered walls after a hurricane, should not be exposed. Her father at last successfully reached the donkey, but he fell in the middle of the rug, while Nancy, on the stair landing, smelling seaweed, asked herself how a murderous child with swollen jaws happened to mention love, if love is not a fever, and the storm-driven sea struck the open reef and went roaring skyward, splashing a tattered gull that clutched at the blast—but if we will all go there immediately it is safe in the Dupré house, because they have this holy candle. There are hidden bone-cold lairs no one knows of, in rock beneath the sea. She shook her bone-white hair.

Rob's whole sensitive face tightened harshly for saying what had to come next, and she thought for a while he wasn't going to make it, but he did. "To hell with it. To absolute hell with it then." He looked stricken, as though he had managed nothing but damaging himself.

"I guess it's just the way I am," Nancy murmured. "I just run off sometimes."

Her voice faded in a deepening glimmer where the human breath is snatched clean away and there are only bubbles, iridescent and pure. When she dove again, they rose in a curving track behind her.

THE FISHING LAKE

She was crossing the edge of the field, along the ridge, walking with a longer, more assured step now; she knew just about where he was. She knew because she had seen the jeep parked just off the road, where it got too soggy to risk and too narrow to go through without a limb batting you between the eyes, and she stopped the car about a stone's throw back from there. Something told her all along he would be at the lake. She cleared the ridge, and there he was just below her, down at the pier, tying up the boat. He didn't look up. She eased herself sidewise down the wet, loamy bank that released the heavy smell of spring with every step, and she was within a few feet of him before he said, still not looking up, "There ought to be a better boat down here. I spent half the time bailing. There used to be another boat."

"I think that's the same one," she said. "It's just that things get run down so in a little while. I bet the Negroes come and use it; there's no way to keep them from it."

"It's got a lock on it."

"Well, you know, they may just sit in it to fish. Either that or let the children play in it."

He had found the mooring chain now; it grated through the metal hook in the prow, and he snapped the lock shut and stepped out on the pier.

"Did you catch anything?"

He leaned down and pulled up a meager string—two catfish, a perch, one tiny goggle-eye. "The lake needs draining and clearing the worst kind. All around the bend there's the worst kind of silt and slime. The stink is going to get worse." He paused. "Or maybe you'd say that I'm the stinker."

"I didn't say that. I didn't say anything about it."

He stood with his back to her, hands hooked on his thighs, like somebody in the backfield waiting for the kickoff, and his hair, still streaked with color—sunburned, yellow and light brown—made him seem a much younger man than he would look whenever he decided to turn around. "I would tell you that I'm going to quit it," he said, "but you know and I know that that just ain't true. I ain't ever going to quit it."

"It wasn't so much getting drunk. . . . I just thought that coming home to visit Mama this way you might have put the brakes on a little bit."

"I intended to. I honestly did."

"And then, if you had to pick somebody out, why on earth did you pick out Eunice Lisles?"

"Who would you have approved of?" he asked. He looked off toward the sunset; it was delicate and pale above the tender, home-made line of her late uncle's fishing lake, which needed draining, had a leaking boat and a rickety pier.

"Well, nobody," she said. "What a damn-fool question. I meant, by the cool, sober light of day, surely you can see that Eunice Lisles—"

"I didn't exactly pick her out," he said. "For all I know, she picked me out." He lit a cigarette, striking the kitchen match on the seat of his trousers. He began to transfer the tackle box, the roach box, the worm can, and the minnow bucket from the boat to the pier. He next took the pole out of the boat and began to wind off the tackle. "Where we made our big mistake is ever saying we'd go out. We came to Mississippi to see your mother, we should have stayed with your mother."

"Well, I mean if it gets to where we can't accept an invitation—"

"It hasn't got to where anything," he said irritably. "I'm exactly the same today as I was yesterday, or a year ago. I'm a day or a year older. I've got a hangover worse than usual. And I would appreciate never having to hear anything more about Eunice Lisles."

—

Her uncle had made a bench near the pier—a little added thought, so very like him. It was for the older ladies to sit on when they brought their grandchildren or nieces and nephews down to swim, and he had had a shelter built over it as well, to shade their heads from the sun, but that had been torn down, probably by Negroes using it for firewood. She remembered playing endlessly around the pier when one of her aunts or her grandfather or Uncle Albert himself brought her down there, and at twilight like this in the summer seeing the men with their Negro rowers come back, solemn and fast, almost processional, heading home from around both bends in the lake, shouting from boat to boat, "Whadyacatch? Hold up yo' string! Lemme *see* 'em, man!" The men would have been secret and quiet all afternoon, hidden in the rich, hot thicket quiet of the brush and stumps, the Negroes paddling softly, holding and backing and easing closer, with hardly a ripple of the dark water. Then, at supper up at Uncle Albert's, there would be the fish dipped in corn meal, spitting and frying in the iron skillets and spewing out the rich-smelling smoke, and platter after platter of them brought in to the table. You ate till you passed out in those days, and there wasn't any drinking to amount to anything—maybe somebody sneaking a swallow or two off out in the yard. Her husband always told her she was wrong about this, that she had been too young to know, but she was there and he wasn't, she said, and ought at least to know better than he did. What she really meant was that her family and their friends and relatives had been the finest people thereabouts, and were noted for their generosity and fair, open dealings, and would never dream of getting drunk all the time, in front of people. He might at least have remembered that this was her home town.

She sat down carefully now on what was left of the bench her uncle had made. She opened her bag. "I brought you something." It was a slug of her sister-in-law's Bourbon she had poured out into a medicine bottle, sneaking as though it were a major theft, and adding a bit of water to the whiskey bottle to bring the level up again, nearly to where it was. She knew that all the family had their opinions. In the house she had kept as quiet as death all day, and so had they. The feeling was that gossip was flying around everywhere, just past the front gate and the back gate, looping and swirling around them.

"That was nice of you. By God, it was." He began to move methodically, slowly, holding back, but his sense of relief gave him a surer touch, so the top of the tackle box came clanging down in a short time, and he came up beside her, taking the small bottle and unscrewing the top. "Ladies first." He offered it to her. She laughed; he could always make her laugh, even if she didn't want to. She shook her head, and the contents of the bottle simply evaporated down his throat. "That's better." He sat companionably beside her; they had to sit close together to get themselves both on the bench.

"I reckon you feel like you get to the end of your rope sometimes," he sympathized. "I think maybe you might."

She had too much of a hangover herself to want even to begin to go into detail about what she felt.

"I don't feel any different toward you," he went on. "In fact, every time you do something like today—go right through your family without batting an eye, steal their whiskey for me out from under their noses, and come down here to get your fussing done in private—I love you that much more. I downright admire you."

She said, after a time, "You know, I just remembered, coming down here up past the sandpit that Uncle dug out to sand the lake with so we could swim without stepping ankle-deep in mud, there was this thing that happened. . . . I did it; I was responsible for it. I used to go there in the afternoons to get a suntan when we used to come and stay with Uncle Albert. And back then they had this wild dog—they thought for a long time it was a wildcat, or some even said a bear—but it turned out to be a wild dog, who used to kill calves. So one day I was lying there sun-bathing and I looked up and there was the dog—that close to the house! It scared me half to death. I just froze. I went tight all over and would have screamed, but I couldn't. I remembered what they said about not getting nervous around animals because it only frightens them, so I didn't say anything and didn't move, I just watched. And after a while, just at the top of the hill where the earth had been busted open to get at the sand, the dog lay down and put its head on its paws—it must have been part bulldog—and watched me. I felt this peaceful feeling—extremely peaceful. It stayed there about an hour and then it went away and I went away. So I didn't mention it. I began to doubt if it had really seen me, because I heard somewhere that dogs' vision is not like humans', but I guessed it knew in its way that I was there. And the next time I went, it came again. I think this went on for about a week, and once I thought I would go close enough to pat its head. I had got so it was the last thing I'd ever be scared of, but when it had watched me climb to within just about from here to the end of the pier away from it, it drew back and got up and backed off. I kept on toward it, and it kept on drawing back and it looked at me—well, in a personal sort of way. It was a sort of dirty white, because of a thin white coat with blue markings underneath. It was the ugliest thing I ever saw.

"Then it killed some more calves, and they had got people out to find it, and more showed up when the word got round, bringing their guns and all, and there was almost a dance on account of it, just because so many people were around. A dollar-pitching, a watermelon-cutting—I don't know what all. I was only about fifteen, and I told on it."

"*Told* on it?"

"Yes, I said that if they would go down to the sandpit at a certain time they would see it come out of the woods to the top of the hill on the side away from the house. And they went out and killed it."

"That's all?"

"That's all."

"And that's the worst thing you ever did?"

"I didn't say that. I mean, I felt the worst about it afterwards."

"You might have thought how those poor calves felt."

"I thought of that. It's not the same thing. The link was me. I betrayed him."

"You worry about this all the time?" He was teasing, somewhat.

"I hadn't thought of it in ten or maybe even fifteen years, until today, coming along the ridge just now. You can still see the sandpit."

At that moment, the bench Uncle Albert had built to make those long-dead ladies comfortable collapsed. They had been too heavy to sit on it, certainly, and shouldn't have tried. As though somebody had reached out of nowhere and jerked a chair from under them, just for a joke, it spilled them both apart, out on the pier.

They began to laugh. "Come out here next year," he said, in his flat-talking Georgia way, "there ain't going to be one splinter hanging on to one nail. Even the bailing can's got a hole rusted in it."

She kept on laughing, for it was funny and awful and absolutely true, and there was nothing to do about it.

THE ADULT HOLIDAY

That day there was a holiday for the college where he taught, but none for the schools, she was alone all day with her husband and he was angry with her. She had really never seen him so angry. A flush of rage had come over him soon after breakfast, and going into his office, just off the kitchen, she ran straight into it at the door, like a fiery wall, though his back was turned, his long hand sorting through some letters. "Oh," she thought, and "Oh," and "Oh," and "Oh . . ." even her thought fading, dissolving out to nothing, and then he turned and let her have it—a white lash of words during which she could only stand, try to catch her breath, try not to turn away, try to last it out, try in the end simply to survive.

Then it was over. It was the kind of thing she had never before experienced, something there was no apologizing for. If she had gone straight upstairs and packed a suitcase to go and get a job someplace, or to go back to her family and call a lawyer for a divorce, there was nothing he could have said to stop her, except possibly "I must be insane, and will go to a psychiatrist immediately." And he was not going to do that at all.

She clung about the house in corners all morning long, and finally fell to dusting the pictures. It had rained in the night, and the big maple on the back lawn stood pale green, enlarging itself in the new season. What did I do to start it, she wondered, as though by thinking of it in a small way, as just like any other quarrel, she might reduce it to being small. Had it been something about his mother? She knew that men were supposed to have deeply hidden sensibilities about their mothers. But all she said at breakfast was something mild about that lady's handwriting's getting worse—a fact they had often remarked upon before. Besides, he had always seemed more deeply aware of things about his father. Had she so much as alluded to his father? She did not think so. Had some chance association brought his father up? Had that arrogant face, ten years gone, intruded above her shoulder at breakfast to let her husband's vision cut through for once upon her, come straight into clear focus on the terrible creature that, for all she knew, she might really be? And had he not been able to bear that?

She didn't know . . . she didn't know. She turned herself all the way into a maid, and got out the silver to polish it. She did not wear her gloves and thought that now her hands would be splotched, which he didn't like but as he had let no stone of herself remain upon another in the general destruction, she felt that lamenting her hands would be like mourning the death of a kitten after the funeral of a child. She turned out a closet and straightened it, taking care to make no noise at all. She could not compose a grocery list, though she tried, and once she peeked down through a crack in the floor abovestairs and saw him eating lunch—he managed well enough alone. She fell to admiring how calmly he could assemble and digest everything. He had not forgotten the butter, nor the two kinds of bread—one for the salad, one for the meat and cheese—nor his favorite pepper mill. She lay hugged to the floor, thinking she would never eat again, but nonetheless admiring him, as a girl in the scullery might admire the lord of the castle. If she stayed on here, she would eventually have to speak to him; a word would have to crack through the voluminous stillness he had created in both their lives. She wondered what it would be. Eeny, meeny, miney, mo: "Did you mail the check for the gas?" "Let's go to the movies tonight." "My dearest wish was only that . . ."

But still she did not cross his path; she did not even cry until their little girl (the youngest, hence the earliest) came home from school and showed her the cutouts. Then her tears rolled down like rain.

"Why are you crying, Mother?"

"Well, I used to make cutouts at school, too," she said, sobbing.

The cutouts—witches, gingerbread men, clowns, and princesses—

got smeared and wet in this torrent, which the child did not like, but grew cautious about. She went in to her father, having gathered up the stack of them. "Mother's crying," she said. "Do you know why?"

"She feels sad because it's my forty-fifth birthday," he said.

"But your birthday is not till tomorrow," said the child.

"I know that," he said, "but she was thinking of it."

There was a long silence. Soon she would have to come alive, to walk on her two numb legs back into his presence and thus concede that the thing had happened indeed and that she could and would go on living there, that dinner would somehow appear for them as usual. She heard the child and her husband building a fire.

"Listen, Daddy," said the child, "how do you feel about getting so old?"

"I don't like it," he said. "I thought that's why they were giving us the holiday, but of course it wasn't."

"The holiday is for Founder's Day."

"That's right, but I didn't go to the ceremony."

"Why didn't you?"

"Because I don't like being forty-five."

The child was silent, thinking all this over. He had a nice way with children—just whimsical enough without exactly trying to fool them; he let them know they were being made to think instead of being made fun of. He was also good at making a child aware of the joins and turns of an adult conversation.

"Does Mother really care *that* much if you're forty-five?" asked the child, and, listening, the mother could all but see just how the child looked when she said that—the downward look of thinking, the crinkle of the brow when she turned up her face. Those sobs had been incongruous with both the reasons given for them; the child would have felt that clearly all along.

He had not answered, but she knew by the crackling sound and the smell of woodsmoke that he had lighted the fire. "Anyway," said the child, to whom the problem still was a dense one, "she's just about thirty-seven herself."

"She should have gone away soon after I met her," he said, in his light, persistent way. "Then I wouldn't be here now."

"But where would you be?"

"Somewhere. Not here."

"Where would it be?" cried the child, gathering a sort of anxious interest, as if he had drawn her into a game.

"Wherever it is, it's not where you are the day before your forty-fifth birthday," he said. "It never is."

"Then where is it, Daddy?"

"If I knew, I'd go there."

"Would you take me?"

"Why would I take you? Of course not." He paused. "To be there I would have had to start going there the day your mother should have gone away."

Caught in a tangle of syntax almost like an enchantment, the child laughed uneasily, and tried to repeat: "To be there you . . . What now?"

"Try it," he said.

———

In the silence of the study, not called for by either of them, she remembered the very day he meant, a quite different spring from this one. He had come down to the office where she worked and waited in the gritty hallway outside for her to finish, had followed her all the way home, talking eagerly about his work, and she knew that he was in love with her, this studious, brilliant, earnest young man who (they said) had the world before him. All the things other people said faded, not mattering, and the two of them, walking together, passed every which way through a world of streams, muddy paths, and flowers, through short cuts that lengthened the way endlessly before them.

It was the deliberate association of that day with this that crushed in upon her, listening, and so all but made up, she felt, the final sum of her life. She put aside the sewing basket—she must have done a month's mending, very skillfully and accurately, in spite of the fact that her glasses were smeared with drying tears and she couldn't see anything. The child was attempting, as with a riddle, to get the syntax right, repeating, "For you to be there now you would have had . . . Wait. For you to be there now you would have had to start going there the day . . . Let me start over. For you to be there now . . ."

In another minute, she thought, the child would not only get it right but understand it, and then they all could vanish. She replaced her cleaned glasses and came to the living room door—a journey into the void. "I didn't leave that day because I didn't want to leave."

He at once said, trembling, "Darling, you didn't leave because I didn't want you to."

The child, greedy for happiness, looked up and smiled at them. Strung between them on a mended web of what they said, she abandoned the puzzle of her father's words forever.

SHARON

Uncle Hernan, my mother's brother (his full name was Hernando de Soto Wirth), lived right near us—a little way down the road, if you took the road; across the pasture, if you didn't—in a house surrounded by thick privet hedge, taller than a man riding by on a mule could see over. He had live oaks around the house, and I don't remember ever going there without hearing the whisper of dry fallen leaves beneath my step on the ground. Sometimes there would be a good many Negroes about the house and yard, for Uncle Hernan worked a good deal of land, and there was always a great slamming of screen doors—people looking for something they couldn't find and hollering about where they'd looked or thought for somebody else to look, or just saying, "What'd you say?" "Huh?" "I said, 'What'd you *say?*'"—or maybe a wrangling noise of a whole clutch of colored children playing off down near the gully. But in spite of all these things, even with all of them going on at one and the same time, Uncle Hernan's place was a still place. That was how it knew itself: it kept its own stillness. When I remember that stillness, I hear again the little resistant veins of a dry oak leaf unlacing beneath my bare foot, so that the sound seems to be heard in the foot's flesh itself.

As a general rule, however, I wasn't barefoot, for Uncle Hernan was a gentleman, and I came to him when I was sent for, to eat dinner, cleaned up, in a fresh dress, and wearing shoes. "Send the child over on Thursday," he would say. Dinner was what we ate in the middle of the day—our big meal. Mama would look me over before I went—ears and nails and mosquito bites—and brush my hair, glancing at the clock. "Tell Uncle Hernan hello for me," she would say, letting me out the side door.

"Marilee?" she would say, when I got halfway to the side gate.

"Ma'am?"

"You look mighty sweet."

"Sweet" was a big word with all of them; I guess they got it from so many flowers and from the night air in South Mississippi, almost all seasons. And maybe I did really look that way when going to Uncle Hernan's.

I would cross a shoulder of pasture, which was stubbled with bitterweed and white with glare under the high sun, go through a slit in the hedge, which towered over me, and wriggle through a gap in the fence. This gap was no haphazard thing but was arranged, the posts placed in such a way that dogs and people could go through but cows couldn't, for Uncle Hernan was a good farmer and not one to leave baggy places in his fences from people crawling over them. He built a gap instead. As I went by, the dogs that were sprawled around dozing under the trees would look up and grin at me, giving a thump or two with their tails in the dust, too lazy to get up and speak. I would go up the steps and stand outside the door and call, looking into the shadowy depths of the hall, like a reflection of itself seen in water. I had always to make my presence known just this way; this was a house that expected behavior. It was simple enough, one-story, with a square front porch, small by Southern standards, opening out from the central doorway. Two stout pillars supported the low classical triangle of white-painted wood, roofed in shingle. The house had been built back before the Civil War. Uncle Hernan and Mama and others who had died or moved away had been brought up here, but they were anxious to let you know right away that they were not pretentious people but had come to Mississippi to continue being what they'd always been—good farming people who didn't consider themselves better or worse than anybody else. Yet somebody, I realized fairly early on, had desired a façade like a Greek temple, though maybe the motive back of the desire had been missing and a prevailing style had been copied without any thought for its effect.

Uncle Hernan, however, was not one of those who protested in this vein any more, if he ever had. He lived the democratic way and had friends in every walk of life, but Sharon—that was the name of the house—had had its heyday once, and he had loved it. It had been livened with more airs and graces than anybody would have patience to listen to, if I knew them all to tell. That was when Uncle Hernan's pretty young wife was there. Mama said that Uncle Hernan used to say that the bright and morning star had come to Sharon. It all sounded very Biblical and right; also, he called her his Wild Irish Rose. She was from Tennessee and brought wagonloads of stuff with her when she came, including a small rosewood piano. Every tasseled, brocaded, gold-leafed, or pearl-inlaid thing in Sharon, you knew at once, had come from Tennessee with Aunt Eileen. At the long windows, for instance, she had put draperies that fastened back with big bronze hooks, the size of a baby's arm bent back, and ending in a lily. Even those lilies were French—the fleur-de-lis. All this was in the best parlor, where nobody ever went very much any more, where the piano was, covered with the tasseled green-and-white throw, and the stern gold-framed portraits (those belonged to our family). It was not that the parlor was closed or that there was anything wrong with going into it. I sometimes got to play in there, and looked at everything to my heart's content. It was just that there was no reason to use it any more. The room opposite, across the hall, was a parlor, too, full of Uncle Hernan's books, and with his big old plantation desk, and his round table, where he sat near the window. The Negroes had worn a path to the window, coming there to ask him things. So life went on here now, in the plain parlor rather than the elegant one, and had since Aunt Eileen died.

She had not lived there very long, only about three or four years, it seems, or anyway not more than five, when she got sick one spring day—the result, they said at first, of having done too much out in the yard. But she didn't get better; one thing led to another, all during the hottest summer Mama said she could ever remember. In September, their hopes flagged, and in the winter she died. This was all before I could remember. Her portrait did not hang in the best parlor with the other, old ones, but there was a daguerreotype of her in a modest oval gold frame hanging in the plain parlor. She had a small face, with her hair done in the soft upswept fashion of the times, and enormous eyes that looked a little of everything—fearful, shy, proud, wistful, happy, adoring, amused, as though she had just looked at Uncle Hernan. She wasn't the angel you might think. Especially when she was sick, she'd make them all jump like grease in a hot skillet, Uncle Hernan said, but he would say it smiling, for everything he felt about her was sheer affection. He was a strong, intelligent man; he had understood her but he had loved her, all the time.

Uncle Hernan never forgot that he'd asked me to dinner, or on which day. He would come to let me in himself. He always put on the same coat, no matter how hot it was—a rumpled white linen coat, faded yellow. He was a large, almost portly man, with a fleshy face, basically light in color but splashed with sunburn, liver spots, and freckles, and usually marked with the line of his hatband. He had untidy, graying, shaggy hair and a tobacco-stained mustache, but he kept his hands and nails scrupulously clean—a matter of pride. I was a little bit afraid of Uncle Hernan. Though I loved to come there, I was careful to do things always the same way, waiting to sit down until I was told, staying interested in whatever he told me, saying, "Yes, thank you, Uncle Hernan," and "No, thank you, Uncle Hernan," when we were at the table. He was fond of me and liked having me, but I was not his heart of hearts, so I had to be careful.

Melissa waited on us. Melissa had originally come there from Tennessee with Aunt Eileen, as her personal maid, so I had got it early through my head that she was not like the rest of the Negroes around home, any more than Aunt Eileen's tasseled, rosewood, pearl-inlaid, gold-leafed, and brocaded possessions were like the plain Wirth house had been before she got there. Melissa talked in a different style from other Negroes; for instance, she said "I'm not" instead of "I ain't" or "I isn't" (which they said when trying to be proper). She even said "He doesn't," which was more than Mama would do very often. It wasn't that she put on airs or was ambitious.

But we all stood in awe of her, a little. You never know for sure when you come into a Negro house, whether you are crossing the threshold of a rightful king or queen, and I felt this way about Melissa's house. It was just Uncle Hernan's cook's cabin, but I felt awkward in it. It was so much her own domain, and there was no set of manners to go by. She had turned scraps of silk and satin into clever doilies for tables and cushion covers and had briar-stitched a spread for her bed with rich dark pieces bound with a scarlet thread; you could tell she had copied all her tastes from Aunt Eileen. The time I discovered that I really liked Melissa was when she came to our house once, the winter Mama had pneumonia. She came and stayed, to help out. She wore a white starched uniform, so then I learned that Melissa, all along, had been a nurse. It seemed that when Aunt Eileen was about to get married, Eileen's father, seeing that Uncle Hernan lived in the wilds of Mississippi, had taken Melissa and had her trained carefully in practical nursing. I guess he thought we didn't have doctors, or if we had we had no roads for them to go and come on; anyway, he wasn't taking any chances. After Mama passed the danger period, Melissa spent a lot of time reading aloud to me. I would sit in her lap by the hour and listen and listen, happy, until one day I went in to see how Mama was and she said, "I wouldn't ask Melissa to read to me too long at the time, Marilee."

"She likes to read," I said.

"I know," she said, "but I'm afraid you'll get to smell like a Negro."

Now that she mentioned it, I realized that I had liked the way Melissa smelled. I wanted to argue, but she looked weak and cross, the way sick people do, so I just said, "Yes, ma'am," and went away.

It is a mighty asset in life to be a good cook, and Melissa never spared to set the best before me when I came to Uncle Hernan's to dinner. If it was fried chicken, the crust would be golden, and as dry as popcorn, with the thinnest skim of glistening fat between the crust and the meat. If it was roast duck or turkey or hen, it would come to the table brown, gushing steam that smelled of all it was stuffed with. There were always hot biscuits—she made tiny hot biscuits, the size of a nickel three inches high—and side dishes of peach pickle, souse, chopped pepper relish, green-tomato pickle,

wild-plum jelly, and blackberry jam. There were iced tea and buttermilk both, with peaches and dumplings for dessert and maybe
homemade ice cream—so cold it hurt your forehead to eat it—and
coconut cake.

Such food as that may have been the main excuse for having me
to dinner, but Uncle Hernan also relished our conversations. After
dinner, I would sit with him in the plain parlor—he with his small
cup of black chicory coffee before him, and I facing him in a chair
that rocked on a stand—telling him whatever he asked me to. About
Mama and Daddy, first; then school—who taught me and what they
said and all about their side remarks and friends and general behavior. Then we'd go into his part, which took the form of hunting
stories, recollections about friends, or stories about his brother,
Uncle Rex, who now lived several miles away, or about books I
ought to be reading. He would enter right into those books he favored as though they were a continuation of life around us. *Les Mis-
érables* was a great favorite of his, not so much because of the poverty
and suffering it depicted but because in spite of all that Valjean was
a man, he said, and one you came a little at a time to see in his full
stature. His stature increased, he would say, and always put his hand
down low and raised it up as high as it would go. I guess he was not
so widely read as he seemed to me at that time to be, but he knew
what he liked and why, and thought that knowing character was the
main reason for reading anything. One day, he took a small gold box
from his pocket and sniffed deftly, with his hand going to each nos-
tril in turn. When I stared at him, startled into wonder, my look in
turn startled him. His hand forgot to move downward and our eyes
met in a lonely, simple way, such as had not happened before.

Then he smiled. "Snuff," he said. He snapped the box to and held
it out. "You want to see? Don't open it, now. You'll sneeze." I took
the box in my hand and turned it—golden, with a small raised cage
of worked gold above the lid. I thought at once I had come on another of Aunt Eileen's tracks, but he said, "I picked that up in New
Orleans a year or so back," and here I had another facet of Uncle
Hernan—a stroll past shops in that strange city I had never seen, a
pause before a window, a decision to enter and buy, cane hooked

over his forearm. The world was large; I was small. He let me out the front door. "You're getting to be a big girl," said Melissa, from halfway back down the hall. "I'm soon going to have to say 'Miss Marilee.'"

———

The one thing I could never do was to go over to Uncle Hernan's without being asked. This was laid down to me, firmly and sternly. It became, of course, the apple in the garden. One summer afternoon when I was alone and bored, getting too big, they said, to play with Melissa's children anymore, I begged Mama to let me go over there. She denied me twice, and threatened to whip me if I asked again, and when Daddy got in from the field she got him to talk to me. They were both sterner and more serious than I ever remembered them being, and made sure I got it straight. I said to Mama, being very argumentative, "You just don't like Melissa." She looked like I had slapped her. She turned white and left the room, but not without a glance at Daddy. I knew he was commissioned to deal with me (he knew it, too), but I also knew that he was not going to treat me as badly as Mama would have if he hadn't been there. He sent me to my room and hoped for the best. There I felt very sorry for myself and told myself I didn't know why I was being treated so harshly, sent to bed in a cold room with no supper, all for making such an innocent remark. I said I would stay in my room till I died, and they'd be sorry, Mama especially. I pictured the sad words that would certainly be exchanged.

Mama relented well before I came to this tragic end. In fact, she came in the room after about an hour. She never could stand any kind of unhappiness for long, and after urging me to come and get supper (I wouldn't reply) she brought me a glass of milk and lighted a little fire to take the chill off the room. But, sweet or not, she was a feline at heart, and at a certain kind of threat her claws came out, ready for blood. She was never nice to Melissa. I overheard them once talking at the kitchen door. Uncle Hernan had sent some plums over and when Mama said, "How are you, Melissa?" in her most grudging and offhand way, Melissa told her. She stood outside the steps, not touching the railing—they had reached their hands out to the farthest limit to give and receive the bucket, and Mama had by now closed the screen door between them—and told her. She had a boil on her leg, she said; no amount of poultices seemed to draw it out and it hurt her all the way up to her hip. She had also been feeling very discouraged in her heart lately, but maybe this was due to the boil.

"I don't see why you don't go on back to Tennessee," Mama said, cold as ice. "You know you ought to, now, don't you?"

"No, ma'am," Melissa answered her politely, "I don't know that I ought to. I promised Miss Eileen I'd stay and care for Sharon."

"You aren't fooling anybody," Mama said. "If Miss Eileen—"

"Good morning, Marilee," said Melissa sweetly.

I said, "Morning, Melissa," and Mama, who hadn't noticed me, whirled around and left without another word.

The day came when I crossed over. Wrong or not, I went to Sharon when nobody had asked me. Mama was away to a church meeting, and Daddy had been called down in the pasture about some cows that had got out. It was late September, still and golden; school hadn't been started very long. I went over barefoot and looked in the window of the plain parlor, but nobody was there, so I circled round to the other side, stopping to pet and silence a dog who looked at me and half barked, then half whined. I looked through the window of the fine parlor, and there they both happened to be, Uncle Hernan and Melissa, talking together and smiling. I could see their lips move, though not hear them, for in my wrongdoing and disobedience I was frightened of being caught, and the blood was pounding in my ears. Melissa looked pretty, and her white teeth flashed with her smiling in her creamy brown face. But it was Uncle Hernan, with the lift of his arm toward her, seated as he was in a large chair with a high back that finished in carved wood above his head, whose gesture went to my heart. That motion, so much a part of him whom I loved, was for her and controlled her, as it had, I knew now, hundreds of times. She came close and they leaned together; he gathered her surely in. She gave him her strength and he drank it; they became one another.

I had forgotten even to tremble and do not remember yet how I reached home from Sharon again. I only remember finding myself in my own room, seated on the edge of my narrow bed, hands folded in my lap, hearing the wrangle of Melissa's children out in the gully playing—they were beating some iron on an old washtub—and presently how her voice shouted out at them from across the back yard at Uncle Hernan's. She had four, and though they could all look nice on Sunday, they were perfect little devils during the week, Mama complained, and Melissa often got so mad she half beat the hide off them. I felt differently about them now. Their awful racket seemed a part of me—near and powerful, realer than itself, like their living blood. That blood was ours, mingling and twining with the other. Mama could kick like a mule, fight like a wildcat in a sack, but she would never get it out. It was there for good.

THE FINDER

Dalton was a pleasant town—still is. Lots of shade trees on residential streets, lots of shrubs in all the front yards, ferns in tubs put outside in the summer, birdbaths well attended, and screen side porches with familiar voices going on through the twilight. Crêpe myrtle lined the uptown streets. The old horse troughs on the square were seen by some in authority to be quite fine, so they were never removed but ran with water even after the last mule had died and the last wagon of the dozens that used to creak into town on Saturday from out in the country had fallen apart in somebody's barn or had been chopped up for kindling. So even on the hottest summer day the persistent murmur of water could be heard through still moments, and the lacy shade of crêpe myrtle lay traced on the sidewalks, on the heads of passing ladies, and on the shoulders of shirt-sleeved men.

There were several strong families in the town, and Gavin Anderson belonged to one of these. In the 1930s, there must have been seven or eight branches of the original Anderson parent stem living in and around there, in addition to others who had been taken North or into cities, according to the professions they picked or the men they married, but all of the Andersons had "kept up" and they came back from time to time. No matter where they went, they always said they felt as if they were living right there in Dalton on the Waukahatchie, where all the good picnics were held, down on the sandbar. Since most of the Andersons were from a little distance alike and since nearly all of them were full of the same cordial sayings and the same way of chuckling with forbearance over what they couldn't help, making it funny if possible, it was hard to remember which of them were dead and which had been more recently born. Not that they lacked personality, but only that together they were like one continuous entity, a long table of a family, rather than a history in which the people might be thought of as different shapes and sizes of beads on a string. And the way they talked of one another—with such clarity and wit about the ones who had passed away—you would think the dead were still right there about to come in any minute.

Gavin Anderson was not different from his family in any discernible way. Looking at him, a stranger would never have guessed what there was about him. It must have started just as a game when he was little, out in the sandpile with all of them. Perhaps somebody had said, "I lost my favorite agate. Now, where is it?" and Gavin's eyes might have been closed just from shutting out the sun as it came too strongly through the cedar limbs, or closed to keep cedar twigs from dropping into them, and maybe the question "Now, where is it?" hadn't been asked of anybody in particular; but lying there with his bright, healthy, tan-colored Anderson hair, dry as spun glass, in the remains of a sand castle, and one short practical Anderson hand thrown over his eyes, Gavin suddenly sat up and said, "It's rolled back behind the kindling box in the kitchen. I saw it there." Or if it was a letter that was lost, he would say, "You left it in the ninth-grade history book." Or if it was a book somebody had borrowed, he would say, "It's on Miss Jamie Whittaker's library shelf; she's put it up with her own by mistake." It got to be noticed he was always right. It was further noticed by an old-maid aunt, who had a sharp ear for picking up the flaws and lapses in what was said to her, that when he said he saw something, he had not, in the ordinary sense, seen it at all. Thereupon she questioned him all one afternoon, announced to the family at supper that it was right uncanny, and returned before day the next morning to a town near Jackson where she had taught Latin for twenty-three years. She herself was known to have second sight, and could generally be counted on "to get a feeling" a few days in advance of a death or disaster. Nobody paid much attention to her discovery about Gavin, as it was a busy fall and too much work to do. None of the Andersons were ever spoiled, because there were too many of them. Still, nothing was ever quite forgotten, either.

When Gavin's gift came to general attention, it was over the incident of the seed-pearl star pin that his father, Robert Anderson, had given to his mother and that had been lost so soon they suspected a servant of taking it. They did not want to suspect anybody, of course, and especially not Lulu, who was such a good cook. It was then that Gavin said right where it was—his mother, in her excitement, having hidden it even from herself. Lulu always said that the Lord spared her through that child. She announced this several times, coming once into the living room, and another time out of the kitchen into the dining room while they were eating. She never mentioned any gratitude to Gavin, and when the story was told in later years Gavin would add this observation with the particular little chuckle of the Andersons.

The story stuck. Even in Gavin's young manhood, somebody uptown would stop to ask him about it. "Was that really true about your mama's pin?" they would ask. He shrugged it off: "Should have gone on the stage, I guess. There was somebody up at the Orpheum in Memphis just the other day. Did you see it in the paper? I missed my chance for ever amounting to anything." But by then he was in his rugged, handsome stage and courting the girl he loved. All the Andersons married for love, and they always loved the right kind. One of the girls married a pharmacist who turned to dope and lost his license, but she stuck to him and he finally got over it. Her character was unbeatable; everyone was proud but none surprised.

It was soon after Gavin turned the insurance agency over to his brother and took the local hardware store over from his father—one of the many Anderson interests—and was every day now up on the town square, the father of two fine children, member of the Kiwanis Club, deacon in the church, with a boat on the lake for fishing every day in the summer with his boys, that the stories about him revived. Every once in so often, somebody would come to see him from out in the country or from a neighboring town, and it got to be known that a peculiar kind of worried look, like a bird dog uncertain of the scent, foretold the sort of errand they were on. Sometimes, too, a letter would arrive. He would get a thick packet, and inside, ink- or pencil-written on lined sheets or on cheap-grade blue stationery from the back counters in dusty drugstores, the entire story would come out in every detail. Something was lost: "Where is it? . . . Where is it? I feel like I just got to know—" Gavin's clerk and the bookkeeper would see him glance through page after page, refold the letter hastily, stuff it in his back pocket, and begin at once to do something else, some kind of straightening up he'd never think of otherwise.

One day in autumn, Gavin made a long-distance call to a neighboring town—a call he did not mention. He closed up the store and drove to that town, thirty miles away. He told his wife he had bank business in that part of the country; he didn't say exactly where. She had "a place" in that direction—something she had inherited. He always saw to it for her. She trusted him so much she never was quite sure where it was, and wouldn't have known how to find it if she had tried. Her name was Ethel. He got in the car and drove.

The minister was watching for his car to enter town, and had already reached the silent weekday church grounds before Gavin could cut off the motor. To reach the minister's study they first had to walk through the church itself. They unlocked the door, opened it, and Gavin stepped into the vestibule and encountered smells he had always, from time immemorial, associated with "religion." Hymnbooks, Sunday School literature, the pulpit Bible, the uncertain cleanliness of aging congregations, the starch of little girls' dresses, the felt in the organ stops, the smell of sunlight filtered by panes of stained glass discoloring the musty maroon carpet. Here there had been flowers sometime recently. He saw some white petals near the stove in passing, and coal dust left scanty by a broom's motion. He passed, following a step or two behind the gray brushed head of the minister—a man he remembered from the time when he had held the pulpit at Dalton but whom he had not seen in twenty-odd years. Dandruff flecked the good brown shoulders of his suit.

"All you all O.K.?" Gavin asked him.

The minister did not turn to answer. "Can't complain. Mrs. Cooper, though, 's got nothing to brag about."

"Serious?"

"Oh no. Hope not."

The door to the Sunday School annex stuck. The minister had to push, then rap the base with his toe. Back there it was cold. Gavin remembered his boyhood. Church-cold. Wasn't it always? Voices returned to him—the all-his-life voices. From last Sunday, from thirty years ago: ". . . not enough money to heat the auditorium, much less the Sunday School annex" . . . "They're only back there a little while; can't they keep their coats on?" And they did, hunched in uncomfortable chairs, sniveling with cold. And voices from those Sunday School classes: "Yes'm, He meant you had to have faith." . . . "Did He mean faith changes things?" Long pause. Somebody had to answer. If nobody answered, there might not be any more Sunday School. There had to be more Sunday School. "Oh, yes'm. That is, it might." "Always?" "It might and it might not, I guess." "Does God answer prayer?" "Yes'm, He does." "You mean God does what I tell Him to?" "Guess He don't always. Don't for me." Laughter. "Well, now, to tell you the truth, Billy, He doesn't for me either." "Sometimes He does, don't He?" "Yes, sometimes He does. So . . . can you summarize?" "Can I what?" "Can you tell me what we've just decided?" Long pause. "Well, uh . . . we decided sometimes He does and sometimes He don't." "There might be a better way to put it. I'd say . . ." The bell rang, a tinkle from the hallway, and the superintendent entered and asked for the collection. The teacher gave it, an envelope already counted and recorded. "We'll be right there. I just want to leave you with this thought for the day. God always answers prayer. Sometimes He says yes, sometimes He says no. And the third answer, we didn't have time to get to. It is this: Wait. Remember that—all week. Now you can go." They would be gone already; there had been a shoving and creaking of chairs from the minute the bell rang.

A country man, a Southern man, a small-town man, not given to book knowledge—he read for entertainment—Gavin Anderson did not recall these things critically. He had a moment's self-doubt—himself and his religion, what did they have to do with one another? If he had once respected, been so impressed by this minister—this Mr. Cooper with the direct sympathies and the earnest plain speech, who could also field in baseball and hit a home run, who had a way of expressing great truths simply and a way of carrying within himself plainly the love of God—why had he waited twenty-odd years to look him up? Gavin noted that what had stirred a boy of twelve and convinced him of deep truth was almost nothing but a memory to a man of thirty-five. Still, he had come there about something.

They entered the study. The minister snapped on an electric heater. "Bought it myself," he explained. "I come over here to get my sermons up. Couldn't live with a cold all winter. It'll just take a minute to heat up." Theological texts, green-black and red, stood in bookcases covered by protective glass panels.

"Let me take your hat. Have a seat. Now." The minister was back of his desk. Gavin Anderson could not see through the frosted windows. The smell of the electric heat seeped into the room.

"Your family all all right? You've married, I understand? Who was it? Don't tell me—that little old Davis girl."

"You've got some memory."

"She O.K.?"

"Yes, oh yes—she is. Two boys. All fine. You thought I'd come about somebody being sick." His bemusement vanished. The Anderson charm, always there to save, made a swift return. He smiled warmly.

The minister glowed with relief. "I was just 'fraid it might be—"

"No. Nothing about illness. No, you'd never guess." He laughed his genial uptown chuckle. "It's something worries me. . . . You may not remember; no reason why you should. You might, though. It's right unusual—I don't recall outside the show-business circuit ever hearing of such a thing, and even that might be a fake. Well, to refresh your mind, I always had this certain gift."

"You weren't the one could find things?" The minister broke out laughing.

You'd think I rode all the way over here to have a tea party, Gavin thought. He was very nearly angry. "It ain't funny, Mr. Cooper. I mean, it's true. I really can. I could then and I can still. I'm telling you the truth, Mr. Cooper. There's a world of people in this state that know about me, and when they lose something they write to me. Recently it's got worse. It's never going to stop. I realized that about six months ago. I got three letters in one day—one from way off in Texas somewhere. It's a gift. I can't give it back. Every time I get a letter, I hesitate to open it. Because I don't like to practice it. I think it's a sin."

"Every good gift and every perfect gift is from above," said Mr. Cooper.

"I thought about that, too."

They were silent. What did I ever see in him? thought Gavin Anderson. "It might be the Devil's gift," he suggested.

"Why, I know your family, Gavin. Everybody knows the Andersons. Nothing you folks have got 's ever been near the Devil."

"It's mighty nice of you to say that," said Gavin. "You've helped me a whole lot."

But really the minister had not told him anything. He thought, I went all the way over there to say out loud what I thought myself.

It was later said in Dalton that Gavin Anderson had gone to see a minister and the minister had told him to give up his finding gift, it was a sin. But this had not happened, as Gavin knew. He let it go as truth, but it was not true. So sometimes still he opened the letters. Sometimes he didn't.

———

Then it was the day of the thunderstorm—a spring day when the sky got black as pitch around about noon. The tree leaves, which were just coming out, turned an incandescent green in the shift of light; they seemed to be burning with green fire. Just back of the square, a wall of velvet black hung flat as a curtain. The girl who came in to keep books half a day twice a week took off an hour early. "Go on," said Gavin Anderson. "I'll stay here. If you run, you can make it." She was out already, going headlong for her car. There was a short warning jab of lightning. The phone rang. It was the clerk's mother. She had been ailing all winter and now she was scared, up on that hill by herself. "Go on home, Percy," said Gavin Anderson. "Yo' mama sounds like it's blowing up Judgment Day." "What about you?" Percy Howell inquired. "Oh, I'll either lock up or stick it out. You're 'bout as safe one place as another." He called home, but no one answered. He had just replaced the receiver and stretched to switch a light on as the dark intensified when the phone rang a second time. He reached his hand toward it, but light snapped and thunder exploded simultaneously within the boxed area of the store. Fire leaped from the black mouth of the phone. He felt himself hurled aside, and lost consciousness for a moment or two—or was it longer? A livid turmoil of air stood at the door, loftier than flame. Rain like a white wall was now in swift advance. Not only leaves but the limbs themselves cross-whipped in crazy ways. He had been thinking of his family when the phone had rung and gone dead; now his thought, like an interrupted current, resumed. Where were they? Why, in his own vision, couldn't he find them? It had never occurred to him before; he had never yet tried to find a person, nor had he ever been asked to.

Then he was hastening to close the door, which had blown wide, and the woman shot through half screaming, a scared rabbit of the storm. It wasn't the bookkeeper back. He never thought it was.

The wild smell of the whole spring rushed terrible and vivid through the door, into his face and nostrils, charged with new life, white and cold. Then he slammed it. She stood in mid-floor, drenched, her face screwed up and her hands to her ears while thunder shook at the walls and ceiling, banged against the high transom.

She opened her eyes just long enough to say, "It's a tornado," then shut them tight again.

He'd never seen her before. The protection he felt toward his family, wherever they were, extended suddenly to her. Alone there, he might not have done anything to make himself safer. "Come here," he said.

He led her with him by the hand—she was not tall, and her hand was like a little wood-wet wild paw, trembling—to the back of the store and, opening a rough wooden door, went down some steps into a storage room, half underground, that his father had built during the Depression for storing potatoes. The walls were earthen and the whole hardly man-high, but as a storm pit he could see it functioning, unless debris fell in to bury them. "Sit down."

He crouched down himself and pulled her down. Drawing herself close to him, she waited in childlike terror, eyes, he could dimly make out, still shut up tight and one hand to her ear, the other hand clutching his hand. "Oh!" and "Oh!" she sobbed, and "Jesus, Jesus!" No woman in his own family said that. She wasn't from around here.

Some minutes later, gently putting her aside, he opened the door. Store air came into the earthen-smelling dark, and with it the steady beat of rain. "Come on," he said. He shook her. "It's O.K. now."

She opened her eyes—they were large and blue—and pushed her dark hair into place. She smiled, climbed the steps after him, and stood before him in the back area of the store among the crates of stock—a small full-breasted woman in her thirties, smartly dressed in black linen with a wide shiny belt, more than a hint of good living about her. She smoothed her hair a second time. "I've always been like that—storms scare me to death."

"Well, that was a bad one," he said, forgiving her. He gestured toward the store, but she took his hand first and turned it.

"I scratched you." She touched the red marks of her nails—there were three of them, one deeper than the rest.

"I see," he said.

He got out a chair for her and offered her a Coke—all he had. They sat together. The rain still lashed, swaying above the town and countryside. The tree limbs blew freely, and some were broken. The rain sluiced against the store windows and closed doors, but there was something domestic and ample about it now.

"You just passing through?" he asked. "You're not from around here."

But she said what he already suspected. She had been looking for a Gavin Anderson, because she had lost something.

It was nothing ordinary. Her grandmother had had it from a man who had died, and some had said he was the real grandfather—here a little laugh—but never mind. The stone was large, and valuable. She had written to Gavin Anderson two weeks ago, but had got no reply. She had the air of a small woman who tried things. If there was a finder to be found, she found him.

"You didn't get my letter."

"I often don't open those letters any more."

"You mean too many people worry you?"

"Something like that."

"You know, I thought that. I really did imagine it."

"I think—" He stopped. His innermost thoughts, his long struggle. Why give it all away, suddenly, to her? Yet he almost had.

"So I thought if I came and told you that it was special, a special case . . ."

"Everybody's case is special," he said. "Some little girl's pencil box is as important to her as a ruby ring is to you."

"How did you know it was a ruby?"

"I didn't know it. Of course I didn't."

He brought matches—store matches to light her cigarette. The rain beat steadily before the door, on the town square, on the town. As the smoke rose, he closed his eyes. He saw the ring. It had fallen in the crevice of some old, dark, broad-boarded floors. A piece of string and the head of a thumbtack lay beside it. The corner of a rug lay over it. He thought, She must have taken it off at night and didn't know she dropped it, going to bed after a party. It lay there in the dark, canted to the side, square-cut, wine red. A little more and he thought he might have seen the silver evening sandals she had probably removed, the stockings fallen beside them. But he opened his eyes. Through the smoke, she was half smiling at him. Now that the danger had come and gone, she looked blue-eyed and young, just out of high school.

He told her where to find the ring.

It was that very evening, after ten, she tried to reach him, but the lines were still down from the storm. She told him this the next morning, excited on the phone, not five minutes after service was resumed. "Right where you said! Can you imagine?"

"Listen," he said. "Please listen. I'm so glad. Yes, I really am, but you've got to listen. I don't want you to tell anybody." For suddenly, vast as an army, scattered out all over the South, maybe all over the country, the numerous connections a woman like that would have stirred to shadowy life in his consciousness. My God, I'll have to explain, he thought, and said, "Listen, are you at home? Will you be at home this evening—afternoon, I mean? Sometime around two or three o'clock?"

"Come to a party tomorrow night! Why don't you? Are you free?"

He was free, but he hesitated. A party was another thing entirely.

"It's nothing fancy," she went on. "Just cocktails and dinner. We'll have a drink or two, then eat. Some friends from Birmingham are bringing me a horse."

"Well, yes, ma'am," he found himself saying. "We'll try. It's sort of far for a party, but maybe we can make it." He hung up.

She would go around saying to everybody, "He has this gift, the most remarkable thing, you can't i*ma*-gine, honey!" and her eyes, no longer clear blue and just out of high school, would burn overbright from alcohol. He wouldn't see her—not the way she seemed in the store just with him. And he would be the traveling magician, the oddity led by the wrist. Then he knew the truth about his fears, too—or were they hopes? Even if she did tell that world of people she knew, to them it would just be another of her stories about the backwoods. Most of them wouldn't even believe it. They'd tell the story maybe, but nobody would come look him up. They wouldn't, after an hour, be able to think of his name. And she—after a week or so, would she be able to?

He did not go to the party.

———

He went to see her instead. He was in that part of the state one afternoon. He got to the town and asked the way from a filling-station attendant. It was out of town, off a side road, over a cattle gap, through a pretty stretch of woods. The fences were all painted white. The house was at the end of a tree-lined path, quite a walk from the car, but the gate to let cars through was closed. He should have telephoned from town. He walked up the path. The trees, though oak, were not imposing, but small instead and rather twisted, as though storm-battered at an early age. And the house, even as it drew closer, was smaller than he had been expecting. It was white with a deep front porch, made private with thickset square pillars and a large bed of azaleas, past their prime. It was hard to get azaleas to bloom in that part of the state. The porch had a swing and white-painted iron furniture with comfortably padded green cushions. There were white-painted iron tables with glass tops, and lamps of wrought iron—all as it should be. No one there. Where was she? Should he stand, like the country man he was, and call? If he called, should he say Mrs. Beris or Naomi? Naomi Beris. It was an odd name. He ascended the front steps and knocked on one of the hollow white pillars. "Anybody home?"

There was a stir from within and a boy came out, tall, in his late teens, with wavy blond hair, wearing beige corduroys and beige suède shoes. The corduroy and suède went with the azaleas in the yard and the shadowy, waxed, thick-carpeted look of the hall. It went with the horses that Gavin Anderson already knew were out back, and would have known about even if she had not mentioned the horse she was getting from Birmingham.

"I'm looking for Mrs. Beris. Is she home?"

"She ought to be back pretty soon." The boy half turned to go inside. "Sit down, if you want to wait." He nodded toward the porch furniture. That was good enough, thought Gavin, feeling himself correctly defined. From a distance, the cattle gap rumbled.

She came in her car through the gate he had thought locked (it was automatic) and, parking in the side yard, got out and started toward the front porch. She was wearing short gloves and a dark cotton dress and carrying, along with her bag, a brown parcel. Near the steps, she paused and, shielding her eyes with one gloved hand, said, "Who is it? Now, don't tell me. It's Mr. Anderson!"

She had a drawling voice that only Southerners who have been away and come to know themselves in another context unconsciously cultivate.

"I was over here on business; just happened to be," he said.

Out back, she had the horses—two of them, a black and a bay. There was a white-fenced area for exercise and mounting, and a building with an open walkway through the middle, two stalls on one side and a tack- and feed-storage room on the other. The horses were small, to scale with everything there, to scale with herself. Perhaps she had a small fortune, Gavin thought. A Negro man who spoke to her pleasantly was cleaning the walkway, humming at his work. Gavin thought maybe the ruby that he had seen only in his vision was the only outsize thing she possessed. He did not ask to see it but, enchanted, listened and watched without seeming to.

"It's mighty pretty here," he said.

"It'd be a shame to part with it, now, wouldn't it?" she asked.

"You going to?"

"What can a lone woman do? My son's here, but after he finishes university he won't want to live here. There's nothing here for him."

"It looks like quite a lot here to me," said Gavin.

"Well, you know. . . . It's sweet of you to say so."

"I didn't know you were a lone woman."

"Divorced," she said. "I could face parting with the house, though it's been in the family a long time. But I couldn't sell a house with a ruby in it, now, could I?" He saw the ridiculous side of it. "Well, now," she pressed on, making him laugh more than ever, "how would you feel?"

She gave him a gin drink in a silver cup, fresh mint amidst the ice, and placed a small hand damp from the sweated silver into his as he stood on the steps, taking his leave.

He didn't get back to Dalton till after dark. He told his wife, Ethel, that he'd been up northeast of there to another county to see about some property he might invest in. It was the property, he said, in the ensuing weeks, that took him back up there, time and again. He asked her not to mention it.

"I think you know somebody up there," his wife said one evening. The boys had gone to a school program. It was autumn, the first cold snap. "I don't think you've bought any property up there at all. Anyway, there's plenty of property around here. So I don't believe it."

She was brushing her bobbed hair at the dresser. She had firm shoulders, had played basketball in school that year the girls' team was so attractive they used to get invited everywhere, and all the men turned out for miles around to whistle at their legs. She had short, strong, capable hands, the nails always breaking from house-work, and knuckles a little large, a perennial cooking burn somewhere—but still attractive. The gas heater hissed in the room.

Gavin didn't answer her. There was no precedent, as far as he knew, for any Anderson's knowing at this point what to say.

"I just think you're trying to tell me not to go through with it about that property," he said at last. "I've been having some doubts myself. I bet you had a dream."

"I don't have to dream. You think I'm dumb? O.K., I never said anything. That's the way I'm going to act, from now on."

———

It was the year of the Anderson reunion—the year the Anderson grandmother was ninety-five, the year an Anderson daughter (Gavin's cousin) had twins, the year the Lord spared an Anderson grandson (Gavin's nephew) in a traffic accident in which four were killed and two cars demolished (the boy himself was pitched into a blackberry thicket and woke up not even scratched by briars), the year Gavin's son's calf won the state-wide blue ribbon, a year of prosperity in which (everybody hoped) there wouldn't be another German war. The reunion was down on the creek, in Indian summer, and a special moon appeared—a swollen oval at the horizon, so orange, so huge, so mysteriously brushed across with one thin black cloud, that one of the aunts kept saying over and over, "If it wasn't so pretty, it'd be downright scary." The night was warm. The Wauka-hatchie Creek curled near the bluff opposite the bar, running shallow after a dry fall over ribbed sand. The sandbar lay white beneath the moon, which had risen, grown smaller and radiant. Dozens of children, far and wide, knew just what they wanted to play, and down the path from the house, which wound through the willows, the women came tripping with plates of trimmed sandwiches, platters of fried chicken, bowls of potato salad, warmers full of rolls. Gavin sat with his brothers, harmonizing. They sang about the moon—a dozen

moon songs—and clapping came up from the women near the tables. Ethel appeared, a ribbon in her hair, looking like a girl. "Thought
you weren't coming," Gavin called to her. She'd had a headache earlier. "Changed my mind," she said, going by. The table spread, they
lighted lanterns—somebody, got fancy and prosperous, had bought
fashionable glass-shielded hurricane lamps, now sparkling grandly
above the food. ("Where'd they come from?" one of the brothers
asked. "Harriet," another answered. "Oh," said the first. You had to
be one of them to get all there was in this.)

Now the brothers, five in all, were sent up to the house, and the
grandmother was carried down in her rocker among them. When
they appeared in her room, she was sitting straight and silent,
dressed and ready. When she saw them, she broke into tears. "Wonderful boys," she kept saying. "Wonderful, wonderful boys." "Hush,
now. Hush, now," they told her. And lightly they bore her down,
among the willows.

On the way home, long after midnight, Ethel said, "Why wouldn't
you find that bowl for them?" It was a silver bowl she meant. The
family had all contributed to give it to the grandmother. Simple,
engraved and beautiful, it was to sit on her dresser, a daily offering
till she died.

"It wasn't lost," he said. "They were teasing."

"They weren't, either. I saw Marvin. He was just about crazy. So
was Pat."

"Well, I didn't b'lieve it. I thought they were kidding. Anyway,
you know I don't like to."

"Not even for Gran's birthday!"

"But they found it."

"But they really thought it was lost. It was just in George's car, but
he went in for some ice and they didn't know it. But you wouldn't."

"I'm not on the midway. You can't just buy a ticket and have the
show commence."

"Seems like if you ever did it in your life you would then. Wasn't
your heart just so full with all the Andersons there? It's what you got
up and said." This was undercutting of the worst kind—flat country-
style.

"Yes, it was. I meant it all. Just like I said."

"You meant it when you said it, that's for sure."

He had got tired. Yet the reunion had finally reached him. His heart, though reluctant at first, had finally filled at that clear spring. The evening had said all the Andersons meant to each other—an eternal table, from the creation onward forever. Now it was plain to him that a tree does not choose to be struck by lightning, and that a plain man—even one who can find a ruby ring and who in consequence is given wine by candlelight and dark nakedness on fine linen—is a plain man still. But who, he thought, knew this better than Ethel? So how could she talk as she had? Well, the answer to that was plain also. He knew how she could, and why.

Next day, he tried all day to write the letter. For two weeks, he stuck strictly around Dalton, and every day he tried to write. At last, he made a phone call.

"I haven't been over," he said. "Listen, I don't think I can any more. You must have guessed that."

"Guessed? No. No, I didn't guess anything."

The conversation locked them in, close as a last embrace, and down, down they sank with it, till, touching bottom at last, they reversed and rose slowly toward the common light. "Just so long as you know how I feel," he was saying. "That I wanted to. Listen. Would you mind if we both came over? Ethel and me. I just want you to meet her." He hesitated. "I want you both to see." It was a crazy idea, but what he felt like. How did you act? How was an Anderson to know? What did it matter as long as Naomi understood?

"Gavin," said the brave, clear, sophisticated voice over the uncertain connection, "I understand perfectly. Y'all come ahead."

When he let himself out of the drugstore phone booth, a daze fell on him. What had he done? What was he blotting out? Whatever the answers, it was too late to stop. The plan, once agreed to, ticked on like a wound clock.

———

Ethel rode all the way that Sunday with her pretty face fixed on the road, back straight, her bag and gloves neat in her lap. It was a cool, dusty, early December day.

"How do you do?" said Naomi Beris. She was standing at the top of the steps, in a dress of thin white wool with a gold chain at the neck. "Sit down," she said. Her son came out and offered them Cokes on ice. Everything was Sunday-quiet. The cattle gap rumbled. "Who on earth?" Naomi said. A car appeared, green, larger and newer than average for those days. It paused to allow the gate to open and drew into the side yard beside Naomi's. A man got out. He was heavy-set, gray-haired, and florid-faced, dressed in khaki and high-laced riding boots, a worn riding coat over a whipcord shirt.

"Mr. Slatton's from Columbus," said Naomi. "He came about the horses. I guess that's right, isn't it, Abe?"

"Are the horses sick?" Ethel asked. Mr. Slatton, certainly not a veterinarian, gave no sign he had heard her.

"No," said Naomi. "I have to sell them eventually, and they show up best before the winter sets in. I didn't mention that, Abe," she said to Slatton. "You see how clever I am."

"Shouldn't mention it now." He did not look at her or at the guests. He drank nothing, not even Coke, and stared out at the avenue of trees.

She was wearing the ruby. Gavin had never seen it before. He had asked her once, and she had said it was in the bank vault; she said the insurance was too expensive to keep up. Now it was just as he had envisioned it. Square-cut, dark as wine, it further shrank her small hand, which rested peacefully on the fine white fabric above her lap. It drank the light, inexhaustibly.

"That's the most beautiful ring," said Ethel, who had never heard of it.

Naomi said, "There's a story about it. My great-grandmother lived in an old house that burned. It was near the Natchez Trace, about a mile over yonder. The road is all fallen in now. Not many people even know that's what it was. This man used to come down it, always going to Jackson and then back to somewhere in Tennessee. He would stop by a spring we had. He was a terrible man—clothes made out of skins, probably smelled like bear grease, nothing to recommend him. My grandmother was a young girl, not but fifteen or sixteen. But he wanted to see her, so he always stopped.

He used to wait on his horse in the woods till she went down to the spring to bring some water up for dinner so it would be cool for the table. And how many times he waited and how many times she had to run away from him nobody knew. Who knew if she *didn't* run away from him? Nobody would answer that. He carried a pack and a small blanket roll behind his saddle.

"One day he came through, and he'd had a fight with some men either the day before or the night before. He'd slipped away from them in the early morning. There was blood on him, so my grandmother said. He told her he would come back if he could. Meantime, he unstrapped the rolled blanket from the cantle and gave it to her. He'd come back for it, he said, if he could; if not, it was hers. And he said he trusted her.

"At the house, she unwrapped it—not a blanket but a dirty shawl such as Indians wore against the wind. Was that all he had to sleep in, or did he stay in inns? It was a small roll of things—a pewter cup, a blue glass bottle that smelled like corn whiskey, and then the ruby. She almost missed it; it was tied up in a rag. And he never came back. She married, or was married to, a Pontotoc boy, soon after. Too soon after, was what they said. So here we are still—and here's the ruby."

All of them were silent.

The man, Abe Slatton, gave no sign that he had listened to her. He had not once looked at her during the story. Finally, still staring out at the line of oak trees, he said, "You got the blood of that *terrible* man flowin' in yo' veins."

"Pete wouldn't be home," she said, nodding toward her son, "but the whole Georgia Tech team came down with flu. They had to cancel the Auburn game."

"Everybody's got it there, too," said Pete.

"Do you-all go to the games?" Naomi asked.

"We go to the high school games," said Ethel. "Our boy is on the team. It keeps us pretty busy, I guess."

Gavin and Ethel Anderson left soon after.

"That man was the rudest thing I ever saw," said Ethel. "He never even said good-by, glad I met you. Nothing. You didn't talk about the property," she added, sly as a fox.

"I told her on the phone I'd decided against it," he said.

"You believe all that about that ring?" she asked, ten miles farther on.

"I don't know."

"I wonder," said Ethel, "if it's even real."

Back in those days, all the roads in Mississippi, with two exceptions, were either dirt or gravel. The road from Naomi Beris's back to Dalton was sixty winding miles, thick-piled with gravel in the center and along the edges, roiling with dust if another car came by. They stopped in a drab little town—a chain of storefronts facing a railroad track, a few houses scattered up rutted roads along broken sidewalks—and had a sandwich in a café.

"Thank you for taking me, Gavin," said Ethel. She was looking at him tenderly, tears in the wide brown eyes that belonged to him; her slyness and undercutting, he knew, were gone. And she wouldn't talk, wouldn't "tell." Things were righted. He was fit once more to bear a grandmother in a rocking chair, feather-light among five strong men, down to the white sandbar. He could sing once more to the moon. What did he need with a wild witch who had blown up out of a thunderstorm, who writhed like a cat, spitting words out that belonged on the walls of a john? What had she wanted with him? A summer had been enough for both of them.

They came out of the restaurant and got into the car. At a curve in the road, the little town vanished like a thought of itself, something that had never been. Now they faced west, drawn straight into a fiery sun, at first so fierce and blinding through the dust that they had to stop until the worst of the glare had muted. It faded beautifully, from a flaming cauldron to blood to wine to deep red velvet, and sank straight ahead of them, removing its deep tinge almost at once from the sky.

His gift was flawed now. It would be like something from boyhood, put aside in a closet. Was he glad or sorry? He didn't know. Driving the harsh gravel, he felt numb somewhere, and placed one hand to his shoulder. Wet blood still thickly stained the dirty leather of his shirt, and the girl with the bucket of spring water, whose waist and lips he knew, reached up to take the rolled shawl, bound with leather strings. The horse shifted beneath him, and her hands, desperate with love, clung along his thigh, which was that of a horseman in his prime, powerful and bold.

THE BUFORDS

There were the windows, high, well above the ground, large, full of
sky. There were the child's eyes, settled back mid-distance in the
empty room. There was the emptiness, the drowsiness of Miss Jackson's own head, tired from tackling the major problems of little
people all day long, from untangling their hair ribbons, their shoe-
laces, their grammar, their arithmetic, their handwriting, their
thoughts. Now there was the silence.

The big, clumsy building was full of silence, stoves cooling off,
great boxy rooms growing cool from the floor up, cold settling
around her ankles. Miss Jackson sat there two or three afternoons a
week, after everybody else had gone, generally with a Buford or
because of a Buford: It was agreed she had the worst grade this year,
because there were Bufords in it. She read a sentence in a theme
four times through. Was it really saying something about a toad-
frog? Her brain was so weary—it was Thursday, late in the week—
she began to think of chipmunks, instead. Suddenly her mouth
began to twitch; she couldn't stand it any longer; she burst out
laughing.

"Dora Mae, *what* are you doing?"

The truth was that Dora Mae was not doing anything. She was
just a Buford. When she was around, you eventually laughed. Miss
Jackson could never resist; but then, neither could anyone. Dora
Mae, being a Buford, did not return her laugh. The Bufords never
laughed unless they wanted to. She drew the book she was supposed
to be studying, but wasn't, slowly downward on the desk; her chin
was resting on it and came gradually down with it. She continued to

stare at Miss Jackson with eyes almost as big as the windows, blue, clear, and loaded with Buford nonsense. She gave Miss Jackson the tiniest imaginable smile.

Miss Jackson continued to laugh. If someone else had been the teacher, she herself would have to be corrected, possibly kept in. It always turned out this way. Miss Jackson dried her eyes. "Sit up straight, Dora Mae," she said.

Once this very child had actually sewed through her own finger, meddling with a sewing machine the high school home-economics girls had left open upstairs. Another time, at recess, she had jumped up and down on a Sears Roebuck catalogue in the dressing room behind the stage, creating such a thunder nobody could think what was happening. She had also shot pieces of broken brick with her brother's slingshot at the walls of the gym, where they were having a 4-H Club meeting. "Head, Heart, Hands, and Health," the signs said. They were inside repeating a pledge about these four things and singing, "To the knights in the days of old, Keeping watch on the mountain height, Came a vision of Holy Grail, And a voice through the waiting night." Some of the chunks of brick, really quite large, came flying through the window.

Dora Mae, of course, had terrible brothers, the Buford boys, and a reputation to live up to—was that it? No, she was just bad, the older teachers in the higher grades would say at recess, sitting on the steps in warm weather or crossing the street for a Coke at the little cabin-size sandwich shop.

"I've got two years before I get Dora Mae," said Miss Martingale.

"Just think," said Mrs. Henry, "I've got four Bufords in my upstairs study hall. At once."

"I've had them already, all but one," said Miss Carlisle. "I've just about graduated."

"I wish they weren't so funny," said Miss Jackson, and then they all began to laugh. They couldn't finish their Cokes for laughing.

Among the exploits of Dora Mae's brothers, there always came to mind the spring day one of them brought a horse inside the school house just before closing bell, leading it with a twist of wire fastened about its lower lip and releasing it to wander right into study hall alone while the principal, Mr. Blackstone, was dozing at his desk.

The thing was, in school, everybody's mind was likely to wander, and the minute it did wander, something would be done to you by a Buford, and you would never forget it. The world you were dozing on came back with a whoosh and a bang; but it was not the same world you had dozed away from, nor was it the one you intended to wake up to or even imagined to be there. Something crazy was the matter with it: a naked horse, unattended, was walking between the rows of seats; or (another day altogether) a little girl was holding her reader up in the air between her feet, her head and shoulders having vanished below desk level, perhaps forever. Had there actually been some strange accident? Were you dreaming? Or were things meant to be this way? That was the part that just for a minute could scare you.

The Bufords lived in a large, sprawled-out, friendly house down a road nobody lived on but them. The grass was never completely cut, and in the fall the leaves never got raked. Somebody once set fire to a sagebrush pasture near their house—one of *them* had done it, doubtless—and the house was threatened, and there were Bufords up all night, stamping the earth and scraping sparks out of the charred fence posts and throwing water into chicken wallows, just in case the fire started again.

When any of the teachers went there to call, as they occasionally had to do, so that the family wouldn't get mad at the extraordinary punishment meted out to one of the children at school—Mr. Blackstone once was driven to give Billy Buford a public whipping with a buggy whip—or (another reason) to try to inform the family just how far the children were going with their devilment and to implore moral support, at least, in doing something about it—when you went there, they all came out and greeted you. They made you sit in a worn wicker rocking chair and ran to get you something— iced tea or lemonade or a Coke, cake, tea cakes, or anything they had.

Then they began to shout and holler and say how glad they were you'd come. They began to say, "Now tell the truth! Tell the truth, now! Ain't Billy Buford the worse boy you ever saw?" . . . "Did you ever see anybody as crazy as that Pete? Now tell me! Now tell the truth!" . . . "Confidentially, Miss Jackson, what on earth are we ever going to do with Dora Mae?"

And Dora Mae would sit and look at you, the whole time. She would sit on a little stool and put her chin on her hands and stare, and then you would say, "I just don't know, Mrs. Buford." And they would all look at you cautiously in their own Buford way, and then in the silence, when you couldn't, couldn't be serious, one of them would say, very quietly, "Ain't you ever going to eat your cake?"

It was like that.

There had once been something about a skunk that had upset not just the school but the whole town and that would not do to think about, just as it didn't do any good, either, to speculate on what might or could or was about to happen on this or any future Halloween.

Was it spring or fall? Dreaming, herself, in the lonely classroom with Dora Mae, Miss Jackson thought of chipmunks and skunks and toad-frogs, words written into themes on ruled paper, the lines of paper passing gradually across her brow and into her brain, until the fine ruling would eventually print itself there. Someday, if they opened her brain, they would find a child's theme inside. Even now she could often scarcely think of herself with any degree of certainty. Was she in love, was she falling in love, or getting restless and disappointed with whomever she knew, or did she want somebody new, or was she recalling somebody gone? Or: Had someone right come along, and she had said all right, she'd quit teaching and marry him, and now had it materialized or had it fallen through, or what?

Children! The Bufords existed in a haze of children and old people: old aunts, old cousins, grandfathers, friends and relatives by marriage of cousins, deceased uncles, family doctors gone alcoholic, people who never had a chance. What did they live on? Oh, enough of them knew how to make enough for everyone to feel encouraged. Enough of them were clever about money, and everybody liked them, except the unfortunate few who had to try to discipline them. A schoolteacher, for instance, was a sort of challenge.

A teacher hung in their minds like the deep, softly pulsing, furry throat in the collective mind of a hound pack. They hardly thought of a teacher as human, you had to suppose. You could get your feelings hurt sadly if you left yourself open to them.

"Dora Mae, let's go," Miss Jackson suddenly said, way too early.

She had recalled that she had a date, but whether it was a spring date (with warm twilight air seeping into the car, filling the street and even entering the stale movie foyer—more excitement in the season than was left for her in this particular person) or whether it was a fall date (when the smell of her new dress brought out sharply by the gas heater she had to turn on in the late afternoon, carried with it the interest of somebody new and the lightness all beginnings have)—which it was, she had to think to say. At this moment, she had forgotten whether she was even glad or not. It was better to be going out with somebody than not; it gave a certain air, for one thing, to supper at the boardinghouse.

Even the regulars, the uptown widows and working wives and the old couples and the ancient widower who came to eat there, held themselves somewhat straighter and took some degree of pride in the matter of Miss Jackson's going out, as going out suggested a progress of sorts and put a tone of freshness and prettiness on things. It was a subject to tease and be festive about; the lady who ran the boardinghouse might even bring candles to light the table. In letting Dora Mae Buford out early, Miss Jackson was responding to that festiveness; she thought of the reprieve as a little present.

She recalled what she had told a young man last year, or maybe the year before, just as they were leaving the movies after a day similar to this one, when she had had to keep another Buford in, how she had described the Bufords to him, so that she got him to laugh about them, too, and how between them they had decided there was no reason, no reason on earth, for Bufords to go to school at all. They would be exactly the same whether they went to school or not. Nothing you told them soaked in; they were born knowing everything they knew; they never changed; the only people they really listened to were other Bufords.

"But I do sometimes wonder," Miss Jackson had said, trying hard to find a foothold that had to do with "problems," "personality," "psychology," "adjustment," all those things she had taken up in detail at teachers' college in Nashville and thought must have a small degree of truth in them—"I wonder if some people don't just feel obligated to be bad."

"There's something in that," the young man had answered. (He had said this often, come to think of it: a good answer to everything.)

Now the child trudged along beside Miss Jackson across the campus. Miss Jackson looked down affectionately; she wanted a child of her own someday—though hardly, she thought (and almost giggled), one like this. It went along on chunky legs and was shaped like cutout paper-doll children you folded the tabs back to change dresses for. Its face was round, its brow raggedly fringed with yellow bangs. Its hands were plump—meddlesome, you'd say on sight. It wore scuffed brown shoes and navy-blue socks and a print dress and carried an old nubby red sweater slung over its books.

"Aren't you cold, Dora Mae?" said Miss Jackson, still in her mood of affection and fun.

"No, ma'am," said Dora Mae, who could and did answer directly at times. "I'm just tired of school."

Well, so am I sometimes, Miss Jackson thought, going home to bathe and dress in her best dress, and then go to the boardinghouse with the other teachers, where, waiting on the porch, if it was warm enough or in the hall if it was not, sitting or standing with hands at rest against the nice material of her frock, she would already be well over the line into her most private domain.

"I don't really like him all that much," she would have confided already—it was what she always said. "I just feel better, you know, when somebody wants to take me somewhere." All the teachers agreed that this was so; they were the same, they said.

What Miss Jackson did not say was that she enjoyed being Lelia. This was her secret, and when she went out, this was what happened: she turned into Lelia, from the time she was dressing in the afternoon until after midnight, when she got in. The next morning, she would be Miss Jackson again.

If it was a weekday.

And if it wasn't a weekday, then she might still feel like Miss Jackson, even on weekends, for they had given her a Sunday School class to teach whenever she stayed in town. If she went home, back fifty miles to the little town she was born in, she had to go to church there, too, and everybody uptown called her "Leel," a nickname. At home they called her "Sister," only it sounded more like Sustah. But Lelia was her name and what she wanted to be; it was what she said was her name to whatever man she met who asked to take her somewhere.

———

One day soon after she had kept Dora Mae Buford after school, she went back into the classroom from recess quite late, having been delayed at a faculty meeting, and Dora Mae was writing "LELIA-JACKSONLELIAJACKSONLELIAJACKSONLELIAJACKSON" over and over in capital letters on the blackboard. She had filled one board and had started on another, going like crazy. All the students were laughing at her.

It became clear to Miss Jackson later, when she had time to think about it, that the reason she became so angry at Dora Mae was that the child, like some diabolical spirit, had seemed to know exactly what her sensitive point was and had gone straight to it, with the purpose of ridiculing her, of exposing and summarizing her secret self in all its foolish yearning.

But at the moment she did not think anything. She experienced a flash of white-faced, passionate temper and struck the chalk from the child's hand. "Erase that board!" she ordered. A marvel she hadn't knocked her down, except that Dora Mae was as solid as a stump, and hitting her, Miss Jackson had almost sprained her wrist.

Dora Mae was shocked half to death, and the room was deadly still for the rest of the morning. Miss Jackson, so gentle and firm (though likely to get worried), had never before struck anyone.

Soon Dora Mae's mother came to see Miss Jackson, after school. She sat down in the empty classroom, a rather tall, dark woman with a narrow face full of slanted wrinkles and eyes so dark as to be almost pitch black, with no discernible white area to them. Miss Jackson looked steadfastly down at her hands.

Mrs. Buford put a large, worn, bulging black purse on the desk before her, and though she did not even remove her coat, the room seemed hers. She did not mean it that way, for she spoke in the most respectful tone, but it was true. "It's really just one thing I wanted to know, Miss Jackson. Your first name is Lelia, ain't it?"

Miss Jackson said that it was.

"So what I mean is, when Dora Mae wrote what she did on the blackboard there, it wasn't nothing like a lie or something dirty, was it?"

"No," said Miss Jackson. "Not at all."

"Well, I guess that's about all I wanted to make sure of."

Miss Jackson did not say anything, and Mrs. Buford finally inquired whether she had not been late coming back to the room that day, when Dora Mae was found writing on the board. Miss Jackson agreed that this was true.

"Churen are not going to sit absolutely still if you don't come back from recess," said Mrs. Buford. "You got to be there to say, 'Now y'all get out your book and turn to page so-and-so.' If you don't they're bound to get into something. You realize that? Well, good! Dora Mae's nothing but a little old scrap. That's all she is."

"Well, I know," said Miss Jackson, feeling very bad.

At this point, Mrs. Buford, alone without any of her children around her, must have got to thinking about them all in terms of Dora Mae; she began to cry.

Miss Jackson understood. She had seen them all, her entire class, heads bent at her command, pencils marching forward across their tablets, and her heart had filled with pity and love.

Mrs. Buford brushed her tears away. "You never meant it for a minute. Anybody can get aggravated, don't you know? You think I can't? I can and do!" She put her handkerchief back in her purse and, straightening her coat, stood up to go. "So, I'm just going right straight and say you're sorry about it and you never meant it."

"Oh," said Miss Jackson, all of a sudden, "but I did mean it. It's true I'm sorry. But I did mean it." Her statement, softly made, threw a barrier across Mrs. Buford's path, like bars through the slots in a fence gap.

Mrs. Buford sat back down. "Miss Jackson, just what have we been sitting here deciding?"

"I don't know," said Miss Jackson, wondering herself. "Nothing that I know of."

"Nothing! You call that nothing?"

"Call what nothing?"

"Why, everything you just got through saying."

"But what do you think I said?" Miss Jackson felt she would honestly like to know. There followed a long silence, in which Miss Jackson, whose room this after all was, felt impelled to stand up. "It's not a good thing to lose your temper. But everyone does sometimes, including me."

Mrs. Buford rose also. "Underneath all that fooling around, them kids of mine is pure gold." Drawn to full height, Mrs. Buford became about twice as tall as Miss Jackson.

"I know! I know that! But you say yourselves—" began Miss Jackson. She started to tremble. Of all the teachers in the school, she was the youngest, and she had the most overcrowding in her room. "Mrs. Buford," she begged, "do please forget about it. Go on home. Please, please go home!"

"You pore child," said Mrs. Buford, with no effort still continuing and even expanding her own authority. "I just never in my life," she added, and left the room.

She proceeded across the campus the way all her dozen or so children went, down toward their lonely road—a good, strong, sincere woman, whose right shoulder sagged lower than the left and who did not look back. From the window, Miss Jackson watched her go.

Uptown a lady gossip was soon to tell her that she was known to have struck a child in a fit of temper and also to have turned out the child's mother when she came to talk about it. Miss Jackson wearily agreed that this was true. She could feel no great surprise, though her sense of despair deepened when one of the Buford boys, Evan, older and long out of school, got to worrying her—calling up at night, running his car behind her on the sidewalk uptown. It seemed there were no lengths he wouldn't go to, no trouble he wouldn't make for her.

When the dove season started, he dropped her. He'd a little rather shoot doves than me, she thought, sitting on the edge of the bed in her room, avoiding the mirror, which said she must be five years older. It's my whole life that's being erased, she thought, mindful that Dora Mae and two of her brothers, in spite of all she could do, were inexorably failing the fourth grade. She got up her Sunday School lesson, washed her hair, went to bed, and fell asleep disconsolate. . . .

———

Before school was out, the Bufords invited Miss Jackson for Sunday dinner. Once the invitation had come—which pleased her about as much as if it had been extended by a tribe of Indians, but which she had to accept or be thought of as a coward—it seemed inevitable to her that they would do this. It carried out to a T their devious and deceptively simple-looking method of pleasing themselves, and of course what she might feel about it didn't matter. But here she was dressing for them, trying to look her best.

The dinner turned out to be a feast. She judged it was no different from their usual Sunday meal—three kinds of meat and a dozen spring vegetables, hot rolls, jams, pickles, peaches, and rich cakes, freshly baked and iced.

The house looked in the airiest sort of order, with hand-crocheted white doilies sprinkled about on the tables and chairs. The whole yard was shaggy with flowers and blooming shrubs; the children all were clean and neatly dressed, with shoes on as well, and the dogs were turned firmly out of doors.

She was placed near Mr. Tom Buford, the father of them all, a tall, spare man with thick white hair and a face burned brick-brown from constant exposure. He plied her ceaselessly with food, more than she could have eaten in a week, and smiled the gentle smile Miss Jackson by now knew so well.

Halfway down the opposite side of the table was Evan Buford, she at last recognized, that terrible one, wearing a spotless white shirt, shaved and spruce, with brown busy hands, looking bland and even handsome. If he remembered all those times he had got her to the phone at one and two and three in the morning, he wasn't letting on. ("Thought you'd be up grading papers, Miss Jackson! Falling down on the job?" . . . "Your family live in Tupelo? Well, the whole town got blown away in a tornado! This afternoon!") Once, in hunting clothes, his dirt-smeared, unshaven face distorted by the rush of rain on his muddy windshield, he had pursued her from the post office all the way home, almost nudging her off the sidewalk with his front fender, his wheels spewing water from the puddles all over her stockings and raincoat, while she walked resolutely on, pretending not to notice.

From way down at the foot of the table, about half a mile away, Dora Mae sat sighting at her steadily through a water glass, her eyes like the magnified eyes of insects.

"'Possum hunting!" Mr. Tom Buford was saying, carving chicken and ham with a knife a foot long, which Miss Jackson sometimes had literally to dodge. "That's where we all went last night. Way up on the ridge. You like 'possum, Miss Jackson?"

"I never had any," Miss Jackson said.

Right from dinner they all went to the back yard to see the 'possum, which had been put in a cage of chicken wire around the base of a small pecan tree. It was now hanging upside down by its tail from a limb. She felt for its helpless, unappetizing shapelessness, grizzly gray, with a long snout, its sensitive eyes shut tight, its tender black petal-like ears alone perceiving, with what terror none could know though she could guess, the presence of its captors.

"Don't smell very good, does it?" Billy Buford said. "You like it, Miss Jackson? Give it to you, you want it." He picked up a stick to punch it with.

She shook her head. "Oh, I'd just let it go back to the woods. I feel sorry for it."

The whole family turned from the creature to her and examined her as if she were crazy. Billy Buford even dropped the stick. There followed one of those long, risky silences.

As they started to go inside, Evan Buford lounged along at her elbow. He separated her out like a heifer from the herd and cornered her before a fence of climbing roses. He leaned his arm against a fence post, blocking any possible escape, and looked down at her with wide, speculative, bright brown eyes. She remembered his laughing mouth behind the car wheel that chill, rainy day, careening after her. Oh, they never got through, she desperately realized. Once they had you, they held on—if they didn't eat you up, they kept you for a pet.

"Now, Miss Jackson, how come you to fail those kids?"

Miss Jackson dug her heels in hard. "I didn't fail them. They failed themselves. Like you might fail to hit a squirrel, for instance."

"Well, now. You mean they weren't good enough. Well, I be darned." He jerked his head. "That's a real good answer."

So at last, after years of trying hard, she had got something across to a Buford, some one little thing that was true. Maybe it had never happened before. It would seem she had stopped him cold. It would seem he even admired her.

"Missed it like a squirrel!" he marveled. "The whole fourth grade. They must be mighty dumb," he reflected, walking along with her toward the house.

"No, they just don't listen," said Miss Jackson.

"Don't listen," he said after her with care, as though to prove that he, at least, did. "You get ready to go, I'll drive you to town, Miss Jackson. Your name is Lelia, ain't it?"

She looked up gratefully. "That's right," she said.

A CHRISTIAN EDUCATION

It was a Sunday like no other, for we were there alone for the first time. I hadn't started to school yet, and he had finished it so long ago it must have been like a dream of something that was meant to happen but had never really come about, for I can remember no story of school that he ever told me, and to think of him as sitting in a class equal with others is as beyond me now as it was then. I cannot imagine it. He read a lot and might conceivably have had a tutor—that I can imagine, in his plantation world.

But this was a town he'd finally come to, to stay with his daughter in his old age, she being also my mother. I was the only one free to be with him all the time and the same went for his being with me—we baby-sat one another.

But that word wasn't known then.

A great many things were known, however; among them, I always had to go to Sunday School.

It was an absolute that the whole world was meant to be part of the church, and if my grandfather seldom went, it was a puzzle no one tried to solve. Sermons were a fate I had only recently got big enough to be included in, but Sunday School classes had had me enrolled in them since I could be led through the door and placed on a tiny red chair, feet not even at that low height connecting to the floor. It was always cold at the church; even in summer, it was cool inside. We were given pictures to color and Bible verses to memorize, and at the end a colored card with a picture of Moses or Jesus or somebody else from the Bible, exotically bearded and robed.

Today I might not be going to Sunday School, and my regret was only for the card. I wondered what it would be like. There was no one to bring it to me. My mother and father were not even in town. They had got into the car right after breakfast and had driven away to a neighboring town. An aunt by marriage had died and they were going to the funeral. I was too little to go to funerals, my mother said.

After they left I sat on the rug near my grandfather. He was asleep in his chair before the fire, snoring. Presently his snoring woke him up. He cut himself some tobacco and put it in his mouth. "Are you going to Sunday School?" he asked me. "I can't go there by myself," I said. "Nobody said I had to take you," he remarked, more to himself than to me. It wasn't the first time I knew we were in the same boat, he and I, we had to do what they said, being outside the main scale of life where things really happened, but by the same token we didn't have to do what they didn't say. Somewhere along the line, however, my grandfather had earned rights I didn't have. Not having to attend church was one; also, he had his own money and didn't have to ask for any.

He looked out the window.

"It's going to be a pretty day," he said.

How we found ourselves on the road downtown on Sunday morning, I don't remember. It was as far to get to town as it was to get to church, though in the opposite direction, and we both must have known that, but didn't remark upon it as we went along. My grandfather walked to town every day except Sunday, when it was considered a sin to go there, for the drugstore was open and the barbershop, too, on occasions, if the weather was fair; and the filling station was open. My parents thought that the drugstore had to be open but should sell drugs only, and that filling stations and barber-shops shouldn't be open at all. There should be a way to telephone the filling station in case you had to have gas for emergency use. This was all worked out between them. I had often heard them talk about it. No one should go to town on Sunday, they said, for it en-couraged the error of the ones who kept their places open.

My grandfather was a very tall man; I had to reach up to hold his hand while walking. He wore dark blue and dark gray herringbone suits, and the coat flap was a long way up, the gold watch chain almost out of sight. I could see his walking cane moving opposite me, briskly swung with the rhythm of his stride: it was my companion. Along the way it occurred to me that we were terribly excited, that the familiar way looked new and different, as though a haze which had hung over everything had been whipped away all at once, like a scarf. I was also having more fun than I'd ever had before.

When he came to the barbershop, my grandfather stepped inside and spoke to the barber and to all who happened to be hanging around, brought out by the sunshine. They spoke about politics, the crops, and the weather. The barber who always cut my hair came over and looked to see if I needed another trim and my grandfather said he didn't think so, but I might need a good brushing; they'd left so soon after breakfast it was a wonder I was dressed. Somebody who'd come in after us said, "Funeral in Grenada, ain't it?" which was the first anybody had mentioned it, but I knew they hadn't needed to say anything, that everybody knew about my parents' departure and why and where. Things were always known about, I saw, but not cared about too much either. The barber's strong arms, fleecy with reddish hair, swung me up into his big chair where I loved to be. He brushed my hair, then combed it. The great mirrors sparkled and everything was fine.

We presently moved on to the drugstore. The druggist, a small, crippled man, hobbled toward us, grinning to see us, and he and my grandfather talked for quite some time. Finally my grandfather said, "Give the child a strawberry cone," and so I had it, miraculous, and the world of which it was the center expanded about it with gracious, silent delight. It was a thing too wondrous actually to have eaten, and I do not remember eating it. It was only after we at last reached home and I entered the house, which smelled like my parents' clothes and their things, that I knew what they would think of what we had done and I became filled with anxiety and other dark feelings.

Then the car was coming up the drive and they were alighting in a post-funeral manner, full of heavy feelings and reminiscence and inclined not to speak in an ordinary way. When my mother put dinner in order, we sat around the table not saying very much.

"Did the fire hold out all right?" she asked my grandfather.

"Oh, it was warm," he said. "Didn't need much." He ate quietly and so did I.

In the afternoons on Sunday we all sat around looking at the paper. My mother had doubts about this, but we all indulged the desire anyway. After the ordeal of dressing up, of Sunday School and the long service and dinner, it seemed almost a debauchery to be able to pitch into those large crackling sheets, especially the funny papers, which were garish with color and loud with exclamation points, question marks, shouting, and all sorts of misdeeds. My grandfather had got sleepy before the fire and retired to his room while my mother and father had climbed out of their graveside feelings enough to talk a little and joke with one another.

"What did you all do?" my mother asked me. "How did you pass the time while we were gone?"

"We walked downtown," I said, for I had been laughing at something they had said to one another and wanted to share the morning's happiness with them without telling any more or letting any real trouble in. But my mother was on it, quicker than anything.

"You didn't go in the drugstore, did you?"

I looked up. Why did she have to ask? It wasn't in my scheme of thinking about things that she would ever do so. My father was looking at me now, too.

"Yes, ma'am," I slowly said. "But not for long," I added.

"You didn't get an ice cream cone, did you?"

And they both were looking. My face must have had astonishment on it as well as guilt. Not even I could have imagined them going this far. Why, on the day of a funeral, should they care if anybody bought an ice cream cone?

"Did you?" my father asked.

The thing to know is that my parents really believed everything they said they believed. They believed that awful punishments were meted out to those who did not remember the Sabbath was holy.

They believed about a million other things. They were terribly honest about it.

Much later on, my mother went into my grandfather's room. I was silently behind her, and I heard her speak to him.

"She says you took her to town while we were gone and got an ice cream."

He had waked up and was reading by his lamp. At first he seemed not to hear; at last, he put his book face down in his lap and looked up. "I did," he said lightly.

A silence fell between them. Finally she turned and went away.

This, so far as I know, was all.

Because of the incident, that certain immunity of spirit my grandfather possessed was passed on to me. It came, I think, out of the precise way in which he put his book down on his lap to answer. There was a lifetime in the gesture, distilled, and I have been a good part of that long growing up to all its meaning.

After this, though all went on as before, there was nothing much my parents could finally do about the church and me. They could lock the barn door, but the bright horse of freedom was already loose in my world. Down the hill, across the creek, in the next pasture—where? Somewhere, certainly: that much was proved; and all was different for its being so.

INDIAN SUMMER

One of my mother's three brothers, Rex Wirth, lived about ten miles from us: he had taken over his wife's family home because her parents had needed somebody on the land to look after it.

Uncle Rex had been wild in youth, had dashed around gambling, among other things, and had not settled down until years after he married. "What Martha's gone through!" was one of Mama's oft-heard remarks. I had a wild boy friend myself back then and I used to reflect that at least Uncle Rex had married Aunt Martha. Furthermore, he did, at last, settle down.

Once stabilized, it became him to be and look like a responsible country gentleman. He was clipped and spare in appearance, scarcely as tall as his horse, and just missed being frail-looking, but he had an almost military air of authority; to me, when I thought of him, I always pictured him as approaching alone. He might be in blue work pants, he might be in a suit; his smart forward step was the same, and his crinkling smile had nothing to beg about. "How you *do*?" was his greeting to everybody, family or stranger. But the place—with its rolling, piny acreage, its big two-story house, its circular drive to the gate—was not his own. He never said this, but his brother, Uncle Hernan, who lived next door to us, said that he never had to mention it because he never forgot it for a minute. "It galls him," was Uncle Hernan's judgment. He was usually right.

The family feeling toward Uncle Rex, which was complicated but filled with reality, had to do, I believe, with his having, when a boy, fallen from a tree into a tractor disk. There was still a scar on his leg and one across his back, but the momentary threat to his manhood, the pity in that, was what gave the family its special tremor about him. If he stood safe it was still a near miss, and gave to his eyes the honest, wide openness of those of our forebears in family daguerreotypes, all the more vulnerable for having died or been killed in the Civil War and yet, at the time of the picture, anyway, not knowing it, that it would happen that way, or happen at all.

To me, even stranger than the tractor disk accident and relating to no photograph of any family member whomsoever, was the time Uncle Rex almost burned alive. He had been sleepy from fox hunting, and out on the place in the afternoon had gone into an abandoned Negro house down in a little hollow with pine and camellia trees around it and built a fire in the empty chimney out of a busted chair and fallen sound asleep on an old pile of cotton—third picking, never ginned. He woke with the place blazing around him and what it came to was that he apparently, from those who saw it, walked out through a solid wall of flame. The house crashed in behind him. He was singed a little but unharmed. Well, he was precious, Mama said, and the Lord had spared him.

Over there where he lived, however, he was a captive of the McClellands; had the Lord spared him for that? A certain way of looking at it made it a predicament. It was better to speak in ordinary terms, that he'd managed the property and taken care of his wife's parents till they died, then had stayed on.

"That farm wouldn't have been anything without you, Rex," I once heard Mama pointing out. "It would have gone to rack and ruin."

"I reckon so," he would say, and brush his hand hard across the sparse hair atop his head, the color having left hold of red for sandy gray, the permanently sun-splotched scalp showing through here and there in slats and angles. "Someday I'll pick up Martha and move in with Hernan." He had as much right, certainly, to live in the old Wirth family home as Uncle Hernan had, for it belonged to all; still, he was joking when he said a thing like that, no matter how many McClellands were always visiting him, making silently clear the place was theirs.

It wouldn't have worked anyway. He was plainer by nature than

Uncle Hernan, who loved his bonded whiskey and gold-trimmed porcelain, silver, table linen, and redolent cigars. Uncle Rex's wild days, even, had had nothing plush about them; his gambling had been done not in the carpeted *maisons* of New Orleans, but around and about with hunting companions; he would hunt in the coldest weather in nothing except an old briar-scratched, dog-clawed, leather jacket, standing bareheaded on deer stands through the long drizzles of winter days. Sometimes he got sick, sometimes not. "Come on, Martha," he would snort from his bed, voice muffled in cold symptoms, up to his neck in blankets, while the poor woman went off in every direction for thermometers and hot water bottles and aspirin and boiled egg and tea and the one book he wanted, which had got mislaid. "Come on! Be good for something!"

It was in the course of nature—that and pleasing the McClellands, who were strict—that Uncle Rex had given all his meanness up; he was a regular churchgoer now, first a deacon, then an elder. So all his hollering at Aunt Martha was understood as no more than prankish. Besides, Aunt Martha had been provably good for something; she'd had a son, a fine boy, so everybody said, including me; he'd gone to military academy and now he taught at one.

—

Once in the winter Mama and Daddy and I drove over to see Uncle Rex and found him alone. It was Sunday. Aunt Martha had gone into town to see some of her folks, who must have had some ailment, else they would have been out there.

"Come on, now," Uncle Rex said, as it was fine weather. "You want to see my filly?" He got up to get his jacket and change into some twill britches for riding in.

"How's she doing?" Daddy asked.

"She's coming on real good, a great big gal. Hope the preacher don't come. Hope Martha's not back early. Just showing a horse, Marilee," he turned to ask me, "ain't that all right on Sunday?" He fancied himself when well mounted and sat as dapper as a cavalry-man. In World War I, he'd trained for that, but had never got to France.

"What's her name?" I asked him.

"Sally," he said. "How's that?" He'd put his arm across my shoulder, walking; he didn't have the mass, the complex drawing power of his brother, Uncle Hernan, but his nature was finely coiled, authentic, within him, you could tell that.

We came out to the barn all together, enwrapped (as all around us was) in the thin winter sunshine which fell without color on the smooth-worn unpainted cattle gate letting into the lot. "Mind your step," said Uncle Rex. The cows were out and grazing; two looked peacefully up; the mare was nowhere in sight. The barn stood Sunday quiet. "She must be back yonder," he said.

At the barn he reached up high to unbolt the lock on the tack room door and fling it back. The steps had rotted but a stump of wood had been upended usefully below the door jamb; if you meant business—and Uncle Rex did—about getting in, it would bear a light climbing step without toppling. Uncle Rex emerged with a bridle over his arm. The woods beyond the fenced lot were winter bare, except for some touches of oak. There were elm, pecan, and walnut, a thick stand along the bluff. Below the bluff was more pasture land, good for playing in, I remembered from childhood, handy for hunting arrowheads. It rolled pleasantly, clumped with plum bushes and one or two shade trees, down to the branch with its sandy banks.

Uncle Rex was leading the mare out now. He had found her back of the barn. He re-entered the harness room for the saddle while she stood quietly, reins flung over an iron hook set in the barn wall. Uncle Rex brushed her thick-set neck, which arched out of her shoulders in one glossy, muscular rise; he tossed on her saddle. He brought the girth under, but she spun back. "I'll hold her," Daddy said, and took the reins. "Whoa, there," he said, while Uncle Rex cinched the girth. He gathered her in then, though she wasn't sure yet that she liked it, tapped her fetlock to bring her lower for the mounting, and up he went. We stood around while he showed her off; she had a smart little singlefoot that he liked, and a long swinging walk. I still remember the straightness of his back as he rode away from us, and the jaunty swing of his elbows.

Afterward we returned to the house and there was Aunt Martha's car, back from her folks in town. She acted glad to see us: it was Uncle Rex she was cool to. The McClelland house was a country place, but it had high, white, important sides with not enough windows, like a house on a city street. The McClellands were nice people, a connection spread over two counties, yet the house was different from what we would have had. It was printed all over Aunt Martha what she was thinking; that Uncle Rex had had that horse out on Sunday. And the beast was female, too; that, I now realized, made a difference to both of them, and had all along.

Aunt Martha was pretty, with an unlined plump face, gray hair she wore curled nicely in place. She was reserved about her feelings, and if Uncle Rex had not come into her life, lighting it up for us to see it, I doubt we'd ever have thought anything about Martha McClelland. That day of the mare, she was wearing brown, but summer would see her turned out in fresh bright cotton dresses she'd made herself, trimmed in eyelet with little pleats and buttons cleverly selected. She also picked out the cars they drove; they were always green or blue. It occurred to me years after that what Aunt Martha liked was owning things. Her ownership, which was not an intrusion—she wanted nothing of anybody else's—extended to all things and persons she had any claim on. When she got to Uncle Rex, then I guess she got a little bit confused; did he belong to her or not? If so, in what way? That question, I thought, would be something like Uncle Rex's own confusion over the McClelland property: he had it, but didn't actually own it. He'd certainly improved it quite a bit. But Aunt Martha also could point to improvements; Uncle Rex was so much better than he used to be. For in former days, freshly married, with promises not to still warmly throbbing in the air, he would come in at dawn, stinking of swamp mud and corn likker, having played poker all night while listening to the fox hounds running way off in the woods—some prefer Grand Opera while playing bezique, Uncle Hernan once remarked. I wondered what bezique was. Whatever it was, it wasn't for Uncle Rex.

As we drove away, Daddy said: "She's probably raising Cain about that mare."

"I don't think so," Mama said. "I don't think Martha raises Cain.

Andrew is coming home at Thanksgiving. That's keeping her happy. She's proud of that boy."

"Rex is proud of him, too," said Daddy.

"Of course he is," Mama said.

———

Andrew was a dark-haired square-set boy, and when we used to play, as children, looking for arrowheads in the pasture, climbing through the fence to the next property where, it was said, the high bump in the ground near the old road was really an Indian mound, I would imagine him an Indian brave or somebody with Indian blood. My effort, I suppose, was to make him mysterious and hence more interesting, but the truth is there was never anything mysterious about Andrew. He was a good boy through and through, the way Aunt Martha wanted him. She would have liked him to go in the ministry but he took up history and played basketball so well he was a wonder. He wasn't so tall but he was fast and well set and had a wondrous way of guarding the ball; he knew how to dribble it and keep it safe. After graduating he got a job teaching and coaching at a military academy run by the church. This was not being a preacher but was in no way acting like his father used to act, and Aunt Martha breathed easy once he decided on it.

He was likely to be home in the summers when not working in some boys' camp.

That was all in the late 1940s, post-war. Andrew was younger than me and unlike the boys my age, he had missed the conflict. He was old enough to play basketball but not to be drafted. Somebody— a man of the town—on seeing him win a whole tournament for Port Claiborne, came up afterward to say: "Boy, it's folks like you that keeps us inter-rested here at home. Don't think you ain't doing your part." Aunt Martha was proud of that; she quoted it often and so did Uncle Rex.

With such a fine boy who'd turned out so well, a place running smoothly and yielding up its harvest year by year, a calmed-down husband with a docile wife, it seemed that Uncle Rex and Aunt Martha could sit on their porch in the summer, in their living room by the gas fire in the winter, smiling and smug and more than content with themselves because of the content they felt about Andrew. Next he would get married, no doubt, and have children, and all would be goodness and love and joy forever. But something happened before that and Aunt Martha lost, I suppose, her holy vision.

———

It happened like this.

One of the summers when Andrew was home sort of puttering around farming and romancing one or two girls in town and reading up for his schoolwork, he and Aunt Martha suddenly got thicker than thieves. They were always out in the family car together, either uptown or driving to Jackson, or out on the place. People leaned in the car window to tell them how much Andrew resembled her side of the family, which was true. The pity (at least to a Wirth) was how pleased they both looked about it. To start really conversing with a parent for the first time must be as strange an experience as falling in love. Daddy and Mama and I love each other but we never say very much about it. Maybe they talk to each other in an unknown tongue when I'm not around. But as for Andrew and Aunt Martha it seemed that somebody had blown up the levee of family reticence, and water and land were mingling to their mutual content.

Late that same summer, Uncle Rex and Uncle Hernan had got together and taken a train trip up to visit their third and older brother, Uncle Andrew, who had lived and worked in Chicago for years, in the law firm of Sanders, Wirth, and Pottle, but who had now retired to a farm he had bought north of Cairo. The trip had renewed the Wirth ties of blood. There is something wonderful about older-type gentlemen on trains. It brings out the good living side of them and makes them relish the table service in the diner, a highball later, and lots of well-seasoned talk. They may even have gambled a little in the club car. The visit with Uncle Andrew must have attained such a joyous and measured richness they would always preserve its privacy.

"It's the property we've looked into these last few days," young Andrew said to his father, on his return. "The possibilities are just great, what with that new highway coming through."

"I think so, too," Aunt Martha said, and served them all the new recipes she was learning. "You've just got to listen to Andrew, Rex."

"I'm still riding the train," said Uncle Rex. "You got to wait awhile before I can listen."

Whether they let him wait awhile or not is doubtful. They were bursting with their plans and designs on the McClelland property. The new highway was coming through. Forty acres given over to real estate was something the farm would never miss. The houses, maybe a shopping center, and even a motel would all be too distant to be seen from the house, yet they glimmered full formed and visible as a mirage in Andrew's talk; and in his thoughts the large pile of money bound to result was already mounding up in the bank.

Andrew had assembled facts and figures, and had borrowed some blueprints of suburban housing from a development firm in Vicksburg. They curled up around his ears when he talked about it all, but nobody had stopped to notice that Uncle Rex had sat the greater part of the time as stiff and straight as if his mare was under him, though the rapport he and that animal shared was not present. He listened and listened and he failed to do justice to the food, and when he couldn't stand it a minute longer he exploded like a firecracker:

"I always knew it!" he jumped up to say. "I never should have moved onto this property."

They looked up with their large brown McClelland eyes, innocent as grazing deer.

"If y'all even think," said Uncle Rex, "that you can sit here and work out all kind of plans the minute I walk out the door you can either un-think 'em or do without me. Which is it?"

"You ought to be open-minded, Father," said Andrew, exactly like he was the oldest one there. He leaned back and let the blueprints roll themselves up with a crackle. "Mother and I have gone to a lot of trouble on this."

"Just listen, Rex," Aunt Martha urged, but her new glow about life was going out like a lamp which has been switched off at the door but doesn't quite know it yet. She spoke timidly.

"I've listened enough already," said Uncle Rex.

He marched out of the room, put on his oldest, most disreputable clothes, and went off in the pickup. He eventually wound up at Uncle Hernan's. We saw him drive up, badly needing a shave. He whammed through the front door of his old home and disappeared. We didn't even dare to telephone. Something, we knew, had happened.

Aunt Martha was so stunned when Uncle Rex hit the ceiling and departed that she shook with nerves all over. She called Mama to come over there (I drove her) and sat and told Mama that everything she had belonged to Rex in her way of thinking, that the Lord had made woman subservient to man, it was put forth that way in the Bible. Did Rex think she would go against the Word of God?

"The land's all yours," Mama said, evidently aware of but not mentioning the wide gap between statements and actions. "I don't think Rex is disputing it. It just comes over him now and then. Maybe Andrew pointed it out to him."

"Andrew ought not to have mentioned it at all," said Aunt Martha. "Oh, I knew that at the time."

"I doubt his coming back to live here now, the way things are," Mama said. "They say the Wirths have got a lot of pride. Especially the men. I just don't know what to tell you. Can you move over to Hernan's with him for a while? Maybe y'all could get more chance to talk things over."

Andrew passed through, knowing everything and not stopping to talk. "He's just hardheaded," he said, in a tone of final authority, and that wasn't smart either. I recalled a saying about the McClellands, that they were so nice they didn't have to be smart. It was widely repeated.

"Hernan's got a whole empty wing," Mama said.

Aunt Martha turned red as a beet and almost cried. She kept twisting her handkerchief, knotting and unknotting it. "Do you imagine a McClelland . . ." she whispered, then she stopped. What she'd started to say was that Uncle Hernan lived with a Negro woman and everybody knew it. It was his young wife's nurse who'd come down from Tennessee with her, nursed her when she got sick and died, then stayed on to keep house. She was Melissa, a good cook—we all took her for granted. But no McClelland could be expected to be under the same roof with that! In fact, Aunt Martha may have thought of herself as sent from God to us, though Mama was also steady at the Ladies Auxiliary and of equal standing.

When we drove back home it was to learn that Uncle Rex had not only departed from Aunt Martha, he had left Uncle Hernan as well, nobody knew for where. He had gone out and loaded his mare in the horse trailer and gone off down the back road unobserved from within, while Aunt Martha was sitting there with Mama and me, crying over him. (We passed a carload of McClellands driving in as we left: at least, we, along with Uncle Rex, had escaped that.)

———

The next day was Sunday and a good chance for all of us over our way to get together in order to worry better.

"I'm glad I never had any children," Uncle Hernan said. Though he'd apparently had any number by Melissa, he didn't have to count them the way Uncle Rex had to count Andrew.

"I don't think for a minute Andrew and Martha calculated the effect something like this was going to have on Rex," Daddy said.

"It's just now worked to a head," Mama said, "about being on her land and all."

"Hadn't been for Rex wouldn't be much of any land to be on," Daddy said. "The McClellands make mighty poor farmers."

"He knew that," said Uncle Hernan. "He knew that everybody knows it. But the facts speak."

"Wonder where he is right now," Mama said, and from her voice I was made to recall the slight lovable man who was her brother, threatened, in her mind, in some perpetual way.

"Down in the swamp somewhere, with that pickup and that mare, living in some hunting camp," was Uncle Hernan's judgment. "I imagine he's near the river; he'll need a road for working the mare out and some free ground not to get bit to death with mosquitoes and gnats."

"This time of year?" said Mama, because fall was coming early; we were into the first cold snap.

"All times of year down in those places."

"I worry about him, I declare I do," Mama said.

"*You* worry about him. Another week of this and Martha's going to be in the hospital," Daddy said.

"That mare," said Uncle Hernan, searching his back pocket. He drew out a gigantic linen handkerchief, blew his nose in a moderate honk, and arranged his bronze mustache. "She must be getting on for ten years old."

"She was nothing but a filly that day we were over there. You remember that, Marilee?" Daddy asked.

"When was that?" Uncle Hernan asked.

"We drove over there one Sunday," said Mama. "Martha was at one of her folks in town. Rex showed off the mare—nothing would do him but for us to see her."

"Martha came back and caught him fresh out of the lot on Sunday," Daddy said.

"Lord have mercy," said Uncle Hernan. Then he said, "How are you, Marilee?"

I was not so much involved in their discussion. I was over in the bay window reading some reports from the real estate office where I had a job now. School teaching, after two years of it, had gone sour on me. I said I was fine. I was keeping quietly in the background for the very good reason that the fault in all this crisis had been partially my own. I had once suggested to Andrew, who sometimes dropped by the office to talk to me, that the McClelland place had a gold mine in real estate if only they'd care to develop it, what with the new highway laid out to run along beside it. He'd asked me a lot of questions and had evidently got the idea well into him, like a fish appreciative of the minnow.

I knew nobody would ever reckon me responsible, simply because I was a girl in business. A girl in business, their assumptions went, was somebody that had no right to be and did not count in thinking or in conversation. I could sit in the window seat reading up on real estate not ten feet away from them, but I might as well have been reading Jane Austen for all it was going to enter their thinking about Uncle Rex.

A log broke in the fireplace while we all, for a most unusually long moment, sat pondering in silence, and a spray of sparks shot out.

"Somebody's *got* to find him," Mama said, and almost cried.

"I'd look myself," said Uncle Hernan, "but I'm down with rheumatism and hardly able to drive, much less take a jeep into a swamp. I might get snake bit into the bargain."

"What about Daddy?" I said, and added that I didn't want to go into any swamp either.

"Oh, my Lord," Daddy said, which was his own admission that the Wirth family had never given him much of a voice in their affairs, though it stirred Mama's indignation to hear about it. Daddy knew he certainly might be successful in any mission they sent him on: he was Jim Summerall—a tough little farming man and a good squirrel shot; but though you could entrust a message to him, how could anybody be sure he'd be listened to when he got there? A wild goose chase would be what he'd probably have to call it, with Mama riled up besides.

"Marilee could find him," Uncle Hernan pronounced, and everybody, including myself, looked up in amazement, but didn't get to ask him why he said it, as he picked up his walking cane and stood up to leave. Daddy walked out with him to go down and look at where the soil conservation people were at work straightening the creek in back of ours and Uncle Hernan's properties. There was going to be a new little three-acre patch on their side to be justly divided, and a neighbor across the way to be treated with satisfaction to all. It was a nice walk.

But Uncle Hernan would have found, if not that, some other reason to leave our house. He never seemed in place there. His own house, or rather the old Wirth home where he lived, was pre–Civil War and classical in design; ours was a sturdy farming house. It was within the power of architecture to let us all know that Uncle Hernan was not in his element sitting in front of our fire in the living room, in spite of Mama's antiques and her hooked rugs and all her pretty things. Then it occurred to me that, whether totally his property by deed or inheritance or purchase or not, that house in turn had claimed Uncle Hernan; that he belonged to it and they were one, and then I knew why Uncle Rex had found no peace there either and had left after two days, as restless in search as a sparrow hawk.

When Daddy got back I walked out to speak to Uncle Hernan at the fence.

"What'd you mean, I could find him?" I asked.

"Well, you've got that fella now, that surveyor," Uncle Hernan said. "'Gully' Richard," he added, giving his nickname.

Joe Richard (pronounced in the French way, accent on the last syllable) was a man with a surveying firm over in Vicksburg whom we'd had out for a couple of jobs. He had got to calling me up lately, always at the office. For some reason, I hadn't mentioned him to anybody.

"You know how he got the name of Gully?" Uncle Hernan asked, looking at the sky.

"No, sir," I said.

"Came up to this country from down yonder in Louisiana and the first job he got to do was survey a tract was nothing but gullies. Like to never got out of there—snakes and kudzu. Says he thinks he's in there yet. Gully's not so bad, Marilee."

"No, sir," I said, and stopped. Let your family know you've seen anybody once or twice and they've already picked out the preacher and decorated the church. But Uncle Hernan wasn't like that. I thought more of him because he'd never commented on anybody I might be going with, except he did say once that the wild boy who had been my first romance could certainly put away a lot of likker. I judged if Uncle Hernan had spoken favorably of Joe Richard, it was because he esteemed him as a man, not because he was hastening to marry me off.

"What's Joe Richard got to do with Uncle Rex?" I asked, but I already knew what the connection was. He'd been surveying some bottom land over toward the river, and, furthermore, he knew people—trappers and squatters and the like. He was a tall, sunburnt, surly-looking man who kept opinions to himself. I had never liked him till I saw his humor. It was like the sun coming out. His grin showed an irregular line of teeth, attractive for some reason, and a good liveliness. He came from a distance, had the air of a divorced man, a name like a Catholic—all this, appealing to me, would be hurdles as high as a steeple to the Summeralls, the McClellands, and the Wirths (except for Uncle Hernan). But any thought that he wanted to get married at all, let alone to me, was pure speculation. Maybe what he would serve for was finding Uncle Rex.

It was a day or so before I saw him. "Will you do it?" I asked him. "Will you try?"

"Hell, he's just goofed off for a while," Joe said. "Anybody can do that. Let him come back by himself."

"He's important to us," I said, "because—" and I stopped and couldn't think of the right thing, but to Joe's credit he didn't do a thing but wait for me to finish. It came to me to put it this way, speaking with Mama's voice, I bet: "Important because he doesn't know he is."

Joe understood that, and said he'd try.

—

One latent truth in all this is that I was mad enough at Andrew McClelland Wirth to kill him. He'd gone about it wrong: snatching authority away from his father was what he'd obviously acted like.

During the second month of Uncle Rex's absence, with Joe Richard still reporting nothing at all, and Aunt Martha meeting with her prayer group all the time (she was sustained also by droves of McClelland relatives who were speculating on divorce), I drove up to the school where Andrew taught and got to see him between class and basketball practice. "You could have had a little more tact," I told him, when more sense was probably nearer to the point, and what I should have said. The night before I had had a dream. I had seen a little cabin in a swamp that was just catching fire, flames licking up the sides, but nobody so far, when I woke, had walked out of it. The dream was still in my head when I drove to find Andrew.

Andrew and I went to a place across the street from his little school, a conglomerate of red-brick serviceable buildings with a football field out back, a gym made out of an army-surplus aluminum airplane hangar off at the side, and a parade ground in the center, with a tall flagpole. It was a sparkling dry afternoon in the fall, chilly in shadow, hot in the sun. "If you haven't noticed anything about the Wirth pride," I continued, "you must be going through life with blinders on."

"You don't understand, Marilee," he said. "It was Mother I was trying to help. She needs something more to interest her than she's got. I thought the real estate idea you had was just about right."

"It would have been if you'd have gone through Uncle Rex."

"You may not know this, Marilee, but after a certain point I can't do a thing with Father, he just won't listen."

"You mean you tried?"

"I tried about other things. He's got an old cultivator out in back that the seat is falling off of, it's so rusty. You'd have to soak it in a swimming pool full of machine oil to get it in shape, but he won't borrow the money to buy a new one."

"He and Daddy and Uncle Hernan are going in together on one for the spring crop," I said. "It was Uncle Rex got them to do it. Didn't you know that?"

"He won't tell me anything anymore; you'd think I wasn't in the world the way he won't talk to me. I've just about quit."

I recalled that Uncle Rex had told Uncle Hernan that Aunt Martha and Andrew had got so thick he was like a stranger at his own table, but there's no use entering into family quarrels. The people themselves all tell a different tale, so how can you judge what's true?

"Promise me one thing," I said.

"What?"

"If he comes back (and you know he's bound to), glad or sad or mean or sweet or dead drunk with one ear clawed off, you go in and talk to him and tell him how it was. Don't even stop to speak to your mama. You go straight to him."

"How do you know he's bound to come back?" Andrew asked.

"I just do," I said. But I didn't; and neither did anybody else.

Andrew said: "You're bound to side with the Wirths, Marilee. You *are* one."

"Well," I said, "are you trying to break up *your* family?"

He thought it over. He was finishing his Coke because he had to go back over to the gym. He wore a coach's cap with a neat bill, a soft knit shirt, gabardine trousers, and gym shoes. He also wore white socks. All told, he looked to have stepped out of the Sears Roebuck catalogue, for he was trim as could be, but he was too regulation to be real.

"You might be right, Marilee," was his final word. "I'll try."

When I got back to Port Claiborne, Joe Richard was waiting for me. His news was that he had finally located Uncle Rex. He was living in a trapper's house down near the Mississippi River. The horse was there, and also a strange woman.

———

Indolent at times, in midday sun still as a turtle on a log which is stuck in the mud near some willows . . . at other times, hasty and hustling, banging away over dried-up mud roads in the pickup with a dozen or so muskrat traps in the back and the chopped bait blood-staining a sack on the floor of the seat beside him . . . at yet other times, fishing the muddy shallows of the little bayous in an old, flat-bottomed rowboat, rowing with one hand tight on a short paddle, hearing the quiet separated sounds of water dripping from paddle, pole, or line, or from the occasional bream or white perch or little mud cat he caught, lifting the string to add another: that's how it was for Rex Wirth. In spring and summer sounds run together but in the fall each is separate; I don't know why. Only insect voices mingle, choiring for a while, then dwindling into single chips of sound. The riverbanks and the bayous seem to have nothing to do with the river itself, which flows magnificently in the background, a whole horizon to itself from the banks, or glimpsed through willow fronds—the Father of Waters not minding its children.

At twilight and in the early morning hours when the dew began to sparkle, he rode the mare. He kept a smudge for her, to ward the insects off, sprayed her, too, and swabbed her with some stuff out of a bucket. The mare had nothing to worry about.

The woman was young—likely in her twenties. She came and went, sometimes with sacks of groceries. At other times she fished; sometimes a child fished with her. Another time a man came and sat talking on the porch. She had blond sunburnt hair, nothing fancy about her. Wore jeans and gingham shirts.

"A nice fanny," Joe said.

"Was it her you were studying or Uncle Rex?" I asked him.

"It's curious," he said. "I stayed longer than I meant to. I've got some good binoculars. That old guy might have found him such a paradise he ain't ever going to show up again. Ever think of that, Marilee? Some folks just looking for an excuse to leave?" I thought of it and it carried its own echo for me: Joe Richard had left Louisiana, or he wouldn't be there talking to me.

I thought that if Uncle Rex had wanted to leave forever he would have gone further than twenty miles away; he had the world to choose from, depending on which temperature and landscape he favored. There must be a reason for his choice, I thought, so I went to talk to Uncle Hernan.

"You were right," I said. "Joe Richard found him." And I told him what he'd seen.

"That would be that Bertis girl," said Uncle Hernan at once.

"Who?" I said.

"Oh, it was back before Rex was married. We all used to go down there with the Meecham brothers and Carter Bankston. It was good duck shooting in the winter and we got some deer too if you could stand the cold—cold is not too bad, but river damp goes right into your bones. Of course, we'd be pretty well fortified.

"There was a family we had, to tend camp for us, a fellow named Bertis, better than a river rat, used to work in construction in Natchez, but lost his arm in an accident, then got into a lawsuit, didn't get a cent out of it, went on relief, found him a river house, got to trapping. Well, he had a wife and a couple of kids to raise. His wife was a nice woman. Ought to have gone back to her folks. She had a college degree, if I recall correctly.

"One year, down there on the camp, Bertis came to cook and skin for us, like he'd always done, but he was worried that year over his wife, who'd come down sick. It was Rex who decided to take her to Natchez to the hospital and let the hunt go on. Some of the bunch had invited some others—a big preacher and a senator: at this late date, I don't quite know myself who all was there. It would have been hard to carry on without Bertis and Bertis needed money, too, though I reckon we might have made up a check.

"Everybody was a little surprised at what Rex offered to take on himself. He stood straight-backed and bright-eyed when he spoke up, like a man who's volunteering for a mission and ready to salute when it's granted. Somebody ought to have offered—that was true. But there's the sort of woman, Marilee, can be around ten to a thousand men all together, and every last one of them will have the same impression of her, but not a one will mention it. So we never spoke of what crossed everybody's mind.

"The funny thing was, Bertis never stirred himself to see about his wife. He was an odd sort of fellow, not mean, but what you'd call life-sick. Some people can endure life, slowly, gradually, all that comes, but with enjoyment and good spirit; but some get lightning struck and something splits off in them. In Bertis's case it was more than an arm he'd lost; it was spirit.

"Rex stayed away and stayed away. Not till the camp was breaking up did Bertis come up to me, and I offered to drive him in. We got to the hospital but his wife wasn't there, she'd gone on to Vicksburg and it was late. The next day, on a street in Vicksburg, in an old house they'd made into apartments, we found her. She was sitting in a nice room with a coal fire burning, looking quiet and at peace. She looked more than that. She looked beautiful. Her hands had turned fine, white, delicate as a lady's in a painting, don't you know. She had an afghan over her.

"When we came in, we heard footsteps out the back hall and a door slamming. 'Hello, Mr. Bertis,' was all she said. I drove them home. As far as I recall they never asked each other's news, never exchanged a word. I put down at the front door of that house out in the wilds, not quite in the swamps but too close to the river to be healthy, not quite a cabin but too run down to call a home—it was just a house, that was all. 'You going to be all right, Mrs. Bertis?' I asked.

"'I reckon I can drive in a day or two,' was what she said. Bertis couldn't do much driving on account of his arm. Though she spoke, it seemed she wasn't really there; she was in a private haze. I remember how she went in the house, like a woman in a dream.

"And there was a little yellow-haired girl in the doorway, waiting for her. That's likely the one's down there now.

"Rex was gone completely for more than a month if I'm not mistaken. He took a trip out West and saw some places he'd always wanted to, though it was a strange time of year to do it, as some pointed out to him when he got back. Married Martha McClelland soon after.

"Marilee, does your mama mind your having a little touch of Bourbon now and then?"

"She minds," I said, "but she's given up."

—

"The next time you have some bright family ideas about real estate," said Joe Richard, "you better count to a hundred-and-two and keep your mouth shut."

"That's the truth," I said.

We were lying facedown on a ridge thick in fallen leaves, side by side, taking turns with the binoculars. I had a blanket under me Joe had dug out of his car to keep me from catching a cold, he said, and I was studying my fill down through the trunks of tall trees— beech, oak, and flaming sycamore—way down to the low fronded willows near the old fishing camp with the weed-grown road and the brown flowing river beyond—and it was all there, just the way he'd said.

I had watched Uncle Rex come up from fishing and moor his boat, had watched a tow-headed child in faded blue overalls enter the field of vision to meet him, and then the blond woman, who'd stood talking in blue jeans and a sweater with the sleeves pushed up—exactly what I had on, truth to tell—taking the string of fish from him, while he walked away and the child ran after him. And I followed with the sights on them, the living field of their life brought as close as my own breath, though they didn't know it—do spirits feel as I did? When he came back, he was leading the mare. She looked well accustomed, and flicked her fine ears, which were fur-ring over for winter, and stood while Uncle Rex lifted the child and set her in the saddle as her mother held the reins. The fish shone silvery on the string against the young woman's leg.

There is such a thing as father, daughter, and grandchild—such a thing as family that is not blood family but a chosen family: I was seeing that. Joe took the glasses out of my hand for his turn and while he looked I thought about Indian summer which isn't summer at all, but something else. There is the long hot summer, heavy and teeming, more real than life; and there is the other summer, pure as gold, as real as hope. Now, not needing glasses, or eyes, either, I saw the problem Rex Wirth must be solving and unsolving every day. If this was the place he belonged and the family that was—though not of blood—in a sense, his, why leave them ever? His life, like a tree drawn into the river and slipping by, must have felt the current pull and turn him every day. Wasn't this where he belonged? Come back, Uncle Rex!—should I run out of the woods and tell him that? No, the struggle was his own. We went away silent, never showing we were there.

—

Uncle Rex did come home.

It was when the weather broke in a big cold front out of the northwest. It must have come ruffling the water, thickening the afternoon sky, then sweeping across the river, a giant black cloak of a cloud, moaning and howling in the night, stripping the little trees and bushes bare of colored leaves and crashing against the willow thickets. It was like a seasonal motion, too, that Uncle Rex should decamp at that time, arrive back at Aunt Martha's with a pickup of frozen fish packed in ice and some muskrat pelts, even a few mink, the mare in her little cart bringing up the rear.

At least I thought he went home, as soon as somebody I knew out on that road called me at the office to say he'd gone by. If he'd gone to Uncle Hernan's that would have been a waste of all his motions, all to do again. I telephoned to Andrew.

"Get on out there," I said. "Don't even stop to coach basketball."

But Andrew couldn't do that. If he had started untying a knot in his shoelace when the last trump sounded, he would keep right on with it, before he turned his attention to anything new. So he started home after basketball practice.

There were giant upheavals of wind and hail and falling temperatures throughout the South, the breakup of Indian summer, but Andrew forged his way homeward, discovering along the road that the car heater needed fixing and that he hadn't got on a warm enough suit, or brought a coat.

He went straight in to Uncle Rex. It seemed to me later than anybody could program Andrew, but I guess on the other hand he'd worried about his father's absence and his mother's abandoned condition a great deal, and nobody except me had told him anything he could do about it. He had gone home a time or two to comfort her, but it hadn't worked miracles.

"I'm sorry for what I said about the land, Father," he said right out, even before he got through shivering. "You're the one ought to decide whatever we do."

Then he stopped. The big, white house was silent, emptied of McClellands, by what method God alone would ever know.

Uncle Rex and Aunt Martha were sitting alone by the gas heater. Aunt Martha had risen to greet him when he came in, but then she'd sat down again, looking subdued.

Uncle Rex rose up and approached Andrew with tears in his eyes. He placed his hands on each of his shoulders. "Son—" he said. "Son—" His face had got bearded during his long time away, grizzled, sun- and wind-burnt, veined, austere, like somebody who has had to deal with Indians and doesn't care to discuss it. His hands had split up in half a dozen places from hard use; his nails had blood and grime under them that no scrubbing would remove. "Son, this property . . . it's all coming to you someday. For now . . ."

If you looked deeply into Andrew's eyes, they did not have very much to tell. He said, "Yes, Father," which was about all that was required. When he told me about it, I could imagine both his parents' faces, how they stole glances at him, glowed with pride the same as ever, on account of his being so fine to look at and their own into the bargain. But I remembered that we are back in the bosom of the real family now—the blood one—and that blood is for spilling, among other things.

"Your mother wanted me on this place, Son," Uncle Rex went on, "and as long as she wants me here the only word that goes is mine. She can tell you now if that's so or not."

"But, Father, you left her worried sick. You never sent word to her! It's been awful!"

"That's not the point, Son," said Uncle Rex. "She wants me here."

"I want him here," Aunt Martha echoed. She looked at Andrew with all her love, but she was looking across a mighty wide river.

"You know how he's acted! You know what he did!"

"That's not the point," Aunt Martha murmured.

"Then what is the point?" Andrew asked, craving to know with as much passion as he'd ever have, I guess.

"That your father—that I want him here." She was studying her hands then—not even looking. They were speakers in a play.

As for Andrew, he said he felt as if he wasn't there anymore, that some force had moved through him and that life was not the same. Figuratively speaking, his voice had been taken from him. Literally, he was coming down with a cold. Aunt Martha gave him supper and poured hot chocolate down him, and he went to bed with nothing but the sounds of a shrieking wind and the ticking clock, in the old room he'd had from childhood on. He felt (he told me later) like nothing and nobody. Nothing . . . nobody: the clock was saying it too. There was an ache at the house's core and at some point he dreamed he rose and dressed and went out into the upstairs hall. There he saw his father's face, white, drawn, and small—a ghost face, floating above the stairwell.

"Why call me 'Son' when you don't mean it?"

There wasn't an answer, and he woke and heard the wind.

———

Uncle Rex—what dream did he have?

"We can't know that," said Uncle Hernan, when I talked to him. "Rex did what he had to. He settled it with those McClellands, once and for all. It was hard for Rex—remember that. Oh yes, Marilee! For Rex it was mighty hard."

THE GIRL WHO LOVED HORSES

———————

She had drawn back from throwing a pan of bird scraps out the door because she heard what was coming, the two-part pounding of a full gallop, not the graceful triple notes of a canter. They were mounting the drive now, turning into the stretch along the side of the house; once before, someone appearing at the screen door had made the horse shy, so that, barely held beneath the rider, barely restrained, he had plunged off into the flower beds. So she stepped back from the door and saw the two of them shoot past, rounding a final corner, heading for the straight run of drive into the cattle gate and the barn lot back of it.

She flung out the scraps, then walked to the other side of the kitchen and peered through the window, raised for spring, toward the barn lot. The horse had slowed, out of habit, knowing what came next. And the white shirt that had passed hugged so low as to seem some strange part of the animal's trappings, or as though he had run under a low line of drying laundry and caught something to an otherwise empty saddle and bare withers, now rose up, angling to an upright posture. A gloved hand extended to pat the lathered neck.

"Lord have mercy," the woman said. The young woman riding the horse was her daughter, but she was speaking also for her son-in-law, who went in for even more reckless behavior in the jumping ring the two of them had set up. What she meant by it was that they were going to kill themselves before they ever had any children, or if they did have children safely they'd bring up the children to be just as foolish about horses and careless of life and limb as they were themselves.

The young woman's booted heel struck the back steps. The screen door banged.

"You ought not to bring him in hot like that," the mother said. "I do know that much."

"Cottrell is out there," she said.

"It's still March, even if it has got warm."

"Cottrell knows what to do."

She ran water at the sink, and cupping her hand, drank primitive fashion out of it, bending to the tap, then wet her hands in the running water and thrust her fingers into the dusty, sweat-damp roots of her sand-colored hair. It had been a good ride.

"I hope he doesn't take up too much time," the mother said. "My beds need working."

She spoke mildly but it was always part of the same quarrel they were in like a stream that was now a trickle, now a still pool, but sometimes after a freshet could turn into a torrent. Such as: "Y'all are just crazy. Y'all are wasting everything on those things. And what are they? I know they're pretty and all that, but they're not a thing in the world but animals. Cows are animals. You can make a lot more money in cattle, than carting those things around over two states and three counties."

She could work herself up too much to eat, leaving the two of them at the table, but would see them just the same in her mind's eye, just as if she'd stayed. There were the sandy-haired young woman, already thirty—married four years and still apparently with no intention of producing a family (she was an only child and the estate, though small, was a fine piece of land)—and across from her the dark spare still young man she had married.

She knew how they would sit there alone and not even look at one another or discuss what she'd said or talk against her; they would just sit there and maybe pass each other some food or one of them would get up for the coffeepot. The fanatics of a strange cult would do the same, she often thought, loosening her long hair upstairs, brushing the gray and brown together to a colorless patina, putting on one of her long cotton gowns with the ruched neck, crawling in between white cotton sheets. She was a widow and if she didn't want to sit up and try to talk to the family after a hard day, she didn't have to. Reading was a joy, lifelong. She found her place in *Middlemarch,* one of her favorites.

But during the day not even reading (if she'd had the time) could shut out the sounds from back of the privet hedge, plainly to be heard from the house. The trudging of the trot, the pause, the low directive, the thud of hoofs, the heave and shout, and sometimes the ring of struck wood as a bar came down. And every jump a risk of life and limb. One dislocated shoulder—Clyde's, thank heaven, not Deedee's—a taping, a sling, a contraption of boards, and pain "like a hot knife," he had said. A hot knife. Wouldn't that hurt anybody enough to make him quit risking life and limb with those two blood horses, quit at least talking about getting still another one while swallowing down pain-killer he said he hated to be sissy enough to take?

"Uh-huh," the mother said. "But it'll be Deborah next. You thought about that?"

"Aw, now, Miss Emma," he'd lean back to say, charming her through his warrior's haze of pain. "Deedee and me—that's what we're hooked on. Think of us without it, Mama. You really want to kill us. We couldn't live."

He was speaking to his mother-in-law but smiling at his wife. And she, Deborah, was smiling back.

———

Her name was Deborah Dale, but they'd always, of course, being from LaGrange, Tennessee, right over the Mississippi border, that is to say, real South, had a hundred nicknames for her. Deedee, her father had named her, and "Deeds" her funny cousins said—"Hey, Deeds, how ya' doin'?" Being on this property in a town of pretty properties, though theirs was a little way out, a little bit larger than most, she was always out romping, swimming in forbidden creeks, climbing forbidden fences, going barefoot too soon in the spring, the last one in at recess, the first one to turn in an exam paper. ("Are you quite sure that you have finished, Deborah?" "Yes, ma'am.")

When she graduated from ponies to that sturdy calico her uncle gave her, bringing it in from his farm because he had an eye for a good match, there was almost no finding her. "I always know she's somewhere on the place," her mother said. "We just can't see it all at once," said her father. He was ailing even back then but he undertook walks. Once when the leaves had all but gone from the trees, on a warm November afternoon, from a slight rise, he saw her down in a little-used pasture with a straight open stretch among some oaks. The ground was spongy and clotted with damp and even a child ought not to have tried to run there, on foot. But there went the calico with Deedee clinging low, going like the wind, and knowing furthermore out of what couldn't be anything but long practice, where to turn, where to veer, where to stop.

"One fine afternoon," he said to himself, suspecting even then (they hadn't told him yet) what his illness was, "and Emma's going to be left with nobody." He remarked on this privately, not without anguish and not without humor.

They stopped her riding, at least like that, by sending her off to boarding school, where a watchful ringmaster took "those girls interested in equitation" out on leafy trails, "at the walk, at the trot, and at the canter." They also, with that depth of consideration which must flourish even among those Southerners unlucky enough to wind up in the lower reaches of hell, kept her young spirit out of the worst of the dying. She just got a call from the housemother one night. Her father had "passed away."

After college she forgot it, she gave it up. It was too expensive, it took a lot of time and devotion, she was interested in boys. Some boys were interested in her. She worked in Memphis, drove home to her mother every night. In winter she had to eat breakfast in the dark. On some evenings the phone rang; on some it was silent. Her mother treated both kinds of evenings just the same.

—

To Emma Tyler it always seemed that Clyde Mecklin materialized out of nowhere. She ran straight into him when opening the front door one evening to get the paper off the porch, he being just about to turn the bell or knock. There he stood, dark and straight in the late light that comes after first dark and is so clear. He was clear as anything in it, clear as the first stamp of a young man ever cast.

"Is Deb'rah here?" At least no Yankee. But not Miss Tyler or Miss Deborah Tyler, or Miss Deborah. No, he was city all right.

She did not answer at first.

"What's the matter, scare you? I was just about to knock."

She still said nothing.

"Maybe this is the wrong place," he said.

"No, it's the right place," Emma Tyler finally said. She stepped back and held the door wider. "Come on in."

"Scared the life out of me," she told Deborah when she finally came down to breakfast the next day, Clyde's car having been heard to depart by Emma Tyler in her upstairs bedroom at an hour she did not care to verify. "Why didn't you tell me you were expecting him? I just opened the door and there he was."

"I liked him so much," said Deborah with grave honesty. "I guess I was scared he wouldn't come. That would have hurt."

"Do you still like him?" her mother ventured, after this confidence.

"He's all for outdoors," said Deborah, as dreamy over coffee as any mother had ever beheld. "Everybody is so indoors. He likes hunting, going fishing, farms."

"Has he got one?"

"He'd like to have. All he's got's this job. He's coming back next weekend. You can talk to him. He's interested in horses."

"But does he know we don't keep horses anymore?"

"That was just my thumbnail sketch," said Deborah. "We don't have to run out and buy any."

"No, I don't imagine so," said her mother, but Deborah hardly remarked the peculiar turn of tone, the dryness. She was letting coast through her head the scene: her mother (whom she now loved better than she ever had in her life) opening the door just before Clyde knocked, so seeing unexpectedly for the first time, that face, that head, that being.... When he had kissed her her ears drummed, and it came back to her once more, not thought of in years, the drumming hoofs of the calico, and the ghosting father, behind, invisible, observant, off on the bare distant November rise.

———

It was after she married that Deborah got beautiful. All LaGrange noticed it. "I declare," they said to her mother or sometimes right out to her face, "I always said she was nice-looking but I never thought anything like that."

———

Emma first saw the boy in the parking lot. He was new. In former days she'd parked in front of nearly any place she wanted to go—hardware, or drugstore, or courthouse: change for the meter was her biggest problem. But so many streets were one-way now and what with the increased numbers of cars, the growth of the town, those days were gone; she used a parking lot back of a café, near the newspaper office. The entrance to the lot was a bottleneck of a narrow drive between the two brick buildings; once in, it was hard sometimes to park.

That day the boy offered to help. He was an expert driver, she noted, whereas Emma was inclined to perspire, crane, and fret, fearful of scraping a fender or grazing a door. He spun the wheel with one hand; a glance told him all he had to know; he as good as sat the car in place, as skillful (she reluctantly thought) as her children on their horses. When she returned an hour later, the cars were denser still; he helped her again. She wondered whether to tip him. This happened twice more.

"You've been so nice to me," she said, the last time. "They're lucky to have you."

"It's not much of a job," he said. "Just all I can get for the moment. Being new and all."

"I might need some help," she said. "You can call up at the Tyler place if you want to work. It's in the book. Right now I'm in a hurry."

———

On the warm June day, Deborah sat the horse comfortably in the side yard and watched her mother and the young man (whose name was Willett? Williams?), who, having worked the beds and straightened a fence post, was now replacing warped fence boards with new ones.

"Who is he?" she asked her mother, not quite low enough, and meaning what a Southern woman invariably means by that question, not what is his name but where did he come from, is he anybody we know? What excuse, in other words, does he have for even being born?

"One thing, he's a good worker," her mother said, preening a little. Did they think she couldn't manage if she had to? "Now don't you make him feel bad."

"Feel bad!" But once again, if only to spite her mother, who was in a way criticizing her and Clyde by hiring anybody at all to do work that Clyde or the Negro help would have been able to do if only it weren't for those horses—once again Deborah had spoken too loudly.

If she ever had freely to admit things, even to herself, Deborah would have to say she knew she not only looked good that June day, she looked sexy as hell. Her light hair, tousled from a ride in the fields, had grown longer in the last year; it had slipped its pins on one side and lay in a sensuous lock along her cheek. A breeze stirred it, then passed by. Her soft poplin shirt was loose at the throat, the two top buttons open, the cuffs turned back to her elbows. The new horse, the third, was gentle, too much so (this worried them); she sat it easily, one leg up, crossed lazily over the flat English pommel, while the horse, head stretched down, cropped at the tender grass. In the silence between their voices, the tearing of the grass was the only sound except for a shrill jay's cry.

"Make him feel bad!" she repeated.

The boy looked up. The horse, seeking grass, had moved forward; she was closer than before, eyes looking down on him above the rise of her breasts and throat; she saw the closeness go through him, saw her presence register as strongly as if the earth's accidental shifting had slammed them physically together. For a minute there was nothing but the two of them. The jay was silent; even the horse, sensing something, had raised his head.

Stepping back, the boy stumbled over the pile of lumber, then fell in it. Deborah laughed. Nothing, that day, could have stopped her laughter. She was beautifully, languidly, atop a fine horse on the year's choice day at the peak of her life.

"You know what?" Deborah said at supper, when they were discussing her mother's helper. "I thought who he looks like. He looks like Clyde."

"The poor guy," Clyde said. "Was that the best you could do?"

Emma sat still. Now that she thought of it, he did look like Clyde. She stopped eating, to think it over. What difference did it make if he did? She returned to her plate.

Deborah ate lustily, her table manners unrestrained. She swabbed bread into the empty salad bowl, drenched it with dressing, bit it in hunks.

"The poor woman's Clyde, that's what you hired," she said. She looked up.

The screen door had just softly closed in the kitchen behind them. Emma's hired man had come in for his money.

It was the next day that the boy, whose name was Willett or Williams, broke the riding mower by running it full speed into a rock pile overgrown with weeds but clearly visible, and left without asking for pay but evidently taking with him in his car a number of selected items from barn, garage, and tack room, along with a transistor radio that Clyde kept in the kitchen for getting news with his early coffee.

Emma Tyler, vexed for a number of reasons she did not care to sort out (prime among them was the very peaceful and good time she had been having with the boy the day before in the yard when Deborah had chosen to ride over and join them), telephoned the police and reported the whole matter. But boy, car, and stolen articles vanished into the nowhere. That was all, for what they took to be forever.

———

Three years later, aged thirty-three, Deborah Mecklin was carrying her fine head higher than ever uptown in LaGrange. She drove herself on errands back and forth in car or station wagon, not looking to left or right, not speaking so much as before. She was trying not to hear from the outside what they were now saying about Clyde, how well he'd done with the horses, that place was as good as a stud farm now that he kept ten or a dozen, advertised and traded, as well as showed. And the money was coming in hard and fast. But, they would add, he moved with a fast set, and there was also the occasional gossip item, too often, in Clyde's case, with someone ready to report first hand; look how quick, now you thought of it, he'd taken up with Deborah, and how she'd snapped him up too soon to hear what his reputation was, even back then. It would be a cold day in August before any one woman would be enough for him. And his father before him? And his father before him. So the voices said.

Deborah, too, was trying not to hear what was still sounding from inside her head after her fall in the last big horse show:

The doctor: You barely escaped concussion, young lady.

Clyde: I just never saw your timing go off like that. I can't get over it.

Emma: You'd better let it go for a while, honey. There're other things, so many other things.

Back home, she later said to Emma: "Oh, Mama, I know you're right sometimes, and sometimes I'm sick of it all, but Clyde depends on me, he always has, and now look—"

"Yes, and 'Now look' is right, he has to be out with it to keep it all running. You got your wish, is all I can say."

Emma was frequently over at her sister-in-law Marian's farm these days. The ladies were aging, Marian especially down in the back, and those twilights in the house alone were more and more all that Deedee had to keep herself company with. Sometimes the phone rang and there'd be Clyde on it, to say he'd be late again. Or there'd be no call at all. And once she (of all people) pressed some curtains and hung them, and once hunted for old photographs, and once, standing in the middle of the little-used parlor among the walnut Victorian furniture upholstered in gold and blue and rose, she had said "Daddy?" right out loud, like he might have been there to answer, really been there. It had surprised her, the word falling out like that as though a thought took reality all by itself and made a word on its own.

And once there came a knock at the door.

All she thought, though she hadn't heard the car, was that it was Clyde and that he'd forgotten his key, or seeing her there, his arms loaded maybe, was asking her to let him in. It was past dark. Though times were a little more chancy now, LaGrange was a safe place. People nearer to town used to brag that if they went off for any length of time less than a weekend and locked the doors, the neighbors would get their feelings hurt; and if the Tylers lived further out and "locked up," the feeling for it was ritual mainly, a precaution.

She glanced through the sidelight, saw what she took for Clyde, and opened the door. There were cedars in the front yard, not too near the house, but dense enough to block out whatever gathering of light there might have been from the long slope of property beyond the front gate. There was no moon.

The man she took for Clyde, instead of stepping through the door or up to the threshold to greet her, withdrew a step and leaned down and to one side, turning outward as though to pick up something. It was she who stepped forward, to greet, help, inquire; for deep within was the idea her mother had seen to it was firmly and forever planted: that one day one of them was going to get too badly hurt by "those things" ever to be patched up.

So it was in outer dark, three paces from the safe threshold and to the left of the area where the light was falling outward, a dim single sidelight near the mantelpiece having been all she had switched on, too faint to penetrate the sheer gathered curtains of the sidelight, that the man at the door rose up, that he tried to take her. The first she knew of it, his face was in hers, not Clyde's but something like it and at Clyde's exact height, so that for the moment she thought that some joke was on, and then the strange hand caught the parting of her blouse, a new mouth fell hard on her own, one knee thrust her legs apart, the free hand diving in to clutch and press against the thin nylon between her thighs. She recoiled at the same time that she felt, touched in the quick, the painful glory of desire brought on too fast—looking back on that instant's two-edged meaning, she would never hear about rape without the lightning quiver of ambivalence within the word. However, at the time no meditation stopped her knee from coming up into the nameless groin and nothing stopped her from tearing back her mouth slathered with spit so suddenly smeared into it as to drag it into the shape of a scream she was unable yet to find a voice for. Her good right arm struck like a hard backhand against a line-smoking tennis serve. Then from the driveway came the stream of twin headlights thrusting through the cedars.

"Bitch!" The word, distorted and low, was like a groan; she had hurt him, freed herself for a moment, but the struggle would have just begun except for the lights, and the screams that were just trying to get out of her. "You fucking bitch." He saw the car lights, wavered, then turned. His leap into the shrubbery was bent, like a hunchback's. She stopped screaming suddenly. Hurt where he lived, she thought. The animal motion, wounded, drew her curiosity for a second. Saved, she saw the car sweep round the drive, but watched the bushes shake, put up her hand to touch but not to close the torn halves of the blouse, which was ripped open to her waist.

Inside, she stood looking down at herself in the dim light. There was a nail scratch near the left nipple, two teeth marks between elbow and wrist where she'd smashed into his mouth. She wiped her own mouth on the back of her hand, gagging at the taste of cigarette smoke, bitterly staled. Animals! She'd always had a special feeling for them, a helpless tenderness. In her memory the bushes, shaking to a crippled flight, shook forever.

She went upstairs, stood trembling in her mother's room (Emma was away), combed her hair with her mother's comb. Then, hearing Clyde's voice calling her below, she stripped off her ravaged blouse and hastened across to their own rooms to hide it in a drawer, change into a fresh one, come downstairs. She had made her decision already. Who was this man? A nothing . . . an unknown. She hated women who shouted Rape! Rape! It was an incident, but once she told it everyone would know, along with the police, and would add to it: they'd say she'd been violated. It was an incident, but Clyde, once he knew, would trace him down. Clyde would kill him.

"Did you know the door was wide open?" He was standing in the living room.

"I know. I must have opened it when I heard the car. I thought you were stopping in the front."

"Well, I hardly ever do."

"Sometimes you do."

"Deedee, have you been drinking?"

"Drinking . . . ? Me?" She squinted at him, joking in her own way; it was a standing quarrel now that alone she sometimes poured one or two.

He would check her breath but not her marked body. Lust with him was mole-dark now, not desire in the soft increase of morning light, or on slowly westering afternoons, or by the night light's glow. He would kill for her because she was his wife. . . .

———

"Who was that man?"

Uptown one winter afternoon late, she had seen him again. He had been coming out of the hamburger place and looking back, seeing her through the street lights, he had turned quickly into an alley. She had hurried to catch up, to see. But only a form was hastening there, deeper into the unlit slit between brick walls, down toward a street and a section nobody went into without good reason.

"That man," she repeated to the owner (also the proprietor and cook) in the hamburger place. "He was in here just now."

"I don't know him. He hangs around. Wondered myself. You know him?"

"I think he used to work for us once, two or three years ago. I just wondered."

"I thought I seen him somewhere myself."

"He looks a little bit like Clyde."

"Maybe so. Now you mention it." He wiped the counter with a wet rag. "Get you anything, Miss Deb'rah?"

"I've got to get home."

"Y'all got yourselves some prizes, huh?"

"Aw, just some good luck." She was gone.

Prizes, yes. Two trophies at the Shelby County Fair, one in Brownsville where she'd almost lost control again, and Clyde not worrying about her so much as scolding her. His recent theory was that she was out to spite him. He would think it if he was guilty about the women, and she didn't doubt any more that he was. But worse than spite was what had got to her, hating as she did to admit it.

It was fear.

She'd never known it before. When it first started she hadn't even known what the name of it was.

Over two years ago, Clyde had started buying colts not broken yet from a stud farm south of Nashville, bringing them home for him and Deborah to get in shape together. It saved a pile of money to do it that way. She'd been thrown in consequence three times, trampled once, a terrifying moment as the double reins had caught up her outstretched arm so she couldn't fall free. Now when she closed her eyes at night, steel hoofs sometimes hung through the dark above them, and she felt hard ground beneath her head, smelled smeared grass on cheek and elbow. To Clyde she murmured in the dark: "I'm not good at it any more." "Why, Deeds, you were always good. It's temporary, honey. That was a bad day."

A great couple. That's what Clyde thought of them. But more than half their name had been made by her, by the sight of her, Deborah Mecklin, out in full dress, black broadcloth and white satin stock with hair drawn trimly back beneath the smooth rise of the hat, entering the show ring. She looked damned good back of the glossy neck's steep arch, the pointed ears and lacquered hoofs which hardly touched earth before springing upward, as though in the instant before actual flight. There was always the stillness, then the murmur, the rustle of the crowd. At top form she could even get applause. A fame for a time spread round them. The Mecklins. Great riders. "Ridgewood Stable. Blood horses trained. Saddle and Show." He'd had it put up in wrought iron, with a sign as well, Old English style, of a horseman spurring.

("Well, you got to make money," said Miss Emma to her son-in-law. "And don't I know it," she said. "But I just hate to think how many times I kept those historical people from putting up a marker on this place. And now all I do is worry one of y'all's going to break your neck. If it wasn't for Marian needing me and all . . . I just can't sleep a wink over here."

("You like to be over there anyway, Mama," Deborah said. "You know we want you here."

("Sure, we want you here," said Clyde. "As for the property, we talked it all out beforehand. I don't think I've damaged it any way."

("I just never saw it as a horse farm. But it's you all I worry about. It's the danger.")

Deborah drove home.

When the workingman her mother had hired three years before had stolen things and left, he had left too on the garage wall inside, a long pair of crossing diagonal lines, brown, in mud, Deborah thought, until she smelled what it was, and there were the blood-stained menstrual pads she later came across in the driveway, dug up out of the garbage, strewed out into the yard.

She told Clyde about the first but not the second discovery. "Some critters are mean," he'd shrugged it off. "Some critters are just mean."

They'd been dancing, out at the club. And so in love back then, he'd turned and turned her, far apart, then close, talking into her ear, making her laugh and answer, but finally he said: "Are you a mean critter, Deedee? Some critters are mean." And she'd remembered what she didn't tell.

But in those days Clyde was passionate and fun, both marvelously together, and the devil appearing at midnight in the bend of a country road would not have scared her. Nothing would have. It was the day of her life when they bought the first two horses.

"I thought I seen him somewhere myself."

"He looks a little bit like Clyde."

———

And dusk again, a third and final time.

The parking lot where she'd come after a movie was empty except for a few cars. The small office was unlighted, but a man she took for the attendant was bending to the door on the far side of a long cream-colored sedan near the back fence. "Want my ticket?"

she called. The man straightened, head rising above the body frame, and she knew him. Had he been about to steal a car, or was he breaking in for whatever he could find, or was it her coming all along that he was waiting for? However it was, he knew her as instantly as she knew him. Each other was what they had, by whatever design or absence of it, found. Deborah did not cry out or stir.

Who knew how many lines life had cut away from him down through the years till the moment when an arrogant woman on a horse had ridden him down with lust and laughter? He wasn't bad-looking; his eyes were beautiful; he was the kind to whom nothing good could happen. From that bright day to this chilly dusk, it had probably just been the same old story.

Deborah waited. Someway or other, what was coming, threading through the cars like an animal lost for years catching the scent of a former owner, was her own.

("You're losing nerve, Deedee," Clyde had told her recently. "That's what's really bothering me. You're scared, aren't you?")

The bitter-stale smell of cigarette breath, though not so near as before, not forced against her mouth, was still unmistakably familiar. But the prod of a gun's muzzle just under the rise of her breast was not. It had never happened to her before. She shuddered at the touch with a chill spring-like start of something like life, which was also something like death.

"Get inside," he said.

"Are you the same one?" she asked. "Just tell me that. Three years ago, Mama hired somebody. Was that you?"

"Get in the car."

She opened the door, slid over to the driver's seat, found him beside her. The gun, thrust under his crossed arm, resumed its place against her.

"Drive."

"Was it you the other night at the door?" Her voice trembled as the motor started, the gear caught.

"He left me with the lot; ain't nobody coming."

The car eased into an empty street.

"Go out of town. The Memphis road."

She was driving past familiar, cared-for lawns and houses, trees and intersections. Someone waved from a car at a stoplight, taking them for her and Clyde. She was frightened and accepting fear, which come to think of it was all she'd been doing for months, working with those horses. ("Don't let him bluff you, Deedee. It's you or him. He'll do it if he can.")

"What do you want with me? What is it you want?"

He spoke straight outward, only his mouth moving, watching the road, never turning his head to her. "You're going out on that Memphis road and you're going up a side road with me. There's some woods I know. When I'm through with you you ain't never going to have nothing to ask nobody about me because you're going to know it all and it ain't going to make you laugh none, I guarantee."

Deborah cleared the town and swinging into the highway wondered at herself. Did she want him? She had waited when she might have run. Did she want, trembling, pleading, degraded, finally to let him have every single thing his own way?

(Do you see steel hoofs above you over and over because you want them one day to smash into your brain?

("Daddy, Daddy," she had murmured long ago when the old unshaven tramp had come up into the lawn, bleary-eyed, face bloodburst with years of drink and weather, frightening as the boogeyman, "raw head and bloody bones," like the Negro women scared her with. That day the sky streamed with end-of-the-world fire. But she hadn't called so loudly as she might have, she'd let him come closer, to look at him better, until the threatening voice of her father behind her, just on the door's slamming, had cried: "What do you want in this yard? What you think you want here? Deborah! You come in this house this minute!" But the mystery still lay dark within her, forgotten for years, then stirring to life again: When I said "Daddy, Daddy?" was I calling to the tramp or to the house? Did I think the tramp was him in some sort of joke or dream or trick? If not, why did I say it? Why?

("Why do you ride a horse so fast, Deedee? Why do you like to do that?" *I'm going where the sky breaks open.* "I just like to." "Why do you like to drive so fast?" "I don't know.")

Suppose he kills me, too, thought Deborah, striking the straight stretch on the Memphis road, the beginning of the long rolling run through farms and woods. She stole a glance to her right. He looked like Clyde, all right. What right did he have to look like Clyde?

("It's you or him, Deedee." All her life they'd said that to her from the time her first pony, scared at something, didn't want to cross a bridge. "Don't let him get away with it. It's you or him.")

Righting the big car into the road ahead, she understood what was demanded of her. She pressed the accelerator gradually downward toward the floor.

————

"And by the time he realized it," she said, sitting straight in her chair at supper between Clyde and Emma, who by chance were there that night together; "—by the time he knew, we were hitting above seventy-five, and he said, 'What you speeding for?' and I said, 'I want to get it over with.' And he said, 'Okay, but that's too fast.' By that time we were touching eighty and he said, 'What the fucking hell'—excuse me, Mama—'you think you're doing? You slow this thing down.' So I said, 'I tell you what I'm doing. This is a rolling road with high banks and trees and lots of curves. If you try to take the wheel away from me, I'm going to wreck us both. If you try to sit there with that gun in my side I'm going to go faster and faster and sooner or later something will happen, like a curve too sharp to take or a car too many to pass with a big truck coming and we're both going to get smashed up at the very least. It won't do any good to shoot me when it's more than likely both of us would die. You want that?'

"He grabbed at the wheel but I put on another spurt of speed and when he pulled at the wheel we side-rolled, skidded back, and another car coming almost didn't get out of the way. I said, 'You see what you're doing, I guess.' And he said, 'Jesus God.' Then I knew I had him, had whipped him down.

"But it was another two or three miles like that before he said, 'Okay, okay, so I quit. Just slow down and let's forget it.' And I said, 'You give me that gun. The mood I'm in, I can drive with one hand or no hands at all, and don't think I won't do it.' But he wanted his gun at least, I could tell. He didn't give in till a truck was ahead and we passed but barely missed a car that was coming (it had to run off the concrete), and he put it down, in my lap."

(Like a dog, she could have said, but didn't. And I felt sorry for him, she could have added, because it was his glory's end.)

"So I said, 'Get over, way over,' and he did, and I coasted from fast to slow. I turned the gun around on him and let him out on an empty stretch of road, by a rise with a wood and a country side road rambling off, real pretty, and I thought, Maybe that's where he was talking about, where he meant to screw hell—excuse me, Mama— out of me. I held the gun till he closed the door and went down in the ditch a little way, then I put the safety catch on and threw it at him. It hit his shoulder, then fell in the weeds. I saw it fall, driving off."

"Oh, my poor baby," said Emma. "Oh, my precious child."

It was Clyde who rose, came round the table to her, drew her to her feet, held her close. "That's nerve," he said. "That's class." He let her go and she sat down again. "Why didn't you shoot him?"

"I don't know."

"He was the one we hired that time," Emma said. "I'd be willing to bet you anything."

"No, it wasn't," said Deborah quickly. "This one was blond and short, red-nosed from too much drinking, I guess. Awful like Mickey Rooney, gone and gotten old. Like the boogeyman, I guess."

"The poor woman's Mickey Rooney. You women find yourselves the damnedest men."

"She's not right about that," said Emma. "What do you want to tell that for? I know it was him. I feel like it was."

"Why'd you throw the gun away?" Clyde asked. "We could trace that."

"It's what I felt like doing," she said. She had seen it strike, how his shoulder, struck, went back a little.

Clyde Mecklin sat watching his wife. She had scarcely touched her food, and now, pale, distracted, she had risen to wander toward the windows, look out at the empty lawn, the shrubs and flowers, the stretch of white-painted fence, ghostly by moonlight.

"It's the last horse I'll ever break," she said, more to herself than not, but Clyde heard and stood up and was coming to her.

"Now, Deedee—"

"When you know you know," she said, and turned, her face set against him: her anger, her victory, held up like a blade against his stubborn willfulness. "I want my children now," she said.

At the mention of children, Emma's presence with them became multiple and vague; it trembled with thanksgiving, it spiraled on wings of joy.

Deborah turned again, back to the window. Whenever she looked away, the eyes by the road were there below her: they were worthless, nothing, but infinite, never finishing—the surface there was no touching bottom for—taking to them, into themselves, the self that was hers no longer.

THE BUSINESS VENTURE

We were down at the river that night. Pete Owens was there with his young wife, Hope (his name for her was Jezzie, after Jezebel in the Bible), and Charlie and me, and both the Houston boys, one with his wife and the other with the latest in a string of new girlfriends. But Nelle Townshend, his steady girl, wasn't there.

We talked and watched the water flow. It was different from those nights we used to go up to the club and dance, because we were older and hadn't bothered to dress, just wore slacks and shorts. It was a clear night but no moon.

Even five years married to him, I was in love with Charlie more than ever, and took his hand to rub the reddish hairs around his wrist. I held his hand under water and watched the flow around it, and later when the others went up to the highway for more whiskey, we kissed like two high school kids and then waded out laughing and splashed water on each other.

The next day Pete Owens looked me up at the office when my boss, Mr. McGinnis, was gone to lunch. "Charlie's never quit, you know, Eileen. He's still passing favors out."

My heart dropped. I could guess it, but wasn't letting myself know I really knew it. I put my hard mask on. "What's the matter? Isn't Hope getting enough from you?"

"Oh, I'm the one for Jezzie. You're the main one for Charlie. I just mean, don't kid yourself he's ever stopped."

"When did any of us ever stop?"

"You have. You like him that much. But don't think you're home free. The funny thing is, nobody's ever took a shotgun to Charlie. So far's I know, nobody's ever even punched him in the jaw."

"It is odd," I said, sarcastic, but he didn't notice.

"It's downright peculiar," said Pete. "But then I guess we're a special sort of bunch, Eileen."

I went back to typing and wished he'd go. He'd be asking me next. We'd dated and done a few things, but that was so long ago, it didn't count now. It never really mattered. I never thought much about it.

"What I wonder is, Eileen. Is everybody else like us, or so different from us they don't know what we're like at all?"

"The world's changing," I said. "They're all getting like us."

"You mean it?"

I nodded. "The word got out," I said. "You told somebody and they told somebody else, and now everybody is like us."

"Or soon will be," he said.

"That's right," I said.

I kept on typing letters, reeling them on and off the platen and working on my electric machine the whole time he was talking, turning his hat over and picking at a straw or two off the synthetic weave. I had a headache that got worse after he was gone.

———

Also at the picnic that night was Grey Houston, one of the Houston brothers, who was always with a different girl. His former steady girlfriend, Nelle Townshend, kept a cleaning and pressing shop on her own premises. Her mother had been a stay-at-home lady for years. They had one of those beautiful old Victorian-type houses—it just missed being a photographer's and tourist attraction, being about twenty years too late and having the wooden trim too ornate for the connoisseurs to call it the real classical style. Nelle had been enterprising enough to turn one wing of the house where nobody went anymore into a cleaning shop, because she needed to make some money and felt she had to be near her mother. She had working for them off and on a Negro back from the Vietnam war who had used his veterans' educational benefits to train as a dry cleaner. She picked up the idea when her mother happened to remark one night after she had paid him for some carpenter work, "Ain't that a dumb nigger, learning dry cleaning with nothing to dry-clean."

Now, when Mrs. Townshend said "nigger," it wasn't as if one of us had said it. She went back through the centuries for her words, back to when "ain't" was good grammar. "Nigger" for her just meant "black." But it was assuming Robin had done something dumb that was the mistake. Because he wasn't dumb, and Nelle knew it. He told her he'd applied for jobs all around, but they didn't offer much and he might have to go to Biloxi or Hattiesburg or Gulfport to get one. The trouble was, he owned a house here. Nelle said, "Maybe you could work for me."

He told her about a whole dry cleaning plant up in Magee that had folded up recently due to the old man who ran it dying on his feet one day. They drove up there together and she bought it. Her mother didn't like it much when she moved the equipment in, but Nelle did it anyway. "I never get the smell out of my hair," she would say, "but if it can just make money I'll get used to it." She was dating Grey at the time, and I thought that's what gave her that much nerve.

Grey was a darling man. He was divorced from a New Orleans woman, somebody with a lot of class and money. She'd been crazy about Grey, as who wouldn't be, but he didn't "fit in," was her complaint. "Why do I have to fit in with her?" he kept asking. "Why shouldn't she fit in with us?" "She was O.K. with us," I said. "Not quite," he said. "Y'all never did relax. You never felt easy. That's why Charlie kept working at her, flirting and all. She maybe ought to have gone ahead with Charlie. Then she'd have been one of us. But she acted serious about it. I said, 'Whatever you decide about Charlie, just don't tell me.' She was too serious."

"Anybody takes it seriously ought to be me," I said.

"Oh-oh," said Grey, breaking out with fun, the way he could do—in the depths one minute, up and laughing the next. "You can't afford that, Eileen."

That time I raised a storm at Charlie. "What did you want to get married for? You're nothing but a goddamn stud!"

"What's news about it?" Charlie wanted to know. "You're just getting worked up over nothing."

"Nothing! Is what we do just nothing?"

"That's right. When it's done with, it's nothing. What I think of you—now, that's something." He had had some problem with a new car at the garage—he had the GM agency then—and he smelled of clean lubricating products and new upholstery and the rough soap where the mechanics cleaned up. He was big and gleaming, the all-over male. Oh, hell, I thought, what can I do? Then, suddenly curious, I asked: "*Did* you make out with Grey's wife?"

He laughed out loud and gave me a sidelong kiss. "Now that's more like it."

Because he'd never tell me. He'd never tell me who he made out with. "Honey," he'd say, late at night in the dark, lying straight out beside me, occasionally tangling his toes in mine or reaching for his cigarettes, "if I'd say I never had another woman outside you, would you believe it?"

I couldn't say No from sheer astonishment.

"Because it just might be true," he went on in the dark, serious as a judge. Then I would start laughing, couldn't help it. Because there are few things in the world which you know are true. You don't know (not anymore: our mamas knew) if there's a God or not, much less if He so loved the world. You don't know what your own native land is up to, or the true meaning of freedom, or the real cost of gasoline and cigarettes, or whether your insurance company will pay up. But one thing I personally know that is *not* true is that Charlie Waybridge has had only one woman. Looked at that way, it can be a comfort, one thing to be sure of.

—

It was soon after the picnic on the river that Grey Houston came by to see me at the office. You'd think I had nothing to do but stop and talk. What he came about was Nelle.

"She won't date me anymore," he complained. "I thought we were doing fine, but she quit me just like that. Hell, I can't tell what's the trouble with her. I want to call up and say, 'Just tell me, Nelle. What's going on?'"

"Why don't you?" I asked.

Grey is always a little worried about things to do with people, especially since his divorce. We were glad when he started dating Nelle. She was hovering around thirty and didn't have anybody, and Grey was only a year or two younger.

"If I come right out and ask her, then she might just say, 'Let's decide to be good friends,' or something like that. Hell, I got enough friends."

"It's to be thought of," I agreed.

"What would you do?" he persisted.

"I'd rather know where I stand," I said, "but in this case I think I'd wait awhile. Nelle's worrying over that business. Maybe she doesn't know herself."

"I might push her too soon. I thought that, too."

"I ought to go around and see old Mrs. Townshend," I said. "She hardly gets out at all anymore. I mean to stop in and say hello."

"You're not going to repeat anything?"

See how he is? Skittery. "Of course not," I said. "But there's such a thing as keeping my eyes and ears open."

I went over to call on old Mrs. Townshend one Thursday afternoon when Mr. McGinnis's law office was closed anyway. The Townshend house is on a big lawn, a brick walk running up from the street to the front step and a large round plot of elephant ears in the front yard. When away and thinking of home, I see right off the Townshend yard and the elephant ears.

I wasn't even to the steps before I smelled clothes just dry-cleaned. I don't guess it's so bad, though hardly what you'd think of living with. Nor would you particularly like to see the sign outside the porte-cochere, though way to the left of the walk and not visible from the front porch. Still, it was out there clearly, saying "Townshend Dry Cleaning: Rapid Service." Better than a funeral parlor, but not much.

The Townshend house is stuffed with things. All these little Victorian tables on tall legs bowed outward, a small lower shelf, and the top covered katy-corner with a clean starched linen doily, tatting around the edge. All these chairs of various shapes, especially one that rocked squeaking on a walnut stand, and for every chair a doily at the head. Mrs. Townshend kept two birdcages, but no birds were in them. There never had been any so far as I knew. It wasn't a dark house, though. Nelle had taken out the stained glass way back when she graduated from college. That was soon after her older sister married, and her mama needed her. "If I'm going to live here," she had said, "that's got to go." So it went.

Mrs. Townshend never raised much of a fuss at Nelle. She was low to the ground because of a humpback, a rather placid old lady. The Townshends were the sort to keep everything just the way it was. Mrs. Townshend was a LeMoyne from over toward Natchez. She was an Episcopalian and had brought her daughters up in that church.

"I'm sorry about this smell," she said in her forthright way, coming in and offering me a Coke on a little tray with a folded linen napkin beside it. "Nelle told me I'd get used to it and she was right: I have. But at first I had headaches all the time. If you get one I'll get some aspirin for you."

"How's the business going?" I asked.

"Nelle will be in in a minute. She knows you're here. You can ask her." She never raised her voice. She had a soft little face and gray eyes back of her little gold-rimmed glasses. She hadn't got to the hearing-aid stage yet, but you had to speak up. We went through the whole rigmarole of mine and Charlie's families. I had a feeling she was never much interested in all that, but around home you have to do it. Then I asked her what she was reading and she woke up. We got off the ground right away, and went strong about the President and foreign affairs, the picture not being so bright but of great interest, and about her books from the library always running out, and all the things she had against book clubs—then Nelle walked in.

Nelle Townshend doesn't look like anybody else but herself. Her face is like something done on purpose to use up all the fine skin, drawing it evenly over the bones beneath, so that no matter at what age, she always would look the same. But that day she had this pinched look I'd never seen before, and her arms were splotched with what must have been a reaction to the cleaning fluids. She rolled down the sleeves of her blouse and sat in an old wicker rocker.

"I saw Grey the other day, Nelle," I said. "I think he misses you."

She didn't say anything outside of remarking she hadn't much time to go out. Then she mentioned some sort of decorating at the church she wanted to borrow some ferns for, from the florist. He's got some he rents, in washtubs. "You can't get all those ferns in our little church," Mrs. Townshend said, and Nelle said she thought two would do. She'd send Robin, she said. Then the bell rang to announce another customer. Nelle had to go because Robin was at the "plant"—actually the old cook's house in back of the property where they'd set the machinery up.

I hadn't said all I had to say to Nelle, so when I got up to go, I said to Mrs. Townshend that I'd go in the office a minute on the way out. But Mrs. Townshend got to her feet, a surprise in itself. Her usual words were, You'll excuse me if I don't get up. Of course, you would excuse her and be too polite to ask why. Like a lot of old ladies, she might have arthritis. But this time she stood.

"I wish you'd let Nelle alone. Nelle is all right now. She's the way she wants to be. She's not the way you people are. She's just not a bit that way!"

———

It may have been sheer surprise that kept me from telling Charlie all this till the weekend. We were hurrying to get to Pete and Hope Owens's place for a dinner they were having for some people down from the Delta, visitors.

"What did you say to that?" Charlie asked me.

"I was too surprised to open my mouth. I wouldn't have thought Mrs. Townshend would express such a low opinion as that. And why does she have it in the first place? Nelle's always been part of our crowd. She grew up with us. I thought they liked us."

"Old ladies get notions. They talk on the phone too much."

To our surprise, Nelle was at the Owenses' dinner, too. Hope told me in the kitchen that she'd asked her, and then asked Grey. But Grey had a date with the little Springer girl he'd brought to the picnic, Carole Springer. "If this keeps up," Hope said to me while I was helping her with a dip, "we're going to have a Springer in our crowd. I'm just not right ready for that." "Me either," I said. The

Springers were from McComb, in lumber. They had money but they never were much fun.

"Did Nelle accept knowing you were going to ask Grey?" I asked.

"I couldn't tell that. She just said she'd love to and would come about seven."

It must have been seven, because Nelle walked in. "Can I help?"

"Your mama," I said, when Hope went out with the tray, "she sort of got upset with me the other day. I don't know why. If I said anything wrong, just tell her I'm sorry."

Nelle looked at her fresh nail polish. "Mama's a little peculiar now and then. Like everybody." So she wasn't about to open up.

"I've been feeling bad about Grey is all," I said. "You can think I'm meddling if you want to."

"Grey's all right," she said. "He's been going around with Carole Springer from McComb."

"All the more reason for feeling bad. Did you know they're coming tonight?"

She smiled a little distantly, and we went out to join the party. Charlie was already sitting up too close to the wife of the guest couple. I'd met them before. They have an antique shop. He is tall and nice, and she is short (wears spike heels) and nice. They are the sort you can't ever remember what their names are. If you get the first names right you're doing well. Shirley and Bob.

"Honey, you're just a doll," Charlie was saying (if he couldn't think of Shirley, Honey would do), and Pete said, "Watch out, Shirley, the next thing you know you'll be sitting on his lap."

"I almost went in for antiques myself," Nelle was saying to Bob, the husband. "I would have liked that better, of course, than a cleaning business, but I thought the turnover here would be too small. I do need to feel like I'm making money if I'm going to work at it. For a while, though, it was fun to go wandering around New Orleans and pick up good things cheap."

"I'd say they'd all been combed over down there," Bob objected.

"It's true about the best things," Nelle said. "I could hardly afford those anyway. But sometimes you see some pieces with really good design and you can see you might realize something on them. Real appreciation goes a long way."

"Bob has a jobber up in St. Louis," Shirley said. "We had enough of all this going around shaking the bushes. A few lucky finds was what got us started."

Nelle said, "I started thinking about it because I went in the living room a year or so back and there were some ladies I never saw before. They'd found the door open and walked in. They wanted to know the price of Mama's furniture. I said it wasn't for sale, but Mama was just coming in from the kitchen and heard them. You wouldn't believe how mad she got. 'I'm going straight and get out my pistol,' she said."

"You ought to just see her mama," said Hope. "This tiny little old lady."

"So what happened?" Shirley asked when she got through laughing.

"Nothing real bad," said Nelle. "They just got out the door as quick as they could."

"Yo' mama got a pistol?" Charlie asked, after a silence. We started to laugh again, the implication being plain that Charlie Waybridge *needs* to know if a woman's mother has a pistol in the house.

"She does have one," said Nelle.

"So watch out, Charlie," said Pete.

Bob remarked, "Y'all certainly don't change much over here."

"Crazy as ever," Hope said proudly. It crossed my mind that Hope was always protecting herself, one way or the other.

Shirley said she thought it was just grand to be back, she wouldn't take anything for it, and after that Grey and Carole arrived. We had another drink and then went in to dinner. Everybody acted like everything was okay. After dinner, I went back in the kitchen for some water, and there was Charlie, kissing Shirley. She was so strained up on tiptoe, Charlie being over six feet, that I thought, in addition to being embarrassed, mad, and backing out before they saw me, What they need is a stepladder to do it right.

On the way home, I told Charlie about catching them. "I didn't know she was within a country mile," he said, ready with excuses. "She just plain grabbed me."

"I've been disgusted once too often," I said. "Tell it to Bob."

"If she wanted to do it right," he said, "she ought to get a stepladder." So then I had to laugh. Even if our marriage wasn't ideal, we still had the same thoughts.

———

It sometimes seemed to me, in considering the crowd we were always part of, from even before we went to school, straight on through, that we were all like one person, walking around different ways, but in some permanent way breathing together, feeling the same reactions, thinking each other's thoughts. What do you call that if not love? If asked, we'd all cry Yes! with one voice, but then it's not our habit to ask anything serious. We're close to religious about keeping everything light and gay. Nelle Townshend knew that, all the above, but she was drawing back. A betrayer was what she was turning into. We felt weakened because of her. What did she think she was doing?

I had to drive Mr. McGinnis way back in the woods one day to serve a subpoena on a witness. He hadn't liked to drive since his heart attack, and his usual colored man was busy with Mrs. McGinnis's garden. In the course of that little trip, coming back into town, I saw Nelle Townshend's station wagon turn off onto a side road. I couldn't see who was with her, but somebody was, definitely.

I must add that this was spring and there were drifts of dogwood all mingled in the woods at different levels. Through those same woods, along the winding roads, the redbud, simultaneous, was spreading its wonderful pink haze. Mr. McGinnis sat beside me without saying much, his old knobby hands folded over a briefcase he held upright on his lap. "A trip like this just makes me think, Eileen, that everybody owes it to himself to get out in the woods this time of year. It's just God's own garden," he said. We had just crossed a wooden bridge over a pretty little creek about a mile back. That same creek, shallower, was crossed by a ford along the road that Nelle's car had taken. I know that little road, too, maybe the prettiest one of all.

Serpents have a taste for Eden, and in a small town, if they are busy elsewhere, lots of people are glad to fill in for them. It still upsets me to think of all the gossip that went on that year, and at the same time I have to blame Nelle Townshend for it, not so much for starting it, but for being so unconscious about it. She had stepped out of line and she didn't even bother to notice.

Once the business got going, the next thing she did was enroll in a class—a "seminar," she said—over at the university at Hattiesburg. It was something to do with art theory, she said, and she was thinking of going on from there to a degree, eventually, and get hold of a subject she could teach at the junior college right up the road. So settling in to be an old maid.

I said this last rather gloomily to Pete's wife, Hope, and Pete overheard and said, "There's all kinds of those." "You stop that," said Hope. "What's supposed to be going on?" I asked. (Some say don't ask, it's better not to, but I think you have to know if only to keep on guard.)

"Just that they're saying things about Nelle and that black Robin works for her."

"Well, they're in the same business," I said.

"Whatever it is, people don't like it. They say she goes out to his house after dark. That they spend too much time over the books."

"Somebody ought to warn her," I said. "If Robin gets into trouble she won't find anybody to do that kind of work. He's the only one."

"Nelle's gotten too independent is the thing," said Pete. "She thinks she can live her own life."

"Maybe she can," said Hope.

Charlie was away that week. He had gone over to the Delta on business, and Hope and Pete had dropped in to keep me company. Hope is ten years younger than Pete. (Pete used to date her sister, Mary Ruth, one of these beauty-queen types, who had gone up to the Miss America pageant to represent Mississippi and come back first runner-up. For the talent contest part of it, she had recited passages from the Bible, and Pete always said her trouble was she was too religious but he hoped to get her over it. She used to try in a nice way to get him into church work, and that embarrassed him.

It's our common habit, as Mary Ruth well knew, to go to morning service, but anything outside that is out. Anyway, around Mary Ruth's he used to keep seeing the little sister Hope, and he'd say, "Mary Ruth, you better start on that girl about church, she's growing up dynamite." Mary Ruth got involved in a promotion trip, something about getting right with America, and met a man on a plane trip to Dallas, and before the seat-belt sign went off they were in love. For Mary Ruth that meant marriage. She was strict, a woman of faith, and I don't think Pete would have been happy with her. But he had got the habit of the house by then, and Mary Ruth's parents had got fond of him and didn't want him drinking too much: they made him welcome. So one day Hope turned seventeen and came out in a new flouncy dress with heels on, and Pete saw the light.)

We had a saying by now that Pete had always been younger than Hope, that she was older than any of us. Only twenty, she worked at making their house look good and won gardening prizes. She gave grand parties, with attention to details.

"I stuck my neck out," I told Hope, "to keep Nelle dating Grey. You remember her mama took a set at me like I never dreamed possible. Nelle's been doing us all funny, but she may have to come back someday. We can't stop caring for her."

Hope thought it over. "Robin knows what it's like here, even if Nelle may have temporarily forgotten. He's not going to tempt fate. Anyway, somebody already spoke to Nelle."

"Who?"

"Grey, of course. He'll use any excuse to speak to her. She got mad as a firecracker. She said, 'Don't you know this is nineteen seventy-*six*? I've got a business to run. I've got a living to make!' But she quit going out to his house at night. And Robin quit so much as answering the phone, up at her office."

"You mean he's keeping one of those low profiles?" said Pete.

Soon after, I ran into Robin uptown in the grocery, and he said, "How do you do, Mrs. Waybridge," like a schoolteacher or a foreigner, and I figured just from that, that he was on to everything and taking no chances. Nelle must have told him. I personally knew what not many people did, that he was a real partner with Nelle, not just her hired help. They had got Mr. McGinnis to draw up the papers. And they had plans for moving the plant uptown, to an empty store building, with some investment in more equipment. So maybe they'd get by till then. I felt a mellowness in my heart about Nelle's effort and all—a Townshend (LeMoyne on her mother's side) opening a dry cleaning business. I thought of Robin's effort, too—he had a sincere, intelligent look, reserved. What I hoped for them was something like a prayer.

———

Busying my thoughts about all this, I had been forgetting Charlie. That will never do.

For one thing, leaving aside women, Charlie's present way of life was very nearly wild. He'd got into oil leases two years before, and when something was going on, he'd drive like a demon over to East Texas by way of Shreveport and back through Pike and Amite counties. At one time he had to sit over Mr. McGinnis for a month getting him to study up on laws governing oil rights. In the end, Charlie got to know as much or more than Mr. McGinnis. He's in and out. The in-between times are when he gets restless. Drinks too much and starts simmering up about some new woman. One thing (except for me), with Charlie it's always a new woman. Once tried, soon dropped. Or so I like to believe. Then, truth to tell, there is really part of me that not only wants to believe but at unstated times does believe that I've been the only one for Charlie Waybridge. Not that I'd begrudge him a few times of having it off down in the hollow back of the gym with some girl who came in from the country, nor would I think anything about flings in New Orleans while he was in Tulane. But as for the outlandish reputation he's acquired now, sometimes I just want to say out loud to all and sundry, "There's not a word of truth in it. He's a big, attractive, friendly guy, O.K.! But he's not the town stud. He belongs to *me*."

All this before the evening along about first dark when Charlie was seen on the Townshend property by Nelle's mother, who went and got the pistol and shot at him.

"Christ, she could have killed me," Charlie said. He was too surprised about it even to shake. He was just dazed. Fixed a stiff drink and didn't want any supper. "She's gone off her rocker," he said. "That's all I could think."

I knew I had to ask it, sooner or later. "What were you doing up there, Charlie?"

"Nothing," he said. "I'd left the car at Wharton's garage to check why I'm burning too much oil. He's getting to it in the morning. It was a nice evening and I cut through the back alley and that led to a stroll through the Townshend pasture. That's all. I saw the little lady out on the back porch. I was too far off to holler at her. She scuttled off into the house and I was going past, when here she came out again with something black weighting her hand. You know what I thought? I thought she had a kitten by the neck. Next thing I knew there was a bullet smashing through the leaves not that far off." He put his hand out.

"Wonder if Nelle was home."

I was nervous as a monkey after I heard this, and nothing would do me but to call up Nelle.

She answered right away. "Nelle," I said, "is your little mama going in for target practice these days?"

She started laughing. "Did you hear that all the way to your place? She's mad 'cause the Johnsons' old cow keeps breaking down our fence. She took a shot in the air because she's tired complaining."

"Since when was Charlie Waybridge a cow?" I asked.

"Mercy, Eileen. You don't mean Charlie was back there?"

"You better load that thing with blanks," I said, "or hide it."

"Blanks is all it's got in it," said Nelle. "Mama doesn't tell that because she feels more protected not to."

"You certainly better check it out," I said. "Charlie says it was a bullet."

There was a pause. "You're not mad or anything, are you Eileen?"

"Oh, no," I warbled. "We've been friends too long for that."

"Come over and see us," said Nelle. "Real soon."

I don't know who told it, but knowing this town like the back of my hand, I know *how* they told it. Charlie Waybridge was up at

Nelle Townshend's and old Mrs. Townshend shot at him. Enough said. At the Garden Club Auxiliary tea, I came in and heard them giggling, and how they got quiet when I passed a plate of sandwiches. I went straight to the subject, which is the way I do. "Y'all off on Mrs. Townshend?" I asked. There was a silence, and then some little cross-eyed bride, new in town, piped up that there was just always something funny going on here, and Maud Varner, an old friend, said she thought Nelle ought to watch out for Mrs. Townshend, she was showing her age. "It's not such a funny goings-on when it almost kills somebody," I said. "Charlie came straight home and told me. He was glad to be alive, but I went and called Nelle. So she does know." There was another silence during which I could tell what everybody thought. The thing is not to get too distant or above it all. If you do, your friends will pull back, too, and you won't know anything. Gradually, you'll just turn into, Poor Eileen, what does she think of all Charlie's carryings-on?

———

Next, the injunction. Who brought it and why? I got the answer to the first before I guessed the second.

It was against the Townshend Cleaners because the chemicals used were a hazard to health and the smell they exuded a public nuisance. But the real reason wasn't this at all.

In order to speed up the deliveries, Nelle had taken to driving the station wagon herself, so that Robin could run in with the cleaning. Some people had begun to remark on this. Would it have been different if Nelle was married or had a brother, a father, a steady boyfriend? I don't know. I used to hold my breath when they went by in the late afternoon together. Because sometimes when the back of the station wagon was full, Robin would be up on the front seat with her, and she with her head stuck in the air, driving carefully, her mind on nothing at all to do with other people. Once the cleaning load got lighter, Robin would usually sit on the back seat, as expected to do. But sometimes, busy talking to her, he wouldn't. He'd be up beside her, discussing business.

Then, suddenly, the business closed.

Nelle was beside herself. She came running to Mr. McGinnis. Her hair was every which way around her head and she was wearing an old checked shirt and no makeup.

She could hardly make herself sit still and visit with me while Mr. McGinnis got through with a client. "Now, Miss Nelle," he said, steering her through the door.

"Just when we were making a go of it!" I heard her say; then he closed the door.

I heard by way of the grapevine that very night that the person who had done it was John Houston, Grey's brother, whose wife's family lived on a property just below the Townshends. They claimed they couldn't sleep for the dry-cleaning fumes and were getting violent attacks of nausea.

"Aren't they supposed to give warnings?" I asked.

We were all at John and Rose Houston's home, a real gathering of the bunch, only Nelle being absent, though she was the most present one of all. There was a silence after every statement, in itself unusual. Finally John Houston said, "Not in cases of extreme health hazard."

"That's a lot of you-know-what," I said. "Rose, your family's not dying."

Rose said: "They never claimed to be dying." And Pete said: "Eileen, can't you sit right quiet and try to use your head?"

"In preference to running off at the mouth," said Charlie, which made me mad. I was refusing, I well knew, to see the point they all had in mind. But it seemed to me that was my privilege.

The thing to know about our crowd is that we never did go in for talking about the "Negro question." We talked about Negroes the way we always had, like people, one at a time. They were all around us, had always been, living around us, waiting on us, sharing our lives, brought up with us, nursing us, cooking for us, mourning and rejoicing with us, making us laugh, stealing from us, digging our graves. But when all the troubles started coming in on us after the Freedom Riders and the Ole Miss riots, we decided not to talk about it. I don't know but what we weren't afraid of getting nervous. We couldn't jump out of our own skins, or those of our parents, grandparents, and those before them. "Nothing you can do about it" was Charlie's view. "Whatever you decide, you're going to act the same way tomorrow as you did today. Hoping you can get Alma to cook for you, and Peabody to clean the windows, and Bayman to cut the grass." "I'm not keeping anybody from voting—yellow, blue, or pink," said Hope, who had got her "ideas" straight from the first, she said. "I don't guess any of us is," said Pete, "them days is gone forever." "But wouldn't it just be wonderful," said Rose Houston, "to have a little colored gal to pick up your handkerchief and sew on your buttons and bring you cold lemonade and fan you when you're hot, and just love you to death?"

Rose was joking, of course, the way we all liked to do. But there are always one or two of them that we seriously insist we know—really *know*—that they love us. Would do anything for us, as we would for them. Otherwise, without that feeling, I guess we couldn't rest easy. You never can really know what they think, what they feel, so there's always the one chance it might be love.

So we—the we I'm always speaking of—decided not to talk about race relations because it spoiled things too much. We didn't like to consider anyone of us really involved in some part of it. Then, in my mind's eye, I saw Nelle's car, that dogwood-laden day in the woods, headed off the road with somebody inside. Or such was my impression. I'd never mentioned it to anybody, and Mr. McGinnis hadn't, I think, seen. Was it Robin? Or maybe, I suddenly asked myself, Charlie? Mysteries multiplied.

"Nelle's got to make a living is the whole thing," said Pete, getting practical. "We can't not let her do that."

"Why doesn't somebody find her a job she'd like?" asked Grey.

"Why the hell," Charlie burst out, "don't you marry her, Grey? Women ought to get married," he announced in general. "You see what happens when they don't."

"Hell, I can't get near her," said Grey. "We dated for six months. I guess I wasn't the one," he added.

"She ought to relocate the plant uptown, then she could run the office in her house, one remove from it, acting like a lady."

"What about Robin?" said Hope.

"He could run back and forth," I said. "They do want to do that," I added, "but can't afford it yet."

"You'd think old Mrs. Townshend would have stopped it all."

"That lady's a mystery."

"If Nelle just had a brother."

"Or even an uncle."

Then the talk dwindled down to silence.

"John," said Pete, after a time, turning around to face him, "we all know it was you—not Rose's folks. Did you have to?"

John Houston was sitting quietly in his chair. He was a little older than the rest of us, turning gray, a little more settled and methodical, more like our uncle than an equal and friend. (Or was it just that he and Rose were the only ones so far to have children— what all our parents said we all ought to do, but couldn't quit having our good times.) He was sipping bourbon. He nodded slowly. "I had to." We didn't ask any more.

"Let's just go quiet," John finally added. "Wait and see."

Now, all my life I'd been hearing first one person then another (and these, it would seem, appointed by silent consensus) say that things were to be taken care of in a certain way and no other. The person in this case who had this kind of appointment was evidently John Houston, from in our midst. But when did he get it? How did he get it? Where did it come from? There seemed to be no need to discuss it.

Rose Houston, who wore her long light hair in a sort of loose bun at the nape and who sat straight up in her chair, adjusted a fallen strand, and Grey went off to fix another drink for himself and Pete and Hope. He sang on the way out, more or less to himself, "For the times they are a-changing . . ." and that, too, found reference in all our minds. Except I couldn't help but wonder whether anything had changed at all.

———

The hearing on the dry cleaning injunction was due to be held in two weeks. Nelle went off to the coast. She couldn't stand the tension, she told me, having come over to Mr. McGinnis's office to see him alone. "Thinking how we've worked and all," she said, "and how just before this came up the auditor was in and told us what good shape we were in. We were just about to buy a new condenser."

"What's that?" I asked.

"Takes the smell out of the fumes," she said. "The very thing they're mad about. I could kill John Houston. Why couldn't he have come to me?"

I decided to be forthright. "Nelle, there's something you ought to evaluate . . . consider, I mean. Whatever word you want." I was shaking, surprising myself.

Nobody was around. Mr. McGinnis was in the next county.

Once when I was visiting a school friend up north, out from Philadelphia, a man at a party asked me if I would have sexual relations with a black. He wasn't black himself, so why was he curious? I said I'd never even thought about it. "It's a taboo, I think you call it," I said. "Girls like me get brainwashed early on. It's not that I'm against them," I added, feeling awkward. "Contrary to what you may think or may even believe," he told me, "you've probably thought a lot about it. You've suppressed your impulses, that's all." "Nobody can prove that," I said, "not even you," I added, thinking I was being amusing. But he only looked superior and walked away.

"It's you and Robin," I said. I could hear myself explaining to Charlie, Somebody had to, sooner or later. "You won't find anybody really believing anything, I don't guess, but it's making people speculate."

Nelle Townshend never reacted the way you'd think she would. She didn't even get annoyed, much less hit the ceiling. She just gave a little sigh. "You start a business, you'll see. I've got no time for anything but worrying about customers and money."

I was wondering whether to tell her the latest. A woman named McCorkle from out in the country, who resembled Nelle so much from the back you'd think they were the same, got pushed off the sidewalk last Saturday and fell in the concrete gutter up near the drugstore. The person who did it, somebody from outside town, must have said something nobody heard but Mrs. McCorkle, because she jumped up with her skirt muddy and stockings torn and yelled out, "I ain't no nigger lover!"

But I didn't tell her. If she was anybody but a Townshend, I might have. Odd to think that, when the only Townshends left there were Nelle and her mother. In cases such as this, the absent are present and the dead are, too. Mr. Townshend had died so long ago you had to ask your parents what he was like. The answer was always the same. "Sid Townshend was a mighty good man." Nelle had had two sisters: one died in her twenties, the victim of a rare disease, and the other got married and went to live on a place out from Helena, Arkansas. She had about six children and could be of no real help to the home branch.

"Come over to dinner," I coaxed. "You want me to ask Grey, I will. If you don't, I won't."

"Grey," she said, just blank, like that. He might have been somebody she met once a long time back. "She's a perpetual virgin," I heard Charlie say once. "Just because she won't cotton up to you," I said. But maybe he was right. Nelle and her mother lived up near the Episcopal church. Since our little town could not support a full-time rector, it was they who kept the church linens and the chalice and saw that the robes were always cleaned and hung in their proper place in the little room off the chancel. Come to think of it, keeping those robes and surplices in order may have been one thing that started Nelle into dry cleaning.

Nelle got up suddenly, her face catching the light from our old window with the wobbly glass in the panes, and I thought, She's a grand-looking woman, sort of girlish and womanish both.

"I'm going to the coast," she said. "I'm taking some books and a sketch pad. I may look into some art courses. You have to have training to teach anything, that's the trouble."

"Look, Nelle, if it's money— Well, you do have friends, you know."

"Friends," she said, just the way she had said "Grey." I wondered just what Nelle was really like. None of us seemed to know.

"Have a good time," I said. After she left, I thought I heard the echo of that blank, soft voice saying, "Good time."

—

It was a week after Nelle had gone that old Mrs. Townshend rang up Mr. McGinnis at the office. Mr. McGinnis came out to tell me what it was all about.

"Mrs. Townshend says that last night somebody tore down the dry cleaning sign Nelle had put up out at the side. Some colored woman is staying with her at night, but neither one of them saw anybody. Now she can't find Robin to put it back. She's called his house but he's not there."

"Do they say he'll be back soon?"

"They say he's out of town."

"I'd get Charlie to go up and fix it, but you know what happened."

"I heard about it. Maybe in daylight the old lady won't shoot. I'll go around with our yardman after dinner." What we still mean by dinner is lunch. So they put the sign up and I sat in the empty office wondering about this and that, but mainly, Where was Robin Byers?

It's time to say that Robin Byers was not any Harry Belafonte calypso-singing sex symbol of a "black." He was strong and thoughtful-looking, not very tall, definitely chocolate, but not ebony. He wore his hair cropped short in an almost military fashion so that, being thick, it stuck straight up more often than not. From one side he could look positively frightening, as he had a long white scar running down the side of his cheek. It was said that he got it in the army, in Vietnam, but the story of just how was not known. So maybe he had not gotten it in the war, but somewhere else. His folks had been in the county forever, his own house being not far out from town. He had a wife, two teenaged children, a telephone, and a TV set. The other side of Robin Byers's face was regular, smooth, and while not especially handsome it was good-humored and likable. All in all, he looked intelligent and conscientious, and that must have been how Nelle Townshend saw him, as he was.

———

I went to the hearing. I'd have had to, to keep Mr. McGinnis's notes straight, but I would have anyway, as all our crowd showed up, except Rose and John Houston. Rose's parents were there, having brought the complaint, and Rose's mama's doctor from over at Hattiesburg, to swear she'd had no end of allergies and migraines, and attacks of nausea, all brought on by the cleaning fumes. Sitting way in the back was Robin Byers, in a suit (a really nice suit) with a blue-and-white-striped "city" shirt and a knit tie. He looked like an assistant university dean, except for the white scar. He also had the look of a spectator, very calm, I thought, not wanting to keep turning around and staring at him, but keeping the image in my mind like an all-day sucker, letting it slowly melt out its meaning. He was holding a certain surface. But he was scared. Half across the courtroom you could see his temple throbbing, and the sweat beads. He was that tense. The whole effect was amazing.

The complaint was read out and Mrs. Hammond, Rose's mother, testified and the doctor testified, and Mr. Hammond said they were both right. The way the Hammonds talk—big Presbyterians—you would think they had the Bible on their side every minute, so naturally everybody else had to be mistaken. Friends and neighbors of the Townshends all these years, they now seemed to be speaking of people they knew only slightly. That is until Mrs. Hammond, a sort of dumpling-like woman with a practiced way of sounding accurate about whatever she said (she was a good gossip because she got all the details of everything), suddenly came down to a personal level and said, "Nelle, I just don't see why if you want to run that thing you don't move it into town," and Nelle said back right away just like they were in a living room instead of a courthouse, "Well, that's because of Mama, Miss Addie. This way I'm in and out with her." At that, everybody laughed, couldn't help it.

Then Mr. McGinnis got up and challenged that very much about Mrs. Hammond's headaches and allergies (he established her age, fifty-two, which she didn't want to tell) had to do with the cleaning plant. If they had, somebody else would have such complaints, but in case we needed to go further into it, he would ask Miss Nelle to explain what he meant.

Nelle got up front and went about as far as she could concerning the type of equipment she used and how it was guaranteed against the very thing now being complained of, that it let very few vapors escape, but then she said she would rather call on Robin Byers to come and explain because he had had special training in the chemical processes and knew all their possible negative effects.

And he came. He walked down the aisle and sat in the chair and nobody had ever seen such composure. I think he was petrified, but so might an actor be who was doing a role to high perfection. And when he started to talk you'd think that dry cleaning was a text and that his God-appointed task was to preach a sermon on it. But it wasn't quite like that, either. More modern. A professor giving a lecture to extremely ignorant students, with a good professor's accuracy, to the last degree. In the first place, he said, the cleaning fluid used was not varsol or carbon tetrachloride, which were known not only to give off harmful fumes but to damage fabrics, but something called "Perluxe" or perchlorethylene (he paused to give the chemical composition), which was approved for commercial cleaning purposes in such and such a solution by federal and state by-laws, of certain numbers and codes, which Mr. McGinnis had listed in his records and would be glad to read aloud upon request. If an operator worked closely with Perluxe for a certain number of hours a day, he might have headaches, it was true, but escaping vapor could scarcely be smelled at all more than a few feet from the exhaust pipes, and caused no harmful effects whatsoever, even to shrubs or "the leaves upon the trees." He said this last in such a lofty, rhythmic way that somebody giggled (I think it was Hope), and he stopped talking altogether.

"There might be smells down in those hollows back there," Nelle filled in from where she was sitting, "but it's not from my one little exhaust pipe."

"Then why," asked Mrs. Hammond right out, "do you keep on saying you need new equipment so you won't have any exhaust? Just answer me that."

"I'll let Robin explain," said Nelle.

"The fact is that Perluxe is an expensive product," Robin said. "At four dollars and twenty-five cents a gallon, using nearly thirty gallons each time the accumulation of the garments is put through the process, she can count on it that the overheads with two cleanings a week will run in the neighborhood of between two and three hundred dollars. So having the condenser machine would mean that the exhaust runs into it, and so converts the vapors back to the liquid, in order to use it once again."

"It's not for the neighbors," Nelle put in. "It's for us."

Everybody had spoken out of order by then, but what with the atmosphere having either declined or improved (depending on how you looked at it) to one of friendly inquiry among neighbors rather than a squabble in a court of law, the silence that finally descended was more meditative than not, having as its most impressive features, like high points in a landscape, Nelle, at some little distance down a front bench, but turned around so as to take everything in, her back straight and her Townshend head both superior and interested; and Robin Byers, who still had the chair by Judge Purvis's desk, collected and severe (he had forgotten the giggle), with testimony faultlessly delivered and nothing more he needed to say. (Would things have been any different if Charlie had been there? He was out of town.)

The judge cleared his throat and said he guessed the smells in the gullies around Tyler might be a nuisance, sure enough, but couldn't be said to be caused by dry cleaning, and he thought Miss Townshend could go on with her business. For a while, the white face and the black one seemed just the same, to be rising up quiet and superior above us all.

The judge asked, just out of curiosity, when Nelle planned to buy the condenser that was mentioned. She said whenever she could find one secondhand in good condition—they cost nearly two thousand dollars new—and Robin Byers put in that he had just been looking into one down in Biloxi, so it might not be too long. Biloxi is on the coast.

Judge Purvis said we'd adjourn now, and everybody stood up of one accord, except Mr. McGinnis, who had dozed off and was almost snoring.

Nelle, who was feeling friendly to the world, or seeming to (we all had clothes that got dirty, after all), said to all and sundry not to worry, "we plan to move the plant uptown one of these days before too long," and it was the "we" that came through again, a slip: she usually referred to the business as hers. It was just a reminder of what everybody wanted not to have to think about, and she probably hadn't intended to speak of it that way.

As if to smooth it well into the past, Judge Purvis remarked that these little towns ought to have zoning laws, but I sat there thinking there wouldn't be much support for that, not with the Gulf Oil station and garage right up on South Street between the Whitmans' and the Binghams', and the small-appliance shop on the vacant lot where the old Marshall mansion had stood, and the Tackett house, still elegant as you please, doing steady business as a funeral home. You can separate black from white but not business from nonbusiness. Not in our town.

Nelle came down and shook hands with Mr. McGinnis. "I don't know when I can afford to pay you." "Court costs go to them," he said. "Don't worry about the rest."

Back at the office, Mr. McGinnis closed the street door and said to me, "The fumes in this case have got nothing to do with dry cleaning. Has anybody talked to Miss Nelle?"

"They have," I said, "but she doesn't seem to pay any attention."

He said I could go home for the day and much obliged for my help at the courthouse. I powdered my nose and went out into the street. It wasn't but eleven-thirty.

Everything was still, and nobody around. The blue jays were having a good time on the courthouse yard, squalling and swooping from the lowest oak limbs, close to the ground, then mounting back up. There were some sparrows out near the old horse trough, which still ran water. They were splashing around. But except for somebody driving up for the mail at the post office, then driving off, there wasn't a soul around. I started walking, and just automatically I went by for the mail because as a rule Charlie didn't stop in for it till noon, even when in town. On the way I was mulling over the hearing and how Mrs. Hammond had said at the door of the courtroom to Nelle, "Aw right, Miss Nellie, you just wait." It wasn't said in any unpleasant way; in fact, it sounded right friendly. Except that she wasn't looking at Nelle, but past her, and except that being older, it wasn't the ordinary thing to call her "Miss," and except that Nelle is a pretty name but Nellie isn't. But Nelle in reply had suddenly laughed in that unexpected but delightful way she has, because something has struck her as really funny. "What am I supposed to wait *for*, Miss Addie?" Whatever else, Nelle wasn't scared. I looked for Robin Byers, but he had got sensible and gone off in that old little blue German car he drives. I saw Nelle drive home alone.

Then, because the lay of my home direction was a shortcut from the post office, and because the spring had been dry and the back lanes nice to walk in, I went through the same way Charlie had that time Mrs. Townshend had about killed him, and enjoyed, the way I had from childhood on, the soft fragrances of springtime, the brown wisps of spent jonquils withered on their stalks, the forsythia turned from yellow to green fronds, but the spirea still white as a bride's veil worked in blossoms, and the climbing roses, mainly wild, just opening a delicate, simple pink bloom all along the back fences. I was crossing down that way when what I saw was a blue car.

It was stopped way back down the Townshend property on a little connecting road that made an entrance through to a lower town road, one that nobody used anymore. I stopped in the clump of bowdarc trees on the next property from the Townshends'. Then I saw Nelle, running down the hill. She still had that same laugh, honest and joyous, that she had shown the first of to Mrs. Hammond. And there coming to meet her was Robin, his teeth white as his scar. They grabbed each other's hands, black on white and white on black. They started whirling each other around, like two schoolchildren in a game, and I saw Nelle's mouth forming the words I could scarcely hear: "We won! We won!" And his, the same, a baritone underneath. It was pure joy. Washing the color out, saying that the dye didn't, this time, hold, they could have been brother and sister, happy at some good family news, or old lovers (Charlie and I sometimes meet like that, too happy at some piece of luck to really stop to talk about it, just dancing out our joy). But, my God, I thought, don't they know they're black and white and this is Tyler, Mississippi? Well, of course they do, I thought next—that's more than half the joy—getting away with it!

Dare and double-dare! Dumbfounded, I just stood, hidden, never seen by them at all, and let the image of black on white and white on black—those pale, aristocratic Townshend hands and his strong, square-cut black ones—linked perpetually now in my mind's eye—soak in.

It's going to stay with me forever, I thought, but what does it mean? I never told. I didn't think they were lovers. But they were into a triumph of the sort that lovers feel. They had acted as they pleased. They were above everything. They lived in another world because of a dry cleaning business. They had proved it when they had to. They knew it.

But nobody could be counted on to see it the way I did. It was too complicated for any two people to know about it.

—

Soon after this we got a call from Hope, Pete's wife. "I've got tired of all this foolishness," she said. "How did we ever get hung up on dry cleaning, of all things? Can you feature it? I'm going to give a party. Mary Foote Williams is coming home to see her folks and bringing Keith, so that's good enough for me. And don't kid yourself. I'm personally going to get Nelle Townshend to come, and Grey Houston is going to bring her. I'm getting good and ready for everybody to start acting normal again. I don't know what's been the matter with everybody, and furthermore I don't want to know."

Well, this is a kettle of fish, I thought: Hope, the youngest, taking us over. Of course, she did have the perspective to see everything whole.

I no sooner put down the phone than Pete called up from his office. "Jezzie's on the warpath," he said. (He calls her Jezzie because she used to tell all kinds of lies to some little high school boy she had crazy about her—her own age—just so she could go out with Pete and the older crowd. It was easy to see through that. She thought she might just be getting a short run with us and would have to fall back on her own bunch when we shoved her out, so she was keeping a foothold. Pete caught her at it, but all it did was make him like her better. Hope was pert. She had a sharp little chin she liked to stick up in the air, and a turned-up nose. "Both signs of meanness," said Mr. Owens, Pete's father, "especially the nose," and buried his own in the newspaper.)

"Well," I said doubtfully, "if you think it's a good idea . . ."

"No stopping her," said Pete, with the voice of a spectator at the game. "If anybody can swing it, she can."

So we finally said yes.

The morning of Hope's party there was some ugly weather, one nasty little black cloud after another and a lot of restless crosswinds. There was a tornado watch out for our county and two others, making you know it was a widespread weather system. I had promised to bring a platter of shrimp for the buffet table, and that meant a whole morning shucking them after driving out to pick up the order at the Fish Shack. At times the lightning was popping so close I had to get out of the kitchen. I would go sit in the living room with the thunder blamming so hard I couldn't even read the paper. Looking out at my backyard through the picture window, the colors of the marigolds and pansies seemed to be electric bright, blazing, then shuddering in the wind.

I was bound to connect all this with the anxiety that had got into things about that party. Charlie's being over in Louisiana didn't help. Maybe all was calm and bright over there, but I doubted it.

However, along about two the sky did clear, and the sun came out. When I drove out to Hope and Pete's place with the shrimp—it's a little way north of town, reached by its own side road, on a hill—everything was wonderful. There was a warm buoyancy in the air that made you feel young and remember what it was like to skip home from school.

"It's cleared off," said Hope, as though in personal triumph over Nature.

Pete was behind her at the door, enveloped in a huge apron. "I feel like playing softball," he said.

"Me, too," I agreed. "If I could just hear from Charlie."

"Oh, he'll be back," said Pete. "Charlie miss a party? Never!"

———

Well, it was quite an affair. The effort was to get us all launched in a new and happy period and the method was the tried and true one of drinking and feasting, dancing, pranking, laughing, flirting, and having fun. I had a new knife-pleated silk skirt, ankle length, dark blue shot with green and cyclamen, and a new off-the-shoulder blouse, and Mary Foote Williams, the visitor, wore a slit skirt, but Hope took the cake in her hoop skirts from her senior-high-school days, and her hair in a coarse gold net.

"The shrimp are gorgeous," she said. "Come look. I called Mama and requested prayer for good weather. It never fails."

"Charlie called," I said. "He said he'd be maybe thirty minutes late and would come on his own."

A car pulled up in the drive and there was Grey circling around and holding the door for Nelle herself. She had on a simple silk dress with her fine hair brushed loose and a pair of sexy new high-heeled sandals. It looked natural to see them together and I breathed easier without knowing I hadn't been doing it for quite a while. Hope was right, we'd had enough of all this foolishness.

"That just leaves John and Rose," said Hope, "and I have my own ideas about them."

"What?" I asked.

"Well, I shouldn't say. It's y'all's crowd." She was quick in her kitchen, clicking around with her skirts swaying. She had got a nice little colored girl, Perline, dressed up in black with a white ruffled apron. "I just think John's halfway to a stuffed shirt and Rose is going to get him all the way there."

So, our crowd or not, she was going right ahead.

"I think this has to do with you-know-what," I said.

"We aren't going to mention you-know-what," said Hope. "From now on, honey, my only four-letter words are 'dry' and 'cleaning.'"

John and Rose didn't show up, but two new couples did, a pair from Hattiesburg and the Kellmans, new in town but promising. Hope had let them in. Pete exercised himself at the bar and there was a strong punch as well. We strolled out to the pool and sat on white-painted iron chairs with cushions in green flowered plastic. Nelle sat with her pretty legs crossed, talking to Mary Foote. Grey was at her elbow. The little maid passed out canapés and shrimp. Light was still lingering in a clear sky barely pink at the edges. Pete skimmed leaves from the pool surface with a long-handled net. Lightning bugs winked and drifted, and the new little wife from Hattiesburg caught one or two in her palm and watched them crawl away, then take wing. "I used to do that," said Nelle. Then she shivered and Grey went for a shawl. It grew suddenly darker and one or two pale stars could be seen, then dozens. Pete, vanished inside, had started some records. Some people began to trail back in. And with another drink (the third, maybe?), it wasn't clear how much time had passed, when there came the harsh roar of a motor from the private road, growing stronger the nearer it got, a slashing of gravel in the drive out front, and a door slamming. And the first thing you knew there was Charlie Waybridge, filling the whole doorframe before Pete or Hope could even go to open it. He put his arms out to everybody. "Well, whaddaya know!" he said.

His tie was loose two buttons down and his light seersucker dress coat was crumpled and open but at least he had it on. I went right to him. He'd been drinking, of course, I'd known it from the first sound of the car—but who wasn't drinking? "Hi ya, baby!" he said, and grabbed me.

Then Pete and Hope were getting their greetings and were leading him up to meet the new people, till he got to the bar, where he dropped off to help himself.

It was that minute that Perline, the little maid, came in with a plate in her hand. Charlie swaggered up to her and said, "Well, if it ain't Mayola's daughter." He caught her chin in his hand. "Ain't that so?" "Yes, sir," said Perline. "I am." "Used to know yo' mama," said Charlie. Perline looked confused for a minute; then she lowered her eyes and giggled like she knew she was supposed to. "Gosh sake, Charlie," I said, "quit horsing around and let's dance." It was hard to get him out of these moods. But I'd managed it more than once, dancing.

Charlie was a good strong leader and the way he danced, one hand firm to my waist, he would take my free hand in his and knuckle it tight against his chest. I could follow him better than I could anybody. Sometimes everybody would stop just to watch us, but the prize that night was going to Pete and Hope, they were shining around with some new steps that made the hoop skirts jounce. Charlie was half drunk, too, and bad on the turns.

"Try to remember what's important about this evening," I said. "You know what Hope and Pete are trying for, don't you?"

"I know I'm always coming home to a lecture," said Charlie and swung me out, spinning. "What a woman for sounding like a wife." He got me back and I couldn't tell if he was mad or not, I guess it was half and half; but right then he almost knocked over one of Hope's floral arrangements, so I said, "Why don't you go upstairs and catch your forty winks? Then you can come down fresh and start over." The music stopped. He blinked, looked tired all of a sudden, and, for a miracle, like a dog that never once chose to hear you, he minded.

I breathed a sigh when I saw him going up the stairs. But now I know I never once mentioned Nelle to him or reminded him right out, him with his head full of oil leases, bourbon, and the road, that she was the real cause of the party. Nelle was somewhere else, off in the back sitting room on a couch, to be exact, swapping family news with Mary Foote, who was her cousin.

Dancing with Charlie like that had put me in a romantic mood, and I fell to remembering the time we had first got serious, down on the coast where one summer we had all rented a fishing schooner. We had come into port at Mobile for more provisions and I had showered and dressed and was standing on deck in some leather sandals that tied around the ankle, a fresh white T-shirt, and some clean navy shorts. I had washed my hair, which was short then, and clustered in dark damp curls at the forehead. I say this about myself because when Charlie was coming on board with a six-pack in either hand, he stopped dead still. It was like it was the first time he'd ever seen me. He actually said that very thing later on after we'd finished with the boat and stayed on an extra day or so with all the crowd, to eat shrimp and gumbo and dance every night. We'd had our flare-ups before, but nothing had ever caught like that one. "I can't forget seeing you on the boat that day," he would say. "Don't be crazy, you'd seen me on that boat every day for a week." "Not like that," he'd rave, "like something fresh from the sea." "A catfish,"

I said. "Stop it, Eileen," he'd say, and dance me off the floor to the dark outside, and kiss me. "I can't get enough of you," he'd say, and take me in so close I'd get dizzy.

I kept thinking through all this in a warm frame of mind while making the rounds and talking to everybody, and maybe an hour, more or less, passed that way, when I heard a voice from the stairwell (Charlie) say: "God Almighty, if it isn't Nelle," and I turned around and saw all there was to see.

Charlie was fresh from his nap, the red faded from his face and his tie in place (he'd even buzzed off his five-o'clock shadow with Pete's electric razor). He was about five steps up from the bottom of the stairs. And Nelle, just coming back into the living room to join everybody, had on a Chinese-red silk shawl with a fringe. Her hair, so simple and shining, wasn't dark or blond either, just the color of hair, and she had on the plain dove-gray silk dress and the elegant sandals. She was framed in the door. Then I saw Charlie's face, how he was drinking her in, and I remembered the day on the boat.

"God damn, Nelle," said Charlie. He came down the steps and straight to her. "Where you been?"

"Oh, hello, Charlie," said Nelle in her friendly way. "Where have *you* been?"

"Honey, that's not even a question," said Charlie. "The point is, I'm *here*."

Then he fixed them both a drink and led her over to a couch in the far corner of the room. There was a side porch at the Owenses', spacious, with a tile floor—that's where we'd all been dancing. The living room was a little off center to the party. I kept on with my partying, but I had eyes in the back of my head where Charlie was concerned. I knew they were there on the couch and that he was crowding her toward one end. I hoped he was talking to her about Grey. I danced with Grey.

"Why don't you go and break that up?" I said.

"Why don't you?" said Grey.

"Marriage is different," I said.

"She can break it up herself if she wants to," he said.

I'd made a blunder and knew it was too late. Charlie was holding both Nelle's hands, talking over something. I fixed myself a stiff drink. It had begun to rain, quietly, with no advance warning. The couple from Hattiesburg had started doing some kind of talking blues number on the piano. Then we were singing. The couch was empty. Nelle and Charlie weren't there. . . .

———

It was Grey who came to see me the next afternoon. I was hung over but working anyway. Mr. McGinnis didn't recognize hangovers.

"I'm not asking her anywhere again," said Grey. "I'm through and she's through. I've had it. She kept saying in the car, 'Sure, I did like Charlie Waybridge, we all liked Charlie Waybridge. Maybe I was in love with Charlie Waybridge. But why start it up all over again? Why?' 'Why did you?' I said. 'That's more the question.' 'I never meant to, just there he was, making me feel that way.' 'You won't let me make you feel any way,' I said. 'My foot hurts,' she said, like a little girl. She looked a mess. Mud all over her dress and her hair gone to pieces. She had sprained her ankle. It had swelled up. That big."

"Oh, Lord," I said. "All Pete and Hope wanted was for you all— Look, can't you see Nelle was just drunk? Maybe somebody slugged her drink."

"She didn't have to drink it."

I was hearing Charlie: "All she did was get too much. Hadn't partied anywhere in months. Said she wanted some fresh air. First thing I knew she goes tearing out in the rain and whoops! in those high-heeled shoes—sprawling."

"Charlie and her," Grey went on. Okay, so he was hurt. Was that any reason to hurt me? But on he went. "Her and Charlie, that summer you went away up north, they were dating every night. Then her sister got sick, the one that died? She couldn't go on the coast trip with us."

"You think I don't know all that?" Then I said: "Oh, Grey!" and he left.

Yes, I sat thinking, unable to type anything: it was the summer her sister died and she'd had to stay home. I was facing up to Charlie Waybridge. I didn't want to, but there it was. If Nelle had been standing that day where I had stood, if Nelle had been wearing those sandals, that shirt, those shorts— Why pretend not to know Charlie Waybridge, through and through? What was he really doing on the Townshend property that night?

Pete, led by Hope, refused to believe anything but that the party had been a big success. "Like old times," said Pete. "What's wrong with new times?" said Hope. In our weakness and disarray, she was moving on in. (Damn Nelle Townshend.) Hope loved the new people; she was working everybody in together. "The thing for you to do about *that*..." she was now fond of saying on the phone, taking on problems of every sort.

When Hope heard that Nelle had sprained her ankle and hadn't been seen out in a day or so, she even got Pete one afternoon and went to call. She had telephoned but nobody answered. They walked up the long front walk between the elephant ears and up the front porch steps and rang the old turning bell half a dozen times. Hope had a plate of cake and Pete was carrying a bunch of flowers.

Finally Mrs. Townshend came shuffling to the door. Humpbacked, she had to look way up to see them, at a mole's angle. "Oh, it's you," she said.

"We just came to see Nelle," Hope chirped. "I understand she hurt her ankle at our party. We'd just like to commiserate."

"She's in bed," said Mrs. Townshend; and made no further move, either to open the door or take the flowers. Then she said, "I just wish you all would leave Nelle alone. You're no good for her. You're no good I know of for anybody. She went through all those years with you. She doesn't want you anymore. I'm of the same opinion." Then she leaned over and from an old-fashioned umbrella stand she drew up and out what could only be called a shotgun. "I keep myself prepared," she said. She cautiously lowered the gun into the umbrella stand. Then she looked up once again at them, touching the rims of her little oval glasses. "When I say you all, I mean all of you. You're drinking and you're doing all sorts of things that waste time, and you call that having fun. It's not my business unless you come here and make me say so, but Nelle's too nice to say so. Nelle never would—" She paused a long time, considering in the mildest sort of way. "Nelle can't shoot," she concluded, like this fact had for the first time occurred to her. She closed the door, softly and firmly.

I heard all this from Hope a few days later. Charlie was off again and I was feeling lower than low. This time we hadn't even quarreled. It seemed more serious than that. A total reevaluation. All I could come to was a question: Why doesn't he reassure me? All I could answer was that he must be in love with Nelle. He tried to call her when I wasn't near. He sneaked off to do it, time and again.

Alone, I tried getting drunk to drown out my thoughts, but couldn't, and alone for a day too long, I called up Grey. Grey and I used to date, pretty heavy. "Hell," said Grey, "I'm fed up to here and so are you. Let's blow it." I was tight enough to say yes and we met out at the intersection. I left my car at the shopping-center parking lot. I remember the sway of his Buick Century, turning onto the Interstate. We went up to Jackson.

———

The world is spinning now and I am spinning along with it. It doesn't stand still anymore to the stillness inside that murmurs to me, I know my love and I belong to my love when all is said and done, down through foreverness and into eternity. No, when I got back I was just part of it all, ordinary, a twenty-eight-year-old attractive married woman with family and friends and a nice house in Tyler, Mississippi. But with nothing absolute.

When I had a drink too many now, I would drive out to the woods and stop the car and walk around among places always known. One day, not even thinking about them, I saw Nelle drive by and this time there was no doubt who was with her—Robin Byers. They were talking. Well, Robin's wife mended the clothes when they were ripped or torn, and she sewed buttons on. Maybe they were going there. I went home.

At some point the phone rang. I had seen to it that it was "out of order" when I went up to Jackson with Grey, but now it was "repaired," so I answered it. It was Nelle.

"Eileen, I guess you heard Mama turned Pete and Hope out the other day. She was just in the mood for telling everybody off." Nelle laughed her clear, pure laugh. You can't have a laugh like that unless you've got a right to it, I thought.

"How's your ankle?" I asked.

"I'm still hobbling around. What I called for, Mama wanted me to tell you something. She said, 'I didn't mean quite everybody. Eileen can still come. You tell her that.'"

Singled out. If she only knew, I thought. I shook when I put down the phone.

———

But I did go. I climbed up to Nelle's bedroom with Mrs. Townshend toiling behind me, and sat in one of those old rocking chairs near a bay window with oak paneling and cane plant, green and purple, in a window box. I stayed quite a while. Nelle kept her ankle propped up and Mrs. Townshend sat in a tiny chair about the size of a twelve-year-old's, which was about the size she was. They told stories and laughed with that innocence that seemed like all clear things—a spring in the woods, a dogwood bloom, a carpet of pine needles along a sun-dappled road. Like Nelle's ankle, I felt myself getting well. It was a new kind of wellness, hard to describe. It didn't have much to do with Charlie and me.

"Niggers used to come to our church," Mrs. Townshend recalled. "They had benches in the back. I don't know why they quit. Maybe they all died out—the ones we had, I mean."

"Maybe they didn't like the back," said Nelle.

"It was better than nothing at all. The other churches didn't even have that. There was one girl going to have a baby. I was scared she would have it right in the church. Your father said, 'What's wrong with that? Dr. Erskine could deliver it, and we could baptize it on the spot.'"

I saw a picture on one of those little tables they had by the dozen, with the starched linen doilies and the bowed-out legs. It was of two gentlemen, one taller than the other, standing side by side in shirt-sleeves and bow ties and each with elastic bands around their upper arms, the kind that used to hold the sleeves to a correct length of cuff. They were smiling in a fine natural way, out of friendship. One must have been Nelle's father, dead so long ago. I asked about the other. "Child," said Mrs. Townshend, "don't you know your own grandfather? He and Sid thought the world of one another." I had a better feeling when I left. Would it last? Could I get it past the elephant ears?

———

I didn't tell Charlie about going there. Charlie got it from some horse's mouth that Grey and I were up in Jackson that time, and he pushed me off the back steps. An accident, he said; he didn't see me when he came whamming out the door. For a minute I thought I, too, had sprained or broken something, but a skinned knee was all it was. He watched me clean the knee, watched the bandage go on. He wouldn't go out—not to Pete and Hope's, not to Rose and John's, not to anywhere—and the whiskey went down in the bottle.

I dreamed one night of Robin Byers, that I ran into him uptown but didn't see a scar on his face. I followed him, asking, Where is it? What happened? Where's it gone? But he walked straight on, not seeming to hear. But it was no dream that his house caught fire, soon after the cleaning shop opened again. Both Robin and Nelle said it was only lightning struck the back wing and burned out a shed room before Robin could stop the blaze. Robin's daughter got jumped on at school by some other black children who yelled about her daddy being a "Tom." They kept her at home for a while to do her schoolwork there. What's next?

Next for me was going to an old lady's apartment for Mr. McGinnis, so she could sign her will, and on the long steps to her door, running into Robin Byers, fresh from one of his deliveries.

"Robin," I said, at once, out of nowhere, surprising myself, "you got to leave here, Robin. You're tempting fate, every day."

And he, just as quick, replied: "I got to stay here. I got to help Miss Nelle."

Where had it come from, what we said? Mine wasn't a bit like me; I might have been my mother or grandmother talking. Certainly not the fun girl who danced on piers in whirling miniskirts and dove off a fishing boat to reach a beach, swimming, they said, between the fishhooks and the sharks. And Robin's? From a thousand years back, maybe, superior and firm, speaking out of sworn duty, his honored trust. He was standing above me on the steps. It was just at dark, and in the first streetlight I could see the white scar, running riverlike down the flesh, like the mark lightning leaves on a smooth tree. When we passed each other, it was like erasing what we'd said and that we'd ever met.

But one day I am walking in the house and picking up the telephone, only to find Charlie talking on the extension. "Nelle . . ." I hear. "Listen, Nelle. If you really are foolin' around with that black bastard, he's answering to *me*." And *blam*! goes the phone from her end, loud as any gun of her mother's.

I think we are all hanging on a golden thread, but who has got the other end? Dreaming or awake, I'm praying it will hold us all suspended.

Yes, praying—for the first time in years.

ITALY

THE WHITE AZALEA

Two letters had arrived for Miss Theresa Stubblefield: she put them in her bag. She would not stop to read them in American Express, as many were doing, sitting on benches or leaning against the walls, but pushed her way out into the street. This was her first day in Rome and it was June.

An enormous sky of the most delicate blue arched overhead. In her mind's eye—her imagination responding fully, almost exhaustingly, to these shores' peculiar powers of stimulation—she saw the city as from above, telescoped on its great bare plains that the ruins marked, aqueducts and tombs, here a cypress, there a pine, and all round the low blue hills. Pictures in old Latin books returned to her: the Appian Way Today, the Colosseum, the Arch of Constantine. She would see them, looking just as they had in the books, and this would make up a part of her delight. Moreover, nursing various Stubblefields—her aunt, then her mother, then her father—through their lengthy illnesses (everybody could tell you the Stubblefields were always sick), Theresa had had a chance to read quite a lot. England, France, Germany, Switzerland, and Italy had all been rendered for her time and again, and between the prescribed hours of pills and tonics, she had conceived a dreamy passion by lamplight, to see all these places with her own eyes. The very night after her father's funeral she had thought, though never admitted to a soul: *Now I can go. There's nothing to stop me now.* So here it was, here was Italy, anyway, and terribly noisy.

In the street the traffic was really frightening. Cars, taxis, buses, and motor scooters all went plunging at once down the narrow length of it or swerving perilously around a fountain. Shoals of tourists went by her in national groups—English schoolgirls in blue uniforms, German boys with cameras attached, smartly dressed Americans looking in shop windows. Glad to be alone, Theresa climbed the splendid outdoor staircase that opened to her left. The Spanish Steps.

Something special was going on here just now—the annual display of azalea plants. She had heard about it the night before at her hotel. It was not yet complete: workmen were unloading the potted plants from a truck and placing them in banked rows on the steps above. The azaleas were as large as shrubs, and their myriad blooms, many still tight in the bud, ranged in color from purple through fuchsia and rose to the palest pink, along with many white ones too. Marvelous, thought Theresa, climbing in her portly, well-bred way, for she was someone who had learned that if you only move slowly enough you have time to notice everything. In Rome, all over Europe, she intended to move very slowly indeed.

Halfway up the staircase she stopped and sat down. Other people were doing it, too, sitting all along the wide banisters and leaning over the parapets above, watching the azaleas mass, or just enjoying the sun. Theresa sat with her letters in her lap, breathing Mediterranean air. The sun warmed her, as it seemed to be warming everything, perhaps even the underside of stones or the chill insides of churches. She loosened her tweed jacket and smoked a cigarette. Content ... excited; how could you be both at once? Strange, but she was. Presently, she picked up the first of the letters.

A few moments later her hands were trembling and her brow had contracted with anxiety and dismay. *Of course, one of them would have to go and do this! Poor Cousin Elec,* she thought, tears rising to sting in the sun, *but why couldn't he have arranged to live through the summer? And how on earth did I ever get this letter anyway?*

She had reason indeed to wonder how the letter had managed to find her. Her Cousin Emma Carraway had written it, in her loose high old lady's script—*t*'s carefully crossed, but *l*'s inclined to wobble like an old car on the downward slope. Cousin Emma had simply put Miss Theresa Stubblefield, Rome, Italy, on the envelope, had walked up to the post office in Tuxapoka, Alabama, and mailed it with as much confidence as if it had been a birthday card to her next-door neighbor. No return address whatsoever. Somebody had scrawled American Express, Piazza di Spagna? across the envelope, and now Theresa had it, all as easily as if she had been the President of the Republic or the Pope. Inside were all the things they thought she ought to know concerning the last illness, death, and burial of Cousin Alexander Carraway.

Cousin Emma and Cousin Elec, brother and sister—unmarried, devoted, aging—had lived next door to the Stubblefields in Tuxapoka from time immemorial until the Stubblefields had moved to Montgomery fifteen years ago. Two days before he was taken sick, Cousin Elec was out worrying about what too much rain might do to his sweetpeas, and Cousin Elec had always preserved in the top drawer of his secretary a mother-of-pearl paper knife which Theresa had coveted as a child and which he had promised she could have when he died. *I'm supposed to care as much now as then, as much here as there,* she realized, with a sigh. *This letter would have got to me if she hadn't even put Rome, Italy, on it.*

She refolded the letter, replaced it in its envelope, and turned with relief to one from her brother George.

But alack, George, when *he* had written, had only just returned from going to Tuxapoka to Cousin Elec's funeral. He was full of heavy family reminiscence. All the fine old stock was dying out, look at the world today. His own children had suffered from the weakening of those values which he and Theresa had always taken for granted, and as for his grandchildren (he had one so far, still in diapers), he shuddered to think that the true meaning of character might never dawn on them at all. A life of gentility and principle such as Cousin Elec had lived had to be known at first hand....

Poor George! The only boy, the family darling. Together with her mother, both of them tense with worry lest things should somehow go wrong, Theresa had seen him through the right college, into the right fraternity, and though pursued by various girls and various mamas of girls, safely married to the right sort, however much in the early years of that match his wife, Anne, had not seemed to understand poor George. Could it just be, Theresa wondered, that Anne had understood only too well, and that George all along was extraordinary only in the degree to which he was dull?

As for Cousin Alexander Carraway, the only thing Theresa could remember at the moment about him (except his paper knife) was that he had had exceptionally long hands and feet and one night about one o'clock in the morning the whole Stubblefield family had been aroused to go next door at Cousin Emma's call—first Papa, then Mother, then Theresa and George. There they all did their uttermost to help Cousin Elec get a cramp out of his foot. He had hobbled downstairs into the parlor, in his agony, and was sitting, wrapped in his bathrobe, on a footstool. He held his long clenched foot in both hands, and this and his contorted face—he was trying heroically not to cry out—made him look like a large skinny old monkey. They all surrounded him, the family circle, Theresa and George as solemn as if they were watching the cat have kittens, and Cousin Emma running back and forth with a kettle of hot water which she poured steaming into a white enameled pan. "Can you think of anything to do?" she kept repeating. "I hate to call the doctor but if this keeps up I'll just have to! Can you think of anything to do?" "You might treat it like hiccups," said Papa. "Drop a cold key down his back." "I just hope this happens to you someday," said Cousin Elec, who was not at his best. "Poor Cousin Elec," George said. He was younger than Theresa: she remembered looking down and seeing his great round eyes, while at the same time she was dimly aware that her mother and father were not unamused. "Poor Cousin Elec."

Now, here they both were, still the same, George full of round-eyed woe, and Cousin Emma in despair. Theresa shifted to a new page.

"Of course [George's letter continued], there are practical problems to be considered. Cousin Emma is alone in that big old house and won't hear to parting from it. Robbie and Beryl tried their best to persuade her to come and stay with them, and Anne and I have told her she's more than welcome here, but I think she feels that she might be an imposition, especially as long as our Rosie is still in high school. The other possibility is to make arrangements for her to let out one or two of the rooms to some teacher of good family or one of those solitary old ladies that Tuxapoka is populated with—Miss Edna Whittaker, for example. But there is more in this than meets the eye. A new bathroom would certainly have to be put in. The wallpaper in the back bedroom is literally crumbling off. . . ." (Theresa skipped a page of details about the house.) "I hope if you have any ideas along these lines you will write me about them. I may settle on some makeshift arrangements for the summer and wait until you return in the fall so we can work out together the best . . ."

I really shouldn't have smoked a cigarette so early in the day, thought Theresa, it always makes me sick. I'll start sneezing in a minute, sitting on these cold steps. She got up, standing uncertainly for a moment, then moving aside to let go past her, talking, a group of young men. They wore shoes with pointed toes, odd to American eyes, and narrow trousers, and their hair looked unnaturally black and slick. Yet here they were obviously thought to be handsome, and felt themselves to be so. Just then a man approached her with a tray of cheap cameos, Parker fountain pens, rosaries, papal portraits. "No," said Theresa. "No, no!" she said. The man did not wish to leave. He knew how to spread himself against the borders of the space that had to separate them. Carrozza rides in the park, the Colosseum by moonlight, he specialized . . . Theresa turned away to escape, and climbed to a higher landing where the steps divided in two. There she walked to the far left and leaned on a vacant section of banister, while the vendor picked himself another well-dressed American lady, carrying a camera and a handsome alligator bag, ascending the steps alone. Was he ever successful, Theresa wondered. The lady with the alligator bag registered interest, doubt, then indignation; at last, alarm. She cast about as though looking for a policeman: this really shouldn't be allowed! Finally, she scurried away up the steps.

Theresa Stubblefield, still holding the family letters in one hand, realized that her whole trip to Europe was viewed in family circles as an interlude between Cousin Elec's death and "doing something" about Cousin Emma. They were even, Anne and George, probably thinking themselves very considerate in not hinting that she really should cut out "one or two countries" and come home in August to get Cousin Emma's house ready before the teachers came to Tuxapoka in September. Of course, it wasn't Anne and George's fault that one family crisis seemed to follow another, and weren't they always emphasizing that they really didn't know what they would do without Theresa? *The trouble is,* Theresa thought, *that while everything that happens there is supposed to matter supremely, nothing here is supposed even to exist. They would not care if all of Europe were to sink into the ocean tomorrow. It never registered with them that I had time to read all of Balzac, Dickens, and Stendhal while Papa was dying, not to mention everything in the city library after Mother's operation. It would have been exactly the same to them if I had read through all twenty-six volumes of Elsie Dinsmore.*

She arranged the letters carefully, one on top of the other. Then, with a motion so suddenly violent that she amazed herself, she tore them in two.

"*Signora?*"

She became aware that two Italian workmen, carrying a large azalea pot, were standing before her and wanted her to move so that they could begin arranging a new row of the display.

"*Mi dispiace, signora, ma ... insomma. . . .*"

"Oh . . . put it there!" She indicated a spot a little distance away. They did not understand. "*Ponere ... la.*" A little Latin, a little French. How one got along! The workmen exchanged a glance, a shrug. Then they obeyed her. "*Va bene, signora.*" They laughed as they returned down the steps in the sun.

Theresa was still holding the torn letters, half in either hand, and the flush was fading slowly from her brow. What a strong feeling had shaken her! She observed the irregular edges of paper, so crudely wrenched apart, and began to feel guilty. The Stubblefields, it was true, were proud and prominent, but how thin, how vulnerable was that pride it was so easy to prove, and how local was that prominence there was really no need to tell even them. But none could ever deny that the Stubblefields meant well; no one had ever challenged that the Stubblefields were good. Now out of their very letters, their sorrowful eyes, full of gentility and principle, appeared to be regarding Theresa, one of their own who had turned against them, and soft voices, so ready to forgive all, seemed to be saying, "Oh, Theresa, how *could* you?"

Wasn't that exactly what they had said when, as a girl, she had fallen in love with Charlie Wharton, whose father had unfortunately been in the pen? Ever so softly, ever so distressed: "Oh, Theresa, how *could* you?" Never mind. That was long ago, over and done with, and right now something clearly had to be done about these letters.

Theresa moved forward, and leaning down she dropped the torn sheets into the azalea pot which the workmen had just left. But the matter was not so easily settled. What if the letters should blow away? One could not bear the thought of that which was personal to the Stubblefields chancing out on the steps where everyone passed, or maybe even into the piazza below to be run over by a motor scooter, walked over by the common herd, spit upon, picked up and read, or—worst of all—returned to American Express by some conscientious tourist, where tomorrow, filthy, crumpled, bedraggled, but still legibly, faithfully relating Cousin Elec's death and Cousin Emma's grief, they might be produced to confront her.

Theresa moved a little closer to the azalea pot and sat down beside it. She covered the letters deftly, smoothing the earth above them and making sure that no trace of paper showed above the ground. The corner of Cousin Emma's envelope caught on a root and had to be shoved under, a painful moment, as if a letter could feel anything—how absurd! Then Theresa realized, straightening up and rubbing dirt off her hand with a piece of Kleenex from her bag, that it was not the letters but the Stubblefields that she had torn apart and consigned to the earth. This was certainly the only explanation of why the whole curious sequence, now that it was complete, had made her feel so marvelously much better.

Well, I declare! Theresa thought, astonished at herself, and in that moment it was as though she stood before the statue of some heroic classical woman whose dagger dripped with stony blood. *My goodness!* she thought, drowning in those blank exalted eyeballs: *Me!*

So thrilled she could not, for a time, move on, she stood noting that this particular azalea was one of exceptional beauty. It was white, in outline as symmetrically developed as an oak tree, and blooming in every part with a ruffled, lacy purity. The azalea was, moreover, Theresa recalled, a Southern flower, one especially cultivated in Alabama. Why, the finest in the world were said to grow in Bellingrath Gardens near Mobile, though probably they had not heard about that in Rome.

Now Miss Theresa Stubblefield descended quickly, down, down, toward the swarming square, down toward the fountain and all the racket, into the Roman crowd. There she was lost at once in the swirl, nameless, anonymous, one more nice rich American tourist lady.

But she cast one last glance back to where the white azalea stood, blooming among all the others. By now the stone of the great staircase was all but covered over. A group of young priests in scarlet cassocks went past, mounting with rapid, forward energy, weaving their way vividly aloft among the massed flowers. At the top of the steps the twin towers of a church rose, standing clearly outlined on the blue air. Some large white clouds, charged with pearly light, were passing overhead at a slow imperial pace.

Well, it certainly is beyond a doubt the most beautiful family funeral of them all! thought Theresa. *And if they should ever object to what I did to them,* she thought, recalling the stone giantess with her dagger and the gouts of blood hanging thick and gravid upon it, *they've only to read a little and learn that there have been those in my position who haven't acted in half so considerate a way.*

THE VISIT

The children were playing through the long empty rooms of the villa, shuttered now against the sunlight during the hottest hour of the day. The great man had gone to take a nap.

Before she had come to Italy, Judy thought that siesta was the word all Latins used for a rest after lunch, but she had learned that you said this only in Spain. In Italy you went to *riposarsi,* and this was exactly what the great man had done.

It was unfortunate because Bill had built up so to this visit. To be invited to see Thompson was, for almost anyone in the academic world, the token of something superior; but in Bill's particular field, it was the treasure, the X mark on the ancient map.

Judy often thought that Bill had an "and-then" sort of career. Graduate courses, a master's degree. A dissertation, a doctorate. A teaching appointment, scholarly articles. And then, and then. Promotion, the dissertation published, and clearly ahead on the upward road they could discern the next goal: a second, solidly important, possibly even definitive book. A grant from the Foundation was a natural forward step, and Bill then got to take his wife to Italy for a year. In Italy, as all knew, was Thompson.

Bill and Judy Owens had arrived in October; now it was June. All year Bill had worked on his book, the ambitious one, all about ancient Roman portraiture; Judy had typed for him, and manuscript had piled up thickly. They went about looking at museums, at ancient ruins and new excavations. They met other attractive young American couples who were abroad on fellowships and scholarships, studied Italian, attended lectures, and frequently complained about not getting to know more of the natives.

But all the time Bill and Judy did not mistake what the real thread was, nor which and-then they were working on now. The book would get written somehow; but what prestige it would gain for Bill if only he had the right to make a personal reference to Thompson even once—and more than once would be overdoing it. Should it go in the introduction, or the preface, or the acknowledgments, or the text itself? This would depend on the nature of what Thompson, at last, yielded; and did it matter so much where the single drop of essence landed, when it would go to work for one anywhere, regardless?

Bill was always thorough—he was anything but aimless, but in this matter he became something he had never been before: he grew crafty as hell. He plotted the right people to write and the best month for them to receive a letter. He considered the number of paragraphs which should go by before Thompson was even mentioned. In some cases Thompson's name was not even allowed to appear; yet his presence (such was Bill's skill) would breathe from every word. Pressure could be brought to bear in some cases: Bill had not been in the academic world fifteen years for nothing; and everything in American life is, in the long run, as we all know, competitive. He poked fun at his scheming mind—yet the goal was important to him, and he pressed forward in an innocent, bloodthirsty way, as if it were a game he had to win.

At last, in May, just when it seemed that nothing would happen, a letter arrived from a Professor Eakins, Bill's mentor in graduate school. "By the way," Eakins wrote (after a certain number of paragraphs had gone by), "I had a letter from Thompson recently saying that if any one of my students would be in the neighborhood of Genoa during June, he would be most welcome at the villa. I could think of no one I would rather have call on him than you, Bill. Of course, if you are planning to be in Sicily at that time, you'll let me know, so that—"

But Bill was not planning to be anywhere near Sicily in June.

—

From Genoa, in June, Bill and Judy had gone straight to the village in the mountains nearest to Thompson's villa. This village was the usual take-off point for people who went to see Thompson. Judy had pointed out that another village nearby had, according to the guidebook, a more interesting church, with a cosmatesque cloister and a work in the baptistry attributed by some to Donatello (Judy loved Donatello), but Bill decided that this was no time for anything unorthodox. So they went to the usual village.

All kind of legends were attached to the place. Some people had waited there for a week or more in the only halfway decent *pensione*, had dispatched all the proper credentials to the villa, but had never received any word at all. They had finally had to leave, looking out of the rear window of the taxi all the way to the station, until the mountain shut out the village forever. But no one could ever be personally encountered to whom anything of the sort had happened, and Bill had decided that it was only a Kafka-like nightmare which had accrued of itself to the Thompson image—he put it out of his mind by force.

He refused to recall it, even after he and Judy had sat waiting in the village for two days. He read the books he had brought to read, and Judy typed the chapter she had brought to type; then they proofread it together. They went out in the evenings and ate outdoors before a little restaurant under a string of colored lights. Here Judy, who got on rather well in Italian, answered all the waiter's questions about their son Henry, who had nine years and was now in care of his aunt in the *Stati Uniti*. The waiter said that she was much too young to have a nine-year-old son, and that her husband was a great scholar—one could see it *subito*. Judy enjoyed herself and drank up most of the wine. Light lingered in the mountains. They walked around and looked down at the view, an aspect of a splendid, darkening valley.

Bill threw himself down on a bench. Perhaps, he reflected aloud, Eakins was the wrong one to recommend him to Thompson. Who, after all, valued Eakins' work as highly as Eakins did? Eakins' large, fleshy, cultivated face all but materialized, with the thin, iron-gray hair and the thin waxed mustaches. It could be that

Thompson thought so little of Eakins that any letter from or about Eakins could easily be tossed aside.

As he sat torturing himself this way, Judy leaned her elbows on the rough wall, looking far down at some twinkling lights. She said that if only they were religious instead of scholastic they would have come off better, since anyone at all could get an audience with the Pope. In fact, the problem seemed to be how to get out of one. In Rome, you might just pull a thread by accident and wind up buying a black veil and checking to see if you had the right gloves and shoes.

Bill said that scholastic was not the right word; it particularly connoted the Middle Ages. As Judy had finished only two years of college, Bill often had to put her right about things.

On their return to the *pensione,* the maid ran out and handed them a letter. *"È arrivata,"* she said. It was somewhat embarrassing to be clearly seen through. Nonetheless, Bill's hour had struck. He and Judy were invited to lunch with Thompson on the following day.

———

Instead of driving their own car up to the villa, they took a taxi, as the proprietor of the *pensione* advised. He said that the way was extremely steep and dangerous. There were falling rocks, sharp curves, few markers. Their tires might be cut to pieces on the stones. Their water might boil away out of the radiator. They might lose the way entirely.

"How symbolic can you get?" Bill remarked. "Besides, his brother probably owns the taxi."

But all the proprietor said proved to be literally true. Bill and Judy were flung against each other several times on the curves. As the road threaded higher and higher, they dared not look out of the windows.

"I have to keep reminding myself," said Bill, shuddering away from a frightful declivity, "that this road may be leading me to the Thrace mosaics."

Judy knew about those mosaics, all from having typed so many letters. She knew as much as anybody. How they had been whatever the polite word was for smuggled out of the Middle East; how large the sums were that had gone for them, some over tables and some under; how museums and authorities of every nation could agree on no one but Thompson to receive them. Now they were at the villa. Some visitors had been allowed to peep at them, some even to have a brief try, as with a jigsaw puzzle, at matching this to that— a foot here, an arm there, and what prestige when the thing was talked about afterward!

"If only you could see them," Judy said.

"I can't think of any reason why I shouldn't," Bill said. The road had stabilized somewhat and he spoke with greater confidence, leaning back and crossing his legs. Judy smoothed her hair and agreed with him, then they were there.

The road flattened; a green plateau appeared before them, and set in it, at a fair distance, the villa. It looked like a photograph of itself. The tawny, bare façade was facing directly toward them. A colonnade ran out toward the left like a strong arm; it broke and softened the long savage drop of the mountain behind and framed in a half-embrace the grassy courtyard. There in the background, a hundred yards or so behind the villa, hung the ruin, the old castle. Rough and craggy, it was unused except artistically, as a backdrop, or to show people through (some visitors had reported being shown through), or perhaps for children to play in. Thompson's daughter, whose husband, the Prince of Gaeta, owned the villa, was said to have two children, and as if to prove that this was so, they at once appeared, a boy and girl, dressed in identical loose gray pinafores and long black stockings. They came out from among the shadows of the colonnade.

The radiator cap on the taxi had been removed for the journey, and Bill and Judy now chugged at a decorous pace into the courtyard, trailing a long plume of smoke. A dark man wearing English flannels came out of the villa and hastened to the colonnade, taking from behind a pillar a large green watering can. He poured water into the radiator of the taxi, then the cab driver handed him the radiator cap through the window, and he screwed it in place. *"È il principe,"* said the driver, over his shoulder. The prince himself!

"Buon giorno," said the prince to the driver, sticking his head through the window.

"*Buon giorno, signor principe,*" returned the driver.

"*Notizie?*"

Judy knew enough to follow that the prince was asking what was new and the driver was saying that nothing much was going on. Then the driver gave the prince a package of letters tied with a string.

The prince greeted his guests in English, opening the car door for them. The children had joined him and were standing nearby, side by side, looking at the newcomers, with dark eyes, brilliant in their pale, inquisitive faces.

"Perhaps," said the prince, "you'd like to see our position before going inside?" He led the way across the courtyard to the right, where they saw the land drop completely away. Portions of a road, perhaps their own, could be seen arranged in broken bits along the sheer slopes, and far below, between boulders, they saw the silent blue and white curling of the sea.

They were received in a small sitting room furnished with much-sat-in overstuffed furniture and opening out on a large terrace. The prince had them sit down and the two children, having been already formally presented in the courtyard, tucked themselves away on stools. Though they did not stare, they certainly watched: two more, they were clearly saying to themselves, had arrived.

Flashing dark, affable smiles, the prince said that he sometimes rode back down to the village with the taxi driver but that it must be hot below. Judy and Bill agreed: the nights were cool but at mid-day especially it was indeed hot below. Presently Madame Thompson came in—one said "Madame" instead of "Mrs." or "Signora" possibly to give her the Continental flavor she deserved, though she was not French but German, and Thompson was American. Her long straight gray hair was screwed into a loose knot at the back. She was wrapped in a coarse white shawl. They should all move out to the terrace, she suggested, because the view was "vunderful." They moved out to the terrace and soon two young women came in. The one with the tray of aperitifs was a servant; the other, the one wearing bracelets and smoking a cigarette, was Thompson's daughter, the princess.

From the opposite end of the terrace, making all turn, Thompson himself strode in.

He was grizzly and vigorous, with heavy brown hands. He wore a cardigan, crumpled trousers that looked about to fall down, and carpet slippers. He advanced to the center of the group and halted, squinting in the strong sun.

Judy dared not look at Bill. She had seen him at many other rungs of the ladder, looking both fearful and hopeful, both nervous and brave, in desperate proportions only Bill could concoct, and her heart had gone out to him. But now, as he confronted the Great Man at last, she looked elsewhere. She knew that he was transferring his glass to his left hand; she knew that his grasp would be damp, shaky, and cold.

Almost as much as for Bill, however, Judy was anxious for herself. Why, she now wondered, had she thought it necessary to look so well? Bill, in carefully pressed flannels, with crisp graying hair and heavy glasses, looked as American as naturally as a Chinaman looked Chinese, but with her the thing had taken some doing, and, inspired by the idea of helping him, she had worked at it hard. Brushes and bottles and God knows what had got into it and what with her best costume, a cream-colored linen sheath with loose matching jacket, a strand of pearls, gold earrings, and shimmering brown hair, she looked ready to be mounted in an enlargement on a handsome page; but what had that to do with scholarship? The princess and her mother, Judy felt certain, did not own one lipstick between them. They dressed like peasants, forgetting the whole thing.

It's only that I know how little I know to talk about, Judy thought. That's why I was so careful. What if they found out about all those books I haven't read? She shook hands with Thompson, but didn't say anything: she only smiled.

Bill, who used to be good at tennis—he and Judy had met one summer on a tennis court—found a means of cutting off the small talk with an opening question like a serve, something about a recent comparison of Byzantine and Roman portraiture. A moment later he was trotting off at Thompson's side, off toward the library, while words like monograph and research grant, Harvard and Cambridge, frothed about in their wake.

Judy was left alone with the family.

She asked them about their daily routine. The princess said she went down each afternoon to bathe in the sea. "But how do you get down?" Judy wanted to know. "Oh, by a stairway in back of the castle. It's quite a walk, but good for my figure." "Then do you walk back up?" "Oh no. There's a ski lift a half-mile from the beach. It lands me on a plateau, a sort of meadow. Beautiful. You've no idea. In the spring it is covered with flowers. I love it. Then I walk back through the castle and home."

"So there's skiing here, too?" she asked the prince.

"Oh no!" said the prince.

"He brought an old ski lift home from the Dolomites," the princess explained. "Just so I could ride up from the beach."

"Do you have a farm here?" Judy asked.

"Oh no!" said the prince.

"He did at one time," said the princess.

"At one time, I did, yes. Then I spent some years in England. In England they are all so kind to the animals. Oh, very kind. When I came back for the first time I saw how cruel our peasants were. Not that they meant to be cruel. Yet they were—they were cruel! I tried to change them. But they would not change. So at last I sold the animals and sent away all the peasants."

"That's one solution," Judy agreed.

"He vill never eat the meat," said Madame Thompson. She smiled, deeply, like the Mona Lisa. "Never!"

"Oh yes, the impression was a strong one. Also I am interested in Moral Rearmament. In England now there are so many thinking in this way. Now I oppose war and I will never eat meat again. *Carne? Mai!*"

It was not surprising, then, that they had pasta for lunch, followed by an omelet. Thompson sat at the head of the table.

"You should go to Greece," Thompson said to Bill. "Don't you plan to?"

"Greece isn't my field," Bill explained. "And of course my fellowship—"

"Fields and fellowships," said Thompson and gulped down some wine. "Fellowships and fields."

Bill remarked with a wry smile that Thompson himself had had one or two grants. "Oh, live on 'em!" Thompson cried. "Absolutely live on 'em. You people keep coming up the mountain—coming up the mountain. We must make it all work. How else?" His eye roved savagely around until it lighted on Judy: she felt as if her clothes were cracking suddenly away at the seams. Still observing her, Thompson said to Bill, "I'll tell you a subject that ten years ago I wouldn't have given a second thought to—at your age I would have derided it. The relation of art to economics."

"Oh, Lord, no," said Bill at once. "Not after 'The Byzantine Aesthetic.'"

"Very odd," said Thompson; "I feel exactly the same about one subject as the other." He sighed. "Well, don't tell Eakins on me, will you?"

"He'd think I was joking," Bill said.

"That summer in Paris," Thompson said, "when we met Eakins. When was that?" He addressed his wife. Madame Thompson had said nothing, it seemed to Judy, since her remark about the meat the prince would not eat; but now she began with patient, devoted, humorless accuracy to trace out what was wanted. Her voice rolled out in heavily muffled phrases, like something amplified through clouds.

"It vas in 1927, the summer Eugene, your secretary for ten years, had died at Cologne of pneumonia on the last day of February. You decided to bring three articles later called 'Some Aspects of the Renaissance'—"

"God!" Bill breathed, showing that he recognized the title.

"—to rewrite in Paris. After Eugene's death you thought alvays of the sculptures in the Louvre."

Memory rushed into Thompson, a back-lashing wave. The wine of that long ago summer seemed to be crisping his tongue. "Oh yes, and there was Eakins wanting all the same books as I in the Bibliothèque Nationale. He carried a sandwich in his briefcase. Very poor. One meal a day. Some *poule* or other was giving him that. No fellowships then. Nothing but fields. Some very green." He gave a short laugh. "I don't say he *read* the books, of course. That might be asking too much of Eakins."

The maid was putting the dessert around, a *crème caramel*. Thompson said he never ate dessert and went shuffling out in his carpet slippers. They all sat eating in silence. The princess said she would soon be going down for a swim if the Owenses would care to join her. "I know I shouldn't so soon after eating, but the walk is good for me." She drew herself in smartly. Bill's refusal included the hint that he intended to have more of a talk with Thompson before the visit was over. "Oh, but he has gone to rest," they all said. "He must have his rest."

Bill looked concerned, and the prince promised to take him into the library, where Thompson would certainly come the moment he got up. Then the prince took Judy out to see his roses. The garden was in back of the castle ruins, in a sheltered area between the mountain and the ruined wall, opening out toward the south. The prince had gone to a great deal of trouble. Roses were especially hard to cultivate in Italy. But he had admired them so in England. His were ravishing—broad blooms of pink, white, red, and yellow. Here they could distinctly hear the sea.

In the pauses between his bits of information the prince looked inquiringly at Judy as if he was wondering if there was something else he could do for himself. His life so far would have been like the sweep of a windshield wiper. Of course, he was a prince; of course, he had a villa and a castle, with the daughter of a famous man for his wife and roses and two beautiful children, and Moral Rearmament and English flannels, and if the peasants did not understand, he sent them away. If that was not enough, he did not eat the meat. Was there something else?

Judy noticed this, but felt the lack of anything to suggest to him. She stood wondering whether, since the peasants and the animals were gone, the roses too were financed by the foundations, but she decided this line of thought was ungracious.

The children appeared from nowhere. "Now they will take you round the castle, if you like," the prince kindly said. "It is mainly in shadow, so you won't grow tired. But mind you don't let them tempt you to climb. They love it, but they are like cats. Say, 'No, no, come down!'"

He turned away, toward nothing.

Clambering around the castle, Judy came on a sort of enclosure, sunlit and quiet. She could smell warm earth beneath the grass. The air was sweet and soft, what Italians called *dolce*. There were some beautiful old broken chunks of ruin lying scattered about. Judy sat down on some ruined steps and rested her chin in her palm. The children called to her out of a tower but she said, "No, no, come down," so they did. The sky was radiant and gentle. She could glimpse the children at intervals, running past empty window gaps, until at last they leaped down on the grass before her.

Suddenly from behind the children, at a notch in the wall, the princess rose up. She was climbing; though as they could not see her feet, she seemed to be rising like a planet. She was rubbing her wet hair with a towel, and the sense and movement of the sea were about her.

Stopping still, she addressed a volley of Italian to the children. It would have been hard to convince anyone that her father was from Minnesota. Judy made out *"Che hai?" "Cattivo, tu!"* and *"Dammelo!"* which meant, she reasoned, that the children had something they shouldn't have which now was to be given to their mother. Then, as they at first hung back with their fists stuffed in the pockets of their pinafores, but finally obeyed, going forward and reaching out toward the princess, Judy glimpsed handful after handful of flashing blue stones, the purest, most vibrant blue she had ever seen. The color seemed to prank about the air for a moment with the freakish skip of lightning.

"Was the ski lift working?" a voice cried. Thompson himself was striding out to find them among the ruins. The princess came down from the wall and sat down quickly on a large fallen cornice. She had taken the stones, like eggs, in her towel, and now she quickly concealed them in it as well.

"It was working but not very well. It goes very *piano*. It also runs at an *angolo*."

"We must send Giuseppe down to look at the motor," Thompson said. "How was the sea?"

"Strong, but right," said the princess.

Judy saw from her watch that it was nearly three. Bill must be going nuts in the library, she knew; and here was Thompson grasping her arm and hustling her along a narrow path. They entered the villa by a side door and were at once standing facing one another in a narrow room with the remains of old frescoes peeling from the walls, a Renaissance chest in the corner, and a cold swept fireplace.

Thompson placed a hand like a bear's paw beneath her chin; his coarse thumb, raking down her cheek from temple to chin, all but left, she felt, a long scar. "Beauty," he remarked. His hand fell away and whatever she was expecting next did not occur.

"My husband," said Judy, "is waiting to see you. You know, don't you, that he is a terribly important scholar?"

"So Eakins said . . . but then I've never especially liked Eakins, do you? He says these things for some purpose. It is rather like playing cards. Perhaps it's all true. How am I to know? I was never a scholar." He confided this last somewhat eagerly, as though it had been the reason for finding her, and having her believe it mattered to him, Judy could not think why. He leaned back against the chest and folded his long arms. "You think I have to go and talk to him?" he debated with her. "You think that is the important thing?"

"I don't know. Oh, I really don't know!" She burst out with this—undoubtedly, the wrong thing—quite unexpectedly, surprising herself.

"Ummm," said Thompson, thinking it over. His eyes—large, pale, old, and, she supposed, ugly—searched hers. Unreasonable pain filled her for a moment: she longed to comfort him, but before she could think of how to, he tilted her head to an angle that pleased him, kissed her brow, and shambled off, though in truth he seemed to trail a length of broken chain.

She was left to lose her way alone.

Corridors, wrongly chosen, led her to a room, a door, a small courtyard, a stretch of gravel, a dry fountain. She walked halfway to the fountain and turned to look back at the façade, which like the other was sunburned and bare. It was surmounted by a noble crest, slightly askew—the prince's doubtless. I should have told Thompson, she thought, that the children had got into the mosaics, but suppose it wasn't true? How could you say such a thing and not make an idiot of yourself if you were wrong?

As she stood, her shadow lying faithfully beside her in the uncompromising sun, a door in the wing to her left swung open and two Hindus, splendidly dressed, the man in a tailored dark suit wearing a scarlet turban, the woman in a delicate spangled sari that prickled over the gravel, walked past the fountain, past Judy, and disappeared through a door in the façade. She had raised her hand to them, she had called, but they had not looked up.

———

Bill was disappointed to the point of despair by his visit, which had yielded him only a scant half-hour with Thompson and a dusty monograph, published in 1928. Even the subject matter—Greek vase painting—was not in Bill's field. Thompson had told him seriously that for a man of his age, he had a wonderful liver. If Eakins had lived in Europe as long as he (Thompson) had, his (Eakins') liver would look like a bloody sponge.

"He's an organized disappointment," Bill complained, "and not very well organized at that. He didn't want to talk to me because he can't compete any more. He's completely out of the swim."

"I liked him," said Judy. "I just loved him, in fact."

"Doubtless. He has a taste for pretty girls. You overdid it, dressing so well. Did he chase you through the upstairs ballroom? That's what it's used for nowadays."

The taxi having reappeared for them promptly at four, they were now speeding down the mountain at a suicidal clip; they clung to straps beside the windows, where many a scholarly pair had clung before. Leaping rocks and whipping around curves, the cab clanged like a factory.

"The children had got into the mosaics," Judy shouted.

"What?" Bill yelled. And when she repeated it, "That can't be true," he answered.

"Did you see the Hindu couple?" she asked, as they sped through a silent green valley.

"No," said Bill. "And please don't describe them." He said that he had a headache and was getting sick. He wondered if they would return alive.

From the corner of her eye, Judy saw a huge boulder, dislodged by their wheels, float out into a white gorge with the leisure of a dream.

THE COUSINS

I could say that on the train from Milan to Florence, I recalled the events of thirty summers ago and the curious affair of my cousin Eric. But it wouldn't be true. I had Eric somewhere in my mind all the time, a constant. But he was never quite definable, and like a puzzle no one could ever solve, he bothered me. More recently, I had felt a restlessness I kept trying without success to lose, and I had begun to see Eric as its source.

The incident that had triggered my journey to find him had occurred while lunching with my cousin Ben in New York, his saying, "I always thought in some way I can't pin down—it was your fault we lost Eric." Surprising myself, I had felt stricken at the remark as though the point of a cold dagger had reached a vital spot. There was a story my cousins used to tell, out in the swing, under the shade trees, about a man found dead with no clues but a bloody shirt and a small pool of water on the floor beside him. Insoluble mystery. Answer: he was stabbed with a Dagger of Ice! I looked up from eating bay scallops. "*My* fault! Why?"

Ben gave some vague response, something about Eric's need for staying indifferent, no matter what. "But he could do that in spite of me," I protested. "Couldn't he?"

"Oh, forget it." He filled my glass. "I sometimes speculate out loud, Ella Mason."

Just before that he had remarked how good I was looking—good for a widow just turned fifty, I think he meant. But once he got my restlessness so stirred up, I couldn't lose it. I wanted calming, absolving. I wanted freeing and only Eric—since it was he I was in some way to blame for, or he to blame for me—could do that. So I came alone to Italy, where I had not been for thirty years.

For a while in Milan, spending a day or so to get over jet lag, I wondered if the country existed anymore in the way I remembered it. Maybe, even back then, I had invented the feelings I had, the magic I had wanted to see. But on the train to Florence, riding through the June morning, I saw a little town from the window in the bright, slightly hazy distance. I don't know what town it was. It seemed built all of a whitish stone, with a church, part of a wall cupping round one side and a piazza with a few people moving across it. With that sight and its stillness in the distance and its sudden vanishing as the train whisked past, I caught my breath and knew it had all been real. So it still was, and would remain. I hadn't invented anything.

From the point of that glimpsed white village, spreading outward through my memory, all its veins and arteries, the whole summer woke up again, like a person coming out of a trance.

Sealed, fleet, the train was rocking on. I closed my eyes with the image of the village, lying fresh and gentle against my mind's eye. I didn't have to try, to know that everything from then would start living now.

———

Once at the hotel and unpacked, with my dim lamp and clean bathroom and view of a garden—Eric had reserved all this for me: we had written and talked—I placed my telephone call. *"Pronto,"* said the strange voice. "Signor Mason," I said. "Ella Mason, is that you?" So there was his own Alabama voice, not a bit changed. "It's me," I said, "tired from the train." "Take a nap. I'll call for you at seven."

Whatever Southerners are, there are ways they don't change, the same manners to count on, the same tone of voice, never lost. Eric was older than I by about five years. I remember he taught me to play tennis, not so much how to play because we all knew that, as what not to do. Tennis manners. I had wanted to keep running after balls for him when they rolled outside the court but he stopped me from doing that. He would take them up himself and stroke them underhand to his opponent across the net. "Once in a while's all right," he said. "Just go sit down, Ella Mason." It was his way of saying there was always a right way to do things. I was only about ten. The next year it was something else I was doing wrong, I guess, because I always had a lot to learn. My cousins had this constant fondness about them. They didn't mind telling what they knew.

Waking in Florence in the late afternoon, wondering where I was, then catching on. The air was still and warm. It had the slight haziness in the brightness that I had seen from the train, and that I had lost in the bother of the station, the hastening of the taxi through the annoyance of crowds and narrow streets, across the Arno. The little hotel, a pensione, really, was out near the Pitti Palace.

Even out so short a distance from the center, Florence could seem the town of thirty years ago, or even the way it must have been in the Brownings' time, narrow streets and the light that way and the same flowers and gravel walks in the gardens. Not that much changes if you build with stone. Not until I saw the stooped gray man hastening through the pensione door did I get slapped by change, in the face. How could Eric look like that? Not that I hadn't had photographs, letters. He at once circled me, embracing, my head right against him, sight of him temporarily lost in that. As was his of me, I realized, thinking of all those lines I must have added, along with twenty extra pounds and a high count of gray among the reddish-brown hair. So we both got bruised by the sight of each other, and hung together, to blot each other out and soothe the hurt.

The shock was only momentary. We were too glad to see each other. We went some streets away, parked his car and climbed about six flights of stone stairs. His place had a view over the river, first a great luxurious room opening past the entrance, then a terrace beyond. There were paintings, dark furniture, divans and chairs covered with good, rich fabric. A blond woman's picture in a silver frame—poised, lovely. Through an alcove, the glimpse of an impressive desk, spread with papers, a telephone. You'd be forced to say he'd done well.

"It's cooler outside on the terrace," Eric said, coming in with drinks. "You'll like it over the river." So we went out there and talked. I was getting used to him now. His profile hadn't changed. It was firm, regular, Cousin Lucy Skinner's all over. That was his mother. We were just third cousins. Kissing kin. I sat answering questions. How long would it take, I wondered, to get around to the heart of things? To whatever had carried him away, and what had brought me here?

—

We'd been brought up together back in Martinsville, Alabama, not far from Birmingham. There was our connection and not much else in that little town of seven thousand and something. Or so we thought. And so we would have everybody else think. We did, though, despite a certain snobbishness—or maybe because of it— have a lot of fun. There were three leading families, in some way "connected." Eric and I had had the same great-grandfather. His mother's side were distant cousins, too. Families who had gone on living around there, through the centuries. Many were the stories and wide-ranged the knowledge, though it was mainly of local interest. As a way of living, I always told myself, it might have gone on for us, too, right through the present and into an endless future, except for that trip we took that summer.

It started with ringing phones.

Eric calling one spring morning to say, "You know, the idea Jamie had last night down at Ben's about going to Europe? Well, why don't we do it?"

"This summer's impossible," I said. "I'm supposed to help Papa in the law office."

"He can get Sister to help him—" That was Eric's sister, Chessie, one way of making sure she didn't decide to go with us. "You all will have to pay her a little, but she wants a job. Think it over, Ella Mason, but not for very long. Mayfred wants to, and Ben sounds serious, and there's Jamie and you makes five. Ben knows a travel agent in Birmingham. He thinks we might even get reduced rates, but we have to hurry. We should have thought this up sooner."

His light voice went racing on. He read a lot. I didn't even have to ask him where we'd go. He and Ben would plan it; both young men who studied things, knew things, read, talked, quoted. We'd go where they wanted to go, love what they planned, admire them. Jamie was younger, my uncle Gale's son, but he was forming that year—he was becoming grown-up. Would he be like them? There was nothing else to be but like them, if at all possible. No one in his right mind would question that.

Ringing phones. . . . "Oh, I'm thrilled to death! What did your folks say? It's not all that expensive what with the exchange, not as much as staying here and going somewhere like the Smokies. You can pay for the trip over with what you'd save."

We meant to go by ship. Mayfred, who read up on the latest things, wanted to fly, but nobody would hear to it. The boat was what people talked about when they mentioned their trip. It was a phrase: "On the boat going over. . . . On the boat coming back. . . ." The train was what we'd take to New York, or maybe we could fly. Mayfred, once redirected, began to plan everybody's clothes. She knew what things were drip-dry and crushproof. On and on she forged through slick-paged magazines.

"It'll take the first two years of law practice to pay for it, but it might be worth it," said Eric. *"J'ai très hâte d'y aller,"* said Ben. The little French he knew was a lot more than ours.

Eric was about twenty-five that summer, just finishing law school, having been delayed a year or so by his army service. I wasn't but nineteen. The real reason I had hesitated about going was a boy from Tuscaloosa I'd been dating up at the university last fall, but things were running down with him, even though I didn't want to admit it. I didn't love him so much as I wanted him to love me, and that's no good, as Eric himself told me. Ben was riding high, having got part of his thesis accepted for publication in the *Sewanee Review*. He had written on "The Lost Ladies of Edgar Allan Poe" and this piece was the chapter on "Ulalume." I pointed out they weren't so much lost as dead, or sealed up half-dead in tombs, but Ben didn't see the humor in that.

The syringa were blooming that year, and the spirea and bridal wreath. The flags had come and gone, but not the wisteria, prettier than anybody could remember. All our mothers doted on their yards, while not a one of us ever raised so much as a petunia. No need to.

We called one another from bower to bower. Our cars kept floating us through soft spring twilights. Travel folders were everywhere and Ben had scratched up enough French grammars to go around so we could practice some phrases. He thought we ought at least to know how to order in a restaurant and ask for stationery and soap in a hotel. Or buy stamps and find the bathroom. He was on to what to say to cab drivers when somebody mentioned that we were spending all this time on French without knowing a word of Italian. What did *they* say for hello, or how much does it cost, or which way to the post office? Ben said we didn't have time for Italian. He thought the people you had to measure up to were the French. What Italians thought of you didn't matter all that much. We were generally over at Eric's house because his mother was away visiting his married sister Edith and the grandchildren, and Eric's father couldn't have cared less if we had drinks of real whiskey in the evening. In fact, he was often out playing poker and doing the same thing himself.

The Masons had a grand house. (Mason was Mama's maiden name and so my middle one.) I loved the house especially when nobody was in it but all of us. It was white, two-story with big high-ceilinged rooms. The tree branches laced across it by moonlight, so that you could only see patches of it. Mama was always saying they ought to thin things out, take out half the shrubs and at least three trees (she would even say which trees), but Cousin Fred, Eric's father, liked all that shaggy growth. Once inside, the house took you over—it liked us all—and we were often back in the big kitchen after supper, fixing drinks, or sitting out on the side porch, making jokes and talking about Europe. One evening it would be peculiar things about the English, and the next, French food, how much we meant to spend on it, and so on. We had a long argument about Mont St. Michel, which Ben had read about in a book by Henry Adams, but everybody else, though coaxed into reading at least part of the book, thought it was too far up there and we'd better stick around Paris. We hoped Ben would forget it: he was bossy when he got his head set. We wanted just to see Ver-sigh and Fontaine-blow.

"We could stop off in the southern part of France on our way to Italy," was Eric's idea. "It's where all the painting comes from."

"I'd rather see the paintings," said Mayfred. "They're mostly in Paris, aren't they?"

"That's not the point," said Ben.

Jamie was holding out for one night in Monte Carlo.

Jamie had shot up like a weed a few years back and had just never filled out. He used to regard us all as slightly opposed to him, as though none of us could possibly want to do what he most liked. He made, at times, common cause with Mayfred, who was kin to us only by a thread so complicated I wouldn't dream of untangling it.

Mayfred was a grand-looking girl. Ben said it once, "She's got class." He said that when we were first debating whether to ask her along or not (if not her, then my roommate from Texas would be invited), and had decided that we had to ask Mayfred or smother her, because we couldn't have stopped talking about our plans if our lives depended on it and she was always around. The afternoon Ben made that remark about her, we were just the three of us—Ben, Eric and me—out to help Mama about the annual lining of the tennis court, and had stopped to sit on a bench, being sweaty and needing some shade to catch our breath in. So he said that in his meditative way, hitting the edge of a tennis racket on the ground between his feet and occasionally sighting down it to see if it had warped during a winter in the press. And Eric, after a silence in which he looked off to one side until you thought he hadn't heard (this being his way), said, "You'd think the rest of us had no class at all." "Of course we have, we just never mention it," said Ben. So we'd clicked again. I always loved that to happen.

Mayfred had a boyfriend named Donald Bailey, who came over from Georgia and took her out every Saturday night. He was fairly nice-looking was about all we knew, and Eric thought he was dumb.

"I wonder how Mayfred is going to get along without Donald," Ben said.

"I can't tell if she really likes him or not," I said. "She never talks about him."

"She just likes to have somebody," Ben said tersely, a thread of disapproval in his voice, the way he could do.

Papa was crazy about Mayfred. "You can't tell what she thinks about anything and she never misses a trick," he said. His unspoken thought was that I was always misjudging things. "Don't you *see*, Ella Mason," he would say. But are things all that easy to see?

"Do you remember," I said to Eric on the terrace, this long after, "much about Papa?"

"What about him?"

"He wanted me to be different someway."

"Different how?"

"More like Mayfred," I said, and laughed, making it clear that I was deliberately shooting past the mark, because really I didn't know where it was.

"Well," said Eric, looking past me out to where the lights were brightening along the Arno, the towers standing out clearly in the dusky air, "I liked you the way you were."

It was good, hearing him say that. The understanding that I wanted might not come. But I had a chance, I thought, and groped for what to say, when Eric rose to suggest dinner, a really good restaurant he knew, not far away; we could even walk.

—

... "Have you been to the Piazza? No, of course, you haven't had time. Well, don't go. It's covered with tourists and pigeon shit. They've moved all the real statues inside except the Cellini. Go look at that and leave quick...."

"You must remember Jamie, though, how he put his head in his hands our first day in Italy and cried, 'I was just being nice to him and he took all the money!' Poor Jamie, I think something else was wrong with him, not just a couple of thousand lire."

"You think so, but what?"

"Well, Mayfred had made it plain that Donald was her choice of a man, though not present. And of course there was Ben. . . ." My voice stopped just before I stepped on a crack in the sidewalk.

"Ben had just got into Yale that spring before we left. He was hitching to a *fu*ture, man!" It was just as well Eric said it.

"So that left poor Jamie out of everything, didn't it? He was young, another year in college to go, and nothing really outstanding about him, so he thought, and nobody he could pair with."

"There were you and me."

"You and me," I repeated. It would take a book to describe how I said that. Half question, half echo, a total wondering what to say next. How, after all, did *he* mean it? It wasn't like me to say nothing. "He might just have wondered what *we* had?"

"He might have," said Eric. In the corner of the white-plastered restaurant, where he was known and welcomed, he was enjoying grilled chicken and artichokes. But suddenly he put down his fork, a pause like a solstice. He looked past my shoulder: Eric's way.

"Ben said it was my fault we 'lost' you. That's how he put it. He told me that in New York, the last time I saw him, six weeks ago. He wouldn't explain. Do you understand what he meant?"

" 'Lost,' am I? It's news to me."

"Well, you know, not at home. Not even in the States. Is that to do with me?"

"We'll go back and talk." He pointed to my plate. "Eat your supper, Ella Mason," he said.

My mind began wandering pleasantly. I fell to remembering the surprise Mayfred had handed us all when we got to New York. We had come up on the train, having gone up to Chattanooga to catch the Southern. Three days in New York and we would board the *Queen Mary* for Southampton. "Too romantic for anything," Mama had warbled on the phone. ("Elsa Stephens says, 'Too romantic for anything,' " she said at the table. "No, Mama, you said that. I heard you." "Well, I don't care who said it, it's true.") On the second afternoon in New York, Mayfred vanished with something vague she had to do. "Well, you know she's always tracking down dresses," Jamie told me. "I think she wants her hair restyled somewhere," I said. But not till we were having drinks in the hotel bar before dinner did Mayfred show up with Donald Bailey! She had, in addition to Donald, a new dress and a new hairstyle, and the three things looked to me about of equal value, I was thinking, when she suddenly announced with an earsplitting smile, "We're married!" There was a total silence, broken at last by Donald, who said with a shuffling around of feet and gestures, "It's just so I could come along with y'all, if y'all don't mind." Another silence followed, broken by Eric, who said he guessed it was one excuse for having champagne.

Mayfred and Donald had actually got married across the state line in Georgia two weeks before. Mayfred didn't want to discuss it because, she said, everybody was so taken up with talking about Europe, she wouldn't have been able to get a word in edgewise. "You better go straight and call yo' Mama," said Ben. "Either you do, or I will."

Mayfred's smile fell to ashes and she sloshed out champagne. "She can't do a thing about it till we get back home! She'll want me to explain everything. Don't y'all make me ... please!"

I noticed that so far Mayfred never made common cause with any one of us, but always spoke to the group: y'all. It also occurred to me both then and now that that was what had actually saved her. If one of us had got involved in pleading for her with Ben, he would have overruled us. But Mayfred, a lesser cousin, was keeping a distance. She could have said—and I thought she was on the verge of it—that she'd gone to a lot of trouble to satisfy us; she might have just brought him along without benefit of ceremony.

So we added Donald Bailey. Unbeknownst to us, reservations had been found for him, and though he had to share a four-berth, tourist-class cabin with three strange men, after a day out certain swaps were effected, and he wound up in second class with Mayfred. Eric overheard a conversation between Jamie and Donald, which he passed on to me. Jamie: "Don't you really think this is a funny way to spend a honeymoon?" Donald: "It just was the best I could do."

He was a polite squarish sort of boy with heavy, dark lashes. He and Mayfred used to stroll off together regularly after the noon meal on board. It was a serene crossing, for the weather cleared two days out of New York, and we could spend a lot of time on deck, playing shuffleboard and betting on races with wooden horses run by the purser. (I forgot to say everybody in our family but Ben's branch were inveterate gamblers and had played poker in the club car all the way up to New York on the train.) After lunch every day Mayfred got seasick, and Donald in true husbandly fashion would take her to whichever side the wind was not blowing against and let her throw up neatly over the rail, like a cat. Then she'd be all right. Later, when you'd see them together, they were always talking and laughing. But with us she was quiet and trim, with her fashion-blank look, and he was just quiet. He all but said "Ma'am" and "Sir." As a result of Mayfred's marriage, I was thrown a lot with Eric, Ben and Jamie. "I think one of you ought to get married," I told them. "Just temporarily, so I wouldn't feel like the only girl." Ben promised to take a look around and Eric seemed not to have heard. It was Jamie who couldn't joke about it. He had set himself to make a pair, in some sort of way, with Mayfred, I felt. I don't know how seriously he took her. Things run deep in our family—that's what you have to know. Eric said out of the blue, "I'm wondering when they had time to see each other. Mayfred spent all her time with us." (We were prowling through the Tate Gallery.) "Those Saturday night dates," I said, studying Turner. At times she would show up with us, without Donald, not saying much, attentive and smooth, making company. Ben told her she looked Parisian.

Eric and Ben were both well into manhood that year, and were so future conscious they seemed to be talking about it even when they weren't saying anything. Ben had decided on literature, had finished a master's at Sewanee and was going on to Yale, while Eric had just stood law-school exams at Emory. He was in some considerable debate about whether he shouldn't go into literary studies, too, for unlike Ben, whose interest was scholarly, he wanted to be a writer, and he had some elaborate theory that actually studying literature reduced the possibility of your being able to write it. Ben saw his point and, though he did not entirely agree, felt that law might just be the right choice—it put you in touch with how things actually worked. "Depending, of course, on whether you tend to fiction or poetry. It would be more important in regard to fiction because the facts matter so much more." So they trod along ahead of us— through London sights, their heels coming down in tandem. They might have been two dons in an Oxford street, debating something. Next to come were Jamie and me, and behind, at times, Donald and Mayfred.

I was so fond of Jamie those days. I felt for him in a family way, almost motherly. When he said he wanted a night in Monte Carlo, I sided with him, just as I had about going at least once to the picture show in London. Why shouldn't he have his way? Jamie said one museum a day was enough. I felt the same. He was all different directions with himself: too tall, too thin, big feet, small head. Once I caught his hand. "Don't worry," I said, "everything good will happen to you." The way I remember it, we looked back just then, and there came Mayfred, alone. She caught up with us. We were standing on a street corner near Hyde Park and, for a change, it was sunny. "Donald's gone home," she said cheerfully. "He said tell you all goodbye."

We hadn't seen her all day. We were due to leave for France the next morning. She told us, for one thing, that Donald had persistent headaches and thought he ought to see about it. He seemed, as far as we could tell, to have limitless supplies of money, and had once taken us all for dinner at the Savoy, where only Mayfred could move into all that glitter with an air of belonging to it. He didn't like to bring up his illness and trouble us, Mayfred explained. "Maybe it was too much honeymoon for him," Eric speculated to me in private. I had to say I didn't know. I did know that Jamie had come out like the English sun—unexpected, but marvelously bright.

———

I held out for Jamie and Monte Carlo. He wasn't an intellectual like Ben and Eric. He would listen while they finished up a bottle of wine and then would start looking around the restaurant. "That lady didn't have anything but snails and bread," he would say, or, of a couple leaving, "He didn't even know that girl when they came in." He was just being a small-town boy. But with Mayfred he must have been different; she laughed so much. "What do they talk about?" Ben asked me, perplexed. "Ask them," I advised. "You think they'd tell me?" "I doubt it," I said. "They wouldn't know what to say," I added. "They would just tell you the last things they said." "You mean like, why do they call it the Seine if they don't seine for fish in it? Real funny."

Jamie got worried about Mayfred in Paris because the son of the hotel owner, a young Frenchman so charming he looked like some-body had made him up whole cloth, wanted to take her out. She fi-nally consented with some trepidation on our part, especially from Ben, who in this case posed as her uncle, with strict orders from her father. The Frenchman, named Paul something, was not disturbed in the least: Ben fitted right in with his ideas of how things ought to be. So Mayfred went out with him, looking, except for her sunny hair, more French than the natives—we all had to admit being proud of her. I, also, had invitations, but none so elegant. "What happened?" we all asked, the next day. "Nothing," she insisted. "We just went to this little nightclub place near some school . . . begins with an 'S.'" "The Sorbonne," said Ben, whose bemusement, at that moment, peaked. "Then what?" Eric asked. "Well, nothing. You just eat something, then talk and have some wine and get up and dance. They dance different. Like this." She locked her hands together in air. "He thought he couldn't talk good enough for me in English, but it was O.K." Paul sent her some *marrons glacés*, which she opened on the train south, and Jamie munched one with happy jaws. Paul had not suited him. It was soon after that, he and Mayfred began their pairing off. In Jamie's mind we were moving on to Monte Carlo, and had been ever since London. The first thing he did was find out how to get to the Casino.

He got dressed for dinner better than he had since the Savoy. Mayfred seemed to know a lot about the gambling places, but her attitude was different from his. Jamie was bird-dogging toward the moment; she was just curious. "I've got to trail along," Eric said after dinner, "just to see the show." "Not only that," said Ben, "we might have to stop him in case he gets too carried away. We might have to bail him out." When we three, following up the rear (this was Ja-mie's night), entered the discreetly glittering rotunda, stepped on thick carpets beneath the giant, multiprismed chandeliers, heard the low chant of the croupier, the click of roulette, the rustle of money at the bank, and saw the bright rhythmic movements of dealers and wheels and stacks of chips, it was still Jamie's face that was the sight worth watching. All was mirrored there. Straight from the bank, he visited card tables and wheels, played the blind dealing machine—chemin-de-fer—and finally turned, a small sum to the good, to his real goal: roulette. Eric had by then lost a hundred francs or so, but I had about made up for it, and Ben wouldn't play at all. "It's my Presbyterian side," he told us. His mother had been one of those. "It's known as 'riotous living,'" he added.

It wasn't riotous at first, but it was before we left, because Jamie, once he advanced on the roulette, with Mayfred beside him—she was wearing some sort of gold blouse with long peasant sleeves and a low-cut neck she had picked up cheap in a shop that afternoon, and was not speaking to him but instead, with a gesture so European you'd think she'd been born there, slipping her arm through his just at the wrist and leaning her head back a little—was giving off the glow of somebody so magically aided by a presence every inch his own that he could not and would not lose. Jamie, in fact, looked suddenly aristocratic, overbred, like a Russian greyhound or a Rumanian prince. Both Eric and I suspended our own operations to watch. The little ball went clicking around as the wheel spun. Black. Red. And red. Back to black. All wins. People stopped to look on. Two losses, then the wins again, continuing. Mayfred had a look of curious bliss around her mouth—she looked like a cat in process of a good purr. The take mounted.

Ben called Eric and me aside. "It's going on all night," he said. We all sat down at the little gold and white marble bar and ordered Perriers.

"Well," said Eric, "what did he start with?"

"Couldn't have been much," said Ben, "if I didn't miss anything. He didn't change more than a couple of hundred at the desk."

"That sounds like a lot to me," said Eric.

"I mean," said Ben, "it won't ruin him to lose it all."

"You got us into this," said Eric to me.

"Oh, gosh, I know it. But look. He's having the time of his life."

Everybody in the room had stopped to watch Jamie's luck. Some people were laughing. He had a way of stopping everybody and saying, "What's *that* mean?" as if only English could or ought to be spoken in the entire world. Some man near us said, *"Le cavalier de l'Okla-hum,*" and another answered, "*Du Texas, plutôt.*" Then he took three more in a row and they were silent.

It was Mayfred who made him stop. It seemed like she had an adding machine in her head. All of a sudden she told him something, whispered in his ear. When he shook his head, she caught his hand. When he pulled away, she grabbed his arm. When he lifted his arm, she came up with it, right off the floor. For a minute I thought they were both going to fall over into the roulette wheel.

"You got to stop, Jamie!" Mayfred said in the loudest Alabama voice I guess they'd ever be liable to hear that side of the ocean. It was curdling, like cheering for 'Bama against Ole Miss in the Sugar Bowl. "I don't have to stop!" he yelled right back. "If you don't stop," Mayfred shouted, "I'll never speak to you again, Jamie Marshall, as long as I live!"

The croupier looked helpless, and everybody in the room was turning away like they didn't see us, while through a thin door at the end of the room, a man in black tie was approaching who could only be called the "management." Ben was already pulling Jamie toward the bank. "Cash it in now. We'll go along to another one . . . maybe tomorrow we can . . ." It was like pulling a stubborn calf across the lot, but he finally made it with some help from Mayfred, who stood over Jamie while he counted everything to the last sou. She made us all take a taxi back to the hotel because she said it was common knowledge when you won a lot they sent somebody out to rob you, first thing. Next day she couldn't rest till she got Jamie to change the francs into traveler's checks, U.S. He had won well over two thousand dollars, all told.

The next thing, as they saw it, was to keep Jamie out of the Casino. Ben haggled a long time over lunch, and Eric, who was good at scheming, figured out a way to get up to a village in the hills where there was a Matisse chapel he couldn't live longer without seeing. And Mayfred took to handholding and even gave Jamie on the sly (I caught her at it) a little nibbling kiss or two. What did they care? I wondered. I thought he should get to go back and lose it all.

It was up in the mountain village that afternoon that I blundered in where I'd rather not have gone. I had come out of the chapel where Ben and Eric were deep in discussion of whether Matisse could ever place in the front rank of French art, and had climbed part of the slope nearby where a narrow stair ran up to a small square with a dry stone fountain. Beyond that, in the French manner, was a small café with a striped awning and a few tables. From somewhere I heard Jamie's voice, saying, "I know, but what'd you do it for?" "Well, what does anybody do anything for? I wanted to." "But what would you want to *for*, Mayfred?" "Same reason you'd want to sometime." "I wouldn't want to except to be with you." "Well, I'm right here, aren't I? You got your wish." "What I wish is you hadn't done it." It was bound to be marrying Donald that he meant. He had a frown that would come at times between his light eyebrows. I came to associate it with Mayfred. How she was running him. When they stepped around the corner of the path, holding hands (immediately dropped), I saw that frown. Did I have to dislike Mayfred, the way she was acting? The funny thing was, I didn't even know.

We lingered around the village and ate there, and the bus was late, so we never made it back to the Casino. By then all Jamie seemed to like was being with Mayfred, and the frown disappeared.

———

Walking back to the apartment, passing darkened doorways, picking up pieces of Eric's past like fragments in the street.

". . . And then you did or didn't marry her, and she died and left you the legacy. . . ."

"Oh, we did get married, all right, the anticlimax of a number of years. I wish you could have known her. The marriage was civil. She was afraid the family would cause a row if she wanted to leave me anything. That was when she knew she hadn't had long to live. Not that it was any great fortune. She had some property out near Pasquallo, a little town near here. I sold it. I had to fight them in court for a while, but it did eventually clear up."

"You've worked, too, for this other family? . . ."

"The Rinaldi. You must have got all this from Ben, though maybe I wrote you, too. They were friends of hers. It's all connections here, like anywhere else. Right now they're all at the sea below Genoa. I'd be there, too, but I'd some business in town, and you were coming. It's the export side I've helped them with. I do know English, and a little law, in spite of all."

"So it's a regular Italian life," I mused, climbing stairs, entering his *salotto*, where I saw again the woman's picture in a silver frame. Was that her, the one who had died? "Was she blond?" I asked, moving as curiously through his life as a child through a new room.

"Giana, you mean? No, part Sardinian, dark as they come. Oh, you mean her. No, that's Lisa, one of the Rinaldi, Paolo's sister . . . that's him up there."

I saw then, over a bookshelf, a man's enlarged photo: tweed jacket, pipe, all in the English style.

"So what else, Ella Mason?" His voice was amused at me.

"She's pretty," I said.

"Very pretty," he agreed.

We drifted out to the terrace once more.

———

It is time I talked about Ben and Eric, about how it was with me and with them and with the three of us.

When I look back on pictures of myself in those days, I see a girl in shorts, weighing a few pounds more than she thought she should, low-set, with a womanly cast to her body, chopped-off reddish hair and a wide, freckled, almost boyish grin, happy to be posing between two tall boys, who happened to be her cousins, smiling their white tentative smiles. Ben and Eric. They were smart. They were fun. They did everything right. And most of all, they admitted me. I was the audience they needed.

I had to run to keep up. I read Poe because of Ben's thesis, and Wallace Stevens because Eric liked his poetry. I even, finding him referred to at times, tried to read Plato. (Ben studied Greek.) But what I did was not of much interest to them. Still, they wanted me around. Sometimes Ben made a point of "conversing" with me— what courses, what books, et cetera—but he made me feel like a high-school student. Eric, seldom bothering with me, was more on my level when he did. To each other, they talked at a gallop. Literature turned them on; their ideas flowed, ran back and forth like a current. I loved hearing them.

I think of little things they did. Such as Ben coming back from Sewanee with a small Roman statue, a copy of something Greek—Apollo, I think—just a fragment, a head, turned aside, shoulders and a part of a back. His professor had given it to him as a special mark of favor. He set it on his favorite pigeonhole desk, to stay there, it would seem, for always, to be seen always by the rest of us—by me.

Such as Eric ordering his "secondhand but good condition" set of Henry James's novels with prefaces, saying, "I know this is corny, but it's what I wanted," making space in his Mama's old upright secretary with glass-front bookshelves above, and my feeling that they'd always be there. I strummed my fingers across the spines lettered in gold. Someday I would draw down one or another to read them. No hurry.

Such as the three of us packing Mama's picnic basket (it seems my folks were the ones with the practical things—tennis court, croquet set; though Jamie's set up a badminton court at one time, it didn't take) to take to a place called Beulah Woods for a spring day in the sun near a creek where water ran clear over white limestone, then plunged off into a swimming hole. Ben sat on a bedspread reading Ransom's poetry aloud and we gossiped about the latest town scandal, involving a druggist, a real-estate deal where some property went cheap to him, though it seemed now that his wife had been part of the bargain, being lent out on a regular basis to the man who sold him the property. The druggist was a newcomer. A man we all knew in town had been after the property and was now threatening to sue. "Do you think it was written in the deed, so many nights a week she goes off to work the property out," Ben speculated. "Do you think they calculated the interest?" It wasn't the first time our talk had run toward sexual things; in a small town, secrets didn't often get kept for long.

More than once I'd dreamed that someday Ben or Eric one would ask me somewhere alone. A few years before the picnic, romping through our big old rambling house at twilight with Jamie, who loved playing hide-and-seek, I had run into the guest room, where Ben was standing in the half dark by the bed. He was looking at something he'd found there in the twilight, some book or ornament, and I mistook him for Jamie and threw my arms around him crying, "Caught you!" We fell over the bed together and rolled for a moment before I knew then it was Ben, but knew I'd wanted it to be; or didn't I really know all along it was Ben, but pretended I didn't? Without a doubt when his weight came down over me, I knew I wanted it to be there. I felt his body, for a moment so entirely present, draw back and up. Then he stood, turning away, leaving. "You better grow up," was what I think he said. Lingering feelings made me want to seek him out the next day or so. Sulky, I wanted to say, "I *am* growing up." But another time he said, "We're cousins, you know."

Eric for a while dated a girl from one of the next towns. She used to ask him over to parties and they would drive to Birmingham sometimes, but he never had her over to Martinsville. Ben, that summer we went to Europe, let it be known he was writing and getting letters from a girl at Sewanee. She was a pianist named Sylvia. "You want to hear music played softly in the 'drawing room,'" I clowned at him. "'Just a song at twilight.'" "Now, Ella Mason, you behave," he said.

I had boys to take me places. I could flirt and I got a rush at dances and I could go off the next to the highest diving board and was good in doubles. Once I went on strike from Ben and Eric for over a week. I was going with that boy from Tuscaloosa and I had begun to think he was the right one and get ideas. Why fool around with my cousins? But I missed them. I went around one afternoon. They were talking out on the porch. The record player was going inside, something of Berlioz's that Ben was onto. They waited till it finished before they'd speak to me. Then Eric, smiling from the depths of a chair, said, "Hey, Ella Mason," and Ben, getting up to unlatch the screen, said, "Ella Mason, where on earth have you been?" I'd have to think they were glad.

Ben was dark. He had straight, dark-brown hair, dry-looking in the sun, growing thick at the brow, but flat at night when he put a damp comb through it, and darker. It fitted close to his head like a monk's hood. He wore large glasses with lucite rims. Eric had sandy hair, softly appealing and always mussed. He didn't bother much with his looks. In the day they scuffed around in open-throated shirts and loafers, crinkled seersucker pants, or shorts; tennis shoes when they played were always dirty white. At night, when they cleaned up, it was still casual but fresh laundered. But when they dressed, in shirts and ties with an inch of white cuff laid crisp against their brown hands: they were splendid!

"Ella Mason," Eric said, "if that boy doesn't like you, he's not worth worrying about." He had put his arm around me coming out of the picture show. I ought to drop it, a tired romance, but couldn't quite. Not till that moment. Then I did.

"Those boys," said Mr. Felix Gresham from across the street. "Getting time they started earning something 'stead of all time settin' around." He used to come over and tell Mama everything he thought, though no kin to anybody. "I reckon there's time enough for that," Mama said. "Now going off to France," said Mr. Gresham, as though that spoke for itself. "Not just France," Mama said, "England, too, and Italy." "Ain't nothing in France," said Mr. Gresham. "I don't know if there is or not," said Mama. "I never have been." She meant that to hush him up, but the truth is, Mr. Gresham might have been to France in World War I. I never thought to ask. Now he's dead.

Eric and Ben. I guess I was in love with both of them. Wouldn't it be nice, I used to think, if one were my brother and the other my brother's best friend, and then I could just quietly and without so much as thinking about it find myself marrying the friend (now which would I choose for which?) and so we could go on forever? At other times, frustrated, I suppose, by their never changing toward me, I would plan on doing something spectacular, finding a Yankee, for instance, so impressive and brilliant and established in some important career that they'd have to listen to him, learn what he was doing and what he thought and what he knew, while I sat silent and poised throughout the conversation, the cat that ate the cream, though of course too polite to show satisfaction. Fantasies, one by one, would sing to me for a little while.

At Christmas vacation before our summer abroad, just before Ben got accepted to Yale and just while Eric was getting bored with law school, there was a quarrel. I didn't know the details, but they went back to school with things still unsettled among us. I got friendly with Jamie then, more than before. He was down at Tuscaloosa, like me. It's when I got to know Mayfred better, on weekends at home. Why bother with Eric and Ben? It had been a poor season. One letter came from Ben and I answered it, saying that I had come to like Jamie and Mayfred so much; their parents were always giving parties and we were having a grand time. In answer I got a long, serious letter about time passing and what it did, how we must remember that what we had was always going to be a part of ourselves. That he thought of jonquils coming up now and how they always looked like jonquils, just absent for a time, and how the roots stayed the same. He was looking forward, he said, to spring and coming home.

Just for fun I sat down and wrote him a love letter. I said he was a fool and a dunce and didn't he know while he was writing out all these ideas that I was a live young woman and only a second cousin and that through the years while he was talking about Yeats, Proust and Edgar Allan Poe that I was longing to have my arms around him the way they were when we fell over in the bed that twilight romping with Jamie and why in the ever-loving world couldn't he see me as I was, a live girl, instead of a cousin-spinster, listening to him and Eric make brilliant conversation? Was he trying to turn me into an old maid? Wasn't he supposed, at least, to be intelligent? So why couldn't he see what I was really like? But I didn't mail it. I didn't because for one thing, I doubted that I meant it. Suppose, by a miracle, Ben said, "You're right, every word." What about Eric? I started dating somebody new at school. I tore the letter up.

Eric called soon after. He just thought it would do him good to say hello. Studying for long hours wasn't his favorite sport. He'd heard from Ben; the hard feelings were over; he was ready for spring holidays already. I said, "I hope to be in town, but I'm really not sure." A week later I forgot a date with the boy I thought I liked. The earlier one showed up again. Hadn't I liked him, after all? How to be sure? I bought a new straw hat, white-and-navy for Easter, with a ribbon down the back, and came home.

———

Just before Easter, Jamie's parents gave a party for us all. There had been a cold snap and we were all inside, with purplish-red punch and a buffet laid out. Jamie's folks had this relatively new house, with new carpets and furnishings, and the family dismay ran to what a big mortgage they were carrying and how it would never be paid out. Meantime his mother (no kin) looked completely unworried as she arranged tables that seemed to have been copied from magazines. I came alone, having had to help Papa with some typing, and so saw Ben and Eric for the first time, though we'd talked on the phone.

Eric looked older, a little worn. I saw something drawn in the way he laughed, a sort of restraint about him. He was standing aside and looking at a point where no one and nothing were. But he came to when I spoke and gave that laugh and then a hug. Ben was busy "conversing" with a couple in town who had somebody at Sewanee, too. He smoked a pipe now, I noticed, smelly when we hugged. He had soon come to join Eric and me, and it was at that moment, the three of us standing together for the first time since Christmas, and change having been mentioned at least once by way of Ben's letter, that I knew some tension was mounting, bringing obscure moments with it. We turned to one another but did not speak readily about anything. I had thought I was the only one, sensitive to something imagined—having "vapors," as somebody called it—but I could tell we were all at a loss for some reason none of us knew. Because if Ben and Eric knew, articulate as they were, they would have said so. In the silence so suddenly fallen, something was ticking.

Maybe, I thought, they just don't like Martinsville anymore. They always said that parties were dull and squirmed out of them when they could. I lay awake thinking, They'll move on soon; I won't see them again.

It was the next morning Eric called and we all grasped for Europe like the drowning, clinging to what we could.

———

After Monte Carlo, we left France by train and came down to Florence. The streets were narrow there and we joked about going single file like Indians. "What I need is moccasins," said Jamie, who was always blundering over the uneven paving stones. At the Uffizi, the second day, Eric, in a trance before Botticelli, fell silent. Could we ever get him to speak again? Hardly a word. Five in number, we leaned over the balustrades along the Arno, all silent then from the weariness of sight-seeing, and the heat, and there I heard it once more, the ticking of something hidden among us. Was it to deny it we decided to take the photograph? We had taken a lot, but this one, I think, was special. I have it still. It was in the Piazza Signoria.

"Which monument?" we kept asking. Ben wanted Donatello's lion, and Eric the steps of the Old Palace. Jamie wanted Cosimo I on his horse. I wanted the *Perseus* of Cellini, and Mayfred the *Rape of the Sabines*. So Ben made straws out of toothpicks and we drew and Mayfred won. We got lined up and Ben framed us. Then we had to find somebody, a slim Italian boy as it turned out, to snap us for a few hundred lire. It seemed we were proving something serious and good, and smiled with our straight family smiles, Jamie with his arm around Mayfred, and she with her smart new straw sun hat held to the back of her head, and me between Ben and Eric, arms entwined. A photo outlasts everybody, and this one with the frantic scene behind us, the moving torso of the warrior holding high the prey while we smiled our ordinary smiles—it was a period, the end of a phase.

Not that the photograph itself caused the end of anything. Donald Bailey caused it. He telephoned the pensione that night from Atlanta to say he was in the hospital, gravely ill, something they might have to operate for any day, some sort of brain tumor was what they were afraid of. Mayfred said she'd come.

We all got stunned. Ben and Eric and I straggled off together while she and Jamie went to the upstairs sitting room and sat in the corner. "Honest to God," said Eric, "I just didn't know Donald Bailey had a brain." "He had headaches," said Ben. "Oh, I knew he had a head," said Eric. "We could see that."

By night it was settled. Mayfred would fly back from Rome. Once again she got us to promise secrecy—how she did that I don't know, the youngest one and yet not even Ben could prevail on her one way or the other. By now she had spent most of her money. Donald, we knew, was rich; he came of a rich family and had, furthermore, money of his own. So if she wanted to fly back from Rome, the ticket, already purchased, would be waiting for her. Mayfred got to be privileged, in my opinion, because none of us knew her family too well. Her father was a blood cousin but not too highly regarded—he was thought to be a rather silly man who "traveled" and dealt with "all sorts of people"—and her mother was from "off," a Georgia girl, fluttery. If it had been my folks and if I had started all this wild marrying and flying off, Ben would have been on the phone to Martinsville by sundown.

One thing in the Mayfred departure that went without question: Jamie would go to Rome to see her off. We couldn't have sealed him in or held him with ropes. He had got on to something new in Italy, or so I felt, because where before then had we seen in gallery after gallery, strong men, young and old, with enraptured eyes, enthralled before a woman's painted image, wanting nothing? What he had got was an idea of devotion. It fitted him. It suited. He would do anything for Mayfred and want nothing. If she had got pregnant and told him she was a virgin, he would have sworn to it before the Inquisition. It could positively alarm you for him to see him satisfied with the feelings he had found. Long after I went to bed, he was at the door or in the corridor with Mayfred, discussing baggage and calling a hotel in Rome to get a reservation for when he saw her off.

Mayfred had bought a lot of things. She had an eye for what she could wear with what, and she would pick up pieces of this and that for putting costumes and accessories together. She had to get some extra luggage and it was Jamie, of course, who promised to see it sent safely to her, through a shipping company in Rome. His two thousand dollars was coming in handy, was all I could think.

Hot, I couldn't sleep, so I went out in the sitting room to find a magazine. Ben was up. The three men usually took a large room together, taking turns for the extra cot. Ever since we got the news, Ben had had what Eric called his "family mood." Now he called me over. "I can't let those kids go down there alone," he said. "They seem like children to me—and Jamie . . . about all he can say is *grazie* and *quanto*." "Then let's all go," I said, "I've given up sleeping for tonight, anyway." "Eric's hooked on Florence," said Ben. "Can't you tell? He counts the cypresses on every knoll. He can spot a Della Robbia a block off. If I make him leave three days early, he'll never forgive me. Besides, our reservations in that hotel can't be changed. We called for Jamie and they're full. He's staying third-class somewhere till we all come. I don't mind doing that. Then we'll all meet up just the way we planned, have our week in Rome and go catch the boat from Naples." "I think they could make it on their own," I said. "It's just that you'd worry every minute." He grinned; "Our father for the duration," was what Eric called him. "I know I'm that way," he said.

Another thing was that Ben had been getting little caches of letters at various points along our trek from his girl friend Sylvia, the one he'd been dating up at Sewanee. She was getting a job in New York that fall that would be convenient to Yale. She wrote a spidery hand on thick rippled stationery, cream colored, and had promised in her last dispatch, received in Paris, to write to Rome. Ben could have had an itch for that. But mainly he was that way, careful and concerned. He had in mind what we all felt, that just as absolutely anything could be done by Mayfred, so could absolutely anything happen to her. He also knew what we all knew: that if the Colosseum started falling on her, Jamie would leap bodily under the rocks.

At 2 A.M. it was too much for me to think about. I went to bed and was so exhausted, I didn't even hear Mayfred leave.

I woke up about ten with a low tapping on my door. It was Eric. "Is this the sleep of the just?" he asked me as I opened the door. The air in the corridor was fresh; it must have rained in the night. No one was about. All the guests, I supposed, were well out into the day's routine, seeing what next tour was on the list. On a trip you were always planning something. Ben planned for us. He kept a little notebook.

Standing in my doorway alone with Eric, in a loose robe with a cool morning breeze and my hair not even combed, I suddenly laughed. Eric laughed, too. "I'm glad they're gone," he said, and looked past my shoulder.

I dressed and went out with him for some breakfast, cappuccino and croissants at a café in the Signoria. We didn't talk much. It was terrible, in the sense of the Mason Skinner Marshall and Phillips sense of family, even to think you were glad they were gone, let alone say it. I took Eric's silence as one of his ironies, what he was best at. He would say, for instance, if you were discussing somebody's problem that wouldn't ever have a solution, "It's time somebody died." There wasn't much to say after that. Another time, when his daddy got into a rage with a next-door neighbor over their property line, Eric said, "You'd better marry her." Once he put things in an extreme light, nobody could talk about them anymore. Saying "I'm glad they're gone" was like that.

But it was a break. I thought of the way I'd been seeing them. How Jamie's becoming had been impressing me, every day more. How Mayfred was a kind of spirit, grown bigger than life. How Ben's dominance now seemed not worrisome, but princely, his heritage. We were into a Renaissance of ourselves, I wanted to say, but was afraid they wouldn't see it the way I did. Only Eric had eluded me. What was he becoming? For once he didn't have to discuss Poe's idea of women, or the Southern code of honor, or Henry James's views of France and England.

As for me, I was, at least, sure that my style had changed. I had bought my little linen blouses and loose skirts, my sandals and braided silver bracelets. "That's great on you!" Mayfred had cried. "Now try this one!" On the streets, Italians passed me too close not to be noticed; they murmured musically in my ear, saying I didn't know just what; waiters leaned on my shoulder to describe dishes of the day.

Eric and I wandered across the river, following narrow streets lined with great stone palaces, seeing them open into small piazzas whose names were not well-known. We had lunch in a friendly place with a curtain of thin twisted metal sticks in the open door, an amber-colored dog lying on the marble floor near the serving table. We ordered favorite things without looking at the menu. We drank white wine. "This is fun," I suddenly said. He turned to me. Out of his private distance, he seemed to be looking down at me. "I think so, too."

He suddenly switched on to me, like somebody searching and finding with the lens of a camera. He began to ask me things. What did you think of that, Ella Mason? What about this, Ella Mason? Ella Mason, did you think Ben was right when he said? . . . I could hardly swing on to what was being asked of me, thick and fast. But he seemed to like my answers, actually to listen. Not that all those years I'd been dumb as a stone. I had prattled quite a lot. It's just that they never treated me one to one, the way Eric was doing now. We talked for nearly an hour, then, with no one left in the restaurant but us, stopped as suddenly as we'd started. Eric said, "That's a pretty dress."

The sun was strong outside. The dog was asleep near the door. Even the one remaining waiter was drowsing on his feet. It was the shutting-up time for everything and we went out into streets blanked out with metal shutters. We hugged the shady side and went single file back to home base, as we'd come to call it, wherever we stayed.

A Vespa snarled by and I stepped into a cool courtyard to avoid it. I found myself in a large yawning mouth, mysterious as a cave, shadowy, with the trickling sound of a fountain and the glimmer in the depths of water running through ferns and moss. Along the interior of the street wall, fragments of ancient sculpture, found, I guess, when they'd built the palazzo, had been set into the masonry. One was a horse, neck and shoulder, another an arm holding a shield and a third at about my height the profile of a woman, a nymph or some such. Eric stopped to look at each, for, as Ben had said, Eric loved everything there, and then he said, "Come here, Ella Mason." I stood where he wanted, by the little sculptured relief, and he took my face and turned it to look at it closer. Then with a strong hand (I remembered tennis), he pressed my face against the stone face and held it for a moment. The stone bit into my flesh and that was the first time that Eric, bending deliberately to do so, kissed me on the mouth. He had held one side of me against the wall, so that I couldn't raise my arm to him, and the other arm was pinned down by his elbow; the hand that pressed my face into the stone was that one, so that I couldn't move closer to him, as I wanted to do, and when he dropped away suddenly, turned on his heel and walked rapidly away, I could only hasten to follow, my voice gone, my pulses all throbbing together. I remember my anger, the old dreams about him and Ben stirred to life again, thinking, *If he thinks he can just walk away,* and knowing with anger, too, *It's got to be now,* as if in the walled land of kinship, thicker in our illustrious connection than any fortress in Europe, a door had creaked open at last. Eric, Eric, Eric. I'm always seeing your retreating heels, how they looked angry. But why? It was worth coming for, after thirty years, to ask that. . . .

"That day you kissed me in the street, the first time," I asked him. Night on the terrace, a bottle of Chianti between our chairs. "You walked away. Were you angry? Your heels looked angry. I can see them still."

"The trip in the first place," he said, "it had to do with you partly. Maybe you didn't understand that. We were outward bound, leaving you, a sister in a sense. We'd talked about it."

"I adored you so," I said. "I think I was less than a sister, more like a dog."

"For a little while you weren't either one." He found my hand in the dark. "It was a wonderful little while."

Memories: Eric in the empty corridor of the pensione. How Italy folds up and goes to sleep from two to four. His not looking back for me, going straight to his door. The door closing, but no key turning and me turning the door handle and stepping in. And he at the window already with his back to me and how he heard the sliding latch on the door—I slid it with my hands behind me—heard it click shut and turned. His face and mine, what we knew. Betraying Ben.

:Walking by the Arno, watching a white-and-green scull stroking by into the twilight, the rower a boy or girl in white and green, growing dimmer to the rhythm of the long oars, vanishing into arrow shape, the pencil thickness, then movement without substance, on. . . .

:A trek the next afternoon through twisted streets to a famous chapel. Sitting quiet in a cloister, drinking in the symmetry, the silence. Holding hands. "'D' is for Donatello," said Eric. "'D' for Della Robbia," I said. "'M' for Michelangelo," he continued. "'M' for Medici." "'L' for Leonardo." "I can't think of an 'L,'" I gave up. "Lumbago. There's an old master." "Worse than Jamie." We were always going home again.

:Running into the manager of the pensione one morning in the corridor. He'd solemnly bowed to us and kissed my hand. *"Bella ragazza,"* he remarked. "The way life ought to be," said Eric. I thought we might be free forever, but from what?

At the train station waiting the departure we were supposed to take for Rome, "Why do we have to go?" I pleaded. "Why can't we just stay here?"

"Use your common sense, Ella Mason."

"I don't have any."

He squeezed my shoulder. "We'll get by all right," he said. "That is, if you don't let on."

I promised not to. Rather languidly I watched the landscape slide past as we glided south. I would obey Eric, I thought, for always. "Once I wrote a love letter to you," I said. "I wrote it at night by candlelight at home one summer. I tore it up."

"You told me that," he recalled, "but you said you couldn't remember if it was to me or Ben."

"I just remembered," I said. "It was you. . . ."

"Why did we ever leave?" I asked Eric in the dead of the night, a blackness now. "Why did we ever decide we had to go to Rome?"

"I didn't think of it as even a choice," he said. "But at that point, how could I know what was there, ahead?"

———

We got off the train feeling small—at least, I did. Ben was standing there, looking around him, tall, searching for us, then seeing. But no

Jamie. Something to ask. I wondered if he'd gone back with May-fred. "No, he's running around Rome." The big smooth station, echoing, open to the warm day. "Hundreds of churches," Ben went on. "Millions. He's checking them off." He helped us in a taxi with the skill of somebody who'd lived in Rome for ten years, and gave the address. "He's got to do something now that Mayfred's gone. It's getting like something he might take seriously, is all. Finding out what Catholics believe. He's either losing all his money, or falling in love, or getting religion."

"He didn't lose any money," said Eric. "He made some."

"Well, it's the same thing," said Ben, always right and not wanting to argue with us. He seemed a lot older than the two of us, at least to me. Ben was tall.

We had mail in Rome; Ben brought it to the table that night. I read Mama's aloud to them: "'When I think of you children over there, I count you all like my own chickens out in the yard, thinking I've got to go out in the dark and make sure the gate's locked because not a one ought to get out of there. To me, you're all my own, and thinking of chickens is my way of saying prayers for you to be safe at home again.'"

"You'd think we were off in a war," said Eric.

"It's a bold metaphor," said Ben, pouring wine for us, "but that never stopped Cousin Charlotte."

I wanted to giggle at Mama, as I usually did, but instead my eyes filled with tears, surprising me, and a minute more and I would have dared to snap at Ben. But, Eric, who had got some mail, too, abruptly got up and left the table. I almost ran after him, but intent on what I'd promised about not letting on to Ben, I stayed and finished dinner. He had been pale, white. Ben thought he might be sick. He didn't return. We didn't know.

Jamie and Ben finally went to bed. "He'll come back when he wants to," said Ben.

I waited till their door had closed, and then, possessed, I crept out to the front desk. "Signor Mason," I said, "the one with the *capelli leggero*—" My Italian came from the dictionary straight to the listener. I found out later I had said that Eric's hair didn't weigh much. Still, they understood. He had taken a room, someone who spoke English explained. He wanted to be alone. I said he might be sick, and I guess they could read my face, because I was guided by a porter in a blue working jacket and cloth shoes, into a labyrinth. Italian buildings, I knew by now, are constructed like dreams. There are passages departing from central hallways, stairs that twist back upon themselves, dark silent doors. My guide stopped before one. *"Ecco,"* he said, and left. I knocked softly, and the door eventually cracked open. "Oh, it's you." "Eric. Are you all right? I didn't know . . ."

He opened the door a little wider. "Ella Mason——" he began. Maybe he was sick. I caught his arm. The whole intensity of my young life in that moment shook free of everything but Eric. It was as though I'd traveled miles to find him. I came inside and we kissed, and then I was sitting apart from him on the edge of the bed and he in a chair, and a letter, official-looking, the top of the envelope torn open in a ragged line, lay on a high black-marble-topped table with bowed legs, between us. He said to read it and I did, and put it back where I found it.

It said that Eric had failed his law exams. That in view of the family connection with the university (his father had gone there and some cousin was head of the board of trustees), a special meeting had been held to grant his repeating the term's work so as to graduate in the fall, but the evidences of his negligence were too numerous and the vote had gone against it. I remember saying something like, "Anybody can fail exams——" as I knew people who had, but knew, also, that those people weren't "us," not one of our class or connection, not kin to the brilliant Ben, or nephew of a governor, or descended from a great Civil War general.

"All year long," he said, "I've been acting like a fool, as if I expected to get by. This last semester especially. It all seemed too easy. It is easy. It's easy and boring. I was fencing blindfold with somebody so far beneath me it wasn't worth the trouble to look at him. The only way to keep the interest up was to see how close I could come without damage. Well, I ran right into it, head on. God, does it serve me right. I'd read books Ben was reading, follow his interests, instead of boning over law. But I wanted the degree. Hot damn, I wanted it!"

"Another school," I said. "You can transfer credits and start over."

"This won't go away."

"Everybody loves you," I faltered, adding, "Especially me."

He almost laughed, at my youngness, I guess, but then said, "Ella Mason," as gently as feathers falling, and came to hold me a while, but not like before, the way we'd been. We sat down on the bed and then fell back on it and I could hear his heart's steady thumping under his shirt. But it wasn't the beat of a lover's heart just then; it was more like the echo of a distant bell or the near march of a clock, and I fell to looking over his shoulder.

It was a curious room, one I guess they wouldn't have rented to anybody if Rome hadn't been, as they told us, so full. The shutters were closed on something that suggested more of a courtyard than the outside as no streak or glimmer of light came through, and the bed was huge, with a great dark tall rectangle of a headboard and a footboard only slightly lower. There were brass sconces set ornamentally around the moldings, looking down, cupids and fawns and smiling goat faces, with bulbs concealed in them, though the only light came from the one dim lamp on the bedside table. There were heavy, dark engravings of Rome—by Piranesi or somebody like that—the avenues, the monuments, the river. And one panel of small pictures in a series showed some familiar scenes in Florence.

My thoughts, unable to reach Eric's, kept wandering off tourist fashion among the myth faces peeking from the sconces, laughing down, among the walks of Rome—the arched bridge over the Tiber where life-size angels stood poised; the rise of the Palatine, mysterious among trees; the horseman on the Campidoglio, his hand outstretched; and Florence, beckoning still. I couldn't keep my mind at any one set with all such around me, and Eric, besides, had gone back to the table and was writing a letter on hotel stationery. When my caught breath turned to a little cry, he looked up and said, "It's my problem, Ella Mason. Just let me handle it." He came to stand by me, and pressed my head against him, then lifted my face by the chin. "Don't go talking about it. Promise." I promised.

I wandered back through the labyrinth, thinking I'd be lost in there forever like a Poe lady. Damn Ben, I thought, he's too above it all for anybody to fall in love or fail an examination. I'm better off lost, at this rate. So thinking, I turned a corner and stepped out into the hotel lobby.

It was Jamie's and Ben's assumption that Eric had picked up some girl and gone home with her. I never told them better. Let them think that.

———

"Your mama wrote you a letter about some chickens once, how she counted children like counting chickens," Eric said, thirty years later. "Do you remember that?"

We fell to remembering Mama. "There's nobody like her," I said. "She has long talks with Papa. They started a year or so after he died. I wish I could talk to him."

"What would you say?"

"I'd ask him to look up Howard. See 'f he's doing all right."

"Your husband?" Eric wasn't sure of the name.

I guess joking about your husband's death isn't quite the thing. I met Howard on a trip to Texas after we got home from abroad. I was visiting my roommate. Whatever else Eric did for me, our time together had made me ready for more. I pined for him alone, but what I looked was ripe and ready for practically anybody. So Howard said. He was a widower with a Texas-size fortune. When he said I looked like a good breeder, I didn't even get mad. That's how he knew I'd do. Still, it took a while. I kept wanting Eric, wanting my old dream: my brilliant cousins, princely, cavalier.

Howard and I had two sons, in their twenties now. Howard got killed in a jeep accident out on his cattle ranch. Don't think I didn't get married again, to a wild California boy ten years younger. It lasted six months exactly.

"What about that other one?" Eric asked me. "Number two."

I had got the divorce papers the same day they called to say Howard's tombstone had arrived. "Well, you know, Eric, I always was a little bit crazy."

"You thought he was cute."

"I guess so."

"You and I," said Eric, smooth as silk into the deep silent darkness that now was ours—even the towers seemed to have folded up and gone home—"we never worked it out, did we?"

"I never knew if you really wanted to. I did, God knows. I wouldn't marry Howard for over a year because of you."

"I stayed undecided about everything. One thing that's not is a marrying frame of mind."

"Then you left for Europe."

"I felt I'd missed the boat for everywhere else. War service, then that law school thing. It was too late for me. And nothing was of interest. I could move but not with much conviction. I felt for you—maybe more than you know—but you were moving on already. You know, Ella Mason, you never are still."

"But you could have told me that!"

"I think I did, one way or another. You sat still and fidgeted." He laughed.

It's true that energy is my middle name.

The lights along the river were dim and so little was moving past by now they seemed fixed and distant, stars from some long-dead galaxy, maybe. I think I slept. Then I heard Eric.

"I think back so often to the five of us—you and Ben, Jamie and Mayfred and me. There was something I could never get out of mind. You remember when we were planning everything about Europe, Europe, Europe before we left, and you'd all come over to my house and we'd sit out on the side porch, listening to Ben mainly, but with Jamie asking some questions like, 'Do they have bathtubs like us?' Remember that? You would snuggle down in one of those canvas chairs like a sling, and Ben was in the big armchair—Daddy's—and Jamie sort of sprawled around on the couch among the travel folders, when we heard the front gate scrape on the sidewalk and heard the way it would clatter when it closed. A warm night and the streetlight filtering in patterns through the trees and shrubs and a smell of honeysuckle from where it was all baled up on the yard fence and a cape jessamine outside, I remember that, too—white flowers in among the leaves. And steps on the walk. They stopped, then they walked again, and Ben got up (I should have) and unlatched the screen. If you didn't latch the screen it wouldn't shut. Mayfred came in. Jamie said, 'Why'd you stop on the walk, Mayfred?' She said, 'There was this toad-frog. I almost stepped on him.' Then she was among us, walking in, one of us. I was sitting back in the corner, watching, and I felt, If I live to be a thousand, I'll never feel more love than I do this minute. Love of these, my blood, and this place, here. I could close my eyes for years and hear the gate scrape, the steps pause, the door latch and unlatch, hear her say, 'There was this toad-frog...' I would want literally to embrace that one minute, hold it forever."

"But you're not there," I said into the dark. "You're here. Where we were. You chose it."

"There's no denying that," was all he answered.

———

We had sailed from Naples, a sad day under mist, with Vesuvius hardly visible and a damp clinging to everything—the end of summer. We couldn't even make out the outlines of the ship, an Italian-line monster from those days called the *Independence*. It towered white over us and we tunneled in. The crossing was rainy and drab. Crossed emotions played around among us, while Ben, noble and aware, tried to be our mast. He read aloud to us, discussed, joked, tried to get our attention.

Jamie wanted to argue about Catholicism. It didn't suit Ben for him to drift that way. Ben was headed toward Anglican belief: that's what his Sylvia was, not to mention T. S. Eliot. But Jamie had met an American Jesuit from Indiana in Rome and chummed around with him; they'd even gone to the beach. "You're wrong about that," I heard him tell Ben. "I'm going to prove it by Father Rogers when we get home."

I worried about Eric; I longed for Eric; I strolled the decks and stood by Eric at the rail. He looked with gray eyes out at the gray sea. He said, "You know, Ella Mason, I don't give a damn if Jamie joins the Catholic Church or not." "Me either," I agreed. We kissed in the dark beneath the lifeboats, and made love once in the cabin while Ben and Jamie were at the movies, but in a furtive way, as if the grown people were at church. Ben read aloud to us from a book on Hadrian's Villa, where we'd all been. There was a half day of sun.

I went to the pool to swim, and up came Jamie, out of the water. He was skinny, string beans and spaghetti. "Ella Mason," he said in his dark croak of a voice, "I'll never be the same again." I was tired of all of them, even Jamie. "Then gain some weight," I snapped, and went pretty off the diving board.

Ben knew about the law-school thing. The first day out, coming from the writing lounge, I saw Eric and Ben standing together in a corner of an enclosed deck. Ben had a letter in his hand, and just from one glance I recognized the stationery of the hotel where we'd stayed in Rome and knew it was the letter Eric had been writing. I heard Ben. "You say it's not important, but I know it is—I knew that last Christmas." And Eric, "Think what you like, it's not to me." And Ben, "What you feel about it, that's not what matters. There's a right way of looking at it. Only to make you see it." And Eric, "You'd better give up. You never will."

What kept me in my tracks was something multiple, yet single, the way a number can contain powers and elements that have gone into its making and can be unfolded, opened up, nearly forever. Ambition and why some had it, success and failure and what the difference was and why you had to notice it at all. These matters, back and forth across the net, were what was going on.

What had stopped me in the first place, though, and chilled me, was that they sounded angry. I knew they had quarreled last Christmas; was this why? It must have been. Ben's anger was attack and Eric's self-defense, defiance. Hadn't they always been like brothers? Yes, and they were standing so, intent, a little apart, in hot debate, like two officers locked in different plans of attack at dawn, stubbornly held to the point of fury. Ben's position, based on rightness, classical and firm. Enforced by what he was. And Eric's wrong, except in and for himself, for holding on to himself. How to defend that? He couldn't, but he did. And equally. They were just looking up and seeing me, and nervous at my intrusion I stepped across the high shipboard sill to the deck, missed clearing it and fell sprawling.

"Oh, Ella Mason!" they cried at once, and picked me up, the way they always had.

One more thing I remember from that ship. It was Ben, finding me one night after dinner alone in the lounge. Everyone was below: we were docking in the morning. He sat down and lighted his pipe. "It's all passed so fast, don't you think?" he said. There was such a jumble in my mind still, I didn't answer. All I could hear was Eric saying, after we'd made love, "It's got to stop now. I've got to find some shape to things. There was promise, promises. You've got to see we're saying they're worthless, that nothing matters." What did matter to me, except Eric? "I wish I'd never come," I burst out at Ben, childish, hurting him, I guess. How much did Ben know? He never said. He came close and put his arm around me. "You're the sister I never had," he said. "I hope you change your mind about it." I said I was sorry and snuffled awhile into his shoulder. When I looked up, I saw his love. So maybe he did know, and forgave us. He kissed my forehead.

———

At the New York pier, who should show up but Mayfred.

She was crisp in black and white, her long blond hair wind shaken, her laughter a wholesome joy. "Y'all look just terrible," she told us with a friendly giggle, and as usual made us straighten up, tuck our tummies in and look like quality. Jamie forgot religion, and Eric quit worrying over a missing bag, and Ben said, "Well, look who's here!" "How's Donald?" I asked her. I figured he was either all right or dead. The first was true. They didn't have to do a brain-tumor operation; all he'd had was a pinched nerve at the base of his cortex. "What's a cortex?" Jamie asked. "It sounds too personal to inquire," said Eric, and right then they brought him his bag.

On the train home, Mayfred rode backward in our large drawing-room compartment (courtesy of Donald Bailey) and the landscape, getting more Southern every minute, went rocketing past. "You can't guess how I spent my time when Donald was in the hospital. Nothing to do but sit."

"Working crossword puzzles," said Jamie.

"Crocheting," said Eric, provoking a laugh.

"Reading *Vogue*," said Ben.

"All wrong! I read Edgar Allan Poe! What's more, I memorized that poem! That one Ben wrote on. You know? That 'Ulalume'!"

Everybody laughed but Ben, and Mayfred was laughing, too, her grand girlish sputters, innocent as sun and water, her beautiful large white teeth, even as a cover girl's. Ben, courteously at the end of the sofa, smiled faintly. It was best not to believe this was true.

> "'*The skies they were ashen and sober;*
>   *The leaves they were crispéd and sere—*
>   *The leaves they were withering and sere:*
> *It was night in the lonesome October*
>   *Of my most immemorial year. . . .*'"

"By God, she's done it," said Ben.

At that point Jamie and I began to laugh, and Eric, who had at first looked quizzical, started laughing, too. Ben said, "Oh, cut it out, Mayfred." But she said, "No, sir, I'm not! I *did* all that. I know *every* word! Just wait, I'll show you." She went right on, full speed, to the "ghoul-haunted woodland of Weir."

Back as straight as a ramrod, Ben left the compartment. Mayfred stopped. An hour later, when he came back, she started again. But it wasn't till she got to Psyche "uplifting her finger" (Mayfred lifted hers) saying, "'Oh, fly!—let us fly!—for we must,'" and all that about the "tremulous light, the crystalline light," et cetera, that Ben gave up and joined in the general merriment. She actually did know it, every word. He followed along open-mouthed through "Astarte" and "Sybillic," and murmured, "Oh, my God," when she got to:

> "'*Ulalume—Ulalume—*
>   '*Tis the vault of thy lost Ulalume!*'"

because she let go in a wail like a hound's bugle and the conductor, who was passing, looked in to see if we were all right.

We rolled into Chattanooga in the best of humor and filed off the train into the waiting arms of my parents, Eric's parents and selected members from Ben's and Jamie's families. There was nobody from Mayfred's, but they'd sent word. They all kept checking us over, as though we might need washing or might have got scarred some way. "Just promise me one thing!" Mama kept saying, just about to cry. "Don't y'all ever go away again, you hear? Not all of you! Just promise you won't do it! Promise me right now!"

I guess we must have promised, the way she was begging us to.

———

Ben married his Sylvia, with her pedigree and family estate in Connecticut. He's a big professor, lecturing in literature, up East. Jamie married a Catholic girl from West Virginia. He works in her father's firm and has sired a happy lot of kids. Mayfred went to New York after she left Donald and works for a big fashion house. She's been in and out of marriages, from time to time.

And Eric and I are sitting holding hands on a terrace in far off Italy. Midnight struck long ago, and we know it. We are sitting there, talking, in the pitch-black dark.

THE LIGHT IN THE PIAZZA

TO JOHN

1

On a June afternoon at sunset, an American woman and her daughter fended their way along a crowded street in Florence and entered with relief the spacious Piazza della Signoria. They were tired from a day of tramping about with a guidebook, often in the sun. The café that faced the Palazzo Vecchio was a favorite spot for them; without discussion they sank down at an empty table. The Florentines seemed to favor other gathering places at this hour. No cars were allowed here, though an occasional bicycle skimmed through, and a few people, passing, met in little knots of conversation, then dispersed. A couple of tired German tourists, all but harnessed in fine camera equipment, sat at the foot of Cellini's triumphant *Perseus,* slumped and staring at nothing.

Margaret Johnson, lighting a cigarette, relaxed over her aperitif and regarded the scene that she preferred before any other, anywhere. She never got enough of it, and now in the clear evening light that all the shadows had gone from—the sun being blocked away by the tight bulk of the city—she looked at the splendid old palace and forgot that her feet hurt. More than that: here she could almost lose the sorrow that for so many years had been a constant of her life. About the crenellated tower where the bells hung, a few swallows darted.

Margaret Johnson's daughter, Clara, looked up from the straw of her orangeade. She, too, seemed quieted from the fretful mood to which the long day had reduced her. "What happened here, Mother?"

"Well, the statue over there, the tall white boy, is by Michelangelo. You remember him. Then—though it isn't a very happy thought—there was a man burned to death right over there, a monk."

Any story attracted her. "Why was he burned?"

"Well, he was a preacher who told them they were wicked and they didn't like him for it. People were apt to be very cruel in those days. It all happened a long while ago. They must feel sorry about it, because they put down a marker to his memory."

Clara jumped up. "I want to see!" She was off before her mother could restrain her. For once Margaret Johnson thought, Why bother? In truth the space before them, so satisfyingly wide, like a pasture, might tempt any child to run across it. To Margaret Johnson, through long habit, it came naturally now to think like a child. Clara, she now saw, running with her head down to look for the marker, had bumped squarely into a young Italian. There went the straw hat she had bought in Fiesole. It sailed off prettily, its broad red ribbon a quick mark in the air. The young man was after it; he contrived to knock it still farther away, once and again, though the day was windless; his final success was heroic. Now he was returning, smiling, too graceful to be true; they were all too graceful to be true. Clara was talking to him. She pointed back toward her mother. Oh, Lord! He was coming back with Clara.

Margaret Johnson, confronted at close range by two such radiant young faces, was careful not to produce a very cordial smile.

"We met him before, Mother. Don't you remember?"

She didn't. They all looked like carbon copies of one another.

He gave a suggestion of a bow. "My—store—" English was coming out. "It—is—near—Piazza della Repubblica—how do you say? The beeg square. Oh, yes, and on Sunday, *si fanno la musica*. Museek, bom, bom." He was a whole orchestra, though his gestures were small. "And the lady—" Now a busty Neapolitan soprano sprang to view, in pink lace, one hand clenched to her heart. Margaret Johnson could not help laughing. Clara was delighted.

Ah, he had pleased. He dropped the role at once. "My store—is there." A chair was vacant. "Please?" He sat. Here came the inevitable card. They were shoppers, after all, or would be. Well, it was better than compliments, offers to guide them, thought Mrs. Johnson. She took the card. It was in English except for the unpronounceable name. "'Via Strozzi 8,'" she read. "'Ties. Borsalino Hats. Gloves. Handkerchiefs. Everything for the Gentlemens.'"

"Not for you. But for your husband," he said to Mrs. Johnson. In these phrases he was perfectly at home.

"He isn't here, unfortunately."

"Ah, but you must take him presents. Excuse me." Now Clara was given a card. "And for your husband, also."

She giggled. "I don't have a husband!"

"Signorina! Ah! Forgive me." He touched his breast. Again the quick suggestion of a bow. "Fabrizio Naccarelli."

It sounded like a whole aria.

"I'm Clara Johnson," the girl said at once. Mrs. Johnson closed her eyes.

"Gian—Gian—" He strained for it.

"No, *Johnson.*"

"Ah! Van Johnson!"

"That's right!"

"He is—*cugino—parente—famiglia?*"

"No," said Mrs. Johnson irritably. She prided herself on her tolerance and interest among foreigners, but she was tired, and Italians are so inquisitive. Given ten words of English they will invent a hundred questions from them. This one at least was sensitive. He withdrew at once. "Clara," he said as if to himself. No trouble there. The girl gave him her innocent smile.

Indeed, she could be remarkably lovely when pleased. The somewhat long lines of her cheek and jaw drooped when she was down-hearted, but happiness drew her up perfectly. Her dark-blue eyes grew serene and clear; her chestnut hair in its long girlish cut shadowed her smooth skin.

Due to an accident years ago, she had the mental age of a child of ten. But anyone on earth, meeting her for the first time, would have found this incredible. Mrs. Johnson had managed in many tactful ways to explain her daughter to young men without wounding them. She could even keep them from feeling too sorry for herself. "Every mother in some way wants a little girl who never grows up. Taken in that light, I do often feel fortunate. She is remarkably sweet, you see, and I find her a great satisfaction." She did not foresee any such necessity with an Italian out principally to sell everything for the "gentlemens." No, he could not offer them anything else. No, he certainly could not pay the check. He had been very kind ... very kind ... yes, yes, very, very kind. ...

2

But Fabrizio Naccarelli, whether Margaret Johnson had cared to master his name or not, was not one to be underestimated. He was very much at home in Florence, where he had been born and his father before him and so on straight back to the misty days before the Medici, and he had given, besides, some little attention to the ways of the *stranieri* who were always coming to his hometown. It seemed in the next few days that he showed up on every street corner. Surely he could not have counted so much on the tie they might decide to buy for Signor Johnson.

Clara invariably lighted up when they saw him, and he in turn communicated over and over his innocent pleasure in this happiest of coincidences. Mrs. Johnson noted that at each encounter he managed to extract from them some new piece of information, foremost among them, how long would they remain? Caught between two necessities, that of lying to him and not lying to her daughter, she revealed that the date was uncertain, and saw the flicker of triumph in his eyes. And the next time they met—well, it was too much. By then they were friends. Could he offer them dinner that evening? He knew a place only for Florentines—good, good, very good. "Oh, yes!" said Clara. Mrs. Johnson demurred. He was very kind, but in the evenings they were always too tired. She was drawing Clara away in a pretense of hurry. The museum might close at noon. At the mention of noon the city bells began clanging all around them. It was difficult to hear. "In the piazza," he cried in farewell, with a gesture toward the Piazza della Signoria, smiling at Clara, who waved her hand, though Mrs. Johnson went on saying, "No, we can't," and shaking her head.

Late that afternoon, they were taking a cup of tea in the big casino near Piazzale Michelangelo, when Clara looked at her watch and said they must go.

"Oh, let's stay a little while longer and watch the sun set," her mother suggested.

"But we have to meet Fabrizio." The odd name came naturally to her tongue.

"Darling, Fabrizio will probably be busy until very late."

It was always hard for Mrs. Johnson to face the troubling-over of her daughter's wide, imploring eyes. Perhaps she should make some pretense, though pretense was the very thing she had constantly to guard against. The doctors had been very firm with her here. As hard as it was to be the source of disappointment, such decisions had to be made. They must be communicated, tactfully, patiently, reasonably. Clara must never feel that she had been deceived. Her whole personality might become confused. Mrs. Johnson sighed, remembering all this, and began her task.

"Fabrizio will understand if we do not come, Clara, because I told him this morning we could not. You remember that I did? I told him that because I don't think we should make friends with him."

"Why?"

"Because he has his own life here and he will stay here always. But we must go away. We have to go back home and see Daddy and Brother and Ronnie—" Ronnie was Clara's collie dog—"and Auntie and all the others. You know how hard it was to leave Ronnie even though you were coming back? Well, it would be very hard to like Fabrizio, wouldn't it, and leave him and never come back at all?"

"But I already like him," said Clara. "I could write him letters," she added wistfully.

"Things are often hard," said Mrs. Johnson in her most cheery and encouraging tone.

It seemed a crucial evening. She did not trust Fabrizio not to call for them at their hotel, or doubt for a moment that he had informed himself exactly where they were staying. So she was careful before dinner to steer Clara to that other piazza—not the Signoria—once the closing hour for the shops had passed. Secure in the pushing crowds of Florentines, she chose one of the less fashionable cafés, settling at a corner table behind a green hedge that grew out of boxes and over the top of which there presently appeared the face of Fabrizio.

She saw him first in Clara's eyes. Next he was beaming upon them. There had been a mistake, of course. He had said only piazza piazza. How could they know? *Difficile*. He was so sorry. Pardon, pardon.

There was simply nothing to be gained by trying to stare him down. His great eyes showed concern, relief, gaiety as clearly as if the words had been written on them, but self-betrayal was unknown to him. Trying to surprise him at his game, one grew distracted and became aware how beautiful his eyes were. His dress gave him away if anything did. Nothing could be neater, cleaner, more carefully or sleekly tailored. His shirt was starched and white; his black hair still gleamed faintly damp at the edges; his close-cut, cuffless gray trousers ended in new black shoes of a pebbly leather with pointed toes. A faint whiff of cologne seemed to come from him. There was something too much here, and a little touching. Well, they would be leaving soon, thought Mrs. Johnson. She decided to relax and enjoy the evening.

But more than this was in it.

When she finally sat back from her excellent meal, lighting a cigarette and setting down her little cup of coffee, she glanced from the distance of her age toward the two young people. It was an advantage that Clara knew no Italian. She smiled sweetly and laughed innocently, so how was Fabrizio to know her dreary secret? Now Clara had taken out all her store of coins, the aluminum five- and ten-lire pieces that amused her, and was setting them on the table in little groups, pyramids and squares and triangles. Fabrizio, his handsome cheek leaning against his palm, was helping her with the tip of one finger, setting now this one, now that one in place. They looked like two children, thought Mrs. Johnson.

It was as if a curtain had lifted before her eyes. The life she had thought forever closed to her daughter spread out its great pastoral vista.

After all, she thought, why not?

3

But, of course, the whole idea was absurd. She remembered it at once when she awoke the next morning, and flinched. I must have had too much wine, she thought.

"I think we must leave for Rome in a day or two," said Mrs. Johnson.

"Oh, Mother!" Clara's face fell.

It was a mistake to set her brooding on a bad day. The rain that had started with a rumble of thunder in the early morning hours was splashing down on the stone city. From their window a curtain of gray hung over the river, dimming the outlines of buildings on the opposite bank. The *carrozza* drivers huddled in chilly bird shapes under their great black umbrellas; the horses stood in crook-legged misery; and water streamed down all the statues. Mrs. Johnson and Clara put on sweaters and went downstairs to the lobby, where Clara was persuaded to write postcards. Once started, the task absorbed her. The selection of which picture for whom, the careful printing of the short sentences. Even Ronnie must have the card picked especially for him, a statue of a Roman dog. Toward lunchtime the sun broke out beautifully. Clara knew the instant it did and startled her mother, who was looking through a magazine.

"It's quit raining!"

Mrs. Johnson was quick. "Yes, and I think if it gets hot again in the afternoon we should go up to the big park and take a swim. You know how you love to swim, and I miss it, too. Wouldn't that be fun?"

She had her difficulties, but when they had walked a short way along streets that were misty from the drying rain, had eaten in a small restaurant but seen no sign of anyone they knew, Clara was persuaded.

Mrs. Johnson enjoyed the afternoon. The park had been refreshed by the rain, and the sun sparkled hot and bright on the pool. They swam and bought ice cream on sticks from the vender, and everyone smiled at them, obviously acknowledging a good sight. Mrs. Johnson, though blond, had the kind of skin that never quite lost the good tan she had once given it, and her figure retained its trim firmness. She showed what she was: the busy American housewife, mother, hostess, cook and civic leader who paid attention to her looks. She sat on a bench near the pool, drying in the sun, smoking, her smart beach bag open beside her, watching her daughter, who swam like a fish, flashing here and there in the pool. She plucked idly at the wet ends of her hair and wondered if she needed another rinse. She observed without the slightest surprise the head and shoulders of Fabrizio surfacing below the diving board, as though he had been swimming underwater the entire time since they had arrived.

Like most Italians he was proud of his body and, having made his appearance, lost no time in getting out of the water. He was in truth slightly bowlegged, but he concealed the flaw by standing in partial profile with one knee bent.

Well, thought Mrs. Johnson, it was just too much for her. She watched them splash water in each other's faces, watched Clara push Fabrizio into the pool, Fabrizio pretend to push Clara into the pool, Clara chase Fabrizio out among the shrubs and down the fall of ground nearby. Endlessly energetic, they flitted like butterflies through the sunlight. Except that butterflies, thought Mrs. Johnson, do not really think very much about sex. The final thing that had happened at home, that had really decided them on another trip abroad, was that Clara had run out one day and flung her arms around the grocery boy.

These problems had been faced; they had been reasoned out, patiently explained; it was understood what one did and didn't do to be good. But impulse is innocent about what is good or bad. A scar on the right side of her daughter's head, hidden by hair, lingered, shaped like the new moon. It was where her Shetland pony, cropping grass, had kicked in a temper at whatever was annoying him. Mrs. Johnson had been looking through the window, and she still remembered the silence that had followed her daughter's sidelong fall, more heart numbing than any possible cry.

Things would certainly take care of themselves sooner or later, Mrs. Johnson assured herself. She had seen the puzzled look commence on many a face, and had begun the weary maneuvering to see yet another person alone before the next meeting with Clara. Right now, for instance—Clara could never play for long without growing hysterical, screaming even. There, she had almost tripped Fabrizio; he had done an exaggerated flip in the air. She collapsed into laughter, gasping, her two hands thrust in her face in a spasm. Poor child, thought her mother. But then Fabrizio came to her and took her hands down. In one quick motion he stood her straight, and she grew quiet. Something turned over in Mrs. Johnson's breast.

They stood before her, panting, their sun-dried skin like so much velvet. "Look," cried Clara, and parted her hair above her ear. "I have a scar over my ear!" She pointed. "A scar. See!"

Fabrizio struck down her hand and put her hair straight. "*No. Ma sono belli.* Your hair—is beautiful."

We must certainly leave for Rome tomorrow, Mrs. Johnson thought. She heard herself thinking it, at some distance, as though in a dream.

She entered thus from that day a conscious duality of existence, knowing what she should and must do and making no motion toward doing it. The Latin temperament may thrive on such subtleties and never find it necessary to conclude them, but to Mrs. Johnson the experience was strange and new. It confused her. She believed, as most Anglo-Saxons do, that she always acted logically and to the best of her ability on whatever she knew to be true. And now she found this quality immobilized and all her actions taken over by the simple drift of the days.

She had, in fact, come face to face with Italy.

4

Something surely would arise to help her.

One had only to sit still while Fabrizio—he of the endless resource—outgeneraled himself and so caught on, or until he tired of them and dreamed of something else. One had only to make sure that Clara went nowhere alone with him. The girl had not a rebellious bone in her, and under her mother's eye she could be kept in tune.

But if Mrs. Johnson had been consciously striving to make a match, she could not have discovered a better line to take. Fabrizio's father was Florentine, but his mother was a Neapolitan, who went regularly to mass and was suspicious of foreigners. She received with approval the news that the *piccola signorina americana* was not allowed to so much as mail a postcard without her mother along. "*Ma sono italiane?* Are they Italian?" She wanted to know. "*No, Mamma, non credo.*" And though Fabrizio declaimed his grand impatience with the *signora americana,* in his heart he was pleased.

A few days later, to the immense surprise of Fabrizio, who was taking coffee with the ladies in the big piazza, they happened to be noticed by an Italian gentleman, rather broad in girth, with a high-bridged Florentine nose and a pair of close-set, keen, cold eyes. "*Ah, Papà!*" cried Fabrizio. "*Fortuna! Signora, signorina, permette.* My father."

Signor Naccarelli spoke English very well indeed. Yes, it was a bit rusty perhaps; he must apologize. He had known many Americans during the war, had done certain small things for them in liaison during the occupation. He had found them very *simpatici,* quite unlike the Germans, whom he detested.

This was a set speech. It gave him time. His face was not at all regular; the jaw went sideways from his high forehead, and his mouth, like Fabrizio's, was somewhat thin. But his eye was pale, and he and Mrs. Johnson did not waste time in taking each other's measure. She sensed his intelligence at once. Now at last, she thought ruefully, between disappointment and relief, the game would be up.

Sitting sideways at the little table, his legs neatly crossed, Signor Naccarelli received his coffee, black as pitch. He downed it in one swallow. The general pleasantries about Florence were duly exchanged. And they were staying? At the Grand. Ah.

"*Domani festa,*" he noted. "I say tomorrow is a holiday, a big one for us here. It is our saint's day, San Giovanni. You have perhaps seen in the Signoria, they are putting up the seats. Do you go?"

Well, she supposed they should really; it was a thing to watch. And the spectacle beforehand? She thought perhaps she could get tickets at the hotel. Signor Naccarelli was struck by an idea. He by chance had extra tickets and the seats were good. She must excuse it if his signora did not come; she was in mourning.

"Oh, I'm very sorry," said Mrs. Johnson.

He waved his hand. No matter. Her family in Naples was a large one; somebody was always dying. He sometimes wore the black band, but then someone might ask him who was dead and if he could not really remember? *Che figura!* His humor and laugh came and were over as fast as something being broken. "And now—you will come?"

"Well—"

"Good! Then my son will arrange where we are to meet and the hour." He was so quickly on his feet. "Signora." He kissed her hand. "Signorina." Clara had learned to put out her hand quite prettily in the European fashion and she liked to do it. With a nod to Fabrizio he was gone.

So the next afternoon they were guided expertly through the packed, noisy streets of the *festa* by Fabrizio, who found them a choice point for watching the parade of the nobles. It seemed that twice a year, and that by coincidence during the tourist season, Florentine custom demanded that titled gentlemen should wedge themselves into the family suit of armor, mount a horse and ride in procession, preceded by lesser men in striped knee breeches beating drums. Pennants were twirled as crowds cheered, and while it was doubtless not as thrilling a spectacle as the Palio in Siena, everyone agreed that it was in much better taste. Who in Florence would dream of bringing a horse into church? Afterward in the piazza, two teams in red and green jerseys would sweat their way through a free-for-all of kicking and running and knocking each other down. This was medieval *calcio;* the program explained that it was the ancestor of American footballs. Fabrizio, whose English was improving, managed to convey that his brother might have been entitled to ride with the nobles, although it was true he was not in direct line for a title. Instead, his cousin, the Marchese della Valle—there he went now, drooping along on that stupid black horse that was not distinguished. "My brother Giuseppe wish so much to ride today," said Fabrizio. "Also he offer to my cousin the marchese much money." He laughed.

Fabrizio wished his English were equal to relating what a figure Giuseppe had made of himself. The marchese, who was fat, slow-witted and greedy, certainly preferred twenty thousand lire to being pinched black and blue by forty pounds of steel embossed with unicorns. He giggled and said, "*Va bene.* All right." He sat frankly admiring the tall, swaying lines of Giuseppe's figure and planning what he would do with the money. Giuseppe was carried away by a glorious prevision of himself prancing about the streets amid fluttering pennants, the beat of drums, the gasp of ladies. He swaggered about the room describing his noble bearing astride a horse of such mettle and spirit as would land his cousin the marchese in the street in five minutes, clanging like the gates of hell. He knew where to find it—just such an animal! Nothing like that dull beast that the marchese kept stalled out in the country all year round and that by this time believed himself to be a cow. . . . Unfortunately the mother of the marchese had been listening all the time behind the door, and took that moment to break in upon them. The whole plan was canceled in no time at all, and Giuseppe was shown to the door. There was not a drop of nobility in his blood, he was reminded, and no such substitution would be tolerated by the council. As Giuseppe had passed down the street, the marchese had flung open the window and called down to him, "Mamma says you only want to impress the American ladies." Everyone in the street had laughed at him and he was furious.

Perhaps it was as well, Fabrizio reflected, not to be able to relate all this to the signora and Clara. What would they think of his family? It was better not to tell too much. Fabrizio's brother Giuseppe

had enjoyed many successes with women and had developed elaborate theories of love, which he would discuss in detail, relating ex-
amples from his own experience, always with the same serious
savor, as if for the first time. No, it was very much wiser not to speak
too much of Giuseppe to nice American ladies.

"My father wait for us in the piazza at this moment," Fabrizio
said.

Sitting beside Mrs. Johnson in the grandstand during the game,
Signor Naccarelli dropped a significant remark or two. Her daughter was charming; his son could think of nothing else. It would be a
sad day for Fabrizio when they went away. How nice to think that
they would not go away at all, but would spend many months in
Florence, perhaps take a small villa. Many outsiders did so. They
wished never to leave.

Mrs. Johnson explained her responsibilities at home—her house,
her husband and family. And what did Signor Johnson do? A busi-
nessman. He owned part interest in a cigarette company and devoted his whole time to the firm. Cigarettes—ah. Signor Naccarelli
rattled off all the name brands until he found the right one. Ah.

And her daughter—perhaps the signorina did not wish to leave
Florence?

"It is clear that she doesn't," said Mrs. Johnson. And then she
thought, I must tell him now. It was the only sensible thing, and
would end this ridiculous dragging on into deeper and deeper com-
plications. She believed that he would understand, even help her to
handle things in the right way. "You see—" she began, but just then
the small medieval cannon that had fired a blank charge to announce the opening of the contest took a notion to fire again. Nobody ever seemed able to explain why. It was hard to believe that it
had ever happened, for in the strong sun the flash of powder, which
must have been considerable by another light, had been all but ne-
gated. All the players stopped and turned to look, and a man who
had been standing between the cannon and the steps of the Palazzo
Vecchio fell to the ground. People rushed in around him.

"Excuse me," said Signor Naccarelli. "I think I know him."

There followed a long series of discussions. Signor Naccarelli could be seen waving his hands as he talked. The game went on and everyone seemed to forget the man, who, every now and then, as the movement around him shifted, could be seen trying to get up. At last two of the drummers from the parade, still dressed in their knee breeches, edged through the crowd with a stretcher and took him away.

Signor Naccarelli returned as the crowds were dispersing. He had apparently been visiting all the time among his various friends and relatives and appeared to have forgotten the accident. He took off his hat to Mrs. Johnson. "My wife and I invite you to tea with us. On Sunday at four. I have a little car and I will come to your hotel. You will come, no?"

5

Tea at the Naccarelli household revealed that they lived in a spacious apartment with marble floors and had more bad pictures than good furniture. They seemed comfortable, nonetheless, and a little maid in white gloves came and went seriously among them.

The Signora Naccarelli, constructed along ample Neapolitan lines, sat staring first at Clara and then at Mrs. Johnson and smiling at the conversation without understanding a word. Fabrizio sat near her on a little stool, let her pat him occasionally on the shoulder and gazed tenderly at Clara. Clara sat with her hands folded and smiled at everyone. She had more and more nowadays a rapt air of not listening to anything.

Giuseppe came in, accompanied by his wife. Sealed dungeons doubtless could not have contained them. He said at once in an accent so middle western as to be absurd, "How do you do? And how arrre you?" It was all he knew except "goodbye"; he had learned it the day before. Yet he gave the impression that he did not speak out of deference to his father, whose every word he followed attentively, making sure to laugh whenever Mrs. Johnson smiled.

Giuseppe's wife was a slender girl with black hair cut short in the new fashion called simply "Italian." She had French blood, though not as much as she led one to believe. She smoked from a short ivory holder clamped at the side of her mouth, and pretended to regard Giuseppe's amours—of which he had been known to boast in front of her, to the distress of his mama—with a knowing side-long glance. Sometimes she would remind him of one of his fail-ures. Now she took a place near Fabrizio and chatted with him in a low voice, casting down on him past the cigarette holder the eye of someone old in the ways of love, amused by the eagerness of the young. She looked occasionally at Clara, who beamed at her.

Signor Naccarelli kept the conversation going nicely and seemed to include everybody in the general small talk. There was family anecdote to draw upon; a word or two in Italian sufficed to give the key to which one he was telling now. Some little mention was made of the family villa in a nearby *paese,* blown up unfortunately by the Allies during the war—the Americans, in fact—but it was indeed a necessary military objective and these things happen in all wars. *Pazienza.* Mrs. Johnson remarked politely on the paintings, but he was quick to admit with a chuckle that they were no good whatso-ever. Only one, perhaps; that one over there had been painted by Ghirlandaio—not the famous one in the guidebooks—on the occa-sion of some ancestor's wedding; he could not quite remember whose.

"In Florence we have too much history. In America you are so free, free—oh, it is wonderful! Here if we move a stone in the street, who comes? The commission on antiquities, the scholars of the middle ages, priests, professors, committees of everything, saying, 'Do not move it. No, you cannot move it.' And even if you say, 'But it has just this minute fallen on my foot,' they show you no pity. In Rome they are even worse. It reminds me, do you remember the man who fell down when the cannon decide to shoot? Well, he is not well. They say the blood has been poisoned by the infection. If someone had given him penicillin. But nobody did. I hear from my friend who is a doctor at the hospital." He turned to his wife. *"No, Mamma? Ti ricordi come ti ho detto. . . ."*

When they spoke of the painting, Clara admired it. It was of course a Madonna and Child, all light-blue and pink flesh tones. Clara had developed a great all-absorbing interest in these recurring ladies with little baby Jesus on their laps. She had a large collection of dolls at home and had often expressed her wish for a real live little baby brother. She did not see why her mother did not have one. The dolls cried only when she turned them over; they wet their pants only when you pushed something rubber, and so on through eye-closing and walking and saying, "Mama." But a real one would do all these things whenever it wanted to. It certainly would, Mrs. Johnson agreed. She was glad those days, at any rate, were over.

Now Clara stared on with parted lips at the painting on which the soft evening light was falling. She had gotten it into her little head recently that Fabrizio and babies were somehow connected. The Signora Naccarelli did not fail to notice the nature of her gaze. On impulse she got up and crossed to sit beside Mrs. Johnson on the couch. She sat facing her and smiling with tears filling her eyes. She was all in black—black stockings, black crepe dress cut in a V at the neck, the small black crucifix on a chain. *"Mio figlio,"* she pronounced slowly, *"è buono. Capisce?"*

Mrs. Johnson nodded encouragingly. *"Si. Capisco."*

"Non lui," said the signora, pointing at Giuseppe, who glanced up with a wicked grin—he was delighted to be bad. The signora shook her finger at him. Then she indicated Fabrizio. *"Ma lui. Si, è buono. Va in chiesa, capisce?"* She put her hands together as if in prayer.

"No, ma Mamma. Che roba!" Fabrizio protested.

"Si, è vero," the signora persisted solemnly; her voice fairly quivered. *"È buono. Capisce, signora?"*

"Capisco," said Mrs. Johnson.

Everyone complimented her on how well she spoke Italian.

6

"Galileo, Dante Alighieri, Boccaccio, Machiavelli, Michelangelo Buonarotti, Donatello, Amerigo Vespucci . . ." Clara chanted, read-

ing the names off the rows of statues of illustrious Tuscans that
flanked the street. Her Italian was sounding more clearly every day.

"Hush!" said Mrs. Johnson.

"Leonardo da Vinci, Benvenuto Cellini, Petracco. . . ." Clara
went right on, like a little girl trailing a stick against the palings of a
picket fence.

Relations between mother and daughter had deteriorated in recent days. In the full flush of pride at the subjugation of Fabrizio to
her every whim, Clara, it is distressing to report, calculated that she
could afford to stick out her tongue at her mother, and she did—at
times, literally. She refused to pick up her clothes or be on time for
any occasion that did not include Fabrizio. She was quarrelsome and
she whined about what she didn't want to do, lying with her elbows
on the crumpled satin bedspread, staring out of the window. Or she
took her Parcheesi board out of the suitcase and sat crosslegged on
the floor with her back to the rugged beauties of the sky line across
the Arno, shaking the dice in the wooden cup, throwing for two sets
of "men" and tapping out the moves. When called she did not hear
or would not answer, and Mrs. Johnson, smoking nervously in the
adjoining room, thought the little sounds would drive her mad. She
had never known Clara to show a mean or stubborn side. Yet the
minute the girl fell beneath the eye of Fabrizio, her rapt, transported
Madonna look came over her, and she sat still and gentle, docile as a
saint, beautiful as an angel. Mrs. Johnson had never beheld such hy-
pocrisy. She had let things go too far, she realized, and whereas before she had been worried, now she was becoming afraid.

Whether she sought advice or whether her need was for somebody to talk things over with, she had gone one day directly after
lunch to the American consulate, where she found, on the second
floor of a palazzo whose marble halls echoed the click and clack of
typing, one of those perpetually young American faces topped by a
crew cut. The owner of it was sitting in a seersucker coat behind a
standard American office desk in a richly paneled room cut to the
noble proportions of the Florentine Renaissance. Memos, documents and correspondence were arranged in stacks before him, and
he looked toward the window while twisting a rubber band repeat-

edly around his wrist. Mrs. Johnson had no sooner got her first statement out—she was concerned about a courtship between her daughter and a young Italian—than he had cut her off. The consulate could give no advice in personal matters. A priest, perhaps, or a minister or doctor. There was a list of such as spoke English. "Gabriella!" An untidy Italian girl wearing glasses and a green crepe blouse came in from her typewriter in the outer office. "There's a services list in the top of that file cabinet. If you'll just find us a copy." All the while he continued looking out of the window and twisting and snapping the rubber band around his wrist. Mrs. Johnson got the distinct impression that but for this activity he would have dozed right off to sleep. By the time she had descended to the courtyard, her disappointment had turned into resentment. We pay for people like him to come and live in a palace, she thought. It would have helped me just to talk, if he had only listened.

The sun's heat pierced the coarsely woven straw of her little hat and prickled sharply at her tears. The hot street was deserted. Feeling foreign, lonely and exposed, she walked past the barred shops.

The shadowy interior of an espresso bar attracted her. Long aluminum chains in bright colors hung in the door and made a pleasant muted jingling behind her. She sat down at a small table and asked for a coffee. Presently, she opened the mimeographed sheets that the secretary had produced for her. There she found, as she had been told, along with a list of tourist services catering to Americans, rates for exchanging money and advice on what to do if your passport was lost, the names and addresses of several doctors and members of the clergy. Perhaps it was worth a try. She found a representative of her ancestral faith and noted the obscure address. With her American instinct for getting on with it, no matter what it was, she found her tears and hurt evaporating, drank her coffee and began fumbling through books and maps for the location of the street. She had never dared to use a telephone in Italy.

She went out into the sun. She had left Clara asleep in the hotel during the siesta hour. A lady professor whose card boasted of a number of university degrees would come and give Clara an Italian lesson at three. Before this was over, Mrs. Johnson planned to have returned. She motioned to a *carrozza* and showed the address to the driver, who leaned far back from his seat, almost into her face, to read it. He needed a shave and reeked of garlic and wine. His whip was loud above the thin rump of the horse, and he plunged with a shout into the narrow, echoing streets so gathered-in at this hour as to make any noise seem rude.

After two minutes of this Mrs. Johnson was jerked into a headache. He was going too fast—she had not said she was in a hurry—and taking corners like a madman. *"Attenzione!"* she called out twice. How did she say "slow down"? He looked back and laughed at her, not paying the slightest attention to the road ahead. The whip cracked like a pistol shot. The horse slid and, to keep his footing, changed from a trot to a desperate two-part gallop that seemed to be wrenching the shafts from the carriage. Mrs. Johnson closed her eyes and held on. It was probably the driver's idea of a good time. Thank God the streets were empty. Now the wheels rumbled; they were crossing the river. They entered the quarter of Oltr'arno, the opposite bank, through a small piazza from which a half-dozen little streets branched out. The paving here was of small, rough-edged stones. Speeding toward one tiny slit of a street, the driver, either through mistake or a desire to show off, suddenly wheeled the horse toward another, almost at right angles to them. The beast plunged against the bit that had flung its head and shoulders practically into reverse, and with a great gasp in which its whole lungs seemed involved as in a bellows, it managed to bring its forelegs in line with the new direction. Mrs. Johnson felt her head and neck jerked as cruelly as the horse's had been.

"Stop! STOP!"

At last she had communicated. Crying an order to the horse, hauling in great lengths of rein, the driver obeyed. The carriage stood swaying in the wake of its lost momentum, and Mrs. Johnson alighted shakily in the narrow street. Heads had appeared at various windows above them. A woman came out of a doorway curtained in knotted cords and leaned in the entrance with folded arms. A group of young men, one of them rolling a motor scooter, emerged from a courtyard and stopped to watch.

Mrs. Johnson's impulse was to walk away without a backward glance. She was mindful always, however, of a certain American responsibility. The driver was an idiot, but his family was probably as poor as his horse. She was drawing a five-hundred-lire note from her purse, when, having wrapped the reins to their post in the *carrozza*, the object of her charity bounded suddenly down before her face. She staggered back, clutching her purse to her. Her wallet had been half out; now his left hand was on it while his right held up two fingers. *"Due! Due mila!"* he demanded, forcing her back another step. The young men around the motor scooter were noticing everything. The woman in the doorway called a casual word to them and they answered.

"Due mila, signora!" repeated the driver, and thrusting his devil's face into hers, he all but danced.

The shocking thing—the thing that was paralyzing her, making her hand close on the wallet as though it contained something infinitely more precious than twenty or thirty dollars in lire—was the overturn of all her values. He was not ashamed to be seen extorting an unjust sum from a lone woman, a stranger, obviously a lady; he was priding himself rather on showing off how ugly about it he could get. And the others, the onlookers, those average people so depended on by an American to adhere to what is good? She did not deceive herself. Nobody was coming to her aid. Nobody was even going to think, It isn't fair.

She thrust two thousand-lire notes into his hand, and folding her purse closely beneath her arm in ridiculous parody of everything Europeans said about Americans, she hastened away. The driver reared back before his audience. He shook in the air the two notes she had given him. *"Mancia! Mancia!"* No tip! Turning aside to mount his carriage, he thrust the money into his inner breast pocket, slanting after her a word that makes Anglo-Saxon curses sound like nursery rhymes. She did not understand what it meant, but she felt the meaning; the foul, cold rat's foot of it ran after her down the street. As soon as she turned a corner, she stopped and stood shuddering against a wall.

Imagine her then, not ten minutes later, sitting on a sofa covered with comfortably faded chintz, steadying her nerves over a cup of tea and talking to a lively old gentleman with a trace of the Scottish highlands in his voice. It had not occurred to her that a Presbyterian minister would be anything but American, but now that she thought of it she supposed that the faith of her fathers was not only Scottish but also French. A memory returned to her, something she had not thought of in years. One Christmas or Thanksgiving as a little girl she had been taken to her grandfather's house in Tennessee. She could reconstruct only a glimpse of something that had happened. She saw herself in the corner of a room with a fire burning and a bay window overlooking an uneven shoulder of side yard partially covered with a light fall of snow. She was meddling with a black book on a little table and an old man with wisps of white hair about his brow was leaning over her: "It's a Bible in Gaelic. Look, I'll show you." And putting on a pair of gold-rimmed glasses he translated strange broken-looking print, moving his horny finger across a tattered page. In this unattractive roughness of things, it was impossible to escape the suggestion of character.

It came to her now in every detail about the man before her. Even the hairs of his gray brows, thick as wire, had each its own almost contrary notion about where to be, and underneath lived his sharp blue eyes, at once humorous and wry. Far from being disinterested in his unexpected visitor, who so obviously had something on her mind, he managed to make Mrs. Johnson feel even more uncomfortable than the specimen of American diplomacy had done. He was, in fact, too interested, alert as a new flame. She had a feeling that compromise was unknown to him, and really, come right down to it, wasn't compromise the thing she kept looking for?

Touching her tea-moistened lip with a small Florentine embroidered handkerchief, she told him her dilemma in quite other terms than the ones that troubled her. She put it to him that her daughter was being wooed by a young Italian of the nicest sort, but naturally a Roman Catholic. This led them along the well-worn paths of theology. The venerable minister, surprisingly, showed little zeal for the workout. An old war-horse, he wearied to hurl himself into so trifling a skirmish. He wished to be tolerant . . . his appointment here after retirement had been a joy to him . . . he had come to love Italy, *but*—one could not help observing. . . . For a moment the sparks flew. Well.

Mrs. Johnson took her leave at the door that opened into a narrow dark stair dropping down to the street.

"Ye'll have written to her faither?"

"Why, no," she admitted. His eyelids drooped ever so slightly. Americans . . . divorce; she could see the suspected pattern. "It's a wonderful idea! I'll do it tonight."

Her enthusiasm did not flatter him. "If your daughter's religion means anything to her," he said, "I urge ye both to make very careful use of your brains."

Well, thought Mrs. Johnson, walking away down the street, what did Clara's religion mean to her? She had liked to cut out and color things in Sunday School, but she had got too big for that department, and no pretense about churchgoing was kept up any longer. She wanted every year, however, to be an angel in the Christmas pageant. She had been, over the course of the years, every imaginable size of angel. Once, long ago, in a breathless burst of adoration, she had reached into the Winston-Salem First Presbyterian Church Ladies' Auxiliary's idea of a manger, a flimsy trough-shaped affair, knocked together out of a Sunkist orange crate, painted gray and stuffed with excelsior. She was looking for the little Lord Jesus, but all she found was a flashlight. Her teacher explained to her, as she stood cheated and tearful, holding this unromantic object in her hands, that it would be sacrilegious to represent the Son of God with a doll. Mrs. Johnson rather sided with Clara; a doll seemed more appropriate than a flashlight.

Now what am I doing? Mrs. Johnson asked herself. Wasn't she employing the old gentleman's warning to reason herself into thinking that Clara's romance was quite all right? More than all right—the very thing? As for writing to Clara's father, why Noel Johnson would be on the transatlantic phone within five minutes after any such suggestion reached him. No, she was alone, really alone.

She sank down on a stone bench in a poor plain piazza with a rough stone paving, a single fountain, a single tree, a bare church façade, a glare of sun, the sound of some dirty little black-headed waifs playing with a ball. Careful use of your brains. She pressed her hand to her head. Outside the interest of conversation, her headache was returning and the shock of that terrible carriage ride. She did not any longer seem to possess her brains, but to stand apart from them as from everything else in Italy. She had got past the guidebooks and still she was standing and looking. And her own mind was only one more thing among the things she was looking at, and what was going on in it was like the ringing of so many different bells. Five to four. Oh, my God! She began to hasten away through the labyrinth, the chill stench of the narrow streets.

She must have taken the wrong turning somewhere, because she emerged too far up the river—in fact, just short of the Ponte Vecchio, which she hastened to cross to reach at any rate the more familiar bank. A swirl of tourists hampered her; they were inching along from one show window to the next of the tiny shops that lined the bridge on both sides, staring at the myriads of baubles, bracelets, watches and gems displayed there. As she emerged into the street, a handsome policeman who, dressed in a snow-white uniform, was directing traffic as though it were a symphony orchestra, smiled into the crowd that was approaching along the Lungarno and brought everything to a dramatic halt.

There, with a nod to him, came Clara! He bowed; she smiled. Why, she looked like an Italian!

Item at a time, mother and daughter had seen things in the shops they could not resist. Mrs. Johnson with her positive, clipped American figure found it difficult to wear the clothes, and had purchased mainly bags, scarves and other accessories. But Clara could wear almost everything she admired. Stepping along now in her handwoven Italian skirt and sleeveless cotton blouse, with leather sandals, smart straw bag, dark glasses and the glint of earrings against her cheek, she would fool any tourist into thinking her a native; and Mrs. Johnson, who felt she was being fooled by Clara in a far graver way, found in her daughter's very attractiveness an added sense of displeasure, almost of disgust.

"Where do you think you're going?" she demanded.

Clara, who was still absorbed in being adored by the policeman, could not credit her misfortune at having run into her mother. Mrs. Johnson took her arm and marched her straight back across the street. Crowds were thronging against them from every direction. A vender shook a fistful of cheap leather bags before them; there seemed no escaping him. Mrs. Johnson veered to the right, entering a quiet street where there were no shops and where Fabrizio would not be likely to pass, returning to work after siesta.

"Where were you going, Clara?"

"To get some ice cream," Clara pouted.

"There's ice cream all around the hotel. Now you know we never tell each other stories, Clara."

"I was looking for you," said Clara.

"But how did you know where I was?" asked Mrs. Johnson.

They had entered the street of the illustrious Tuscans. "Galileo, Dante Alighieri, Boccaccio, Machiavelli, Michelangelo . . ." chanted Clara.

This is not my day, sighed Mrs. Johnson to herself.

She was right about this; alighting from her taxi with Clara before the Grand Hotel, she heard a cry behind her.

"Why, Mar-gar-et John-son!"

Two ladies from Winston-Salem stood laughing before her. They were sisters—Meg Kirby and Henrietta Mulverhill—a chatty, plumpish pair whose husbands had presented them both with a summer abroad.

Now they were terribly excited. They had no idea she would be here still. They had heard she was in Rome by now. What a coincidence! They simply couldn't get over it! Wasn't it wonderful what you could buy here? Linens! Leather-lined bags! So cheap! If only she could see what just this morning—! And how was Clara?

Constrained to go over to the Excelsior—their hotel, just across the street—for tea, Margaret Johnson sat like a creature in a net and felt her strength ebb from her. The handsome salon echoed with Winston-Salem news, gossip, exact quotations, laughter, and during it all, Clara became again her old familiar little lost self, oblivious, searching through her purse, leafing for pictures in the guidebooks on the tea table, only looking up to say, "Yes, ma'am," and "No, ma'am."

"Well, it's just so difficult to pick out a hat for Noel without him here to try it on," said Mrs. Johnson. "I tried it once in Washington, and—" I've been blinded, she thought, the image of her daughter constant in the corner of her vision. Blinded—by what? By beauty, art, strangeness, freedom. By romance, by sun—yes, by hope itself.

By the time she had shaken the ladies, making excuses about dinner but with a promise to call by for them tomorrow, and had reached at long last her hotel room, her headache had grown steadily worse. She yearned to shed her street clothes, take aspirin and soak in a long bath. Clara passed sulking ahead of her through the anteroom, through the larger bedroom, the bath and into her own small room. Mrs. Johnson tossed her bag and hat on the bed and, slipping out of her shoes, stepped into a pair of scuffs. A rap at the outer door revealed a servant with a long florist's box. Carrying the box, Mrs. Johnson crossed the bath to her daughter's room.

Through the weeks that they had dallied here, Clara's room had gradually filled with gifts from Fabrizio. A baby elephant of green china, its howdah enlarged to contain brightly wrapped sweets, grinned from a tabletop. A stuffed dog, Fabrizio's idea of Ronnie, sat near Clara's pillow. On her wrist a charm bracelet was slowly filling with golden miniature animals and tiny musical instruments. She did not have to be told that another gift had arrived, but observed from a glance at the label, as her mother had not, that the flowers were for both of them. Then she filled a tall vase with water. Chores of this sort fell to her at home.

Mrs. Johnson sat down on the bed.

Clara happily read the small card. "It says, 'Naccarelli,'" she announced.

Then she began to arrange the flowers in the vase. They were rather remarkable flowers, Mrs. Johnson thought—a species of lily apparently highly regarded here, though with their enormous naked stamens, based in a back-curling, waxen petal, they had always struck her as being rather blatantly phallic. Observing some in a shop window soon after they had arrived in Florence, it had come to her to wonder then if Italians took sex so much for granted that they hardly thought about it at all, as separate, that is, from anything else in life. Time had passed, and the question, more personal now, still stood unanswered.

The Latin mind—how did it work? What did it think? She did not know, but as Clara stood arranging the flowers one at a time in the vase (there seemed to be a great number of them—far more than a dozen—in the box and all very large), the bad taste of the choice seemed, in any language, inescapable. The cold eye of Signor Naccarelli had selected this gift, she felt certain, not Fabrizio, and that thought, no less than the flowers themselves, was remarkably effective in short-circuiting romance. Could she be wrong in perceiving a kind of Latin logic at work—its basic quality factual, hard, direct? Even if nobody ever *put* it that way, it was there. And no matter what *she* might think, it was, like the *carrozza* driver, not in the least ashamed. A demand was closer to being made than she liked to suppose. Exactly where, it seemed to say, did she think all this was leading? She looked at the stuffed dog, at the baby elephant who carried sweets so coyly, at the charm bracelet dancing on Clara's wrist as her hand moved, setting in place one after another the stalks with their sensual bloom.

It's simply that they are facing what I am hiding from, she thought.

"Come here, darling."

She held out her hands to Clara and drew her down to the edge of the bed beside her. Unable to think of anything else to do, she lied wildly.

"Clara, I have just been to the doctor. That is where I went. I didn't tell you—you've been having such a good time—but I'm not feeling well at all. The doctor says the air is very bad for me here and that I must leave. We will come back, of course. As soon as I feel better. I'm going to call for reservations and start packing at once. We will leave for Rome tonight."

Later she nervously penned a note to the ladies at the Excelsior. Clara was not feeling well, she explained, and the doctor had advised their leaving. They would leave their address at American Express in Rome, though there was a chance they might have to go to the lakes for cooler weather.

7

To the traveler coming down from Florence to Rome in the summertime, the larger, more ancient city is bound to be a disappointment. It is bunglesome; nothing is orderly or planned; there is a tangle of electric wires and tramlines, a ceaseless clamor of traffic. The distances are long; the sun is hot. And if, in addition, the heart has been left behind as positively as a piece of baggage, the tourist is apt to suffer more than tourists generally do. Mrs. Johnson saw this clearly in her daughter's face. To make things worse, Clara never mentioned Florence or Fabrizio. Mrs. Johnson had only to think of those flowers to keep herself from mentioning either. They had come to see Rome, hadn't they? Very well, Rome would be seen.

At night, after dinner, Mrs. Johnson assembled her guidebooks and mapped out strenuous tours. Cool cloisters opened before them, and the gleaming halls of the Vatican galleries. They were photographed in the spray of fountains and walking through the parks were trailed by pairs of *pappagalli*—flashy young men who tried picking up anything in skirts, especially, Mrs. Johnson thought, those who looked able to pay for things. At Tivoli, Clara had a sunstroke in the ruin of a Roman villa. A goatherd came and helped her to the shade, fanned her with his hat and brought her some water. Mrs. Johnson was afraid for her to drink it. At dusk they walked out the hotel door and saw the whole city in the sunset from the top of the Spanish Steps. Couples stood linked and murmuring together, leaning against the parapets.

"When are we going back, Mother?" Clara asked in the dark.

"Back where?" said Mrs. Johnson vaguely.

"Back to Florence."

"You want to go back?" said Mrs. Johnson, more vaguely still.

Clara did not reply. To a child, a promise is a promise, a sacred thing, the measure of love. "We will come back," her mother had said. She had told Fabrizio so when he came to the station, called unexpectedly out of his shop with this thunderbolt tearing across his heart, clutching a demure mass of wild chrysanthemums and a tin of *caramelle*. While the train stood open-doored in the station, he had drawn Clara behind a post and kissed her. "We are coming back," said Clara, and threw her arms around him. When he forced down her arms, he was crying, and there stood her mother.

Day by day, Clara followed after Mrs. Johnson's decisive heels, always at the same silent distance, like a good little dog. In the Roman Forum, urged on by the guidebook, Mrs. Johnson sought out the ruins of "an ancient basilica containing the earliest known Christian frescoes." They may have been the earliest, but to Mrs. Johnson they looked no better than the smeary pictures of Clara's Sunday School days. She studied them one at a time, consulting her book. When she looked up, Clara was gone. She called once or twice and hastened out into the sun. The ruins before her offered many a convenient hiding place. She ran about in a maze of paths and ancient pavings, until finally, there before her, not really very far away, she saw her daughter sitting on a fallen block of marble with her back turned. She was bent forward and weeping. The angle of her head and shoulders, her gathered limbs, though pained was not pitiful. And arrested by this, Mrs. Johnson did not call again, but stood observing how something of a warm, classic dignity had come to this girl, and no matter whether she could do long division or not, she was a woman.

To Mrs. Johnson's credit she waited quietly while Clara straightened herself and dried her eyes. Then the two walked together through the ruin of an open court with a quiet rectangular pool. They went out of the Forum and crossed a busy street to a sidewalk café, where they both had coffee. In all the crash and clang of the tramlines and the hurry of the crowds there was no chance to speak.

A boy came by, a beggar, scrawny, in clothing deliberately oversized and poor, the trousers held up by a cord, rolled at the cuffs, the bare feet splayed and filthy. A jut of black hair set his swart face in a frame, and the eyes, large, abject, imploring, did not meet now, perhaps had never met, another's. He mumbled some ritualistic phrases and put out a hand that seemed permanently shriveled into the wrist; the tension, the smear and fear that money was, was in it. In Italy, especially in Rome, Mrs. Johnson had gone through many states of mind about beggars, all the way from, Poor things, why doesn't the church do something? to, How revolting, why don't they ever let us alone? So she had been known to give them as much as a thousand lire or spurn them like dogs. But something inside her had tired. Clara hardly noticed the child at all; exactly like an Italian, she took a ten-lire piece out of the change on the table and dropped it in his palm. And Mrs. Johnson, in the same way that people crossed themselves with a dabble of holy water in the churches, found herself doing the same thing. He passed on, table by table, and then entered the ceaseless weaving of the crowd, hidden, reappearing, vanishing, lost.

She closed her eyes and, with a sigh that was both qualm and relief, she surrendered.

A lull fell in the traffic. "Clara," she said, "we will go back to Florence tomorrow."

8

It wasn't that simple, of course. Nobody with a dream should come to Italy. No matter how dead and buried the dream is thought to be, in Italy it will rise and walk again. Margaret Johnson had a dream, though she thought reality had long ago destroyed it. The dream was that Clara would one day be perfectly well. It was here that Italy had attacked her, and it was this that her surrender involved.

Then "surrender" is the wrong word, too. Women like Margaret Johnson do not surrender; they simply take up another line of campaign. She would go poised into combat, for she knew already that the person who undertakes to believe in a dream pursues a course that is dangerous and lonely. She knew because she had done it before.

The truth was that when Clara was fourteen and had been removed from school two years previously, Mrs. Johnson had decided to believe that there was not anything the matter with her. It was September, and Noel Johnson was away on a business trip and conference that would last a month. Their son was already away at college. The opportunity was too good to be missed. She chose a school in an entirely new section of town; she told a charming pack of lies and got Clara enrolled there under most favorable conditions. The next two weeks were probably the happiest of her life. With other mothers, she sat waiting in her car at the curb until the bright crowd came breasting across the campus: Clara's new red tam was the sign to watch for. At night the two of them got supper in the kitchen while Clara told all her stories. Later they did homework, sitting on the sofa under the lamp.

Three teachers came to call at different times. They were puzzled, but were persuaded to be patient. Two days before Noel Johnson was due to come home, Mrs. Johnson was invited to see the principal. Some inquiries, he said, had been felt necessary. He had wished to be understanding, and rather than take the evidence from other reports had done some careful testing of his own under the most favorable circumstances: the child had suspected nothing.

He paused. "I understand that your husband is away." She nodded. "So you have undertaken this—ah—experiment entirely on your own." She nodded again, dumbly. Her throat had tightened. The word "experiment" was damning; she had thought of it herself. No one, of course, should experiment with any human being, much less one's own daughter. But wasn't the alternative, to accept things as they were, even worse? It was all too large, too difficult to explain.

The principal stared down at his desk in an embarrassed way. "These realities are often hard for us to face," he said. "Yet from all I have been able to learn, you did know. It had all been explained to you, along with the best techniques, the limits of her capabilities—"

"Yes," she faltered. "I did know. But I know so much else besides.

I know that in so many ways she is as well as you and I. I know that the doctors have said that no final answers have been arrived at in these things." She was more confident now. Impressive names could be quoted; statements, if need be, could be found in writing. "Our mental life is not wholly understood as yet. Since no one knows the extent to which a child may be retarded, so no one can say positively that Clara's case is a hopeless one. We know that she is not one bit affected physically. She will continue to grow up just like any other girl. Even if marriage were ever possible to her, the doctors say that her children would be perfectly all right. Everyone sees that she behaves normally most of the time. Do I have to let the few ways she is slow stand in the way of all the others to keep her from being a whole person, from having a whole life?" She could not go on.

"But those 'few ways,'" he said, consenting, it was obvious, to use her term, "are the main ones we are concerned with here. Don't you see that?"

She agreed. She did see. And yet . . .

At the same moment, in another part of the building, trivial, painful things were happening to Clara—no one could possibly want to hear about them.

The serene fall afternoon, as she left the school, was as disjointed as if hurricane and earthquake had been at it. Toward nightfall, Mrs. Johnson telephoned to Noel to come home. At the airport, with Clara waiting crumpled like a bundle of clothes on the backseat of the car, she confessed everything to him. When he said little, she realized he thought she had gone out of her mind. Clara was sent to the country to visit an aunt and uncle, and Mrs. Johnson spent a month in Bermuda. Strolling around the picture-postcard landscape of the resort, she said to herself, I was out of my mind, insane. As impersonal as advertising slogans, or skywriting, the words seemed to move out from her, into the golden air.

Courage, she thought now, in a still more foreign landscape, riding the train back to Florence. *Coraggio.* The Italian word came easily to mind. Mrs. Johnson belonged to various clubs, and campaigns to clean up this or raise the standards of that were frequently turned over to committees headed by her. She believed that women in their way could accomplish a great deal. What was the best way to handle Noel? How much did the Naccarellis know? As the train drew into the station, she felt her blood race, her whole being straighten and poise to the fine alertness of a drawn bow. Whether Florence knew it or not, she invaded it.

As for how much the Naccarelli family knew or didn't know or cared or didn't care, no one not Italian had better undertake to say. It was never clear. Fabrizio threatened suicide when Clara left. The mother of Clara had scorned him because he was Italian. No other reason. Everyone had something to say. The household reeled until nightfall, when Fabrizio plunged toward the central open window of the *salotto*. The serious little maid, who had been in love with him for years, leaped in front of him with a shriek, her arms thrown wide. Deflected, he rushed out of the house and went tearing away through the streets. The Signora Naccarelli collapsed in tears and refused to eat. She retired to her room, where she kept a holy image that she placed a great store by. Signor Naccarelli alone enjoyed his meal. He said that Fabrizio would not commit suicide and that the ladies would probably be back. He had seen Americans take fright before; no one could ever explain why. But in the end, like everyone else, they would serve their own best interests. If he did not have some quiet, he would certainly go out and seek it elsewhere.

He spent the pleasantest sort of afternoon locked in conversation with Mrs. Johnson a few days after her return. It was all an affair for juggling, circling, balancing, very much to his liking. He could not really say she had made a conquest of him: American women were too confident and brisk. But he could not deny that encounters with her had a certain flavor.

The lady had consented to go with him on a drive up to San Miniato, stopping at the casino for a cup of tea and a pastry. Signor Naccarelli managed to get in a drive to Bello Sguardo, as well, and many a remark about young love and many a glance at his companion's attractive legs and figure. Margaret Johnson achieved a cool but not unfriendly position while folding herself into and out of a car no bigger than an enclosed motorcycle. The management of her skirt alone was enough to occupy her entire attention.

"They are in the time of life," Signor Naccarelli said, darting the car through a narrow space between two motor scooters, "when each touch, each look, each sigh arises from the heart, the heart alone." He removed his hands from the wheel to do his idea homage, flung back his head and closed his eyes. Then he snapped to and shifted gears. "For them love is without thought, as to draw breath, to sleep, to walk. You and I—we have come to another stage. We have known all this before—we think of the hour, of some business—so we lose our purity, who knows how? It is sad, but there is nothing to do. But we can see our children. I do not say for Fabrizio, of course—it would be hard to find a young Florentine who has had no experience. I myself at a younger age, at a much younger age—do you know my first love was a peasant girl? It was at the villa where I had gone out with my father. A *contadina*. The spring was far along. My father stayed too long with the animals. I became, how shall I say—bored, yes, but something more also. She was very beautiful. I still can dream of her, only her—I never succeed to dream of others. I do not know if your daughter will be for Fabrizio the first, or will not be. I would say not, but still—he is *figlio di mamma,* a good boy—I do not know." He frowned. They turned suddenly and shot up a hill. When they gained the crest, he came to a dead stop and turned to Mrs. Johnson. "But for her he has the feeling of the first woman! I am Italian and I tell you this. It is unmistakable! That, *cara signora,* is what I mean to say." Starting forward again, the car wound narrowly between tawny walls richly draped with vines. They emerged on a view and stopped again. Cypress, river, hill and city like a natural growth among them—they looked down on Tuscany. The air was fresher here, but undoubtedly very hot below. There was a slight haze, just enough to tone away the glare, but even on the distant blue hills outlines of a tree or a tower were distinct to the last degree—one had the sense of being able to see everything exactly as it was.

"There is no question with Clara," Mrs. Johnson murmured. "She has been very carefully brought up."

"Not like other American girls, eh? In Italy we hear strange things. Not only hear. *Cara signora*, we *see* strange things, also. You can imagine. Never mind. The signorina is another thing entirely. My wife has noticed it at once. Her innocence." His eyes kept returning to Mrs. Johnson's knee, which in the narrow silk skirt of her dress it was difficult not to expose. Her legs were crossed and her stocking whitened the flesh.

"She is very innocent," said Mrs. Johnson.

"And her father? How does he feel? An Italian for his daughter? Well, perhaps in America you, too, hear some strange words about us. We are no different from others, except we are more—well, you see me here—we are here together—it is not unpleasant—I look to you like any other man. And yet perhaps I feel a greater—how shall I say? You will think I play the Italian when I say there is a greater..."

She did think just that. She had been seriously informed on several occasions recently that Anglo-Saxons knew very little about passion, and now Signor Naccarelli, for whom she had a real liking, was about to work up to the same idea. She pulled down her skirt with a jerk. "There are plenty of American men who appreciate women just as much as you do," she told him.

He burst out laughing. "Of course! We make such a lot of foolishness, signora. But on such an afternoon—" His gesture took in the landscape. "I spoke of your husband. I think to myself, He is in cigarettes, after all. A very American thing. When you get off the boat, what do you say? 'Where is Clara?' says Signor Johnson. 'Where is my leetle girl?' 'Clara, ah!' you say. 'She is back in Italy. She has married with an Italian. I forgot to write you—I was so busy.'"

"But I write to him constantly!" cried Mrs. Johnson. "He knows everything. I have told him about you, about Fabrizio, the signora, Florence, all these things."

"But first of all you have considered your daughter's heart. For yourself, you could have left us, gone, gone. Forever. Not even a postcard." He chuckled. Suddenly he took a notion to start the car. It backed at once, as if a child had it on a string, then leaping forward, fairly toppled over the crest of a steep run of hill down into the city, speeding as fast as a roller skate. Mrs. Johnson clutched her hat. "When my son was married," she cried, "my husband wrote out a check for five thousand dollars. I have reason to think he will do the same for Clara."

"Ma che generoso!" cried Signor Naccarelli, and it seemed he had hardly said it before he was jerking the hand brake to prevent their entering the hotel lobby.

She asked him in for an aperitif. He leaned flirtatiously at her over a small round marble-topped table. The plush decor of the Grand Hotel, with its gilt and scroll-edged mirrors that gave back wavy reflections, reminded Mrs. Johnson of middle-aged adultery, one party only being titled. But neither she nor Signor Naccarelli was titled. It was a relief to know that sin was not expected of them. If she were thinking along such lines, heaven only knew what was running in Signor Naccarelli's head. Almost giggling, he drank down a red, bitter potion from a fluted glass.

"So you ran away," he said, "upset. You could not bear the thought. You think and you think. You see the signorina's unhappy face. You could not bear her tears. You return. It is wise. There should be a time for thought. This I have said to my wife, to my son. But when you come back, they say to me, 'But if she leaves again?' But I say, 'The signora is a woman who is without caprice. She will not leave again.'"

"I do not intend to leave again," said Mrs. Johnson, "until Clara and Fabrizio are married."

As if on signal, at the mention of his name, Fabrizio himself stepped before her eyes, but at some distance away, outside the archway of the salon, which he had evidently had the intention of entering if something had not distracted him. His moment of distraction itself was pure grace, as if a creature in nature, gentle to one word only, had heard that word. There was no need to see that Clara was somewhere within his gaze.

Signor Naccarelli and Mrs. Johnson rose and approached the

door. They were soon able to see Clara above stairs—she had promised to go no farther—leaning over, her hair falling softly past her happy face. *"Ciao,"* she said finally, *"come stai?"*

"Bene. E tu?"

"Bene."

Fabrizio stood looking up at her for so long a moment that Mrs. Johnson's heart had time almost to break. Gilt, wavy mirrors and plush decor seemed washed clean, and all the wrong, hurt years of her daughter's affliction were not proof against the miracle she saw now.

Fabrizio was made aware of the two in the doorway. He had seen his father's car and stopped by. A cousin kept his shop for him almost constantly nowadays. It was such a little shop, while he—he wished to be everywhere at once. Signor Naccarelli turned back to Mrs. Johnson before he followed his son from the lobby. There were tears in her eyes; she thought perhaps she observed something of the same in his own. At any rate, he was moved. He grasped her hand tightly, and his kiss upon it as he left her said to her more plainly than words, she believed, that they had shared together a beautiful and touching moment.

9

Letters, indeed, had been flying; the air above the Atlantic was thick with them. Margaret Johnson sat up nights over them. A shawl drawn round her, she worked at her desk near the window overlooking the Arno, her low night-light glowing on the tablet of thin airmail stationery. High diplomacy in the olden days perhaps proceeded thus, through long cramped hours of weighing one word against another, striving for just the measure of language that would sway, persuade, convince.

She did not underestimate her task. In a forest of question marks, the largest one was her husband. With painstaking care, she tried to consider everything in choosing her tone: Noel's humor, the season, their distance apart, how busy he was, how loudly she would have to speak to be heard.

Frankly, she recalled the time she had forced Clara into school; she admitted her grave error. Point at a time, she contrasted that disastrous sequence with Clara's present happiness. One had been a plan, deliberately contrived, she made clear; whereas here in Florence, events had happened of their own accord.

"The thing that impresses me most, Noel," she wrote, "is that nothing beyond Clara ever seems to be required of her here. I do wonder if anything beyond her would ever be required of her. Young married girls her age, with one or two children, always seem to have a nurse for them; a maid does all the cooking. There are mothers and mothers-in-law competing to keep the little ones at odd hours. I doubt if these young wives ever plan a single meal.

"Clara is able to pass every day here, as she does at home, doing simple things that please her. But the difference is that here, instead of being always alone or with the family, she has all of Florence for company, and seems no different from the rest. Every afternoon she dresses in her pretty clothes and we walk to an outdoor café to meet with some young friends of the Naccarellis. You would be amazed how like them she has become. She looks more Italian every day. They prattle. About what? Well, as far as I can follow—Clara's Italian is so much better than mine—about movie stars, pet dogs, some kind of car called Alfa Romeo and what man is handsomer than what other man.

"I understand that usually in the summer all these people go to the sea, where they spend every day for a month or two swimming and lying in the sun. They would all be there now if Fabrizio's courtship had not so greatly engaged their interest. Courtship is the only word for it. If you could see how he adores Clara and how often he mentions the very same things that we love in her: her gentleness, her sweetness and goodness. I had expected things to come to some conclusion long before now, but nothing of the sort seems to occur, and now the thought of separating the two of them begins to seem more and more wrong to me, every day. . . ."

This letter provoked a transatlantic phone call. Mrs. Johnson went to the lobby to talk so Clara wouldn't hear her. She knew what the first words would be. To Noel Johnson, the world was made of brass tacks, and coming down to them was his specialty.

"Margaret, are you thinking that Clara should marry this boy?"

"I'm only trying to let things take their natural course."

"*Natural* course!" Even at such a distance, he could make her jump.

"I'm with her constantly, Noel. I don't mean they're left to themselves. I only mean to say I can't wrench her away from him now. I tried it. Honestly I did. It was too much for her. I saw that."

"But surely you've talked to these people, Margaret. You must have told them all about her. Don't any of them speak English?" It would seem unbelievable to Noel Johnson that she or anyone related to him in any way would have learned to communicate in any language but English. He would be sure they had got everything wrong.

"I've tried to explain everything fully," she assured him. Well, hadn't she? Was it her fault a cannon had gone off just when she meant to explain?

Across the thousands of miles she heard his breath and read its quality: he had hesitated. Her heart gave a leap.

"Would I encourage anything that would put an ocean between Clara and me?"

She had scored again. Mrs. Johnson's deepest rebellion against her husband had occurred when he had wanted to put Clara in a sort of "school" for "people like her." The rift between them on that occasion had been a serious one, and though it was smoothed over in time and never mentioned subsequently, Noel Johnson might still not be averse to putting distances between his daughter and him.

"They're just after her money, Margaret."

"No, Noel—I wrote you about that. They *have* money." She shut her eyes tightly. "And nobody wants to come to America, either."

When she put down the phone a few minutes later, Mrs. Johnson had won a concession. Things should proceed along their natural course, very well. But she was to make no permanent decision until

Noel himself could be with her. His coming, at the moment, was next to impossible. Business was pressing. One of the entertainers employed to advertise the world's finest smoke on a national network had been called up by the Un-American Activities Committee. The finest brains in the company were being exercised far into the night. It would not do for the American public to conclude they were inhaling Communism with every puff on a well-known brand. This could happen; it could ruin them. Noel would go to Washington in the coming week. It would be three weeks at least until he could be with her. Then—well, she could leave the decision up to him. If it involved bringing Clara home with them, he would take the responsibility of it on himself.

Noel and Margaret Johnson gravely wished each other good luck over the transatlantic wire, and each resumed the burden of his separate enterprise.

—

"Where'd you go, Mother?" Clara wanted to know as soon as Mrs. Johnson returned.

"You'll never guess. I've been talking with Daddy on the long-distance phone!"

"Oh!" Clara looked up. She had been sitting on a footstool shoved back against the wall of her mother's room, writing in her diary. "Why didn't you tell me?"

"I didn't know that's who it was," she lied.

"But I wanted to talk to him, too!"

"What would you have said?"

"I would have said . . ." She hesitated, thinking hard, staring past her mother into the opposite wall, her young brow contracting faintly. "I would have said, *'Ciao. Come stai?'*"

"Would Daddy have understood?"

"I would have told him," Clara said faithfully.

After that she said nothing more but leaned her head against the wall, and forgetful of father, mother and diary, she stared before her with parted lips, dreaming.

Oh, my God, Margaret Johnson thought. How glad I am that Noel is coming to get me out of this!

10

After her husband's telephone call, Margaret Johnson went to bed in as dutiful and obedient a frame of mind as any husband of whatever nationality could wish for. She awoke flaming with new anxiety, confronted by the simplest truth in the world.

If Noel Johnson came to Florence, he would spoil everything. She must have known that all along.

He might not mean to—she gave him the benefit of the doubt. But he would do it. Given a good three days, her dream would all lie in little bright bits on the floor like the remains of the biggest and most beautiful Christmas-tree ornament in the world.

For one thing, there was nothing in the entire Florentine day that would not seem especially designed to irritate Noel Johnson. From the coffee he would be asked to drink in the morning, right through the siesta, when every shop, including his prospective son-in-law's, shut up at the very hour when they could be making the most money, up through midnight, when mothers were still abroad with their babies in the garrulous streets—he would have no time whatsoever for this inefficient way of life. Was there any possible formation of stone and paint hereabout that would not remind him uncomfortably of the Catholic church? In what frame of mind would he be cast by Fabrizio's cuffless trousers, little pointed shoes and carefully dressed hair? No, three days was a generous estimate; he would send everything sky-high long before that. And though he might regret it, he would never be able to see what he had done that was wrong.

His wife understood him. She sat over her *caffè latte* at her by-now-beloved window above the Arno, and while she thought of him, a peculiarly tender and generous smile played about her face. "Clara," she called gently, "have you written to Daddy recently?" Clara was splashing happily in the bathtub and did not hear her.

Soon Mrs. Johnson rose to get her cigarettes from the dresser, but stopped in the center of the room, where she stood with her hand to her brow for a long time, so enclosed in thought she could not have told where she was.

If she went back on her promise to Noel to do nothing until he came, the whole responsibility of action would be her own, and in the very moment of taking it, she would have to begin to lie. To lie in Winston-Salem was one thing, but to start lying to everybody in Italy—why, Italians were past masters at this sort of thing. Wouldn't they see through her at once? Perhaps they already had.

She could never quite get it out of her mind that perhaps, indeed, they already had. Her heart had occasionally quite melted to the idea—especially after a glass of wine—that the Italian nature was so warm, so immediate, so intensely personal, that they had all perceived at once that Clara was a child and had loved her anyway, for what she was. They had not, after all, gone the dreary round from doctor to doctor, expert to expert, in the dwindling hope of finding some way to make the girl "normal." They did not *think,* after all, in terms of IQ, "retarded mentality" and "adult capabilities." And why, oh, why, Mrs. Johnson had often thought, since she, too, loved Clara for herself, should anyone think of another human being in the light of a set of terms?

But though she might warm to the thought—and since she never learned the answer she never wholly discarded it—she always came to the conclusion that she could not act upon it, and had to put it aside as being, for all practical purposes, useless. "Ridiculous," she could almost hear Noel Johnson say. Mrs. Johnson came as near as she ever had in her life to wringing her hands. Oh, my God, she thought, if he comes here!

But she did not, that morning, seek out advice from any crew-cut diplomat or frosty-eyed Scot. At times she came flatly to the conclusion that she would stick to her promise to Noel because it was right to do so—she believed in doing right—and that since it was right, no harm could come of it. At other times, she wished she could believe this.

In the afternoon, she accompanied Clara to keep an appointment at a café with Giuseppe's wife, Franca, and another girl. She left the three of them enjoying pretty pastries and chattering happily of movie stars, dogs and the merits of the Alfa Romeo. Clara had learned so much Italian that Mrs. Johnson could no longer understand her.

Walking distractedly, back of the hotel, away from the river, she soon left the tourist-ridden areas behind her. She went thinking, unmindful of the people who looked up with curiosity as she passed. Her thought all had one center: her husband.

Never before had it seemed so crucial that she see him clearly. What was the truth about him? It had to be noted first of all, she believed, that Noel Johnson was in his own and everybody else's opinion a good man. Meaning exactly what? Well, that he believed in his own goodness and the goodness of other people, and would have said, if asked, that there must be good people in Italy, Germany, Tasmania, even Russia. On these grounds he would reason correctly that the Naccarelli family might possibly be as nice as his wife said they were.

Still, he did not think—fundamentally, he doubted, and Margaret had often heard him express something of the sort—that Europeans really had as much sense as Americans. Intellect, education, art and all that sort of thing—well, maybe. But ordinary sense? Certainly he was in grave doubts here when it came to the Latin races. And come right down to it—in her thoughts she slipped easily into Noel's familiar phrasing—didn't his poor afflicted child have about as much sense already as any Italian? His first reaction would have been to answer right away: Probably she does.

Other resentments sprang easily to his mind when touched on this sensitive point. Americans had had to fight two awful wars to get Europeans out of their infernal messes. He had a right to some sensitivity, anyone must admit. In the first war he had risked his life; his son had been wounded in the second; and if that were not enough, he could always remember his income tax. But there was no use getting really worked up. Some humor would prevail here, and he was not really going to lose sleep over something he couldn't help.

But Clara, now—she could almost hear him saying—this thing of Clara. There Margaret Johnson could grieve for Noel almost more than for herself. Something had happened here that he was powerless to do anything about; a chance accident had turned into a persisting and delicate matter, affecting his own pretty little daughter in this final way. An ugly finality, and no decent way of disposing of it. A fact he had to live with, day after day. An abnormality; hence, to a man like himself, a source of horror. For wasn't he dedicated, in his very nature, to "doing something about" whatever was not right?

How, she wondered, had Noel spent yesterday afternoon after he had replaced the telephone in his study at home? She could tell almost to a T, no crystal-ball gazing required. He would have wandered, thinking, about the rooms for a time, unable to put his mind on the next morning's committee meeting. As important as it was that no Communist crooner should leave a pink smear on so American an outfit as their tobacco company, he would not have been able to concentrate. He likely would have entered the living room, only to find Clara's dog, Ronnie, lying under the piano, a spot he favored during the hot months. They would have looked at each other, the two of them, disputing something. Then he would presently have found himself before the icebox, making a ham sandwich, perhaps, snapping the cap from a cold bottle of beer. Tilting beer into his mouth with one hand, eating with the other, he might later appear strolling about the yard. It might occur to him—she hoped it had—that he needed to speak to the yardman about watering the grass twice a week so it wouldn't look like the Sahara Desert when they returned. When *they* returned! With Clara, or without her? Qualms swept her. Her heart went down like an elevator.

"Signora! Attenzione!"

The voice was from above. A window had been pushed wide and a woman was leaning out to shake a carpet into the street. Margaret Johnson stopped, stepping back a few paces. Dust flew down, then settled. An arm came out and closed the shutters. She went on.

And quite possibly Noel, then, as dusk fell, his mind being still unsettled, would have walked over three blocks and across the park to his sister Isabel's apartment. Didn't he, in personal matters, always turn to women? Isabel, yes, would be the first to hear the news from abroad. She would not be as satisfactory a listener as Margaret, for being both a divorcée and something of a businesswoman—she ran the hat department in Winston-Salem's largest department store—she was inclined to be entirely too casual about everybody's affairs except her own. She would be beautifully dressed in one of her elaborate lounging outfits, for nobody appreciates a Sunday evening at home quite so much as a working woman. She would turn off the television to accommodate Noel, and bring him a drink of the very best Scotch. When she had heard the entire story of the goings-on in Florence, she would as likely as not say, "Well, after all, why not?" Hadn't she always advanced the theory that Clara had as much sense as most of the women she sold hats to? "They're going to want a dowry," she might add.

Now mentioning a dowry that way would be all to the good. Noel would feel a great relief. He disliked being taken advantage of, and he was obviously uneasy that the Naccarellis were only after Clara's money. Wouldn't Margaret be staying in the best hotel, eating at the best restaurants, shopping in the best shops? The Italians had "caught on," of course, from the first that she was well off. But now, through Isabel, he would have a name for all this. Dowry. It was customary. "Of course, they're all Catholics," he would go on to complain. Isabel would not be of any use at all there. Religion was of no interest to her whatever. She could not see why it was of interest to anybody.

Later as they talked, Isabel would ask Noel about the Communist scare. She would be in doubt that the crooner was actually such a threat to the nation or the tobacco company that a song or two would ruin them all. And was all this trouble and upset necessary—trips to Washington, committee meetings, announcements of policy and what not? Noel would not be above reminding her that she liked her dividend checks well enough not to want them put in any jeopardy. He might not come right out and say this, but it would cross his mind. More and more in recent years, Noel's every experience found immediate reference in his business. Or had he always been this way, if, in his younger years, less obviously so? Yet Mrs. Johnson remembered once on a summer vacation they had taken at

Myrtle Beach during the Depression, Noel playing ball on the sand with the two children, when a wind had driven them inside their cottage and for a short time they had been afraid a hurricane was starting. How they had saved to make that trip! That was all Noel could recall about it in later years. But at the time he had remarked as the raw wind streamed sand against the thin tremulous walls—he was holding Clara in his lap, "Well, at least we're all together." The wind had soon dropped, and the sea had enjoyed a quiet green dusk; their fear had gone, too, but she could not forget the steadying effect of his words. When, at what subtle point, had money come to seem to him the very walls that kept out the storm? Or was the trouble simply that with Clara and her problem always before him at home, he had found business to be a thing he could at least handle success-fully, as he could not, in common with all mankind (poor Noel!), ultimately "handle" life? And business was, after all, so "normal."

Whatever the answer to how it had happened—and perhaps the nature of the times had had a lot to do with it: depression, the New Deal, the war—the fact was that it had happened, and Margaret knew now that nothing on earth short of the news of the imminent death of her or Clara or both, could induce Noel Johnson to Flor-ence until the business in hand was concluded to the entire satisfac-tion of the tobacco company, whose future must, at all personal cost, be secure. On the other hand, since she had already foreseen that if he came here he would spoil everything, wasn't this an advantage?

She had wandered, in this remote corner of the city, into a small, poor bar. She lighted a cigarette and asked for a coffee. Since there was no place to sit, she stood at the counter. Two young men were working back of the bar, and seeing that she only stared at her coffee without drinking it, they became extremely anxious to make her happy. They wondered whether the coffee was hot enough, if she wanted more sugar or some other thing perhaps. She shook her head, smiling her thanks, seeing as though from a distance their great dim eyes, their white teeth and their kindness. "*Simpatica,*" one said, more about her than to her. "*Si, simpatica,*" the other agreed. They had exchanged a nod. One had an inspiration. "*Americana?*" he asked.

"*Si,*" said Mrs. Johnson.

They stood back, continuing to smile like adults who watch a child, while she drank her coffee down. At this moment, she had the feeling that if she had requested their giant espresso machine, which seemed, besides a few cheap cups and saucers and a pastry stand, to be their only possession, they would have ripped it up bodily and given it to her. And perhaps, for a moment, this was true.

What is it, to reach a decision? It is like walking down a long Florentine street where, at the very end, a dim shape is waiting until you get there. When Mrs. Johnson finally reached this street and saw what was ahead, she moved steadily forward to see it at long last up close. What was it? Well, nothing monstrous, it seemed, but human, with a face much like her own, that of a woman who loved her daughter and longed for her happiness.

"I'm going to do it," she thought. "Without Noel."

11

Signor Naccarelli was late coming home for lunch the next day; the water in the pasta pot had boiled away once and had to be replenished. He was not as late, however, as he had been many times before, or as late as he would have preferred to be that day. And though his news was good, his temper was short. Signora Johnson had talked with her husband on the telephone from America. Signor Johnson could not come to Italy from America. He could not leave his business. They were to proceed with the wedding without Signor Johnson. He neatly baled mouthfuls of spaghetti on his fork, mixed mineral water with a little wine and found ways of cutting off the effusive rejoicing his family was given to. The real fact was that he was displeased with the American signora. Why, after dressing herself in the new Italian costume of printed white silk, which must have cost at least 60,000 lire in the Via Tornabuoni—and with the chic little hat, too—should she give him her news and then leave him in the café after thirty minutes, saying "lunch" and "time to go" and "Clara"? American women were at the mercy of their children. It was shocking and disgusting. She had made the appointment with him, well and good. In the most fashionable café in Florence; they had been observed talking deeply together over an aperitif in the shadow of a great green umbrella. It would not be the first time he had been observed with this lady about the city. And then, after thirty minutes—! An Italian man would see to manners of this sort. This bread was stale. Were they all eating it, or was it saved from last week, especially for him?

Signora Naccarelli, meanwhile, from the mention of the word "wedding," had quietly taken over everything. She had been more or less waiting up to this time, neither impatient nor anxious, but, like a natural force, quite aware of how inevitable she was, while the others debated and decided superficial affairs. The heart of the matter in Signora Naccarelli's view was so overwhelmingly enormous that she did not have to decide to heed it, because there was nothing outside of it to make this decision. She simply *was* the heart—that great pulsing organ that could bleed with sorrow or make little fishlike leaps of joy and that always knew just what it knew. What it knew in Signora Naccarelli's case was very little and quite sufficient. Her son Fabrizio was handsome and good, and Clara, the little American flower, so sweet and gentle, would bear children for him. The signora's arms had yearned for some time for Clara and were already beginning to yearn for her children, and this to the signora was exactly the same thing as saying that the arms of the Blessed Virgin yearned for Clara and for Clara's children, and this in turn was the same as saying that the Holy Mother Church yearned likewise. It was all very simple and true.

Informed with such certainties, Signora Naccarelli had not been inactive. A brother of a friend of her nephew's was a priest who had studied in England. She had fixed on him already, since he spoke English, as the very one for Clara's instruction. That same afternoon she set about arranging a time for them to meet. Within a few days, the priest was reporting to her that Clara had a real devotion to the Virgin. The signora had known all along that this was true. A distant cousin of Signor Naccarelli's was secretary to a *monsignore* at the Vatican, and through him special permission was obtained for Clara to be married in a full church ceremony. At this the signora's joy could not be contained, and she went so far as to telephone Mrs. Johnson and explain these developments to her, a word at a time, in Italian, at the top of her voice, with tears.

"*Capisce, signora? In chiesa! Capisce?*"

Mrs. Johnson did not *capisce*. She thought from the tears that something must have gone wrong.

But nothing had, or did, until the morning in the office of the *parroco*, where they gathered a little more than two weeks before the wedding to fill out the appropriate forms.

12

What had happened was not at all clear for some time; it was not even clear that anything had.

The four of them—Clara and Fabrizio, with Margaret Johnson and Signor Naccarelli for witnesses—were assembled in the office of the *parroco*, a small dusty room with a desk, a few chairs and several locked cabinets that reached to the ceiling and one window looking down on a cloister. In the center of the cloister was a hexagonal medieval well. It was nearing noon. Whatever noise there was seemed to gather itself together and drowse in the sun on the stone pavings below, so that Mrs. Johnson experienced the reassuring tranquillity of silence. Signor Naccarelli, hat in hand, took a nervous turn or two around the office, looked at a painting that was propped in the back corner and, with a sour downturning of his mouth, said something uncomplimentary about priests, which Mrs. Johnson did not quite catch. Fabrizio sat by Clara and twirled a clever straw ornament attached to her bag. So much stone was all that kept them cool. The chanting in the church below had stopped, but the priest did not come.

The hours ahead were planned: they would go to lunch to join Giuseppe and Franca, his wife, and two or three other friends. Of course, Mrs. Johnson was explaining to herself, this smell of candle smoke, stone dust and oil painting is to them just what blackboards, chalk and old Sunday School literature are to us; there's probably no difference at all if you stay open-minded. To be ready for the questions that they were there to answer, she made sure that she had brought her passport and Clara's. She drew them out of their appropriate pocket in the enormous bag Winston-Salem's best department store had advised for European travel and held them ready.

Signor Naccarelli decided to amuse her. He sat down beside her. Documents, he explained in a jaunty tone, were the curse of Italy. You could not become a corpse in Italy without having filled in the proper document. There were people in offices in Rome still sorting documents filed there before the war. What war? they would say if you told them. But, Mrs. Johnson assured him, all this kind of thing went on in America, too. The files were more expensive, perhaps. She got him to laugh. His quick hands picked up the passports. Clara and Fabrizio were whispering to each other. Their voices, too, seemed to go out into the sun, like a neighborhood sound. Signor Naccarelli glanced at Mrs. Johnson's passport picture—how terrible! She was much more beautiful than this. Clara's next—this of the signorina was better, somewhat. A page turned beneath his thumb.

A moment later, Signor Naccarelli had leaped up as though stung by a bee. He hastened to Fabrizio, to whom he spoke rapidly in Italian. Then he shot from the room. Fabrizio leaped up, also. *"Ma Papà! Non possiamo fare nulla—!"* The priest came, but it was too late. He and Fabrizio entered into a long conversation. Clara retreated to her mother's side. When Fabrizio turned to them at last, he seemed to have forgotten all his English. "My father—forget—remember—the appointments," he blundered. Struck by an idea, he whirled back to the priest and embarked on a second conversation, which he finally summarized to Clara and her mother, "To-morrow."

At that, precisely as though he were a casual friend who hoped to see them again sometime, he bowed over Mrs. Johnson's hand, made an appropriate motion to Clara and turned away. They were left alone with the priest.

"Tomorrow" . . . *domani*. Mrs. Johnson knew by now to be the word in Italy most likely to signal the finish of everything. She felt, indeed, without the ghost of an idea how or why it had happened, that everything was trembling, tottering about her, had perhaps, without her knowledge, already collapsed. She looked out on the priest like someone seen across a gulf. As if to underscore the impression, he spread his hands with a little helpless shrug and said, "No Eeenglish."

Mrs. Johnson zipped the passports back into place and went out into the corridor, down the steps and into the sun. *"Domani,"* the priest said after them.

Holding Clara by the hand, she made her way back to the hotel.

The instant she was alone she had the passports out, searching through them. Would nothing give her a clue to what had struck Signor Naccarelli? She remembered stories: the purloined letter; the perfect crime, marred only by the murderer's driver's license left carelessly on the hotel dresser. What had she missed? She thought her nerves would fly apart in all directions.

Slowly, with poise and majesty, the beautiful afternoon went by. A black cloud crossed the city, flashed two or three fierce bolts, rumbled halfheartedly and passed on. The river glinted under the sun, and the boys and fishermen who had not been frightened inside shouted and laughed at the ones who had. Everything stood strongly exposed in sunlight and cast its appropriate shadow: in Italy there is the sense that everything is clear and visible, that nothing is withheld. Fabrizio, when Margaret Johnson had touched his arm to detain him in the office of the *parroco*, had drawn back like recoiling steel. When Clara had started forward with a cry, he had set her quickly back, and silent. If they were to be rejected, had they not at least the right to common courtesy? What were they being given to understand? In Florence, at four o'clock, everything seemed to take a step nearer, more distinctly, more totally to be seen.

When the cloud came up, Mrs. Johnson and Clara clung together, pretending that was what they were afraid of. Later they got out one of Clara's favorite books: Nancy Drew, the lady detective, turned airline hostess to solve the murder of a famous explorer. Nancy Drew had so far been neglected. Clara was good and did as she was told about everything, but could not eat. Late in the evening, around ten, the telephone rang in their suite. A gentleman was waiting below for the signora.

Coming down alone, Mrs. Johnson found Signor Naccarelli awaiting her, but how changed! If pleasant things had passed between them, he was not thinking of them now; one doubted that they had actually occurred. Grave, gestureless, as though wrapped in a black cape, he inclined to her deeply. Margaret Johnson had trouble keeping herself from giggling. Wasn't it all a comedy? If somebody would only laugh out loud with enough conviction, wouldn't it all crumble? But she recalled Clara, her eye feasting on Fabrizio's shoulder, her finger exploring the inspired juncture of his neck and spine, and so she composed herself and allowed herself to be escorted from the hotel.

She saw at once that his object was to talk and that he had no destination—they walked along the river. The heat had been terrible for a week, but a breeze was blowing off the water now, and she wished she had brought her shawl.

"I saw today," Signor Naccarelli began in measured tones, but when Mrs. Johnson suddenly sneezed, "Why did not you tell me?" he burst out, turning on her. "What can you be thinking of?"

Stricken silent, she walked on beside him. Somehow, then, he had found out. Certain dreary, familiar feelings returned to her. Meeting Noel at the airport, Clara behind in the car, wronged again, poor little victim of her own or her mother's impulses. Well, if Signor Naccarelli was to be substituted for Noel, she thought with relief that anyway she could at last confess. Instead of Bermuda, they could go to the first boat sailing from Naples.

"It is too much," went on Signor Naccarelli. "Two, three years, where there is love, where there is agreement, I say it is all right. But, no, it is too much. It is to make the fantastic."

"Years?" she repeated.

"Can it be possible! But you must have understood! My son Fabrizio is twenty years old, no more. Whereas, your daughter, I see with my two eyes, written in the passport today in the office of the *parroco*—twenty-six! Six years difference! It cannot be. In that moment I ask myself, What must I say, what can I do? Soon it will be too late. What to do? I make the excuse, an appointment. I see often in the cinema this same excuse. It was not true. I have lied. I tell you frankly."

"I had not thought of her being older," said Mrs. Johnson. Weak with relief, she stopped walking. When she leaned her elbow against the parapet, she felt it trembling. "Believe me, Signor Naccarelli, they seemed so much the same age to me, it had not entered my mind that there was any difference."

"It cannot be," said Signor Naccarelli positively, scowling out toward the noble skyline of his native city. "I pass an afternoon of torment, an inferno. As I am a man, as I am a Florentine, as I am a father, as I long for my son's happiness, as—" Words failed him.

"But surely the difference between them is not as great as that," Mrs. Johnson reasoned. "In America we have seen many, many happy marriages with an even greater difference. Clara—she has been very carefully brought up. She had a long illness some years ago. To me she seemed even younger than Fabrizio."

"A long illness." He whirled on her scornfully. "How am I to know that she is cured of it?"

"You see her," countered Mrs. Johnson. "She is as healthy as she seems."

"It cannot be." He turned away.

"Don't you realize," Mrs. Johnson pleaded, "that they are in love? Whatever their ages are, they are both young. This is a deep thing, a true thing. To try to stop what is between them now—"

"*Try* to stop? My dear lady, I will stop whatever I wish to stop."

"Fabrizio—" she began.

"Yes, yes. He will try to kill himself. It is only to grow up. I, also, have sworn to take my life—can you believe? With passion I shake like this—and here I am today. No, no. To talk is one thing, to do another. Do not make illusions. He will not."

"But Clara—" she began. Her voice faltered. She thought she would cry in spite of herself.

Signor Naccarelli scowled out toward the dark river. "It cannot be," he repeated.

Mrs. Johnson looked at him and composure returned to her. Because whether this was comedy or tragedy, he had told her the truth. He could and would stop everything if he chose, and Fabrizio would not kill himself. If Mrs. Johnson had thought it practical, she would have murdered Signor Naccarelli. Instead she suggested that they cross over to a small bar. She was feeling that perhaps a brandy . . .

The bar was a tourist trap, placed near to American Express and crowded during the day. At night few people wandered in. Only one table was occupied at present. In the far corner, what looked to Mrs. Johnson exactly like a girl from Winston-Salem was conversing with an American boy who was growing a beard. Mrs. Johnson chose a table at equidistance between the pair and the waiter. She gave her order and waited, saying nothing till the small glass on the saucer was set before her. It was her last chance and she knew it. It helped her timing considerably to know how much she detested Signor Naccarelli.

"This is all too bad," said Mrs. Johnson softly. "I received a letter from my husband today. Instead of five thousand dollars, he wants to make Clara and Fabrizio a present of fifteen thousand dollars."

"That is nine million three hundred and seventy-five thousand lire," said Signor Naccarelli. "So now you will write and explain everything, and that this wedding cannot be."

"Yes," said Mrs. Johnson, and sipped her brandy.

Presently Signor Naccarelli ordered a cup of coffee.

Later on they might have been observed in various places, strolling about quiet, less frequented streets. Their talk ran on many things. Signor Naccarelli recalled her sneeze and wondered if she was cold. Mrs. Johnson was busily working out in the back of her mind how she was going to get fifteen thousand dollars without her husband, for the moment, knowing anything about it.

It would take most of a family legacy, invested in her own name; and the solemn confidence of a lawyer, an old family friend; a long-distance request for him to trust her and cooperate; a promise that Noel would know everything anyway, within the month. Later, explaining to Noel, "In the U.S. you would undoubtedly have wanted to build a new house for your daughter and her husband. . . ." A good point.

"You must forgive me," said Signor Naccarelli, "if I ask a most personal thing of you. The Signorina Clara, she would like to have children, would she not? My wife can think of nothing else."

"Oh, Clara longs for children!" said Mrs. Johnson.

Toward midnight they stopped in a bar for a final brandy. Signor Naccarelli insisted on paying, as always.

When she returned to her room, Margaret Johnson sat on her bed for a while. Then she stood at the window for a while and looked down on the river. With one finger, she touched her mouth where there lingered an Italian kiss.

How had she maneuvered herself out of further, more prolonged and more intimately staged embraces without giving the least impression that she hadn't enjoyed the one he had surprised her with? In the shadow of a handsome façade, before the stout, lion-mouth crested arch where he had beckoned her to stop—"Something here will interest you, perhaps"—how, oh, how, had she managed to manage it well? Out of practice in having to for, she shuddered to think, how many years. Nor could anything erase, remove from her the estimable flash of his eye, so near her own, so near.

"Mother!"

Why, I had forgotten *her,* thought Mrs. Johnson.

"Yes, darling, I'm coming!" In Clara's room she switched on a dim Italian lamp. "There, now, it's all going to be all right. We're going to meet them tomorrow, just as we did today. But tomorrow it will be all right. Go to sleep now. You'll see."

It's true, she thought, smoothing Clara's covers, switching out the light. No doubt of it now. And to keep down the taste of success, she bit hard on her lip (so lately kissed). If he let me out so easily, it means he doesn't want to risk anything. It means he wants this wedding. He wants it, too.

13

In that afternoon's gentle decline, Fabrizio had found himself restless and irritable. Earlier he had deliberately ignored his promise to meet Giuseppe, who was doubtless burning to find out why the luncheon had not come off. That day he traveled unfamiliar paths, did not return home for lunch and spent the siesta hours sulking about the Boboli Gardens, where an unattractive American lady with a guidebook flattered herself that he was pursuing her. Every emotion seemed stronger than usual. If anyone he knew should see him here! He all but dashed out at the thought, entered narrow streets and, in a poor quarter, gnawed a workingman's sandwich—a hard loaf with a paper-thin slice of salami. When the black cloud blew up he waited in the door of a church he had never seen before.

About six he entered his own little shop, where he had been seldom seen of late and then always full of jokes and laughter. Now he asked for the books and, finding that some handkerchief boxes had got among the gloves, imagined that everything was in disorder and that the cousin was busy ruining his business and robbing him. The cousin, who had been robbing him, but only mildly—they both understood almost to the lira exactly how much—insisted that Fabrizio should pay him his wages at once and he would leave and never return voluntarily as long as he lived. They both became bored with the argument.

Fabrizio thought of Clara. When he thought of her thighs and breasts he sighed; weakness swept him; he grew almost ill. So he thought of her face instead. Gentle, beautiful, it rose before him. He saw it everywhere, that face. No lonely villa on a country hillside, yellow in the sun, oleanders on the terrace, but might have inside a chapel, closed off, unused for years, on the wall a fresco, work of some ancient name known in all the world, a lost work—Clara. He loved her. She looked up at him now out of the glass-enclosed counter for merchandise, but the face was only his, framed in socks.

At evening, at dark, he went the opposite way from home, down the Arno, walking sometimes along the streets, descending wherever he could to walk along the bank itself. He saw the sun set along the flow, and stopping in the dark at last he said aloud, "I could walk to Pisa." At another direction into the dark, he said, "Or Vallombrosa." Then he turned, ascended the bank to the road and walked back home. Possessed by an even deeper mood, the strangest he had ever known, he wandered about the city, listening to the echo of his own steps in familiar streets and looking at towering shapes of stone. The night seemed to be moving along secretly, but fast; the earth, bearing all burdens lightly, spinning, and racing ahead—just as a Florentine had said, so it did. The silent towers tilted toward the dawn.

He saw his father the next morning. "It is all right," said Signor Naccarelli. "I have talked a long time with the signora. We will go today as yesterday to the office of the *parroco*."

"But Papà!" Fabrizio spread all ten fingers wide and shook his hands violently before him. "You had me sick with worry. My heart almost stopped. Yesterday I was like a crazy person. I have never spent such a day."

"Yes, well. I am sorry. The signorina is a bit older than I thought. Not much, but—Did you know?"

"Of course I knew. I told you so. Long ago. Did you forget it?"

"Perhaps I did. Never mind. And you, my son. You are twenty-one years, *vero*?"

"Papà!" Here Fabrizio all but left the earth itself. "I am twenty-three! The sun has cooked your brain. I should be the one to act like this."

"All right, all right. I was mistaken. But my instinct was right." He tapped his brow. "It is always better to discuss everything in great detail. I felt that we were going too quickly. You cannot be too careful in these things. But my son—" He caught the boy's shoulder. "Remember to say nothing to the Americans. Do you want them to think we are crazy?"

"You are *innamorato* of the signora. I understand it all."

14

At the wedding Margaret Johnson sat quietly while a dream unfolded before her. She watched closely and missed nothing.

She saw Clara emerge like a fresh flower out of the antique smell of candle smoke, incense and damp stone, and advance in white Venetian lace with so deep a look shadowing out the hollow of her cheek, she might have stood double for a Botticelli. As for Fabrizio, he who had such a gift for appearing did not fail them. His beauty was outshone only by his outrageous pride in himself; he saw to it that everybody saw him well. Like an angel appearing in a painting, he seemed to face outward to say, This is what I look like, see? But his innocence protected him like magic.

Clara lifted her veil like a good girl exactly when she had been told to. Fabrizio looked at her and love sprang up in his face. The priest went on intoning, and since it was twelve o'clock all the bells from over the river and nearby began to ring at slightly different intervals—the deep-throated ones and the sweet ones, muffled and clear—one could hear them all.

The Signora Naccarelli had come into her own that day. She obviously believed that she had had difficulties to overcome in bringing about this union, but having gotten the proper heavenly parties well informed, she had brought everything into line. Her bosom had sometimes been known to heave and her eye to dim, but that day she was serene. She wore flowers and an enormous medallion of her dead mother outlined in pearls. That unlikely specimen, a middle-class Neapolitan, she now seemed both peasant and goddess. Her hair had never been more smoothly bound, and natural color touched her large cheeks. Before the wedding, the wicked Giuseppe had seen her and run into her arms. Smiling perpetually at no one, it was as though she had created them all.

Signor Naccarelli had escorted Margaret Johnson to her place and sat beside her. He kept his arms tightly folded across his chest, and his face wore an odd, unreadable expression, mouth somewhat pursed, his high, cold Florentine nose drawn toughly across the bridge. Perhaps his collar was too tight.

Yes, Margaret Johnson saw everything, even the only person to cry, Giuseppe's wife, who had chosen to put her sophisticated self into a girlish, English-type summer frock of pale blue with a broad white collar.

I will not be needed anymore, thought Margaret Johnson with something like a sigh, for before her eyes the strongest maternal forces in the world were taking her daughter to themselves. I have stepped out of the picture forever, she thought, and as if to bear her out, as the ceremony ended and everyone started moving toward the church door, no one noticed Margaret Johnson at all. They were waiting to form the wedding cortege, which would wind over the river and up the hill to the restaurant and the long luncheon.

She did not mind not being noticed. She had done her job, and she knew it. She had played, single-handed and unadvised, a tricky game in a foreign country, and she had managed to realize from it the dearest wish of her heart. Signora Naccarelli was passing—one had to pause until the suction of that lady in motion had faded. Then Mrs. Johnson moved through the atrium and out to the colonnaded porch, where, standing aside from the others, she could observe Clara stepping into a car, her white skirts dazzling in the sun. Clara saw her mother: they waved to each other. Fabrizio was made to wave, as well. Over everybody's head a bronze fountain in the piazza jetted water into the sunlight, and nearby a group of tourists had stopped to look.

Clara and Fabrizio were driving off. So it had really happened! It was done. Mrs. Johnson found her vision blotted out. The reason was simply that Signor Naccarelli, that old devil, had come between her and whatever she was looking at; now he was smiling at her. The money again. There it was, forever returning, the dull moment of exchange.

Who was fooling whom, she longed to say, but did not. Or rather, since we both had our little game to play, which of us came off better? Let's tell the truth at last, you and I.

It was a great pity, Signor Naccarelli was saying, that Signor Johnson could not have been here to see so beautiful a wedding. Mrs. Johnson agreed.

Though no one knew it but her, Signor Johnson at that very moment was winging his way to Rome. She had cut things rather fine; it made her shudder to realize how close a schedule she had had to work with. Tomorrow she would rise early to catch the train to Rome, to wait at the airport for Noel to land, but wait alone this time, and, no matter what he might think or say, triumphant.

He was going to think and say a lot, Noel Johnson was, and she knew she had to brace herself. He was going to go on believing for the rest of his life, for instance, that she had bought this marriage, the way American heiresses used to engage obliging titled gentlemen as husbands. No use telling him that sort of thing was out of date. Was money ever out of date? he would want to know.

But Margaret Johnson was going to weather the storm with Noel, or so at any rate she had the audacity to believe. Hadn't he in some mysterious way already, at what point she did not know, separated his own life from that of his daughter's? A defective thing must go. She had seen him act upon this principle too many times not to feel that in some fundamental, unconscious way he would, long ago, have broken this link. Why had he done so? Why, indeed? Why are we all and what are we really doing? Who was to say when *he*, in turn, had irritated the selfish, greedy nature of things and been kicked on the head in all the joyousness of his playful ways? No, it would be pride alone that was going to make him angry: she had gone behind his back. At least so she believed.

Though weary of complexities and more than ready to take a long rest from them all, Mrs. Johnson was prepared on the strength of her belief to make one more gamble yet, namely, that however Noel might rage, no honeymoon was going to be interrupted, that Signor Naccarelli was not going to be searched out and told the truth, and that the officials of the great Roman church could sleep peacefully in rich apartments or poor damp cells, undisturbed by Noel Johnson. He would grow quiet at last, and in the quiet, even Margaret Johnson had not yet dared to imagine what sort of life, what degree of delight in it, they might not be able to discover (rediscover?) together. This was uncertain. What was certain was that in that same quiet she would begin to miss her daughter. She would go on missing her forever.

She was swept by a strange weakness. Signor Naccarelli was offering her his arm, but she could not move to take it. Her head was spinning and she leaned, instead, against the cool stone column. She did not feel able to move. Beyond them, the group of tourists were trying to take a picture, but were unable to shield their cameras from the light's terrible strength. A scarf was tried, a coat; would some person cast a shadow?

"Do you remember," it came to Mrs. Johnson to ask Signor Naccarelli, "the man who fell down when the cannon fired that day? What happened to him?"

"He died," said Signor Naccarelli.

She saw again, as if straight into her vision, painfully contracting it, the flash that the sun had all but blurred away to nothing. She heard again the momentary hush under heaven, followed by the usual noise's careless resumption. In desperate motion through the flickering rhythms of the "event," he went on and on in glimpses, trying to get up, while near him, silent in bronze, Cellini's *Perseus,* in the calm repose of triumph, held aloft the Medusa's head.

"I did the right thing," she said. "I know I did."

Signor Naccarelli made no reply. "The right thing": what was it?

Whatever it was, it was a comfort to Mrs. Johnson, who presently felt strong enough to take his arm and go with him, out to the waiting car.

UP NORTH

I, MAUREEN

On the sunny fall afternoon, I (Maureen) saw the girl sitting in the oval-shaped park near the St. Lawrence River. She was sitting on green grass, bent lovingly, as though eternally, over her guitar. They are always like that, absorbed, hair falling past their faces, whether boys or girls: there seems little difference between them: they share the tender absorption of mother with child. The whole outside world regards them, forms a hushed circle about them.

I, Maureen, perceived this while driving by on an errand for Mr. Massimo.

I used to live out there, on what in Montreal we call the Lakeshore. I did nothing right then, so returning to that scene is painful. I sought relief from the memories of five years ago by letting the girl with the guitar—bending to it, framed in grass, the blue river flowing by—redeem my memories, redeem me, I could only hope, also. Me, Maureen, stung with the identity of bad memories.

Everything any woman in her right mind could want—that was my life. Denis Partham's wife, and not even very pretty or classy: I never had anything resembling looks or background. I was a bit run-down looking, all my life. From the age of two, I looked run-down. People used to say right out to me: "You've just had luck, that's all." But Denis said the luck was his. He really thought that, for years and years. Until the day I thought he was dead. After that he had to face it that luck can run out, even for a Partham.

We had a house on the river and it was beautiful, right on the water. It was in Baie d'Urfé, one of the old townships, and you can describe it for yourself, if you so desire. There can be rugs of any texture, draperies of any fabric, paneling both painted and stained, shelves to put books in, cupboards to fill with china and linen. The choice of every upholstery sample or kitchen tile was a top-level decision; the struggle for perfection had a life-and-death quality about it. If my interest was not wholly taken up in all this, if I was play-acting, I did not know it. Are people when measuring and weighing and pondering names for a crown prince, serious? I was expecting the prince; that was why the Parthams gave us the house. Sure enough, the baby was a boy. Two years and another one arrived, a girl. (Isn't Nature great? She belongs to the Parthams.)

In the winter we had cocktails before dinner in a spacious room overlooking the frozen lake, watching the snow drift slowly down, seeing the skaters stroking outward. We had sherry between church services and Sunday lunch. Then the ice boats raced past, silent, fast as dreams.

Our children were beautiful, like children drawn with a pencil over and again in many attitudes, all pure, among many Canadian settings. Denis was handsome, a well-built man, younger than I, with dark hair and a strong, genuine smile. In his world, I was the only dowdy creature. Yet he loved me, heart and soul. And why? I used to sit in a big chair in a corner of the library hunched up like a crow, and wonder this. In summer I sat on the terraces, and there, too, I wondered.

All I knew was that aged twenty-five, a plain, single girl, I had come to the Parthams' big stone house high in Westmount with some friends. It was late, a gathering after a local play. A woman who worked at the library with me had a younger sister in the play and had asked me to come. One of the Parthams was in it, too, so we all got invited up for drinks. Somebody graciously learned that I was living way out in N.D.G., that area of the unnumbered middle class, and Denis, who had been talking to me about the library, offered to drive me home. When we reached the house, he turned off the motor, then the lights, and turning to me began to kiss me hungrily. He had fallen silent along the way, and I had felt he was going to do something like this. I simply judged that he was a rich boy out for more sexual experience, seeking it outside his own class, the way privileged people often do. Yet he was moved and excited way beyond the average: so I put him down as a boy with problems, and squirmed my way out of his arms and his Oldsmobile as best I could. Next day he telephoned me at the library, longing to see me again. He was that way from then on. He said he could never change. Through all our dates, then through season after season, year after year, I saw how his voice would take on a different note when he saw me, how his eyes would light up. I knew his touch, his sexual currents, his eager kisses, his talk, his thoughts, his tastes. At some point, we got married. But the marriage, I helplessly realized, had taken place already, in the moment he had seen me in the corner of one of the many Partham living rooms in their great stone house, me (Maureen), completely out of place. Before I knew it, he had enveloped me all over, encased me like a strong vine. My family could believe my good fortune no more than I could. It was too good to last, but it did; too good to be true, but it was. We had, in addition to the Lakeshore house at Baie d'Urfé, an apartment on Drummond Street in Montreal, servants, two cars, wonderful friends, a marvelous life.

Then, one summer day, it happened. It could never unhappen.

Denis was out sailing and in passing under a bridge, the metal mast of the boat struck a live wire. His hand was on the mast and the voltage knocked him down. When they brought him in they had rolled him onto the sail and were carrying him by four improvised corners, like somebody asleep in a hammock. His head was turned to one side. Everyone on our lawn and dock seemed to know from the minute the boat appeared, unexpectedly returned, that something terrible had happened. We crowded forward together, all the family and friends not sailing, left behind on the lawns to swim, sun, play, or talk, and though I was among the first, I felt just as one of them, not special. I saw his face turned to one side, looking (the eyes shut and the skin discolored blue and red) like a face drowned through a rift in ice. I thought he was dead, and so did we all, even, I later learned, those who were carrying him. They laid him on the lawn and someone said: "Stay back," while another, running from the moment the boat touched the dock, was already at the telephone. But by that time there were arms around me, to hold me back from rushing to him. They encountered no forward force. I was in retreat already, running backward from the moment, into another world which had been waiting for me for some time. All they did was hasten me into it. My fierce sprinting backward plus the force of their normal human attention—that of trying to keep a wife from hurling herself with all the velocity of human passion toward her husband, so unexpectedly served up before her as (so it seemed) a corpse—outdid possibility. But we leave the earth with difficulty, and I wasn't up to that. I fell backward, sprawling awkwardly; I lay observing the bluest of July skies in which white clouds had filled in giant areas at good distances from the sun. Sky, cloud, and sun completed me, while ambulances wailed and bore away whomever they would.

Denis did not die; he recovered nicely. All life resumed as before. A month later I made my first attempt at suicide.

———

It was finally to one of the psychiatrists I saw that I recounted how all of this had started, from a minor event, meaningless *to all but me*. (To me alone the world had spoken.)

I had been sunbathing on the pier a week or so before Denis's accident when two of the children whose parents owned a neighboring property began to throw things into the water. I could see them—two skinny boys on the neighboring pier—and know that while they pretended to be hurling rocks and bottles straight out into the lake, they were in reality curving them closer into land, striking near our docking area. I was thinking of getting up to shout at them when it happened. A bit of blue-green glass arching into the sun's rays, caught and trapped an angle of that light, refracting it to me. It struck, a match for lightning. My vision simply for a moment was by this brilliance extinguished; and in the plunge of darkness that ensued I could only see the glass rock reverse its course and speed toward me. It entered my truest self, my consciousness, reverberating with silent brilliance. From that point I date my new beginning. It was a nothing point, an illusion, but an illusion that had happened to me, if there is such a thing. . . .

"If there is such a thing," the doctor repeated.

"If there is such a thing," I said again, sounding, I knew, totally mad.

Doctors wait for something to be said that fits a pattern they have learned to be true, just as teachers wait for you to write English or French. If you wrote a new and unknown language they wouldn't know what to do with you—you would fail.

"It explains to me," I went on, realizing I was taking the risk of being consigned to the asylum at Verdun for an indefinite period, "why I ran backward instead of forward when I thought Denis was dead. I want my own world. I have been there once. I want to return. If I can't, I might as well be dead."

"Your attempts to take your own life might be thought of as efforts to join your husband, whom you believed to have reached death," the doctor suggested. He had a thick European accent, and an odd name, Miracorte. God knows where he was from.

I said nothing.

One day I left home. I had done this before but they had always come for me, tranquilized me, hospitalized me, removed things from me that might be handy ways of self-destruction, talked to me, loved me, nurtured me back to being what they wanted me to be—somebody, in other words, like themselves. This time they didn't come. A doctor came, a new one, younger than the first. He asked from the intercom system in the apartment building in East Montreal which I had fled to, taking the first furnished place I could find, whether he could see me. I let him in.

He was plain English-Canadian from Regina, named Johnson.

"Everyone is a little schizoid," he said. They had told me that, told me and told me that. "You choose the other side of the coin, the other side of yourself. You have to have it. If you don't have it, you will die. Don't you know that some people drink themselves into it, others hit drugs, some run off to the bush, some kill or steal or turn into religious freaks? You're a mild case, comparatively speaking. All you want is to be with it, calmly, like a lover."

I was crying before I knew it, tears of relief. He was the first to consent to my line of feeling. Why had it been so hard, why were they all reluctant to do so? We allow people to mouth platitudes to us one after another, and agree to them blandly, knowing they aren't true, just because there's no bite to them, no danger. The truth is always dangerous, so in agreeing to what I felt, he was letting me in for danger. But it was all that was left to try.

"There's a bank account for you at this address." He gave me the chequebook and the deposit slip. "If you need more, call me. Your husband has agreed to this plan."

I took the chequebook silently, but was vowing already that I would never use it. I was going to get a job.

The young doctor sat frowning, eyes on the floor.

"Denis feels awful," I said, reading his thoughts aloud. "This has made him suffer."

"I didn't say that," Dr. Johnson said. "It makes you suffer to stay with him. Maybe—well, maybe he can get through better without you than you can with him."

———

From then on I was on my own, escaping into the mystery that is East Montreal, a fish thrown barely alive back into water. Not that I had ever lived there. But to Westmount families who own houses in Baie d'Urfé, East Montreal presents even more of an opaque surface than N.D.G. It is thought to be French, and this is so, but it is also Greek, Italian, Oriental, and immigrant Jewish. I was poor, unattractive as ever; I ached for my children and the sound of Denis's voice, his love, everything I had known. I went through an agony of missing what I could have, all back, and whole as ever, just by picking up the phone, just by taking a taxi and saying, "Take me home."

But when I gave in (and I did give in every time the world clicked over and I saw things right side up instead of upside down), odd consequences resulted. I would call a number but strange voices out of unknown businesses or residences would answer, or someone among the Partham friends would say hello, and I would begin to talk about myself—me, *me*, ME—relating imagined insults, or telling stories that were only partly true, and though I knew I was doing this, though my mind stood by like a chance pedestrian at the scene of an accident, interested, but a little sickened, with other things to do, still my voice, never lacking for a word, went on. Once

I took a taxi home with all my possessions loaded inside, but directed the driver to the wrong turning, overshot the mark and wound up at the wrong driveway. The people who came out the door knew me; oh, this was horrible; I crouched down out of sight and shouted, "Go back, go back! Take me home!" (The meaning of home had shifted, the world had flipped once more.)

Again I came on the bus in the middle of a fine afternoon, calm and right within myself, to "talk things over," sanely to prepare for my return to the family. I found no one there, the house open, the living room empty. I sat down to wait. At a still center, waiting for loved ones' faces to appear through a radiance of outer sunlight, I stared too hard at nothing, closed my eyes and heard it from the beginning: a silent scream, waxing unbearably. I had come to put out my arms, to say, I have failed to love, but now I know this. I love you, I love you all. What was there in this to make the world shrink back, flee, recede, rock with agony to its fair horizons? I could bear it no longer, and so fled. I ran past one of them, one of the Partham women (my mother-in-law, sister-in-law, aunt-in-law, a cousin?— they look alike, all of them) coming in from the garden in her white work gloves with shears in hand, a flat of cut flowers on her arm. *She* must have screamed also, I saw her mouth make the picture of a scream, but that is unimportant except to her. For if she was Denis's mother she must have wanted to scream ever since I had first walked into her presence, hand in hand with Denis, and then there I was back again, crazy and fleeing with a bruised forehead all purple and gold (in my haste to reach them I had slammed into a door).

My journey back on one rattling bus after another, threading streets under an overcast sky, seemed longer than I could have imagined. I wondered then and since if I had dreamed that journey, if I would not presently wake up in the dark room where my resolution had taken place at 3 A.M. (the hour of weakness and resolve), if the whole matter of getting up, dressing, taking the taxi, were not all a dream of the soul's motion upon deciding, while I myself, like a chained dog, lay still held to sleep and darkness. On the other hand, I wondered whether I had made that same decision and that same trip not once or twice but twenty or thirty times, as though the split side of myself were carrying on a life it would not tell me about. Denis had a brother who was a physicist and used to talk about a "black hole in space," where matter collapses of its own gravity, ceases to exist in any form that we know of as existence. Yet some existence must continue. Was this myself, turned inside-out like a sleeve, whirled counterclockwise to a vacuum point? When I disappeared would I (Maureen) know it? Confusion thickened in my head.

I thought I saw Denis at the end of a snowy street in East Montreal near Dorchester Boulevard, a child holding to either hand, and so sprang up my fantasy that they often came to watch silently from somewhere just to see me pass, but often as I thought I glimpsed them, I never hastened to close the distance and find the answer.

"You prefer the fantasy to the reality," Dr. Johnson said.

"What made me the way I am? Why have I caused all this?"

"Becoming is difficult."

"Becoming what?"

"Your alter ego. Your other self."

"You've said it a hundred times."

"So what?"

"It makes no sense, my other self. None whatever."

"You feel it's irrational?"

We both fell silent and looked down as if this self had fallen like an object between us on the floor.

"No one is wholly rational," Dr. Johnson said.

I still sat looking. Rational or not, could it live, poor thing? If I nudged it with my toe, would it move?

"Basically, you are happier now," he told me.

"I am lonely," I said. The words fell out, without my knowing it. Perhaps the self on the floor had spoken.

"You like it, or you wouldn't be," he said at once.

I was surprised by this last remark and returned home with something like an inner smile. For the first time in months I thought of buying something new and pretty and I looked in shop windows along the way. I stopped in a drugstore and got a lipstick. That night I washed my hair. Sitting out on my balcony, watching the people drift by, smoking, the way I always like to do, I put a blanket over my still damp head, for it was only March, and the world was still iced, crusted in decaying snow. I sat like a squaw woman, but inside I felt a little stir of green feeling. I would be happy in this world I'd come to, not just an exile, a maverick that had jumped the fence. I would feel like a woman again.

———

A woman invisible, floating softly through a June day, I went to church when my daughter was confirmed. I sat far in the back in the dim church, St. James on Bishop Street. Seeing her so beautiful, I felt exalted, meaning all the hymns, all the words. But as I was leaving I heard a murmuring behind me and my name spoken. Then a curate was chasing me, calling out my name. I knew him from the old days, didn't I? Wasn't he the one I'd asked to dinner and sherry and tea? He meant everything that was good; he wanted to grasp my hand and speak to me, about forgiveness, love, peace, the whole catalogue. But who stood back of him? Not the kingdom, the power, and the glory, but Parthams, Parthams, and Parthams. I ran like the wind. The air blew white in my face, white as my daughter's communion dress, white as a bridal veil. I stopped at last to gasp it down. No footsteps sounded from behind. I was safe once more. Running backward, I had broken records: forward, I'm unbeatable. This was the grim joke I told myself, skulking home.

"It was a big risk," Dr. Johnson warned me. "How did you even know about the service?"

"A maid I used to have. She told me."

"The trouble I've gone to. . . . Don't you realize they want to commit you? If they succeed, you may never get out again."

"Nobody could keep me from seeing her," I said. "Not on that day."

"To them you're a demon in the sacred place." He was smiling, but I heard it solemnly. Maybe they were right.

Such, anyway, were my forays into enemy land.

———

But some were also made to me, in my new country. For I saw them, at times, and at others I thought I saw them, shadows at twilight on the edge of their forest, or real creatures venturing out and toward me; it was often impossible to tell which.

Carole Partham really came, graceful and hesitant, deerlike, and I let her come, perceiving that it was not curiosity or prying that brought her over, but an inner need to break away, to copy me, in some measure.

There she was one twilight, waiting in the pizza restaurant near my entrance. Carole was born a Partham, but her husband was Jim O'Brien, a broker. He was away in Europe, she said. Now's your big chance, she had doubtless told herself.

A smart-looking girl, up to the latest in clothes, a luxury woman, wearing suède with a lynx collar, tall brown rain boots, brushed brown hair.

"Come in," I urged her, getting her out of that place where, dressed like that, she was making them nervous. "I'm safe to be with. You can see my place."

Then she was sitting, smoking, loosening her coat, eyes coasting about here and there, from floor to wall to ceiling. My apartment wasn't much to see. I would have set the dogs on her—dogs of my inner rages—if I hadn't seen her realness. Instead I saw it well: she was frightened. Happy or not? She didn't know. What does life mean? There was panic in the question, if you asked it often enough. She had no answer and her husband was away for quite some time.

"Come work here for a month," I advised. "You can get a job, or loaf, or think, or see what happens."

But her eyes were restless; they stopped at closed drawers, probed at closet doors. Sex! Oh, certainly, I thought. Oh, naturally. I remembered Jim O'Brien with his ready talk and his toothy grin flashing over an ever-present, ever-tilted tumbler of martini on the rocks, and the glitter and swagger in his stroll from guest to guest, his intimate flattering talk, and now I knew what I had thought all along: who would marry Jim O'Brien but a woman with a childhood terror still behind the door? And now she'd done it, how could she escape?

"Don't tell them where you are," I advised. "I can find a room for you maybe. Somewhere near if you want me to. You can see I've no space here."

"Oh, I didn't want—"

"Just tell them you've gone away. What about Florida? You can say that."

Helpless, the eyes roved.

"I've no one here," I told her. "No lover, no friend. I work in a photographer's studio. That's all there is to know. You'll see it at the corner. My boss is Mr. Massimo. He owns it. There's nothing to know."

After a long silence, she said, looking down at herself, "These clothes are wrong."

"Who cares? Just face it that nobody cares."

"Nobody cares? Nobody *cares*?" She kept repeating this. It was what she couldn't swallow, had got hung up on, I guess, all by herself. I had hit it by accident.

"I mean," I said, "nobody over *here* cares. Over there . . . I don't know about that."

"Nobody . . . nobody. . . ." Her voice now had gone flat. She got up to go, headed for the terrace window rather than the door, fell through the glass, stumbled over the terrace railing, her fashionable boots flailing the air, skirts sliding up to her neck. . . . But, no, this didn't happen. That wasn't the end of Carole. She went out the door, like anybody else.

She did move to the street for a time; I forget for how long. She brought plain old clothes and tied her head in a scarf. She worked some afternoons for a kind, arthritic Frenchman with white hair who ran a magazine shop. There was also the dark young man who stared down daily from a window four floors up; he descended to trail her home, offering to carry her grocery sack. How nice this tableau looked and how charming it would have been if only his I.Q. had been halfway average. He was once a doorman, I understood, but had kept falling asleep on his feet, like a horse.

She got drunk on resin-tasting wine one night in a Greek restaurant and lured eleven Greek waiters into a cheap hotel room. How sweet and eager and passionate they had seemed! They milled around—or so I was told—not knowing what to do. A humiliation to end all mental nymphomania: Carole escaped unmolested.

She had found a room with a woman whose mother had died and who baby-sat for pin money. On long evenings when she didn't baby-sit she told Carole the story of her life. Otherwise, Carole read, and drank, and told herself the story of her own life. She was happy in the butcher shop once and sat madonna-like with the butcher's cat purring in her lap, but the butcher's Spanish wife did not like her and kicked the cat to say so. Mr. Massimo pondered about her. "How did you know her?" he asked. "She once knew my sister," is all I answered.

Old clothes or not, Carole did one thing she didn't intend: she gave out the indefinable air of class. Surely, the street began to say, she was the forerunner of an "in" group which would soon discover us and then we would all make money and turn into background to be glanced at. So some thought. But when I saw her, knowing better, I saw a host of other women—pretty, cared-for women—walking silently with her, rank on rank, women for whom nothing will ever quite add up. Every day, I guess, she wrote down her same old problems, in different combinations, and every day she got the same sum.

Suddenly, one day, she was before me. "My month is up. It's been a wonderful experience."

"I'm glad you thought so."

We both sat smoking thoughtfully, occasionally glancing at each other. I knew her room had been rifled twice by thieves and that she could not sleep at night when the baby-sitter baby-sat. The faces of those Greek waiters would, I imagine, press on her memory forever. If the world is one, what was the great secret to make those faces accessible to her own self? The answer had escaped her.

"It's been a great experience," she repeated, smiling brightly, her mouth like painted wood, like a wound.

———

A voice, another voice, in that same room is talking . . . Vinnie Partham and her husband Charles? It can't be.

". . . I knew it was safe to see you again when Carole confessed that she had and you were all right. Carole's gone into social work, she got over her crisis whatever it was, and now we're thinking it's time you got through with yours, for you may not be able even to imagine how desolate Denis still is, Maureen. Can you, can you?

"We thought for a long time the problem was sexual but then we decided you were out to destroy us and then we thought your mental condition would make you incapable of anything at all by way of job or friends. But all our theories are wrong, I guess."

On she goes, with Charles dozing in his chair after the manner of British detectives in the movies, who look dumb but are actually intelligent and wide awake, solving the perfect crime, the difference being that Charles really is both half-asleep and stupid and has never been known to solve anything at all. Vinnie knows it. The phrases have started looping out of her mouth like a backward spaghetti-eating process. Luminous cords reach up and twine with others, grow into patterns of thought. The patterns are dollar signs. I see them forming.

"With Denis having no heart for the estate affairs, what chance have Charles and I for the consideration he's always extended us? And if you think who, out of a perfect grab bag of women now getting interested, he might actually take it in his head to marry—"

Something dawns on me. Vinnie Partham is never going to stop talking!

I stare at her and stare, feeling cross-eyed with wonder and helpless and hypnotized, like someone watching a force in nature take its course. What can I do? She'll be there forever.

"I'm tired, Vinnie," I tell her. "I'm terribly tired."

They melt away, her mouth is moving still.... Did I dream them? Do women still wear long beads? Can it really be they wanted me back for nothing but money? No, money is their name for something else. That chill place, that flaw in the world fabric, that rift in the Partham world about the size of Grand Canyon—they keep trying to fill it, trying to fill it, on and on, throwing everything in to fill it up. It was why Denis wanted me.

Oh, my poor children! Could they ever grow up to look like Aunt Vinnie and Uncle Charles?

At the thought of them, so impossibly beautiful, so possibly doomed, noises like cymbals crash in my ears, my eyes blur and stream. If my visitors were there I could not see them.

But they must be gone, I think, squinting around the room, if they were there at all. If they were ever alive at all . . . if they were ever anywhere.

Through all this, night was coming on; and summer—that, too, was coming on. Vinnie and Charles were dreams. But love is real.

———

I first saw Michel when he came to the photographer's shop for some application-size pictures. He was thin and ravaged, frowning, worried, *pressé*. I had learned to do routine requests as Mr. Massimo was often away taking wedding pictures or attending occasions such as christenings and retirements. Mr. Massimo thrived on these events, which included fancy food and lots to drink and dressed-up women. It was when Michel and I got in the semi-dark of the photographing room together that I received his full impact. I stirred about among the electrical cords, the lamp stands; I wielded the heavy-headed camera into focus; I directed his chin to lift, then found him in the lenses, dark and straight. Indian blood? I snapped the shutter.

He said he was new in the neighborhood, lived up the street, and would come back next day to see the proofs.

But I passed him again, not an hour later, on my way home. He was sitting outdoors at the pizza parlor talking volubly to the street cleaner who had stopped there for a beer. He saw me pass, go in my building, and I felt his regard in my senses.

Who was he? What would he do?

Something revolutionary was what I felt to be in his bones. Political? Then he would be making contacts and arguing for the liberation of the province.

I was wrong. No passion for Quebec but the rent of an empty barbershop was what had brought him there, one on the lower floor of a small building with a tree in front. He was going to put in one of those shops that sold hippie costumes, Indian shirts, long skirts, built-up shoes, some papier-mâché decorators' items, and some artwork. This would incidentally give him a chance to show some of his own artwork, which had failed to interest the uptown galleries. He was going to leave the barber chairs and mirrors, using them all as décor, props, for the things he sold.

He told me all this when he came to see the photographs. Mr. Massimo had gone to a reunion of retired hockey players. Michel looked over the proofs and selected one. He wanted it enlarged, a glossy finish he could reproduce to make ads for his shop. He was telling me how in some detail and I thought that a little more would find him back in Mr. Massimo's darkroom, doing it for himself.

"I hope your business works," I said.

The day before, skirting about among the photographic equipment, we had entangled face to face among some electrical cords, which we had methodically to unplug and unwind to find release from a near embrace. Now, he turned from a scrutiny of his own face to a minute examination of my own.

"If you hope so, then you think it could. *Vous le croyez*, eh?"

"*Moi? J'en sais pas, moi.* What does it matter?"

His elbow skidded on the desk. His face beetled into my own. It was his eyes that were compelling, better than good, making an importance out of themselves, out of my opinions, out of me.

"Your thinking so . . . why, that's strong. You have power. *Vous êtes formidable.* That's it, madame. *C'est ça.*"

A tilt of the head, an inch or two more, and our mouths, once more, might have closed together. My own was dry and thirsty, it woke to tell me so.

He straightened, gathered up his pictures, and neatly withdrew. His step left the doorway empty. I filled the order blank carefully.

It had turned much warmer and after work now I sat on the balcony with the windows open behind me and what I had to call curtains even stirred a bit, a dreamy lift of white in a dusk-softened room. I was moved to put a Mozart record on. I remembered that Mozart had died a pauper and been carried by cart to the outskirts of Vienna in winter and dumped in a hole. To me, that made the music tenderer still. Michel! From the day I'd seen him a private tower had begun to rise about me; its walls were high and strong. I might gnaw toast and jam and gulp coffee standing in my closet-sized kitchen, wriggle into the same old skirt, blouse, sweater, and leather coat (now put away), and walk to work, a drab, square-set, middle-aged woman going past at an accustomed time, but, within myself, a princess came to life and she leaned from high-set window sills. Did Michel know, she kept on asking, as she studied the horizon and admired the blue sky.

He passed the shop twice, once for his enlargement, once to talk; he went by daily on the street. A stir went up about his footsteps. He would change us all. At the very least, I reasoned, he kept my mind off the divorce papers.

One night there was a shouting in the street and a clang of fire engines. I rushed to the balcony and saw where it was: Michel's, up on the corner. A moment later I heard his voice from the shadows, down in the street below, and I hurried to let him in, climbed back with him unseen, opened my door to him for the first time.

He had caught my hands, holding them together in his own, in a grasp warm with life. His explanations blundered out . . . coming back from somewhere, tired, smoking in bed, fell asleep, the stuff collected for the shop catching fire. "But if they know I'm back, that I set the fire, then the shop will never open. Nobody saw me. Nobody. Will you let me stay? Will you?"

"Smoking in bed, that's crazy."

"Correct." He leaned wearily toward me, smiling, sallow cheekbone sharp against my cheek, then holding closer, his mouth searching, and mine searching, too, finding and holding. The will to have him there was present already: it was he who'd set the tower up, and furnished it, for this very thing, for his refuge. But for such enfoldment as we found, the binding of my thought was needed, the total silent agreement that a man and woman make, a matched pattern for love. The heart of his gamble was there. He won it.

Left alone while I worked, Michel sat in the corner and read all day.

"What do you do when you're not reading?" I would ask, coming in from work.

"Je pense."

"À quoi?"

"À toi."

"Tu pense à toi. Et tu le sais bien, toi." I was putting down my bag, I was emptying my grocery sack, but always I was turning to him. And I was moving to him. And he to me.

There was talk on the street of the fire, how the whole house had almost caught, and about the strange absence of Michel, whose inflammable junk had caused it all, but for whom nobody had an address or a telephone number.

One day I came from work and the tower stood empty. I knew it before I opened the door; Michel was gone. Through empty space I moved at last to the balcony and there up the street a taxi was pulling up before the rooming house. Out stepped Michel, as though home from a long journey, even carrying a suitcase! For the first time, it seemed, he was discovering his charred quarters, calling out the building superintendent, raising a commotion on the steps for all to hear. Quarreling, shouting, and multiple stories—they went on till nightfall.

Michel tried, at least, to collect the insurance on damages to his property. I never knew for certain if it worked. He said that it did, but he seldom told the truth. It was not his nature. If the fire was accidental, he escaped without a damage suit. But if he did it on purpose, hoping for insurance money to buy a better class of junk, and counting in advance on me to shelter him, then he was a fool to take so much risk. But why begin to care? Liar, cheat, thief, and lover—he stays unchanged and unexplaining. We have never had it out, or made it up, or parted. The tower is dissolving as his presence fades from it, leaves as water drying from a fabric, thread by thread. It floats invisible, but at least undestroyed. I felt this even after his shop opened—even after a dark young girl with long hair and painted eyes came to work there.

He comes and goes. Summer is over. *C'est ça.*

———

To think the Parthams ever let go is a serious mistake.

I recall a winter night now, lost in driving snow. There is a madness of snow, snow everywhere, teeming, shifting, lofty as curtains in the dream of a mad opera composer, cosmic, yet intimate as a white thread caught in an eyelash. The buses stall on Côte des Neiges: there is a moaning impotence among them, clouds of exhaust and a dimming of their interior lights as they strain to ascend the long hill, but some already have given up and stand dull and bulky, like great animals in herd awaiting some imminent extinction. The passengers file from them. I toil upward from Sherbrooke through a deepening tunnel, going toward the hospital. My son's name has become the sound of my heart. The receptionist directs me to a certain floor.

I think of everyone inside as infinitely small because of the loftiness of the night outside, its mad whiteness, chaotic motion, insatiable teeming. The hospital is a toy with lights, set on the mountain, a bump like a sty. The night will go on forever, it seems to be saying; it will if it wants to and it wants to and it will. So I (human) am small beneath this lofty whim. Perhaps I think like this to minimize the dull yet painful edge of guilt. My son may die; I abandoned him years ago. Yet he wants to see me, and they have thought that he should be permitted to. And I have thought, Why think it is good of them, nobody is that bad? and Why think it is good of me either, no mother is that cold? (But they might have been, and so might I.) Under realms of snow I progress at snail pace, at bug size, proving that great emotion lives in tiny hearts. On the floor, a passing aide, little as a sparrow, indicates the way. At the desk, a nurse, a white rabbit, peers at a note that has been left. Snow at the window, furious, boils. "Mr. Partham regrets he cannot be here. . . . You wish to see the boy? It's number ten." Swollen feelings lift me down the corridor. I crack the door. "Mother, is that you?" "Yes." "I knew you'd come." "Of course, I came." His hand, at last, is mine. It is the world.

Night after night I come, through blizzard, through ice and sleet, once in a silenced snow-bound city walking more than half the way into a wind with a −40° wind chill against my face, ant-sized under the glitter of infinite distances, at home with the derision of stars. So I push my stubborn nightly way. "You are sleepy," says Mr. Massimo at work. "Why are you so sleepy lately?" I tell him nothing. I can't for yawning.

Bundled in my dark coat, in the shadowy corridor, I sometimes, when Parthams are present, doze. They walk around me, speak to one another, are aware of my presence but do not address it. Denis, once, appearing, stands directly before me; when I lift my head our eyes meet, and they speak and we know it, yes we do. But there is a wall clear as glass between us and if we should fling ourselves through it, it would smash and let us through. Still, we would hurtle past each other. For the glass has a trick in it, a layer at the center seems to place us face to face but really angles us apart. He knows it, I know it. We have been shown the diagram. He nods and turns away.

Several times I see his wife. I recognize her by the newspaper photographs. She is quietly, expensively dressed, with soft shining hair, the one he should have married in the first place. I do not need the coat. Sitting there in the warm room, why do I wear it? The minute the Parthams leave, I shed it. Its dropping from me is real but a symbol also. I am in the room in the same moment.

We hardly talk at all, my son and I. We know everything there is to know already. I sense the hour, almost the minute, when his health begins to flow back again.

We are sitting together on a Saturday morning. Dawn has come to a clear spotless frozen sky. Smoke from the glittering city beneath us, laid out below the windows, turns white. It plumes upward in windless purity. I have been here through the night. We are talking. It is the last time; I know that, too. The needles have been withdrawn from his arms. Soon the morning routine of the hospital will begin to crackle along the hallway and some of it will enter here. I look around me and see what things the Parthams have filled the room with—elegant little transistor radios, sports books and magazines, a lovely tropical aquarium where brilliant fish laze fin and tail among the shells and water plants. Nothing has been spared. He is smiling. His nightmare with the long name—peritonitis—is over. His gaze is weak no longer, but has entered sunlight, is penetrating and can judge.

So much drops away from a sick person; ideas, personality, ambition, interests—all the important Partham baggage. When the pressures of the body turn eccentric and everything is wrong, then they find their secret selves. But once the Partham body returns, it's a sign of laziness not to look around, discriminate, find life "interesting," activities "meaningful"; it would be silly not to be a Partham since a Partham is what one so fortunately is. "Can I come to find you when I get out of here?" my son begs. "Can I, Mother?" "Of course, of course, you can." "I promise to." I am on my way, before the nurse comes with her thermometers or the elephantine gray wagon of trays lumbers in. I am into my coat again, retreating from the Partham gaze. But my insect heart in the unlikely shape of me, almost permanently bent, like a wind-blasted tree, by the awful humors of that phenomenal winter, is incandescent with inextinguishable joy. He will live, he will live. Nothing, nobody, can take that away. I stumble, slip, list, slide down frozen pavements, squeaking over surfaces of impacted snow. In the crystal truth of the day world, the night is done. He will live.

(His name? My son's name? I won't tell you.)

I wing, creep, crawl, hop—what you will—back into my world.

———

Denis, eventually, seeks me. He comes to find me. A third Partham. I see him at a street end.

He is gray; the winter has made everybody's skin too pale, except, I suppose, the habitual skiers who go up on peaks where the sun strikes. Denis used to ski, but not this year. There he is, gray at the street's end. All has been blown bare and lean by the awful winter. He is himself lean, clean, with gray overcoat and Persian lamb hat, darker gray trousers, brown, fur-lined gloves. "Maureen? Can we go somewhere? Just have a coffee . . . talk a little?" We go to the "bar-b-q" place. It's impersonal there, being on a busy corner; at the pizza restaurant they would want to know who Denis was, and why he'd come and do I have a new boy friend. Also Michel might pass by.

"He thinks you saved him," Denis tells me. "For all I know, it's true. But he thinks more than that. He's obsessed with you . . . can't talk of anything else at times. I don't know what to do, Maureen. He thinks you're a saint, something more than human. Your visits were

only half-real to him. They were like—appearances, apparitions."
He stops, hesitant. It is the appealing, unsure Denis, absent, I imagine, for most of the time, that I see again as I saw him when we first met, seeking out my eyes, begging for something.

"It must be easy to disillusion him," I say. "You, of all people, could best do that."

"Oh, he's heard all the facts. Not so much from me, mind you . . ."

From his grandmother, I think, and his grandfather and his aunts. Heard all those things he "ought to know."

"I didn't know you went there so often, sat for whole nights at a time, it seems." He is speaking out of a deepening despair, floundering.

"But you saw me there."

"I know, but I—"

"Didn't you know I loved him, too?"

"You loved—" At the mention of love, his face seems about to shatter into a number of different planes, a face in an abstract painting, torn against itself. "To me your love was always defective. You—Maureen, when we were first married, I would think over and over, Now is forever; forever is now. Why did you destroy it all? It frightens me to think of you sitting, in the dark hours, with that boy. You could have pinched his life out like a match."

"I wouldn't do that, Denis. I couldn't hurt what's hurt already." I could have told him what light is like, as I had seen its illusion that day before his accident, how the jagged force tore into my smoothly surfaced vision. I had tried to tell him once: he thought I was raving. Later I smashed a set of his mother's china, and tore up a beautifully tiled wall with my nails, until they split and the blood ran down.

"I thought I had some force that would help him. That's not why I went but it's why I stayed."

"It might not have worked," Denis reflected. "He might have died anyway."

"Then you could have blamed me," I pointed out. "Then I could have been a witch, an evil spirit."

"I don't know why you ever had to turn into a spirit at all! Just a woman, a wife, a mother, a human being—! That's all I ever wanted!"

"Believe me, Denis," I said, *"I don't know either."*

We'd had it out that way, about a million times. Making no real progress, returning to our old familiar dead end, our hovel, which, in a way, was the only home we had.

I was then inspired to say: "It just may be, Denis, that if I'd never left, I could never have returned, and if I never had returned, it just may be that he would never have lived, he would have died, Denis, think of that, he would be dead."

For a moment, I guess he did consider it. His face turned to mine, mouth parted. He slipped little by little into the idea, let himself submerge within it. I will say for Denis: at least, he did that. "The doctors," he said at last, "they were terribly good, you know. The major credit," he said, finishing his coffee, "goes to them."

"Undoubtedly," I said. He had come to the surface, and turned back into a Partham again.

It had been a clear, still, frozen afternoon when we met, but holding just that soft touch of violet which said that winter would at last give over. Its grip was terrible, but a death grip no longer.

I tried to recall my old routine, to show my Partham side myself. "I imagine he will find new interests, once he gets more active. He won't think so much about me. But, Denis, if he does want to hold on to something about me, can't you let him?"

"I wouldn't dream of stopping him. It's a matter of proportion, that's all." He was pulling on his beautiful gloves. "He's practically made a religion of you."

As we were going out, I saw it all more clearly and began to laugh. "Then that's your answer, Denis."

"What is?"

"If I'm to be a 'religion,' then there are ways of handling me. Confine me to one hour a week, on Sunday morning. . . . I need never get out of bounds. Don't worry about him, Denis. He's a Partham, after all."

"Maureen? You're bitter, aren't you? People *have* to live, even Parthams. Life *has* to go on."

We were standing outside by then, at the intersection with my street. He wouldn't enter there, I thought; it was not in accord with his instincts to do so.

"I'm not bitter," I said. "I'm helpless."

"It didn't have to be that way."

It was like a final exchange; it had a certain ring. He leaned to touch my face, then drew back, moving quickly away, not looking behind.

And now I am waiting for the fourth visitor, my son. I think I will see him, at some street corner, seeking me, find him waiting for me in the pizza shop, hear a voice say, "Mother? I promised you. . . ." And before I know it, I will have said his name. . . .

I am waiting still.

———

Mr. Massimo, one day, leans at me over his portrait camera. "I hear you were married to a wealthy man in Westmount," he says.

"I am a princess in a silver tower," I reply. "Golden birds sing to me. I drift around in a long silk gown. What about you?"

"My father was Al Capone's brother. We rode around when young in a secondhand Rolls-Royce with a crest of the House of Savoia painted on the door. Then we got run out of Italy. The family took another name." He is smiling at me. It is not the story that reaches me, true or false, but the outpouring sun of Italy.

———

"You'll get me fired," I tell Michel.

"Come work for me," he says. "You can tell fortunes in the back. I'll make you rich."

He's using me again, working in collage—photography plus painting—he needs Mr. Massimo's darkroom. I telephone him when Mr. Massimo is gone and he comes to run a print through, or make an enlargement. When this phase passes, he will go again.

But he creates a picture before that, half-photo, half-drawing. He photographs my hands over a blood-red glass globe, lighted from within. I think the fortune-telling idea has given him the image. He makes the light strong; the veins of my hands stand out in great detail; the bones are almost X-ray visible. "Let me wash my hands," I say, because dirt shows under the nail tips. "No, I like it that way, leave it." So it stays. Watching Michel, I forget to feel anything else, and he is busy timing, setting, focusing. So the hands stay in place as my feelings rock with the sense of the light, and when he shuts it off, finished, we lock the shop up and go home together. Only the next day do I notice that my palm is burned so badly I have to bandage it and go for days in pain. Is the pain for Michel? Damn Michel! The pain is mine, active and virulent. It is mine alone.

The picture, with its background drawing of a woman in evening dress turned from a doorway, and its foreground of hands across a glowing glass, catches on. Michel has others in his package, but none is so popular as this one. He makes enlargements, sells them, makes others, sells those. They go out by the hundreds.

"What is it you carry? *Qu'est-ce que tu as,* Maureen?" Now he is after me, time and again, intense, volpine, impossible, begging from doorways, brushing my shoulder as he passes in the dark. *"Qu'est-ce tu as?"*

"I don't know. *Que t'importe, toi?"*

Among his pictures, a U.S. distributor chooses this one, one of three. If I go to certain shops in New York where cheap exotic dress is sold, incense, and apartment decorations of the lowlier sort, bought for their grass-scented pads by homosexual pairs, or by students or young lovers, or by adventurous young people with little taste for permanence, I will see that picture somewhere among them, speaking its silent language. I will look at my hands, see the splash of red that lingers. The world over, copies of it will eventually stick up out of garbage cans, or will be left in vacated apartments. Held to the wall by one thumb tack, it will hang above junk not thought to be worth moving. It celebrates life as fleeting as a dance.

Yet it was created, it happened, and that, in its smallness must pass for everything—must, in this instance, stand for all.

JACK OF DIAMONDS

One April afternoon, Central Park, right across the street, turned green all at once. It was a green toned with gold and seemed less a color of leaves than a stained cloud settled down to stay. Rosalind brought her bird book out on the terrace and turned her face up to seek out something besides pigeons. She arched, to hang her long hair backward over the terrace railing, soaking in sunlight while the starlings whirled by.

The phone rang, and she went inside.

"I just knew you'd be there, Rosie," her father said. "What a gorgeous day. Going to get hotter. You know what I'm thinking about? Lake George."

"Let's go right now," Rosalind said.

The cottage was at Bolton Landing. Its balconies were built out over the water. You walked down steps and right off into the lake, or into the boat. In a lofty beamed living room, shadows of water played against the walls and ceiling. There was fine lake air, and chill pure evenings . . .

The intercom sounded. "Gristede's, Daddy. They're buzzing."

Was it being in the theater that made her father, whenever another call came, exert himself to get more into the first? "Let's think about getting up there, Rosie. Summer's too short as it is. You ask Eva when she comes in. Warm her up to it. We'll make our pitch this evening. She's never even seen it . . . can you beat that?"

"I'm not sure she'll even like it," Rosalind said.

"Won't like it? It's hardly camping out. Of course she'll love it. Get it going, Rosie baby. I'm aiming for home by seven."

The grocer's son who brought the order up wore jeans just like Rosalind's. "It's getting hot," he remarked. "It's about melted my ass off."

"Let's see if you brought everything." She had tried to give up presiding over the food after her father remarried, but when her stepmother turned out not to care much about what happened in the kitchen, she had cautiously gone back to seeing about things.

"If I forgot, I'll get it. But if you think of something—"

"I know, I'll come myself. You think you got news?"

They were old friends. They sassed each other. His name was Luis—Puerto Rican.

It was after the door to the service entrance closed with its hollow echo, and was bolted, and the service elevator had risen, opened, and closed on Luis, that Rosalind felt the changed quality in things, a new direction, like the tilt of an airliner's wing. She went to the terrace and found the park's greenness surer of itself than ever. She picked up her book and went inside. A boy at school, seeing her draw birds, had given it to her. She stored it with her special treasures.

Closing the drawer, she jerked her head straight, encountering her own wide blue gaze in her bedroom mirror. From the entrance hall, a door was closing. She gathered up a pack of cards spread out for solitaire and slid them into a gilded box. She whacked at her long brown hair with a brush; then she went out. It was Eva.

Rosalind Jennings's stepmother had short, raven-black glossy hair, a full red mouth, jetty brows and lashes. Shortsighted, she handled the problem in the most open way, by wearing great round glasses trimmed in tortoiseshell. All through the winter—a winter Rosalind would always remember as The Stepmother: Year I—Eva had gone around the apartment in gold wedge-heeled slippers, pink slacks, and a black chiffon blouse. Noiseless on the wall-to-wall carpets, the slippers slapped faintly against stockings or flesh when she walked—spaced, intimate ticks of sound. "Let's face it, Rosie," her father said, when Eva went off to the kitchen for a fresh drink as he tossed in his blackjack hand. "She's a sexy dame."

Sexy or not, she was kind to Rosalind. "I wouldn't have married anybody you didn't like," her father told her. "That child's got *the* most heavenly eyes," she'd overheard Eva say.

Arriving now, having triple-locked the apartment door, Eva set the inevitable Saks parcels down on the foyer table and dumped her jersey jacket off her arm onto the chair with a gasp of relief. "It's turned so hot!" Rosalind followed her to the kitchen, where she poured orange juice and soda over ice. Her nails were firm, hard, perfectly painted. They resembled, to Rosalind, ten small creatures who had ranked themselves on this stage of fingertips. Often they ticked off a pile of poker chips from top to bottom, red and white, as Eva pondered. "Stay . . ." or "Call . . ." or "I'm out . . ." then, "Oh, damn you, Nat . . . that's twice in a row."

"I've just been talking on the phone to Daddy," Rosalind said. "I've got to warn you. He's thinking of the cottage."

"Up there in Vermont?"

"It's in New York, on Lake George. Mother got it from her folks. You know, they lived in Albany. The thing is, Daddy's always loved it. He's hoping you will too, I think."

Eva finished her orange juice. Turning to rinse the glass in the sink, she wafted out perfume and perspiration. "It's a little far for a summer place. . . . But if it's what you and Nat like, why, then . . ." She affectionately pushed a dark strand of Rosalind's hair back behind her ear. Her fingers were chilly from the glass. "I'm yours to command." Her smile, intimate and confident, seemed to repeat its red picture on every kitchen object.

Daughter and stepmother had got a lot chummier in the six months since her father had married. At first, Rosalind was always wondering what they thought of her. For here was a new "they," like a whole new being. She had heard, for instance, right after the return from the Nassau honeymoon:

Eva: "I want to be sure and leave her room just the way it is."

Nat: "I think that's right. Change is up to her."

But Rosalind could not stop her angry thought: *You'd just better try touching my room!* Her mother had always chosen her decor, always the rose motif, roses in the wallpaper and deeper rose valances and matching draperies. This was a romantic theme with her parents, accounting for her name. Her father would warble "Sweet Rosie O'Grady" while downing his whiskey. He would waltz his little girl around the room. She'd learned to dance before she could walk, she thought.

"Daddy sets the music together with what's happening on the stage. He gets the dancers and actors to carry out the music. That's different from composing or writing lyrics." So Rosalind would explain to new friends at school, every year. Now she'd go off to some other school next fall, still ready with her lifelong lines. "You must have heard of some of his shows. Remember So-and-So, and then there was . . ." Watching their impressionable faces form their cries. "We've got the records of that!" "Was your mother an actress?" "My stepmother used to be an actress—nobody you'd know about. My mother died. She wasn't ever in the theater. She studied art history at Vassar." Yes, and married the assistant manager of his family firm: Jennings' Finest Woolen Imports; he did not do well. Back to his first love, theater. From college on they thought they'd never get him out of it, and they were right. Some purchase he had chosen in West Germany turned out to be polyester, sixty percent. "I had a will to fail," Nat Jennings would shrug, when he thought about it. "If your heart's not in something, you can't succeed" was her mother's reasoning, clinging to her own sort of knowing, which had to do with the things you picked, felt about, what went where. Now here was another woman with other thoughts about the same thing. She'd better not touch my room, thought Rosalind, or I'll . . . what? Trip her in the hallway, hide her glasses, throw the keys out the window?

"What are you giggling at, Rosie?"

Well might they ask, just back from Nassau at a time of falling leaves. "I'm wondering what to do with this leg of lamb. It's too long and skinny."

"Broil it like a great big chop." Still honeymooning, they'd be holding hands, she bet, on the living-room sofa.

"Just you leave my room alone," she sang out to this new Them. "Or I won't cook for you!"

"Atta girl, Rosie!"

—

Now, six months later in the balmy early evening with windows wide open, they were saying it again. Daddy had come in, hardly even an hour later than he said, and there was the big conversation, starting with cocktails, lasting through dinner, all about Lake George and how to get there, where to start, but all totally impossible until day after tomorrow at the soonest.

"One of the few unpolluted lakes left!" Daddy enthused to Eva. It was true. If you dropped anything from the boat into the water, your mother would call from the balcony, "It's right down there, darling," and you'd see it as plainly as if it lay in sunlight at your feet and you could reach down for it instead of diving. The caretaker they'd had for years, Mr. Thibodeau, reported to them from time to time. Everything was all right, said Mr. Thibodeau. He had about fifteen houses on his list, for watching over, especially during the long winters. He was good. They'd left the cottage empty for two summers, and it was still all right. She remembered the last time they were there, June three years back. She and Daddy were staying while Mother drove back to New York, planning to see Aunt Mildred from Denver before she put out for the West again. "What a nuisance she can't come here!" Mother had said. "It's going to be sticky as anything in town, and when I think of that Thruway!"

"Say you've got food poisoning," said Daddy. "Make something up."

"But Nat! Can't you understand? I really *do* want to see Mildred!" It was Mother's little cry that still sounded in Rosalind's head. "Whatever you do, please don't go to the apartment," Daddy said. He hadn't washed dishes for a week; he'd be ashamed for an in-law to have an even lower opinion of him, though he thought it wasn't possible. "It's a long drive," her mother pondered. "Take the Taconic, it's cooler." "Should I spend one night or two?"

Her mother was killed on the Taconic Parkway the next day by a man coming out of a crossover. There must have been a moment of terrible disbelief when she saw that he was actually going to cross in front of her. Wasn't he looking, didn't he see? They would never know. He died in the ambulance. She was killed at once.

Rosalind and her father, before they left, had packed all her mother's clothing and personal things, but that was all they'd had the heart for. The rest they walked off and left, just so. "Next summer," they had said, as the weeks wore on and still they'd made no move. The next summer came, and still they did not stir. One day they said, "Next summer." Mr. Thibodeau said not to worry, everything was fine. So the Navaho rugs were safe, and all the pottery, the copper and brass, the racked pewter. The books would all be lined in place on the shelves, the music in the Victorian music rack just as it had been left, Schumann's "Carnaval" (she could see it still) on top. And if everything was really fine, the canoe would be dry, though dusty and full of spiderwebs, suspended out in the boathouse, and the roof must be holding firm and dry, as Mr. Thibodeau would have reported any leak immediately. All that had happened, he said, was that the steps into the water had to have new uprights, the bottom two replaced, and that the eaves on the northeast corner had broken from a falling limb and been repaired.

Mention of the fallen limb recalled the storms. Rosalind remembered them blamming away while she and her mother huddled back of the stairway, feeling aimed at by the thunderbolts; or if Daddy was there, they'd sing by candlelight while he played the piano. He dared the thunder by imitating it in the lower bass. . . .

"Atta girl, Rosie."

She had just said she wasn't afraid to go up there alone tomorrow, take the bus or train, and consult with Mr. Thibodeau. The Thibodeaus had long ago taken a fancy to Rosalind; a French Canadian, Mrs. Thibodeau had taught her some French songs, and fed her on *tourtière* and beans.

"That would be wonderful," said Eva.

"I just can't let her do it," Nat said.

"I can stay at Howard Johnson's. After all, I'm seventeen."

While she begged, her father looked at her steadily from the end of the table, finishing coffee. "I'll telephone the Thibodeaus," he finally said. "One thing you aren't to do is stay in the house alone. Howard Johnson's is okay. We'll get you a room there." Then, because he knew what the house had meant and wanted to let her know it, he took her shoulder (Eva not being present) and squeezed it, his eyes looking deep into hers, and Irish tears rising moistly. "Life goes on, Rosie," he whispered. "It has to."

She remembered all that, riding the bus. But it was for some unspoken reason that he had wanted her to go. And she knew that it was right for her to do it, not only to see about things. It was an important journey. For both of them? Yes, for them both.

———

Mr. Thibodeau himself met her bus, driving up to Lake George Village.

"Not many people yet," he said. "We had a good many on the weekend, out to enjoy the sun. Starting a baseball team up here. The piers took a beating back in the winter. Not enough ice and too much wind. How's your daddy?"

"He's fine. He wants to come back here now."

"You like your new mother? Shouldn't ask. Just curious."

"She's nice," said Rosalind.

"Hard to be a match for the first one."

Rosalind did not answer. She had a quietly aware way of closing her mouth when she did not care to reply.

"Pretty?" pursued Mr. Thibodeau. Not only the caretaker, Mr. Thibodeau was also a neighbor. He lived between the property and the road. You had to be nice to the Thibodeaus; so much depended on them.

"Yes, she's awfully pretty. She was an actress. She had just a little part in the cast of the show he worked with last year."

"That's how they met, was it?"

To Rosalind, it seemed that Eva had just showed up one evening in her father's conversation at dinner. "There's somebody I want you to meet, Rosie. She's—well, she's a she. I've seen her once or twice. I think you'll like her. But if you don't, we'll scratch her, Rosie. That's a promise."

"Here's a list, Mr. Thibodeau," she said. "All the things Daddy wants done are on it. Telephone, plumbing, electricity . . . maybe Mrs. Thibodeau can come in and clean. I've got to check the linens for mildew. Then go through the canned stuff and make a grocery list."

"We got a new supermarket since you stopped coming, know that?"

"I bet."

"We'll go tomorrow. I'll take you."

The wood-lined road had been broken into over and over on the lake side, the other side, too, by new motels. Signs about pools, TV, vacancy came rudely up and at them, until, swinging left, they entered woods again and drew near the cutoff to the narrow, winding drive among the pines. "Thibodeau" the mailbox read in strong, irregular letters, and by its side a piece of weathered plywood nailed to the fence post said "Jennings," painted freshly over the ghost of old lettering beneath.

She bounced along with Mr. Thibodeau, who, his black hair grayed over, still had his same beaked nose, which in her mind gave him his Frenchness and his foreignness. Branches slapped the car window. The tires squished through ruts felted with fallout from the woods. They reached the final bend. "Stop," said Rosalind, for something white that gave out a sound like dry bones breaking had passed beneath the wheels. She jumped out. It was only birch branches, half rotted. "I'll go alone." She ran ahead of his station wagon, over pine needles and through the fallen leaves of two autumns, which slowed her motion until she felt the way she did in dreams.

The cottage was made of natural wood, no shiny lacquer covering it; boughs around it, pine and oak, pressed down like protective arms. The reach of the walls was laced over with undergrowth, so that the house at first glance looked small as a hut, not much wider than the door. Running there, Rosalind tried the knob with the confidence of a child running to her mother, only to find it locked, naturally; then with a child's abandon, she flung out her arms against the paneling, hearing her heart thump on the wood until Mr. Thibodeau gently detached her little by little as though she had got stuck there.

"Now there . . . now there . . . just let me get hold of this key." He had a huge wire ring for his keys, labels attached to each. His clientele. *"Des clients, vous en avez beaucoup,"* Rosalind had once said to him as she was starting French in school. But Mr. Thibodeau was unregretfully far from his Quebec origins. His family had come there from northern Vermont to get a milder climate. Lake George was a sun trap, a village sliding off the Adirondacks toward the lake, facing a daylong exposure.

The key ground in the lock. Mr. Thibodeau kicked the base of the door, and the hinges whined. He let her enter alone, going tactfully back to his station wagon for nothing at all. He gave her time to wander before he followed her.

She would have had to come someday, Rosalind thought, one foot following the other, moving forward: the someday was this one. It wasn't as if anything had actually "happened" there. The door frame that opened from the entrance hall into the living room did not face the front door but was about ten feet from it to the left. Thus the full scope of the high, shadowy room, which was the real heart of the cottage, opened all at once to the person entering. Suddenly, there was an interior world. The broad windows opposite, peaked in an irregular triangle at the top, like something in a modernistic church, opened onto the lake, and from the water a rippling light, muted by shade, played constantly on the high-beamed ceiling. Two large handwoven Indian rugs covered the central area of floor; on a table before the windows, a huge pot of brown-and-beige pottery was displayed, filled with money plant that had grown dusty and ragged. There were coarse-fibered curtains in off-white monk's cloth, now dragging askew, chair coverings in heavy fabric, orange-and-white cushions, and the piano, probably so out of tune now with the damp it would never sound right, which sat closed and silent in the corner. An open stairway, more like a ladder than a stair, rose to the upper-floor balcony, with bedrooms in the wing. "We're going to fall and break our silly necks someday," she could hear her mother saying. "It's pretty, though." The Indian weaving of the hawk at sunrise, all black and red, hung on the far left wall.

She thought of her mother, a small, quick woman with bronze, close-curling hair cut short, eager to have what she thought of as "just the right thing," wandering distant markets, seeking out things for the cottage. It seemed to Rosalind when she opened the door past the stairwell into the bedroom that her parents had used, that surely she would find that choosing, active ghost in motion over a chest or moving a curtain at the window, and that surely, ascending the dangerous stair to look into the two bedrooms above, she would hear the quick voice say, "Oh, it's you, Rosalind, now you just tell me . . ." But everything was silent.

Rosalind came downstairs. She returned to the front door and saw that Mr. Thibodeau had driven away. Had he said something about going back for something? She closed the door quietly, reentered the big natural room, and let the things there speak.

For it was all self-contained, knowing and infinitely quiet. The lake gave its perpetual lapping sound, like nibbling fish in shallow water, now and then splashing up, as though a big one had flourished. Lap, lap against the wooden piles that supported the balcony. Lap against the steps, with a swishing motion on the lowest one, a passing-over instead of an against sound. The first steps were replaced, new, the color fresh blond instead of worn brown. The room heard the lapping, the occasional splash, the swish of water.

Rosalind herself was being got through to by something even less predictable than water. What she heard was memory: voices quarreling. From three years ago they woke to life. A slant of light—that had brought them back. Just at this time of day, she had been coming in from swimming. The voices had climbed the large, clear windows, clawing for exit, and finding none, had fled like people getting out of a burning theater, through the door to the far right that opened out onto the balcony. She had been coming up the steps from the water when the voices stampeded over her, frightening, intense, racing outward from the panic within. "You know you do and you know you will . . . there's no use to lie, I've been through all that. Helpless is all I can feel, all I can be. That's the awful part . . . !" "I didn't drive all this way just to get back into that. Go on, get away to New York with dear Aunt Mildred. Who's to know, for that matter, if it's Mildred at all?" "You hide your life like a card in the deck and then have the nerve—! Oh, you're a great magician, aren't you?" "Hush, she's out there . . . hush, now . . . you must realize—" "I do nothing but realize—" "Hush . . . just . . . no . . ." And their known selves returned to them as she came in, dripping, pretending nothing had happened, gradually believing her own pretense.

The way she'd learned to do, all the other times. Sitting forgotten, for the moment, in an armchair too big back in New York, listening while her heart hurt until her mother said, "Darling, go to your room, I'll be there in a minute." Even on vacation, it was sometimes the same thing. And Mother coming in later, as she half slept, half waited, to hold her hand and say, "Just forget it now, tomorrow it won't seem real. We all love each other. Tomorrow you won't even remember." Kissed and tucked in, she trusted. It didn't happen all the time. And the tomorrows were clear and bright. The only trouble was, this time there hadn't been any tomorrow, only the tomorrow of her mother's driving away. Could anybody who sounded like that, saying those things, have a wreck the very next morning and those things have nothing to do with it?

Maybe I got the times mixed up.

("She had just a little part in the cast of the show he worked with last year." "That's how they met, was it?") ("Your mother got the vapors sometimes. The theater scared her." She'd heard her father say that.)

I dreamed it all, she thought, and couldn't be sure this wasn't true, though wondered if she could dream so vividly that she could see the exact print of her wet foot just through the doorway there, beside it the drying splash from the water's runnel down her leg. But it could have been another day.

Why not just ask Daddy?

At the arrival of this simple solution, she let out a long sigh, flung her hands back of her head, and stretched out on the beautiful rug her mother had placed there. Her eyes dimmed; she felt the lashes flutter downward. . . .

A footstep and a voice awakened her from how short a sleep she did not know. Rolling over and sitting up, she saw a strange woman—short, heavyset, with faded skin, gray hair chopped off around her face, plain run-down shoes. She was wearing slacks. Then she smiled and things about her changed.

"You don't remember me, do you? I'm Marie Thibodeau. I remember you and your mom and your dad. That was all bad. *Gros dommage*. But you're back now. You'll have a good time again, eh? We thought maybe you didn't have nothing you could eat yet. You come back with me. I going make you some nice lunch. My husband said to come find you."

She rose slowly, walked through shadows toward the woman, who still had something of the quality of an apparition. Did she think that because of her mother, others must have died too? She followed. The lunch was the same as years before: the meat pie, the beans, the catsup and relish and the white bread taken sliced from its paper. And the talk, too, was nearly the same: kind things said before, repeated now; chewed, swallowed.

———

"You don't remember me, but I remember you. You're *the* Nat Jennings's daughter, used to come here with your folks." This was what the boy said, in Howard Johnson's.

"We're the tennis ones—Dunbar," said the girl, who was his sister, not his date; for saying "tennis" had made Rosalind remember the big house their family owned—"the villa," her father called it—important grounds around it, and a long frontage on the lake. She remembered them as strutting around smaller then, holding rackets that looked too large for their bodies. They had been allowed on the court only at certain hours, along with their friends, but even then they had wished to be observed. Now here they were before her, grown up and into denim, like anybody else. Paul and Elaine. They had showed up at the entrance to the motel restaurant, tan and healthy. Paul had acquired a big smile; Elaine a breathless hesitating voice, the kind Daddy didn't like, it was so intended to tease.

"Let's all find a booth together," Paul Dunbar said.

Rosalind said, "I spent half the afternoon with the telephone man, the other half at the grocery. Getting the cottage opened."

"You can come up to our house after we eat. Not much open here yet. We're on spring holidays."

"They extended it. Outbreak of measles."

"She made that up," said the Dunbar boy, who was speaking

straight and honestly to Rosalind. "We told them we had got sick and would be back next week."

"It's because we are so in-tell-i-gent. . . . Making our grades is not a prob-lem," Elaine said in her trick voice.

"We've got the whole house to ourselves. Our folks won't be coming till June. Hey, why don't you move down with us?"

"I can't," said Rosalind. "Daddy's coming up tomorrow. And my stepmother. He got married again."

"Your parents split?"

"No . . . I mean, not how you think. My mother was killed three years ago, driving to New York. She had a wreck."

"Jesus, what a break. I'm sorry, Rosalind."

"You heard about it, Paul. We both did."

"It's still a tough break."

"Mr. Thibodeau's been helping me. Mrs. Thibodeau's cleaning up. They're coming tomorrow." If this day is ever over.

She went with them after dinner. . . .

The Dunbar house could be seen from the road, a large two-story house on the lake, with white wood trim. There were two one-story wings, like smaller copies of the central house, their entrances opening at either side, the right one on a flagstone walk, winding through a sloping lawn, the left on a porte-cochere, where the Dunbars parked. Within, the large rooms were shuttered, the furniture dust-covered. The three of them went to the glassed-in room on the opposite wing and put some records on. They danced on the tiled floor amid the white wicker furniture.

Had they heard a knocking or hadn't they? A strange boy was standing in the doorway, materialized. Elaine had cried, "Oh goodness, Fenwick, you scared me!" She moved back from Paul's controlling rhythm. They were all facing the stranger. He was heavier than Paul; he was tall and grown to the measure of his big hands and feet. He looked serious and easily detachable from the surroundings; it wasn't possible to guess by looking at him where he lived or what he was doing there.

"Fenwick . . ." Paul was saying to him. What sort of name was that? He strode over to the largest chaise longue, and fitted himself into it. Paul introduced Rosalind to Fenwick.

"I have a mile-long problem to solve before Thursday," Fenwick said. "I'm getting cross-eyed. You got a beer?"

"Fenwick is a math-uh-mat-i-cul gene-i-yus," Elaine told Rosalind. The record finished and she switched off the machine.

"Fenwick wishes he was," said Fenwick.

It seemed that they were all at some school together, called Wakeley, over in Vermont. They knew people to talk about together. "I've been up about umpteen hours," Rosalind said. "I came all the way from New York this morning."

"Just let me finish this beer, and I'll take you home," said Fenwick.

"It's just Howard Johnson's," she said.

"There are those that call it home," said Fenwick, downing beer.

They walked together to the highway, where Fenwick had left his little old rickety car. The trees were bursting from the bud, you could practically smell them grow, but the branches were still dark, and cold-looking and wet, because it had rained while they were inside. The damp road seamed beneath the tires. There were not many people around. She hugged herself into her raincoat.

"The minute I saw you I remembered you," Fenwick said. "I just felt like we were friends. You used to go to that little park with all the other kids. Your daddy would put you on the seesaw. He pushed it up and down for you. But I don't guess you'd remember me."

"I guess I ought to," Rosalind said. "Maybe you grew a lot."

"You can sure say that. They thought I wasn't going to stop." The sign ahead said "Howard Johnson's." "I'd do my problem better if we had some coffee."

"Tomorrow maybe," she said. "I'm dead tired." But what she thought was, He likes me.

At the desk she found three messages, all from Daddy and Eva. "Call when you come in." "Call as soon as you can." "Call even if late." She called.

"So it'll be late tomorrow, maybe around dinner. What happened was . . ." He went on and on. With Nat Jennings, you got used to postponements, so her mother always said. "How's it going, Rosie? I've thought about you every minute."

"Everything's ready for you, or it will be when you come."

"Don't cook up a special dinner. We might be late. It's a long road."

—

In a dream her mother was walking with her. They were in the library at Lake George. In the past her mother had often gone there to check out books. She was waiting for a certain book she wanted, but it hadn't come back yet. "But you did promise me last week," she was saying to somebody at the desk; then she was walking up the street with Rosalind, and Rosalind saw the book in her shopping bag. "You got it after all," she said to her mother. "I just found it lying there on the walk," her mother said, and then Rosalind remembered how she had leaned down to pick up something. "That's nice," said Rosalind, satisfied that things could happen this way. "I think it's nice, too," said her mother, and they went along together.

—

By noon the next day her work was done, but she felt bad because she had found something—a scarf in one of the dresser drawers. It was a sumptuous French satin scarf in a jagged play of colors, mainly red, a shade her mother, with her coppery hair, had never worn. It smelled of Eva's perfume. So they had been up here before, she thought, but why—this far from New York? And why not say so? Helpless was what her mother said she felt. Can I, thought Rosalind, ask Daddy about this, too?

In the afternoon she drove up into the Adirondacks with Elaine and Paul Dunbar. They took back roads, a minor highway that crossed from the lakeshore road to the Thruway; another beyond that threaded along the bulging sides of the mountains. They passed one lake after another: some small and limpid; others half-choked with water lilies and thickly shaded where frogs by the hundreds were chorusing, invisible amid the fresh lime-green; and some larger still, marked with stumps of trees mysteriously broken off. From one of these, strange birdcalls sounded. Then the road ran upward. Paul pulled up under some tall pines and stopped.

"We're going to climb," he announced.

It suited Rosalind because Elaine had just asked her to tell her "all about the theater, every single thing you know." She wouldn't have to do that, at least. Free of the car, they stood still in deserted air. There was no feel of houses near. The brother and sister started along a path they apparently knew. It led higher, winding through trees, with occasional glimpses of a rotting lake below and promise of some triumphant view above. Rosalind followed next to Paul, with Elaine trailing behind. Under a big oak they stopped to rest.

Through the leaves a small view opened up; there was a little valley below, with a stream running through it. The three of them sat hugging their knees and talking, once their breath came back. "Very big deal," Paul was saying. "Five people sent home, weeping parents outside offices, and everybody tiptoeing past. About what? The whole school smokes pot, everybody knows it. Half the profs were on it. Remember old Borden?"

Elaine's high-pitched laugh. "He said, 'Just going for a joint,' when he pushed into the john one day. Talking back over his shoulder."

"What really rocked the boat was when everybody started cheating. Plain and fancy."

"What made them start?" Rosalind asked. Pot was passed around at her school, too, in the Upper Eighties, but you could get into trouble about it.

"You know Miss Hollander was heard to say out loud one day, 'The dean's a shit.'"

"That's the source of the whole fucking mess," said Paul. "The stoopid dean's a shit."

"Is he a fag?" asked Rosalind, not too sure of language like this.

"Not even that," said Paul, and picked up a rock to throw. He put down his hand to Rosalind. "Come on, we got a little farther to climb."

The path snaked sharply upward. She followed his long legs and brown loafers, one with the stitching breaking at the top, and stopping for breath, she looked back and discovered they were alone. "Where's Elaine?"

"She's lazy." He stopped high above to wait for her. She looked up to him and saw him turn to face her, jeans tight over his narrow thighs and flat waist. He put a large hand down to pull her up, and grinned as she came unexpectedly too fast; being thin and light, she sailed up so close they bumped together. His face skin was glossy with sweat. "Just a little farther," he encouraged her. His front teeth were not quite even. Light exploded from the tips of his ears. Grappling at roots, avoiding sheer surfaces of rock, gaining footholds on patches of earth, they burst finally out on a ledge of rough but fairly flat stone, chiseled away as though in a quarry, overlooking a dizzying sweep of New York countryside. "Oh." Rosalind caught her breath. "How gorgeous! We live high up with a terrace over Central Park," she confided excitedly. "But that's nothing like this!"

Paul put his arm around her. "Don't get too close. You know some people just love heights. They love 'em to death. Just show them one and off they go."

"Not me."

"Come here." He led her a little to the side, placing her—"Not there, here"—at a spot where two carved lines crossed, as though Indians had marked it for something. Then, his arm close around her, he pressed his mouth down on hers. Her long brown hair fell backward over his shoulder. If she struggled, she might pull them both over the edge. "Don't." She broke her mouth away. His free hand was kneading her.

"Why? Why not?" The words burrowed into her ear like objects.

"I hadn't thought of you . . . not for myself."

"Think of me now. Let's just stay here a minute."

But she slipped away and went sliding back down. Arriving in the level space with a torn jacket and a skinned elbow she found Elaine lying back against a rock, apparently sleeping. A camera with a telescope lens was resting on the canvas shoulder bag she had carried up the hill.

Elaine sat up, opening her eyes. Rosalind stopped, and Paul's heavy stride, overtaking, halted close behind her. She did not want to look at him, and was rubbing at the blood speckled out on her scratched arm where she'd fallen against a limb.

"Paul thinks he's ir-ree-sisty-bul," Elaine said. "Now we know it isn't so."

Looking up, Rosalind could see the lofty ledge where she and Paul had been. Elaine picked up the camera, detached the lens, and fitted both into the canvas bag. "Once I took a whole home movie. That was the time he was screwing the waitress from the pizza place."

"Oh, sure, get funny," said Paul. He had turned an angry red.

In the car, Elaine leaned back to speak to Rosalind. "We're known to be a little bit crazy. Don't you worry, Ros-uh-lind."

Paul said nothing. He drove hunched forward over the wheel.

"Last summer was strictly crazy, start to finish," said Elaine. "Wasn't that true, Paul?"

"It was pretty crazy," said Paul. "Rosalind would have loved it," he added. He was getting mad at her now, she thought.

She asked to hop out at the road to the cottage, instead of going to the motel. She said she wanted to see Mr. Thibodeau.

"Sorry you didn't like the view," said Paul from the wheel. He was laughing now; his mood had changed.

Once they'd vanished, she walked down the main road to the Fenwick mailbox.

———

From the moment she left the road behind she had to climb again, not as strenuously as up to the mountain ledge, but a slow, winding climb up an ill-tended road. The house that finally broke into view after a sharp turn was bare of paint and run-down. There was a junk car in the wide yard, the parts just about picked off it, one side sitting on planks, and a litter of household odds and ends nearby. A front porch, sagging, was covered with a tangle of what looked to be hunting and camping things. From behind, a dog barked, a warning sound to let her know who was in charge. There was mud in the path to the door.

Through the window of a tacked-on wing to the right, there was Fenwick, sure enough, at a table with peeling paint, in a plain kitchen chair, bending over a large notebook. Textbooks and graph papers were scattered around him. She rapped on the pane and summoned his attention, as though from another planet. He came to the door.

"Oh, it's you, Rose."

"Rosalind."

"I'm working on my problem." He came out and joined her. Maybe he was a genius, Rosalind thought, to have got a fellowship to that school, making better grades than the Dunbars.

"I've been out with Paul and Elaine."

"Don't tell me Paul took you up to that lookout."

She nodded. They sat down on a bench that seemed about to fall in.

"Dunbar's got a collection of pictures—girls he's got to go up there. It's just a dumb gimmick."

"He thinks it's funny," she said, and added, "I left."

"Good. They're on probation, you know. All that about school's being suspended's not true. I'm out for another reason, studying for honors. But—"

A window ran up. A woman's voice came around the side of the house. "Henry, I told you—"

"But I need a break, Mother," he said, without turning his head.

"Is your name Henry?" Rosalind asked.

"So they tell me. Come on, I'll take you back where you're staying."

"I just wanted to see where you lived." He didn't answer. Probably it wasn't the right thing. He walked her down the hill, talking all the way, and put her into his old Volkswagen.

"The Dunbars stick too close together. You'd think they weren't kin. They're like a couple dating. They make up these jokes on people. I was there the other night to help them through some math they failed. But it didn't turn out that way. Know why? They've got no mind for work. They think something will happen, so they won't have to." He hesitated, silent, as the little car swung in and out of the wooded curves. "I think they make love," he said, very low. It was a kind of gossip. "There's talk at school. . . . Now don't go and tell about it."

"You're warning me," she said.

"That's it. There's people living back in the woods, no different from them. Mr. Thibodeau and Papa—they hunt bear together, way off from here, high up. Last winter I went, too, and there was a blizzard. We shot a bear but it looked too deep a snow to get the carcass out, but we did, after a day or so. We stayed with these folks, brother and sister. Some odd little kids running around.

"If they get thrown out of Wakeley, they can go somewhere else. Their folks have a lot of money. So no problem."

"But I guess anywhere you have to study," said Rosalind.

He had brought her to the motel, and now they got out and walked to a plot where shrubs were budding on the slant of hill above the road. Fenwick had speculative eyes that kept to themselves, and a frown from worry or too many figures, just a small thread between his light eyebrows.

"When I finish my problem, any minute now, I'll go back to school."

"My mother died three years ago, in June," said Rosalind.

"I knew that. It's too bad, Rosalind. I'm sorry."

"Did you know her?" Rosalind experienced an eagerness, expectation, as if she doubted her mother's ever having been known.

"I used to see her with you," said Fenwick. "So I guess I'd know her if I saw her." His hand had appeared on her shoulder. She was at about the right height for that.

"Nobody will ever see her again," she said. He pulled her closer.

"If I come back in the summer, I'd like to see you, Rosalind."

"Me, too," she said.

"I've got some stuff you can read." He was squinting. The sun had come through some pale clouds.

"Things you wrote?" She wondered at him.

"I do a lot of things. I'll have this car." He glanced toward it doubtfully. "It's not much of a car, though."

"It's a fine car," she said, so he could walk off to it, feeling all right, and wave to her.

———

Rosalind was surprised and obscurely hurt by the message she received at the motel: namely, that her father and stepmother had already arrived and had called by for her. She had some money left over from what her father had given her, and not wanting to call, she took a taxi down to the cottage.

Her hurt sprang from thwarted plans. She had meant to prepare for them, greet them, have dinner half done, develop a festive air. Now they would be greeting her.

In the taxi past Mr. Thibodeau's house, she saw a strange car coming toward them that made them draw far to one side, sink treacherously among loose fallen leaves. A Chevrolet sedan went past; the man within, a stranger, was well dressed and wore a hat. He looked up to nod at the driver and glance keenly within at his passenger.

"Who was that?" Rosalind asked.

"Griffin, I think his name is," the driver said. "Real estate," he added.

There had been a card stuck in the door when she had come, Rosalind recalled, and a printed message: "Thinking of selling? Griffin's the Guy."

Then she was alighting, crying, "Daddy! Eva! It's me!" And they were running out, crying, "There she is! You got the call?" Daddy was tossing her, forgetting she'd grown; he almost banged her head against a beam. "You nearly knocked my three brains out," she laughed. "It's beautiful!" Eva cried, about the cottage. She spread her arms wide as wings and swirled across the rugs in a solo dance. "It's simply charming!"

Daddy opened the piano with a flourish. He began thumping the old keys, some of which had gone dead from the damp. But "Sweet Rosie O'Grady" was unmistakably coming out. They were hugging and making drinks and going out to look at the boat, kneeling down to test the still stone-chill water.

"What good taste your mother had!" Eva told her, smiling. "The apartment . . . now this!" She was kind.

———

In the late afternoon Rosalind and her father lowered and launched the canoe, and finding that it floated without a leak and sat well in the water, they decided to test it. Daddy had changed his gray slacks and blazer for gabardine trousers and a leather jacket. He wore a denim shirt. Daddy glistened with life, and what he wore was more important than what other people wore. He thought of clothes, evidently, but he never, that she could remember, discussed them. They simply appeared on him, like various furs or fleece that he could shed suddenly and grow just as suddenly new. Above button-down collars or open-throated knit pullovers or turtlenecks or black bow ties, his face, with its slightly ruddy look, even in winter, its cleft chin and radiating crinkles, was like a law of attraction, drawing whatever interested, whatever lived. In worry or grief, he hid it, that face. Then the clothes no longer mattered. Rosalind had sometimes found him in a room alone near a window, still, his face bent down behind one shoulder covered with some old faded shirt, only the top of his head showing and that revealed as startlingly gray, the hair growing thin. But when the face came up, it would seem to resume its livingness as naturally as breath, his hair being the same as ever, barely sprinkled with gray. It was the face for her, his gift.

"Did you see the real estate man?" Rosalind asked over her shoulder, paddling with an out-of-practice wobble.

"Griffin? Oh, yes, he was here. Right on the job, those guys."

They paddled along, a stone's throw from the shore. To their right the lake stretched out wide and sunlit. One or two distant fishing boats dawdled near a small island. The lake, a creamy blue, flashed now and again in air that was still sharp.

"Daddy, did you know Eva a long time?"

There was a silence from behind her. "Not too long." Then he said what he'd said before. "She was a member of the cast. Rosie, we shouldn't have let you go off by yourself. I realized that this morning. I woke up early thinking it, and jumped straight out of bed. By six I'd packed. Who've you been seeing?"

"I ran into the Dunbars, Paul and Elaine, down in the big white house, you know. They're here from school. I have to run from Mrs. Thibodeau. She wants to catch and feed me. And then there's Fenwick."

"Some old guy up the hill who sells junk . . . is that the one?"

"No, his son. He's a mathematical genius, Daddy."

"Beware of mathematical geniuses," her father said, "especially if their fathers sell junk."

"You always told me that," said Rosalind. "I just forgot."

When they came in they were laughing. She and Eva cooked the meals. Daddy played old records, forgoing gin rummy for once. That was the first day.

———

"Wait! Look now! Look!"

It was Eva speaking while Daddy blindfolded Rosalind. They had built a fire. Somebody had found in a shop uptown the sort of stuff you threw on it to make it sparkle. The room on a gloomy afternoon, though shut up tight against a heavy drizzle, was full of warmth and light. Elaine and Paul Dunbar were there, sitting on the couch. Fenwick was there, choosing to crouch down on a hassock in the corner like an Indian, no matter how many times he was offered a chair. He had been followed in by one of the Fenwick dogs, a huge German shepherd with a bushy, perfectly curling tail lined with white, which he waved at times from side to side like a plume, and when seated, furled about his paws. He smelled like a wet dog owned by a junk dealer.

At the shout of "Look now!" Daddy whipped off the blindfold. The cake had been lighted—eighteen candles—a shining delight. They had cheated a little to have a party for Rosalind; her birthday wasn't till the next week. But the idea was fun. Eva had thought of it because she had found a box full of party things in the unused bedroom: tinsel, sparklers, masks, and a crepe-paper tablecloth with napkins. She had poured rum into some cherry Kool-Aid and floated orange slices across the top. She wore a printed off-the-shoulder blouse with a denim skirt and espadrilles. Her big glasses glanced back fire and candlelight. The young people watched her lighting candles for the table with a long, fancy match held in brightly tipped fingers. Daddy took the blue bandanna blindfold and wound it pirate-fashion around his forehead. He had contrived an eye patch for one eye. "Back in the fifties these things were a status symbol," he said, "but I forget what status they symbolized."

"Two-car garage but no Cadillac," Paul said.

Daddy winked at Elaine. "My daughter's friends get prettier every day."

"So does your daughter," Paul said.

Eva passed them paper plates of birthday cake.

"*She's* getting to the dangerous age, not me. Hell, I was there all the time."

Everyone laughed but Fenwick. He fed small bites of cake to the dog and large ones to himself, while Rosalind refilled his glass.

The friends had brought her presents. A teddy bear dressed in blue jeans from Elaine. A gift-shop canoe in birchbark from Paul. The figure of an old man carved in wood from Fenwick. His father had done it, he said. Rosalind held it up. She set it down. He watched her. He was redeeming his father, whom nobody thought much of. "It's grand," she said, "I love it." Fenwick sat with his hand buried in the dog's thick ruff. His nails, cleaned up for coming there, would get grimy in the dog's coat.

Rosalind's father so far had ignored Fenwick. He was sitting on a stool near Elaine and Paul, talking about theater on campuses, how most campus musicals went dead on Broadway, the rare one might survive, but usually . . . Eva approached the dog, who growled at her. "He won't bite," said Fenwick.

"Is a mathematician liable to know whether or not a dog will bite?" Eva asked.

"Why not?" asked Fenwick.

"You've got quite a reputation to live up to," Eva pursued. She was kneeling near him, close enough to touch, holding her gaze, like her voice, very steady. "I hear you called a genius more often than not."

"You can have a genius rating in something without setting the world on fire," said Fenwick. "A lot of people who've got them are just walking around doing dumb things, the same as anybody."

"I'll have to think that over," Eva said.

There came a heavy pounding at the door, and before anybody could go to it, a man with a grizzled beard, weathered skin, battered clothes, and a rambling walk entered the room. He looked all around until he found Fenwick. "There you are," he said.

Rosalind's father had risen. Nobody said anything. "I'm Nat Jennings." Daddy put out his hand. "This is my wife. What can we do for you?"

"It's my boy," said Fenwick's father, shaking hands. "His mother was looking for him, something she's wanting him for. I thought if he wasn't doing nothing . . ."

"Have a drink," said Nat.

"Just pour it straight out of the bottle," said Fenwick's father, who had taken the measure of the punch.

Fenwick got up. "That's O.K., Mr. Jennings. I'll just go on with Papa."

The dog had moved to acknowledge Mr. Fenwick, who had downed his drink already. Now the boy came to them both, the dog being no longer his. He turned to the rest of the room, which seemed suddenly to be of a different race. "We'll go," he said. He turned again at the living-room entrance. "Thanks."

Rosalind ran after them. She stood in the front door, hidden by the wall of the entrance from those in the room, and leaned out into the rain. "Oh, Mr. Fenwick, I love the carving you did!"

He glanced back. "Off on a bear hunt, deep in the snow. Had to do something."

"Goodbye, Fenwick. Thanks for coming!"

He stopped to answer, but said nothing. For a moment his look was like a voice, crying out to her from across something. For the first time in her life, Rosalind felt the force that pulls stronger than any other. Just to go with him, to be, even invisibly, near. Then the three of them—tall boy, man, and dog, stair-stepped together—were walking away on the rainy path.

When she went inside, she heard Paul Dunbar recalling how Nat Jennings used to organize a fishing derby back in one of the little lakes each summer. He would get the lake stocked, and everybody turned out with casting rods and poles to fish it out. (Rosalind remembered; she had ridden on his shoulder everywhere, till suddenly, one summer, she had got too big for that, and once it had rained.) "And then there were those funny races down in the park—you folks put them on. One year I won a prize!" (Oh, that too, she remembered, her mother running with two giant orange bows like chrysanthemums, held in either hand, orange streamers flying, her coppery hair in the sun.) "You ought to get all that started again."

"It sounds grand, but I guess you'd better learn how yourselves," Eva was saying. "We'll probably not be up here at all."

"Not be here!" Rosalind's cry as she returned from the door was like an alarm. "Not be here!" A silence was suddenly on them.

Her father glanced up, but straightened out smoothly. "Of course we'll be here. We'll have to work on it together."

It had started raining harder. Paul and Elaine, though implored to stay, left soon.

When the rain chilled the air, Eva had got out a fringed Spanish shawl, embroidered in bright flowers on a metallic gold background. Her glasses above this, plus one of the silly hats she'd found, made her seem a many-tiered fantasy of a woman, concocted by Picasso, or made to be carried through the streets for some Latin holiday parade.

Light of movement, wearing a knit tie, cuff links on his striped shirt ("In your honor," he said to Rosalind), impeccable blue blazer above gray slacks, Nat Jennings played the country gentleman with pleasure to himself and everyone. His pretty daughter at her birthday party was his delight. This was what his every move had been saying. And now she had gone to her room. He was knocking on its door. "Rosie?"

"I'm drunk," said Rosalind.

He laughed. "We're going to talk at dinner, Rosie. When you sober up, come down. Did you enjoy your birthday party, baby?"

"Sure I did."

"I like your friends."

"Thank you."

"Too bad about Fenwick's father. That boy deserves better."

"I guess so."

She was holding an envelope Paul had slipped into her hand when he left. It had a photo and its negative enclosed, the one on the high point, the two of them kissing. The note said, "We're leaving tomorrow, sorry if I acted stupid. When we come back, maybe we can try some real ones. Paul."

There won't be any coming back for me, she lay thinking, dazed. But this was your place, Mother. Mother, what do I do now?

———

He was waiting for her at the bottom of the stairs and treated her with delightful solemnity, as though she were the visiting daughter of an old friend. He showed her to her place and held the chair for her. Eva, now changed into slacks, a silk shirt, and nubby sweater, came in with a steaming casserole. The candles were lighted again.

"I'm not a grand cook, as Rose knows." She smiled. "But you couldn't be allowed, on your birthday . . ."

"She's read a hole in the best cookbook," said Daddy.

"I'm sure it's great," Rosalind said in a little voice, and felt tension pass from one of them to the other.

"I'm in love with Fenwick," Eva announced, and dished out coq au vin.

"Won't get you anywhere," Daddy said. "I see the whole thing: he's gone on Rosie, but she's playing it cool."

"They're all going back tomorrow," Rosalind said. "Elaine and Paul were just on suspension, and Fenwick's finished his problem."

They were silent, passing dishes. Daddy and Eva exchanged glances.

"Rosie," said Daddy, filling everyone's wineglass, "we've been saving our good news till after your party. Now we want you to know. You remember the little off-Broadway musical I worked with last fall? Well, Hollywood is picking it up at quite a hefty sum. It's been in negotiation for two months. Now all's clear, and they're wanting to hire me along with the purchase. Best break I ever had."

"I'm so happy I could walk on air," said Eva.

"Are we going to *move* there!" Rosalind felt numb.

"Of course not, baby. There'll be trips, some periods out there, nothing permanent."

Before Rosalind suddenly, as she glanced from one of them to the other, they grew glossy in an extra charge of flesh and beauty. A log even broke in the fireplace, and a flame reached to some of the sparkler powder that was unignited, so that it flared up as though to hail them. They grew great as faces on a drive-in movie screen, seen

floating up out of nowhere along a highway; they might mount skyward any minute and turn to constellations. He had wanted something big to happen, she knew, for a long time. "They never give me
any credit" was a phrase she knew by heart. Staying her own human
size, Rosalind knew that all they were saying was probably true.
They had shoved her birthday up by a week to tidy her away, but
they didn't look at it that way, she had to guess.

"Let's drink a toast to Daddy!" she cried, and drained her wineglass.

"Rosalind!" her father scolded happily. "What does anyone do
with an alcoholic child?"

"Straight to AA," Eva filled in, "the minute we return."

"Maybe there's a branch in Lake George," Daddy worried.

"I'll cause spectacles at the Plaza," Rosalind giggled through the
dizziness of wine. "I'll dance on the bar and jump in the fountain.
You'll be so famous it'll make the *Daily News.*"

"I've even got some dessert," said Eva, who, now the news was
out, had the air of someone who intends to wait on people as seldom as possible. The cottage looked plainer and humbler all the
time. How could they stand it for a single other night? Rosalind
wondered. They would probably just explode out of there by some
chemical process of rejection that not even Fenwick could explain.

"If things work out," Daddy was saying, "we may get to make
Palm Beach winters yet. No use to plan ahead."

"Would you like that?" Rosalind asked Eva, as if she didn't know.

"Why, I just tag along with the family," Eva said. "Your rules are
mine."

———

That night Rosalind slipped out of her upstairs room. In order to
avoid the Thibodeaus, whose house had eyes and ears, she skirted
through the woods and ran into part of the lake, which appeared
unexpectedly before her, like a person. She bogged in spongy loam
and slipped on mossy rocks, and shivered, drenched to the knees, in
the chill night shade of early foliage. At last she came out of shadow
onto a road, but not before some large shape, high up, had startled
her, blundering among the branches. A car went past and in the

glancing headlights she saw the mailbox and its lettering and turned to climb the steep road up to the Fenwicks'. What did she expect to happen there? Just whom did she expect to find? Fenwick himself, of course, but in what way? To lead her out of here, take her somewhere, take her off for good? Say she could stay on with him, and they'd get the cottage someday and share it forever? That would be her dream, even if Fenwick's daddy camped on them and smelled up the place with whiskey.

She climbed with a sense of the enveloping stillness of the woods, the breath of the lake, the distant appeal of the mountains. The road made its final turn to the right, just before the yard. But at that point she was surprised to hear, as if growing out of the wood itself, murmurous voices, not one or two, but apparently by the dozen, and the sound of a throbbing guitar string, interposing from one pause to the next. She inched a little closer and stopped in the last of the black shade. A fire was burning in a wire grating near the steps. Tatters of flame leaped up, making the shadows blacker. High overhead, the moon shone. Fenwick, too, was entitled to a last night at home, having finished some work nobody else could have understood. He would return that summer. He was sitting on the edge of the porch, near a post. Some others were on the steps, or on chairs outside, or even on the ground.

They were humming some tune she didn't know and she heard a voice rise, Mrs. Thibodeau's beyond a doubt! "Now I never said I knew that from a firsthand look, but I'd have to suppose as much." Then Mr. Thibodeau was joining in: "Seen her myself . . . more than a time or two." The Thibodeaus were everywhere, with opinions to express, but about what and whom? All went foundering in an indistinct mumble of phrases until a laugh rose and then another stroke across the strings asked them to sing together, a song she'd never heard. "Now that's enough," a woman's voice said. "I ain't pitching no more tunes." "I've sung all night, many's the time." "Just you and your jug."

From near the steps a shape rose suddenly; it was one of the dogs, barking on the instant of rising—there had been a shift of wind. He trotted toward her. She stood still. Now the snuffling muzzle ranged over her. The great tail moved its slow white fan. It was the one she knew. She patted the intelligent head. Someone whistled. It was Fenwick, who, she could see, had risen from his seat.

Something fell past him, out of the thick-bunched human shapes on the porch. It had been pushed or shoved and was yelling, a child. "Stealing cake again," some voice said, and the body hit the ground with a thump. The mother in the chair, not so much as turning, said, "Going to break ever' bone in her one o' these days." "Serve her right" came from the background—Mr. Fenwick. It was young Fenwick himself who finally went down to pick her up (by the back of her shirt, like a puppy), Mrs. Thibodeau who came to dust her off. The yelling stopped. "Hush now," said Mrs. Thibodeau. Rosalind turned and went away.

"Who's there?" Fenwick was calling toward the road. "Nobody," a man's voice, older, said. "Wants his girlfriend," said the father. "Go and git her, fella."

The mountain went on talking. Words faded to murmurs, losing outline; as she stumbled down turns of road, they lost even echoes. She was alone where she had not meant to be, but for all that, strangely detached, elated.

Back on the paved road, she padded along in sneakers. Moonlight lay bright in patterns through the trees. Finally the Dunbar house rose up, moonlight brightening one white portico, while the other stood almost eclipsed in darkness. In a lighted interior, through a downstairs window, she could see them, one standing, the other looking up, graceful hands making gestures, mouths moving— together and alone. Great white moths circling one another, planning, loving maybe. She thought they were like the photographs they took. The negative is me, she thought.

Far up the road, so far it tired her almost as much to think of it as to walk it, the old resort hotel looked out on Lake George with hundreds of empty windows, eyes with vision gone, the porticoes reaching wide their outspread arms. Water lapped with none to hear. "No Trespassing," said the sign, and other signs said "For Sale," like children calling to one another.

Rosalind looked up. Between her and the road, across the lawn, a brown bear was just standing up. He was turning his head this way and that. The head was small, wedge-shaped. The bear's pelt moved when he did, like grass in a breeze. Pointing her way, the head stopped still. She felt the gaze thrill through her with long foreverness, then drop away. On all fours, he looked small, and moved toward the lake with feet shuffling close together, rather like a rolling ball, loose and tumbling toward the water. The moon sent a shimmering golden path across the lake. She was just remembering that her mother, up here alone with her, claimed to have seen a bear late at night, looking through the window. Daddy didn't doubt she'd dreamed it. He didn't think they came so close. Rosalind knew herself as twice seen and twice known now, by dog and bear. She walked the road home.

———

Voices sounding in her head, Rosalind twisted and turned that night, sleepless. She got up once, and taking the red scarf she had found from the drawer, she put it down on the living-room table near the large vase of money plant. Then she went back up and slept, what night was left of it.

———

Daddy came in for Eva's coffee and then they both appeared, he freshly shaved and she perfect in her smooth makeup, a smartly striped caftan flowing to her ankles. Rosalind had crept down in wrinkled pajamas, her bare feet warping back from the chill floor.

"Today's for leaving," her father said. When Rosalind dropped her gaze, he observed her. They were standing in the kitchen before the stove. They were alone. He was neat, fit, in slacks, a beige shirt checked in brown and blue, and a foulard—affected for anyone but him. His amber eyes fixed on her blue ones, offered pools of sincerity for her to plunge into.

"What's this?" Eva asked. She came in with the scarf.

"I found it," said Rosalind. "Isn't it yours?"

Eva looked over her head at Nat. "It must have been your mother's."

"No," said Rosalind. "It wasn't."

———

After breakfast, by common consent, Rosalind and her father rose from the table and went down to the boat. Together they paddled out to the island. They had done this often in the past. The island was inviting, slanted like a turtle's back, rich with clumps of birch and bushes, trimmed with gray rock. Out there today, their words emerged suddenly, like thoughts being printed on the air.

"We aren't coming back," said Rosalind. "This is all."

"I saw you come in last night."

A bird flew up out of the trees.

"Did you tell Eva?"

"She was asleep. Why?"

"She'll think I just sneaked off to see Fenwick. But I didn't. I went off myself . . . by myself."

He played with rocks, seated, forearms resting on his knees, looking at the lake. "I won't tell."

"I wanted to find Mother."

"Did you?"

"In a way . . . I know she's here, all around here. Don't you?"

"I think she might be most everywhere."

Maybe what he was saying was something about himself. The ground was being shifted; they were debating without saying so, and he was changing things around without saying so.

"I let you come up here alone," he went on, "because I thought you needed it—your time alone. Maybe I was wrong."

"If you'd just say you see it too."

"See what?"

"What I was saying. That she's here. No other places. Here."

The way he didn't answer her was so much a silence she could hear the leaves stir. "You didn't love her." The words fell from her, by themselves, you'd have to think, because she hadn't willed them to. They came out because they were there.

"Fool! Of course I did!"

Long after, she realized he had shouted, screamed almost. She didn't know it at the moment, because her eyes had blurred with what she'd accused him of, and her hearing, too, had gone with her sight. She was barely clinging to the world.

When her vision cleared, she looked for him and saw that he was lying down on gray rock with his eyes closed, facing upward, exactly as though exhausted from a task. Like the reverse picture on a face card, he looked to be duplicating an opposite image of his straight-up self; only the marked cleft in his chin was more visible at that angle, and she recalled her mother's holding up a card when they were playing double solitaire once while waiting for him for dinner: "Looks like Daddy...." "Let me see ... sure does...." She had seen the florid printed face often enough, the smile affable, the chin cleft. "Jack of Diamonds," her mother said. For hadn't the two of them also seen the father's face turn fixed and mysterious as the painted image, unchanging from whatever it had changed to? The same twice over: she hadn't thought that till now. He reached up and took her hand. The gesture seemed to say they had blundered into the fire once, but maybe never again.

The scent of pine, the essence of oak scent, too, came warm to her senses, assertive as animals. She rubbed with her free hand at the small debris that hugged the rock. In former times she had peeled away hunks of moss for bringing back. The rock was old enough to be dead, but in school they said that rocks lived.

"You're going to sell it, aren't you? The cottage, I mean."

"I have to. I need the money."

"I thought you were getting money, lots."

"I'm getting some. But not enough."

So he had laid an ace out before her. There was nothing to say. The returned silence, known to trees, rocks, and water, went agelessly on.

Nat Jennings sat up lightly, in one motion. "What mysteries attend my Rosalind, wandering through her forest of Arden?"

"I was chased by a bear," said Rosalind, attempting to joke with him, but remembering she had almost cried just now, she blew her nose on a torn Kleenex.

"Sleeping in his bed, were you? Serves you right."

He scratched his back where something bit. "I damned near fell asleep." He got to his feet. "It's time." It's what he'd said when they left that other time, three years ago. He put out his hand.

Pulling her up, he slipped on a mossy patch of rock and nearly fell. But dancing was in his bones; if he hadn't been good at it, they both would have fallen. As it was they clung and held upright.

Rosalind and her father got into the boat and paddled toward the cottage, keeping perfect time. Eva, not visible, was busy inside. They found her in the living room.

She had the red scarf wound about her head gypsy-fashion. Above her large glasses, it looked comical, but right; sexy and friendly, the way she was always being. She had cleared up everything from breakfast and was packing.

"You two looked like a picture coming in. I should have had a camera."

"Oh, we're a photogenic pair," Nat said.

"Were you ever tempted to study theater?" Eva asked her.

"I was, but— Not now. Oh, no, not now!" She stood apart, single, separate, ready to leave.

Startled by her tone, Nat Jennings turned. "I think it was her mother," he quickly said. "She didn't like the idea."

THE SKATER

Haloed in lynx hats that gleamed with softly falling snow, wrapped in fur-lined raincoats, the two Westmount women went gossiping past the Ritz, until somewhere between "Then she said" and "So I wondered" a small figure crossing with the light on Mountain Street passed before them, wearing the red beret. The woman on the right began suddenly, wordlessly, to run after her, around the corner, down the street, half falling on a streak of snow-hidden ice, only to right herself and race ahead, as though silently calling, Oh, wait!

"What's the matter? Sara! You were running!"

She stood panting, smiling at the friend in weak apology. "It's just that I gave Nan's old red beret to the char's daughter. I thought that might be her." A lie. They both stood looking down Mountain Street to where, a block away, the red beret marched steadily on.

Another time Sara dreamed it. It was all the same except that in the dream she caught up, pulled the child around to face her, saw an ugly, coarse young stranger who spit out icicles at her like a mouthful of teeth, while Sara cried, You stole that hat, and raised her hand to strike.

It was like my daughter's beret, exactly, she heard herself tell some unknown confidante, who would reply, *But that was years ago, fifteen at least.* Then I once followed a boy with his arm in a slate-blue sling exactly like Rob's, the time he broke his arm playing soccer. If only he'd turn and have a face like Rob's. Couldn't that happen, too? And there was Jeff. *Your youngest?* Blond and small once, a tiny, brave boy. In Westmount Park this child I saw—

Forget the confidante, she told herself, lecturing the mirror.

They're safe, they're alive, they're married and gone. They just aren't here. You're not making sense.

———

Then there was summer air, filling the whole strange room. "I wondered so much about you, right from the first. Finding it all out—won't that be great?"

Sara didn't bother to answer. She turned her head, moving it slowly, comfortably, against his shoulder. She, too, had been full of questions. Now, languid, she didn't summon the energy to ask them. It was enough that he was actually there, with his mid-European accent, his learned English, and the one cry brought from a long distance. She rubbed a lock of his black hair between her fingers, like fine cloth.

Day was fading from the windows, slowly, smoothly, like honey being poured carefully. The tree outside the hotel window was at its fullest green. Her eye turned to his watch on the bedside table. It lay beside her own diminutive one with the gold linked bracelet, and the gold shell-shaped earrings, smooth as glass, curved like a snail's back. He liked to stroke them. Time, said the watches. Time.

To go home to Westmount. Stop on the way for groceries. Change to robe and slippers. Cook. Drinks with husband. Dinner. TV. For the man beside her, another world was out there. He picked up the watch and strapped it on.

"Everything seems to run better with us these days," her husband remarked at dinner. "Hard to understand."

"What's hard about it?"

He spooned out veau Marengo. "We used to be always worrying over the children."

"It's change of life," she suggested. "I'm changing for the better."

"You've got used to them being gone. At first that was too much for you."

She finished eating first, and sat with cheek resting on her palm, regarding him, smoking. The images of thirty years were in her memory: his walking through crowds at a station to meet her; her running forward over a lawn to find him; his worried frown at her first flare-ups; his proudly watchful smile above the bow of a wrapped present. She put out her cigarette.

"Something happened today," he said.

He finished his coffee deliberately. Evidently, as though taking a case to court, he was arranging what he had to tell in his mind before he started. He seldom mentioned his cases; he "left the work load at the office." He ate in shirtsleeves and leather house shoes. The dark vest—he was a man who liked vests—cut its usual pattern into the white clarity of his shirt.

"I was just leaving for the day when a young man came in, without an appointment, looking frantic. So I turned back. I saw him."

"And?"

"His problem all spilled out in a hurry. His father had died, but before he died, he had sent him (the son, an only child) a copy of his will. The will left him everything, a considerable estate. But when the funeral was over, another will entirely was produced, and he found himself disinherited. A psychic group is now supposed to get everything, including the house. It seemed to him like a dirty trick, his father jeering at him 'from beyond the grave,' was how he put it. On the other hand, maybe it wasn't the father, but someone else who had forged it."

"Who, for instance?"

"The will the boy had was an informal document—a holograph copy—handwritten. The lawyer who drew up will number two may have been up to some fancy footwork on the date."

"It's not clear which was first?"

"They were dated the same day. That's the odd part. What the boy has is just a photocopy, the original of that one is God knows where. No lockbox has turned it up; the father could be assumed to have destroyed it in favor of will number two. That's certainly what the psychic's lawyer will argue."

"A psychic group. That sounds crazy. Was he?"

"The deceased? Well, he was over seventy, alone in one of those big old mansions way up the mountain. Found dead of a stroke. The boy wasn't living there."

"He's just a young boy?"

"What do I call a boy these days? He may even be thirty. Way behind you and me."

She got up to bring him coffee. Any mention of youth made her wince a little. It was the weak point, bound to surface, in the affair she had stumbled into. Her lover was younger. Safe in the kitchen, she touched the corner of her mouth. Bruised from kissing, it was preciously sore. She took in the coffee.

"Why wasn't the son living there? Was he married?"

"No, he's alone. There had been some hard feeling, some quarreling over his not having work. He assumed that was done with when he got the first will. Anyone would." He folded his napkin on this. He often said that as intelligent as you wanted to be about it, life was never solved. "Haven't you heard of him—old Phil McIvor? He made a pile in mining up in northern Ontario. I won't go snooping around old mansions, but there are certainly matters to explore." He glanced at his watch. It was time for one of his political talk shows on TV.

She felt he had given her a puzzle to play with. "The son might have written the will himself."

"Then why would he have only a Xerox? It was notarized, however. We're checking on that."

She was still clearing the table when the telephone rang. Her husband answered. "Oh," she heard him say, and, "But I make it a strict practice never to see clients at home. Yes, I know I said we would need more time, but I gave you an appointment for next week. I understand. . . . Just a minute." He placed a hand over the receiver. "Sara, by coincidence, it's that boy I was just talking about. He's wandering around alone, got our address, wants to come in for a few minutes. . . ." He paused, looking at her. Such things didn't happen.

"Let him come," she said.

He smiled. "You mean it?"

"Why not?"

They did, of course, both miss the children.

———

"You're keeping something," her lover said.

"I know," she said, "but it's nothing really to do with me. I mean, it has to do with a case, something legal. A confidence."

"I think it's more than that. You must have legal confidences to burn."

"There's a young man, a client of my husband's, who did a strange thing. He asked to stop in the other night and talk to Ted. He was odd."

"Gay, you mean? Queer?"

She shook her head. "He was intense, troubled. On the raw edge with nerves. Yet in spite of that, or maybe because of it, appealing. It's hard to describe."

He turned her face to his. "He attracts you?"

"Karl, I didn't mean that."

"It's how you make it sound."

"If I meant anything like that, I'd say Ted attracts him. I think he wants to attach Ted in some way."

Attractions . . . attachments. She lived with such thoughts now, enchantment-circled, in a spell. She no longer tracked strange children through streets and parks. That night with Ted and his client, she had sat deciding the boy's real need was not for any will but for caring, making contact. His hair was carrot-red. Long, spiraling scars marked his cheek and neck. She shuddered.

"There should be something gratifying to Ted," she mused, "in such dependence. When he left, he grabbed Ted's hand and squeezed it. I thought he might kneel." She laughed softly, wanting to be done with it, turning her face to Karl's.

"Mysteries are everywhere." He smiled quick kisses against her cheek, into her ear. "Beware the RCMP, watch out for the CIA. Are the KGB as far away as we think?" The kisses found her mouth; the client left her mind completely. It was Karl—Karl Darcas was his name, shortened from something long and difficult, Polish-Hungarian-Jewish—who brought him up again later while buttoning his shirt. "What does he look like?"

"Who?"

"The mysterious client."

"He has bright red hair and thin legs."

"Oh, that's really sinister!" He stroked her hair so that she had to arrange it again. She looked around the room—a neat, plain hotel in the far East End of the city—saw the green leaves of Montreal's short, precious summer. This time, too, they held their midsummer fullness.

———

The very thought of her husband, Ted Mangham, forming some new attachment had not entered Sara's mind before. "Ted's ex*clu*sively yours, my dear," some old aunt had said, ages ago. But since Karl Darcas had burst in on her, she had been full of new thoughts and feelings; she was like fresh earth turned up in spring. Every entry into the Metro going from West to East seemed a long underwater plunge from which she could shoot upward into new air, hurrying toward further change. Maybe, she thought, Ted needs to get involved. She was smiling at the idea when she came like a rainwashed flower up out of the Metro exit on her way home and noticed the red-haired young man with his back to her, leaning forward to look in a shop window. Her walk's rhythm broke at once; there was a chill moment of hesitance in her heart's pulsing. He's been hired to watch me, she thought. Ted's having me watched. . . .

As a girl, Sara had been fantastic, crystalline. Guarded, reared, schooled, feted, presented. Her marriage to a promising young lawyer had been the natural step to take. Unnaturally—with shock, even—bride and groom had fallen in love. For years they had wanted nothing but an excuse to travel, "to get off by themselves." Family minds were soon to grow impatient. Relatives and friends were enlisted to put a word in; but pregnancy, once, twice, and thrice, laid fears to rest. Ted's shoulder wound up firmly set to the wheel, and passion bloomed more rarely. Sara and Ted, from beautiful and wanton, turned handsome and acceptable. ("Don't talk so much about the children," he warned her. She complied.) Ted-and-Sara: around their Westmount circle it was said like one word. Over Karl's bare shoulder Sara confided to the green leaves: "Ted's forgotten all that silly way we used to be. I haven't. That's the trouble.

It's not what people call real trouble, I suppose." "It's real," he corrected, "as trouble goes."

Karl Darcas was one of the bright new TV producers on the national network. In his job he was wary as a badger in the bush, eyes in the back of his head. He had plans for moving on to Toronto; she guessed that from the first, though he never said—playing it close, as Ted would have put it.

She had met him at a large benefit at the Château Champlain, the kick-off party for an annual charity drive. Her Christmas mink, so new she still thrilled to the smell of it, was not even checked at the hotel cloakroom while she cast around for Ted, who had got there ahead of her, and felt someone watching her. Not that she knew him. As his eyes fell away, hers lingered for a moment on his thick black hair, growing low on his forehead but making the face for some reason—the strong nose maybe—not less but more intelligent, as if the brain matter had sent up this rich growth. My fur, his hair, she thought and almost smiled when the eyes whipped back to her own, surprising her. He moved toward her.

"Karl Darcas. Have we met?"

"I don't think so. I'm Sara Mangham."

"Mangham." He drew a paper from his coat pocket. "The chairman . . . just who I was looking for. The CBC is running a spot—"

"Oh, no, not me. It's my husband you want. I'm looking for him, too."

This time the eyes did not waver. "Too bad it wasn't you."

Outside later, in minus-twenty weather, they waited before the hotel, together by coincidence, he for a cab, she for Ted to bring the car around. The mink hood was up. When he stroked the rich fur across her back and shoulders, it seemed the most natural move in the world. Drawn from within, she turned her face up to his. "You look like a northern Madonna," he said. Then, dropping his arm as the car drew up, "Where can I find you?" "I'll let you know," she astonished herself in reply, as the tiny snowflakes of deep cold twinkled between their faces.

Now it was summer, and as he said, they were finding things out.

He questioned her—fact after fact, with an outsider's curiosity—but the information he gave her in return was mainly about ideas: Montreal and the French ("Just another ethnic struggle—they think they're different, but they're not"), Canada ("The States will get the whole country someday, piece at a time"), Europe under Communism, writers, political currents, topics she had never heard of, though she had lived through the same global scrambles as he. She thought he might have talked about his childhood or his native landscape, but he didn't; he lived in his mind and his body, not accounting for much in the past. She had to ignore his turtlenecks and scuffed shoes; she'd not the right to change him. He takes me for a sample of Westmount, she thought. But there were plenty of those to choose from, she reflected, and observed the iron-hard line between his brows, the dark cast of beard confined beneath the skin.

"Back to the red-haired man. Did your husband follow up?"

"I guess he's still a client. I'd forgotten about him."

But what she said wasn't true. He had called that very morning. . . .

"I'm watching the house," the strange voice on the phone had said.

"What house do you mean? Who are you?" Blackmail crept another step forward, out of the corners of her mind.

"You know who this is. You were there the night I came. It's my father's house I mean, my house. You know the reason I came up there to you? I had to see what you were like. Once I'd seen you, I knew. Knew I could have hopes. Your husband is not going to listen to me, not in a million years. He thinks I'm a kook. He's a common-sense man. Did you know I've got binoculars? The house is being searched. I'm up above it in the park every afternoon. No, it's not the caretaker. It's one of that stinking psychic group. There's an original copy of the will somewhere—the one I have. Don't you get it? They're after it!" Hysteria. He was tumbling off the edge.

"Leave me out of it. Just don't you bother me."

"I'm alone," the calmed voice said. "I'm alone in the world."

("Before I met you I felt lonely," she had said to Karl Darcas. "The children are gone, you see. I was going mad." "Without you the place is empty as a tomb," her husband told her once when she came back from Barbados. But "alone in the world"—that was another thing.)

"Don't you have a girlfriend?" she asked him.

"When I was young I had a rare bone disease. I was in a cast so long after the transplants the skin atrophied. I had a lot of skin grafts. It's why I look funny. No woman could stand to look at that."

"Some women are forgiving . . . gentle," she said.

"Who wants pity?"

I'll be arguing with him all day, she thought. "Why pick me out? You must know other people."

"It's dangerous to talk. My father was rich. The world is all joined up. I might fall through a trapdoor. I might just disappear. I see you ride the Metro. Women like you take cabs, don't they?"

"I take it shopping. It's quicker."

"Shopping? Over in the East?"

"Fabrics," she groped. "There are places—"

"Now you're explaining."

"Go get a job," she urged. "Something that interests you."

"Things are going on," he said. "Things are going on."

Sara had hung up. . . .

"Your mind is wandering again," her lover said. "Come on, what's it about?"

"Just that boy again," she smiled. "I lied."

"So not forgotten, after all?"

"It's not Ted he's bothering now. It's me."

"Could he be the one who had an estate snatched by a bunch of psychic nuts? I read about it."

"I never said that!" Her astonishment gave her away.

"It was in the paper; you must have seen it. The types seemed to match, that's all. Oh, come on. I'd never say you told me." He lit a cigarette and passed it to her. "Lots of angles there." Meditative, he let his hand wander over her. "Obscure psychic society, old Westmount mansion, people who communicate with departed spirits. The old guy thought his house was loaded with them—tables that walked, rumblings from the attic, creaking doors, groans from the basement, blue outlines of the walking dead."

"You come from Dracula land. Old castles dripping blood. Bats swarming at twilight."

"That's Rumania. Quiet. The old guy decides he's been selected by the dark powers. Either that or he called the psychic bunch and they decided it for him. Their leader's from the States, by the way. Ruttlestern by name. Talks like he's always making a speech: 'Now, my dee-ah, we shall soon have clearly demonstrated . . .' I got this girl to call him up. She recorded what he said—"

"What girl?"

"Somebody on the staff. Nobody special. I was thinking of doing a TV spot newscast on it, really not sufficient for a feature. Just 'City at Six' stuff. A contested will, unusual circumstances . . ."

"If anything led back to Ted. If anything led to you and me—"

"Don't worry. Sara! Don't worry!"

"Then tell me, whatever you do. Promise that, at least."

"On my Westmount honor."

"No. Seriously."

"I promise."

When she emerged into a cloudy summer twilight and went toward the Metro station she saw the red-haired young man sitting in a coffee bar. She was miles from home; he could only be tracking her. She passed him nonstop, but when the phone rang the next morning, at exactly the same time as before, she knew who it was, beyond a doubt.

"When your father was alive," she asked, "did you sneak up in the attic to sleep?"

"How'd you know that? I haven't even told your husband." Off balance. Well, better him than me.

"The story in the paper. Tales of strange noises."

"He had turned me out. We'd had a quarrel over a job. He said I could come back when I had money of my own. But how to make any? I had to stay somewhere. I'm alone. I told you."

"Your father never suspected, caught you?"

"What *is* all this?"

Sara felt stronger, cleverer than before. "Don't be discouraged," her doctor had told her. "When children leave, women often discover hidden facets of their personality." But, she had wanted to ask, do they see their children coming back, pursue them for the sake of a red beret, a plaid skirt, a hockey helmet, hoping to find those very faces just once more? To say that might well land her in some psychiatrist's appointment book. Instead she had landed in Karl's, who'd lightly said, "The world's a mask. It's my job to strip it off, look at what's underneath, get to the point." This lonely boy's mask now seemed so flimsy it was no more than tissue paper.

"Meet me," she said. "Let's talk."

———

Before they could meet the next afternoon, there came a spell of cold rain. Wind crashed against leaves that had hardly yet thought of turning. Summer would come back, but not fiercely. In the new chill, she went belted in garbardine, a green satin scarf wound around her head. A cab took her far afield into a neighborhood of delicatessens and shoe repair, souvlaki restaurants and mini-lotto tickets. She entered a walk-down coffee shop way out on Saint-Laurent. The boy was there, knuckled up over a table in a booth, and had scarcely heard her order coffee when he came at her with his question. "How did you know I stayed in the attic?"

"I didn't. I guessed."

"I should have denied it. You caught me off guard. I shouldn't have let on."

She said nothing to comfort him. It's what he gets for intruding on me, she thought.

"You think it was so wrong of me to do that, then not to want it known? If people found out— They'd size me up for a nut, somebody not worth an inheritance."

"Who knows but me? All I did was guess. You went there and lived there unbeknownst to him and he thought the house was haunted. You must have sneaked down at midnight to raid the pantry."

"He was a mile away and snoring. He had a silly old Quebec cook who blabbed to him about missing food, doors ajar, God knows what. Some of it she probably invented."

"She never saw you?"

"You have to understand. The place is as big as Parliament. Whole wings closed off. It's a castle."

"Couldn't you tell him you were there?"

"If you knew how it was! I got thrown out of this job he got me. I had to let the room I was living in, just one room, to a fat Italian woman out of work. She answered the phone for me. Then I'd nowhere to stay. He said I wasn't worth anything. I had to prove myself, get a 'position.'"

"Did you find it?"

He had been facing sideways, looking at a wall painted a faded watery yellow and hung with a dusty bullfight poster. "Who would hire me?" he bleakly asked.

Her own response amazed her. She felt, as if beside her, the myth presence of her lover, and she put her hand out to him in a moment's tender understanding. "You're desperate, aren't you?"

He was sniveling. Nail biting had made cushions of his finger ends, and it was these that pressed her wrist.

"I thought he cared for me—finally, at last, that he felt something for me. I imagined when I got the will—registered mail—that he'd had a change of heart. That he'd decided to overlook it if I couldn't get the sort of work he had in mind. That out of benevolence, like God on high, he'd finally accepted me. I even went to see him. 'Thank you, thank you. You'll be proud of me yet.' He looked vague. He had these funny blue eyes, never precisely looked at you. 'It was nothing,' he said and walked out in his slippers, looking for a book. Then he dies and I hear about the change of mind like that, on the same day. With nobody to tell me, nobody to explain. Was it a joke he was playing? Was that what he meant by 'It was nothing'—that 'nothing' was what it was? I'll never know."

Sara imagined the half-mocking response Karl might make to the boy: "You can ask the psychic society to look him up." It went against her sympathizing ear.

They were alone in the shop, which was overheating, the door not having opened since she arrived. She slipped out of her raincoat, tucking the skirts up from the trashy floor.

"Don't you think your father may have been more than a little dotty before he died?"

"Suppose he was completely sane, sane as the devil." He turned on her his clear, tear-washed eyes, pale, rimmed with stubby reddish lashes. First God, now the devil. But how could she dream of letting the poor child down?

"Why did you call this morning?"

"I meant to say something. That you aren't riding any Metro to shop for fabrics."

"But now you're not going to say it," she firmly advised.

"Why not?"

"You're not going to throw away the only person who really wants to help."

"Then I won't say it." He was round-eyed with dawning relief.

She took a pen from her bag. "Give me your number."

——

Karl was away on assignment in Halifax. Sara fought off the impulse to get out the children's toys; she did not even look through their old pictures. She went out instead, in settled weather, and looked at the small hotel, and the tree beside it.

She was learning a lot about Montreal she had never known. She had never eaten in small restaurants where food native to everywhere from Greece to the Argentine was good and spicy, and rich coffees arrived, variously brewed and hot, and unlikely pastries.

"I've joined the psychic society!" She almost burst with laughter at her daring when telling Goss McIvor, the redheaded boy, pulling back a tweed jacket from her shoulders. "It was an idea I had, a good one. They meet down in Old Montreal, a big bare room reached by a creaky doorway off a street that probably keeps icicles straight through July. They've got your father's will there, under glass. It's funny, but I thought they might. It's their founding document. The leader is American and so are some of the members. Americans believe in founding documents."

"It's bound to be a copy, like mine."

"That's the tempting part. It isn't."

"The original."

She nodded. "I heard it from one of the members." She laughed so much she could hardly get it out. "With a copy, the spirits wouldn't respond."

"There's a higher court for you," said Goss. "Well," he added, "steal it."

"I thought of that, but I don't see how I could even try, much less succeed. Anything they could trace to me— There's Ted to consider."

"Then don't get traced."

"I'd be suspected. It might come out in court. What, then?"

"What a situation!" But he couldn't stop seeing the funny side. He had got human by degrees. From bitten nails to sense of humor. Then she saw that a whole area of his left cheek would not smile. Irregular as an island, it was dead. It continued downward past the neck of his shirt.

"You're cured, aren't you? Of that old illness, old trouble?"

"If you call it cured. It didn't kill me."

"It's not that bad, you know—the scar. Not bad enough."

"Enough for what?"

"To make you want to get your own back at the world. To make you think that spying on me was okay."

"But now you're getting something out of it. When else would you get an excuse to join a psychic society?"

"Last night we pulled a long curl of mist in through the window. It refused to take a shape, though."

"That was after it rained. Does your husband wonder where you are?"

"I tell him it's bridge night. He doesn't play."

"I thought lawyers liked bridge. Aren't you ever at home?"

Ted Mangham was cognizant of about fifty percent of his wife's venturings, and the rest he might have drawn up with a fair degree of accuracy if he had cared to do so. But he saw Sara in a perpetual present, a lovely woman seated in his living room, dressed for afternoon, talking with someone he could not at the moment, from the corridor, see, radiating rightness, kindness. How could she really find herself anywhere else for very long? No, not possible, thought Ted. Yet in earlier days, opening the nursery door, he used to discover her down on the floor, crawling about to play with the children and their toys. More than once she was suckling a baby until the very bell announcing guests had made her button up her hostess gown.

"Funny thing," Ted mentioned at dinner. "You know that psychic society I mentioned, the one old Phil McIvor left his house to, or so they claim? Well, there's going to be a TV item on them. The son called to ask me to stop it. They wanted to bring a camera crew inside the house, then move on to that meeting place they have now. Well, we can keep them out of the house. The property is in escrow until probate is over."

"What's his objection?"

"He thinks it's a plot of that bunch of crazies to find the original of the will he has and destroy it. That would leave him without a hope of finding it. Of course, he's more than a little obsessed. Sees threats everywhere."

———

In quite another setting than Ted had ever seen her, Karl Darcas extracted a document from his briefcase. He handed it to her. "Here it is."

There was an early snowfall. Large flakes drifted through the tree limbs outside.

What she held on her knees was the original of the will the psychic society had had. He had managed to steal it. How? It was like him not to want to fill in many details. She saw a dark-haired ghetto waif in shabby clothes, sent out for bread, moving through smelly streets. She saw a young boy traveling alone through the nights, from contact to contact, scavenging for food in the dark; smuggled by plane out of Poland to Italy, thence to France; handing over money for forged documents; accepting a new name; never looking back. From Montreal, too, he would move on. He had told her so.

She did learn the excuse he gave for getting his hands on the document—the camera would not photograph through glass. With all that wired equipment, a blown fuse was the natural next step. No magic was evoked to repair it as quickly as they might have liked. But there must at least have been a magic Xerox? He didn't explain.

They burned it page by page in a large ashtray. It came to her out of the small flames and oft-struck matches that his risk had been a gift to her. But I'm risking, too, she thought, thinking that if such conniving became known, her own life might well be downgraded forever by people she had always lived among, or, like something useless, thrown out. She walked to the edge of that possibility and took one dizzy look downward. Was even falling as hard as leaving this room? She could join Karl in Toronto, of course (he kept saying it), but she grew silent on the thought, only next to be twisting in a grasp so strong her arms stayed bruised for weeks. "Leave Ted for you?" she heard herself saying. "How could you even want that?" She could never make herself believe him, though she tried.

He sat on the edge of the bed, smoking, staring across the room at her with heavy-lidded eyes. "Your beautiful satin slip," he brooded. "Your shining gold. How to live without them?" "I'm not like that!" was her protest, heartfelt.

She wanted to praise the daring intelligence she had always honored—especially now that he had proved it. But his scorn met her; that quality which went with his defiant shabbiness was raised up before her like a shield. She'd not the strength to strike it down. She murmured something Ted might have said, though scarcely with tear-filled eyes: "I've no method for doing that." For going away with him, was what she meant. "Some women," he said, "have no such problem." What women did he mean? She had picked up bits and pieces of his past: that there was, or once had been, a wife, still in France; that acquaintance in Montreal was not hard to come by. But she had wanted deeper confidence without requesting it; she thought that trust should come and curl up in her lap like a cat. Later, she would think of East European mysteries when she thought of him, and know they had never found a really common language. Nothing in her experience gave him so much as a sentence to start with. Everything he said to describe her life failed to ring true.

"Anyway," he went brutally on, "I did your dirty work for you."

And that, at least, got through.

———

Still hoarding her bruises like souvenirs, still shaking her head like an old woman to the beat of remembered phrases, she went, some days later, to meet Goss McIvor in a small bar on Crescent Street. They had got into each other's continued stories.

"My mother was a lot younger than my father. We were such pals. She ran off with somebody else, but even then she didn't forget about me. She wanted me with her. He hated her for leaving. He hated me for knowing why. I think that was the source of what he did. I stayed with her a lot."

"Where is she now?"

"Out in B.C. She's happy. I came back for treatments. He could afford them; she couldn't. It was back before Medicare, when it started. It went on and on. All that pain. After the worst of it, I saw that he didn't have anybody with him. So I stayed."

"Then—rejection?"

"You never know how terrible people can be. Until they are."

They wandered into a used bookshop. "You don't ride the Metro anymore," said Goss.

"No need to." She tried to smile but nearly cried, and then confessed, without giving Karl a name or any work, much less telling what he'd done for Goss.

Goss was prompt to summarize. "You didn't really love him or you'd be with him."

"That's easy to say."

They wondered at life, standing among the murder mysteries.

———

"It's that silly will case again," Ted told her. "It's just taken a new turn. The will those psychic people have is only a photocopy, too. I could have sworn the original was what they had, because their lawyer was so cocksure. They claim the TV crew took it. But the man who did the show has gone to work in Toronto."

"Can't they contact him?"

"My understanding is that they did. I think they've no proof of theft or they'd bring charges. Of course, that would attract a 'bad press,' as it's called."

"But what did the TV man say?"

"He said they were crazy."

"There's scarcely news in that," Sara said. "Everybody knows they are."

He smiled. "They burn rose petals to invite the departed to speak. Once they sacrificed a budgerigar." He paused. His level stare was on her. "Yet you joined yourself for a while."

She jumped, then braced. There might be more to come. "Yes . . . I was curious. I've been depressed at times over the children. There was Nan—I kept remembering her as a child. And Rob, too."

"Let's not forget Jeff," he added.

"Oh, not for a minute!"

Over his shoulder, she glimpsed her face in a mirror. The eyes seemed lambent, too bright, larger than they should be, like some oversize moth in a sort of fantasy film her sons had once loved to see. If Ted pushed her . . .

"Nobody could have known who I was. I wore plain clothes, just an old skirt and sweater. I went only twice, that was all. It was dark, and people just sat on folding chairs in the background. They passed out leaflets with funny chants on them. I didn't sign anything," she hastened on; "or give my real name."

"A girl from our office we sent to check out the scene—she saw you there."

His paper was there to read and he read it, until she said, "You remember when that red-haired boy first showed up that night? I could have sworn he was trying to attach himself to you, in some serious way."

"I thought that, too. I think he was after a father, one way or another. Maybe a mother was what he found."

She made no answer, but sat twisting her rings. "I suppose he'll win the case now."

"It certainly begins to look that way."

She watched him resettle his glasses, which he habitually removed to speak, and resume reading the paper. His gestures had come through the years to be where he himself lived and was defined; she could in no way imagine her own life without them to give it shape, like a mold she was poured into.

No need to tell him (was there?) that she had gone with Goss McIvor that very afternoon actually to see the father's house. It was part of the western mountain's outline, as though along with the mountain it had been discovered there—a grand castellated bulk, rising violet-colored through the snow-dimmed afternoon. "In mining camps, half freezing," he said, "my father dreamed of such a place. Then, just when he hit it big, this came on the market." It had belonged to some railroad owners, a prodigiously wealthy family whose descendants had sold out and gone to Nassau to live out their lives escaping taxes.

"I've got a job," said Goss. "He might like me better now." Leaving, she kissed him on the scarred cheek.

No way or reason to tell Ted either that coming home, down steep streets past tall houses, she remembered her own childhood and the skating rinks of Westmount. Calls from somewhere near came to her, and the click and urgent rush of blades. Had that old McIvor man once looked down from some turret window and seen the skaters racing, twirling, and spinning through slants of snow? She felt herself among them still, a red scarf flying. As dark came on, how far outward she would go, inscribing wide parabolas, while known voices grew distant through the dark.

NEW STORIES

THE LEGACY

_____

In the stillness, from three blocks over, Dottie Almond could hear a big diesel truck out on the highway, climbing the grade up to the stoplight, stopping, shifting gears, and passing on.

She went and brushed her hair that was whiter than pull candy and rubbed a little dime-store lipstick on her mouth. In the bathroom window, her cousin Tandy's big white buckskin shoes all but covered the sill. They were outlined with swirling perforated leather strips, toe and heel and nest for laces, and had been placed there to dry. When he got back from Memphis, he would probably be going out on a date or out on the highway someplace or "just out," which was what he said when you never knew. He never asked Dottie anywhere, never told her anything, never talked to her once. She kept notes on him from such things as cleaned-up shoes.

She had heard them—Aunt Hazel and Tandy—out in the living room the night she came. They had thought she was asleep, she had been so dead tired when she'd gone to bed.

"One more mouth to feed, huh?" Tandy said. Whatever he said, it was always as if he were telling jokes, the subject of this present joke being what his mother had got into about Dottie.

"You don't have to look at it that way," Aunt Hazel said. "She had to be somewhere."

"Just keep her out of my things. She gets in my things, she's going to know it."

"Try and be nice to her."

"Not paying us a cent."

"Well, I know, but try your best. Be nice to her."

"Oh, I'll be nice to her." The tone went up; it was an unpromising voice, off center. If it made a promise, the promise might be its opposite because a word had got twisted around. "I'll be nice to her, all right."

Dottie's father worked in Birmingham and did not make much money. She'd had to go somewhere, which was why Aunt Hazel had taken her in. There was also a Great-aunt Maggie Lee Asquith, who (she had said) would have done the same and that she ought to, but she was too old, all alone in a big house in the middle of a Delta "place." A young girl like that—gull, she called it—a young gull like that ought to have young people around. Aunt Hazel and Tandy lived in a town with young people in it. They were the ones to take her in.

———

"How long you been with Miss Hazel?" The speaker was a Mr. Avery Donelson, to whose law office Dottie had just been summoned.

"About a year."

Hanging down from the straight chair one foot couldn't quite touch the floor. She crossed her legs, in order to resemble any other girl, though the man at the desk gave no sign of noticing. She had heard her father once say that Mr. Avery Donelson was a high-class fellow.

"Your family has a high mortality rate," he remarked, and seemed almost prepared to be amused about it.

Dottie didn't laugh. Death to her had nothing to do with anybody except her mother (who had held her hand when she hurt from polio and who was right there, everything they did to her. "When you hurt, I hurt, baby. Just think about that. Only I hurt twice as bad." Nobody else who had died—or lived either—had ever said that). However, Aunt Hazel's husband, Uncle Jack, had died of a stroke uptown one hot day three years ago, and Aunt Maggie Lee had gone quick, from cancer, just last spring. Dottie hadn't attended the funeral. Her daddy wouldn't let her. He had come over from Birmingham to stay with her while Aunt Hazel went. Aunt Maggie Lee was on her mother's side of the family. "You go on,

Hazel," Daddy said. "My little ole sugar's not going to any more ole funerals." He had taken her out to eat in a restaurant and then, as they couldn't find anything to talk about, he took her to the picture show. The show was sad, so she got to cry in it. What she was thinking about was her mother's funeral. Maybe he had known that because he held her hand. When they got home Aunt Hazel and Tandy had got back from the Delta, where Aunt Maggie Lee's funeral was held that afternoon, and Daddy gave Dottie a lot of wet, smacking kisses and called her his little old honey bun, and went off back to Birmingham, late as it was. She thought that Aunt Hazel made him nervous. "He's always got business somewhere," was what Aunt Hazel said . . .

"I knew your aunt Miss Maggie Lee pretty well," Mr. Avery Donelson said. "She was quite a stepper." He seemed to be enjoying himself.

"What's a stepper?" Dottie asked. So far she hadn't smiled; feeling herself observed, she kept her blue eyes steady, thought of her skin, which was darker than her taffy-white hair.

"She was a fine lady," he said. "Knew how to dress, how to talk. Kept a good house, set a good table. Lived in good circumstances. Husband was a planter. Left her well-fixed."

Dottie had herself known Aunt Maggie Lee. She and her mother had gone once or twice to visit her and stayed overnight, in the Delta, a long way from Birmingham. Mother was a little nervous and hoped Dottie and she were behaving all right, especially at the table. Aunt Maggie Lee sat up straight in graceful antique chairs; yet on the second day she lay down on the sofa for a while. ("Maggie Lee's tired," Mother said to someone when they returned. "I think something's wrong.") She had a kind of cosmetics Dottie had never seen in stores, and her bathrooms were rosy, her house soft with rugs and dim lights because the Delta in the summer was full of glare; air-conditioning was essential and curtains had to stay drawn. With her mother out of the room, Aunt Maggie Lee questioned Dottie extensively on a number of subjects. "Do you have a hobby?" she asked. "I collect things," Dottie said. "What, for instance?" "Bird cards from Arm and Hammer soda boxes, for one thing." "What else?" "Pencils, all different colors." When she was sick, for some reason, everybody had started giving her boxes of pencils. She had all colors now. If she got one the same color as another she would go out and exchange it for a color she didn't have. "Birds are of some interest," said Aunt Maggie Lee. "But pencils . . ."

"She kept up with you," Mr. Avery Donelson went on. "She knew about your making good grades in school. She thought you must have a little bit of what it took. I wanted to see you alone because of what she did for you. She made a special bequest for you before she died."

"Bequest?"

"A settlement . . . money . . . all yours. But—a secret."

Dottie was quaking again now; another one had known of her, thought and spoken of her, made her a secret and formal gift. It sounded like something God might do.

"You're not interested in how much?" Mr. Avery Donelson finally said.

"Five hundred dollars?" Then she blushed. Greedy was what she knew she'd sounded like.

"How about ten thousand?"

"Ten thousand? What? Pennies?" A wisecrack was not the right thing. She had just reached the conclusion that it was all a big joke.

"Dollars, young lady. And if you don't want 'em, there's plenty that will."

"I didn't mean that. It seemed like—. It was a surprise, that's all."

"Don't you like surprises?"

"It was a big surprise."

"You sing in school, I hear."

So he knew that, too. Her contralto voice had a rich thrill in it when she let go with a song. She and everybody else had found out about this by accident, trying out songs. They all liked to hear her, even the teachers, and they got her to sing at school programs sometimes. There would be dances, too, to sing at, but she wouldn't go to them. If you were crippled, it was better not to go. But on rainy days she could hold the student body in the auditorium at recess, singing almost anything anybody wanted to play for her. Her mother had never known she could sing, not like that.

"What do you want to be?" Mr. Avery Donelson pressed her. "That's a good sum of money, you know. Set up in trust until you turned eighteen, it could see you some of the way through college. Your Aunt Hazel wouldn't be able to afford to send you to college."

"Tandy doesn't like it because I live there free of charge," said Dottie. "He thinks I ought to pay. Maybe Aunt Hazel would think it, too, if she knew I could."

"Then don't mention it," he said at once. "You don't have to. We can say it's in trust for you, just for college."

"But it's not, is it?"

"She wanted you to decide, that's all. Me to administrate, advise. You to decide."

Through slats in the venetian blinds Dottie could see the town water tank, painted silver, the tops of the trees, see the still, hot, morning sky. The window air conditioner purred. Mr. Avery Donelson had brown-and-white horizontally striped curtains, a rug, a desk, some black leather chairs. His secretary was outside and the door was closed. He would never call a daughter "little old honey bun," and if he took her to dinner he would know what to talk about. He had known Aunt Maggie Lee, who was a stepper like himself and who had picked Dottie out for possible entry into a world different from Aunt Hazel's.

But did she *have* to be what they had decided, whatever it was? They had taken her consent for granted. She was dazed.

"I get to think it over, don't I?"

The carpet took her halting walk. The man at the desk—gray, unmoving, nicely suited but casually rumpled—had stopped smiling, sat watching instead, his attention all finally upon her. He rose to open the door. She was a small girl, came hardly to his top vest button.

"It's in the bank for you. I'm supposed to do anything you say, young lady." He pressed her hand.

Then she was through the office, down the stairs, and on the hot sidewalk that led back to Aunt Hazel's, hot and chill together in the scald of sun, a jerky progress through the dazzle.

All that money poured out on me, *me*, ME! She almost struck herself on the forehead. Transparent as a locust's wing, the frail self within tried to stir, to take up whatever was meant by it; since it was recognized, it ought to emerge and fly. But all it was was Dorothy Almond, plodding back toward her few small treasures and necessities, toward pencils and bird cards no two the same, her four or five cotton dresses, her slacks and blouses, her new white sandals.

When she came in the front door the phone was ringing. "I called you twice," said Aunt Hazel, on the other end.

"I was in the bathtub."

"You must have stayed till you shriveled. I have to work through dinner. Just fix yourself something."

"Yessum."

"Did the paper ever come?"

"Yessum."

"Did Tandy call?"

"No'm. I don't guess he did."

"I don't reckon so. I'll see you this evening, honey."

Dottie went and looked to see if the big white male shoes were still on the bathroom windowsill. They were. There was nowhere else they could have gone. Men's shoes, white, heavy, secretive, knowledgeable—they derided her as much after as before Mr. Avery Donelson's call had smashed into her silence. All else had changed and diminished; *they* were the same. What did she expect? She had heard of a distant cousin who had stuck his finger up an empty socket to see whether, since the bulb would not work, the lamp was broken. It wasn't. Was it a shock she had expected when she put her hand out and put her fingers over those shoes, heel to vamp to toe? Shoes like these, only brown, were now treading pavement in Memphis, Tennessee, with Tandy in them. He was going to know the minute he looked that something had happened to her, and he would find out what it was, right away. Now she was scared. A call to life was one thing, but getting the first breath kicked straight out of you—. It would happen if she wasn't careful. She called up Avery Donelson.

"You said I could have anything, any time."

"That's right."

"Can I have five hundred dollars, then?"

"Certainly."

"Can I get it at two o'clock?"

"That's possible."

"Will you put all the rest where nobody can get it, just tell them if they ask you that five hundred dollars was all there was, that was all?"

A hesitance. "If you say so."

She had climbed his answers like stair steps, one by one; they had taken her higher and higher, to the very top, and at that top—like saying "Walk!" the way they had in the hospital and she had held her breath and walked, the leg feeling liquid at first and numb, then thin as a toothpick but holding—so at this final moment in what was happening now, she had to jump, which was more than walk; and the jump was trust.

"Do you promise?" She clutched the receiver. Her eyes were squinched up tight.

"I promise." She was held, so far, unfalling.

———

The bus to Birmingham had left, as Dottie had known it would from visiting her father, at two-thirty. She was on it. Near a window, bolt upright with five hundred dollars—less the price of the ticket—in her purse, she was drawn forward above the landscape like a pulled-out string. In the Birmingham bus station, she dialed Daddy on the pay telephone, holding her finger on his number in the book. A woman's voice answered "Hell-o?" too loud. Dottie asked for Mr. Almond, then added, for some reason, "I'm his daughter," but the woman said she had the wrong number. She tried again, but though she let the phone ring six times, nobody answered it. Maybe he was still at work. She tried Southern Railway, where he had his office, but only got the ticket counter, and when she tried to explain, they couldn't hear her, there was such a lot of noise at the other end, and then she was out of dimes. She walked out of the station, which smelled of frying hamburgers, still remembering the woman's voice on the phone. She attained to an enormous lack of conviction about things involved in finding Daddy, and seeing a bus with MIAMI on the front, she bought a ticket and climbed into it. On the bus, at intervals, she slept. Miami was not till the next day. When she got there, she didn't know what to do, so took another bus that said KEY WEST. In Key West there was nothing to do either, but it was the end. Dottie went to a motel of separate cabins in a shady park full of plants, rented one, and fell asleep.

It was the end of running; that she knew. Like a small planet, she had set.

Another day, freshly risen, she sat in a newly bought bathing suit on a sandy beach with one leg tucked under her, looking out at the sea. There were large clouds above her, all the same color as her hair, which made them seem more personal than they might have been to brunettes or redheads.

There was a boy circling round, a man, really, though younger than Tandy and certainly better to look at. He was all bronze and gold, like a large, well-formed wasp, she thought, and he had the same copper hair on his head, chest, arms, and legs. And his drift— the way he spoke to her, looked at her—was something like that of a wasp, which might or might not be thinking favorably of you. He asked her if she wanted to swim, and she told him no.

"You're getting sunburned," he said.

"I'm all right," she said.

"Where are you staying?"

"The Hibiscus."

"Walk you home?"

She shook her head, gazing up at the clouds. But he was right. She *was* getting sunburned. She wished he'd go. She wished he'd leave her alone. Then he did.

Dottie had told him the truth about the Hibiscus because she had done nothing lately but tell lies. The first night away, for instance, at a bus stop, she had phoned Aunt Hazel so Aunt Hazel wouldn't call out the FBI, or the highway patrol, or whatever you called out, to look for her. She had said:

"Aunt Hazel, I hope you found the letter I left."

What followed was such a volley of words that Dottie felt sorry for Aunt Hazel, who when she got to worrying about things there

was no stopping her. "Let me tell you something, honey. It's just ridiculous for you to go off like that. If Maggie Lee had known you'd
be spending all her money at the beach, she never would have left
you a dime, let alone five hundred dollars. But there you are throwing it away, *five hundred dollars,* and with any number of things you
really need, and I can't think of why anybody would be that incon-
siderate, as good as Tandy and I have been to you. Why didn't you
at least go to see your daddy in Birmingham?"

"I tried to call him, but he wasn't there."

"You ain't *with* anybody?"

"No'm."

"Well, you'd just better mind out," Aunt Hazel said. And when
Dottie didn't answer she said, "You'll phone me every night until
you get home? I'm going to worry about you every single night."

———

Dottie stayed in the shady little cabin she had rented at Hibiscus
Cottages All Conveniences Pool TV. You reached the cabins
through winding paved paths bordered by plants and flowering
shrubs, shaded by palms. It was a pretty place, and not many people
were there. Not that many people came to Key West in the summer,
so they said. If you swam in the pool, the water felt like you could
just as well take a bath in it. She read some movie magazines, then a
paperback mystery book, then made a ham sandwich and ate it, ate
a tomato whole with salt, ate some coconut marshmallow cookies,
some pink, some white, and drank a glass of milk. Then she lay
down and looked at TV and fell asleep with the air conditioner
purring. At four o'clock she went walking. It was still hot all over
town, hot as an oven, but the clouds had got bigger, and from somewhere off she heard a tumble of thunder.

At the end of a street, she could look at the gulf, and way out
there she saw the big clouds piled higher than ever before, the silver
color darkening from the top downward. She turned her back on
them and walked into town, past houses with plants round them,
oleanders, a stubby sort of grass, pale faded green or artificial
funeral-parlor green, not like the grass up home, and always palms,
some bent and low as plants, some the size of real trees. The trees

she liked the best were—she'd been told by an old lady on the bus coming down—royal palms. The trunks of the palms were round, swelled out at mid-height but narrow at top and bottom, and looked to be made of stone, with a bunch of thick palm fronds coming out of the top, as though stuck in a too-tall vase. They were pretty trees, Dottie decided, and when the afternoon rain hit Key West and she had no idea which way to go to get back, she went and sat under one of them, at the corner of somebody's property. It was probably the most dangerous place to be, as the tree was high and would attract a lightning bolt possibly, but its top was waving in such an impressive way she thought she'd rather be there than elsewhere. She crouched there as the rain fell in ropes. Soon she was soaked to the skin.

When the sun burst out again she started returning by trial and error and so came into the Hibiscus from the back, before she knew it. Standing in the garden, also wet, wearing beige cotton trousers, a T-shirt, and a dripping slicker was the copper-haired boy she had met at the beach. She ran right into him and then, seeing it wasn't just a coincidence, that he was coming toward her, she turned around and started off through the paths. He had to run to catch her arm. She stopped, head down and shuddering, like she'd seen wild animals do in the country the minute some boy would get his hands on them. She drooped like that and didn't look.

"What'd you come for?" she said.

"You're not from around here, are you?"

She shook her head.

"What are you limping about?"

"Something fell on me."

The boy looked around at the maze of paths, the village of cottages spotted out among the dripping foliage. "Where's yours?"

"Number ten."

He was half holding her up, but before he got to the door he thought it simpler to carry her, and so did. "Give me your key." She took out the key, but being let down, stood holding herself upright by the door, downcast still, and tremulous. "Nothing really fell on me," she said.

"But you're hurt, obviously."

"I'm crippled."

"Is that why you wouldn't go swimming?"

"Please."

She felt his large warm hand drop from her arm. "Okay." He drew back, looking at her with a different air altogether. Was she glad or not? She didn't know. She thought she must have looked terrible after the rain. Like a drowned white rat, she thought, closing the door on him, leaning against it.

She was still hearing his voice and not answering it. New feelings—fresh, sharp, hurting—had sprung up as though branches of her blood had turned into vines that were determined all by themselves to flourish in her. It was what she thought it would never do any good to look for. She fell face down across the bed. She might have known, but hadn't. She could have said that in addition to being lame, her mother had died, and that the lawyer Mr. Avery Donelson had sent for her, and that her aunt Miss Maggie Lee Asquith, well known in the Delta, had left her a legacy of ten thousand dollars, a part of which, in the opinion of Aunt Hazel, she was now throwing away in Florida. She was somebody picked out. Being lame in *itself* was being picked out. But he wouldn't see any of that. He wasn't from where she was. All that traveled with her was a short leg.

And her white hair, whiter than taffy, born white, said the streak of sun coming through the one slat of blinds that had got twisted.

—

Late in the afternoon, her hair brushed and combed, face washed, she walked down the main street of Key West, past the big square hotel. She was looking for somewhere to eat and went past a big open bar where a sign said Ernest Hemingway used to sit and drink. Among palms, and near a large spreading tree with red flowers, she saw a barnlike building painted brick red whose sign, also outside, said it was a playhouse. Another sign, of hastily lettered green on white cardboard, said that tryouts for a play were being held. Dottie hobbled to the door and found it open. She went through an empty foyer plastered with posters, and through a second large heavy door into an auditorium with a stage before it and rows of folding chairs, some disarranged, some open and placed in regular lines, others closed and propped against the walls.

A tall dark woman like the statue of a goddess, wearing a crumpled linen dress and leather sandals, was standing near the center of the stage, which was lighted artificially, with a large bound sheaf of pages in her hand, open half the way through, back folded on itself. Her hands were long, and tanned, and aware of themselves; her whole self was aware and nurtured; her black hair tumbled the way she wanted it to around her face. She was pointing out to three or four others on the stage with her, younger than she, what they ought to do, what she thought they ought to do, how this, how that. She turned, walked away, leaned back against a table, and picked up a half-smoked cigarette from an ashtray, inhaling, pluming smoke; her body gave life to the clinging linen. At the lift of her fingers, the young actors, all about Dottie's age, holding smaller books, began to read aloud. Dottie hated the large woman of authority in linen and sandals . . . she was afraid of her by instinct. She turned to go away, but was called to.

"Hey, blondie!"

Obedient, not showing what she felt, she turned back and limped forward, down between the raggedly arranged chairs. The woman had come to the footlights, and as Dottie approached, the former went down on one knee, as though kneeling by the edge of a pool to retrieve something. She did it like poetry. Dottie's face was a mask, looking up at her.

"You want to try out? What can you do?"

"Sing," said Dottie.

"Sing what?"

The boys were talking now, over the footlights, the words falling toward her lifted face: "Rock? . . . Revival? . . . Country-western?"

"Just sing," Dottie said. "Popular mostly."

"There's all kinds of popular," one of the boys said. "But, hey—stick around. We expected more people. . . . Take a script."

"Take mine," another boy said.

"You know this play? It's *Picnic.* There's a song in it somewhere, at least I think there is."

"Or we'll put one in," somebody said, and another: "She looks like Kim Novak."

"I'm crippled," Dottie said, right out. "I can sing, that's all."

There was a quick silence, like a whole orchestra gone dead. Then they reached their arms down and pulled her up over the footlights, out of the dark and onto the bright stage. She hobbled over to the piano and a girl about her age came and sat down to play for her. She sang one of the songs she liked, and they clapped, saying with astonished voices how wonderful she was, and she knew it, too.

She had bought herself a little cap, like a sailor's cap, at an open-air shop along the way where things were all displayed, and when she sang her song she held this in her small hands and knew it made a good effect. When they shot a spotlight on her face she didn't mind a bit. A sissy boy at school used to turn his spotlight on her: she was used to it. Her face and voice went floating away from her legs, off from the part they could forget while she sang. She heard them applaud again and she heard what they said and then she sang again and told them that was all.

The light switched off. The large woman seemed to her to have gone completely, but this was not so; she had gone out of the circle of light to sit on the edge of a table.

Then they were leaving. Dottie was moving with them, or they with her, as she was not going with them in spirit, but only moving alone though among them, through the disarray of chairs in the big dusky barnlike room, and feeling not so far from home, for it resembled the high school auditorium where she had held many more people for an even longer time. She heard them speaking to her but was not answering; and then the daylight struck through the second door they opened, not glaring as when she had entered, but softened by evening. There was a car freshly pulled up beside a yellow Pontiac that had been parked there when Dottie went in, and the boy was in it, the one from the beach and the storm, just getting out when he saw them come through the door. She saw him get out, turning as he closed the door the way she had seen good basketball players turn without seeming to move at all, the way dancers follow each other. He was there for them, she knew at once: his approach said so. And she knew too why she had been afraid of the dark woman.

Dottie left the crowd and walked across the street.

"Hi." The boy was following her.

"Hi." She didn't stop walking.

"You're in the play?"

"Ask them," she said and kept limping on.

—

The pool was a quiet rectangle with no one swimming in it, and the people who circled, stood, wound, and twined and drank and talked with one another moved like columns, slowly revolving and changing place, one to another, in long dresses, in white jackets, reflecting in the water. The house was built around this open area, with a balustrade above in white painted wood such as Dottie thought she'd seen in pictures or paintings. There were brick-colored urns of geraniums and a long twining plant with purplish blue blooms as if a head of hair had decked itself that way, and there were others, yellow and pink and white. No one walked on the balustrades, or climbed the stairs. They turned, columnar and decorous, with muted voices, around the still pool. They sipped from glasses that sparkled with amber whiskey or white gin or crystal ice.

"No, thank you," said Dottie. "Just some water," she said.

She refused not from righteousness or inexperience but simply because she was drunk already, having earlier ordered three martinis in a restaurant somewhere near the Hibiscus. Later, she'd been found wandering around the old Spanish fort, jumping off and onto the parapet, pretending nothing was the matter with her while all sorts of wild ideas somersaulted through her head—been found by the copper-haired boy and another, his friend.

In the friend's car, all of Key West had looped and dived around her like a dolphin. If you got drunk, how long did you have to stay drunk? She was wondering this when the friend stopped before a

Spanish-type house and, once inside, began pulling evening skirts out of a closet.

"Try any one you want."

"You got a sister?" Dottie said.

"She's not here. Besides, she wouldn't mind. She swaps clothes all the time," he said with a laugh to the boy Dottie knew, the copper-haired boy. Johnny was his name.

The phone rang and Johnny's friend went to answer it. Johnny threw his arms around Dottie and tumbled her back on the bed. She lay there a little while with his arms around her. Then they heard the other boy coming back and she got up to try the skirts on. In the long skirt she felt uncrippled. She moved her built-up sandal in a different way, just like her hips were swaying. Pretty, pretty, she thought, looking in the mirror. I can be like magic.

Then they drove to another house, the big one with the drive. There Dottie saw the dark woman whom in linen she had hated, only she was columnar now, standing by the still pool in a bold drop of yellow with great white wings or fronds and a white binding against the tan of her bare arms and her hair in rich careless coils.

"They tell me you sing, young lady."

The speaker was a man, the host here, with dark thinning hair combed straight back. He smiled at Dottie and showed teeth that looked false.

"Yes, sir," she said.

He asked her where she'd come from, where she went to school, where she wanted to go to college. She must have been saying things back.

"Can you sing for us?" he said. "Sometime this evening, I mean."

"I'm sorry."

"Oh, you must," he said.

"I got drunk," Dottie said.

The beautiful dark head above the bare brown back showed it had heard her and was turning. The carefully painted mask hung perfectly. Dottie wanted to be with people who wouldn't notice her too much. Nobody would have cared what she said except the dark woman, who was, of course, her enemy, and said nothing.

Dottie started climbing the flight of stairs. A Cuban-looking man in a white jacket had said she would find the bathroom up there. In passing she saw that a pottery urn filled with blooms was just above the head of the hostess, the dark woman, Pam, the enemy who did not want her to live. Dottie placed her hands, one on either side of the urn, and gazed, calculating, as one might along the barrel of a cousin's BB gun. She drank up the possibility of the action as she might another martini. This was what she needed to do, but couldn't. A door opened off in the shadowy passageway behind her, and she turned, surprised, unable to see anyone.

Later, coming out of the bathroom, she thought about the urn again but in a distant way. Johnny met her at the foot of the stairs with a banana daiquiri and somebody from above screamed, "Watch out!" They all looked up. An old woman with too bright blond hair, too scarlet a mouth was clutching at that same terra-cotta urn, and everyone leaped aside as it swung, tottered, slipped past her painted nails and long pink chiffon handkerchief, smashing on the marble paving near the pool.

"Grandmother!"

The old woman, like a mad witch entered on a balcony during a play, leaned far out into the velvet air, calling, "I hit it by mistake! It just fell!"

To Dottie, who could not stop gazing above, it was like seeing herself sixty years from now, a grotesque double. Was it the old lady's door she had heard a while ago?

The Cuban, a servant it seemed, was picking up pieces of broken pottery that had scattered near Pam's skirt. Pam's husband, whom someone had jerked from the falling urn's path, mounted the stairs toward the old woman.

Conversation resumed. There was a drift toward a table of food. Someone remarked that half of Key West was there. Many of them were young, the age of Johnny, more or less.

I'll just sneak out, Dottie thought. I'll go home alone.

———

But she didn't go home alone, because Johnny reappeared to drive her, and not with the boy whose sister's skirt she wore, but Johnny alone and driving like the wind, racing out from Key West up the long highway that arrowed toward Marathon, then swirling off along back shell roads because he was high on something maybe liquor maybe not and talking a blue streak, and she was piecing it out the best she could, she Dottie Almond, to whom all of life was gradually reducing itself to one single problem: How to Stay Awake Another Minute. The day must have already been sixty-four hours long. She could hear him the way she might hear the sea rustling when asleep by it, or the way you'd hear prayers in church.

"Morrissey knew about it from the first and that I wasn't any killer, not a thief, and certainly that if I went too far that time, it was out of my own principles . . . how they got out of bounds. He had some good inside stuff about them, but when they put on the pressure, he was even able to swing a position elsewhere, it's how he got the big appointment . . . oh, Pam's money . . . you saw that house . . . where'd he be without it, nobody can say, only it's not so much money . . . just that he saw a way of getting me out, out of the country till it blew over . . . that was when Pam came looking. It was her idea . . . I'd swear to it anytime . . ."

"Out of the country where?" she mumbled, her mouth sticky inside from being sleepy.

"Think of anywhere. Mexico. Think of Canada."

She thought of Canada, but only saw polar bears. They had got back. He turned at the Hibiscus sign and, drifting in, stopped the car. Hundred-pound weights sat on her eyelids. "Look." He held his hands forward and turned up the dash light, then showed her his fingers, palms up. She could discern by the dim light what she'd seen before, the healed skin over fingertips that had been cut or burnt. She was still hearing the soft crush of shells beneath the tires, and then she felt the broken fingertips like pieces of screen printing her cheek and neck, then her mouth pressed and opened with his own. She remembered earlier how he'd pushed her down, knew her body had taken a note of it, like a secretary might write down a call to be made at a later moment, which had now arrived. She was dead for sleep, opened the door herself to stumble out and find her cabin but instead was being carried, floating, skimming silently down along a smooth and swollen stream, face rising up above the surface, eyes closed, branches of oleander, vines of bougainvillea, hibiscus like trumpets, crisp and red.

———

She woke with the sun coming in through the blinds, the long borrowed skirt crumpled on a chair, herself a trampled field with a game over, the score standing.

She lay there till she got hungry. No one came in the door and no message was to be found. She dressed, folded up the skirt, and put it in a grocery sack. Outside, it was clear and hot, without a cloud. The breathless immensity of the Florida day entered her breathing self and made it light and pure. She could find him. The skirt was her excuse.

He wasn't at play practice, nor was anyone. A tolling bell reminded her: This was Sunday. She turned strange corners until she saw—far down a street in the ever-heating sunlight—a couple of shore patrols in white uniforms struggling with a man they were dragging out of a front walk between red flowers. All down the street she could hear their heaving breath but no words . . . nothing to say.

She grew faint and around eleven-thirty went into a drugstore, sat down at the lunch counter, and ate a sandwich. A fan was turning overhead. In a jar of pickling brine, some large eggs were floating. The man at the counter was darkly thinking of things not before him. The whiteness of the eggs in the huge jar frightened Dottie vaguely. From the mirror a smooth little face, her own, watched and noted that she looked about the same.

Move closer, or go far, she thought and folded up her paper napkin. She knew which already. She paid her check and gathered up her bundle as responsibly as if it bore a child inside. She had wandered in; now, committed and compelled, she went a chosen way. She was lame, yes, and motherless, yes, and she'd been left with a legacy greater than she needed, but the one thing she knew she bore was a right to be seen, to be answered.

———

Everything, she guessed, was in the precise look of that big luxurious white stucco house when she finally found it by the blaze of the afternoon sun. She trudged in through the gate, her footsteps making unequal crushes into the gravel, her height not reaching halfway up the square sentinel posts of the entrance drive. The house looked blank, green-shuttered, sheltered and curtained and cool within. She remembered the patio, the pond, the trailing vines, thick as a head of hair, a house with a woman inside whom she didn't like, an intricate mystery. In one sense she drove herself forward; in another, it was all she could possibly do. Her vital thread, whose touch was her life, was leading her.

From the upper-floor windows, she supposed, you could see the water. The entrance was recessed into the shadow of an arch, and a grillwork gate of iron stood ajar before a closed front door of dark-stained wood. A fanlike spread of steps led down to the gravel drive, and above them and below, a paving of square yellow tiles gave off a flat gloss to the sun. At either end of the tiled area below, large cement urns of verbena stood on square pedestals.

Clambering upward, step by halting step, she gained the entrance, but before approaching the door, she turned and looked around her. Out at the side where the pool was situated, she could see the coconut head of the Cuban, motionless, out of hearing. She walked three steps backward, and looked up to where, on a balcony above, the dark woman stood. She shielded her face from the sun.

"I thought you'd be at play practice," Dottie said.

"Not on Sunday. Wait there. I'm coming down."

Sandals on the long white walkways, the white-railed stairs, the marble floors, approaching expensively.

Then Dottie heard the sound of a car turning into the drive. She dropped the sack and ran.

Hidden behind a large stone urn full of verbena, Dottie watched as her enemy greeted Johnny at the door. Where did she go? Pam was probably asking him. Where did *who* go? You know, that girl you brought. The lame one. The *singer,* dopey.

Dottie looked up to where, gazing down from an upper window, the drunk blond grandmother was regarding her silently. When Pam and Johnny went inside, Dottie remained behind the verbena pot, alone and miserable, for even the old lady had closed the window, and the Cuban was out there asleep. He had to be asleep. Nobody could sit that still.

I want! I want! thought Dottie Almond; and alone, not just in that place but in the world, in the grand presence of her wishes, she turned and put her arms around the verbena urn and wet the harsh cement surface with streaming tears. Not only for Johnny but for herself, outside like that, and for her grand aplomb in seeing herself the possessor of the cool lovely house alone with him there in it, sometimes hidden from each other, wandering shadowy passages, sometimes discovering by chance or by search the other that each sought constantly, bedding for whole afternoons, and at night gathering moonlight in through windows, joining like twin divers in the pool, tangling like vines from sunny breakfasts onward, lords to the last fence corner and rock of gravel at the drive's head of all. All. *All.*

A drapery slid across a distant window, and Dottie limped out and away. Home. Nothing was merited; that, she knew. Nothing was ever deserved.

———

When, two days later, she saw him on the beach, he asked her where she'd been. "I thought about you," he said. "About the other night."

"What were you thinking?"

"How sweet you were." He touched her cheek, then caught her hand, and sat, holding it. "Why don't you come up to the university?" he said. "School's not far off. Morrissey can get you in."

"Pam's husband."

"Sure, Pam's husband. You met him. Morrissey."

"Pam—" she started, then gave out.

"What about Pam?" he asked.

"You're something—to her."

"I know I did a lot of talking the other night. Maybe I said things—things you didn't understand."

"Or maybe I did." Some force she didn't know the name of was pushing her on to the next thing to say. "Ron Morrissey—"

"What about him?"

"He got you out of something bad."

The boy did not answer.

"Is Johnny even your real name?"

He dropped his arm away, and whereas before they had been blending warm with each other while one breath did for both, he was now sitting separate from her, stonily silent. Dottie felt exhausted, like a sea creature who had struggled up on the beach, then to a rock, attaining, while the damp dried from its panting sides, a visible, singular identity. There wasn't any need to go further.

"Come to practice," he said, and bent to kiss her.

———

"Be glad you're just crippled," they used to say, "you might be dead."

"But why be either one?" she had asked.

From the beach she watched jet streams like scars fade into the sky. There was nothing left to do but pack her clothes, say good-bye to the room, get ready to take the bus all the way up Florida, across Alabama, all the way to north Mississippi in unbroken silence. And once on the road, she would drift in and out of sleep, thinking, Aunt Maggie Lee Asquith, it's you I'm riding with; Mr. Avery Donelson, I am traveling with you.

THE MASTER OF SHONGALO

We have it now before us and know at least that it isn't any dream. The name is plain enough, written down in the old guidebook of the state I just yesterday found by accident on the shelves. The book was done by a WPA commission back in the Depression. But where did that name come from? Out of the Bible, like Sharon (rose of), Mizpah, Gennesaret, Galilee, or Gilead (balm in)? No, probably an Indian name—what tribe? Read further. We find that it was an old Mississippi town, long since absorbed into another one. I know no one who remembers it. But the name, though I dream about it, is a real name. In the dream I know its reality without doubt, though when waking I doubt and am glad to have it proved. Once I see it proved, I can return to the dream. I can see it all.

There is a large house of mellow old red brick trimmed in white, still in the baking afternoon sun, and an entrance at the side with a small portico. Seldom used, it matches in a minor modest way the imposing front portico. Here wasps may have built in the overhang, or large bright colored flies, trapped, may have died and fallen in the space between the outer door and the screen. The door is hard to pull inward, the wood having swollen after many rains, and the screen sticks at the bottom, so that a sharp kick is needed to help it along.

Now go into the garden. It is like this. A sunken garden laid out in a rectangle, slightly shorter and narrower than a tennis court. A low slope of grass, trimly mowed, frames it on every side. There are four sets of three steps each, with low balustrades. Each terminates in a square flagstone plateau, a place for setting out pairs of clay pots for flowering plants, or ornamental urns in a classical design. On one side there is a small statue of a goat figure, dancing, about two feet high, a copy of something Roman. He has no mate; the space for one is bare. There is a fountain in the center, composed only of four equal spray heads, slanting upward, not often turned on. But there is water in the shallow rectangular pool, and lily pads at one end, at the other a few lazy goldfish, with one ordinary lake fish, gray among their brilliance, dropped there from the sky or by someone who caught it and judged it too small to eat. Life spared, it swims with a strange race. Such is its destiny.

At the far end of the sunken garden there is a stone bench with scrolled arms. It looks to be for ornament only, as if no one had ever actually sat on it. But I go and sit on it anyway. This visit must be complete.

Let me say who I am. I said "we" at first because I wanted to include you, whoever you are. And because, though not everyone should go to Shongalo, you may be among those who should. It is mysterious. It is beautiful. Even in the full glare of Mississippi July afternoon sun, it raises questions no one will remember to ask, and if they do, and if someone begins to answer, an interruption will occur and no one will recall afterward what was being said.

There, I have done it too. Started to say who I am, then got interrupted by another train of thought. Well, I'll start again.

I'm nobody really. A teacher from the town. One of the children here, a girl in my class during the school year, which concluded two months ago, admired me, favored me, liked being my student. Nothing would do but an invitation here, where before I had been invited only once, for Sunday dinner, nothing so exciting as a dinner party. She persisted. Miss Weldon must have a chance to visit during the summer. We would read some more, we could go swim at the country club pool, we could talk some more, and I could get to know her brother, home from school, her parents, and maybe even a cousin or two, some well known, even from as far away as Washington. They came in the summer, at intervals.

My thoughts were wary. I wondered how I would be treated. A student's enthusiasm in no way makes a haughty family democratic.

Wouldn't the favored-teacher role set me in a category: poor relation? The decision to chunk me whole into that box would be so immediate they would never stop to think about it. Not saying it, but making me feel it. Yet my clothes were in good taste, and my manners beyond criticism. Money? Was that what gave me pause? It was obviously not plentiful or I wouldn't be teaching in a Mississippi high school. And what about my single status? Matter of choice—mine or others'? Who does she "go with"? These were the questions that no one would bring up, but everyone would think them anyway. Better they would be asked openly, like some impossibly bad visiting boy cousin who belched at the table, or jumped out of stairwell closets in the dark.

Nevertheless, the following was true: I had gone back for the summer to my hometown, a hundred miles to the south. I was completing work on a thesis for a graduate degree. The town was named Stubbins, Mississippi. It was dull and hot and tiresome. So I accepted Maida's invitation. Her mother had written as well—swirling initials engraved on ivory notepaper, confidently scrawling script. Using plain but decent drugstore notepaper, I replied. I could drive there as suggested on a Thursday, planning to stay for the weekend. I tried not to pack my misgivings with my clothes. I came.

So why was I all alone on a hot Friday afternoon, out in the sunken garden, sitting on the stone bench, observing the pool? Everyone was taking a nap—that was one reason. I had gone to my room (air conditioner in the window, cool high ceilings, four-poster bed, ruffled snow-white pillow shams), agreeing to nap also, but wanting a book, any book, I drifted downstairs. If there were bookshelves, a library somewhere, it was hard to find. The house was silent, as though they'd all gone off and died. Far out on a corner of the front porch, under the shade of the portico, beyond the line of ferns, a large dog was sleeping. A stranger, I hesitated to go that way. He might rouse up, bark, disturb them all. My books were in my car, parked somewhere out back on a large sweep of gravel near the yawning mouth of a garage. I had come out the side door, seen the garden, been tempted to wander and explore.

What lingers in some of us, in me, of the child exploring the mysterious castle, the château we took refuge in from a twilight storm, the sudden looming structure at the end of a winding road that a mistaken turn has led us on to follow? Once it is seen there, the feeling comes: "I am no stranger here." I mean to say that houses like this were part of my heritage, and since I had never lived in one, they were to be possessed only in this way of wandering, a native not to be told she wasn't to explore. For what was I exploring in this case but my own spiritual property?

But, hindering, there was the heat. Just like Stubbins. Something stung my ankle, sweat glazed my eyes. The nap here was a required ritual I should be observing. I would try it tomorrow. From the sunken garden I went toward the back, where the cars were parked, crunching through gravel as softly as possible, for one or two windows, high up above, were open. I sorted out a couple of books from the back seat of my own modest Ford and returned, entering on tiptoe through the side door.

Something seen out of the corner of my eye as I passed now was developing. Could it have been the tail end of a strange car? I thought so. I thought I had seen the sleekly tapered rear of something decidedly foreign. I didn't go back to check on it. The sight gave me, for no good reason, a start, a qualm, as if someone had come on purpose to unsettle things. To threaten?

Maybe I was wrong. Even if right, why feel it as disturbing? I tiptoed through the dining room, its windows shuttered against the heat, the long cherry table polished and quiet, not yet set for dinner. The chairs were arranged symmetrically back against the walls. The doors throughout the house towered high above my head. I pushed open the door between the dining room and the hall. There was the stair, ready to lead me up to my room. But still wondering where they kept their books, thinking that I remembered Maida, my student, mentioning "the library," I wandered across into the formal living room. Last night before dinner we had sat in the less formal room, adjacent to the dining room. Chairs and sofas there were slipcovered in cool faded fabric; furniture in the formal room wore satin, draperies were in lustrous brocade.

Perhaps my real reason was just to see the room once more, meditatively, alone. Its proportions had struck me as beautiful. There was ornamental scrollwork around the moldings; and a medallion of similar design on the ceiling surrounded the hanging point of the chandelier. A round table of inlaid polished wood stood central to the room beneath the chandelier, and a man was bending over it, his back to me. He was pulling out one of the drawers, or closing it. He turned: a stranger. We looked at each other. He was tall and rather messily dressed in a long-sleeved shirt but no tie, rumpled tan trousers, loafers. His hair was light, fading to gray. His expression, however, was dark, annoyed.

"Who are you?"

It seemed he had every right to ask that.

"Just a visitor," I said. "I'm sorry. I didn't mean . . ." Just what didn't I mean? "I mean, I didn't know you were here."

He laughed in an odd way, somewhere between amused and scornful. "You still don't, do you? *I* mean, you don't know who I am."

"That's true," I said. I supposed he wanted me to go, but when I reached for the door he said, "Wait." I turned back and he said, "Come here . . . closer."

"What is it?" I said, moving halfway toward him.

"No one . . . nobody knows I'm here. I'd rather they didn't." Then he smiled. Charming. He wanted something. "I'd rather you didn't mention it." That was it.

"Then just tell me who you are. I ought to know; that is, if I'm not supposed to mention you."

"I'm just a cousin," he said. "That will have to do."

"Wouldn't they want to see you?"

"Well, sometimes they might. It depends." He glanced up and around, as though regarding the whole large structure: Shongalo. Its vast shoulders sturdily asleep in the full afternoon light. "Nap time," he remarked, returning his gaze to me. "It never fails. Come at nap time, you won't see anybody. You, too—you're supposed to be napping."

"I just wanted something to read. Do you know where they keep the books?"

The smile again. "You've got some in your hand."

"I mean theirs. These are mine."

"The books—oh, yes." He swung away, quickly, on his heel. "Come here. I've just a minute." He opened a door I hadn't noticed; it adjoined the small fireplace, with its cold grate protected by curved bars. "Here." He beckoned. I came and looked inside. The room was oblong, running along the right flank of the house, with two shuttered windows set equidistant from the center of the outer wall. The shelves were all around, between the windows, covering the walls, on either side of the door. A table with a reading lamp was central and two straight chairs were drawn up to it, facing. Two others stood in the corners. I stepped across the threshold, following, and looked admiringly up at the shelves, which were pressed to overflowing with row after row of books.

I went farther inside. He pulled at a shutter, letting in a tilt of light. I could see the side yard, the drive, and a few shrubs just beyond. I was turning to stare all around, upward at the sets of Dickens and Scott, medium height to biographies and novels, then downward to an encyclopedia in rows and piled-up *National Geographic*s, when I noticed he had moved away from the window. Leaving? Well, he had mentioned haste.

But then I sensed him right behind me and turned directly into him, astonished, but with a sense of rightness in being exactly there. His smile up close had a quality I was wanting without knowing it to find—that of letting himself be just himself. The scorn was out of it.

"A pretty woman here." Marveling, he almost laughed, the way he might at sudden luck—that being how he meant it, I had to conclude.

The room needed airing. The book smell was dense. I stood still as he raked a careful finger around my hairline, damp from the heat, just as my lip would be beaded.

"What are you, besides a visitor? Did you fall out of a plane? Wander off the road?"

"Teacher," I said; one word was all I had breath for. The pull of kissing had come to both of us at once. It was what we did. "Maida's," I murmured, my hand resting naturally on his shoulder. "You must know her."

"Lord, that little brat. Well . . . it's all for the best." I didn't ask what he meant. Later, I pondered it through the years. It may be that it was just a phrase. It didn't have to mean anything. What was for the best? Something to do with Maida or with himself? "Please tell me . . ." I began, about to ask him any number of things. But all he did was kiss me again. The only time I moved was to set the books down on the table, so as to free my arms. I still have no idea how much time passed before he made that slight movement that could only mean looking at his watch. "What a cryin' shame."

He moved away, going toward the door, but turned to me again, looking as intent as anyone ever had since time began. "Remember, you're not to mention me, please, ma'am." Then he smiled in a different way. "Can you possibly help it?" He had brought his distance back, gathered it all in. Then he left.

I stood stock-still for long moments in the sought-for room full of books, but after hearing the muted rustle of gravel as his car backed cautiously and turned, the roll of tires past the windows and their dwindling sound, I still could not break with the room itself where this unexpected magic had occurred, but circled about it like a trapped bee. I might well have buzzed but didn't know how. I heard the afternoon house waking, the creak of beds, the shuffle of footsteps. Leave? Yes, I must.

———

"I found the library," I told Maida in the hallway, seeing her come pattering down the stairs.

"Oh, there you are. I was calling you."

"I hope you don't mind if I explored."

"Course not. Want to get your suit? We'll drive in and swim."

"Where?" I was dazed and languid, as if more had happened.

"At the club. You know. It's not all that far. I told you."

Maida Stratton was blond and plump, a bouncy girl, always looking about ready to laugh. When I'd first seen her last September at the start of school, I had put her down in my mental notes as possibly dumb, or one of those students with native intelligence but who, try as I might, would not be induced to proper study. Later, when the students were discussing stories and poems that we read together, assigned or introduced in class, her perceptions astonished me. They were quick and sure. "Wouldn't that mean she was just uncertain what to do?" ... "Didn't he feel he was lots better than the girl he was with?" ... "Aren't they really trying to hide something?" She would get the point, quick as a blink. And make it sound easy. Her hair was long and untidy; she wore it bound back in a little scarf. Pieces kept slipping through and getting in the way as she bent to write something. But her homework was neat, brief, intelligent. High school English was her favorite class, she told me with a blush, turning a paper in. "Hasn't it always been your favorite?" I asked. A gulp. Then, "Mainly just since you came." That touched me. The Sunday dinner invitation came not long after. Mrs. Stratton, her mother, sent a note to me at school. "Mother sent you this," Maida said. She turned and almost ran away. It is painful to be young.

We drove to the club in one of the family cars. The minute we left the entrance gates, Maida, silent till then, began to talk rapidly. She was reading the Ibsen play I had given her. She loved reading plays. She could visualize how the scene might look before her on the stage. "Or a movie screen," I said.

"No! I'd rather imagine the stage ... me in the audience." That refreshing giggle. "You could be there, too, long as I'm imagining."

"Why not on the stage ... you, I mean?"

"Maybe later I'll think about it. But in Norway they have a lot of old dark furniture. They have stuffy old parlors, I bet."

"Why stuffy?"

"It's cold there. They'd have to keep the windows closed, wouldn't they? I bet they all have colds."

At the pool, she dove and splashed, greeted her friends, laughed a lot. But her delight, I had to recognize, was in having me there, her teacher now becoming her friend. A breathless change. "Yes, I'm from Stubbins," I kept saying, to some I hadn't met, home for the summer. Then I had to explain where it was. These south Mississippi towns might have been out West as far as the Delta mentality went. "Isn't that near Wimbly?" one boy asked, and everyone laughed. I said that it was. He had only said that because the names were funny. What did they recognize except each other? Maida confided on the way home that her father had wanted to have a swimming pool put in at Shongalo, but gave up the idea. "He didn't know how he would keep the poor children out. He'd hate not to be democratic. We're all democratic," she added. I wondered if she thought the Glenwood country club was democratic. We went riding happily home. Home was Shongalo.

—

"Somebody was here this afternoon," Bobby said at dinner. Bobby was Maida's brother, a husky boy, freckled and friendly, home from his first year in college. A bath before dinner, strenuously urged upon him by his mother, had reddened the mosquito bites along his arms. The water had darkened and subdued his light hair.

Mrs. Stratton laughed. "Lots of people were here." Her gaze on him was almost doting. Her children were her idols. Missing him through the school year had made her twice as fond. "The four of us, at least."

"Don't leave Miss Weldon out," Mr. Stratton said kindly.

"Milly, please," I said.

"All right. Milly. Is that for Mildred?"

"Yes, but I like it better. I never liked Mildred."

"I'm telling you there was this car here." Bobby was getting cross at them, but I could imagine it happened quite a lot—they had a strange habit of talking past or around a point somebody was trying to make.

"Lots of cars," his father teased.

"Aw 'ight, y'all don't wanna listen." Now he was mocking country speech, another trick. "What if I said it was a Jaguar?"

That stopped them. Now they paid attention. "I was coming back from the creek. Down there fishing with R.C. I came up the bank by the tennis court and saw it drive off. I swear I did."

"Well," his mother said after a pause, "who was it?"

"Don't know. Just told you what I saw." He shut up, sealed up tight, getting them back. He finished his plate.

Nothing was quite the same since he'd mentioned a Jaguar. "How did you know that's what it was?" Mr. Stratton pursued.

"Saw it."

"I guess it's all right to have a Jaguar," Mrs. Stratton meditated. "I just don't know anyone who owns one."

"Came for Milly," Mr. Stratton bantered. "Down in Stubbins they all drive around in 'em. Yes, sir."

"In Stubbins they raise pickles," I laughed.

"Lots of money in pickles," Mr. Stratton said. "Maida, you must have seen it. You never go to sleep."

"I was trying on bathing suits," Maida said. "It wasn't at the club," she added. It would naturally be there.

"I bet it was Edward," Mrs. Stratton suddenly said.

Mr. Stratton looked sharply up. Bobby and Maida stopped eating. Everyone but me knew who Edward was.

"Well," Mrs. Stratton explained, "the time before it was a Mercedes, wasn't it?"

"He'd borrowed that one from some friend," Mr. Stratton said drily. "With friends like that, anything is possible."

"You always think the worst," Mrs. Stratton said. She was not wanting to quarrel.

"Edward got some money out of that old place of theirs. Finally sold it, I understand. Maybe he just came to visit in his brand-new car."

"But nobody really saw him," Maida complained. "You don't know it was him." She sounded like what she was, a bright student arguing a firm point.

Mrs. Stratton smiled at her. "It just seems like it would have to be Edward."

Mr. Stratton turned to me. "Edward, Miss Weldon—Milly, I mean—is a cousin of ours. He—well, how *do* we explain Edward?"

"He does unexpected things," Mrs. Stratton said. "Going off to Mexico, for instance. I was always fond of Edward," she added, and looked a little wistfully, I thought, down at her wedge of icebox pie.

"He *wants* unexpected things," Mr. Stratton continued. "All sorts of records on this house, for instance."

"That you won't give him," Mrs. Stratton almost flared. "No reason on earth not to."

"None of his business. The Glenns sold it. George Glenn preferred not to hold on. So it's finished."

"You like refusing," his wife returned. "Jeannie never meant the slightest harm." Strange names were flying, tempers close behind.

"I like minding my own business."

"It's a simple request. You like defeating him. You won't admit it."

"I want some more tea," said Bobby. Mrs. Stratton rang the bell.

As for me, I said nothing. No more than Bobby did I know for sure that the man I'd seen was Edward. I wanted to know and yet didn't want to speak of it. Yet didn't they have a right to find out that a stranger was in the house, looking for something? I guessed they did, but still I never said. I went floating through the encounter once again, moment by moment.

———

"It's the funniest thing! I can't help laughing out loud. It's just most awfully funny." Maida was reading Noël Coward, *Hay Fever.*

"You're sounding British already," I said.

"We could go there someday."

"Go where?"

"To England."

"Maybe." I had to be vague. I had gotten into her plans; her future delights included me.

"I used to love reading," Mrs. Stratton volunteered from across the room, putting aside the paper. "But, you know, when I met Robert and married . . . well, it's foolish to say so, but all the things I was reading *for* were all around me, right near instead of somewhere else. I mean I read about these girls who admired some man and then found he liked them too, and so finally they had some sort of romance or got married after a lot of hitches and all that. But wasn't there always a big estate in it somewhere? A wonderful house and all that? Well, all of a sudden I had Shongalo. Why read about some place I might not even like? This one was good enough." Her little laugh was young, a lot like Maida's. "I saw lots of splendid old houses on a trip to England. You know, I wouldn't take any of them for this place right here. Did you know Maida started there?"

"Oh, Mama, don't tell that."

"We rode somewhere I forget, a little bit out from the center of London, Robert and I. We were trying out the 'tube,' as they call it there. I looked up and saw this station that said 'Maida Vale.' It sounded so pretty, I just couldn't get over how pretty that did sound. So I said to Robert, 'If we ever have our little girl, I'm going to name her that. Maida Vale.' We just don't use all of it, though I think double names are nice. They're often very melodic, don't you think so, Milly?"

"Well, I don't think much of Mildred Carrothers Weldon."

"A family name. That's different. They're often awkward. Mine is double, too. Linda May. I always liked both, but to Robert I'm just Linda—or Lin. Only then you'd spell it different."

"Differently," Maida corrected.

"I'm going to spank you," Mrs. Stratton said without meaning it.

It was late on Saturday morning, nearly lunchtime. Among the rooms at Shongalo trivial conversations could spin on forever. They were like iced tea, cold in tall glasses packed with ice cubes, pale with a moon-shaped slice of lemon. Outside the heat almost audibly prickled on the lawn, baked hot the flagstone path to the sunken garden; within, a breeze stirred through the tall windows, the blade fan turned slowly above, taking it up, passing it on. Maida ran out of the room—seeking bathroom or dictionary or following some whim about what to read next.

Mrs. Stratton put down the paper with a definite gesture.

"You can't know how pleased I am with this interest you've stirred in Maida Vale. She's always been so active. I get worried sometimes when she gets active in the wrong direction. You can imagine. We joined the club for her. Bobby too, of course. Robert and I couldn't care less about all those meetings and club doings. He never golfs. But the children . . . socially, I suppose . . ." She trailed off. She was about to say, I think, that social affairs didn't interest her much. The lack of interest went with her inward air, her absence of any detailed care for clothes or looks. It made sense that she would be content in her place as Robert Stratton's wife at Shongalo, not needing to seek anything to fill her time. There were relatives they spoke of, not only the mysterious Edward but others, some in the North, and others in Alabama who had "needed them" for a time but now were "straightening up again." I never inquired. I listened.

"Maida," I began, but did not know how to follow up.

"Yes?" said Mrs. Stratton.

"Maida may be getting too fond of me." I felt awkward and blushed.

"Oh yes, I know what you mean." Mrs. Stratton should have been sewing. Her speech went like that. She could have stopped from time to time to smooth out fabric, straighten thread, inspect her work, then continue. She smiled. "Things of that sort pass. Maybe it's a phase. Can you stay?"

"Stay?" I was surprised. I had meant to leave the next morning.

"Robert will speak to you. We have to be away on Monday. It's some business over near Leland. I want to go along with him to see about Maggie Lee . . . I don't suppose you know her . . . Maggie Lee Asquith?" Linda Stratton lived in a world where everybody knew Maggie Lee Asquith. I said that I didn't. "Well, she's just this wonderful person, an aunt of ours by marriage. She doesn't have long, they tell us." Here, I thought she should have been drawing a thread through an intricate turn. By "have long" she meant, I guessed, that the aunt was dying. "Leaving Maida Vale here just with Bobby. Just boy like, he won't pay her a bit of attention except when he feels like it. And besides, she's just wild for you to stay."

"Well, I—"

"Robert will speak to you." At that she did their strange trick of turning into someone else. Laid aside the imaginary sewing, rising, efficient. "Excuse me a minute. I've just got to see about—" The chatelaine. I had learned that word, somewhere along the way. It suited her. Her reading now—romances from the sound of them, but maybe not the cheap kind. Magazines were her choice at present, probably. Or mysteries. TV had not caught such a firm hold here, scarcely into the fifties. Bobby was showing signs of interest. There was a set with rabbit ears such as people had back then, in the upstairs hall. He would sit there in an old wicker armchair covered in faded cretonne, looking at the images. In those days before color they often looked grayish, and the frames would jump around depending on the weather. "You're going to ruin your eyes," Mrs. Stratton would say, passing him on the way to her own room. I could glimpse its spaciousness when she opened her door. Sparsely furnished with a large oval rug on the dark-stained, wide-boarded floor, the huge hexagonal mahogany posts of the bed. On two sides, tall windows let in light, which seemed to bring in the color blue, like the sky.

—

Robert did speak to me, as she had said.

"We want you to stay on a day or two, Milly," he earnestly told me.

He had asked me out for a stroll just before dinner to see his new plan for a terrace with chairs and tables near the tennis court. "The children are always eating out here. No place to put things." Was he asking my advice? I thought it only a pretense, a preface to something important. But was it so important to stay with Maida? He raised a hand, like someone warding off an interruption. "I've no right to ask for your time. Only if you could."

"I never dreamed it was so crucial." I wanted to ask why.

"Oh, I wouldn't undertake to say crucial. Maida is at a time when things are shaping up for her future. We're looking at colleges. We feel the presence of someone she respects—and loves"—he said it right out: loves—"would be the best thing for her. Besides, she's got her heart set on your staying. Maida. . . . There can't be a better gift to the world, Milly, than a woman who just goes into life with all that wonderful wildness about her. Right now, she's just a sight to behold, all her reading this, and thinking that. I confess none of it gets me worked up, not at my age. But she's just plain head over heels about it. Your going off . . . it would seem like leaving her high and dry. We'd have a regular crybaby. No telling how we'd manage."

We were walking side by side in a vague semicircle around the empty tennis court. It was after the ritual nap, also after the trip to the pool, cut short because there was such a crowd. Saturday after-noon. There had also been the ritual bath.

Mr. Stratton was not an imposing man. He might have been at-tractive, in a boyish way, when younger. He had discerning gray eyes, fair skin, and an open way of talking, his regard traveling all about you as he spoke. Evaluating, noting, though never staring ex-actly . . . kindly, I supposed. He always seemed to know much more than he chose to say. His business in town, for instance. I knew he ran an insurance company and went in daily on its affairs. He kept "some few head of cattle," as he once remarked, at Shongalo, though where they were escaped me, never having heard them so much as moo. He was glad to be through with row-farming, he had also once remarked.

He had asked me questions before, but always in company, had never spoken to me alone. Yet now we strolled together amiably, like old friends, possibly relatives. The feeling was of having known him since childhood. My thoughts drifted around him.

He was rapidly becoming more bald than any man would have liked. A pale, high forehead crowned him, made his eyes prominent. He was scarcely taller than I; though not frail exactly, he was not rugged either. His regard was for his property. Wherever those cows were, they were being cared for. Careful, he picked up a fallen pecan branch and looked at it before he hurled it aside into some weeds in an untended part of the yard beyond us. His property in-cluded Maida; he was looking after her. But she was more than that, of course, and he next let me know it.

"There was all that trouble last year."

I turned in surprise. "What trouble?"

"Some boy she got crazy about here. I say 'some boy.' Let's just say he wasn't anybody who would do for her. We'll leave it there."

"Is he in school?" I thought I might as well know who.

"No . . . gone. Well, not exactly gone. He has some sort of local job." It had a dark ring to it, the way he said it, and I knew I wasn't to learn any more from him.

As we walked back to the house, he talked about what kind of chairs and tables we might like best for the terrace. His saying "we" that way made me feel a little alarmed. He asked again if I would stay. Looking up at the house, mysterious in the westering light that slanted before us, I marveled at how weightless its presence before us seemed. I could suddenly not imagine being anywhere else. "I kissed a strange man in the library," I almost said, almost adding, "I live here." I had found in the thought a different meaning for that simple phrase, *I live here.* I turned it in my mind, just as in an exercise I had often had my students do. *Here, I live.*

I told Robert Stratton I would stay for a day or so longer.

"Good," he answered, and having gained the front steps, he ran up them to the porch. In that motion I saw him become imposing. He had the air of the owner of Shongalo. He held the door for me.

———

Monday morning.

"They've gone!" Maida said, gloating, full of jumps and twirls, running to fetch me coffee, make me toast, find the special jar of peach preserves.

Sunday had passed in a jumble of decisions about church. I went to the service with Mrs. Stratton, and Maida, dressing in a topsy-turvy rush, trying to find some good shoes and a piece of something she called a hat, went with us at the last minute. She sat close beside me in the pew; we read the responses in unison. In the afternoon, a clutch of chattering people came and went—relatives, friends. Names went up around them like a flock of birds. Who knew anything about me? That day, I did decide on napping. I dreamed.

Then Sunday was gone, like a day misplaced.

"They've gone!" said Maida.

Bobby, sleeping late, was soon to be seen plodding downstairs, a firm hand on the bannister. He passed squint-eyed into the kitchen. The cook was off also, let go for the day. Bobby soon came to the table with a plate of cold fried potatoes and some leftover apple pie. He poured coffee and picked his fork up with his fist. Boys were often like that, pretending to be workmen or cowboys out of a movie. Maida ignored him. Whenever someone else was with us, she was waiting for them to leave. Since the evening before, we had been reading Tennyson aloud.

When I asked Bobby's plans for the day, he said he meant to go off fishing with R.C. and Clayton, whoever they were, but that it looked like rain. "I'll just go over there anyway," he concluded. He gave a look that plainly said any place was better than here in the house with us. I asked him, teacher fashion, if he'd seen any more Jaguars.

"Naw. I know it was Edward though."

"How'd you know that?" Maida was a great one for probing. She always had her curiosity working, one thing that made her such a good student. "I mean," she added, "nobody saw him."

"I just think it was," said Bobby, shoveling pie into his mouth.

"But who," I asked, "is Edward?"

There was a small silence, and Bobby said, "A cousin."

I laughed. "You said that before. Isn't everybody your cousin?"

Bobby was already heading out the door. Maida began to clear the table. She was thinking already of *Idylls of the King*. "He just comes and goes so funny," she said.

"Why 'funny'?" I asked. How to get to know without seeming to want to know?

She came back from the kitchen for more of the breakfast things, but stopped to look out the window of the smaller dining room, where we sat. The family hardly ever breakfasted together. They, too, came and went. "It's so pretty out there," she remarked, seeing the morning yard with its rose garden, its birdbath, its shrubs. She all but clapped her hands. Bobby was gone. We had the place to ourselves. "I want to always live at Shongalo!"

"I can't say I blame you."

"Don't you love it?"

"I love it," I said, sincere as ever I could be. "Can I come and go," I ventured, "like this Edward person?"

Maida whirled on me, jumping forward in a little rabbitlike spring, throwing slightly sticky arms around my neck. "You can come and *never* go! We'll read and read! Everything there is! I'll know as much as you!"

"Lots more, I hope."

"Promise?"

"Promise what?"

"You'll never leave."

"I promise we'll find our book wherever we left it yesterday."

"You won't promise?"

"Now, Maida. I'll come and go, whenever you let me. Soon you'll be saying I come and go 'funny,' like Edward."

She sat down; her bouncing fit was passing. "But Edward just comes without telling anybody. He just shows up. Daddy says Edward thinks he belongs here."

"What do you think of that?"

"Just that you wouldn't. I don't guess you would. Mother likes to see him, though. He makes Daddy mad."

"Why?"

"Oh . . . he thinks she likes him."

"Do you like to see him?"

"I would . . . but he calls me a brat. And I'm not. Am I?" The question was a tease, but before I could answer she was off at a run, leaving the breakfast things to me.

A brat. . . . Yes, he had said that.

Gently, the rain had started.

———

All that long day while the rain plunged us both into our separate dreams, we read in the library, in the family room, in the formal living room at the round inlaid table beneath the chandelier. Curious as Maida, but for different reasons, I pulled a drawer a little way out. "Look," I noted. "The table's like a pie." Indeed it was: The five drawers with bronze pulls were triangular, ending in a point at the center. Maida hardly noticed. In one brief glimpse I had seen that the drawer was empty. Bad manners were something I could not afford to let her notice my having. Were the other drawers empty, too? We had reached the magical story of Sir Gawain's vision. The rain continued.

It hadn't started in the usual rush of wind and flash-bang of thunder, but only as a rustle, muted as a whisper, then growing louder. It seemed to have put out gray arms and enveloped the day. The interiors of Shongalo were shadowy, dim. At night we might have found strong light in corners, not the cloudy mist that permeated every room, drank up the lamplight, and left us sometimes unable to make out the words on the page. In the corner of a sofa, Maida leaned against my shoulder as I read. We were about to go on to Mordred's betrayal of Lancelot and Guinevere to Arthur. I finished a long descriptive passage.

"You know," Maida remarked, "it's pretty, but it makes me sleepy."

"Later on," I promised, "it will make you cry."

"Let's skip to that," she said. Maida and I had talked of it one day: Why do people like to read what makes them cry? "Emotions get to show themselves," I explained. "You can sympathize and cry over people you never met, so it does your own feelings good." She puzzled over it, and really it wasn't a very good answer. Why do teachers think they have to answer things that students ask?

One thing I was glad about: the rain made it impossible to go in and swim. Maida was always taking chances, diving, chasing somebody underwater. She had some of the boys there daring her. One of them called her at times. He asked her to go with him to a picnic or the movies. She would tell him that Miss Weldon was still here, though to her I'd long since become just Milly. "Go on if you want to see him." "Maybe I don't," was all she'd say. She'd let it out that a boy she'd liked last year was always around wherever she went with somebody else. "You don't want to see him?" She was vague in replying. So that must have been the one her father spoke of. One day, leaving the pool, I had seen him too. He was lingering out near the entrance, a tall, rather swart boy, with thick hair of a color that habitually looked dirty, a serious face half turned away. Maida had given a little wave and he had nodded. "That's Garth," she'd told me. "Who?" "You know . . . the one they didn't like."

The rain was shifting around, blowing softly in through an open window. Maida jumped up to close it. "I know. Let's go upstairs. There's a good lamp in the little room. You haven't seen the little room, I bet." She was running already, up the stairs. I followed.

The door to the "little room" was between the one opening on her parents' bedroom and another, farther up the hall, that was Bobby's. No telling what was behind that one, though I could imagine pennants and posters, a jumble of everything and nothing. In the little room there was a jumble, too.

Sewing! Not for nothing had I connected Mrs. Stratton with that. She had obviously put everything pertaining to it here. There stood her dress form, armless, chastely plastered over with brown paper, though her own lines were visible, low-set and full-fleshed, a friendly shape. An old quilt was folded, lying on top of a large oval basket, woven from broad withes. Mending must be inside. Both a hanging lamp and a standing one were fitted with strong bulbs. Maida had switched them on already. The one window looked down to the lawn far below and the path that led to the sunken garden. "Now . . ." A sofa bed against the wall was waiting for us to sit and read more. But though she sat down as though waiting for me, she did not open the book or offer it to me. She just sat holding it, frowning and thinking of something very hard. The rain stood at the window, a gray presence, but here it was full of secluded light. An armchair too big for the small space was opposite. When I sat in it, our knees were almost touching. "Are you tired of reading?" I asked. She didn't answer.

Maida Vale had a charming face, mainly, I had often thought, because it was so changeable. Serious, she might almost seem to sulk; her thoughts were inward, running over something that puzzled, maybe even offended her. She had chubby cheeks when she smiled, lighting up at something from the outside world, small teeth, bursts of crinkles, upturning lips when she laughed, her eyes half-shut with all-out fun. A boy might want to kiss her a lot, I thought. I felt she wanted to confide something in me, so was waiting; but then the telephone rang. It rang persistently, five times or more. Maida, not especially wanting to go, finally went out to the extension near the TV in the upper hall. She came back distractedly.

"It's for you."

"For me?"

My mother, of course, knew where I was. I had called to tell her that I would stay longer, but why would she call me now? Sickness, maybe, or an accident.

Of course, there was Willie.

I had kept Willie under wraps because there was nothing much to say about him, the necessary escort in the small town, the one you went to the movies with, asked to parties, gave routine good-night kisses to. There'd been others before him, one at college I'd rather not think about, but others, too, here and there, no more than average. Willie would hardly call.

"Hello," the voice said in answer to mine. Then I knew. "Still there?"

"A little longer," I stumbled.

"I've thought of you. But . . . what's your name—?"

"My name?"

"Yes, your name. I didn't get it."

"Mildred . . . I mean, Milly. . . . What's yours?"

"Can't hear." There was a sputtering on the line, then a crackle. "Can't hear you," he said again.

"Who are you?" I all but shouted. Some word began to form, but the sound mangled and the line went dead.

I returned slowly.

"Who was it?" Maida asked me.

"I don't know. The wrong number, I suppose."

"But you said your name."

"It's how he knew it was wrong, I guess."

She gave me the kind of look that comes out of knowing a friend has told a lie. Her mouth was slightly open; a thinking went on. "He said 'that pretty woman staying there.' It's what he said."

"I guess women stay everywhere," I said lightly. I picked up *Idylls of the King*. "I lost the place," I said, searching.

But Maida was not listening. She was staring at me, her mood so altered that mentioning the book seemed totally irrelevant. "Did you ever fall in love?" she suddenly inquired.

"Everybody does," I said, "sooner or later."

"I was in love last year. It was Garth. They said it wouldn't do."

"Who said so?"

"Mother did and Daddy. Daddy was the worst."

"They think of you," I said firmly. I couldn't be ganging up against them. Nor did I want to deny her confidence. It was danger-ous ground.

"It was when his mother came. She came here and wanted to talk to Mother." She suddenly picked up a cushion and held it on her lap, lifting and shaking it. "Mother said it was awful."

"You mean, his mother was awful? Then you saw what they meant—your parents, I mean."

"I don't know if I saw what they meant. I just don't know. It was all such a big lot of talking all of a sudden." She hit the cushion. "I just hated everything."

I smiled. "It's all behind you, isn't it? Back there last year some-where?" At her age a year was a long time.

"I don't know," she said, still thinking. "I guess."

I had found the place in *Idylls of the King*.

"Do you think sex is bad? Making love, I mean. Is that so bad?"

"Well, no, but I think you ought to get older before you decide about it."

"Do you know about it?"

I began to read on from where we had stopped. Not a doubt that she wasn't listening, but like someone walking ahead on a path I hoped she'd follow.

"Somebody wanted you," Maida insisted. "They wanted to talk to you."

"Why don't you read for a change?" I held out the book.

She stared a moment, then got up and ran from the room, stum-bling over the large basket, which tilted open, spilling its contents. Between friends, what lie will ever do? The answer is: none.

I knew that I didn't care quite enough what Maida thought. I knew that. I sat with my heart beating like a drum. He had remem-bered me. He had called. "What's your name?" It kept chanting. I could even hear again the snarled static on the phone. Rumbling thunder shook the house softly, like a dog worrying a worn-out toy. Then there was the rumble of the cattle gap, from far off at the entrance. The Strattons had returned.

As the car drew up, stopping near the front, I wondered where Maida had gone. I searched, intending, I suppose, to take her hands, to say I was sorry for whatever had upset her. But I didn't find her. She would reappear. Open and frank always, she would tell me what was wrong. We would find another book, a different sort, snappy satire or hard-surfaced mystery. Things would resume as before.

From an upstairs window I saw the sky clearing, long broken clouds turning to pink scarves, light gleaming on the wet trees. There was evening still left, and part of the late afternoon. Shoes were crunching the gravel, tapping up the wooden steps. "Maida! Bobby? Milly! We're home!"

I dressed for dinner with more care than usual. I brushed my hair till it shone, a mix of blond and brown, sun-streaked in summer. I dampened it and fastened it with a brown clasp like tortoiseshell. I put on a full flowered skirt I had not worn before, and a blouse in ivory cotton latticed with embroidery, cut low. In my Stubbins vision of what might happen at Shongalo, I had prepared for a possible party, a dance at the country club, who knew what? But these were not to be, and so far I had not dared to appear in such a getup. But now I didn't care.

Where was Maida? The heavy steps I heard battering up and down the stairs were Bobby's. First he was explaining something, then his father called him back, he was quarreling with his mother, from the sound of water pouring out he was taking a shower, he was hollering from the door that he couldn't hear what they were saying. He was much too big for the house, for any house. Something fell and crashed in his room. He was mad. He was furious. A few minutes later, the smell of ham and biscuits drifting up from below, he was dressed in slacks and a fresh shirt and smiled with calm beatitude when we encountered each other at the top of the stairs.

At dinner no one even mentioned the trip to Leland, or the aunt Maggie Lee. Robert Stratton, responding to my dressed-up state, drew my chair out for me. He waited a moment to start serving the plates, as Maida was not present but could be heard descending the stairs. She came in quietly and sat with her head tucked, her face quiet and pale, not looking my way. "Are you all right, honey?" asked her mother. She said that she was.

"We drove through some awful weather," Robert Stratton said. "Coming back between here and Leland. The worst was over when we arrived."

"A whole roof blown off and some trees down. The house was dark when we came. Didn't you all have sense enough to turn the lights on?" She was asking Bobby.

"I thought it was like that other time we lost power," Mr. Stratton recalled. "Candlelight and lamps, I thought."

"It was pretty," said Mrs. Stratton. "But everything got cold."

"We've got no old range anymore to build a fire with stove wood. I well remember that other time. I went out back and found that son of Annie's. Or was it Delia's?"

"No, sir, it was Annie's," Delia said from the kitchen.

"I said, 'Can you bring us in some stove wood.' He had just got home from Chicago for a visit. He didn't know what stove wood was. What happened to that old range, Lin?"

"Gave it away. One of Annie's daughters wanted it."

"Now she's got electricity too. Time marches on."

"Speaking of time," I said, "I think it's time for me to be going home tomorrow."

Maida looked up, startled. They were all silent.

"Oh? Make it the day after." Robert Stratton put it that way, for reasons he knew best. He didn't say, Stay on and on. He didn't say, What could we do without you? I found out why the next evening, when we talked in the sunken garden, out near the lily pool.

———

We sat on the stone bench. It had grown warm again that day, though the freshness from the rain had lingered.

"Maida isn't so taken up," he remarked. I had got to know his train of thought. His conversation up to then had seemed to absorb him, changes in the Delta, more to come, things his little trip had brought to mind. But this was his real subject, now appearing.

"'Taken up'?" I repeated. I could already guess what he meant.

"All this reading . . . you, the marvelous teacher. It's slacked off."

"So you thought it was a bad thing?" I saw that, unconsciously, I had used the past tense. Maida and I had talked, but had not mentioned a book all day long. We had talked about movies, one we had missed in town. Some friends of Bobby's had showed up and she had wanted to go out to play tennis with them. I had to join, she insisted, so as to have another girl.

"I think," said Robert Stratton, and crossed his ankle over his knee, "that anything done to exclusion is not such a good thing." He glanced at me through the late lingering light. "Don't you agree?"

"I never thought it was forever," I said. "It's been such fun—her enthusiasm, I mean. To think I stirred it up. I love books, too, you know." I thought I should point that out.

"Oh, I'm sure she won't forget. Nor will we." He leaned against me, pressed my knee, took my hand. He was a great one for patting. "We'll always thank you, Milly." And time, as he had so lightly mentioned it at table, had not marched; it had jumped right out at us.

I saw how neatly he had taken everything away from me. I wanted to protest. But I knew whatever I said to him would leave me biting my lip, feeling it was wrong at that moment, as in the future I would feel it, looking back.

I said something anyhow. "Thank me for what? What is it you think I did?"

"Oh, I expect you see that, or will if you don't now. She had to live through it, you see. So one day . . . why, you'll see."

Angry! But how, if I didn't have words to say why, could I flash out at him? I murmured something about having to pack and walked away, inside. My planned speech—how wonderful it had been at Shongalo, getting to know them, make friends, plan a return visit. . . . What was the use of going through a useless exchange? I left Robert Stratton sitting meditatively, smoking a pipe, which he would presently knock out against the stone bench before he went inside. It was another ritual, a habit he had.

Mrs. Stratton heard me come in and called from the living room. Would I have coffee? I pleaded a headache. I went trembling up the stairs. Wasn't it part of my perception of them that they were different from the ordinary run of people? Not to be easily, if ever, completely seen into? But I'd been used! It was that that hurt, more than if they'd coarsely scorned me at the beginning, or given me a caretaker's shed room at the back.

I looked around the room, at the muted luster of its polished walnut and mahogany, its wide dark-stained floorboards, its rugs a little worn, a little sun-stained. My things were all around, more confident than I. I drew my suitcase from the big closet and set it open on the bed. That headache was no lie. I took two aspirin and lay down beside the open case. I fell asleep.

When I woke I wondered what time it was. Everything was quiet. I found my watch: two o'clock. Tiptoeing to the broad hall outside, I knew I had gained control again. I would have this place, in memory at least, from now on. I moved to the front of the central upper hall, where the broad curved windows looked down on the lawns below. I could see the path to the sunken garden and part of the garden itself, not the pool but an urn and the one small statue, clearly visible in the moonlight.

Someone was out there. A shadow moved, going toward the line of shrubs between the house and the garden, returning with the deliberate rhythm of a tall man walking slowly, hands thrust in pockets. It was not Robert Stratton.

I knew who it was.

I floated downward, drawn through the silence of thinking about it. I found no obstacle, not a creaking floorboard or a resistant door. The path to the garden was plain; I turned the corner by the hedge. There lay the pool, smooth as carbon paper. The grass had been mowed that day and the fresh smell lingered. I had noticed it earlier, mingling with the scent of Robert Stratton's whiskey. No one was about. I circled outward, moving toward the heavy line of trees, dense in their dew-wet mystery. I went to them and peered into the wood. The insects had stopped chanting, but I heard no footstep, no breath or rustle. I saw no one. Nothing. I returned to the house. On the path, the old dog snuffled up beside me. He put a damp nose in my palm, and we walked up the front steps together. On the porch he went to his accustomed corner and lay down. He was not allowed inside.

—

All that was forty years ago.

For years I received a Christmas message from the Strattons, a card with a letter enclosed, telling me about Bobby and Maida, also about themselves and what had gone on during the year at Shongalo. The children went off to school, had various mishaps and triumphs. Bobby barely missed having to go to Vietnam. After finishing school and college at Duke, Maida almost moved to New York to work. Instead, she married a Charleston boy, a young doctor. Maida wrote me, too, for a time, but the correspondence faded into postcards and finally vanished. I sent a wedding present.

Before I left, I took something. I went into the little room to find the book we had been reading. It was lying face down where we'd left it. The woven basket had turned over with Maida's rush from the room. Scraps of fabric had spilled out, and a packet of letters. They had been held together with a rubber band, but it had broken. I saw at once, among all the others, a long envelope, faded yellow, with "Edward Glenn" written across it in black ink in an old-fashioned flowing hand. There was no address, just the name, so it was meant to be given by hand. It was by instinct that I picked it up, without thought. Perhaps what I had in mind was a sort of revenge.

Once away, I opened it, but found nothing surprising. A wish from an elderly man, some aging relative, that "my boy," the young Edward, would have a profitable time at school, and would make the family proud, as they had always been of him heretofore. It was handsomely stated, with feeling as real as heartbeats. It was such as this he felt worth returning to search for in the crevices of Shongalo. And Linda Stratton thought worth saving for him? Yes, and so did I; and I would tell him, "This is yours," if the chance came my way.

THE RUNAWAYS

Every day Edward walked down to the village. Joclyn saw him go, usually with a list from her in his pocket. It was a long walk. If she was going to walk, she said, staying near the ridge was preferable. She could stop and talk to some of the children in the native houses, out of sight but not so far away. She could practice her Spanish. She had learned it wasn't wise to hand out favors. Even when she did go to town, she did not go with Edward, as a rule. He always asked her, "Anything from below?" It would be hot there. Up here on the ridge, cool nights, temperate afternoons.

The Hacienda Sol y Agua was not really a hacienda, but rather a cluster of cottages, recently built, spaced out along a ridge above a long green valley. Perhaps there would be a hacienda some day, the guests speculated. Or perhaps there had been one in the past. The ruins of a mining project far down the eastern drop of the hill made them think that. Crumbling walls down that way were grown up in vines, a jungle of bloom. Some said copper was mined here once, some said silver. No one knew for sure. As for *agua*, there was nothing to swim in either; they were far inland from the ocean, with no lake in sight. The theory ran that the new swimming pool, now only a red gash down the western slope, looking abandoned, was what was meant. The feeling was that its not being finished was what made the rents so reasonable. Others gave credit to the recent struggles of the peso. But the level ridge top where the little houses stood was beautifully laid out with winding walks and rock-bordered beds. And the sun, at least, was certainly there. The nights were velvety, starlit, clear, and calm. Days, the path to the village beckoned downward.

But Joclyn seldom felt like the climb back. She did her graphics, a series of them, promised for book illustrations. The mail was important to her. Edward had her written permission to pick it up. The packets with the San Francisco postmark, he knew those were the ones she waited for. She had told him.

When she had gone, a time or two, she had discovered a long winding path, in addition to the sharp climb he preferred. She could dawdle and rest, coming up by stages. She had not been well. She was thin, and as with many very thin people, it was hard to tell her age. She didn't volunteer to reveal it. Mystery in Mexico, a mysterious country. She felt it part of being here not to come right out with everything. And unlike the other renters, he didn't inquire.

"You can come if you want to." He always said that, but on the climb the one time she came along, he seldom spoke. One evening, though, he waited till after sunset to see that she did indeed return up the longer path. He met her. "What took you so long? I was worried." "I ran into a woman and talked to her. She's got three children and another one coming. She's hardly older than twenty, if that. Her husband needs a job. I guess it's a common story." "You see where practicing Spanish can get you? Into sympathizing." It seemed a harsh comment, but she let it pass. It was the slurred way he spoke, Southern obviously, that made irony seem like sarcasm or even contempt. Leaning back slightly, talking down. Maybe just joking. "Come sit," he offered. He'd placed a chair before his entrance door. "Take the weight off yo' feet." She had so little weight, she thought that might be a joke, too. She shook her head. "Another time." She walked back to her own cottage, at the far end.

———

It was an unspoken code among the renters that they either met for drinks separately, in households or alone, or all together, gathering. "Our time next." It was said easily, two or three times weekly. There were seven of the units, five occupied at present. The month was about to terminate, meaning a turnover for a number of them. The hilltop had been laid out amply; the beds held jacarandas, pepper trees, lemon trees, oleanders, hibiscuses, geraniums. Footsteps crunched on the gravel walks that branched off to individual cottages. "Efficiencies," somebody had said early on, during drinks. "I hate that word," Edward had said under his breath, and Joclyn had heard him, being accidentally nearby.

Later on the day of the long climb, her supper finished, she was about to shower and go to bed, legs aching from the effort of the afternoon, when she heard a knock at the windowpane toward the back. It was Edward, the only name for him that she knew. "I forgot to give you the mail." She let him in. "But I went down today. I was at the post office." "I got there first. They passed it over without asking. I just forgot." He handed her two letters. Family mail, a bill. She put them aside. He was standing there rather awkwardly, not like his usual way. "Well, come in." She was irritated. The feeling was that he had gotten her mail, then kept it from her. Was he finally losing his distance? Why should she mind? Certainly, he was attractive, sensitive looking, his intelligence communicated without any particular proof needed, and he too was mysterious. Unasked and unanswered questions about him doubtless had occurred to everyone there, and had actually been put to him by the less reticent ones, like that Hartley couple, for instance. "Now, just what brought you down all this way?" they wanted to know. "I saw an ad." (Period.) Mussed brown hair, well-set, fairly tall. Late thirties? Hard to tell. Tan trousers usually, T-shirt and dirty tennis shoes, not very good for walking. But as he stood there with her mail in hand, she noticed that he had bathed and smelled like good soap. His shirt was clean.

"I get tired very easily," she said, by way of getting him out of there after the one drink she was now going to fetch for him. "I was recently sick."

"That's too bad. Are you better?" Memory stirred for her, out of the soap smell: tub baths in the slow, soft California twilight, clean pajamas, the murmur of a family talking on the side porch.

"It's slow."

He sat down and was a leisurely while taking the first swallow from his glass. "It was breaking up my marriage is the trouble with me," he said. "Ten years of it and all over. Gone. I had to get off and think."

"Is that what you do here?" she asked him. "Think?"

"I call it that. Really it's just going over it again. Like hitting yourself where it hurts the most. The first time you can't stand it, the second time you think you'll die, the third time is worst of all, but then by the tenth or twelfth or twentieth time, being still alive, you get surprised at yourself. By the hundredth time, you're numb."

"And finally you don't care?"

"I must be getting there. But lately I've wondered if I want to."

"Ever?"

"I believe I never really want not to care."

With that, to her surprise, he got up and left. Then why had he dressed? she wondered. Maybe just for himself.

———

At week's end the company changed. The inquisitive Hartleys left, as did the retired minister Mr. Telfair and his wife, with talk of their "kiddies," meaning grandchildren, and the Maynards, who wondered the whole time if their Labrador was all right at the vet's, and if the lawn was being watered, what with a drought all over the Midwest.

Edward and Joclyn were the only ones still there. The new list had gone up in the guardhouse, as they called the caretaker's unit, but the names—though one seemed Russian and another distinctly Jewish—meant little or nothing, Edward and Joclyn agreed, as long as the people who owned them were okay.

"I'm fairly antisocial," he told her, having wandered into the office while she was studying over the notice. "Some good nasty characters might be interesting." He then knocked on the caretaker's door to say in Spanish that his stove needed repair.

Those who had cars or had rented jeeps, which were more common, took the road down the back side of the mountain to sightsee, explore, shop, or dine. There was a small convenience store connected with the cottages, but it was often locked up, the old senora and her daughter who ran it gone somewhere best known to themselves. They always said any absence was for washing clothes down below at the river, and maybe it was. "It's where they meet and talk to everybody," Edward explained. "They gossip." Still, it got to be a saying among the renters: "Gone to wash clothes."

"I think you'd better go and wash clothes," was what Edward had the misfortune to say to the blond wife of one of the new arrivals. She had made a dead set for him right away the first evening. The next day, having found a window open, she was into his quarters when he came back up the hill from town. The newcomers' arrival party, held regularly for a get-together drink, had been her first appearance. After a couple of drinks, she had draped her arm around Edward and had pushed her head up under his chin. Her name was Gail Loftis. Her husband, Bill, said he was in investments. Edward told him that he had no money to invest, and then he had to reveal to the wife that he had no wish to invest in her either. The clothes-washing remark offended her, however, so she went around the next morning telling everyone how insulting he was.

"It's a saying we have," Joclyn explained. "An 'in' joke. About the little shop that's never open."

"God, does he think everything on two legs is after him?" Evidently, Gail Loftis wanted to start dropping in for coffee or beer or just anything anybody had. It was Joclyn's turn for her visit. "Most of us have some little work to develop here," Joclyn explained. "Mr. Rotovsky is a writer, isn't he? So he must work, too, for one." "It's what he said," Gail sulked, and finished the cup of instant coffee. She was not offered more. "You can take some nice trips," Joclyn counseled. "I'd like to myself, but I have a commission for some graphics to finish. I have a deadline." Her voice had gotten firmer, and finally even Gail Loftis understood that she was supposed to leave. "Bill's such a bore," she said. "He's keeping us on this awful budget. We ought to see more of the country." She got up. "He's not gay, is he?" It was Edward she meant. Joclyn sensed the trap. "I wouldn't think so," she was quick enough to reply.

———

After lunch, Edward talked with Mr. Rotovsky. They sat on lawn chairs, looking out over the back slope toward a low mountain range behind. A blue fringe of light hung evenly over the summit.

"But if you go existential," Edward said, "you plunge toward something new, and then how're you to know you'll wind up any better than at first?"

"Well, then you must feel so strongly that you plunge anyway. There is no time for the questions of this nature."

Joclyn heard all this while passing behind them. She was off to pick some wildflowers for her rooms, as the beds near the walkways were off-limits. Knee-deep in weeds—something like sedge—she picked blue flowers whose name she didn't know. She saw an iguana stretched on a rock in the sun. She straightened and looked toward the blue mountains.

———

After dark that evening, Edward came to see her for the second time. "It's that damn woman," he said when she let him in. "She waits around after dinner. If she gets in again, I'm going to throw her out bodily. Then there'll be a big row. At least I speak enough Spanish so they'll let me explain, possibly even believe me."

"Her husband's gone all around explaining already," Joclyn said. "You didn't hear him? 'It's just when she's drinking,' was what he said. He thinks she undergoes a female Jekyll-Hyde personality shift."

"It doesn't do me much good," Edward said. "She's not apt to stop."

The knock at the door was her, of course. Joclyn went and cracked it open. The hectic face, hair streaming half across it, peered out of the dark. "I knew it! He's here! Well, you two little bugs in a rug! . . . Have fun!" The door slammed in her face. Joclyn had got mad enough for that.

She turned to Edward. "I don't care if you don't."

He didn't answer. His glass was empty. She got him another drink.

Presently, she went over to the large folding table she kept set up in one corner and switched on her work light, the one she had brought with her. A white sheet, held down with steel rulers on either side, was half covered with the black outlines of what might be just a design but was really a half-formed picture. He did not come closer or inquire.

"I killed my wife," he said into the semidark of his side of the room. She did not look up. "She was a crazy wild one, too, a nuisance every way you'd care to imagine. I had loved her too long. It all ran dry. She wasn't living in the family home with us anymore. She'd rented an apartment for herself. I had to go there for something she wanted to talk about. The argument—well, who'd want to hear about it? I hit her. She fell and died. The weapon was a heavy piece of green Venetian glass my sister got on a summer trip. She'd liked it, so took it. She had taking ways."

"Weren't you arrested?"

"It looked like an accident. Everybody knew she was on whatever it took to have one. Nobody knew I was even in town. I spent a lot of time off fishing last summer. I think, though, that maybe everybody knows but doesn't blame me. We—my family is well known, prominent—. What can I say? In a Southern small town—. No way to explain just how it is. If you didn't do it, you didn't do it, no matter if you and everybody else knows that you did, including your mother."

"Most of all your mother," was what came to her to say. She leaned forward to smudge a line. Her hand was shaking. It wouldn't stop. She turned out the light.

In the newly dark room she crossed the floor and came to him. Groping, she pulled a hassock forward and sat near him.

"I'm going to die," she said.

He put his hand on her head. "I know. I thought so." She leaned forward and laid her head on his knee. Close and warm, his hand moved on her hair.

He said: "Today, down in the village, I saw this Mexican, an older guy, riding a bicycle in a muddy street, holding this kid, a little girl, before him on the seat. She had grabbed onto the handlebars, close to the middle. They were both laughing. I never saw two people so happy. I guess it was his granddaughter—it would have to be. I think I'll remember it forever. There in a muddy street of a dirt-poor town on a half-broke old bicycle—pure happiness. You don't see it often."

"You didn't kill your wife," she said.

"I was walking the steep way back and sat down to rest at that turn, you remember, from the first time you tried it."

"The only time. It's too taxing."

"There's a path I hadn't noticed before, it slopes off down to the left if you're coming up, to the right otherwise. Down there, I heard something move and a girl came up, a Mexican girl, Indian I would think, old skirt, black hair, broad face with no expression on it. When she left I walked down a piece and saw where this spring was welling up, just a thread of water trickling down, and some kind of little statue there, I couldn't tell of what. A face, half worn off, but whose? Surrounded by flowers, bunches tied together. About ten or a dozen bunches, some dead, some fresh, some wilted. I wondered if she'd left some flowers, and if that's their way of saying prayers. Do you know?"

"You didn't kill your wife," said Joclyn.

"No, I didn't kill her. I wanted to, but I didn't. I was lying."

"I wasn't."

"I know."

She stayed where she was, cheek laid on his knee, head silently beneath his hand. This was the happiest she had felt, in such a long time.

THE WEEKEND TRAVELERS

_____

It was midafternoon, hardly later than three, when Anna and Karl came to the house. They were following a sign they had seen by the roadside a mile or so back: POTTERY. They were not collectors, but the leafy Vermont roads, cool on this midsummer day, had so far been a pleasure to go along, winding, rising, gently falling, curving, and rising again. They could only lead to pleasurable things. However, the side road since the sign and the turnoff was little used. It was rutted, with weeds grown up so high they concealed the potholes and rattled beneath the fenders. Something crashed in the undergrowth to their right, running away. They never saw what it was. "Some animal," Karl summarized. But she thought it was somebody. She thought just now in terms of people, being hopeful of pregnancy, though he didn't quite know that.

A mile went by, then another. No further sign appeared.

Down from Canada on a long weekend holiday, married only a scant year, lovers (again) that very morning, they both experienced New England as pastoral, with a cool, uncrowded loveliness they remarked on, and were happy just to breathe its air. Maybe the place will be the charm, she thought, babies on her mind.

—

"Are you sure this was the right road?"

"I guess we'd better turn back."

Which one of them said these things scarcely mattered. They seemed the only thoughts to be had, and so the only things to say. The woods, they noticed as they stopped and wondered how to turn, had got thicker, stranger, wilder. Trees here had grown to fantastic heights, with long bare trunks and fronded crests that took out large portions of the sky. Close by the road's tracks there was a thick encroachment of sumac and elderberry tangled with some other bushes Anna couldn't name. Looking down from the car window, Anna judged the growth as masking a declivity of uncertain depth. Now they were stuck for a place to turn. Karl went into gear again and inched forward, hoping for a wider opening. Then at the road's next curve there it was, the house.

It was weatherworn, unpainted, with broad steps running up to the porch. A couple of wooden tables displayed pottery. No one was about. Not a soul.

———

Karl and Anna Wallens had met at a Montreal business colloquium where the prevailing language was French. Stumbling through a conversation at the social hour that followed, they discovered an absurd truth—they both were fluent in English. He was Polish, born there, but had stayed with relatives in Toronto to attend college. Anna Mendoza, born and reared in Spain, had an English mother, and had been sent off to school in the U.K. So it started between them. Later it was easy to drop the -ky off Wallensky. With marriage and rechristening, they had the feeling of rebirth. "In Canada," she observed to Karl, "one could be just anybody from anywhere—Iranian or Finnish or Czech." "What does it matter?" Karl would say. "We'll just be from nowhere." "Oh, but you must see Spain." "Maybe sometime," he would say. "Promise?" "Yes, promise." Anna often wore white, unsuitable for Montreal, but recalling to her the dry hills and flowering courtyards near Jerez. *I'll go back someday.* So she devoutly thought. At work Karl was simply Wallens. His slight accent merged with others.

———

For a little while they sat looking at what seemed an empty house. Finally they got out. Now the air was darker, shading toward twilight. From off in the woods behind the house, a little to the left by the sound of it, a dog was howling and barking urgently. Howl, then bark. Bark, then howl. It seemed ready to continue, for minutes or hours.

But here they were and there on the porch was pottery. Together they mounted the steps. Knocking at the door, which stood open, brought no one. Within the depths of one large room, they could see more pottery displayed on a banquet-sized table, filling most of the space between windows and fireplace.

Someone came. A girl with an aging plain face, long sand-colored hair that looked never to have been either cut or combed, stained jeans, and a man's shirt.

"Want something?"

"Oh, just to look. We saw your sign."

She did not reply; she only waved a hand at the display, then stood there, behind the table. Anna picked up a plate. The price, fifteen dollars, was scrawled on the bottom. Either could have told that neither of them was comfortable here. There was something odd about it, though what, except for the unkempt road and the raucous dog, it would have pressed them to say. The girl stood looking at a broken fingernail with curiosity, as though it had nothing to do with her. The plate was a gray crater, the diameter of a large dinner plate, balanced, smooth to the touch, in its plain way perfect.

"If you want it, get it," Karl said. He looked at the other objects with distaste. They were all marred by clumsy attempts to embellish them, some with animal motifs, Disney-like, and some with lettering of the HIS and HER sort. MARY'S MUG with a funny face beneath. BILL'S MUG, etc. There were vases made of upended fish with open mouths, bookends of back-to-back squirrels, an endless succession of pitchers in every size, resembling frogs.

Anna decided to buy the plate and leave. Karl had no change for twenty dollars, nor did the girl. Karl and Anna made the sum up between them. "Do you have many customers?" Anna decided on conversation, a humanizing effort.

The girl did not glance up, but pulled at the ragged nail. "We take a lot of stuff into town."

"So you don't do it all alone here?"

"Oh, no." Out back, the dog abruptly fell silent. The room seemed still as midnight.

"Well . . . thanks."

Karl and Anna began, as though by common consent, to back away, moving toward the door.

"I'll wrap it," the girl said, coming out of her distraction.

"It's okay." Anna felt suddenly that any delay in getting out of there was not to be considered.

As they reached the car, a noise from the road signaled the arrival of someone else, and before they could turn to leave, a pickup came jolting out of the woods and stopped just behind them. Two men got out. They were bearded, dressed like the girl. Only their beards distinguished them from each other, one being black and thick, the other a coppery, thin scraggle needing a trim. They were going past, toward the house, scarcely giving a glance. Karl and Anna might have been invisible, not there at all.

"Excuse me, but you've blocked our way," Karl said. He spoke too loudly, in the tone of someone making an arrest.

Still, they did not look. One of them said, passing up the steps with something like urgency, "Just in a minute." They went inside.

The Wallens waited in the car. When insects drifted toward them out of the dusky air, they rolled up the windows. From out back of the house, the dog resumed barking. It was close in the car. Anna held the plate on her lap. It was rather heavy.

Karl finally got out and went up the steps. Anna leaned out the window and saw him banging on the door. "You're blocking our way," he called. "Hallo! We can't get out." There was no answer. The place could have been deserted. It seemed now to be getting later than it actually was. Karl came back down the steps. "The damnedest thing," he said.

"Let's try to drive past the truck," Anna suggested. "It can't be that impossible."

He walked around the pickup, and looked into the bushes. Anna got out and looked, too. The growth seemed too thick to deal with except with an axe perhaps, a two-man saw, a machine for land clearing. She even checked the back of the pickup to see if any of those items were available. She felt that if there had been, they would have seized them at once and plunged into clearing the jungle, but nothing was visible except a pile of cloths, huddled together like old bedding, and several empty crates made of plywood.

"Shit." Karl said it with finality. He had started for the steps when the red-bearded man emerged from around the corner of the house. He was grinning, reaching in his jeans pocket, evidently for the key. A dog was trailing at his heels. It was a police-type dog, small for the breed. It went snuffling, as though in an unfamiliar place.

"Sorry. I just forgot."

Karl stepped back, smiling now. Everything was okay. "We couldn't get out," he said, with a cordial note of understanding.

"I know, I know." Ramming his hand in one pocket after another, the man began to frown. "Hell, I guess he's got it."

"The key?"

"Yeah, the key." He turned around and moved off. "I'll be right back. Won't take a minute." He passed the corner of the house, the dog trailing. Again they sat and waited.

—

"Damn all this." Karl got out and slammed the door.

For some reason she said, "Don't."

"I've got to—" he began but did not finish. He strode angrily up the steps and into the house. She noticed the wet patches in his black hair, as he went away. Sweat from irritation ... nerves. . . . From the car Anna heard him calling. "Hey! We need the key! Hey!" She pushed up the blond gathering of hair from her neck. It was damp from the heat.

There was never such a surrounding silence. In it, she heard his footsteps stamp through the house to the back, then a slamming door. Descending steps, then silence again. She sat in the car and wondered, *Why am I so frightened?* She didn't know. And that was the frightening part.

By the time she at last got from the car and walked toward the steps, she had the curious feeling of not knowing her own size. She could have been walking on stilts, nine feet tall; she could have been the squashed-down height of a midget. Just as they had remarked about origins, she could have been not only anybody, but any size of anybody. She mounted the steps as he had done. She passed through the door, the large silent room with the animal pots. She pushed through the back door. It gave onto a porch, high from the ground, identical with the front, so that except for the display tables, the house could have been swung back to front on a swivel and no difference would have appeared.

The backyard stretched out before her, sloping sharply down to an ill-kept-up fence with a sagging gate, standing open. No one was in sight. The sun was moving below the treetops. Anna called Karl by name, but her voice was taken up by the expanse of yard, and struck the line of trees and growth just beyond the fence too faintly even to echo. She tried again, but the echo was meager.

Why not go on, through the sagging gate, follow the path into the woods? She shook herself sternly. No, the thing to do was find a telephone inside, call that number (nine one one), the police (she didn't know how), the operator (that should be easy). He had been gone too long, but how long? The day was lowering fast; yet her watch showed an early hour. It might have stopped, but did she know? Could she say positively? On the phone, she would invent something, exaggerate. She rose.

Just then, from the long fall of the woods to the right she heard voices. The words were indistinguishable. Their rise and fall had the rhythm of a discussion; their quality seemed male, with only the occasional higher note of what might have been a woman. She called again. "Karl!"

She would run down the steps, she would run toward the voices. They stopped suddenly.

Anna was standing on the steps. From somewhere in the woods toward the left the dog began to bark again, then howl. Howl, then bark. Was it the same dog they had seen? Why hadn't it gone where the people were?

Will I scream? she wondered.

Halfway up the steps or halfway down them (as it might equally well be described) Anna sat down. To her surprise she saw that she had brought along the plate. It rested heavily on her lap. She rubbed her fingers on the smooth gray surface. It felt cool.

From nearby in the woods a number of birds, gathered together, were twittering mildly in a rhythm much like conversation. The sound was soothing because it was so companionable, like questions and answers around a favored child who might be sleeping. The voices began again and so did the dog, but both had receded to a farther distance than before. The birds seemed nearer.

Anna sat quietly on the steps, listening. A small eternity caught and held, as strong as life or death.

"The key fell among the leaves," said the birds. "They are searching for it. The dog is barking at a squirrel. Soon he will go to them. They will all come back to you. Wait and see . . . wait . . . see . . ."

FIRST CHILD

The station wagon had eased into the cottage drive a little past three. The man and woman got out, each turning to reach back for the child. The storekeeper across the highway noted them and wondered if he could recall them from the summer before. He concluded that they were new, and when after an hour they came across the road in the sun glare to shop, he proved to be right.

"We've rented from the Stimsons. Just for this weekend," the man said. "Do you know them?"

"Sure thing," the storekeeper said.

"How's fishing?"

"Catching some, but mainly far out."

"I'll stick to shore. You got minnows?"

"Some. Take a look."

A barrel stood in the cool back of the store. It was past the end of the glass-front counters and the shelves loaded with canned goods and specialty items. A net hung on a hook near the barrel.

"You got dinosaurs?" the child asked.

"Haven't noticed any today," the storekeeper said. "In the hot weather, they mainly stay out in the swamp."

The woman laughed. "He means rubber ones, I think. The kind you can blow up and float in the water."

"You'll have to go up the road for those. K-mart maybe."

"So you'll have to wait," the woman said to the boy, who looked uncertain about it.

The boy's name was Cooper. He was not her son. His mother was her brother's wife, only her brother had left for other parts, some-where out West, and remarried. Had anyone told him his ex-wife was in the hospital, gravely ill? Had anyone told him the mother of his son was ill?

Questions like these might float around in the atmosphere, might come in on the repetitive waves of thought. But no one asked, so no one answered.

———

Packard, who was neither the boy's father nor the woman's husband, sat out on the porch and watched the sea. He had already brought poles up from the basement and strung the lines, but still he made no move toward going out. He let the sea sound, the salt air invade him, like water permeating dry fabric. He had brought work with him, but he did not think about it. He wondered if they had done the right thing. The Stimsons' unexpected offer was hard to refuse. A vacant weekend for their cottage at Ocean Isle. But there was this illness. The tide was out and the waves reached the long sand beach in a slow measure, unfurling, retreating, but not breaking open. The water seemed like satin, glossy, swelling and shrinking.

Inside, Elsa was taking the few staples from the store out of sacks, stocking the cabinets and the refrigerator. "I'm sorry," she had told Packard back in Eltonville, "but we'll have to take Cooper. There's nobody else to keep him."

"Aren't you going to fish?" her voice floated through the open window.

"Later. Where's Cooper?"

"Watching TV."

Packard snorted. "If I had a kid . . ."

"You'd what?"

"I'd take that damn box five miles out and dump it."

"There'd just be more, more, more. You'd never stop them. Nothing will."

"But don't you watch it, too?" He hadn't learned a lot about her.

"Some things. Don't you?"

"Mighty few."

"But some."

He dropped the argument. Reading was always Packard's preference. Only there was too much to read.

"TV and dinosaurs," he muttered, half to himself. "Just proves he's a normal kid." He was learning about Cooper, too.

The refrigerator door closed with a definitive sound. "I have to drive up for more groceries. Are you coming?"

"I'm staying. See if they're biting."

"Cooper! Come and shop." She had to call twice.

There was a burst from the spare bedroom. Packard turned to look. Cooper was a nice brown little boy, about seven. He went to grammar school, not the high school where Packard worked as assistant administrator. "TV is a tool," he often lectured students. "An educational crutch. It's not for you to devote your life to. If you're not learning anything, switch it off. Go play basketball."

"You're not making a dent, I bet," Elsa told him.

"Maybe not. Maybe some of them listen."

Cooper was barefoot. "Better put your sneakers on," Packard advised. Elsa agreed. "You'll have dinosaurs stepping on your toes."

Cooper giggled. He believed in them and he didn't at the same time.

Packard dropped his magazine and went inside. He helped Cooper tie his sneakers. They were red with a white rubber rim around the soles. Cooper ran back in the room to get something. Before he came back, Packard kissed the back of Elsa's neck. "We're going to get through it somehow," he assured her.

She made a face. "Just like Margery to get sick."

—

Elsa and Cooper drove the highway to the shopping mall. They stopped at the fish market for shrimp, in case Packard didn't catch anything. Elsa had a feeling that he wouldn't. She kept her eyes on the road with almost too much concentration, a frown between her eyes. Margery was no kin to her was what she was thinking. Whatever Cooper said she answered yes and no. He rode beside her, his feet in red sneakers stuck straight out.

"Wish you taught at the school," Packard had told her. She

worked at the county tax office, collating answers to particular surveys, sending out notices.

"I wouldn't try to control those brats for anything," had been her answer. Cooper, fallen silent, kept pulling at a rip in the vinyl upholstery. "Don't," Elsa told him, twice. Then she slapped his hand. He tried not to cry. "I'm sorry, Cooper," she said. "Where's Mommy?" he asked, though he knew very well. She told him again. "She's in the hospital. She'll be all right." He said nothing, his round little face shut up tight.

Cooper trailed Elsa through the supermarket without saying anything, but when they had hauled the sacks out to the car, he said "K-mart."

Oh Lord, Elsa thought, and supposed that she had to. Women her age, twenty-eight, were supposed to have kids already. She sometimes wondered why she hadn't. It was that early marriage maybe. It was that liquid regard and ripe no-nonsense mouth that showed her cool to motherhood. But now she had to buy a dinosaur.

———

They came in large plastic envelopes, each with a colored picture of the one waiting within. Cooper chose a brontosaurus. As he knew already, the next step was the filling station to have it blown up. Elsa knew she had to do that too and pulled in under a Texaco sign.

The attendant, who came out to help, spread the large expanse of rubber on the pavement. He then found the entry valve and plugged in the air nozzle. A hissing sound continued for several minutes, and when he turned around he said, "My God!"

Elsa was astounded and Cooper was delighted. The creature, in all its painted glory, soared up in the air above them. Cooper jumped up to circle its lofty neck, but couldn't reach it. It smiled down with a stupid lizard grin. All lizards grin, thought Elsa, and looking at the massive feet, the long, tapering tail, wondered how to get it in the station wagon.

But there was no parting Cooper from it now. He was jumping with delight and looking ready to wet his pants, though he said he didn't need to go.

The attendant helped Elsa squeeze the creature through the

back: a tight fit. Not much more than a boy himself, he was obviously having fun. They laid it on its side. They had to bend and fold the tail across its back. When they sat in the front seat, the tiny head reached over and stuck itself between them. Elsa shoved at it. A glance showed her not only that lizard grin but eyelashes painted on. One eye was staring into hers. "It has funny ears," said Cooper.

———

"What you got there, sport?" Packard wanted to know. But this was just when they started unloading. "Jesus," he next remarked.

"You're mighty right," said Elsa. They set the dinosaur upright on the lawn and stood staring at it.

Like all the houses so near the sea, the cottage had living quarters on the second floor, utility and storage space below. There was no way to get the dinosaur up the outside stairs. They circled the house to the beach side and managed to get him into the porch. He filled most of the floor space, where they placed him, huge feet planted, tail hanging out the door, foolish head nudging the ceiling. "His name is Billy," said Cooper.

It was getting late. "We'll have to hurry if you want to swim," said Packard.

Cooper said that Billy didn't want to swim.

"I thought that's why you bought him," Packard said to Elsa.

"Don't ask me why I bought him," said Elsa. "Forty damn dollars' worth of rubber monster."

"Come on, Coop," said Packard. "Let's take him in the water for a ride. Let's see if Billy can swim."

Elsa went inside. She heard Cooper say again that Billy didn't want to.

———

By the next afternoon, however, they had all gone swimming with Billy and they had walked with Billy on the beach. They had tied a rope around the rise of the neck, painted like the rest of him all gray, green, and orange. They had pulled and nudged him along. His lengthy tail wagged across the sand. He was light with all the air inside, but also awkward. He towered over them, grinning at people, grinning at the sea. People pointed and laughed. Some had taken pictures.

The three had had lunch in the cottage. Packard had even caught a fish. And though they had made love in the night, it hadn't been the best ever. Elsa kept dreaming about dinosaurs. "I'm fucking with the damned things," she confided. "Better stop it," Packard advised. But now it was afternoon. One thing they had always agreed on: Love in the afternoon was the best. Since they didn't live together, it was why they liked to go away. Now it was afternoon.

"All parents have the problem," Elsa said to Packard. "We can't send him out to swim. He might drown."

"Just leave him with the TV," said Packard.

She laughed. "It's what you're against."

"Maybe this is all it's good for."

"He'll see more sex on that than if he sat and watched."

"Don't be so graphic," Packard said. He was squeamish. He didn't like talking about sexy behavior. When he got going he would let out little cries and whispers. Elsa liked to talk dirty, once she got into it.

Out on the porch, Cooper was sitting in the swing with the dinosaur beside him on the floor. He had to hold it by one arm to keep it from sliding away from him. Sometimes he put his arm all the way around it. He was swinging and singing something tuneless.

"Let's give it up," Elsa said.

They then stared at each other as though someone else, invisible, had spoken. For desire was with them now, knocking about in the blood.

For the first time, since they came, the phone rang.

It took them both a while to quit looking at it and answer it. They both knew why.

Elsa finally went to it. All she said was Yes and No and Of course. She straightened up and bit her lip.

Packard went out on the porch. He sat in a rocker very near Cooper and the dinosaur. "Did Billy like his swim?" he asked.

"He'd rather walk with us," said Cooper.

Packard forbade himself even to look at the creature. He thought maybe he hated all this dinosaur craze as much as he hated TV. It's off the same bolt of cloth, he thought.

He had an inspiration. "If I give you ten dollars, will you go across the street and buy something?"

"Like what?"

"Something I might want and something you might want—two things or one thing for us both. Will you?"

"What about Billy?"

"Something for Billy too. I'll look after him. I promise." He held out the money.

Cooper put Billy in the living room. He left for the store. "Look both ways when you cross the road," Packard advised. Then he turned to Elsa. "When he comes back in, we'll hear the door."

"You hope," said Elsa, but she was already ahead of him, hurrying to the bedroom, shedding her jeans, getting out of her blouse.

"A quickie," she said, head flung back against the pillows, eagerly and happily, laughing. She was stripped to her bikini briefs and bra, leaving them for Packard, who liked taking them off.

He turned her and smoothed her, he murmured to her. He really was good at it. Now he was over her once again, and she could draw her fingers down the V of black chest hair. ("You've got brown hair," she had told him the first time she saw it. "Do you dye all this?") Her firm fingers explored the black thicket below. She watched his sex emerge to stand all white and sturdy, ready to lean right in. "Ooh!" said Elsa. "Oh-ohhh!" she said.

Better than nothing at all, Packard said, when the short time passed. They lay a little apart and listened. "He should be back by now," said Elsa. "The door squeaks," Packard had assured her. "We'll be certain to hear him."

But the whole house was silent.

———

From the first time they met, they had known what they wanted. Packard, still in his twenties, felt he had plenty of time to think about marriage, for the truth was he was hesitant about it. He took responsibility too seriously. At the high school, he was always fretting the details. Marriage meant smaller kids than those, with their interminable demands. But he liked sex.

He had run into Elsa, literally run into her at the door of the gym one night before a basketball game. She was hurrying not to miss the start. She had Cooper with her, and her sister-in-law was trailing behind. She had bumped straight into him, though it wouldn't have happened if he hadn't been looking back over his shoulder and talking with someone. "Oh, sorry." "My fault." Packard had stepped on Cooper's foot. Cooper was saying, "You hurt my foot."

Later on, Packard went and found them. "Is your little boy all right?" "He's not mine," said Elsa, "but he's all right. I've got no kids," she continued amiably. "I know how to keep out of that," she found herself going on to say, and not exactly without knowing what she was saying, for he had attracted her from the bumping point. Just the right height for her, and lean in the bargain. *Umm,* she was already thinking.

Elsa had run off and got married at sixteen, but had got her fill of it in less than a year. She'd discovered the unconscious selfishness of men, and furthermore that she had no intention of getting used to it. She left as abruptly as she had come. He had to claim desertion. So that was over with. But she liked sex.

Wasn't there just enough time for a little more? She leaned her thigh into Packard's, touching again, starting him up. There was a persistent whisper in her mind, like a little night wind.

"What was that phone call about?" asked Packard.

She had to tell him. "Margy."

"Better?" he asked, turning his head to her on the pillow, frowning when she didn't answer, then finally said,

"No."

He came up suddenly on his elbow. "Very serious then?" Again she didn't answer. "Why didn't you say?"

But he knew why she hadn't and that it was the same reason that he, when the call came, had gone out on the porch.

"Jesus," she flared up, "I can't do miracles."

But what miracle did she mean? She didn't know, she only felt accused.

He flung back the fold of sheet he had drawn partway over his legs and, rising off the bed, began grabbing for his clothes.

"Don't you realize . . . ?"

A fight was in the air. They had been careful, all these past months, never to get quarreling, as, they both assured each other, all they wanted was the same thing, nothing to quarrel over. Now he was going to accuse her. She knew it.

But he didn't, unless his sudden cutoff of feeling, his urgency, was an accusation.

"I'll go get him from the store," he said.

"If he's there," she flung after him, making him turn back.

"What on earth do you mean?"

"I mean that he hasn't come back, so he must have gone somewhere else."

"God in heaven," Packard said, and plunged through the living room. He ran to the top of the steps that ran to ground level.

Cooper, she thought, *I'm doing something to you. But then Margy wanted us to take you. What could she do with him, was what she said. And now I'm supposed to be. . . .* What? What was she supposed to be? She remembered the exact words of the call, though she hadn't told them to Packard. "We'd urge you to come as soon as possible. She's not improving." But Packard hadn't wanted to hear. It's why he'd gone on the porch. Like a signal that had told her. And they both knew it. Yes, both of them.

———

Packard was still on the steps when a man in blue jeans and a faded T-shirt walked into the yard.

"Oh, hello," said Packard.

"Hi yer doin'. Say, is one of you over here named Billy?"

"No . . . well, yes and no. He's a . . . well, he's our . . . relative."

"A kid was over to the store. He was talking about Billy."

"Where's he now?"

"He just struck out."

"Struck out?"

"Preston over there, he come to the conclusion the kid was with you. But he just wasn't sure."

"You mean he left? For where?" He was gazing hard into a country face, sun-reddened, with sun-scaled skin and eyebrows speckled gray under a cap bill.

"Beats me, if he ain't here."

Packard was stricken. He stood fixed on the stair, feeling his feet grow numb as if set in cement. Elsa, all dressed, came out beside him. "Don't tell me he's lost." He turned on her in something like the start of an outburst, but then said hurriedly, "We're going to the store."

They crossed the road together.

———

Preston had no more to offer than what they'd heard already. "Just struck out. Kept talking about Billy. Are you Billy?"

"No," said Packard.

A woman came from the back of the store. She was well-informed. "How come you letting him out like that? How old is he?"

"Seven," said Elsa.

"You ought not to let him out like that."

"He was supposed to come right back," said Packard.

"He said something about his mother, too," said the storekeeper, Preston. "You his mother? He was talking about her and Billy."

Elsa and Packard got in the station wagon and rode up and down the highway. They stopped at every place of business to inquire about Cooper. They described him so much they knew him by heart. The last phrase was always red tennis shoes.

They went back to the beach house and called the police. Then they sat and tried not to look at each other. It seemed like the first bad afternoon in Eden.

———

It was after dark that a car pulled up in the yard below. Packard and Elsa rushed to the stair. An elderly couple were alighting from their car, and here came Cooper.

"We should have stopped and called," they said. "But we decided to hurry back instead."

The story was simple enough. They had filled up with gas at Preston's store and Cooper had heard them say they were heading to Eltonville. He wanted to see his mother and tell her about Billy. She was sick and he thought it would be good for her to know. He had crawled into the back seat. What happened next was never quite clear because everybody started talking at once. Did they notice him there before they heard the announcement on the radio, or afterward? The man had judged he had got in at the store, only place they'd stopped for gas. He'd turned right around to come back. And then the radio.... But there—after all was said, and never to be understood—there was Cooper, standing so small and so separate from Packard and herself. Separate from the others too. So separate he was almost nameless, like a kid without a name, Elsa thought. She cried out "Cooper!" and suddenly closed the distance. She threw her arms around him and burst into tears. Cooper hugged her back.

"Golly, sport," said Packard. "You sure scared us silly."

"How's Billy?" Cooper asked.

The elderly couple said they were glad to have been a help. It was their little adventure, they said. They gave their name and address and telephone number and Packard, giving his, said "we"— "we live at," etc. Letting out they weren't married seemed not quite the thing. Probably he would never see them again, except maybe in the grocery.

In the dew-damp early night, the three of them stood in the dark, waving good-bye to the nice people as they backed away and moved into the highway.

Then Packard and Elsa turned and followed Cooper up the stairs to where the brontosaurus waited in the living room.

"We're leaving now," Packard said firmly. "We've got to get to Margery."

———

Packard and Elsa never went away together again. Elsa kept remembering what she had felt about Cooper, how she had seen and seen and seen again, in her mind's vivid memory, the hurt face when she'd slapped him, the firm little shoulders trudging ahead of her, eagerly leading her down the aisles at K-mart, the two smudges of blood on his legs from mosquito bites, the march of the red tennis shoes. And her inward cry in the awful afternoon of "Come back, my darling, please." It had all surprised her. She had never thought of Cooper as her darling. She never cried. She didn't know she could. Once, long ago, she had cried. It was not long after her mother died and had to do with something about some roller skates, but what she couldn't remember. She thought it didn't matter anymore.

—

Margery didn't die, she just almost did.

Elsa got married and moved away to Oklahoma. She had children one after another. She even had twins. Packard got a better job up in Maryland, and he got married too. Soon he had a son. He would stare at him in loving amazement.

But wherever they were, Packard and Elsa always thought of Cooper as their first child. They didn't know that they each thought this. One day Packard drove down to Raleigh on some school business. Being near Eltonville, he went over and looked Cooper up.

He had grown into a great boy, rather brusk, but friendly. He didn't remember much about Ocean Isle, only going off somewhere in a car. But when Packard mentioned Billy, he grinned. "He stayed blown up for a long time," said Cooper. "But the air finally faded right out of him." He turned to his mother, Margery. "It was that dinosaur I had once," he explained. "Oh, yes," she said. "It went down a little at a time. There was nothing left but his little old head." Cooper was laughing. "That silly grin just wouldn't go away."

Packard wanted to tell that to Elsa.

OWL

What was she doing at the window?

She had just been sleeping. Lying pencil straight in the narrow guest-room bed, she had heard it only once, or so it seemed. Once was all that got through. Drawn up, she had gone to the window and stood looking out, or trying to. She knew what it was: owl.

On that moonless night, the second-floor window revealed only the dark presence of trees outside, branches of elm and sycamore melted indistinctly together.

It spoke again. *Oooo....* Deep sound drawn up out of feathers. Feathery deep ... then a rustle. She thought she could make out a large moving shape and could hear a rustle in the branches. The motion stopped. There had been something clumsy about it, as though the wings were too large for the spaces between branches. Then a righting, a folding down, suspended silence. It was all so near.

Ooooo ...

Ginia was alone. Two children grown, moved away, married, husband away. She never minded the empty house, even after the cat had got run over and the dog had died of age. She had things to do. Guy's trips never lasted long: fishing, golfing, hunting, out with the "club." *Club* was his word; she thought of it as "the gang." But not resentfully. Life was easy for this older woman on this late-spring night.

The owls she'd seen were large and gray, a sort of striated gray, a very dark stippled edge, next a stripe of medium dark, then a paler one still, and start again. There was the tiny curved beak, set dead center under glowing golden eyes, night-seeing. Could it see her?

I wish I could see you, she thought. She whispered it. "Why can't we see each other?" She leaned closer to the screen, peering, and then began to raise it. But what a blunder that was, for she at once heard the branches shake, a whoosh of wings, a large shadow, and a presence fled. Which direction? It seemed to have gone straight up.

Night silence.

Had she dreamed it? Drowsy back in bed, she was fading into sleep when a chill, glacial in the warm night, a thought-shadow, close to palpable, fell across her. Owl calls meant death. She had heard that from childhood. So their cook had told her often. And three times could only mean three days. She saw again the round black face in the warm kitchen on a midsummer morning, kindly telling her this. Nonsense. Childish nonsense.

But gray and feathery, the presence lingered, and so did the exact, seeking sound of the call. A call was meant to say something to some other being. Person? Bird? Beast? Another owl? Who was to know?

Sleep, returning, tumbled her like surf.

———

Ginia did accounts for a local charity and one afternoon a week kept the desk at a shelter for the homeless. She served on committees and talked to friends. Her daughter urged her to get a regular job. She said she didn't want to.

"Guy's coming back next week," she told a caller. "They're playing several courses in Florida."

That was the first day. She read the obituaries, but found no name she knew.

On the second an entire family of friends she had not seen in twenty years called while passing through. She asked them to stop by. The husband and wife, getting gray and overly cheerful, had brought their daughter with two grandchildren. They had been traveling in the mountains.

As they sat at the dining table with coffee, Cokes, and cookies, the little girl bent double with a terrible stomach pain. The visit ended in the emergency room at the hospital, where Ginia sat in a row with the family, trying to amuse the little boy. He wanted to be sick, too, finding it interesting. She thought of the owl. Appendicitis? Even so, there was no real danger. Unless peritonitis. . . . The doctor called them in. Acute gastritis. Take these. The trouble passed.

———

Alone again in a night so silent, the silence seemed a presence she might speak to. She leaned to the window. Nothing was there.

———

The third day. She kept a lunch date with a friend. The friend was tearful. Her little spaniel had had a fierce fight with a neighbor's Doberman and was now at the vet's. He might not survive. "Why, that's terrible," said Ginia. Back home in the afternoon, she left her chores to telephone. Great news. The dog was improving. It wouldn't have to be "put down." That awful phrase.

Restless, she finished dinner alone and telephoned her children. Everybody was well. "He's coming back early next week," she said. Another still twilight faded toward another silent night. She locked up the house and went to a movie.

On the drive home a thin scythe of moon was just shyly showing over the treetops. She lowered the window to breathe night air. The glare of headlights appeared very close in the rearview mirror. A man in a white T-shirt was driving the car behind. It kept pressing nearer. The face was expressionless, pale, nondescript, below a jut of short-cropped spiky blond hair. The bumper touched hers, a jolt like a shudder.

For the first time, she thought: *Maybe it meant me.*

She did not want to lead him home with no one there. She spun out to the highway. He followed close behind. She knew what the next move should be—the police station, sitting outside and honking out a call. The empty highway climbed. The frail moon looked toward a far horizon. Abruptly, the pursuer swung left, crossed the meridian, and vanished into a side road, thick with dark trees.

She drove some minutes longer, but he did not return.

Entering her house from the driveway, she saw she had left a light on in the kitchen.

When she entered, Guy stood from searching the refrigerator to greet her. "Got rained out. Should have called. Had to run for the plane. Hey, what's the matter?" She had almost screamed. "You look like you've seen a ghost."

She sank into a chair. "I feel like it."

His face was florid. His bourbon glass sat half-empty on the table. His booming voice filled the room. "I'm not one yet, sweetheart. You'll have to wait awhile." He squeezed her hand and planted a kiss.

Once he was asleep and snoring happily, she returned to the guest-room window and searched the darkness. "Where are you?" she whispered, as though to a friend. "Come back. You're nothing bad, nothing bad. Only let me hear you once again."

ABOUT THE AUTHOR

Born in Carrollton, Mississippi, in 1921, ELIZABETH SPENCER has been one of America's most acclaimed fiction writers for much of the second half of the twentieth century. For more than three decades her stories appeared in a number of publications, including *The New Yorker, The Atlantic,* and *The Southern Review.* Recipient of five O. Henry Awards, Spencer has earned a number of other awards, including the Rosenthal Award from the American Academy of Arts and Letters, the Award of Merit Medal from the Academy, and a senior grant in literature from the National Endowment for the Humanities. She was elected to membership in the American Academy in 1985.

Elizabeth Spencer grew up in a rural, agrarian society rooted in the Southern tradition and lore that informs much of her early fiction. After publishing two novels, *Fire in the Morning* in 1948 and *This Crooked Way* in 1952, she went to Italy on a Guggenheim Fellowship to write *The Voice at the Back Door,* published in 1956.

She lived in Italy for five years, and some of her finest work was inspired by this sojourn, including *The Light in the Piazza* (1960). That book, reprinted around the world, sold more than two million copies and solidified Spencer's reputation as a writer admired by critics and fellow writers. About Elizabeth Spencer, James Dickey once wrote, "She is a writer one puts on the 'permanent' shelf. [Her] stories will be read and reread."

In 1958 she returned to North America, settling in Montreal with her English husband, John Rusher. "From 1960 on," she once said, "[I began] to come to terms with, not the Southern world, but the world of modern experience." Her books from this period include the novels *Knights & Dragons* (1965), *No Place for an Angel* (1967), *The Snare* (1972), and *The Salt Line* (1984), and the collection *Ship Island and Other Stories* (1968). As her reputation continued to grow, she earned praise from a number of contemporary writers, including the Canadian short-story writer Alice Munro, who wrote, "What [her] stories do wonderfully, for me, is explore the ties that bind—in families, friendships, communities, marriages—how mysterious, twisted, chafing, inescapable, and life-supporting such ties are."

In 1986 she returned to the South, moving with her husband to Chapel Hill, North Carolina. In 1988 she published her third collection of short stories, *Jack of Diamonds,* and in 1991 her most recent novel, *The Night Travellers,* was released.

In her foreword to *The Stories of Elizabeth Spencer* (1981), Eudora Welty praised Spencer as one of the South's masters. She wrote, "It is as her fellow writer that I see so well what is *unerring* about her writing. The good South, bestowing blessings at the cradle of storytellers, touches her most tenderly with the sense of place. Elizabeth evokes place and evokes it acutely in that place's own terms."

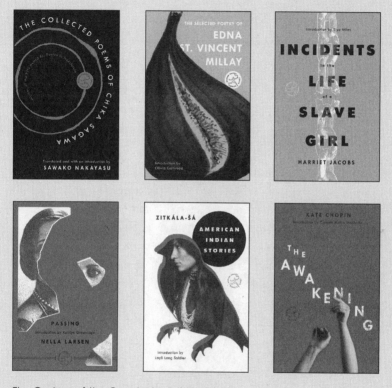